From a portrait by E. O. Hoppé

JOHN GALSWORTHY

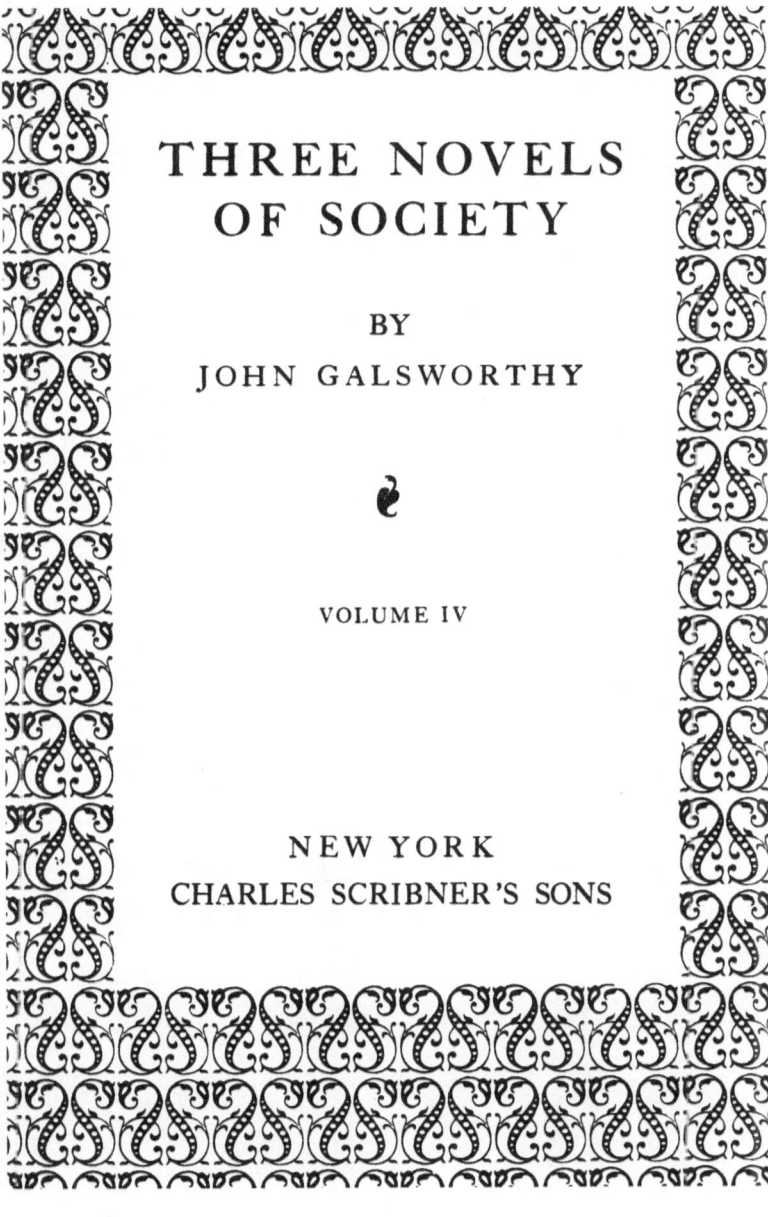

THREE NOVELS OF SOCIETY

BY

JOHN GALSWORTHY

VOLUME IV

NEW YORK

CHARLES SCRIBNER'S SONS

CONTENTS

BOOK I

THE COUNTRY HOUSE

Part I

Part II

PART III

BOOK II

FRATERNITY

CONTENTS

BOOK III

THE PATRICIAN

BOOK I

THE COUNTRY HOUSE

"... 't is an unweeded garden"
—*Hamlet.*

TO

W. H. HUDSON

For love of "The Purple Land"
and all his other books

PART I

CHAPTER I

A PARTY AT WORSTED SKEYNES

THE year was 1891, the month October, the day Monday. In the dark outside the railway-station at Worsted Skeynes Mr. Horace Pendyce's omnibus, his brougham, his luggage-cart, monopolised space. The face of Mr. Horace Pendyce's coachman monopolised the light of the solitary station lantern. Rosygilled, with fat close-clipped grey whiskers and inscrutably pursed lips, it presided high up in the easterly air like an emblem of the feudal system. On the platform within, Mr. Horace Pendyce's first footman and second groom in long livery coats with silver buttons, their appearance slightly relieved by the rakish cock of their top-hats, awaited the arrival of the 6.15.

The first footman took from his pocket a half-sheet of stamped and crested notepaper covered with Mr. Horace Pendyce's small and precise calligraphy. He read from it in a nasal, derisive voice:

"Hon. Geoff. and Mrs. Winlow, blue room and dress; maid, small drab. Mr. George, white room. Mrs. Jaspar Bellew, gold. The Captain, red. General Pendyce, pink room; valet, back attic. That's the lot."

The groom, a red-cheeked youth, paid no attention.

"If this here Ambler of Mr. George's wins on Wednesday," he said, "it's as good as five pounds in my pocket. Who does for Mr. George?"

"James, of course."

The groom whistled.

"I'll try an' get his loadin' to-morrow. Are you on, Tom?"

The footman answered:

"Here's another over the page. Green room, right wing—that Foxleigh; he's no good. 'Take all you can and give nothing' sort! But can't he shoot just! That's why they ask him!"

From behind a screen of dark trees the train ran in.

Down the platform came the first passengers—two cattlemen

with long sticks, slouching by in their frieze coats, diffusing an odour of beast and black tobacco; then a couple, and single figures, keeping as far apart as possible, the guests of Mr. Horace Pendyce. Slowly they came out one by one into the loom of the carriages, and stood with their eyes fixed carefully before them, as though afraid they might recognise each other. A tall man in a fur coat, whose tall wife carried a small bag of silver and shagreen, spoke to the coachman:

"How are you, Benson? Mr. George says Captain Pendyce told him he wouldn't be down till the 9.30. I suppose we'd better——"

Like a breeze tuning through the frigid silence of a fog, a high, clear voice was heard:

"Oh, thanks; I'll go up in the brougham."

Followed by the first footman carrying her wraps, and muffled in a white veil, through which the Hon. Geoffrey Winlow's leisurely gaze caught the gleam of eyes, a lady stepped forward, and with a backward glance vanished into the brougham. Her head appeared again behind the swathe of gauze.

"There's plenty of room, George."

George Pendyce walked quickly forward and disappeared beside her. There was a crunch of wheels; the brougham rolled away.

The Hon. Geoffrey Winlow raised his face again.

"Who was that, Benson?"

The coachman leaned over confidentially, holding his podgy white-gloved hand outspread on a level with the Hon. Geoffrey's hat.

"Mrs. Jaspar Bellew, sir. Captain Bellew's lady, of the Firs."

"But I thought they weren't——"

"No, sir; they're not, sir."

"Ah!"

A calm rarefied voice was heard from the door of the omnibus:

"Now, Geoff!"

The Hon. Geoffrey Winlow followed his wife, Mr. Foxleigh, and General Pendyce into the omnibus, and again Mrs. Winlow's voice was heard:

"Oh, do you mind my maid? Get in, Tookson!"

Mr. Horace Pendyce's mansion, white and long and low, standing well within its acres, had come into the possession of his great-great-great-grandfather through an alliance with the last of the Worsteds. Originally a fine property let in smallish holdings to tenants who, having no attention bestowed on them, did very well and paid excellent rents, it was now farmed on model lines at a slight loss. At stated intervals Mr. Pendyce imported a new kind of cow, or partridge, and built a wing to the schools. His income was fortunately independent of this estate. He was in complete accord with the Rector and the sanitary authorities, and not infrequently complained that his tenants did not stay on the land. His wife was a Totteridge, and his coverts admirable. He had been, needless to say, an eldest son. It was his individual conviction that individualism had ruined England, and he had set himself deliberately to eradicate this vice from the character of his tenants. By substituting for their individualism his own tastes, plans, and sentiments, one might almost say his own individualism, and losing money thereby, he had gone far to demonstrate his pet theory that the higher the individualism the more sterile the life of the community. If, however, the matter was thus put to him he grew both garrulous and angry, for he considered himself not an individualist, but what he called a " Tory Communist." In connection with his agricultural interests he was naturally a Fair Trader; a tax on corn, he knew, would make all the difference in the world to the prosperity of England. As he often said: "A tax of three or four shillings on corn, and I should be farming my estate at a profit."

Mr. Pendyce had other peculiarities, in which he was not too individual. He was averse to any change in the existing order of things, made lists of everything, and was never really so happy as when talking of himself or his estate. He had a black spaniel dog called John, with a long nose and longer ears, whom he had bred himself till the creature was not happy out of his sight.

In appearance Mr. Pendyce was rather of the old school, upright and active, with thin side-whiskers, to which, however, for some years past he had added moustaches which drooped and were now grizzled. He wore large cravats and square-tailed coats. He did not smoke.

At the head of his dining-table loaded with flowers and plate, `he sat between the Hon. Mrs. Winlow and Mrs. Jaspar Bellew, nor could he have desired more striking and contrasted supporters. Equally tall, full-figured, and comely, Nature had fixed between these two women a gulf which Mr. Pendyce, a man of spare figure, tried in vain to fill. The composure peculiar to the ashen type of the British aristocracy wintered permanently on Mrs. Winlow's features like the smile of a frosty day. Expressionless to a degree, they at once convinced the spectator that she was a woman of the best breeding. Had an expression ever arisen upon these features, it is impossible to say what might have been the consequences. She had followed her nurse's adjuration: "Lor, Miss Truda, never you make a face! You might grow so!" Never since that day had Gertrude Winlow, an Honourable in her own right and in that of her husband, made a face, not even, it is believed, when her son was born. And then to find on the other side of Mr. Pendyce that puzzling Mrs. Bellew with the green-grey eyes, at which the best people of her own sex looked with instinctive disapproval! A woman in her position should avoid anything conspicuous, and Nature had given her a too-striking appearance. People said that when, the year before last, she had separated from Captain Bellew, and left the Firs, it was simply because they were tired of one another. They said, too, that it looked as if she were encouraging the attentions of George, Mr. Pendyce's eldest son.

Lady Malden had remarked to Mrs. Winlow in the drawing-room before dinner:

"What is it about that Mrs. Bellew? I never liked her. A woman situated as she is ought to be more careful. I don't understand her being asked here at all, with her husband still at the Firs, only just over the way. Besides, she's very hard up. She doesn't even attempt to disguise it. I call her almost an adventuress."

Mrs. Winlow had answered:

"But she's some sort of cousin to Mrs. Pendyce. The Pendyces are related to everybody! It's so boring. One never knows——"

Lady Malden replied:

"Did you know her when she was living down here? I dislike those hard-riding women. She and her husband were perfectly reckless. One heard of nothing else but what she had jumped and how she had jumped it; and she bets and goes racing. If George Pendyce is not in love with her, I'm very much mistaken. He's been seeing far too much of her in town. She's one of those women that men are always hanging about!"

At the head of his dinner-table, where before each guest was placed a menu carefully written in his eldest daughter's hand-writing, Horace Pendyce supped his soup.

"This soup," he said to Mrs. Bellew, "reminds me of your dear old father; he was extraordinarily fond of it. I had a great respect for your father—a wonderful man! I always said he was the most determined man I'd met since my own dear father, and *he* was the most obstinate man in the three kingdoms!"

He frequently made use of the expression "in the three kingdoms," which sometimes preceded a statement that his grandmother was descended from Richard III., while his grandfather came down from the Cornish giants, one of whom, he would say with a disparaging smile, had once thrown a cow over a wall.

"Your father was too much of an individualist, Mrs. Bellew. I have a lot of experience of individualism in the management of my estate, and I find that an individualist is never contented. My tenants have everything they want, but it's impossible to satisfy them. There's a fellow called Peacock, now, a most pig-headed, narrow-minded chap. I don't give in to him, of course. If he had his way, he'd go back to the old days, farm the land in his own fashion. He wants to buy it from me. Old vicious system of yeoman farming. Says his grandfather had it. He's that sort of man. I hate individualism; it's ruining England. You won't find better cottages, or better farm-buildings anywhere than on my estate. I go in for centralisation. I dare say you know what I call myself—a 'Tory Communist.' To my mind, that's the party of the future. Now, your father's motto was: 'Every man for himself!' On the land that would never do. Landlord and tenant must work together. You'll come over to Newmarket with us on Wednesday? George has a very fine horse running in the Rutlandshire—a very fine horse. He doesn't bet, I'm glad to say. If there's one thing I hate more than another, it's gambling!"

Mrs. Bellew gave him a sidelong glance, and a little ironical smile peeped out on her full red lips. But Mr. Pendyce had been called away to his soup. When he was ready to resume the conversation she was talking to his son, and the Squire, frowning, turned to the Hon. Mrs. Winlow. *Her* attention was automatic, complete, monosyllabic; she did not appear to fatigue herself by an over-sympathetic comprehension, nor was she subservient. Mr. Pendyce found her a competent listener.

"The country is changing," he said, "changing every day.

Country houses are not what they were. A great responsibility rests on us landlords. If *we* go, the whole thing goes."

What, indeed, could be more delightful than this country-house life of Mr. Pendyce; its perfect cleanliness, its busy leisure, its combination of fresh air and scented warmth, its complete intellectual repose, its essential and professional aloofness from suffering of any kind, and its soup—emblematically and above all, its soup—made from the rich remains of pampered beasts?

Mr. Pendyce thought this life the one right life; those who lived it the only right people. He considered it a *duty* to live this life, with its simple, healthy, yet luxurious curriculum, surrounded by creatures bred for his own devouring, surrounded, as it were, by a sea of soup! And that people should go on existing by the million in the towns, preying on each other, and getting continually out of work, with all those other depressing concomitants of an awkward state, distressed him. While suburban life, that living in little rows of slate-roofed houses so lamentably similar that no man of individual taste could bear to see them, he much disliked. Yet, in spite of his strong prejudice in favour of country-house life, he was not a rich man, his income barely exceeding ten thousand a year.

The first shooting-party of the season, devoted to spinneys and the outlying coverts, had been, as usual, made to synchronise with the last Newmarket Meeting, for Newmarket was within an uncomfortable distance of Worsted Skeynes; and though Mr. Pendyce had a horror of gaming, he liked to figure there and pass for a man interested in sport for sport's sake, and he was really rather proud of the fact that his son had picked up so good a horse as the Ambler promised to be for so little money, and was racing him for pure sport.

The guests had been carefully chosen. On Mrs. Winlow's right was Thomas Brandwhite (of Brown and Brandwhite), who had a position in the financial world which could not well be ignored, two places in the country, and a yacht. His long, lined face, with very heavy moustaches, wore habitually a peevish look. He had retired from his firm, and now only sat on the Boards of several companies. Next to him was Mrs. Hussell Barter, with that touching look to be seen on the faces of many English ladies, that look of women who are always doing their duty, their rather painful duty; whose eyes, above cheeks creased and withered, once rose-leaf hued, now over-coloured by strong weather, are starry and anxious; whose speech is simple, sympathetic, direct, a little shy, a little hopeless, yet always hopeful; who are ever surrounded by children, invalids, old people, all looking to them for support; who have never known the luxury of breaking down—of these was Mrs. Hussell Barter, the wife of the Reverend Hussell Barter, who would shoot to-morrow, but would not attend the race-meeting on the Wednesday. On her other hand was Gilbert Foxleigh, a lean-flanked man with a long, narrow head, strong white teeth, and hollow, thirsting eyes. He came of a county family of Foxleighs, and was one of six brothers, invaluable to the owners of coverts or young, half-broken horses in days when, as a Foxleigh would put it, "hardly a Johnny of the lot could shoot or ride for nuts." There was no species of beast, bird, or fish, that he could not and did not destroy with equal skill and enjoyment. The only thing against him was his income, which was very small. He had taken in Mrs. Brandwhite, to whom, however, he talked but little, leaving her to General Pendyce, her neighbour on the other side.

Had he been born a year before his brother, instead of a year after, Charles Pendyce would naturally have owned Worsted Skeynes, and Horace would have gone into the Army instead. As it was, having almost imperceptibly become a Major-General, he had retired, taking with him his pension. The third brother, had he chosen to be born, would have gone into the Church, where a living awaited him; he had elected otherwise, and the living had passed perforce to a collateral branch. Between Horace and Charles, seen from behind, it was difficult to distinguish. Both were spare, both erect, with the least inclination to bottle shoulders, but Charles Pendyce brushed his hair, both before and behind, away from a central parting, and about the back of his still active knees there was a look of feebleness. Seen from the front they could readily be differentiated, for the General's whiskers broadened down his cheeks till they reached his moustaches, and there was in his face and manner a sort of formal, though discontented, effacement, as of an individualist who has all his life been part of a system, from which he has issued at last, unconscious indeed of his loss, but with a vague sense of injury. He had never married, feeling it to be comparatively useless, owing to Horace having gained that year on him at the start, and he lived with a valet close to his club in Pall Mall.

In Lady Malden, whom he had taken in to dinner, Worsted

Skeynes entertained a good woman and a personality, whose teas to Working Men in the London season were famous. No Working Man who had attended them had ever gone away without a wholesome respect for his hostess. She was indeed a woman who permitted no liberties to be taken with her in any walk of life. The daughter of a Rural Dean, she appeared at her best when seated, having rather short legs. Her face was well-coloured, her mouth, firm and rather wide, her nose well-shaped, her hair dark. She spoke in a decided voice, and did not mince her words. It was to her that her husband, Sir James, owed his reactionary principles on the subject of woman.

Round the corner at the end of the table the Hon. Geoffrey Winlow was telling his hostess of the Balkan Provinces, from a tour in which he had just returned. His face, of the Norman type, with regular, handsome features, had a leisurely and capable expression. His manner was easy and pleasant; only at times it became apparent that his ideas were in perfect order, so that he would naturally not care to be corrected. His father, Lord Montrossor, whose seat was at Coldingham six miles away, would ultimately yield to him his place in the House of Lords.

And next him sat Mrs. Pendyce. A portrait of this lady hung over the sideboard at the end of the room, and though it had been painted by a fashionable painter, it had caught a gleam of that "something" still in her face these twenty years later. She was not young, her dark hair was going grey; but she was not old, for she had been married at nineteen and was still only fifty-two. Her face was rather long and very pale, and her eyebrows arched and dark and always slightly raised. Her eyes were dark grey, sometimes almost black, or the pupils dilated when she was moved; her lips were the least thing parted, and the expression of those lips and eyes was of a rather touching gentleness, of a rather touching expectancy. And yet all this was not the "something"; *that* was rather the outward sign of an inborn sense that she had no need to ask for things, of an instinctive faith that she already had them. By that "something," and by her long, transparent hands, men could tell that she had been a Totteridge. And her voice, which was rather slow, with a little, not unpleasant, trick of speech, and her eyelids by second nature just a trifle lowered, confirmed this impression. Over her bosom, which hid the heart of a lady, rose and fell a piece of wonderful old lace.

Round the corner again Sir James Malden and Bee Pendyce

(the oldest daughter) were talking of horses and hunting—Bee seldom from choice spoke of anything else. Her face was pleasant and good, yet not quite pretty, and this little fact seemed to have entered into her very nature, making her shy and ever willing to do things for others.

Sir James had small grey whiskers and a carved, keen visage. He came of an old Kentish family which had migrated to Cambridgeshire; his coverts were exceptionally fine; he was also a Justice of the Peace, a Colonel of Yeomanry, a keen Churchman, and much feared by poachers. He held the reactionary views already mentioned, being a little afraid of Lady Malden.

Beyond Miss Pendyce sat the Reverend Hussell Barter, who would shoot to-morrow, but would not attend the race-meeting on Wednesday.

The Rector of Worsted Skeynes was not tall, and his head had been rendered somewhat bald by thought. His broad face, of very straight build from the top of the forehead to the base of the chin, was well-coloured, clean-shaven, and of a shape that may be seen in portraits of the Georgian era. His cheeks were full and folded, his lower lip had a habit of protruding, and his eyebrows jutted out above his full, light eyes. His manner was authoritative, and he articulated his words in a voice to which long service in the pulpit had imparted remarkable carrying-power—in fact, when engaged in private conversation, it was with difficulty that he was not overheard. Perhaps even in confidential matters he was not unwilling that what he said should bear fruit. In some ways, indeed, he was typical. Uncertainty, hesitation, toleration—except of such opinions as he held—he did not like. Imagination he distrusted. He found his duty in life very clear, and other people's perhaps clearer, and he did not encourage his parishioners to think for themselves. The habit seemed to him a dangerous one. He was outspoken in his opinions, and when he had occasion to find fault, spoke of the offender as " a man of no character," " a fellow like that," with such a ring of conviction that his audience could not but be convinced of the immorality of that person. He had a bluff jolly way of speaking, and was popular in his parish—a good cricketer, a still better fisherman, a fair shot, though, as he said, he could not really afford time for shooting. While disclaiming interference in secular matters, he watched the tendencies of his flock from a sound point of view, and especially encouraged them to support the existing order of things—the

British Empire and the English Church. His cure was hereditary, and he fortunately possessed some private means, for he
had a large family. His partner at dinner was Norah, the
younger of the two Pendyce girls, who had a round, open face,
and a more decided manner than her sister Bee.

Her brother George, the eldest son, sat on her right. George
was of middle height, with a red-brown, clean-shaved face and
solid jaw. His eyes were grey; he had firm lips, and darkish,
carefully brushed hair, a little thin on the top, but with that
peculiar gloss seen on the hair of some men about town. His
clothes were unostentatiously perfect. Such men may be seen
in Piccadilly at any hour of the day or night. He had been
intended for the Guards, but had failed to pass the necessary
examination, through no fault of his own, owing to a constitu-
tional inability to spell. Had he been his younger brother
Gerald, he would probably have fulfilled the Pendyce tradition,
and passed into the Army as a matter of course. And had
Gerald (now Captain Pendyce) been George the elder son, he
might possibly have failed. George lived at his club in town
on an allowance of six hundred a year, and sat a great deal in
a bay-window reading Ruff's "Guide to the Turf."

He raised his eyes from the menu and looked stealthily round.
Helen Bellew was talking to his father, her white shoulder
turned a little away. George was proud of his composure, but
there was a strange longing in his face. She gave, indeed, just
excuse for people to consider her too good-looking for the position in which she was placed. Her figure was tall and supple
and full, and now that she no longer hunted was getting fuller.
Her hair, looped back in loose bands across a broad low brow,
had a peculiar soft lustre. There was a touch of sensuality
about her lips. The face was too broad across the brow and
cheekbones, but the eyes were magnificent—ice-grey, sometimes
almost green, always luminous, and set in with dark lashes.

There was something pathetic in George's gaze, as of a man
forced to look against his will.

It had been going on all that past summer, and still he did
not know where he stood. Sometimes she seemed fond of him,
sometimes treated him as though he had no chance. That which
he had begun as a game was now deadly earnest. And this in
itself was tragic. That comfortable ease of spirit which is
the breath of life was taken away; he could think of nothing
but her. Was she one of those women who feed on men's

admiration, and give them no return? Was she only waiting to make her conquest more secure? These riddles he asked of her face a hundred times, lying awake in the dark. To George Pendyce, a man of the world, unaccustomed to privation, whose simple creed was " Live and enjoy," there was something terrible about a longing which never left him for a moment, which he could not help any more than he could help eating, the end of which he could not see. He had known her when she lived at the Firs, he had known her in the hunting-field, but his passion was only of last summer's date. It had sprung suddenly out of a flirtation started at a dance.

A man about town does not psychologise himself; he accepts his condition with touching simplicity. He is hungry; he must be fed. He is thirsty; he must drink. Why he is hungry, when he became hungry, these inquiries are beside the mark. No ethical aspect of the matter troubled him; the attainment of a married woman, not living with her husband, did not impinge upon his creed. What would come after, though full of unpleasant possibilities, he left to the future. His real disquiet, far nearer, far more primitive and simple, was the feeling of drifting helplessly in a current so strong that he could not keep his feet.

" Ah yes; a bad case. Dreadful thing for the Sweetenhams! That young fellow's been obliged to give up the Army. Can't think what old Sweetenham was about. He must have known his son was hit. I should say Bethany himself was the only one in the dark. There's no doubt Lady Rose was to blame! " Mr. Pendyce was speaking.

Mrs. Bellew smiled.

" My sympathies are all with Lady Rose. What do you say, George "

George frowned.

" I always thought," he said, " that Bethany was an ass."

" George," said Mr. Pendyce, " is immoral. All young men are immoral. I notice it more and more. You've given up your hunting, I hear."

Mrs. Bellew sighed.

" One can't hunt on next to nothing! "

" Ah, you live in London. London spoils everybody. People don't take the interest in hunting and farming they used to. I can't get George here at all. Not that I'm a believer in apron-strings. Young men will be young men! "

Thus summing up the laws of Nature, the Squire resumed his knife and fork.

But neither Mrs. Bellew nor George followed his example; the one sat with her eyes fixed on her plate and a faint smile playing on her lips, the other sat without a smile, and his eyes, in which there was such a deep resentful longing, looked from his father to Mrs. Bellew, and from Mrs. Bellew to his mother. And as though down that vista of faces and fruits and flowers a secret current had been set flowing, Mrs. Pendyce nodded gently to her son.

CHAPTER II

THE COVERT SHOOT

AT the head of the breakfast-table sat Mr. Pendyce, eating methodically. He was somewhat silent, as became a man who has just read family prayers; but about that silence, and the pile of half-opened letters on his right, was a hint of autocracy.

" Be informal—do what you like, dress as you like, sit where you like, eat what you like, drink tea or coffee, but——" Each glance of his eyes, each sentence of his sparing, semi-genial talk, seemed to repeat that "but."

At the foot of the breakfast-table sat Mrs. Pendyce behind a silver urn which emitted a gentle steam. Her hands worked without ceasing amongst cups, and while they worked her lips worked too in spasmodic utterances that never had any reference to herself. Pushed a little to her left and entirely neglected, lay a piece of dry toast on a small white plate. Twice she took it up, buttered a bit of it, and put it down again. Once she rested, and her eyes, which fell on Mrs. Bellew, seemed to say: " How very charming you look, my dear ! " Then, taking up the sugar-tongs, she began again.

On the long sideboard covered with a white cloth reposed a number of edibles only to be found amongst that portion of the community which breeds creatures for its own devouring. At one end of this row of viands was a large game pie with a tri-angular gap in the pastry; at the other, on two oval dishes, lay four cold partridges in various stages of decomposition. Behind them a silver basket of openwork design was occupied by three bunches of black, one bunch of white grapes, and a silver grape-cutter, which performed no function (it was so blunt), but had once belonged to a Totteridge and wore their crest.

No servants were in the room, but the side-door was now and again opened, and something brought in, and this suggested that behind the door persons were collected, only waiting to be called upon. It was, in fact, as though Mr. Pendyce had said: " A butler and two footmen at least could hand you things, but this is a simple country house."

At times a male guest rose, napkin in hand, and said to a

15

lady: "Can I get you anything from the sideboard?" Being refused, he went and filled his own plate. Three dogs—two fox-terriers and a decrepit Skye—circled round uneasily, smelling at the visitors' napkins. And there went up a hum of talk in which sentences like these could be distinguished: "Rippin' stand that, by the wood. D'you remember your rockettin' wood-cock last year, Jerry?" "And the dear old Squire never touched a feather! Did you, Squire?" "Dick—Dick! Bad dog!—come and do your tricks. Trust—trust! Paid for! Isn't he rather a darling?"

On Mr. Pendyce's foot, or by the side of his chair, whence he could see what was being eaten, sat the spaniel John, and now and then Mr. Pendyce, taking a small portion of something between his finger and thumb, would say:

"John!—Make a good breakfast, Sir James; I always say a half-breakfasted man is no good!"

And Mrs. Pendyce, her eyebrows lifted, would look anxiously up and down the table, murmuring: "Another cup, dear; let me see—are you sugar?"

When all had finished a silence fell, as if each sought to get away from what he had been eating, as if each felt he had been engaged in an unworthy practice; then Mr. Pendyce, finishing his last grape, wiped his mouth.

"You've a quarter of an hour, gentlemen; we start at ten-fifteen."

Mrs. Pendyce, left seated with a vague, ironical smile, ate one mouthful of her buttered toast, now very old and leathery, gave the rest to "the dear dogs," and called:

"George! You want a new shooting tie, dear boy; that green one's quite faded. I've been meaning to get some silks down for ages. Have you had any news of your horse this morning?"

"Yes, Blacksmith says he's fit as a fiddle."

"I do so hope he'll win that race for you. Your Uncle Hubert once lost four thousand pounds over the Rutlandshire. I remember perfectly; my father had to pay it. I'm so glad you don't bet, dear boy!"

"My dear mother, I do bet."

"Oh, George, I hope not much! For goodness' sake, don't tell your father: he's like all the Pendyces, can't bear a risk."

"My dear mother, I'm not likely to; but, as a matter of fact, there is no risk. I stand to win a lot of money to nothing."

"But, George, is that right?"

"Of course it's all right."

"Oh, well, I don't understand." Mrs. Pendyce dropped her eyes, a flush came into her white cheeks; she looked up again and said quickly: "George, I *should* like just a little bet on your horse—a *real* bet, say about a sovereign."

George Pendyce's creed permitted the show of no emotion. He smiled.

"All right, mother, I'll put it on for you. It'll be about eight to one."

"Does that mean that if he wins I shall get eight?"

George nodded.

Mrs. Pendyce looked abstractedly at his tie.

"I think it might be two sovereigns; one seems very little to lose, because I do so want him to win. Isn't Helen Bellew perfectly charming this morning! It's delightful to see a woman look her best in the morning."

George turned, to hide the colour in his cheeks.

"She looks fresh enough, certainly."

Mrs. Pendyce glanced up at him; there was a touch of quizzicality in one of her lifted eyebrows.

"I mustn't keep you, dear; you'll be late for the shooting."

Mr. Pendyce, a sportsman of the old school, who still kept pointers, which, in the teeth of modern fashion, he was unable to employ, set his face against the use of two guns.

"Any man," he would say, "who cares to shoot at Worsted Skeynes must do with one gun, as my dear old father had to do before me. He'll get a good day's sport—no barndoor birds" (for he encouraged his pheasants to remain lean, that they might fly the better), "but don't let him expect one of these battues—sheer butchery, I call them."

He was excessively fond of birds—it was, in fact, his hobby, and he had collected under glass cases a prodigious number of specimens of those species which are in danger of becoming extinct, having really, in some Pendycean sort of way, a feeling that by this practice he was doing them a good turn, championing them, as it were, to a world that would soon be unable to look upon them in the flesh. He wished, too, that his collection should become an integral part of the estate, and be passed on to his son, and his son's son after him.

"Look at this Dartford Warbler," he would say; "beautiful little creature—getting rarer every day. I had the greatest difficulty in procuring this specimen. You wouldn't believe me if I told you what I had to pay for him!"

Some of his unique birds he had shot himself, having in his youth made expeditions to foreign countries solely with this object, but the great majority he had been compelled to purchase. In his library were row upon row of books carefully arranged and bearing on this fascinating subject; and his collection of rare, almost extinct, birds' eggs was one of the finest in the "three kingdoms." One egg especially he would point to with pride as the last obtainable of that particular breed. "This was procured," he would say, "by my dear old gillie Angus out of the bird's very nest. There was just the single egg. The species," he added, tenderly handling the delicate, porcelain-like oval in his brown hand covered with very fine, blackish hairs, "is now extinct." He was, in fact, a true bird-lover, strongly condemning cockneys, or rough, ignorant persons who, with no collections of their own, wantonly destroyed kingfishers, or scarce birds of any sort, out of pure stupidity. "I would have them flogged," he would say, for he believed that no such bird should be killed except on commission, and for choice— barring such extreme cases as that Dartford Warbler—in some foreign country or remoter part of the British Isles. It was indeed illustrative of Mr. Pendyce's character and whole point of view that whenever a rare, winged stranger appeared on his own estate it was talked of as an event, and preserved alive with the greatest care, in the hope that it might breed and be handed down with the property; but if it were personally known to belong to Mr. Fuller or Lord Quarryman, whose estates abutted on Worsted Skeynes, and there was grave and imminent danger of its going back, it was promptly shot and stuffed, that it might not be lost to posterity. An encounter with another landowner having the same hobby, of whom there were several in his neighbourhood, would upset him for a week, making him strangely morose, and he would at once redouble his efforts to add something rarer than ever to his own collection.

His arrangements for shooting were precisely conceived. Little slips of paper with the names of the "guns" written thereon were placed in a hat, and one by one drawn out again, and this he always did himself. Behind the right wing of the house he held a review of the beaters, who filed before him out of the yard, each with a long stick in his hand, and no expression on his face. Five minutes of directions to the keeper, and then

the guns started, carrying their own weapons and a sufficiency
of cartridges for the first drive in the old way.

A misty radiance clung over the grass as the sun dried the
heavy dew; the thrushes hopped and ran and hid themselves,
the rooks cawed peacefully in the old elms. At an angle the
game cart, constructed on Mr. Pendyce's own pattern, and drawn
by a hairy horse in charge of an aged man, made its way slowly
to the end of the first beat.

George lagged behind, his hands deep in his pockets, drinking
in the joy of the tranquil day, the soft bird sounds, so clear
and friendly, that chorus of wild life. The scent of the coverts
stole to him, and he thought:

'What a ripping day for shooting!'

The Squire, wearing a suit carefully coloured so that no bird
should see him, leather leggings, and a cloth helmet of his own
devising, ventilated by many little holes, came up to his son;
and the spaniel John, who had a passion for the collection of
birds almost equal to his master's, came up too.

"You're end gun, George," he said; "you'll get a nice high
bird!"

George felt the ground with his feet, and blew a speck of
dust off his barrels, and the smell of the oil sent a delicious
tremor darting through him. Everything, even Helen Bellew,
was forgotten. Then in the silence rose a far-off clamour; a
cock pheasant, skimming low, his plumage silken in the sun,
dived out of the green and golden spinney, curled to the right,
and was lost in undergrowth. Some pigeons passed over at a
great height. The tap-tap of sticks beating against trees began;
then with a fitful rushing noise a pheasant came straight out.
George threw up his gun and pulled. The bird stopped in
mid-air, jerked forward, and fell headlong into the grass sods
with a thud. In the sunlight the dead bird lay, and a smirk of
triumph played on George's lips. He was feeling the joy of
life.

During his covert shoots the Squire had the habit of recording
his impressions in a mental note-book. He put special marks
against such as missed, or shot birds behind the waist, or placed
lead in them to the detriment of their market value, or broke
only one leg of a hare at a time, causing the animal to cry like
a tortured child, which some men do not like; or such as,

"wiped an important neighbour's eye," or shot too many beaters in the legs. Against this evidence, however, he unconsciously weighed the more undeniable social facts, such as the title of Winlow's father; Sir James Malden's coverts, which must also presently be shot; Thomas Brandwhite's position in the financial world; General Pendyce's relationship to himself; and the importance of the English Church. Against Foxleigh alone he could put no marks. The fellow destroyed everything that came within reach with utter precision, and this was perhaps fortunate, for Foxleigh had neither title, coverts, position, nor cloth! And the Squire weighed one thing else besides—the pleasure of giving them all a good day's sport, for his heart was kind.

The sun had fallen well behind the home wood when the guns stood waiting for the last drive of the day. From the keeper's cottage in the hollow, where late threads of crimson clung in the brown network of Virginia creeper, rose a mist of wood smoke, dispersed upon the breeze. Sound there was none, only that faint stir—the far, far callings of men and beasts and birds—that never quite dies of a country evening. High above the wood some startled pigeons were still wheeling, no other life in sight; but a gleam of sunlight stole down the side of the covert and laid a burnish on the turned leaves till the whole wood seemed quivering with magic. Out of that quivering wood a wounded rabbit had stolen and was dying. It lay on its side on the slope of a tussock of grass, its hind legs drawn under it, its forelegs raised like the hands of a praying child. Motionless as death, all its remaining life was centred in its black soft eyes. Uncomplaining, ungrudging, unknowing, with that poor soft wandering eye, it was going back to Mother Earth. There Foxleigh, too, some day must go, asking of Nature why she had murdered him.

CHAPTER III

THE BLISSFUL HOUR

IT was the hour between tea and dinner, when the spirit of the country house was resting, conscious of its virtue, half asleep.

Having bathed and changed, George Pendyce took his betting-book into the smoking-room. In a nook devoted to literature, protected from draught and intrusion by a high leather screen, he sat down in an armchair and fell into a doze.

With legs crossed, his chin resting on one hand, his comely figure relaxed, he exhaled a fragrance of soap, as though in this perfect peace his soul were giving off its natural odour. His spirit, on the borderland of dreams, trembled with those faint stirrings of chivalry and aspiration, the outcome of physical well-being after a long day in the open air, the outcome of security from all that is unpleasant and fraught with danger. He was awakened by voices.

" George is not a bad shot ! "

" Gave a shocking exhibition at the last stand; Mrs. Bellew was with him. They were going over him like smoke; he couldn't touch a feather."

It was Winlow's voice. A silence, then Thomas Brandwhite's:

" A mistake, the ladies coming out. I never will have them myself. What do you say, Sir James ? "

" Bad principle—very bad "

A laugh—Thomas Brandwhite's laugh, the laugh of a man never quite sure of himself.

" That fellow Bellew is a cracked chap. They call him the ' desperate character ' about here. Drinks like a fish, and rides like the devil. *She* used to go pretty hard, too. I've noticed there's always a couple like that in a hunting country. Did you ever see him ? Thin, high-shouldered, white-faced chap, with little dark eyes and a red moustache."

" She's still a young woman ? "

" Thirty or thirty-two."

" How was it they didn't get on ? "

The sound of a match being struck.

21

" Case of the kettle and the pot."

"It's easy to see she's fond of admiration. Love of admiration plays old Harry with women ! "

Winlow's leisurely tones again:

" There was a child, I believe, and it died. And after that —I know there was some story; you never could get to the bottom of it. Bellew chucked his regiment in consequence. She's subject to moods, they say, when nothing's exciting enough; must skate on thin ice, must have a man skating after her. If the poor devil weighs more than she does, in he goes."

" That's like her father, old Cheriton. I knew him at the club—one of the old sort of squires; married his second wife at sixty and buried her at eighty. Old ' Claret and Piquet,' they called him; had more children under the rose than any man in Devonshire. I saw him playing half-crown points the week before he died. It's in the blood. What's George's weight? —ah, ha ! "

" It's no laughing matter, Brandwhite. There's time for a hundred up before dinner if you care for a game, Winlow? "

The sound of chairs drawn back, of footsteps, and the closing of a door. George was alone again, a spot of red in either of his cheeks. Those vague stirrings of chivalry and aspiration were gone, and gone that sense of well-earned ease. He got up, came out of his corner, and walked to and fro on the tiger-skin before the fire. He lit a cigarette, threw it away, and lit another.

Skating on thin ice! That would not stop him! Their gossip would not stop him, nor their sneers; they would but send him on the faster!

He threw away the second cigarette. It was strange for him to go to the drawing-room at this hour of the day, but he went.

Opening the door quietly, he saw the long, pleasant room' lighted with tall oil-lamps, and Mrs. Bellew seated at the piano, singing. The tea-things were still on a table at one end, but every one had finished. As far away as might be, in the embrasure of the bay-window, General Pendyce and Bee were playing chess. Grouped in the centre of the room, by one of the lamps, Lady Malden, Mrs. Winlow, and Mrs. Brandwhite had turned their faces towards the piano, and a sort of slight unwillingness or surprise showed on those faces, a sort of " We were having a most interesting talk; I don't think we ought to have been stopped" expression.

Before the fire, with his long legs outstretched, stood Gerald Pendyce. And a little apart, her dark eyes fixed on the singer, and a piece of embroidery in her lap, sat Mrs. Pendyce, on the edge of whose skirt lay Roy, the old Skye terrier.

> "But had I wist, before I kist,
>   That love had been sae ill to win;
> I had lockt my heart in a case of gowd
>   And pinn'd it with a siller pin. . . .
> O waly waly, but love be bonny
>   A little time while it is new,
> But when 'tis auld, it waxeth cauld
>   And fades awa' like morning dew."

This was the song George heard, trembling and dying to the chords of the fine piano that was a little out of tune.

He gazed at the singer, and though he was not musical, there came a look into his eyes that he quickly hid away.

A slight murmur occurred in the centre of the room, and from the fireplace Gerald called out, "Thanks; that's rippin'!"

The voice of General Pendyce rose in the bay-window: "Check!"

Mrs. Pendyce, taking up her embroidery, on which a tear had dropped, said gently:

"Thank you, dear; most charming!"

Mrs. Bellew left the piano, and sat down beside her. George moved into the bay-window. He knew nothing of chess—indeed, he could not stand the game; but from here, without attracting attention, he could watch Mrs. Bellew.

The air was drowsy and sweet-scented; a log of cedar-wood had just been put on the fire; the voices of his mother and Mrs. Bellew, talking of what he could not hear, the voices of Lady Malden, Mrs. Brandwhite, and Gerald, discussing some neighbours, of Mrs. Winlow dissenting or assenting in turn, all mingled in a comfortable, sleepy sound, clipped now and then by the voice of General Pendyce calling, "Check!" and of Bee saying, "Oh, uncle!"

A feeling of rage rose in George. Why should they all be so comfortable and cosy while this perpetual fire was burning in himself? And he fastened his moody eyes on her who was keeping him thus dancing to her pipes.

He made an awkward movement which shook the chess-table. The General said behind him: "Look out, George! What— what!"

George went up to his mother.

"Let's have a look at that, Mother."

Mrs. Pendyce leaned back in her chair and handed up her work with a smile of pleased surprise.

"My dear boy, you won't understand it a bit. It's for the front of my new frock."

George took the piece of work. He did not understand it, but turning and twisting it he could breathe the warmth of the woman he loved. In bending over the embroidery he touched Mrs. Bellew's shoulder; it was not drawn away, a faint pressure seemed to answer his own. His mother's voice recalled him:

"Oh, my needle, dear! It's so sweet of you, but perhaps——"

George handed back the embroidery. Mrs. Pendyce received it with a grateful look. It was the first time he had ever shown an interest in her work.

Mrs. Bellew had taken up a palm-leaf fan to screen her face from the fire. She said slowly:

"If we win to-morrow I'll embroider you something, George."

"And if we lose?"

Mrs. Bellew raised her eyes, and involuntarily George moved so that his mother could not see the sort of slow mesmerism that was in them.

"If we lose," she said, "I shall sink into the earth. We must win, George."

He gave an uneasy little laugh, and glanced quickly at his mother. Mrs. Pendyce had begun to draw her needle in and out with a half-startled look on her face.

"That's a most haunting little song you sang, dear," she said.

Mrs. Bellew answered: "The words are so true, aren't they?"

George felt her eyes on him, and tried to look at her, but those half-smiling, half-threatening eyes seemed to twist and turn him about as his hands had twisted and turned about his mother's embroidery. Again across Mrs. Pendyce's face flitted that half-startled look.

Suddenly General Pendyce's voice was heard saying very loud: "Stale? Nonsense, Bee, nonsense! Why, damme, so it is!"

A hum of voices from the centre of the room covered up that outburst, and Gerald, stepping to the hearth, threw another cedar log upon the fire. The smoke came out in a puff.

Mrs. Pendyce leaned back in her chair smiling, and wrinkling her fine, thin nose.

"Delicious!" she said, but her eyes did not leave her son's face, and in them was still that vague alarm.

CHAPTER IV

THE HAPPY HUNTING-GROUND

OF all the places where, by a judicious admixture of whip and spur, oats and whisky, horses are caused to place one leg before another with unnecessary rapidity, in order that men may exchange little pieces of metal with the greater freedom, Newmarket Heath is " the topmost, and merriest, and best."

This museum of the state of flux—the secret reason of horseracing being to afford an example of perpetual motion (no proper racing-man having ever been found to regard either gains or losses in the light of an accomplished fact)—this museum of the state of flux has a climate unrivalled for the production of the British temperament.

Not without a due proportion of that essential formative of character, east wind, it has at once the hottest sun, the coldest blizzards, the wettest rain, of any place of its size in the " three kingdoms." It tends—in advance even of the City of London —to the nurture and improvement of individualism, to that desirable " I'll see you d——d " state of mind which is the proud objective of every Englishman, and especially of every country gentleman. In a word—a mother to the self-reliant secretiveness which defies intrusion and forms an integral part in the Christianity of this country—Newmarket Heath is beyond all others the happy hunting-ground of the landed classes.

In the Paddock half an hour before the Rutlandshire Handicap was to be run numbers of racing-men were gathered in little knots of two and three, describing to each other with every precaution the points of strength in the horses they had laid against, the points of weakness in the horses they had backed, or vice versa, together with the latest discrepancies of their trainers and jockeys. At the far end George Pendyce, his trainer Blacksmith, and his jockey Swells, were talking in low tones. Many people have observed with surprise the close-buttoned secrecy of all who have to do with horses. It is no matter for wonder. The horse is one of those generous and somewhat careless animals that, if not taken firmly from the first, will surely give itself away. Essential to a man who has to do with horses is a complete closeness of physiognomy, otherwise the animal will never know what is expected of him. The more that is expected of him, the closer must be the expression of his friends, or a grave fiasco may have to be deplored.

It was for these reasons that George's face wore more than its habitual composure, and the faces of his trainer and his jockey were alert, determined, and expressionless. Blacksmith, a little man, had in his hand a short notched cane, with which, contrary to expectation, he did not switch his legs. His eyelids drooped over his shrewd eyes, his upper lip advanced over the lower, and he wore no hair on his face. The jockey Swells' pinched-up countenance, with jutting eyebrows and practically no cheeks, had under George's racing-cap of "peacock blue" a subfuse hue like that of old furniture.

The Ambler had been bought out of the stud of Colonel Dorking, a man opposed on high grounds to the racing of two-year-olds, and at the age of three had never run. Showing more than a suspicion of form in one or two home trials, he ran a bye in the Fane Stakes, when obviously not up to the mark, and was then withdrawn from the public gaze. The Stable had from the start kept its eye on the Rutlandshire Handicap, and no sooner was Goodwood over than the commission was placed in the hands of Barney's, well known for their power to enlist at the most appropriate moment the sympathy of the public in a horse's favour. Almost coincidentally with the completion of the Stable Commission it was found that the public were determined to support the Ambler at any price over seven to one. Barney's at once proceeded judiciously to lay off the Stable Money, and this having been done, George found that he stood to win four thousand pounds to nothing. If he had now chosen to bet this sum against the horse at the then current price of eight to one, it is obvious that he could have made an absolute certainty of five hundred pounds, and the horse need never even have started. But George, who would have been glad enough of such a sum, was not the man to do this sort of thing. It was against the tenets of his creed. He believed, too, in his horse, and had enough of the Totteridge in him to like a race for a race's sake. Even when beaten there was enjoyment to be had out of the imperturbability with which he could take that beating, out of a sense of superiority to men not quite so sportsmanlike as himself.

"Come and see the nag saddled," he said to his brother Gerald.

In one of the long line of boxes the Ambler was awaiting his toilette, a dark-brown horse, about sixteen hands, with well-placed shoulders, straight hocks, a small head, and what is known as a rat-tail. But of all his features, the most remarkable was his eye. In the depths of that full, soft eye was an almost uncanny gleam, and when he turned it, half-circled by a moon of white, and gave bystanders that look of strange comprehension, they felt that he saw to the bottom of all this that was going on around him. He was still but three years old, and had not yet attained the age when people apply to action the fruits of understanding; yet there was little doubt that as he advanced in years he would manifest his disapproval of a system whereby men made money at his expense. And with that eye half-circled by the moon he looked at George, and in silence George looked back at him, strangely baffled by the horse's long, soft, wild gaze. On this heart beating deep within its warm, dark satin sheath, on the spirit gazing through that soft, wild eye, too much was hanging, and he turned away.

"Mount, jockeys!"

Through the crowd of hard-looking, hatted, muffled, two-legged men, those four-legged creatures in their chestnut, bay, and brown, and satin nakedness, most beautiful in all the world, filed proudly past, as though going forth to death. The last vanished through the gate, the crowd dispersed.

Down by the rails of Tattersall's George stood alone. He had screwed himself into a corner, whence he could watch through his long glasses that gay-coloured, shifting wheel at the end of the mile and more of turf. At this moment, so pregnant with the future, he could not bear the company of his fellows.

"They're off!"

He looked no longer, but hunched his shoulders, holding his elbows stiff, that none might see what he was feeling. Behind him a man said:

"The favourite's beat. What's that in blue on the rails?"

Out by himself on the far rails, out by himself, sweeping along like a home-coming bird, was the Ambler. And George's heart leaped, as a fish leaps of a summer evening out of dark pool.

"They'll never catch him. The Ambler wins! It's a walk-over! The Ambler!"

Silent amidst the shouting throng, George thought: 'My horse! my horse!' and tears of pure emotion sprang into his eyes. For a full minute he stood quite still; then, instinctively adjusting hat and tie, made his way calmly to the Paddock. He left it to his trainer to lead the Ambler back, and joined him at the weighing-room.

The little jockey was seated, nursing his saddle, negligent and saturnine, awaiting the words: "All right."

Blacksmith said quietly:

"Well, sir, we've pulled it off. Four lengths. I've told Swells he does no more riding for me. There's a gold-mine given away. What on earth was he about to come in by himself like that? We shan't get into the 'City' now under nine stone. It's enough to make a man cry!"

And, looking at his trainer, George saw the little man's lips quiver.

In his stall, streaked with sweat, his hind-legs outstretched, fretting under the ministrations of the groom, the Ambler stayed the whisking of his head to look at his owner, and once more George met that long, proud, soft glance. He laid his gloved hand on the horse's lather-flecked neck. The Ambler tossed his head and turned it away.

George came out into the open, and made his way towards the Stand. His trainer's words had instilled a drop of poison into his cup. "A gold-mine given away!"

He went up to Swells. On his lips were the words: "What made you give the show away like that?" He did not speak them, for in his soul he felt it would not become him to ask his jockey why he had not dissembled and won by a length. But the little jockey understood at once.

"Mr. Blacksmith's been at me, sir. You take my tip: he's a queer one, that 'orse. I thought it best to let him run his own race. Mark my words, *he knows what's what*. When they're like that, they're best let alone."

A voice behind him said:

"Well, George, congratulate you! Not the way I should have ridden the race myself. He should have lain off to the distance. Remarkable turn of speed that horse. There's no riding nowadays!"

The Squire and General Pendyce were standing there. Erect and slim, unlike and yet so very much alike, the eyes of both of them seemed saying:

'I shall differ from you: there are no two opinions about it. I shall differ from you!'

Behind them stood Mrs. Bellew. Her eyes could not keep still under their lashes, and their light and colour changed continually. George walked on slowly at her side. There was a look of triumph and softness about her; the colour kept deepening in her cheeks, her figure swayed. They did not look at each other.

Against the Paddock railings stood a man in riding-clothes, of spare figure, with a horseman's square, high shoulders, and thin long legs a trifle bowed. His narrow, thin-lipped, freckled face, with close-cropped sandy hair and clipped red moustache, was of a strange dead pallor. He followed the figures of George and his companion with little fiery dark-brown eyes, in which devils seemed to dance. Someone tapped him on the arm.

"Hallo, Bellew! had a good race?"

"Devil take you, no! Come and have a drink?"

Still without looking at each other, George and Mrs. Bellew walked towards the gate.

"I don't want to see any more," she said. "I should like to get away at once."

"We'll go after this race," said George. "There's nothing running in the last."

At the back of the Grand Stand, in the midst of all the hurrying crowd, he stopped.

"Helen?" he said.

Mrs. Bellew raised her eyes and looked full into his.

Long and cross-country is the drive from Royston Railway Station to Worsted Skeynes. To George Pendyce, driving the dog cart, with Helen Bellew beside him, it seemed but a minute—that strange minute when the heaven is opened and a vision shows between. To some men that vision comes but once, to some men many times. It comes after long winter, when the blossom hangs; it comes after parched summer, when the leaves are going gold; and of what hues it is painted—of frost-white and fire, of wine and purple, of mountain flowers, or the shadowy green of still deep pools—the seer alone can tell. But this is certain—the vision steals from him who looks on it all images of other things, all sense of law, of order, of the living past, and the living present. It is the future, fair-scented, singing, jewelled, as when suddenly between high banks a bough of apple-blossom hangs quivering in the wind loud with the song of bees.

George Pendyce gazed before him at this vision over the grey mare's back, and she who sat beside him muffled in her fur was touching his arm with hers. And back to them the second groom, hugging himself above the road that slipped away beneath, saw another kind of vision, for he had won five pounds, and his eyes were closed. And the grey mare saw a vision of her warm light stall, and the oats dropping between her manger bars, and fled with light hoofs along the lanes where the side-lamps shot two moving gleams over dark beech-hedges that rustled crisply in the northeast wind. Again and again she sneezed in the pleasure of that homeward flight, and the light foam of her nostrils flicked the faces of those behind. And they sat silent, thrilling at the touch of each other's arms, their cheeks glowing in the windy darkness, their eyes shining and fixed before them.

The second groom awoke suddenly from his dream.

"If I owned that 'orse, like Mr. George, and had such a topper as this 'ere Mrs. Bellew beside me, would I be sittin' there without a word?"

CHAPTER V

MRS. PENDYCE'S DANCE

MRS. PENDYCE believed in the practice of assembling county society for the purpose of inducing it to dance, a hardy enterprise in a county where the souls, and incidentally the feet, of the inhabitants were shaped for more solid pursuits. Men were her chief difficulty, for in spite of really national discouragement, it was rare to find a girl who was not "fond of dancing."

"Ah, dancing; I did so love it! Oh, *poor* Cecil Tharp!" And with a queer little smile she pointed to a strapping red-faced youth dancing with her daughter. "He nearly trips Bee up every minute, and he hugs her so, as if he were afraid of falling on his head. Oh, dear, what a bump! It's lucky she's so nice and solid. I like to see the dear boy. Here come George and Helen Bellew. Poor George is not quite up to her form, but he's better than most of them. Doesn't she look lovely this evening?"

Lady Malden raised her glasses to her eyes by the aid of a tortoise-shell handle.

"Yes, but she's one of those women you never can look at without seeing that she has a—a—body. She's too—too—d'you see what I mean? It's almost—almost like a Frenchwoman!"

Mrs. Bellew had passed so close that the skirt of her sea-green dress brushed their feet with a swish, and a scent as of a flower-bed was wafted from it. Mrs. Pendyce wrinkled her nose.

"Much nicer. Her figure's so delicious," she said.

Lady Malden pondered.

"She's a dangerous woman. James quite agrees with me."

Mrs. Pendyce raised her eyebrows; there was a touch of scorn in that gentle gesture.

"She's a very distant cousin of mine," she said. "Her father was quite a wonderful man. It's an old Devonshire family. The Cheritons of Bovey are mentioned in Twisdom. I like young people to enjoy themselves."

A smile illumined softly the fine wrinkles round her eyes. Beneath her lavender satin bodice, with strips of black velvet

32

banding it at intervals, her heart was beating faster than usual. She was thinking of a night in her youth, when her old playfellow, young Trefane of the Blues, danced with her nearly all the evening, and of how at her window she saw the sun rise, and gently wept because she was married to Horace Pendyce.

"I always feel sorry for a woman who can dance as she does. I should have liked to have got some men from town, but Horace will only have the county people. It's not fair to the girls. It isn't so much their dancing, as their conversation—all about the first meet, and yesterday's cubbing, and to-morrow's covert-shooting, and their fox-terriers (though I'm awfully fond of the dear dogs), and then that new golf course. Really, it's quite distressing to me at times." Again Mrs. Pendyce looked out into the room with her patient smile, and two little lines of wrinkles formed across her forehead between the regular arching of her eyebrows that were still dark-brown. "They don't seem able to be gay. I feel they don't really care about it. They're only just waiting till to-morrow morning, so that they can go out and kill something. Even Bee's like that!"

Mrs. Pendyce was not exaggerating. The guests at Worsted Skeynes on the night of the Rutlandshire Handicap were nearly all county people, from the Hon. Gertrude Winlow, revolving like a faintly coloured statue, to young Tharp, with his clean face and his fair bullety head, who danced as though he were riding at a bullfinch. In a niche old Lord Quarryman, the Master of the Gaddesdon, could be discerned in conversation with Sir James Malden and the Reverend Hussell Barter.

Mrs. Pendyce said:

"Your husband and Lord Quarryman are talking of poachers; I can tell that by the look of their hands. I can't help sympathising a little with poachers."

Lady Malden dropped her eyeglasses.

"James takes a very just view of them," she said. "It's such an insidious offence. The more insidious the offence the more important it is to check it. It seems hard to punish people for stealing bread or turnips, though one must, of course; but I've no sympathy with poachers. So many of them do it for sheer love of sport!"

Mrs. Pendyce answered:

"That's Captain Maydew dancing with her now. He *is* a good dancer. Don't their steps fit? Don't they look happy? I *do* like people to enjoy themselves! There is such a dreadful lot of unnecessary sadness and suffering in the world. I think it's really all because people won't make allowances for each other."

Lady Malden looked at her sideways, pursing her lips; but Mrs. Pendyce, by race a Totteridge, continued to smile. She had been born unconscious of her neighbours' scrutinies.

"Helen Bellew," she said, "was such a lovely girl. Her grandfather was my mother's cousin. What does that make her? Anyway, my cousin, Gregory Vigil, is her first cousin once removed—the Hampshire Vigils. Do you know him?"

Lady Malden answered:

"Gregory Vigil? The man with a lot of greyish hair? I've had to do with him in the S.R.W.C."

But Mrs. Pendyce was dancing mentally.

"Such a good fellow! What is that—the——?"

Lady Malden gave her a sharp look.

"Society for the Rescue of Women and Children, of course. Surely you know about that?"

Mrs. Pendyce continued to smile.

"Ah, yes, that is nice! What a beautiful figure she has! It's so refreshing. I envy a woman with a figure like that; it looks as if it would never grow old. 'Society for the Regeneration of Women'? Gregory's so good about that sort of thing. But he never seems quite successful, have you noticed? There was a woman he was very interested in this spring. I think she drank."

"They all do," said Lady Malden; "it's the curse of the day."

Mrs. Pendyce wrinkled her forehead.

"Most of the Totteridges," she said, "were great drinkers. They ruined their constitutions. Do you know Jaspar Bellew?"

"No."

"It's such a pity he drinks. He came to dinner here once, and I'm afraid he must have come intoxicated. He took me in; his little eyes quite burned me up. He drove his dog cart into a ditch on the way home. That sort of thing gets about so. It's such a pity. He's quite interesting. Horace can't stand him."

The music of the waltz had ceased. Lady Malden put her glasses to her eyes. From close beside them George and Mrs. Bellew passed by. They moved on out of hearing, but the breeze of her fan had touched the arching hair on Lady Malden's forehead, the down on her upper lip.

"Why isn't she with her husband?" she asked abruptly.

Mrs. Pendyce lifted her brows.

"Do you concern yourself to ask that which a well-bred woman leaves unanswered?" she seemed to say, and a flush coloured her cheeks.

Lady Malden winced, but, as though it were forced through her mouth by some explosion in her soul, she said:

"You have only to look and see how dangerous she is!"

The colour in Mrs. Pendyce's cheeks deepened to a blush like a girl's.

"Every man," she said, "is in love with Helen Bellew. She's so tremendously alive. My cousin Gregory has been in love with her for years, though he *is* her guardian or trustee, or whatever they call them now. It's quite romantic. If I were a man I should be in love with her myself." The flush vanished and left her cheeks to their true colour, that of a faded rose.

Once more she was listening to the voice of young Trefane, "Ah, Margery, I love you!"—to her own half-whispered answer, "Poor boy!" Once more she was looking back through that forest of her life where she had wandered so long, and where every tree was Horace Pendyce.

"What a pity one can't always be young!" she said.

Through the conservatory door, wide open to the lawn, a full moon flooded the country with pale gold light, and in that light the branches of the cedar-trees seemed printed black on the grey-blue paper of the sky; all was cold, still witchery out there, and not very far away an owl was hooting.

The Reverend Hussell Barter, about to enter the conservatory for a breath of air, was arrested by the sight of a couple half-hidden by a bushy plant; side by side they were looking at the moonlight, and he knew them for Mrs. Bellew and George Pendyce. Before he could either enter or retire, he saw George seized her in his arms. She seemed to bend her head back, then bring her face to his. The moonlight fell on it, and on the full, white curve of her neck. The Rector of Worsted Skeynes saw, too, that her eyes were closed, her lips parted.

CHAPTER VI

INFLUENCE OF THE REVEREND HUSSELL BARTER

ALONG the walls of the smoking-room, above a leather dado, were prints of horsemen in night-shirts and night-caps, or horsemen in red coats and top-hats, with words underneath such as:

> "'Yeoicks!' says Thruster, 'Yeoicks!' says Dick.
> 'My word! these d——d Quornites shall now see the trick!'"

Two pairs of antlers surmounted the hearth, mementoes of Mr. Pendyce's deer-forest, Strathbegally, now given up, where, with the assistance of his dear old gillie Angus McBane, he had secured the heads of these monarchs of the glen. Between them was the print of a personage in trousers, with a rifle under his arm and a smile on his lips, while two large deerhounds worried a dying stag, and a lady approached him on a pony.

The Squire and Sir James Malden had retired; the remaining guests were seated round the fire. Gerald Pendyce stood at a side-table, on which was a tray of decanters, glasses, and mineral water.

"Who's for a dhrop of the craythur? A wee dhrop of the craythur? Rector, a dhrop of the craythur? George, a dhrop——"

George shook his head. A smile was on his lips, and that smile had in it a quality of remoteness, as though it belonged to another sphere, and had strayed on to the lips of this man of the world against his will. He seemed trying to conquer it, to twist his face into its habitual shape, but, like the spirit of a strange force, the smile broke through. It had mastered him, his thoughts, his habits, and his creed; he was stripped of fashion, as on a thirsty noon a man stands stripped for a cool plunge from which he hardly cares if he come up again.

And this smile, not by intrinsic merit, but by virtue of its strangeness, attracted the eye of each man in the room; so, in a crowd, the most foreign-looking face will draw all glances. The Reverend Hussell Barter with a frown watched that smile, and strange thoughts chased through his mind.

"Uncle Charles, a dhrop of the craythur—a wee dhrop of the craythur?"

General Pendyce caressed his whisker.

"The least touch," he said, "the least touch! I hear that our friend Sir Percivil is going to stand again."

Mr. Barter rose and placed his back before the fire.

"Outrageous!" he said. "He ought to be told at once that we can't have him."

The Hon. Geoffrey Winlow answered from his chair:

"If he puts up, he'll get in; they can't afford to lose him." And with a leisurely puff of smoke: "I must say, sir, I don't quite see what it has to do with his public life."

Mr. Barter thrust forth his lower lip.

"An impenitent man," he said.

"But a woman like that! What chance has a fellow if she once gets hold of him?"

"When I was stationed at Halifax," began General Pendyce, "she was the belle of the place——"

Again Mr. Barter thrust out his lower lip.

"Don't let's talk of her—the jade!" Then suddenly to George: "Let's hear your opinion, George. Dreaming of your victories, eh?" And the tone of his voice was peculiar.

But George got up.

"I'm too sleepy," he said; "good-night." Curtly nodding, he left the room.

Outside the door stood a dark oak table covered with silver candlesticks; a single candle burned thereon, and made a thin gold path in the velvet blackness. George lighted his candle, and a second gold path leaped out in front; up this he began to ascend. He carried his candle at the level of his breast, and the light shone sideways and up over his white shirt-front and the comely, bulldog face above it. It shone, too, into his eyes, grey and slightly bloodshot, as though their surfaces concealed passions violently struggling for expression. At the turning platform of the stairs he paused. In darkness above and in darkness below the country house was still; all the little life of its day, its petty sounds, movements, comings, goings, its very breathing, seemed to have fallen into sleep. The forces of its life had gathered into that pool of light where George stood listening. The beating of his heart was the only sound; in that small sound was all the pulse of this great slumbering space. He stood there long, motionless, listening to the beating of his heart, like a man fallen into a trance. Then floating up through the darkness came the echo of a laugh. George started. "The d——d parson!" he muttered, and turned up the stairs again; but now he moved like a man with a purpose, and held his candle high so that the light fell far out into the darkness. He went beyond his own room, and stood still again. The light of the candle showed the blood flushing his forehead, beating and pulsing in the veins at the side of his temples; showed, too, his lips quivering, his shaking hands. He stretched out that hand and touched the handle of a door, then stood again like a man of stone, listening for the laugh. He raised the candle, and it shone into every nook; his throat clicked, as though he found it hard to swallow. . . .

It was at Barnard Scrolls, the next station to Worsted Skeynes, on the following afternoon, that a young man entered a first-class compartment of the 3.10 train to town. The young man wore a Newmarket coat, natty white gloves, and carried an eyeglass. His face was well coloured, his chestnut moustache well brushed, and his blue eyes with their loving expression seemed to say, "Look at me—come, look at me—can anyone be better fed?" His valise and hat-box, of the best leather, bore the inscription, "E. Maydew, 8th Lancers."

There was a lady leaning back in a corner, wrapped to the chin in a fur garment, and the young man, encountering through his eyeglass her cool, ironical glance, dropped it and held out his hand.

"Ah, Mrs. Bellew, great pleasure t'see you again so soon. You goin' up to town? Jolly dance last night, wasn't it? Dear old sort, the Squire, and Mrs. Pendyce such an awf'ly nice woman."

Mrs. Bellew took his hand, and leaned back again in her corner. She was rather paler than usual, but it became her, and Captain Maydew thought he had never seen so charming a creature.

"Got a week's leave, thank goodness. Most awf'ly slow time of year. Cubbin's pretty well over, an' we don't open till the first."

He turned to the window. There in the sunlight the hedge-rows ran golden and brown away from the clouds of trailing train smoke. Young Maydew shook his head at their beauty.

" The country's still very blind," he said. " Awful pity you've given up your huntin'."

Mrs. Bellew did not trouble to answer, and it was just that certainty over herself, the cool assurance of a woman who has known the world, her calm, almost negligent eyes, that fascinated this young man. He looked at her quite shyly.

' I suppose you will become my slave,' those eyes seemed to say, ' but I can't help you, really.'

" Did you back George's horse? I had an awf'ly good race. I was at school with George. Charmin' fellow, old George."

In Mrs. Bellew's eyes something seemed to stir down in the depths, but young Maydew was looking at his glove. The handle of the carriage had left a mark that saddened him.

" You know him well, I suppose, old George? "

" Very well."

" Some fellows, if they have a good thing, keep it so jolly dark. You fond of racin', Mrs. Bellew? "

" Passionately."

" So am I." And his eyes continued, ' It's ripping to like what you like,' for, hypnotised, they could not tear themselves away from that creamy face, with its full lips and the clear, faintly smiling eyes above the high collar of white fur.

At the terminus his services were refused, and rather crestfallen, with his hat raised, he watched her walk away. But soon, in his cab, his face regained its normal look, his eyes seemed saying to the little mirror, ' Look at me—come, look at me—can anyone be better fed? '

CHAPTER VII

SABBATH AT WORSTED SKEYNES

In the white morning-room which served for her boudoir Mrs. Pendyce sat with an opened letter in her lap. It was her practice to sit there on Sunday mornings for an hour before she went to her room adjoining to put on her hat for church. It was her pleasure during that hour to do nothing but sit at the window, open if the weather permitted, and look over the home paddock and the squat spire of the village church rising among a group of elms. It is not known what she thought about at those times, unless of the countless Sunday mornings she had sat there with her hands in her lap waiting to be roused at 10.45 by the Squire's entrance and his " Now, my dear, you'll be late ! " She had sat there till her hair, once dark-brown, was turning grey; she would sit there until it was white. One day she would sit there no longer, and, as likely as not, Mr. Pendyce, still well preserved, would enter and say, " Now, my dear, you'll be late ! " having for the moment forgotten.

But this was all to be expected, nothing out of the common ; the same thing was happening in hundreds of country houses throughout the " three kingdoms," and women were sitting waiting for their hair to turn white, who, long before, at the altar of a fashionable church, had parted with their imaginations and all the changes and chances of this mortal life.

Round her chair " the dear dogs " lay—this was their practice too, and now and again the Skye (he was getting very old) would put out a long tongue and lick her little pointed shoe. For Mrs. Pendyce had been a pretty woman, and her feet were as small as ever.

Beside her on a spindley table stood a china bowl filled with dried rose-leaves, whereon had been scattered an essence smelling like sweetbriar, whose secret she had learned from her mother in the old Warwickshire home of the Totteridges, long since sold to Mr. Abraham Brightman. Mrs. Pendyce, born in the year 1840, loved sweet perfumes, and was not ashamed of using them.

The Indian summer sun was soft and bright; and wistful,

soft, and bright were Mrs. Pendyce's eyes, fixed on the letter in her lap. She turned it over and began to read again. A wrinkle visited her brow. It was not often that a letter demanding decision or involving responsibility came to her hands past the kind and just censorship of Horace Pendyce. Many matters were under her control, but were not, so to speak, connected with the outer world. Thus ran the letter:

> " S.R.W.C., HANOVER SQUARE,
> " *November* 1, 1891.

" DEAR MARGERY,

" I want to see you and talk something over, so I'm running down on Sunday afternoon. There is a train of sorts. Any loft will do for me to sleep in if your house is full, as it may be, I suppose, at this time of year. On second thoughts I will tell you what I want to see you about. You know, of course, that since her father died I am Helen Bellew's only guardian. Her present position is one in which no woman should be placed; I am convinced it ought to be put an end to. That man Bellew deserves no consideration. I cannot write of him coolly, so I won't write at all. It is two years now since they separated, entirely, as I consider, through his fault. The law has placed her in a cruel and helpless position all this time; but now, thank God, I believe we can move for a divorce. You know me well enough to realise what I have gone through before coming to this conclusion. Heaven knows if I could hit on some other way in which her future could be safeguarded, I would take it in preference to this, which is most repugnant; but I cannot. You are the only woman I can rely on to be interested in her, and I must see Bellew. Let not the fat and just Benson and his estimable horses be disturbed on my account; I will walk up and carry my toothbrush.

" Affectionately your cousin,
" GREGORY VIGIL."

Mrs. Pendyce smiled. She saw no joke, but she knew from the wording of the last sentence that Gregory saw one, and she liked to give it a welcome; so smiling and wrinkling her forehead, she mused over the letter. Her thoughts wandered. The last scandal—Lady Rose Bethany's divorce—had upset the whole county, and even now one had to be careful what one said.

Horace would not like the idea of another divorce-suit, and that so close to Worsted Skeynes. When Helen left on Thursday he had said:

"I'm not sorry she's gone. Her position is a queer one. People don't like it. The Maldens were quite——"

And Mrs. Pendyce remembered with a glow at her heart how she had broken in:

"Ellen Malden is too bourgeoise for anything!"

Nor had Mr. Pendyce's look of displeasure effaced the comfort of that word.

Poor Horace! The children took after him, except George, who took after her brother Hubert. The dear boy had gone back to his club on Friday—the day after Helen and the others went. She wished he could have stayed. She wished——The wrinkle deepened on her brow. Too much London was bad for him! Too much—— Her fancy flew to the London which she saw now only for three weeks in June and July, for the sake of the girls, just when her garden was at its best, and when really things were such a whirl that she never knew whether she was asleep or awake. It was not like London at all—not like that London under spring skies, or in early winter lamplight, where all the passers-by seemed so interesting, living all sorts of strange and eager lives, with strange and eager pleasures, running all sorts of risks, hungry sometimes, homeless even—*so* fascinating, *so* unlike——

"Now, my dear, you'll be late!"

Mr. Pendyce, in his Norfolk jacket, which he was on his way to change for a black coat, passed through the room, followed by the spaniel John. He turned at the door, and the spaniel John turned too.

"I hope to goodness Barter'll be short this morning. I want to talk to old Fox about that new chaff-cutter."

Round their mistress the three terriers raised their heads; the aged Skye gave forth a gentle growl. Mrs. Pendyce leaned over and stroked his nose.

"Roy, Roy, how *can* you, dear?"

Mr. Pendyce said:

"The old dog's losing all his teeth; he'll have to be put away."

His wife flushed painfully.

"Oh no, Horace—oh no!"

The Squire coughed.

"We must think of the dog!" he said.

Mrs. Pendyce rose, and crumpling the letter nervously, followed him from the room.

A narrow path led through the home paddock towards the church, and along it the household were making their way. The maids in feathers hurried along guiltily by twos and threes; the butler followed slowly by himself. A footman and a groom came next, leaving trails of pomatum in the air. Presently General Pendyce, in a high square-topped bowler hat, carrying a malacca cane, and Prayer-Book, appeared walking between Bee and Norah, also carrying Prayer-Books, with fox-terriers by their sides. Lastly, the Squire in a high hat, six or seven paces in advance of his wife, in a small velvet toque.

The rooks had ceased their wheeling and their cawing; the five-minutes bell, with its jerky, toneless tolling, alone broke the Sunday hush. An old horse, not yet taken up from grass, stood motionless, resting a hind-leg, with his face turned towards the footpath. Within the churchyard wicket the Rector, firm and square, a low-crowned hat tilted up on his bald forehead, was talking to a deaf old cottager. He raised his hat and nodded to the ladies; then, leaving his remark unfinished, disappeared within the vestry. At the organ Mrs. Barter was drawing out stops in readiness to play her husband into church, and her eyes, half-shining and half-anxious, were fixed intently on the vestry door.

The Squire and Mrs. Pendyce, now almost abreast, came down the aisle and took their seats beside their daughters and the General in the first pew on the left. It was high and cushioned. They knelt down on tall red hassocks. Mrs. Pendyce remained over a minute buried in thought, Mr. Pendyce rose sooner, and looking down, kicked the hassock that had been put too near the seat. Fixing his glasses on his nose, he consulted a worn old Bible, then rising, walked to the lectern and began to find the Lessons. The bell ceased; a wheezing, growling noise was heard. Mrs. Barter had begun to play; the Rector, in a white surplice, was coming in. Mr. Pendyce, with his back turned, continued to find the Lessons. The service began.

Through a plain glass window high up in the right-hand aisle the sun shot a gleam athwart the Pendyces' pew. It found its last resting-place on Mrs. Barter's face, showing her soft crumpled cheeks painfully flushed, the lines on her forehead, and those shining eyes, eager and anxious, travelling ever from her husband to her music and back again. At the least fold or frown on his face the music seemed to quiver, as to some spasm in the player's soul. In the Pendyces' pew the two girls sang loudly and with a certain sweetness. Mr. Pendyce, too, sang, and once or twice he looked in surprise at his brother, as though he were not making a creditable noise. Mrs. Pendyce did not sing, but her lips moved, and her eyes followed the millions of little dust atoms dancing in the long slanting sunbeam. Its gold path canted slowly from her, then, as by magic, vanished. Mrs. Pendyce let her eyes fall. Something had fled from her soul with the sunbeam; her lips moved no more.

The Squire sang two loud notes, spoke three, sang two again; the Psalms ceased. He left his seat, and placing his hands on the lectern's sides, leaned forward and began to read the Lesson. He read the story of Abraham and Lot, and of their flocks and herds, and how they could not dwell together, and as he read, hypnotised by the sound of his own voice, he was thinking:

'This Lesson is well read by me, Horace Pendyce. I am Horace Pendyce—Horace Pendyce. Amen, Horace Pendyce!'

And in the first pew on the left Mrs. Pendyce fixed her eyes upon him, for this was her habit, and she thought how, when the spring came again, she would run up to town, alone, and stay at Green's Hotel, where she had always stayed with her father when a girl. George had promised to look after her and take her round the theatres. And forgetting that she had thought this every autumn for the last ten years, she gently smiled and nodded. Mr. Pendyce said:

"'And I will make thy seed as the dust of the earth; so that if a man can number the dust of the earth, then shall thy seed also be numbered. Arise, walk through the land in the length of it and in the breadth of it; for I will give it unto thee. Then Abram removed his tent, and came and dwelt in the plain of Mamre, which is in Hebron, and built there an altar unto the Lord.' Here endeth the first Lesson."

The sun, reaching the second window, again shot a gold pathway athwart the church; again the millions of dust atoms danced, and the service went on.

There came a hush. The spaniel John, crouched close to the ground outside, poked his long black nose under the churchyard gate; the fox-terriers, seated patient in the grass, pricked their ears. A voice speaking on one note broke the hush. The spaniel John sighed, the fox-terriers dropped their ears, and lay down

heavily against each other. The Rector had begun to preach.
He preached on fruitfulness, and in the first right-hand pew
six of his children at once began to fidget. Mrs. Barter, sideways and unsupported on her seat, kept her starry eyes fixed on
his cheek; a line of perplexity furrowed her brow. Now and
again she moved as though her back ached. The Rector quartered his congregation with his gaze, lest any amongst them
should incline to sleep. He spoke in a loud-sounding voice.

God—he said—wished men to be fruitful, intended them to
be fruitful, commanded them to be fruitful. God—he said—
made men, and made the earth; He made man to be fruitful
in the earth; He made man neither to question nor answer nor
argue; He made him to be fruitful and possess the land. As
they had heard in that beautiful Lesson this morning, God had
set bounds, the bounds of marriage, within which man should
multiply; within those bounds it was his duty to multiply, and
that exceedingly—even as Abraham multiplied. In these days
dangers, pitfalls, snares, were rife; in these days men went
about and openly, unashamedly advocated shameful doctrines.
Let them beware. It would be his sacred duty to exclude such
men from within the precincts of that parish entrusted to his
care by God. In the language of their greatest poet, " Such men
were dangerous "—dangerous to Christianity, dangerous to their
country, and to national life. They were not brought into this
world to follow sinful inclination, to obey their mortal reason.
God demanded sacrifices of men. Patriotism demanded sacrifices of men, it demanded that they should curb their inclinations and desires. It demanded of them their first duty as men
and Christians, the duty of being fruitful and multiplying, in
order that they might till this fruitful earth, not selfishly, not
for themselves alone. It demanded of them the duty of multiplying in order that they and their children might be equipped
to smite the enemies of their Queen and country, and uphold
the name of England in whatever quarrel, against all who rashly
sought to drag her flag in the dust.

The Squire opened his eyes and looked at his watch. Folding
his arms, he coughed, for he was thinking of the chaff-cutter.
Beside him Mrs. Pendyce, with her eyes on the altar, smiled
as if in sleep. She was thinking, ' Skyward's in Bond Street
used to have lovely lace. Perhaps in the spring I could——
Or there was Goblin's, their *Point de Venise*——'

Behind them, four rows back, an aged cottage woman, as

upright as a girl, sat with a rapt expression on her carved old face. She never moved, her eyes seemed drinking in the movements of the Rector's lips, her whole being seemed hanging on his words. It is true her dim eyes saw nothing but a blur, her poor deaf ears could not hear one word, but she sat at the angle she was used to, and thought of nothing at all. And perhaps it was better so, for she was near her end.

Outside the churchyard, in the sun-warmed grass, the foxterriers lay one against the other, pretending to shiver, with their small bright eyes fixed on the church door, and the rubbery nostrils of the spaniel John worked ever busily beneath the wicket gate.

CHAPTER VIII

GREGORY VIGIL PROPOSES

ABOUT three o'clock that afternoon a tall man walked up the avenue at Worsted Skeynes, in one hand carrying his hat, in the other a small brown bag. He stopped now and then, and took deep breaths, expanding the nostrils of his straight nose. He had a fine head, with wings of grizzled hair. His clothes were loose, his stride was springy. Standing in the middle of the drive, taking those long breaths, with his moist blue eyes upon the sky, he excited the attention of a robin, who ran out of a rhododendron to see, and when he had passed began to whistle. Gregory Vigil turned, and screwed up his humorous lips, and, except that he was completely lacking in *embonpoint,* he had a certain resemblance to this bird, which is supposed to be peculiarly British.

He asked for Mrs. Pendyce in a high, light voice, very pleasant to the ear, and was at once shown to the white morning-room.

She greeted him affectionately, like many women who have grown used to hearing from their husbands the formula " Oh! *your* people! "—she had a strong feeling for her kith and kin.

" You know, Grig," she said, when her cousin was seated, " your letter was rather disturbing. Her separation from Captain Bellew has caused such a lot of talk about here. Yes; it's very common, I know, that sort of thing, but Horace is so——! All the squires and parsons and county people we get about here are just the same. Of course, I'm very fond of her, she's so charming to look at; but, Gregory, I really don't dislike her husband. He's a desperate sort of person—I think that's rather refreshing; and you know I *do* think she's a little like him in that! "

The blood rushed up into Gregory Vigil's forehead; he put his hand to his head, and said:

" Like him? Like that man? Is a rose like an artichoke? "

Mrs. Pendyce went on:

" I enjoyed having her here immensely. It's the first time she's been here since she left the Firs. How long is that? Two

47

years? But you know, Grig, the Maldens were quite upset about her. Do you think a divorce is really necessary?"

Gregory Vigil answered: "I'm afraid it is."

Mrs. Pendyce met her cousin's gaze serenely; if anything, her brows were uplifted more than usual; but, as at the stirring of secret trouble, her fingers began to twine and twist. Before her rose a vision of George and Mrs. Bellew side by side. It was a vague maternal feeling, an instinctive fear. She stilled her fingers, let her eyelids droop, and said:

".Of course, dear Grig, if I can help you in any way—Horace does so dislike anything to do with the papers."

Gregory Vigil drew in his breath.

"The papers!" he said. "How hateful it is! To think that our civilisation should allow women to be cast to the dogs! Understand, Margery, I'm thinking of her. In this matter I'm not capable of considering anything else."

Mrs. Pendyce murmured: "Of course, dear Grig, I quite understand."

"Her position is odious; a woman should not have to live like that, exposed to everyone's foul gossip."

"But, dear Grig, I don't think she minds; she seemed to me in such excellent spirits."

Gregory ran his fingers through his hair.

"Nobody understands her," he said; "she's so plucky!"

Mrs. Pendyce stole a glance at him, and a little ironical smile flickered over her face.

"No one can look at her without seeing her spirit. But, Grig, perhaps you don't quite understand her either!"

Gregory Vigil put his hand to his head.

"I must open the window a moment," he said.

Again Mrs. Pendyce's fingers began twisting, again she stilled them.

"We were quite a large party last week, and now there's only Charles. Even George has gone back; he'll be so sorry to have missed you!"

Gregory neither turned nor answered, and a wistful look came into Mrs. Pendyce's face.

"It was so nice for the dear boy to win that race! I'm afraid he bets rather! It's such a comfort Horace doesn't know."

Still Gregory did not speak.

Mrs. Pendyce's face lost its anxious look, and gained a sort of gentle admiration.

"Dear Grig," she said, "where do you go about your hair? It *is* so nice and long and wavy!"

Gregory turned with a blush.

"I've been wanting to get it cut for ages. Do you really mean, Margery, that your husband can't realise the position she's placed in?"

Mrs. Pendyce fixed her eyes on her lap.

"You see, Grig," she began, "she was here a good deal before she left the Firs, and, of course, she's related to me—though it's very distant. With those horrid cases, you never know what will happen. Horace is certain to say that she ought to go back to her husband; or, if that's impossible, he'll say she ought to think of Society. Lady Rose Bethany's case has shaken everybody, and Horace *is* nervous. I don't know how it is, there's a great feeling amongst people about here against women asserting themselves. You should hear Mr. Barter and Sir James Malden, and dozens of others; the funny thing is that the women take their side. Of course, it seems odd to me, because so many of the Totteridges ran away, or did something funny. I can't help sympathising with her, but I have to think of—of——In the country, you don't know how things that people do get about before they've done them! There's only that and hunting to talk of."

Gregory Vigil clutched at his head.

"Well, if this is what chivalry has come to, thank God I'm not a squire!"

Mrs. Pendyce's eyes flickered.

"Ah!" she said, "I've thought like that so often."

Gregory broke the silence.

"I can't help the customs of the country. My duty's plain. There's nobody else to look after her."

Mrs. Pendyce sighed, and, rising from her chair, said: "Very well, dear Grig; do let us go and have some tea."

Tea at Worsted Skeynes was served in the hall on Sundays, and was usually attended by the Rector and his wife. Young Cecil Tharp had walked over with his dog, which could be heard whimpering faintly outside the front-door.

General Pendyce, with his knees crossed and the tips of his fingers pressed together, was leaning back in his chair and staring at the wall. The Squire, who held his latest bird's-egg in his hand, was showing its spots to the Rector.

In a corner by a harmonium, on which no one ever played,

Norah talked of the village hockey club to Mrs. Barter, who sat with her eyes fixed on her husband. On the other side of the fire Bee and young Tharp, whose chairs seemed very close together, spoke of their horses in low tones, stealing shy glances at each other. The light was failing, the wood logs crackled, and now and then over the cosy hum of talk there fell short, drowsy silences—silences of sheer warmth and comfort, like the silence of the spaniel John asleep against his master's boot.

"Well," said Gregory softly, "I must go and see this man."

"Is it really necessary, Grig, to see him at all? I mean— if you've made up your mind——"

Gregory ran his hand through his hair.

"It's only fair, I think!" And crossing the hall, he let himself out so quietly that no one but Mrs. Pendyce noticed he had gone.

An hour and a half later, near the railway-station, on the road from the village back to Worsted Skeynes, Mr. Pendyce and his daughter Bee were returning from their Sunday visit to their old butler, Bigson. The Squire was talking.

"He's failing, Bee—dear old Bigson's failing. I can't hear what he says, he mumbles so; and he forgets. Fancy his forgetting that I was at Oxford. But we don't get servants like him nowadays. That chap we've got now is a sleepy fellow. Sleepy! he's—— What's that in the road? They've no business to be coming at that pace. Who is it? I can't see."

Down the middle of the dark road a dog cart was approaching at top speed. Bee seized her father's arm and pulled it vigorously, for Mr. Pendyce was standing stock-still in disapproval. The dog cart passed within a foot of him and vanished, swinging round into the station. Mr. Pendyce turned in his tracks.

"Who was that? Disgraceful! On Sunday, too! The fellow must be drunk; he nearly ran over my legs. Did you see, Bee, he nearly ran over——"

Bee answered:

"It was Captain Bellew, Father; I saw his face."

"Bellew? That drunken fellow? I shall summons him. Did you see, Bee, he nearly ran over my——"

"Perhaps he's had bad news," said Bee. "There's the train going out now; I do hope he caught it!"

"Bad news! Is that an excuse for driving over me? You hope he *caught* it? I hope he's thrown himself out. The ruffian! I hope he's killed himself."

In this strain Mr. Pendyce continued until they reached the church. On their way up the aisle they passed Gregory Vigil leaning forward with his elbows on the desk and his hand covering his eyes. . . .

At eleven o'clock that night a man stood outside the door of Mrs. Bellew's flat in Chealsea violently ringing the bell. His face was deathly white, but his little dark eyes sparkled. The door was opened, and Helen Bellew in evening dress stood there holding a candle in her hand.

"Who are you? What do you want?"

The man moved into the light.

"Jaspar! You? What on earth——"

"I want to talk."

"Talk? Do you know what time it is?"

"Time—there's no such thing. You might give me a kiss after two years. I've been drinking, but I'm not drunk."

Mrs. Bellew did not kiss him, neither did she draw back her face. No trace of alarm showed in her ice-grey eyes. She said: "If I let you in, will you promise to say what you want to say quickly, and go away?"

The little brown devils danced in Bellew's face. He nodded. They stood by the hearth in the sitting-room, and on the lips of both came and went a peculiar smile.

It was difficult to contemplate too seriously a person with whom one had lived for years, with whom one had experienced in common the range of human passion, intimacy, and estrangement, who knew all those little daily things that men and women living together know of each other, and with whom in the end, without hatred, but because of one's nature, one had ceased to live. There was nothing for either of them to find out, and with a little smile, like the smile of knowledge itself, Jaspar Bellew and Helen his wife looked at each other.

"Well," she said again; "what have you come for?"

Bellew's face had changed. Its expression was furtive; his mouth twitched; a furrow had come between his eyes.

"How—are—you?" he said in a thick, muttering voice.

Mrs. Bellew's clear voice answered:

"Now, Jaspar, what is it that you want?"

The little brown devils leaped up again in Jaspar's face.

"You look very pretty to-night!"

His wife's lips curled.

"I'm much the same as I always was," she said.

A violent shudder shook Bellew. He fixed his eyes on the floor a little beyond her to the left; suddenly he raised them. They were quite lifeless.

"I'm perfectly sober," he murmured thickly; then with startling quickness his eyes began to sparkle again. He came a step nearer.

"You're my wife!" he said.

Mrs. Bellew smiled.

"Come," she answered, "you must go!" and she put out her bare arm to push him back. But Bellew recoiled of his own accord; his eyes were fixed again on the floor a little beyond her to the left.

"What's that?" he stammered. "What's that — that black——?"

The devilry, mockery, admiration, bemusement, had gone out of his face; it was white and calm, and horribly pathetic.

"Don't turn me out," he stammered; "don't turn me out!"

Mrs. Bellew looked at him hard; the defiance in her eyes changed to a sort of pity. She took a quick step and put her hand on his shoulder.

"It's all right, old boy—all right!" she said. "There's nothing there!"

CHAPTER IX

MR. PARAMOR DISPOSES

MRS. PENDYCE, who, in accordance with her husband's wish, still occupied the same room as Mr. Pendyce, chose the ten minutes before he got up to break to him Gregory's decision. The moment was auspicious, for he was only half awake.

"Horace," she said, and her face looked young and anxious, "Grig says that Helen Bellew ought not to go on in her present position. Of course, I told him that you'd be annoyed, but Grig says that she can't go on like this, that she simply must divorce Captain Bellew."

Mr. Pendyce was lying on his back.

"What's that?" he said.

Mrs. Pendyce went on:

"I knew it would worry you; but really "—she fixed her eyes on the ceiling—"I suppose we ought only to think of her."

The Squire sat up.

"What was that," he said, "about Bellew?"

Mrs. Pendyce went on in a languid voice and without moving her eyes:

"Don't be angrier than you can help, dear; it *is* so wearing. If Grig says she ought to divorce Captain Bellew, then I'm sure she ought."

Horace Pendyce subsided on his pillow with a bounce, and he too lay with his eyes fixed on the ceiling.

"Divorce him!" he said—"I should think so! He ought to be hanged, a fellow like that. I told you last night he nearly drove over me. Living just as he likes, setting an example of devilry to the whole neighbourhood! If I hadn't kept my head he'd have bowled me over like a ninepin, and Bee into the bargain."

Mrs. Pendyce sighed.

"It *was* a narrow escape," she said.

"Divorce him!" resumed Mr. Pendyce—"I should think so! She ought to have divorced him long ago. It was the nearest thing in the world; another foot and I should have been knocked off my feet!"

53

Mrs. Pendyce withdrew her glance from the ceiling.

"At first," she said, "I wondered whether it was quite—but I'm very glad you've taken it like this."

"Taken it! I can tell you, Margery, that sort of thing makes one think. All the time Barter was preaching last night I was wondering what on earth would have happened to this estate —if——" And he looked round with a frown. "Even as it is, I barely make the two ends of it meet. As to George, he's no more fit at present to manage it than you are; he'd make a loss of thousands."

"I'm afraid George is too much in London. That's the reason I wondered whether—I'm afraid he sees too much of——"

Mrs. Pendyce stopped; a flush suffused her cheeks; she had pinched herself violently beneath the bedclothes.

"George," said Mr. Pendyce, pursuing his own thoughts, "has no gumption. He'd never manage a man like Peacock—and you encourage him! He ought to marry and settle down."

Mrs. Pendyce, the flush dying in her cheeks, said:

"George is very like poor Hubert."

Horace Pendyce drew his watch from beneath his pillow.

"Ah!" But he refrained from adding, "Your people!" for Hubert Totteridge had not been dead a year. "Ten minutes to eight! You keep me talking here; it's time I was in my bath."

Clad in pyjamas with a very wide blue stripe, grey-eyed, grey-moustached, slim and erect, he paused at the door.

"The girls haven't a scrap of imagination. What do you think Bee said? 'I hope he hasn't lost his train.' Lost his train! Good God! and I might have—I might have——" The Squire did not finish his sentence; no words but what seemed to him violent and extreme would have fulfilled his conception of the danger he had escaped, and it was against his nature and his training to exaggerate a physical risk.

At breakfast he was more cordial than usual to Gregory, who was going up by the first train, for as a rule Mr. Pendyce rather distrusted him, as one would a wife's cousin, especially if he had a sense of humour.

"A very good fellow," he was wont to say of him, "but an out-and-out Radical." It was the only label he could find for Gregory's peculiarities.

Gregory departed without further allusion to the object of his visit. He was driven to the station in a brougham by the first groom, and sat with his hat off and his head at the open window, as if trying to get something blown out of his brain. Indeed, throughout the whole of his journey up to town he looked out of the window, and expressions half humorous and half puzzled played on his face. Like a panorama slowly unrolled, country house after country house, church after church, appeared before his eyes in the autumn sunlight, among the hedgerows and the coverts that were all brown and gold; and far away on the rising uplands the slow ploughman drove, outlined against the sky.

He took a cab from the station to his solicitors' in Lincoln's Inn Fields. He was shown into a room bare of all legal accessories, except a series of Law Reports and a bunch of violets in a glass of fresh water. Edmund Paramor, the senior partner of Paramor and Herring, a clean-shaven man of sixty, with iron-grey hair brushed in a cockscomb off his forehead, greeted him with a smile.

"Ah, Vigil, how are you? Up from the country?"

"From Worsted Skeynes."

"Horace Pendyce is a client of mine. Well, what can we do for *you?* Your Society up a tree?"

Gregory Vigil, in the padded leather chair that had held so many aspirants for comfort, sat a full minute without speaking; and Mr. Paramor, too, after one keen glance at his client that seemed to come from very far down in his soul, sat motionless and grave. There was at that moment something a little similar in the eyes of these two very different men, a look of kindred honesty and aspiration. Gregory spoke at last.

"It's a painful subject to me."

Mr. Paramor drew a face on his blotting-paper.

"I have come," went on Gregory, "about a divorce for my ward."

"Mrs. Jaspar Bellew?"

"Yes; her position is intolerable."

Mr. Paramor gave him a searching look.

"Let me see: I think she and her husband have been separated for some time."

"Yes, for two years."

"You're acting with her consent, of course?"

"I have spoken to her."

"You know the law of divorce, I suppose?"

Gregory answered with a painful smile:

"I'm not very clear about it; I hardly ever look at those cases in the paper. I hate the whole idea."

Mr. Paramor smiled again, became instantly grave, and said:

"We shall want evidence of certain things. Have you got any evidence?"

Gregory ran his hand through his hair.

"I don't think there'll be any difficulty," he said. "Bellew agrees—they both agree!"

Mr. Paramor stared.

"What's that to do with it?"

Gregory caught him up.

"Surely, where both parties are anxious, and there's no opposition, it can't be difficult."

"Good Lord!" said Mr. Paramor.

"But I've seen Bellew; I saw him yesterday. I'm sure I can get him to admit anything you want!"

Mr. Paramor drew his breath between his teeth.

"Did you ever," he said drily, "hear of what's called collusion?"

Gregory got up and paced the room.

"I don't know that I've ever heard anything very exact about the thing at all," he said. "The whole subject is hateful to me. I regard marriage as sacred, and when, which God forbid, it proves unsacred, it is horrible to think of these formalities. This is a Christian country; we are all flesh and blood. What is this slime, Paramor?"

With this outburst he sank again into the chair and leaned his head on his hand. And oddly, instead of smiling, Mr. Paramor looked at him with haunting eyes.

"Two unhappy persons must not seem to agree to be parted," he said. "One must be believed to desire to keep hold of the other, and must pose as an injured person. There must be evidence of misconduct, and in this case of cruelty or of desertion. The evidence must be impartial. This is the law."

Gregory said without looking up:

"But why?"

Mr. Paramor took his violets out of the water, and put them to his nose.

"How do you mean—why?"

"I mean, why this underhand, roundabout way?"

Mr. Paramor's face changed with startling speed from its haunting look back to his smile.

"Well," he said, "for the preservation of morality. What do you suppose?"

"Do you call it moral so to imprison people that you drive them to sin in order to free themselves?"

Mr. Paramor obliterated the face on his blotting-pad.

"Where's your sense of humour?" he said.

"I see no joke, Paramor."

Mr. Paramor leaned forward.

"My dear friend," he said earnestly, "I don't say for a minute that our system doesn't cause a great deal of quite unnecessary suffering; I don't say that it doesn't need reform. Most lawyers and almost any thinking man will tell you that it does. But that's a wide question which doesn't help us here. We'll manage your business for you, if it can be done. You've made a bad start, that's all. The first thing is for us to write to Mrs. Bellew, and ask her to come and see us. We shall have to get Bellew watched."

Gregory said:

"That's detestable. Can't it be done without that?"

Mr. Paramor bit his forefinger.

"Not safe," he said. "But don't bother; we'll see to all that."

Gregory rose and went to the window. He said suddenly:

"I can't bear this underhand work."

Mr. Paramor smiled.

"Every honest man," he said, "feels as you do. But, you see, we must think of the law."

Gregory burst out again:

"Can no one get a divorce, then, without making beasts or spies of themselves?"

Mr. Paramor said gravely:

"It is difficult, perhaps impossible. You see, the law is based on certain principles."

"Principles?"

A smile wreathed Mr. Paramor's mouth, but died instantly.

"Ecclesiastical principles, and according to these a person desiring a divorce *ipso facto* loses caste. That they should have to make spies or beasts of themselves is not of grave importance."

Gregory came back to the table, and again buried his head in his hands.

"Don't joke, please, Paramor," he said; "it's all so painful to me."

Mr. Paramor's eyes haunted his client's bowed head.

"I'm not joking," he said. "God forbid! Do you read poetry?" And opening a drawer, he took out a book bound in red leather. "This is a man I'm fond of:

> "'Life is mostly froth and bubble;
> Two things stand like stone—
> KINDNESS in another's trouble,
> COURAGE in your own.'

That seems to me the sum of all philosophy."

"Paramor," said Gregory, "my ward is very dear to me; she is dearer to me than any woman I know. I am here in a most dreadful dilemma. On the one hand there is this horrible underhand business, with all its publicity; and on the other there is her position—a beautiful woman, fond of gaiety, living alone in this London, where every man's instincts and every woman's tongue look upon her as fair game. It has been brought home to me only too painfully of late. God forgive me! I have even advised her to go back to Bellew, but that seems out of the question. What am I to do?"

Mr. Paramor rose.

"I know," he said—"I know. My dear friend, I know!" And for a full minute he remained motionless, a little turned from Gregory. "It will be better," he said suddenly, "for her to get rid of him. I'll go and see her myself. We'll spare her all we can. I'll go this afternoon, and let you know the result."

As though by mutual instinct, they put out their hands, which they shook with averted faces. Then Gregory, seizing his hat, strode out of the room.

He went straight to the rooms of his Society in Hanover Square. They were on the top floor, higher than the rooms of any other Society in the building—so high, in fact, that from their windows, which began five feet up, you could practically only see the sky.

A girl with sloping shoulders, red cheeks, and dark eyes, was working a typewriter in a corner, and sideways to the sky at a bureau littered with addressed envelopes, unanswered letters, and copies of the Society's publications, was seated a grey-haired lady with a long, thin, weather-beaten face and glowing eyes, who was frowning at a page of manuscript.

"Oh, Mr. Vigil," she said, "I'm so glad you've come. This paragraph mustn't go as it is. It will never do."

Gregory took the manuscript and read the paragraph in question.

"This case of Eva Nevill is so horrible that we ask those of our women readers who live in the security, luxury perhaps, peace certainly, of their country homes, what they would have done, finding themselves suddenly in the position of this poor girl—in a great city, without friends, without money, almost without clothes, and exposed to all the craft of one of those fiends in human form who prey upon our womankind. Let each one ask herself: Should I have resisted where she fell?"

"It will never do to send that out," said the lady again.

"What is the matter with it, Mrs. Shortman?"

"It's too personal. Think of Lady Malden, or most of our subscribers. You can't expect them to imagine themselves like poor Eva. I'm sure they won't like it."

Gregory clutched at his hair.

"Is it possible they can't stand that?" he said.

"It's only because you've given such horrible details of poor Eva."

Gregory got up and paced the room.

Mrs. Shortman went on:

"You've not lived in the country for so long, Mr. Vigil, that you don't remember. You see, I know. People don't like to be harrowed. Besides, think how difficult it is for them to imagine themselves in such a position. It'll only shock them, and do our circulation harm."

Gregory snatched up the page and handed it to the girl who sat at the typewriter in the corner.

"Read that, please, Miss Mallow."

The girl read without raising her eyes.

"Well, is it what Mrs. Shortman says?"

The girl handed it back with a blush.

"It's perfect, of course, in itself, but I think Mrs. Shortman is right. It might offend some people."

Gregory went quickly to the window, threw it up, and stood gazing at the sky. Both women looked at his back.

Mrs. Shortman said gently:

"I would only just alter it like this, from after 'country

homes': 'whether they do not pity and forgive this poor girl in a great city, without friends, without money, almost without clothes, and exposed to all the craft of one of those fiends in human form who prey upon our womankind,' and just stop there."

Gregory returned to the table.

"Not 'forgive,'" he said, "not 'forgive'!"

Mrs. Shortman raised her pen.

"You don't know," she said, "what a strong feeling there is. Mind, it has to go to numbers of parsónages, Mr. Vigil. Our principle has always been to be very careful. And you *have* been plainer than usual in stating the case. It's not as if they really could put themselves in her position; that's impossible. Not one woman in a hundred could, especially among those who live in the country and have never seen life. I'm a squire's daughter myself."

"And I a parson's," said Gregory, with a smile.

Mrs. Shortman looked at him reproachfully.

"Joking apart, Mr. Vigil, it's touch and go with our paper as it is; we really can't afford it. I've had lots of letters lately complaining that we put the cases unnecessarily strongly. Here's one:

"'BOURNEFIELD RECTORY,
"'*November* 1.

"'DEAR MADAM,

"'While sympathising with your good work, I am afraid I cannot become a subscriber to your paper while it takes its present form, as I do not feel that it is always fit reading for my girls. I cannot think it either wise or right that they should become acquainted with such dreadful aspects of life, however true they may be.

"'I am, dear madam,
"'Respectfully yours,
"'WINIFRED TUDDENHAM.

"'P.S.—I could never feel sure, too, that my maids would not pick it up, and perhaps take harm.'

I had that only this morning."

Gregory buried his face in his hands, and sitting thus he looked so like a man praying that no one spoke. When he raised his face it was to say:

"Not 'forgive,' Mrs. Shortman, not 'forgive'!"

Mrs. Shortman ran her pen through the word.

"Very well, Mr. Vigil," she said; "it's a risk."

The sound of the typewriter, which had been hushed, began again from the corner.

"That case of drink, Mr. Vigil—Millicent Porter—I'm afraid there's very little hope there."

Gregory asked:

"What now?"

"Relapsed again; it's the fifth time."

Gregory turned his face to the window, and looked at the sky.

"I must go and see her. Just give me her address."

Mrs. Shortman read from a green book:

"'Mrs. Porter, 2 Bilcock Buildings, Bloomsbury.' Mr. Vigil!"

"Yes."

"Mr. Vigil, I do sometimes wish you would not persevere so long with those hopeless cases; they never seem to come to anything, and your time is *so* valuable."

"How can I give them up, Mrs. Shortman? There's no choice."

"But, Mr. Vigil, why is there no choice? You must draw the line somewhere. Do forgive me for saying that I think you sometimes waste your time."

Gregory turned to the girl at the typewriter.

"Miss Mallow, is Mrs. Shortman right? do I waste my time?"

The girl at the typewriter blushed vividly, and without looking round, said:

"How can I tell, Mr. Vigil? But it does worry one."

A humorous and perplexed smile passed over Gregory's lips.

"Now I know I shall cure her," he said. "2 Bilcock Buildings." And he continued to look at the sky. "How's your neuralgia, Mrs. Shortman?"

Mrs. Shortman smiled.

"Awful!"

Gregory turned quickly.

"You feel that window, then; I'm so sorry."

Mrs. Shortman shook her head.

"No, but perhaps Molly does."

The girl at the typewriter said:

"Oh no; please, Mr. Vigil, don't shut it for me."

"Truth and honour?"

"Truth and honour," replied both women. And all three

for a moment sat looking at the sky. Then Mrs. Shortman said:
"You see, you can't get to the root of the evil—that husband of hers."

Gregory turned.

"Ah," he said, "that man! If she could only get rid of him!
That ought to have been done long ago, before he drove her to
drink like this. Why didn't she, Mrs. Shortman, why didn't
she?"

Mrs. Shortman raised her eyes, which had such a peculiar
spiritual glow.

"I don't suppose she had the money," she said; "and she
must have been such a nice woman then. A nice woman doesn't
like to divorce——"

Gregory looked at her.

"What, Mrs. Shortman, you too, you too among the Phari-
sees?"

Mrs. Shortman flushed.

"She wanted to save him," she said; "she must have wanted
to save him."

"Then you and I——" But Gregory did not finish, and
turned again to the window. Mrs. Shortman, too, biting her
lips, looked anxiously at the sky.

Miss Mallow at the typewriter, with a scared face, plied her
fingers faster than ever.

Gregory was the first to speak.

"You must please forgive me," he said gently. "A personal matter; I forgot myself."

Mrs. Shortman withdrew her gaze from the sky.

"Oh, Mr. Vigil, if I had known——"

Gregory smiled.

"Don't, don't!" he said; "we've quite frightened poor Miss
Mallow!"

Miss Mallow looked round at him, he looked at her, and all
three once more looked at the sky. It was the chief recreation
of this little society.

Gregory worked till nearly three, and walked out to a bun-
shop, where he lunched off a piece of cake and a cup of coffee.
He took an omnibus, and getting on the top, was driven West
with a smile on his face and his hat in his hand. He was
thinking of Helen Bellew. It had become a habit with him to
think of her, the best and most beautiful of her sex—a habit in
which he was growing grey, and with which, therefore, he could

not part. And those women who saw him with his uncovered head smiled, and thought:

'What a fine-looking man!'

But George Pendyce, who saw him from the window of the Stoics' Club, smiled a different smile; the sight of him was always a little unpleasant to George.

Nature, who had made Gregory Vigil a man, had long found that he had got out of her hands, and was living in celibacy, deprived of the comfort of woman, even of those poor creatures whom he befriended; and Nature, who cannot bear that man should escape her control, avenged herself through his nerves and a habit of blood to the head. Extravagance, she said, I cannot have, and when I made this man I made him quite extravagant enough. For his temperament (not uncommon in a misty climate) had been born seven feet high; and as a man cannot add a cubit to his stature, so neither can he take one off. Gregory could not bear that a yellow man must always remain a yellow man, but trusted by care and attention some day to see him white. There lives no mortal who has not a philosophy as distinct from every other mortal's as his face is different from their faces; but Gregory believed that philosophers unfortunately alien must gain in time a likeness to himself if he were careful to tell them often that they had been mistaken. Other men in this Great Britain had the same belief.

To Gregory's reforming instinct it was a constant grief that he had been born refined. A natural delicacy *would* interfere and mar his noblest efforts. Hence failures deplored by Mrs. Pendyce to Lady Malden the night they danced at Worsted Skeynes.

He left his bus near to the flat where Mrs. Bellew lived; with reverence he made the tour of the building and back again. He had long fixed a rule, which he never broke, of seeing her only once a fortnight; but to pass her windows he went out of his way most days and nights. And having made this tour, not conscious of having done anything ridiculous, still smiling, and with his hat on his knee, perhaps really happier because he had not seen her, was driven East, once more passing George Pendyce in the bow-window of the Stoics' Club, and once more raising on his face a jeering smile.

He had been back at his rooms in Buckingham Street half an hour when a club commissionaire arrived with Mr. Paramor's promised letter.

He opened it hastily.

" THE NELSON CLUB,
" TRAFALGAR SQUARE.

" MY DEAR VIGIL,

" I've just come from seeing your ward. An embarrassing complexion is lent to affairs by what took place last night. It appears that after your visit to him yesterday afternoon her husband came up to town, and made his appearance at her flat about eleven o'clock. He was in a condition bordering on delirium tremens, and Mrs. Bellew was obliged to keep him for the night. 'I could not,' she said to me, 'have refused a dog in such a state.' The visit lasted until this afternoon—in fact, the man had only just gone when I arrived. It is a piece of irony, of which I must explain to you the importance. I think I told you that the law of divorce is based on certain principles. One of these excludes any forgiveness of offences by the party moving for a divorce. In technical language, any such forgiveness or overlooking is called condonation, and it is a complete bar to further action for the time being. The Court is very jealous of this principle of nonforgiveness, and will regard with grave suspicion *any conduct on the part of the offended party* which might be construed as amounting to condonation. I fear that what your ward tells me will make it altogether inadvisable to apply for a divorce on any evidence that may lie in the past. It is too dangerous. In other words, the Court would almost certainly consider that she has condoned offences so far. Any further offence, however, will in technical language 're-vive' the past, and under these circumstances, though nothing can be done at present, there may be hope in the future. After seeing your ward, I quite appreciate your anxiety in the matter, though I am *by no means sure* that you are right in advising this divorce. If you remain in the same mind, however, I will give the matter my best personal attention, and my counsel to you is not to worry. This is no matter for a layman, especially not for one who, like you, judges of things rather as they ought to be than as they are.

" I am, my dear Vigil,
" Very sincerely yours,
EDMUND PARAMOR.

" GREGORY VIGIL, ESQ.

" If you want to see me, I shall be at my club all the evening.—E. P."

When Gregory had read this note he walked to the window, and stood looking out over the lights on the river. His heart beat furiously, his temples were crimson. He went downstairs, and took a cab to the Nelson Club.

Mr. Paramor, who was about to dine, invited his visitor to join him.

Gregory shook his head.

"No, thanks," he said; "I don't feel like dining. What is this, Paramor? Surely there's some mistake? Do you mean to tell me that because she acted like a Christian to that man she is to be punished for it in this way?"

Mr. Paramor bit his finger.

"Don't confuse yourself by dragging in Christianity. Christianity has nothing to do with law."

"You talked of principles," said Gregory—"ecclesiastical——"

"Yes, yes; I meant principles imported from the old ecclesiastical conception of marriage, which held man and wife to be undivorceable. That conception has been abandoned by the law, but the principles still haunt——"

"I don't understand."

Mr. Paramor said slowly:

"I don't know that anyone does. It's our usual muddle. But I know this, Vigil—in such a case as your ward's we must tread very carefully. We must 'save face,' as the Chinese say. We must pretend we don't want to bring this divorce, but that we have been so injured that we are obliged to come forward. If Bellew says nothing, the Judge will have to take what's put before him. But there's always the Queen's Proctor. I don't know if you know anything about him?"

"No," said Gregory, "I don't."

"Well, if he can find out anything against our getting this divorce, he will. It is not my habit to go into Court with a case in which anybody can find out anything."

"Do you mean to say——"

"I mean to say that she must not ask for a divorce merely because she is miserable, or placed in a position that no woman should be placed in, but only if she has been offended in certain technical ways; and if—by condonation, for instance—she has given the Court technical reason for refusing her a divorce, that divorce will be refused her. To get a divorce, Vigil, you must be as hard as nails and as wary as a cat. Now do you understand?"

Gregory did not answer.

Mr. Paramor looked searchingly and rather pityingly in his face.

"It won't do to go for it at present," he said. "Are you still set on this divorce? I told you in my letter that I am not sure you are right."

"How can you ask me, Paramor? After that man's conduct last night, I am more than ever set on it."

"Then," said Mr. Paramor, "we must keep a sharp eye on Bellew, and hope for the best."

Gregory held out his hand.

"You spoke of morality," he said. "I can't tell you how inexpressibly mean the whole thing seems to me. Good-night."

And, turning rather quickly, he went out.

His mind was confused and his heart torn. He thought of Helen Bellew as of the woman dearest to him in the coils of a great slimy serpent, and the knowledge that each man and woman unhappily married was, whether by his own, his partner's, or by no fault at all, in the same embrace, afforded him no comfort whatsoever. It was long before he left the windy streets to go to his home.

CHAPTER X

AT BLAFARD'S

THERE comes now and then to the surface of our modern civilisation one of those great and good men who, unconscious, like all great and good men, of the goodness and greatness of their work, leave behind a lasting memorial of themselves before they go bankrupt.

It was so with the founder of the Stoics' Club.

He came to the surface in the year 187–, with nothing in the world but his clothes and an idea. In a single year he had floated the Stoics' Club, made ten thousand pounds, lost more, and gone down again.

The Stoics' Club lived after him by reason of the immortal beauty of his idea. In 1891 it was a strong and corporate body, not perhaps quite so exclusive as it had been, but, on the whole, as smart and aristocratic as any club in London, with the exception of that one or two into which nobody ever got. The idea with which its founder had underpinned the edifice was, like all great ideas, simple, permanent, and perfect—so simple, permanent, and perfect that it seemed amazing no one had ever thought of it before. It was embodied in No. 1 of the members' rules:

" No member of this club shall have any occupation whatsoever."

Hence the name of a club renowned throughout London for the excellence of its wines and cuisine.

Its situation was in Piccadilly, fronting the Green Park, and through the many windows of its ground-floor smoking-room the public were privileged to see at all hours of the day numbers of Stoics in various attitudes reading the daily papers or gazing out of the window.

Some of them who did not direct companies, grow fruit, or own yachts, wrote a book, or took an interest in a theatre. The greater part eked out existence by racing horses, hunting foxes, and shooting birds. Individuals among them, however, had been known to play the piano, and take up the Roman Catholic religion. Many explored the same spots of the Continent year after year at stated seasons. Some belonged to the Yeomanry; others called themselves barristers; once in a way one painted a picture or devoted himself to good works. They were, in fact, of all sorts and temperaments, but their common characteristic was an independent income, often so settled by Providence that they could not in any way get rid of it.

But though the principle of no occupation overruled all class distinctions, the Stoics were mainly derived from the landed gentry. An instinct that the spirit of the club was safest with persons of this class guided them in their elections, and eldest sons, who became members almost as a matter of course, lost no time in putting up their younger brothers, thereby keeping the wine as pure as might be, and preserving that fine old country-house flavour which is nowhere so appreciated as in London.

After seeing Gregory pass on the top of a bus, George Pendyce went into the card-room, and as it was still empty, set to contemplation of the pictures on the walls. They were effigies of all those members of the Stoics' Club who from time to time had come under the notice of a celebrated caricaturist in a celebrated society paper. Whenever a Stoic appeared, he was at once cut out, framed, glassed, and hung alongside his fellows in this room. And George moved from one to another till he came to the last. It was himself. He was represented in very perfectly cut clothes, with slightly crooked elbows, and race-glasses slung across him. His head, disproportionately large, was surmounted by a black billycock hat with a very flat brim. The artist had thought long and carefully over the face. The lips and cheeks and chin were moulded so as to convey a feeling of the unimaginative joy of life, but to their shape and complexion was imparted a suggestion of obstinacy and choler. To the eyes was given a glazed look, and between them set a little line, as though their owner were thinking:

'Hard work, hard work! *Noblesse oblige.* I must keep it going!'

Underneath was written: "The Ambler."

George stood long looking at the apotheosis of his fame. His star was high in the heavens. With the eye of his mind he saw a long procession of turf triumphs, a long vista of days and nights, and in them, round them, of them—Helen Bellew; and by an odd coincidence, as he stood there, the artist's glazed look came over his eyes, the little line sprang up between them.

He turned at the sound of voices and sank into a chair. To have been caught thus gazing at himself would have jarred on his sense of what was right.

It was twenty minutes past seven, when, in evening dress, he left the club, and took a shilling's-worth to Buckingham Gate. Here he dismissed his cab, and turned up the large fur collar of his coat. Between the brim of his opera-hat and the edge of that collar nothing but his eyes were visible. He waited, compressing his lips, scrutinising each hansom that went by. In the soft glow of one coming fast he saw a hand raised to the trap. The cab stopped; George stepped out of the shadow and got in. The cab went on, and Mrs. Bellew's arm was pressed against his own.

It was their simple formula for arriving at a restaurant together.

In the third of several little rooms, where the lights were shaded, they sat down at a table in a corner, facing each a wall, and, underneath, her shoe stole out along the floor and touched his patent leather boot. In their eyes, for all their would-be wariness, a light smouldered which would not be put out. An habitué, sipping claret at a table across the little room, watched them in a mirror, and there came into his old heart a glow of warmth, half ache, half sympathy; a smile of understanding stirred the crow's-feet round his eyes. Its sweetness ebbed, and left a little grin about his shaven lips. Behind the archway in the neighbouring room two waiters met, and in their nods and glances was that same unconscious sympathy, the same conscious grin. And the old habitué thought:

'How long will it last?' . . . "Waiter, some coffee and my bill!"

He had meant to go to the play, but he lingered instead to look at Mrs. Bellew's white shoulders and bright eyes in the kindly mirror. And he thought:

'Young days at present. Ah, young days!' . . . "Waiter, a Benedictine!" And hearing her laugh, his old heart ached. 'No one,' he thought, 'will ever laugh like that for me again!' . . . "Here, waiter, how's this? You've charged me for an ice!" But when the waiter had gone he glanced back into the mirror, and saw them clink their glasses filled with golden bubbling wine, and he thought: 'Wish you good luck! For a flash of those teeth, my dear, I'd give——'

But his eyes fell on the paper flowers adorning his little table

—yellow and red and green; hard, lifeless, tawdry. He saw them suddenly as they were, with the dregs of wine in his glass, the spill of gravy on the cloth, the ruin of the nuts that he had eaten. Wheezing and coughing, 'This place is not what it was,' he thought; 'I shan't come here again!'

He struggled into his coat to go, but he looked once more in the mirror, and met their eyes resting on himself. In them he read the careless pity of the young for the old. His eyes answered the reflection of their eyes, 'Wait, wait! It is young days yet! I wish you no harm, my dears!' and limping—for one of his legs was lame—he went away.

But George and his partner sat on, and with every glass of wine the light in their eyes grew brighter. For who was there now in the room to mind? Not a living soul! Only a tall, dark young waiter, a little cross-eyed, who was in consumption; only the little wine-waiter, with a pallid face, and a look as if he suffered. And the whole world seemed of the colour of the wine they had been drinking; but they talked of indifferent things, and only their eyes, bemused and shining, really spoke. The dark young waiter stood apart, unmoving, and his cross-eyed glance, fixed on her shoulders, had all unconsciously the longing of a saint in some holy picture. Unseen, behind the serving screen, the little wine-waiter poured out and drank a glass from a derelict bottle. Through a chink of the red blinds an eye peered in from the chill outside, staring and curious, till its owner passed on in the cold.

It was long after nine when they rose. The dark young waiter laid her cloak upon her with adoring hands. She looked back at him, and in her eyes was an infinite indulgence. 'God knows,' she seemed to say, 'if I could make you happy as well, I would. Why should one suffer? Life is strong and good!'

The young waiter's cross-eyed glance fell before her, and he bowed above the money in his hand. Quickly before them the little wine-waiter hurried to the door, his suffering face screwed into one long smile.

"Good-night, madam; good-night, sir. Thank you very much!"

And he, too, remained bowed over his hand, and his smile relaxed.

But in the cab George's arm stole round her underneath the cloak, and they were borne on in the stream of hurrying hansoms, carrying couples like themselves, cut off from all but each other's eyes, from all but each other's touch; and with their eyes turned in the half-dark they spoke together in low tones.

PART II

CHAPTER I

GREGORY REOPENS THE CAMPAIGN

AT one end of the walled garden which Mr. Pendyce had formed in imitation of that at dear old Strathbegally, was a virgin orchard of pear and cherry trees. They blossomed early, and by the end of the third week in April the last of the cherries had broken into flower. In the long grass, underneath, a wealth of daffodils, jonquils, and narcissus, came up year after year, and sunned their yellow stars in the light which dappled through the blossom.

And here Mrs. Pendyce would come, tan gauntlets on her hands, and stand, her face a little flushed with stooping, as though the sight of all that bloom was restful. It was due to her that these old trees escaped year after year the pruning and improvements which the genius of the Squire would otherwise have applied. She had been brought up in an old Totteridge tradition that fruit-trees should be left to themselves, while her husband, possessed of a grasp of the subject not more than usually behind the times, was all for newer methods. She had fought for those trees. They were as yet the only things she *had* fought for in her married life, and Horace Pendyce still remembered with a discomfort robbed by time of poignancy how she had stood with her back to their bedroom door and said, " If you cut those poor trees, Horace, I won't live here!" He had at once expressed his determination to have them pruned; but, having put off the action for a day or two, the trees still stood unpruned thirty-three years later. He had even come to feel rather proud of the fact that they continued to bear fruit, and would speak of them thus: " Queer fancy of my wife's, never been cut. And yet, remarkable thing, they do better than any of the others ! "

This spring, when all was so forward, and the cuckoos already in full song, when the scent of young larches in the New Plantation (planted the year of George's birth) was in the air like the

73

perfume of celestial lemons, she came to the orchard more than usual, and her spirit felt the stirring, the old, half-painful yearning for she knew not what, that she had felt so often in her first years at Worsted Skeynes. And sitting there on a green-painted seat under the largest of the cherry-trees, she thought even more than her wont of George, as though her son's spirit, vibrating in its first real passion, were calling to her for sympathy.

He had been down so little all that winter, twice for a couple of days' shooting, once for a week-end, when she had thought him looking thinner and rather worn. He had missed Christmas for the first time. With infinite precaution she had asked him casually if he had seen Helen Bellew, and he had answered, "Oh yes, I see her once in a way!"

Secretly all through the winter she consulted the *Times* newspaper for mention of George's horse, and was disappointed not to find any. One day, however, in February, discovering him absolutely at the head of several lists of horses with figures after them, she wrote off at once with a joyful heart. Of five lists in which the Ambler's name appeared, there was only one in which he was second. George's answer came in the course of a week or so.

"MY DEAR MOTHER,
"What you saw were the weights for the Spring Handicaps. They've simply done me out of everything. In great haste,
"Your affectionate son,
"GEORGE PENDYCE."

As the spring approached, the vision of her independent visit to London, which had sustained her throughout the winter, having performed its annual function, grew mistier and mistier, and at last faded away. She ceased even to dream of it, as though it had never been, nor did George remind her, and as usual, she ceased even to wonder whether he would remind her. She thought instead of the season visit, and its scurry of parties, with a sort of languid fluttering. For Worsted Skeynes, and all that Worsted Skeynes stood for, was like a heavy horseman guiding her with iron hands along a narrow lane; she dreamed of throwing him in the open, but the open she never reached.

She woke at seven with her tea, and from seven to eight made little notes on tablets, while on his back Mr. Pendyce snored lightly. She rose at eight. At nine she poured out coffee. From half-past nine to ten she attended to the housekeeper and her birds. From ten to eleven she attended to the gardener and her dress. From eleven to twelve she wrote invitations to persons for whom she did not care, and acceptances to persons who did not care for her; she drew out also and placed in due sequences cheques for Mr. Pendyce's signature; and secured receipts, carefully docketed on the back, within an elastic band; as a rule, also, she received a visit from Mrs. Hussell Barter. From twelve to one she walked with her and "the dear dogs" to the village, where she stood hesitatingly in the cottage doors of persons who were shy of her. From half-past one to two she lunched. From two to three she rested on a sofa in the white morning-room with the newspaper in her hand, trying to read the Parliamentary debate, and thinking of other things. From three to half-past four she went to her dear flowers, from whom she was liable to be summoned at any moment by the arrival of callers; or, getting into the carriage, was driven to some neighbour's mansion, where she sat for half an hour and came away. At half-past four she poured out tea. At five she knitted a tie, or socks, for George or Gerald, and listened with a gentle smile to what was going on. From six to seven she received from the Squire his impressions of Parliament and things at large. From seven to seven-thirty she changed to a black low dress, with old lace about the neck. At seven-thirty she dined. At a quarter to nine she listened to Norah playing two waltzes of Chopin's, and a piece called "Serenade du Printemps" by Baff, and to Bee singing "The Mikado," or the "Saucy Girl." From nine to. ten-thirty she played a game called piquet, which her father had taught her, if she could get anyone with whom to play; but as this was seldom, she played as a rule patience by herself. At ten-thirty she went to bed. At eleven-thirty punctually the Squire woke her. At one o'clock she went to sleep. On Mondays she wrote out in her clear Totteridge hand, with its fine straight strokes, a list of library books, made up without distinction of all that were recommended in the *Ladies' Paper* that came weekly to Worsted Skeynes. Periodically Mr. Pendyce would hand her a list of his own, compiled out of the *Times* and the *Field* in the privacy of his study; this she sent too.

Thus was the household supplied with literature unerringly adapted to its needs; nor was it possible for any undesirable book to find its way into the house—not that this would have mattered much to Mrs. Pendyce, for as she often said with gentle regret, "My dear, I have no time to read."

This afternoon it was so warm that the bees were all around among the blossoms, and two thrushes, who had built in a yew-tree that watched over the Scotch garden, were in a violent flutter because one of their chicks had fallen out of the nest. The mother bird, at the edge of the long orchard grass, was silent, trying by example to still the tiny creature's cheeping, lest it might attract some large or human thing.

Mrs. Pendyce, sitting under the oldest cherry-tree, looked for the sound, and when she had located it, picked up the baby bird, and, as she knew the whereabouts of all the nests, put it back into its cradle, to the loud terror and grief of the parent birds. She went back to the bench and sat down again.

She had in her soul something of the terror of the mother thrush. The Maldens had been paying the call that preceded their annual migration to town, and the peculiar glow which Lady Malden had the power of raising had not yet left her cheeks. True, she had the comfort of the thought, 'Ellen Malden is so bourgeoise,' but to-day it did not still her heart.

Accompanied by one pale daughter who never left her, and two pale dogs forced to run all the way, now lying under the carriage with their tongues out, Lady Malden had come and stayed full time; and for three-quarters of that time she had seemed, as it were, labouring under a sense of duty unfulfilled; for the remaining quarter Mrs. Pendyce had laboured under a sense of duty fulfilled.

"My dear," Lady Malden had said, having told the pale daughter to go into the conservatory, "I'm the last person in the world to repeat gossip, as you know; but I think it's only right to tell you that I've been hearing things. You see, my boy Fred" (who would ultimately become Sir Frederick Malden) "belongs to the same club as your son George—the Stoics. All young men belong there of course—I mean, if they're anybody. I'm sorry to say there's no doubt about it; your son has been seen dining at—perhaps I ought not to mention the name—Blafard's, with Mrs. Bellew. I dare say you don't know what sort of a place Blafard's is—a lot of little rooms where people go when they don't want to be seen. I've never been there, of course; but I can imagine it perfectly. And not once, but frequently. I thought I would speak to you, because I do think it's so scandalous of her in her position."

An azalea in a blue and white pot had stood between them,
and in this plant Mrs. Pendyce buried her cheeks and eyes;
but when she raised her face her eyebrows were lifted to their
utmost limit, her lips trembled with anger.

"Oh," she said, "didn't you know? There's nothing in that;
it's the latest thing!"

For a moment Lady Malden wavered, then duskily flushed;
her temperament and principles had recovered themselves.

"If that," she said with some dignity, "is the latest thing,
I think it is quite time we were back in town."

She rose, and as she rose, such was her unfortunate conforma-
tion, it flashed through Mrs. Pendyce's mind:

'Why was I afraid? She's only——' And then as quickly:
'Poor woman! how can she help her legs being short?'

But when she was gone, side by side with the pale daughter,
the pale dogs once more running behind the carriage, Margery
Pendyce put her hand to her heart.

And out here amongst the bees and blossom, where the blackbirds were improving each minute their new songs, and the air
was so fainting sweet with scents, her heart would not be stilled,
but throbbed as though danger were coming on herself; and
she saw her son as a little boy again in a dirty holland suit with
a straw hat down the back of his neck, flushed and sturdy, as
he came to her from some adventure.

And suddenly a gush of emotion from deep within her heart
and the heart of the spring day, a sense of being severed from
him by a great, remorseless power, came over her; and taking
out a tiny embroidered handkerchief, she wept. Round her the
bees hummed carelessly, the blossom dropped, the dappled sunlight covered her with a pattern as of her own fine lace. From
the home farm came the lowing of the cows on their way
to milking, and, strange sound in that well-ordered home, a
distant piping on a penny flute. . . .

"Mother, Mother, Mo-o-ther!"

Mrs. Pendyce passed her handkerchief across her eyes, and
instinctively obeying the laws of breeding, her face lost all trace
of its emotion. She waited, crumpling the tiny handkerchief in
her gauntleted hand.

"Mother! Oh, there you are! Here's Gregory Vigil!"

Norah, a fox-terrier on either side, was coming down the
path; behind her, unhatted, showed Gregory's sanguine face
between his wings of grizzled hair.

"I suppose you're going to talk. I'm going over to the Rectory. Ta-ta!"

And preceded by her dogs, Norah went on.

Mrs. Pendyce put out her hand:

"Well, Grig," she said, "this is a surprise."

Gregory seated himself beside her on the bench.

"I've brought you this," he said. "I want you to look at it before I answer."

Mrs. Pendyce, who vaguely felt that he would want her to see things as he was seeing them, took a letter from him with a sinking heart.

"*Private.*

"LINCOLN'S INN FIELDS,
"*April* 21, 1892.

"MY DEAR VIGIL,

"I have now secured such evidence as should warrant our instituting a suit. I've written your ward to that effect, and am awaiting her instructions. Unfortunately, we have no act of cruelty, and I've been obliged to draw her attention to the fact that, should her husband defend the suit, it will be very difficult to get the Court to accept their separation in the light of desertion on *his* part—difficult indeed, even if he doesn't defend the suit. In divorce cases one has to remember that what has to be kept out is often more important than what has to be got in, and it would be useful to know, therefore, whether there is likelihood of opposition. I do not advise any direct approaching of the husband, but if you are possessed of the information you might let me know. I hate humbug, my dear Vigil, and I hate anything underhand, but divorce is always a dirty business, and while the law is shaped as at present, and the linen washed in public, it will remain impossible for anyone, guilty or innocent, and even for us lawyers, to avoid soiling our hands in one way or another. I regret it as much as you do.

"There is a new man writing verse in the *Tertiary,* some of it quite first-rate. You might look at the last number. My blossom this year is magnificent.

"With kind regards, I am,
"Very sincerely yours,
"Gregory Vigil, Esq.   EDMUND PARAMOR."

Mrs. Pendyce dropped the letter in her lap, and looked at her cousin.

"He was at Harrow with Horace. I *do* like him. He is one of the very nicest men I know."

It was clear that she was trying to gain time.

Gregory began pacing up and down.

"Paramor is a man for whom I have the highest respect. I would trust him before anyone."

It was clear that he, too, was trying to gain time.

"Oh, mind my daffodils, *please!*"

Gregory went down on his knees, and raised the bloom that he had trodden on. He then offered it to Mrs. Pendyce. The action was one to which she was so unaccustomed that it struck her as slightly ridiculous.

"My dear Grig, you'll get rheumatism, and spoil that nice suit; the grass comes off so terribly!"

Gregory got up, and looked shamefacedly at his knees.

"The knee is not what it used to be," he said.

Mrs. Pendyce smiled.

"You should keep your knees for Helen Bellew, Grig. I was always five years older than you."

Gregory rumpled up his hair.

"Kneeling's out of fashion, but I thought in the country you wouldn't mind!"

"You don't notice things, dear Grig. In the country it's still more out of fashion. You wouldn't find a woman within thirty miles of here who would like a man to kneel to her. We've lost the habit. She would think she was being made fun of. We soon grow out of vanity!"

"In London," said Gregory, "I hear all women intend to be men; but in the country I thought——"

"In the country, Grig, all women would like to be men, but they don't dare to try. They trot behind."

As if she had been guilty of thoughts too insightful, Mrs. Pendyce blushed.

Gregory broke out suddenly:

"I can't bear to think of women like that!"

Again Mrs. Pendyce smiled.

"You see, Grig dear, you are not married."

"I detest the idea that marriage changes our views, Margery; I loathe it."

"Mind my daffodils!" murmured Mrs. Pendyce.

She was thinking all the time: 'That dreadful letter! What am I to do?'

And as though he knew her thoughts, Gregory said:

"I shall assume that Bellew will not defend the case. If he has a spark of chivalry in him he will be only too glad to see her free. I will never believe that any man could be such a soulless clod as to wish to keep her bound. I don't pretend to understand the law, but it seems to me that there's only one way for a man to act—and after all Bellew's a gentleman. You'll see that he will act like one!"

Mrs. Pendyce looked at the daffodil in her lap.

"I have only seen him three or four times, but it seemed to me, Grig, that he was a man who might act in one way to-day and another to-morrow. He is so very different from all the men about here."

"When it comes to the deep things of life," said Gregory, "one man is much as another. Is there any man you know who would be so lacking in chivalry as to refuse in these circumstances?"

Mrs. Pendyce looked at him with a confused expression—wonder, admiration, irony, and even fear, struggled in her eyes.

"I can think of dozens."

Gregory clutched his forehead.

"Margery," he said, "I hate your cynicism. I don't know where you get it from."

"I'm so sorry; I didn't mean to be cynical—I didn't, really. I only spoke from what I've seen."

"Seen?" said Gregory. "If I were to go by what I saw daily, hourly, in London in the course of my work I should commit suicide within a week."

"But what else can one go by?"

Without answering, Gregory walked to the edge of the orchard, and stood gazing over the Scotch garden, with his face a little tilted towards the sky. Mrs. Pendyce felt he was grieving that she failed to see whatever it was he saw up there, and she was sorry. He came back, and said:

"We won't discuss it any more."

Very dubiously she heard those words, but as she could not express the anxiety and doubt torturing her soul, she told him tea was ready. But Gregory would not come in just yet out of the sun.

In the drawing-room Beatrix was already giving tea to young Tharp and the Reverend Hussell Barter. And the sound of these well-known voices restored to Mrs. Pendyce something of her tranquillity. The Rector came towards her at once with a teacup in his hand.

" My wife has got a headache," he said. " She wanted to come over with me, but I made her lie down. Nothing like lying down for a headache. We expect it in June, you know. Let me get you your tea."

Mrs. Pendyce, already aware even to the day of what he expected in June, sat down, and looked at Mr. Barter with a slight feeling of surprise. He was a very good fellow; it was nice of him to make his wife lie down! She thought his broad, red-brown face, with its projecting, not unhumorous, lower lip, looked very friendly. Roy, the Skye terrier at her feet, was smelling at the reverend gentleman's legs with a slow movement of his tail.

"The old dog likes me," said the Rector; "they know a dog-lover when they see one—wonderful creatures, dogs! I'm sometimes tempted to think they may have souls! "

Mrs. Pendyce answered:

"Horace says he's getting too old."

The dog looked up in her face, and her lip quivered.

The Rector laughed.

"Don't you worry about that; there's plenty of life in *him*." And he added unexpectedly: "I couldn't bear to put a dog away, the friend of man. No, no; let Nature see to that."

Over at the piano Bee and young Tharp were turning the pages of the "Saucy Girl"; the room was full of the scent of azaleas; and Mr. Barter, astride of a gilt chair, looked almost sympathetic, gazing tenderly at the old Skye.

Mrs. Pendyce felt a sudden yearning to free her mind, a sudden longing to ask a man's advice.

"Oh, Mr. Barter," she said, "my cousin, Gregory Vigil, has just brought me some news; it is confidential, please. Helen Bellew is going to sue for a divorce. I wanted to ask you whether you could tell me——" Looking in the Rector's face, she stopped.

"A divorce! H'm! Really !"

A chill of terror came over Mrs. Pendyce.

" Of course you will not mention it to anyone, not even to Horace. It has nothing to do with us."

Mr. Barter bowed; his face wore the expression it so often wore in school on Sunday mornings.

"H'm !" he said again.

It flashed through Mrs. Pendyce that this man with the heavy jowl and menacing eyes, who sat so square on that flimsy chair, knew something. It was as though he had answered:

"This is not a matter for women; you will be good enough to leave it to me."

With the exception of those few words of Lady Malden's, and the recollection of George's face when he had said, "Oh, yes, I see her now and then," she had no evidence, no knowledge, nothing to go on; but she knew from some instinctive source that her son was Mrs. Bellew's lover.

So, with terror and a strange hope, she saw Gregory entering the room.

"Perhaps," she thought, "he will make Grig stop it."

She poured out Gregory's tea, followed Bee and Cecil Tharp into the conservatory, and left the two men together.

CHAPTER II

CONTINUED INFLUENCE OF THE REVEREND HUSSELL BARTER

To understand and sympathise with the feelings and action of the Rector of Worsted Skeynes, one must consider his origin and the circumstances of his life.

The second son of an old Suffolk family, he had followed the routine of his house, and having passed at Oxford through certain examinations, had been certificated at the age of twenty-four as a man fitted to impart to persons of both sexes rules of life and conduct after which they had been groping for twice or thrice that number of years. His character, never at any time undecided, was by this fortunate circumstance crystallised and rendered immune from the necessity for self-search and spiritual struggle incidental to his neighbours. Since he was a man neither below nor above the average, it did not occur to him to criticise or place himself in opposition to a system which had gone on so long and was about to do him so much good. Like all average men, 'he was believer in authority, and none the less because authority placed a large portion of itself in his hands. It would, indeed, have been unwarrantable to expect a man of his birth, breeding, and education to question the machine of which he was himself a wheel.

He had dropped, therefore, at the age of twenty-six, insensibly, on the death of an uncle, into the family living at Worsted Skeynes. He had been there ever since. It was a constant and natural grief to him that on his death the living would go neither to his eldest nor his second son, but to the second son of his elder brother, the Squire. At the age of twenty-seven he had married Miss Rose Twining, the fifth daughter of a Huntingdonshire parson, and in less than eighteen years begotten ten children, and was expecting the eleventh, all healthy and hearty like himself. A family group hung over the fireplace in the study, under the framed and illuminated text, " Judge not, that ye be not judged," which he had chosen as his motto in the first years of his cure, and never seen any reason to change. In that family group Mr. Barter sat in the centre with his dog between his legs; his wife stood behind him, and on both sides the children spread out like the wings of a fan or butterfly. The bills of their schooling were beginning to weigh rather heavily, and he complained a good deal; but in principle he still approved of the habit into which he had got, and his wife never complained of anything.

The study was furnished with studious simplicity; many a boy had been, not unkindly, caned there, and in one place the old Turkey carpet was rotted away, but whether by their tears or by their knees, not even Mr. Barter knew. In a cabinet on one side of the fire he kept all his religious books, many of them well worn; in a cabinet on the other side he kept his bats, to which he was constantly attending; a fishing-rod and a gun-case stood modestly in a corner. The archway between the drawers of his writing-table held a mat for his bulldog, a prize animal, wont to lie there and guard his master's legs when he was writing his sermons. Like those of his dog, the Rector's good points were the old English virtues of obstinacy, courage, intolerance, and humour; his bad points, owing to the circumstances of his life, had never been brought to his notice.

When, therefore, he found himself alone with Gregory Vigil, he approached him as one dog will approach another, and came at once to the matter in hand.

"It's some time since I had the pleasure of meeting you, Mr. Vigil," he said. "Mrs. Pendyce has been giving me in confidence the news you've brought down. I'm bound to tell you at once that I'm surprised."

Gregory made a little movement of recoil, as though his delicacy had received a shock.

"Indeed!" he said, with a sort of quivering coldness.

The Rector, quick to note opposition, repeated emphatically:

"More than surprised; in fact, I think there must be some mistake."

"Indeed?" said Gregory again.

A change came over Mr. Barter's face. It had been grave, but was now heavy and threatening.

"I have to say to you," he said, "that somehow—somehow, this divorce must be put a stop to."

Gregory flushed painfully.

"On what grounds? I am not aware that my ward is a parishioner of yours, Mr. Barter, or that if she were——"

The Rector closed in on him, his head thrust forward, his lower lip projecting.

"If she were doing her duty," he said, "she would be. I'm not considering her—I'm considering her husband; *he* is a parishioner of mine, and I say this divorce must be stopped."

Gregory retreated no longer.

"On what grounds?" he said again, trembling all over.

"I've no wish to enter into particulars," said Mr. Barter, "but if you force me to, I shall not hesitate."

"I regret that I must," answered Gregory.

"Without mentioning names, then, I say that she is not a fit person to bring a suit for divorce!"

"You say that?" said Gregory. "You——"

He could not go on.

"You will not move me, Mr. Vigil," said the Rector, with a grim little smile. "I have my duty to do."

Gregory recovered possession of himself with an effort.

"You have said that which no one but a clergyman could say with impunity," he said freezingly. "Be so good as to explain yourself."

"My explanation," said Mr. Barter, "is what I have seen with my own eyes."

He raised those eyes to Gregory. Their pupils were contracted to pin-points, the light-grey irises around had a sort of swimming glitter, and round these again the whites were injected with blood.

"If you must know, with my own eyes I've seen her in that very conservatory over there kissing a man."

Gregory threw up his hand.

"How dare you!" he whispered.

Again Mr. Barter's humorous under-lip shot out.

"I dare a good deal more than that, Mr. Vigil," he said, "as you will find; and I say this to you—stop this divorce, or I'll stop it myself!"

Gregory turned to the window. When he came back he was outwardly calm.

"You have been guilty of indelicacy," he said. "Continue in your delusion, think what you like, do what you like. The matter will go on. Good-evening, sir."

And turning on his heel, he left the room.

Mr. Barter stepped forward. The words, "You have been guilty of indelicacy," whirled round his brain till every blood-vessel in his face and neck was swollen to bursting, and with a hoarse sound like that of an animal in pain he pursued Gregory to the door. It was shut in his face. And since on taking Orders he had abandoned for ever the use of bad language, he was very near an apoplectic fit. Suddenly he became aware that Mrs. Pendyce was looking at him from the conservatory door. Her face was painfully white, her eyebrows lifted, and before that look Mr. Barter recovered a measure of self-possession.

"Is anything the matter, Mr. Barter?"

The Rector smiled grimly.

"Nothing, nothing," he said. "I must ask you to excuse me, that's all. I've a parish matter to attend to."

When he found himself in the drive, the feeling of vertigo and suffocation passed, but left him unrelieved. He had, in fact, happened on one of those psychological moments which enable a man's true nature to show itself. Accustomed to say of himself bluffly, "Yes, yes; I've a hot temper, soon over," he had never, owing to the autocracy of his position, had a chance of knowing the tenacity of his soul. So accustomed and so able for many years to vent displeasure at once, he did not himself know the wealth of his old English spirit, did not know of what an ugly grip he was capable. He did not even know it at this minute, conscious only of a sort of black wonder at this monstrous conduct to a man in his position, doing his simple duty. The more he reflected, the more intolerable did it seem that a woman like this Mrs. Bellew should have the impudence to invoke the law of the land in her favour—a woman who was no better than a common baggage—a woman he had seen kissing George Pendyce. To have suggested to Mr. Barter that there was something pathetic in this black wonder of his, pathetic in the spectacle of his little soul delivering its little judgments, stumbling its little way along with such blind certainty under the huge heavens, amongst millions of organisms as important as itself, would have astounded him; and with every step he took the blacker became his wonder, the more fixed his determination to permit no such abuse of morality, no such disregard of Hussell Barter.

"You have been guilty of indelicacy!" This indictment had a wriggling sting, and lost no venom from the fact that he could in no wise have perceived where the indelicacy of his conduct lay. But he did not try to perceive it. Against himself, clergyman and gentleman, the monstrosity of the charge was clear. This was a point of morality. He felt no anger against George; it was the woman that excited his just wrath. For so long he had been absolute among women, with the power, as it were, over them of life and death. This was flat immorality! He had never approved of her leaving her husband; he had never approved of her at all! He turned his steps toward the Firs.

From above the hedges the sleepy cows looked down; a yaffle laughed a field or two away; in the sycamores, which had come out before their time, the bees hummed. Under the smile of the spring the innumerable life of the fields went carelessly on around that square black figure ploughing along the lane with head bent down under a wide-brimmed hat.

George Pendyce, in a fly drawn by an old grey horse, the only vehicle that frequented the station at Worsted Skeynes, passed him in the lane, and leaned back to avoid observation. He had not forgotten the tone of the Rector's voice in the smoking-room on the night of the dance. George was a man who could remember as well as another. In the corner of the old fly, that rattled and smelled of stables and stale tobacco, he fixed his moody eyes on the driver's back and the ears of the old grey horse, and never stirred till they set him down at the hall door.

He went at once to his room, sending word that he had come for the night. His mother heard the news with feelings of joy and dread, and she dressed quickly for dinner that she might see him the sooner. The Squire came into her room just as she was going down. He had been engaged all day at Sessions, and was in one of the moods of apprehension as to the future which but seldom came over him.

"Why didn't you keep Vigil to dinner?" he said. "I could have given him things for the night. I wanted to talk to him about insuring my life; he knows about that. There'll be a lot of money wanted, to pay my death-duties. And if the Radicals get in I shouldn't be surprised if they put them up fifty per cent."

"I wanted to keep him," said Mrs. Pendyce, "but he went away without saying good-bye."

"He's an odd fellow!"

For some moments Mr. Pendyce made reflections on this breach of manners. He had a nice standard of conduct in all social affairs.

"I'm having trouble with that man Peacock again. He's

the most pig-headed—— What are you in such a hurry for,
Margery?"

"George is here!"

"George? Well, I suppose he can wait till dinner. I have
a lot of things I want to tell you about. We had a case of arson
to-day. Old Quarryman was away, and I was in the chair. It
was that fellow Woodford that we convicted for poaching—a
very gross case. And this is what he does when he comes out.
They tried to prove insanity. It's the rankest case of revenge
that ever came before me. We committed him, of course. He'll
get a swinging sentence. Of all dreadful crimes, arson is the
most——"

Mr. Pendyce could find no word to characterise his opinion
of this offence, and drawing his breath between his teeth, passed
into his dressing-room. Mrs. Pendyce hastened quietly out, and
went to her son's room. She found George in his shirt-sleeves,
inserting the links of his cuffs.

"Let me do that for you, my dear boy! How dreadfully
they starch your cuffs! It *is* so nice to do something for you
sometimes!"

George answered her:

"Well, Mother, and how have you been?"

Over Mrs. Pendyce's face came a look half sorrowful, half
arch, but wholly pathetic. 'What! is it beginning already?
Oh, don't put me away from you!' she seemed to say.

"Very well, thank you, dear. And you?"

George did not meet her eyes.

"So-so," he said. "I took rather a nasty knock over the
'City' last week."

"Is that a race?" asked Mrs. Pendyce.

And by some secret process she knew that he had hurried
out that piece of bad news to divert her attention from another
subject, for George had never been a "cry-baby."

She sat down on the edge of the sofa, and though the gong
was about to sound, incited him to dawdle and stay with her.

"And have you any other news, dear? It seems such an age
since we've seen you. I think I've told you all our budget in
my letters. You know there's going to be another event at the
Rectory?"

"Another? I passed Barter on the way up. I thought he
looked a bit blue."

A look of pain shot into Mrs. Pendyce's eyes.

"Oh, I'm afraid that couldn't have been the reason, dear." And she stopped, but to still her own fears hurried on again. "If I'd known you'd been coming, I'd have kept Cecil Tharp. Vic has had such dear little puppies. Would you like one? They've all got that nice black smudge round the eye."

She was watching him as only a mother can watch—stealthily, minutely, longingly, every little movement, every little change of his face, and more than all, that fixed something behind which showed the abiding temper and condition of his heart.

'Something is making him unhappy,' she thought. 'He is changed since I saw him last, and I can't get at it. I seem to be so far from him—so far!'

And somehow she knew he had come down this evening because he was lonely and unhappy, and instinct had made him turn to her.

But she knew that trying to get nearer would only make him put her farther off, and she could not bear this, so she asked him nothing, and bent all her strength on hiding from him the pain she felt.

She went downstairs with her arm in his, and leaned very heavily on it, as though again trying to get close to him, and forget the feeling she had had all that winter—the feeling of being barred away, the feeling of secrecy and restraint.

Mr. Pendyce and the two girls were in the drawing-room.

"Well, George," said the Squire dryly, "I'm glad you've come. How you can stick in London at this time of year! Now you're down you'd better stay a couple of days. I want to take you round the estate; you know nothing about anything. I might die at any moment, for all you can tell. Just make up your mind to stay."

George gave him a moody look.

"Sorry," he said; "I've got an engagement in town."

Mr. Pendyce rose and stood with his back to the fire.

"That's it," he said: "I ask you to do a simple thing for your own good—and—you've got an engagement. It's always like that, and your mother backs you up. Bee, go and play me something."

The Squire could not bear being played to, but it was the only command likely to be obeyed that came into his head.

The absence of guests made little difference to a ceremony esteemed at Worsted Skeynes the crowning blessing of the day. The courses, however, were limited to seven, and champagne was not drunk. The Squire drank a glass or so of claret, for, as he said, "My dear old father took his bottle of port every night of his life, and it never gave him a twinge. If I were to go on at that rate it would kill me in a year."

His daughter drank water. Mrs. Pendyce, cherishing a secret preference for champagne, drank sparingly of a Spanish burgundy, procured for her by Mr. Pendyce at a very reasonable price, and corked between meals with a special cork. She offered it to George.

"Try some of my burgundy, dear; it's so nice."

But George refused and asked for whisky-and-soda, glancing at the butler, who brought it in a very yellow state.

Under the influence of dinner the Squire recovered equanimity, though he still dwelt somewhat sadly on the future.

"You young fellows," he said, with a friendly look at George, "are such individualists. You make a business of enjoying yourselves. With your piquet and your racing and your billiards and what not, you'll be used up before you're fifty. You don't let your imaginations work. A green old age ought to be your ideal, instead of which it seems to be a green youth. Ha!"

Mr. Pendyce looked at his daughters till they said:

"Oh, Father, how *can* you!"

Norah, who had the more character of the two, added:

"Isn't Father rather dreadful, Mother?"

But Mrs. Pendyce was looking at her son. She had longed so many evenings to see him sitting there.

"We'll have a game of piquet to-night, George."

George looked up and nodded with a glum smile.

On the thick, soft carpet round the table the butler and second footman moved. The light of the wax candles fell lustrous and subdued on the silver and fruit and flowers, on the girls' white necks, on George's well-coloured face and glossy shirt-front, gleamed in the jewels on his mother's long white fingers, showed off the Squire's erect and still spruce figure; the air was languorously sweet with the perfume of azaleas and narcissus bloom. Bee, with soft eyes, was thinking of young Tharp, who to-day had told her that he loved her, and wondering if father would object. Her mother was thinking of George, stealing timid glances at his moody face. There was no sound save the tinkle of forks and the voices of Norah and the Squire, talking of little things. Outside, through the long opened windows, was the still, wide country; the full moon, tinted apricot and figured like a coin, hung above the cedar-trees, and by her light the whispering stretches of the silent fields lay half enchanted, half asleep, and all beyond that little ring of moonshine, unfathomed and unknown, was darkness—a great darkness wrapping from their eyes the restless world.

CHAPTER III

THE SINISTER NIGHT

On the day of the big race at Kempton Park, in which the Ambler, starting favourite, was left at the post, George Pendyce had just put his latch-key in the door of the room he had taken near Mrs. Bellew, when a man, stepping quickly from behind, said:

"Mr. George Pendyce, I believe."

George turned.

"Yes; what do you want?"

The man put into George's hand a long envelope.

"From Messrs. Frost and Tuckett."

George opened it, and read from the top of a slip of paper:

"'Admiralty, Probate, and Divorce.

"'The humble petition of Jaspar Bellew——'"

He lifted his eyes, and his look, uncannily impassive, unresenting, unangered, dogged, caused the messenger to drop his gaze as though he had hit a man who was down.

"Thanks. Good-night!"

He shut the door, and read the document through. It contained some precise details, and ended in a claim for damages, and George smiled.

Had he received this document three months ago, he would not have taken it thus. Three months ago he would have felt with rage that he was caught. His thoughts would have run thus: 'I have got her into a mess; I have got myself into a mess. I never thought this would happen. This is the devil! I must see someone—I must stop it. There must be a way out.' Having but little imagination, his thoughts would have beaten their wings against this cage, and at once he would have tried to act. But this was not three months ago, and now——

He lit a cigarette and sat down on the sofa, and the chief feeling in his heart was a strange hope, a sort of funereal gladness. He would have to go and see her at once, that very night; an excuse—no need to wait in here—to wait—wait on the chance of her coming.

He got up and drank some whisky, then went back to the sofa and sat down again.

'If she is not here by eight,' he thought, 'I will go round.'

Opposite was a full-length mirror, and he turned to the wall to avoid it. There was fixed on his face a look of gloomy determination, as though he were thinking, 'I'll show them all that I'm not beaten yet.'

At the click of a latch-key he scrambled off the sofa, and his face resumed its mask. She came in as usual, dropped her opera cloak, and stood before him with bare shoulders. Looking in her face, he wondered if she knew.

"I thought I'd better come," she said. "I suppose you've had the same charming present?"

George nodded. There was a minute's silence.

"It's really rather funny. I'm sorry for you, George."

George laughed too, but his laugh was different.

"I will do all I can," he said.

Mrs. Bellew came close to him.

"I've seen about the Kempton race. What shocking luck! I suppose you've lost a lot. Poor boy! It never rains but it pours."

George looked down.

"That's all right; nothing matters when I have you."

He felt her arms fasten behind his neck, but they were cool as marble; he met her eyes, and they were mocking and compassionate.

Their cab, wheeling into the main thoroughfare, joined in the race of cabs flying as for life toward the East—past the Park, where the trees, new-leafed, were swinging their skirts like ballet-dancers in the wind; past the Stoics' and the other clubs, rattling, jingling, jostling for the lead, shooting past omnibuses that looked cosy in the half-light with their lamps and rows of figures solemnly opposed.

At Blafard's the tall dark young waiter took her cloak with reverential fingers; the little wine-waiter smiled below the suffering in his eyes. The same red-shaded lights fell on her arms and shoulders, the same flowers of green and yellow grew bravely in the same blue vases. On the menu were written the same dishes. The same idle eye peered through the chink at the corner of the red blinds with its stare of apathetic wonder.

Often during that dinner George looked at her face by stealth, and its expression baffled him, so careless was it. And, unlike her mood of late, that had been glum and cold, she was in the wildest spirits.

People looked round from the other little tables, all full now that the season had begun, her laugh was so infectious; and George felt a sort of disgust. What was it in this woman that made her laugh, when his own heart was heavy? But he said nothing; he dared not even look at her, for fear his eyes should show his feeling.

'We ought to be squaring our accounts,' he thought—'looking things in the face. Something must be done; and here she is laughing and making everyone stare!' Done! But what could be done, when it was all like quicksand?

The other little tables emptied one by one.

"George," she said, "take me somewhere where we can dance!"

George stared at her.

"My dear girl, how can I? There is no such place!"

"Take me to your Bohemians!"

"You can't possibly go to a place like that."

"Why not? Who cares where we go, or what we do?"

"I care!"

"Ah, my dear George, you and your sort are only half alive!"

Sullenly George answered:

"What do you take me for? A cad?"

But there was fear, not anger, in his heart.

"Well, then, let's drive into the East End. For goodness' sake, let's do something not quite proper!"

They took a hansom and drove East. It was the first time either had ever been in that unknown land.

"Close your cloak, dear; it looks odd down here."

Mrs. Bellew laughed.

"You'll be just like your father when you're sixty, George."

And she opened her cloak the wider. Round a barrel-organ at the corner of a street were girls in bright colours dancing.

She called to the cabman to stop.

"Let's watch those children!"

"You'll only make a show of us."

Mrs. Bellew put her hands on the cab door.

"I've a good mind to get out and dance with them!"

"You're mad to-night," said George. "Sit still!"

He stretched out his arm and barred her way. The passers-by looked curiously at the little scene. A crowd began to collect.

"Go on!" cried George.

There was a cheer from the crowd; the driver whipped his horse, they darted East again.

It was striking twelve when the cab put them down at last near the old church on Chelsea Embankment, and they had hardly spoken for an hour.

And all that hour George was feeling:

'This is the woman for whom I've given it all up. This is the woman to whom I shall be tied. This is the woman I cannot tear myself away from. If I could, I would never see her again. But I can't live without her. I must go on suffering when she's with me, suffering when she's away from me. And God knows how it's all to end!'

He took her hand in the darkness; it was cold and unresponsive as a stone. He tried to see her face, but could read nothing in those greenish eyes staring before them, like a cat's, into the darkness.

When the cab was gone they stood looking at each other by the light of a street lamp. And George thought:

'So I must leave her like this, and what then?'

She put her latch-key in the door, and turned round to him. In the silent, empty street, where the wind was rustling and scraping round the corners of tall houses, and the lamplight flickered, her face and figure were so strange, motionless, Sphinx-like. Only her eyes seemed alive, fastened on his own.

"Good-night!" he muttered.

She beckoned.

"Take what you can of me, George!" she said.

CHAPTER IV

MR. PENDYCE'S HEAD

MR. PENDYCE's head, seen from behind at his library bureau, where it was his practice to spend most mornings from half-past nine to eleven or even twelve, was observed to be of a shape to throw no small light upon his class and character. Its contour was almost national. Bulging at the back, and sloping rapidly to a thin and wiry neck, narrow between the ears and across the brow, prominent in the jaw, the length of a line drawn from the back headland to the promontory at the chin would have been extreme. Upon the observer there was impressed the conviction that here was a skull denoting, by surplusage of length, great precision of character and disposition to action, and, by deficiency of breadth, a narrow tenacity which might at times amount to wrongheadedness. The thin cantankerous neck, on which little hairs grew low, and the intelligent ears, confirmed this impression; and when his face, with its clipped hair, dry rosiness, into which the east wind had driven a shade of yellow and the sun a shade of brown, and grey, rather discontented eyes, came into view, the observer had no longer any hesitation in saying that he was in the presence of an Englishman, a landed proprietor, and, but for Mr. Pendyce's rooted belief to the contrary, an individualist. His head, indeed, was like nothing so much as the Admiralty Pier at Dover—that strange long narrow thing, with a slight twist or bend at the end, which first disturbs the comfort of foreigners arriving on these shores, and strikes them with a sense of wonder and dismay.

He sat very motionless at his bureau, leaning a little over his papers like a man to whom things do not come too easily; and every now and then he stopped to refer to the calendar at his left hand, or to a paper in one of the many pigeon-holes. Open, and almost out of reach, was a back volume of *Punch,* of which periodical, as a landed proprietor, he had an almost professional knowledge. In leisure moments it was one of his chief recreations to peruse lovingly those aged pictures, and at the image

96

of John Bull he never failed to think: 'Fancy making an Englishman out a fat fellow like that!'

It was as though the artist had offered an insult to himself, passing him over as the type, and conferring that distinction on someone fast going out of fashion. The Rector, whenever he heard Mr. Pendyce say this, strenuously opposed him, for he was himself of a square, stout build, and getting stouter.

With all their aspirations to the character of typical Englishmen, Mr. Pendyce and Mr. Barter thought themselves far from the old beef and beer, port and pigskin types of the Georgian and early Victorian era. They were men of the world, abreast of the times, who by virtue of a public school and 'Varsity training had acquired a manner, a knowledge of men and affairs, a standard of thought on which it had really never been needful to improve. Both of them, but especially Mr. Pendyce, kept up with all that was going forward by visiting the Metropolis six or seven or even eight times a year. On these occasions they rarely took their wives, having almost always important business in hand—old College, Church, or Conservative dinners, cricket-matches, Church Congress, the Gaiety Theatre, and for Mr. Barter the Lyceum. Both, too, belonged to clubs—the Rector to a comfortable, old-fashioned place where he could get a rubber without gambling, and Mr. Pendyce to the Temple of things as they had been, as became a man who, having turned all social problems over in his mind, had decided that there was no real safety but in the past.

They always went up to London grumbling, but this was necessary, and indeed salutary, because of their wives; and they always came back grumbling, because of their livers, which a good country rest always fortunately reduced in time for the next visit. In this way they kept themselves free from the taint of provincialism.

In the silence of his master's study the spaniel John, whose head, too, was long and narrow, had placed it over his paw, as though suffering from that silence, and when his master cleared his throat he fluttered his tail and turned up an eye with a little moon of white, without stirring his chin.

The clock ticked at the end of the long, narrow room; the sunlight through the long, narrow windows fell on the long, narrow backs of books in the glassed book-case that took up the whole of one wall; and this room, with its slightly leathery smell,

seemed a fitting place for some long, narrow ideal to be worked
out to its long and narrow ending.

But Mr. Pendyce would have scouted the notion of an ending
to ideals having their bases in the hereditary principle.

" Let me do my duty and carry on the estate as my dear old
father did, and hand it down to my son enlarged if possible,"
was sometimes his saying, very, very often his thought, not
seldom his prayer. " I want to do no more than that."

The times were bad and dangerous. There was every chance
of a Radical Government being returned, and the country going
to the dogs. It was but natural and human that he should pray
for the survival of the form of things which he believed in and
knew, the form of things bequeathed to him, and embodied in
the salutary words " Horace Pendyce." It was not his habit
to welcome new ideas. A new idea invading the country of the
Squire's mind was at once met with a rising of the whole population, and either prevented from landing, or if already on shore
instantly taken prisoner. In course of time the unhappy creature, causing its squeaks and groans to penetrate the prison walls,
would be released from sheer humaneness and love of a quiet
life, and even allowed certain privileges, remaining, however,
" that poor, queer devil of a foreigner." One day, in an inattentive moment, the natives would suffer it to marry, or find
that in some disgraceful way it had caused the birth of children
unrecognised by law ; and their respect for the accomplished fact,
for something that already lay in the past, would then prevent
their trying to unmarry it, or restoring the children to an un-
born state, and very gradually they would tolerate this intrusive
brood. Such was the process of Mr. Pendyce's mind. Indeed,
like the spaniel John, a dog of conservative instincts, at the
approach of any strange thing he placed himself in the way,
barking and showing his teeth ; and sometimes truly he suffered
at the thought that one day Horace Pendyce would no longer be
there to bark. But not often, for he had not much imagination.

All the morning he had been working at that old vexed subject of Common Rights on Worsted Scotton, which his father
had fenced in and taught him once for all to believe was part
integral of Worsted Skeynes. The matter was almost beyond
doubt, for the cottagers—in a poor way at the time of the fencing, owing to the price of bread—had looked on apathetically
till the very last year required by law to give the old Squire
squatter's rights, when all of a sudden that man, Peacock's

father, had made a gap in the fence and driven in beasts, which had reopened the whole unfortunate question. This had been in '65, and ever since there had been continual friction bordering on a law suit. Mr. Pendyce never for a moment allowed it to escape his mind that the man Peacock was at the bottom of it all; for it was his way to discredit all principles as ground of action, and to refer everything to facts and persons; except, indeed, when he acted himself, when he would somewhat proudly admit that it was on principle. He never thought or spoke on an abstract question; partly because his father had avoided them before him, partly because he had been discouraged from doing so at school, but mainly because he temperamentally took no interest in such unpractical things.

It was, therefore, a source of wonder to him that tenants of his own should be ungrateful. He did his duty by them, as the Rector, in whose keeping were their souls, would have been the first to affirm; the books of his estate showed this, recording year by year an average gross profit of some sixteen hundred pounds, and (deducting raw material incidental to the upkeep of Worsted Skeynes) a net loss of three.

In less earthly matters, too, such as non-attendance at church, a predisposition to poaching, or any inclination to moral laxity, he could say with a clear conscience that the Rector was sure of his support. A striking instance had occurred within the last month, when, discovering that his underkeeper, an excellent man at his work, had got into a scrape with the postman's wife, he had given the young fellow notice, and cancelled the lease of his cottage.

He rose and went to the plan of the estate fastened to the wall, which he unrolled by pulling a green silk cord, and stood there scrutinising it carefully and placing his finger here and there. His spaniel rose too, and settled himself unobtrusively on his master's foot. Mr. Pendyce moved and trod on him. The spaniel yelped.

"D——n the dog! Oh, poor fellow, John!" said Mr. Pendyce. He went back to his seat, but since he had identified the wrong spot he was obliged in a minute to return again to the plan. The spaniel John, cherishing the hope that he had been justly treated, approached in a half-circle, fluttering his tail; he had scarcely reached Mr. Pendyce's foot when the door was opened, and the first footman brought in a letter on a silver salver.

Mr. Pendyce took the note, read it, turned to his bureau, and said: "No answer."

He sat staring at this document in the silent room, and over his face in turn passed anger, alarm, distrust, bewilderment. He had not the power of making very clear his thought, except by speaking aloud, and he muttered to himself. The spaniel John, who still nurtured a belief that he had sinned, came and lay down very close against his leg.

Mr. Pendyce, never having reflected profoundly on the working morality of his times, had the less difficulty in accepting it. Of violating it he had practically no opportunity, and this rendered his position stronger. It was from habit and tradition rather than from principle and conviction that he was a man of good moral character.

And as he sat reading this note over and over, he suffered from a sense of nausea.

It was couched in these terms:

> "THE FIRS,
> "May 20.

"DEAR SIR,

"You may or may not have heard that I have made your son, Mr. George Pendyce, co-respondent in a divorce suit against my wife. Neither for your sake nor your son's, but for the sake of Mrs. Pendyce, who is the only woman in these parts that I respect, I will withdraw the suit if your son will give his word not to see my wife again.

"Please send me an early answer.

> "I am,
> "Your obedient servant,
> "JASPAR BELLEW."

The acceptance of tradition (and to accept it was suitable to the Squire's temperament) is occasionally marred by the impingement of tradition on private life and comfort. It was legendary in his class that young men's peccadilloes must be accepted with a certain indulgence. They would, he said, be young men. They must, he would remark, sow their wild oats. Such was his theory. The only difficulty he now had was in applying it to his own particular case, a difficulty felt by others in times past, and to be felt again in times to come. But, since he was not a philosopher, he did not perceive the inconsistency between his theory and his dismay. He saw his universe reeling

before that note, and he was not a man to suffer tamely; he felt
that others ought to suffer too. It was monstrous that a fellow
like this Bellew, a loose fish, a drunkard, a man who had nearly
run over him, should have it in his power to trouble the serenity
of Worsted Skeynes. It was like his impudence to bring such
a charge against his son. It was like his d——d impudence!
And going abruptly to the bell, he trod on his spaniel's ear.

"D——n the dog! Oh, poor fellow, John!" But the spaniel
John, convinced at last that he had sinned, hid himself in a
far corner whence he could see nothing, and pressed his chin
closely to the ground.

"Ask your mistress to come here."

Standing by the hearth, waiting for his wife, the Squire displayed to greater advantage than ever the shape of his long and
narrow head; his neck had grown conspicuously redder; his
eyes, like those of an offended swan, stabbed, as it were, at everything they saw.

It was not seldom that Mrs. Pendyce was summoned to the
study to hear him say: "I want to ask your advice. So-and-so
has done such and such . . . I have made up my mind."

She came, therefore, in a few minutes. In compliance with
his "Look at that, Margery," she read the note, and gazed at
him with distress in her eyes, and he looked back at her with
wrath in his. For this was tragedy.

Not to everyone is it given to take a wide view of things—
to look over the far, pale streams, the purple heather, and moonlit pools of the wild marches, where reeds stand black against the
sundown, and from long distance comes the cry of a curlew—
nor to everyone to gaze from steep cliffs over the wine-dark,
shadowy sea—or from high mountainsides to see crowned chaos,
smoking with mist, or gold-bright in the sun.

To most it is given to watch assiduously a row of houses, a
back-yard, or, like Mr. and Mrs. Pendyce, the green fields, trim
coverts, and Scotch garden of Worsted Skeynes. And on that
horizon the citation of their eldest son to appear in the Divorce
Court loomed like a cloud, heavy with destruction.

So far as such an event could be realised—imagination at
Worsted Skeynes was not too vivid—it spelled ruin to an harmonious edifice of ideas and prejudice and aspiration. It would
be no use to say of that event, "What does it matter? Let people
think what they like, talk as they like." At Worsted Skeynes
(and Worsted Skeynes was every country house) there was but

one set of people, one church, one pack of hounds, one everything. The importance of a clear escutcheon was too great. And they who had lived together for thirty-four years looked at each other with a new expression in their eyes; their feelings were for once the same. But since it is always the man who has the nicer sense of honour, their thoughts were not the same, for Mr. Pendyce was thinking: 'I won't believe it—disgracing us all!' and Mrs. Pendyce was thinking: 'My boy!'

It was she who spoke first.

"Oh, Horace!"

The sound of her voice restored the Squire's fortitude.

"There you go, Margery! D'you mean to say you believe what this fellow says? He ought to be horsewhipped. He knows my opinion of him. It's a piece of his confounded impudence! He nearly ran over me, and now——"

Mrs. Pendyce broke in:

"But, Horace, I'm afraid it's true! Ellen Malden——"

"Ellen Malden?" said Mr. Pendyce. "What business has she——" He was silent, staring gloomily at the plan of Worsted Skeynes, still unrolled, like an emblem of all there was at stake. "If George has really," he burst out, "he's a greater fool than I took him for! A fool? He's a knave!"

Again he was silent.

Mrs. Pendyce flushed at that word, and bit her lips.

"George could never be a knave!" she said.

Mr. Pendyce answered heavily:

"Disgracing his name!"

Mrs. Pendyce bit deeper into her lips.

"Whatever he has done," she said, "George is sure to have behaved like a gentleman!"

An angry smile twisted the Squire's mouth.

"Just like a woman!" he said.

But the smile died away, and on both their faces came a helpless look. Like people who have lived together without real sympathy—though, indeed, they had long ceased to be conscious of that—now that something had occurred in which their interests were actually at one, they were filled with a sort of surprise. It was no good to differ. Differing, even silent differing, would not help their son.

"I shall write to George," said Mr. Pendyce at last. "I shall believe nothing till I've heard from him. He'll tell us the truth, I suppose."

There was a quaver in his voice.

Mrs. Pendyce answered quickly:

"Oh, Horace, be careful what you say! I'm sure he is suffering!"

Her gentle soul, disposed to pleasure, was suffering, too, and the tears stole up in her eyes. Mr. Pendyce's sight was too long to see them. The infirmity had been growing on him ever since his marriage.

"I shall say what I think right," he said. "I shall take time to consider what I shall say; I won't be hurried by this ruffian."

Mrs. Pendyce wiped her lips with her lace-edged handkerchief.

"I hope you will show me the letter," she said.

The Squire looked at her, and he realised that she was trembling and very white, and, though this irritated him, he answered almost kindly:

"It's not a matter for you, my dear."

Mrs. Pendyce took a step towards him; her gentle face expressed a strange determination.

"He is my son, Horace, as well as yours."

Mr. Pendyce turned round uneasily.

"It's no use your getting nervous, Margery. I shall do what's best. You women lose your heads. That d——d fellow's lying! If he isn't——"

At these words the spaniel John rose from his corner and advanced to the middle of the floor. He stood there curved in a half-circle, and looked darkly at his master.

"Confound it!" said Mr. Pendyce. "It's—it's damnable!"

And as if answering for all that depended on Worsted Skeynes, the spaniel John deeply wagged that which had been left him of his tail.

Mrs. Pendyce came nearer still.

"If George refuses to give you that promise, what will you do, Horace?"

Mr. Pendyce stared.

"Promise? What promise?"

Mrs. Pendyce thrust forward the note.

"This promise not to see her again."

Mr. Pendyce motioned it aside.

"I'll not be dictated to by that fellow Bellew," he said. Then, by an afterthought: "It won't do to give him a chance. George must promise me that in any case."

Mrs. Pendyce pressed her lips together.

"But do you think he will?"

"Think—think who will? Think he will what? Why can't you express yourself, Margery? If George has really got us into this mess he must get us out again."

Mrs. Pendyce flushed.

"He would never leave her in the lurch!"

The Squire said angrily:

"Lurch! Who said anything about lurch? He owes it to *her*. Not that she deserves any consideration, if she's been—— You don't mean to say you think he'll refuse? He'd never be such a donkey!"

Mrs. Pendyce raised her hands and made what for her was a passionate gesture.

"Oh, Horace!" she said, "you don't understand. *He's in love with her!*"

Mr. Pendyce's lower lip trembled, a sign with him of excitement or emotion. All the conservative strength of his nature, all the immense dumb force of belief in established things, all that stubborn hatred and dread of change, that incalculable power of imagining nothing, which, since the beginning of time, had made Horace Pendyce the arbiter of his land, rose up within his sorely tried soul.

"What on earth's that to do with it?" he cried in a rage. "You women! You've no sense of anything! Romantic, idiotic, immoral—I don't know what you're at. For God's sake don't go putting ideas into his head!"

At this outburst Mrs. Pendyce's face became rigid; only the flicker of her eyelids betrayed how her nerves were quivering. Suddenly she threw her hands up to her ears.

"Horace!" she cried, "do—— Oh, *poor* John!"

The Squire had stepped hastily and heavily on to his dog's paw. The creature gave a grievous howl. Mr. Pendyce went down on his knees and raised the limb.

"Damn the dog!" he stuttered. "Oh, poor fellow, John!"

And the two long and narrow heads for a moment were close together.

CHAPTER V

RECTOR AND SQUIRE

THE efforts of social man, directed from immemorial time towards the stability of things, have culminated in Worsted Skeynes. Beyond commercial competition—for the estate no longer paid for living on it—beyond the power of expansion, set with tradition and sentiment, it was an undoubted jewel, past need of warranty. Cradled within it were all those hereditary institutions of which the country was most proud, and Mr. Pendyce sometimes saw before him the time when, for services to his party, he should call himself Lord Worsted, and after his own death continue sitting in the House of Lords in the person of his son. But there was another feeling in the Squire's heart—the air and the woods and the fields had passed into his blood a love for this, his home and the home of his fathers.

And so a terrible unrest pervaded the whole household after the receipt of Jaspar Bellew's note. Nobody was told anything, yet everybody knew there was something; and each after his fashion, down to the very dogs, betrayed their sympathy with the master and mistress of the house.

Day after day the girls wandered about the new golf course knocking the balls aimlessly; it was all they could do. Even Cecil Tharp, who had received from Bee the qualified affirmative natural under the circumstances, was infected. The off foreleg of her grey mare was being treated by a process he had recently discovered, and in the stables he confided to Bee that the dear old Squire seemed " off his feed; " he did not think it was any good worrying him at present. Bee, stroking the mare's neck, looked at him shyly and slowly.

" It's about George," she said; " I know it's about George! Oh, Cecil! I do wish I had been a boy ! "

Young Tharp assented in spite of himself:

" Yes; it must be beastly to be a girl."

A faint flush coloured Bee's cheeks. It hurt her a little that he should agree; but her lover was passing his hand down the mare's shin.

"Father *is* rather trying," she said. "I wish George would marry."

Cecil Tharp raised his bullet head; his blunt, honest face was extremely red from stooping.

"Clean as a whistle," he said; "*she's* all right, Bee. I expect George has too good a time."

Bee turned her face away and murmured:

"*I* should loathe living in London." And she, too, stooped and felt the mare's shin.

To Mrs. Pendyce in these days the hours passed with incredible slowness. For thirty odd years she had waited at once for everything and nothing; she had, so to say, everything she could wish for, and—nothing, so that even waiting had been robbed of poignancy; but to wait like this, in direct suspense, for something definite was terrible. There was hardly a moment when she did not conjure up George, lonely and torn by conflicting emotions; for to her, long paralysed by Worsted Skeynes, and ignorant of the facts, the proportions of the struggle in her son's soul appeared Titanic; her mother instinct was not deceived as to the strength of his passion. Strange and conflicting were the sensations with which she awaited the result; at one moment thinking, 'It is madness; he *must* promise—it is too awful!' at another, 'Ah! but how can he, if he loves her so? It is impossible; and she, too—ah! how awful it is!'

Perhaps, as Mr. Pendyce had said, she was romantic; perhaps it was only the thought of the pain her boy must suffer. The tooth was too big, it seemed to her; and, as in old days, when she took him to Cornmarket to have an aching tooth out, she ever sat with his hand in hers while the little dentist pulled, and ever suffered the tug, too, in her own mouth, so now she longed to share this other tug, so terrible, so fierce.

Against Mrs. Bellew she felt only a sort of vague and jealous aching; and this seemed strange even to herself—but, again, perhaps she was romantic.

Now it was that she found the value of routine. Her days were so well and fully occupied that anxiety was forced below the surface. The nights were far more terrible; for then, not only had she to bear her own suspense, but, as was natural in a wife, the fears of Horace Pendyce as well. The poor Squire found this the only time when he could get relief from worry; he came to bed much earlier on purpose. By dint of reiterating dreads and speculation he at length obtained some rest. Why had not George answered? What was the fellow about? And so on and so on, till, by sheer monotony, he caused in himself the need for slumber. But his wife's torments lasted till after the birds, starting with a sleepy cheeping, were at full morning chorus. Then only, turning softly for fear she should awaken him, the poor lady fell asleep.

For George had not answered.

In her morning visits to the village Mrs. Pendyce found herself, for the first time since she had begun this practice, driven by her own trouble over that line of diffident distrust which had always divided her from the hearts of her poorer neighbours. She was astonished at her own indelicacy, asking questions, prying into their troubles, pushed on by a secret aching for distraction; and she was surprised how well they took it—how, indeed, they seemed to like it, as though they knew that they were doing her good. In one cottage, where she had long noticed with pitying wonder a white-faced, black-eyed girl, who seemed to crouch away from everyone, she even received a request. It was delivered with terrified secrecy in a back-yard, out of Mrs. Barter's hearing.

"Oh, ma'am! Get me away from here! I'm in trouble—it's comin', and I don't know what I shall do."

Mrs. Pendyce shivered, and all the way home she thought: 'Poor little soul—poor little thing!' racking her brains to whom she might confide this case and ask for a solution; and something of the white-faced, black-eyed girl's terror and secrecy fell on her, for she found no one—not even Mrs. Barter, whose heart, though soft, belonged to the Rector. Then, by a sort of inspiration, she thought of Gregory.

'How can I write to him,' she mused, 'when my son——'

But she did write, for, deep down, the Totteridge instinct felt that others should do things for her; and she craved, too, to allude, however distantly, to what was on her mind. And, under the Pendyce eagle and the motto: *Strenuus aureâque pennâ,* thus her letter ran:

"DEAR GRIG,

"Can you do anything for a poor little girl in the village here who is 'in trouble'?—you know what I mean. It is such a terrible crime in this part of the country, and she looks so wretched and frightened, poor little thing! She is twenty years old. She wants a hiding-place for her misfortune, and some-

where to go when it is over. Nobody, she says, will have anything to do with her where they know; and, really, I have noticed
for a long time how white and wretched she looks, with great
black frightened eyes. I don't like to apply to our Rector, for
though he is a good fellow in many ways, he has such strong
opinions; and, of course, Horace could do nothing. I *would*
like to do something for her, and I could spare a little money,
but I can't find a place for her to go, and that makes it difficult.
She seems to be haunted, too, by the idea that wherever she goes
it will come out. Isn't it dreadful? Do do something, if you
can. I am rather anxious about George. I hope the dear boy
is well. If you are passing his club some day you might look
in and just ask after him. He is sometimes so naughty about
writing. I wish we could see you here, dear Grig; the country
is looking beautiful just now—the oak-trees especially—and
the apple-blossom isn't over, but I suppose you are too busy.
How is Helen Bellew? Is she in town?

> "Your affectionate cousin,
> "MARGERY PENDYCE."

It was four o'clock this same afternoon when the second groom,
very much out of breath, informed the butler that there was a
fire at Peacock's farm. The butler repaired at once to the
library. Mr. Pendyce, who had been on horseback all the morning, was standing in his riding-clothes, tired and depressed,
before the plan of Worsted Skeynes.

"What do you want, Bester?"

"There is a fire at Peacock's farm, sir."

Mr. Pendyce stared.

"What?" he said. "A fire in broad daylight! Nonsense!"

"You can see the flames from the front, sir."

The worn and querulous look left Mr. Pendyce's face.

"Ring the stable-bell!" he said. "Tell them all to run with
buckets and ladders. Send Higson off to Cornmarket on the
mare. Go and tell Mr. Barter, and rouse the village. Don't
stand there—God bless me! Ring the stable-bell!" And
snatching up his riding-crop and hat, he ran past the butler,
closely followed by the spaniel John.

Over the stile and along the footpath which cut diagonally
across a field of barley he moved at a stiff trot, and his spaniel,
who had not grasped the situation, frolicked ahead with a certain surprise. The Squire was soon out of breath—it was twenty

years or more since he had run a quarter of a mile. He did not, however, relax his speed. Ahead of him in the distance ran the second groom; behind him a labourer and a footman. The stable-bell at Worsted Skeynes began to ring. Mr. Pendyce crossed the stile and struck into the lane, colliding with the Rector, who was running, too, his face flushed to the colour of tomatoes. They ran on side by side.

"You go on!" gasped Mr. Pendyce at last, "and tell them I'm coming."

The Rector hesitated—he, too, was very out of breath—and started again, panting. The Squire, with his hand to his side, walked painfully on; he had run himself to a standstill. At a gap in the corner of the lane he suddenly saw pale-red tongues of flame against the sunlight.

"God bless me!" he gasped, and in sheer horror started to run again. Those sinister tongues were licking at the air over a large barn, some ricks, and the roofs of stables and outbuildings. Half a dozen figures were dashing buckets of water on the flames. The true insignificance of their efforts did not penetrate the Squire's mind. Trembling, and with a sickening pain in his lungs, he threw off his coat, wrenched a bucket from a huge agricultural labourer, who resigned it with awe, and joined the string of workers. Peacock, the farmer, ran past him; his face and round red beard were the colour of the flames he was trying to put out; tears dropped continually from his eyes and ran down that fiery face. His wife, a little dark woman with a twisted mouth, was working like a demon at the pump. Mr. Pendyce gasped to her:

"This is dreadful, Mrs. Peacock—this is dreadful!"

Conspicuous in black clothes and white shirt-sleeves, the Rector was hewing with an axe at the boarding of a cow-house, the door end of which was already in flames, and his voice could be heard above the tumult shouting directions to which nobody paid any heed.

"What's in that cow-house?" gasped Mr. Pendyce.

Mrs. Peacock, in a voice harsh with rage and grief answered: "It's the old horse and two of the cows!"

"God bless me!" cried the Squire, rushing forward with his bucket.

Some villagers came running up, and he shouted to these, but what he said neither he nor they could tell. The shrieks and snortings of the horse and cows, the steady whirr of the flames, drowned all lesser sounds. Of human cries, the Rector's voice alone was heard, between the crashing blows of his axe upon the woodwork.

Mr. Pendyce tripped; his bucket rolled out of his hand; he lay where he had fallen, too exhausted to move. He could still hear the crash of the Rector's axe, the sound of his shouts. Somebody helped him up, and trembling so that he could hardly stand, he caught an axe out of the hand of a strapping young fellow who had just arrived, and placing himself by the Rector's side, swung it feebly against the boarding. The flames and smoke now filled the whole cow-house, and came rushing through the gap that they were making. The Squire and the Rector stood their ground. With a furious blow Mr. Barter cleared a way. A cheer rose behind him, but no beast came forth. All three were dead in the smoke and flames.

The Squire, who could see in, flung down his axe, and covered his eyes with his hands. The Rector uttered a sound like a deep oath, and he, too, flung down his axe.

Two hours later, with torn and blackened clothes, the Squire stood by the ruins of the barn. The fire was out, but the ashes were still smouldering. The spaniel John, anxious, panting, was licking his master's boots, as though begging forgiveness that he had been so frightened, and kept so far away. Yet something in his eye seemed to be saying:

" Must you really have these fires, master? "

A black hand grasped the Squire's arm, a hoarse voice said: " I shan't forget, Squire! "

" God bless me, Peacock! " returned Mr. Pendyce, " that's nothing! You're insured, I hope? "

" Aye, I'm insured; but it's the beasts I'm thinking of! "

" Ah! " said the Squire, with a gesture of horror.

The brougham took him and the rector back together. Under their feet crouched their respective dogs, faintly growling at each other. A cheer from the crowd greeted their departure.

They started in silence, deadly tired. Mr. Pendyce said suddenly :

" I can't get those poor beasts out of my head, Barter! "

The Rector put his hand up to his eyes.

" I hope to God I shall never see such a sight again! Poor brutes, poor brutes! "

And feeling secretly for his dog's muzzle, he left his hand

against the animal's warm, soft, rubbery mouth, to be licked again and again.

On his side of the brougham Mr. Pendyce, also unseen, was doing precisely the same thing.

The carriage went first to the Rectory, where Mrs. Barter and her children stood in the doorway. The Rector put his head back into the brougham to say:

"Good-night, Pendyce. You'll be stiff to-morrow. I shall get my wife to rub me with Elliman!"

Mr. Pendyce nodded, raised his hat, and the carriage went on. Leaning back, he closed his eyes; a pleasanter sensation was stealing over him. True, he would be stiff to-morrow, but he had done his duty. He had shown them all that blood told; done something to bolster up that system which was—himself. And he had a new and kindly feeling towards Peacock, too. There was nothing like a little danger for bringing the lower classes closer; then it was they felt the need for officers, for something!

The spaniel John's head rose between his knees, turning up eyes with a crimson touch beneath.

'Master,' he seemed to say, 'I am feeling old. I know there are things beyond me in this life, but you, who know all things, will arrange that we shall be together even when we die.'

The carriage stopped at the entrance of the drive, and the Squire's thoughts changed. Twenty years ago he would have beaten Barter running down that lane. Barter was only forty-five. To give him fourteen years and a beating was a bit too much to expect. He felt a strange irritation with Barter—the fellow had cut a very good figure! He had shirked nothing. Elliman was too strong! Homocea was the thing. Margery would have to rub him! And suddenly, as though springing naturally from the name of his wife, George came into Mr. Pendyce's mind, and the respite that he had enjoyed from care was over. But the spaniel John, who scented home, began singing feebly for the brougham to stop, and beating a careless tail against his master's boot.

It was very stiffly, with frowning brows and a shaking under-lip, that the Squire descended from the brougham, and began sorely to mount the staircase to his wife's room.

CHAPTER VI

THE PARK

THERE comes a day each year in May when Hyde Park is possessed. A cool wind swings the leaves; a hot sun glistens on Long Water, on every bough, on every blade of grass. The birds sing their small hearts out, the band plays its gayest tunes, the white clouds race in the high blue heaven. Exactly why and how this day differs from those that came before and those that will come after, cannot be told; it is as though the Park said: 'To-day I live; the Past is past. I care not for the Future!'

And on this day they who chance in the Park cannot escape some measure of possession. Their steps quicken, their skirts swing, their sticks flourish, even their eyes brighten—those eyes so dulled with looking at the streets; and each one, if he has a Love, thinks of her, and here and there among the wandering throng he has her with him. To these the Park and all sweet-blooded mortals in it nod and smile.

There had been a meeting that afternoon at Lady Malden's in Prince's Gate to consider the position of the working-class woman. It had provided a somewhat heated discussion, for a person had got up and proved almost incontestably that the working-class woman had no position whatsoever.

Gregory Vigil and Mrs. Shortman had left this meeting together, and, crossing the Serpentine, struck a line over the grass.

"Mrs. Shortman," said Gregory, "don't you think we're all a little mad?"

He was carrying his hat in his hand, and his fine grizzled hair, rumpled in the excitement of the meeting, had not yet subsided on his head.

"Yes, Mr. Vigil. I don't exactly——"

"We *are* all a little mad! What did that woman, Lady Malden, mean by talking as she did? I detest her!"

"Oh, Mr. Vigil! She has the best intentions!"

"Intentions?" said Gregory. "I loathe her! What did we go to her stuffy drawing-room for? Look at that sky!"

Mrs. Shortman looked at the sky.

"But, Mr. Vigil," she said earnestly, "things would never get done. Sometimes I think you look at everything too much in the light of the way it ought to be!"

"The Milky Way," said Gregory.

Mrs. Shortman pursed her lips; she found it impossible to habituate herself to Gregory's habit of joking.

They had scant talk for the rest of their journey to the S.R.W.C., where Miss Mallow, at the typewriter, was reading a novel.

"There are several letters for you, Mr. Vigil."

"Mrs. Shortman says I am unpractical," answered Gregory. "Is that true, Miss Mallow?"

The colour in Miss Mallow's cheeks spread to her sloping shoulders.

"Oh no. You're most practical, only—perhaps—I don't know, perhaps you do try to do rather impossible things, Mr. Vigil."

"Bilcock Buildings!"

There was a minute's silence. Then Mrs. Shortman at her bureau beginning to dictate, the typewriter started clicking.

Gregory, who had opened a letter, was seated with his head in his hands. The voice ceased, the typewriter ceased, but Gregory did not stir. Both women, turning a little in their seats, glanced at him. Their eyes caught each other's and they looked away at once. A few seconds later they were looking at him again. Still Gregory did not stir. An anxious appeal began to creep into the women's eyes.

"Mr. Vigil," said Mrs. Shortman at last, "Mr. Vigil, do you think——"

Gregory raised his face; it was flushed to the roots of his hair.

"Read that, Mrs. Shortman."

Handing her a pale grey letter stamped with an eagle and the motto *Strenuus aureâque pennâ* he rose and paced the room. And as with his long, light stride he was passing to and fro, the woman at the bureau conned steadily the writing, the girl at the typewriter sat motionless with a red and jealous face.

Mrs. Shortman folded the letter, placed it on the top of the bureau, and said without raising her eyes:

"Of course, it is very sad for the poor little girl; but surely, Mr. Vigil, it must *always* be, so as to check, to check——"

Gregory stopped, and his shining eyes disconcerted her; they

seemed to her unpractical. Sharply lifting her voice, she went
on:

"If there were no disgrace, there would be no way of stopping it. I know the country better than you do, Mr. Vigil."

Gregory put his hands to his ears.

"We must find a place for her at once."

The window was fully open, so that he could not open it any
more, and he stood there as though looking for that place in the
sky. And the sky he looked at was very blue, and large white
birds of clouds were flying over it.

He turned from the window, and opened another letter.

"LINCOLN'S INN FIELDS,
"May 24, 1892.

"MY DEAR VIGIL,

"I gathered from your ward when I saw her yesterday that
she has not told you of what, I fear, will give you much pain.
I asked her point-blank whether she wished the matter kept
from you, and her answer was, 'He had better know—only I'm
sorry for him.' In sum it is this: Bellew has either got wind
of our watching him, or someone must have put him up to it;
he has anticipated us and brought a suit against your ward,
joining George Pendyce in the cause. George brought the citation to me. If necessary he's prepared to swear there's nothing
in it. He takes, in fact, the usual standpoint of the 'man
of honour.'

"I went at once to see your ward. She admitted that the
charge is true. I asked her if she wished the suit defended,
and a counter-suit brought against her husband. Her answer
to that was: 'I absolutely don't care.' I got nothing from
her but this, and, though it sounds odd, I believe it to be true.
She appears to be in a reckless mood, and to have no particular
ill-will against her husband.

"I want to see you, but only after you have turned this matter over carefully. It is my duty to put some considerations
before you. The suit, if brought, will be a very unpleasant matter for George, a still more unpleasant, even disastrous one, for
his people. The innocent in such cases are almost always the
greatest sufferers. If the cross-suit is instituted, it will assume
at once, considering their position in Society, the proportions
of a *cause célèbre,* and probably occupy the court and the daily
press anything from three days to a week, perhaps more, and

you know what that means. On the other hand, not to defend the suit, considering what we know, is, apart from ethics, revolting to my instincts as a fighter. My advice, therefore, is to make every effort to prevent matters being brought into court at all.

"I am an older man than you by thirteen years. I have a sincere regard for you, and I wish to save you pain. In the course of our interviews I have observed your ward very closely, and at the risk of giving you offence, I am going to speak out my mind. Mrs. Bellew is a rather remarkable woman. From two or three allusions that you have made in my presence, I believe that she is altogether different from what you think. She is, in my opinion, one of those very vital persons upon whom our judgments, censures, even our sympathies, are wasted. A woman of this sort, if she comes of a county family, and is thrown by circumstances with Society people, is always bound to be conspicuous. If you would realise something of this, it would, I believe, save you a great deal of pain. In short, I beg of you not to take her, or her circumstances, too seriously. There are quite a number of such men and women as her husband and herself, and they are always certain to be more or less before the public eye. Whoever else goes down, she will swim, simply because she can't help it. I want you to see things as they are.

"I ask you again, my dear Vigil, to forgive me for writing thus, and to believe that my sole desire is to try and save you unnecessary suffering.

"Come and see me as soon as you have reflected.
"I am,
"Your sincere friend,
"EDMUND PARAMOR."

Gregory made a movement like that of a blind man. Both women were on their feet at once.

"What is it, Mr. Vigil? Can I get you anything?"

"Thanks; nothing, nothing. I've had some rather bad news. I'll go out and get some air. I shan't be back to-day."

He found his hat and went.

He walked towards the Park, unconsciously attracted towards the biggest space, the freshest air; his hands were folded behind him, his head bowed. And since, of all things, Nature is ironical, it was fitting that he should seek the Park this day when it was gayest. And far in the Park, as near the centre as might be, he lay down on the grass. For a long time he lay without moving, his hands over his eyes, and in spite of Mr. Paramor's reminder that his suffering was unnecessary, he suffered.

And mostly he suffered from black loneliness, for he was a very lonely man, and now he had lost that which he had thought he had. It is difficult to divide suffering, difficult to say how much he suffered, because, being in love with her, he had secretly thought she must love him a little, and how much he suffered because his private portrait of her, the portrait that he, and he alone, had painted, was scored through with the knife. And he lay first on his face, and then on his back, with his hand always over his eyes. And around him were other men lying on the grass, and some were lonely, and some hungry, and some asleep, and some were lying there for the pleasure of doing nothing and for the sake of the hot sun on their cheeks; and by the side of some lay their girls, and it was these that Gregory could not bear to see, for his spirit and his senses were a-hungered. In the plantations close by were pigeons, and never for a moment did they stop cooing; never did the blackbirds cease their courting songs; the sun its hot, sweet burning; the clouds above their love-chase in the sky. It was the day without a past, without a future, when it is not good for man to be alone. And no man looked at him, because it was no man's business, but a woman here and there cast a glance on that long, tweed-suited figure with the hand over the eyes, and wondered, perhaps, what was behind that hand. Had they but known, they would have smiled their woman's smile that he should so have mistaken one of their sex.

Gregory lay quite still, looking at the sky, and because he was a loyal man he did not blame her, but slowly, very slowly, his spirit, like a spring stretched to the point of breaking, came back upon itself, and since he could not bear to see things as they were, he began again to see them as they were not.

'She has been forced into this,' he thought. 'It is George Pendyce's fault. To me she is, she must be, the same!'

He turned again on to his face. And a small dog who had lost its master sniffed at his boots, and sat down a little way off, to wait till Gregory could do something for him, because he smelled that he was that sort of man.

CHAPTER VII

DOUBTFUL POSITION AT WORSTED SKEYNES

WHEN George's answer came at last, the flags were in full bloom round the Scotch garden at Worsted Skeynes. They grew in masses and of all shades, from deep purple to pale grey, and their scent, very penetrating, very delicate, floated on the wind.

While waiting for that answer, it had become Mr. Pendyce's habit to promenade between these beds, his hand to his back, for he was still a little stiff, followed at a distance of seven paces by the spaniel John, very black, and moving his rubbery nostrils uneasily from side to side.

In this way the two passed every day the hour from twelve to one. Neither could have said why they walked thus, for Mr. Pendyce had a horror of idleness, and the spaniel John disliked the scent of irises; both, in fact, obeyed that part of themselves which is superior to reason. During this hour, too, Mrs. Pendyce, though longing to walk between her flowers, also obeyed that part of her, superior to reason, which told her that it would be better not.

But George's answer came at last.

" STOICS' CLUB.

" DEAR FATHER,

" Yes, Bellew is bringing a suit. I am taking steps in the matter. As to the promise you ask for, I can give no promise of the sort. You may tell Bellew I will see him d——d first.

" Your affectionate son,
" GEORGE PENDYCE."

Mr. Pendyce received this at the breakfast-table, and while he read it there was a hush, for all had seen the handwriting on the envelope.

Mr. Pendyce read it through twice, once with his glasses on and once without, and when he had finished the second reading he placed it in his breast pocket. No word escaped him; his eyes, which had sunk a little the last few days, rested angrily on his wife's white face. Bee and Norah looked down, and,

as if they understood, the four dogs were still. Mr. Pendyce
pushed his plate back, rose, and left the room.

Norah looked up.

"What's the matter, Mother?"

Mrs. Pendyce was swaying. She recovered herself in a moment.

"Nothing, dear. It's very hot this morning, don't you think?
I'll just go to my room and take some sal volatile."

She went out, followed by old Roy, the Skye; the spaniel John,
who had been cut off at the door by his master's abrupt exit,
preceded her. Norah and Bee pushed back their plates.

"I can't eat, Norah," said Bee. "It's horrible not to know
what's going on."

Norah answered:

"It's perfectly brutal not being a man. You might just as
well be a dog as a girl, for anything anyone tells you!"

Mrs. Pendyce did not go to her room; she went to the library.
Her husband, seated at his table, had George's letter before him.
A pen was in his hand, but he was not writing.

"Horace," she said softly, "here is poor John!"

Mr. Pendyce did not answer, but put down the hand that
did not hold his pen. The spaniel John covered it with kisses.

"Let me see the letter, won't you?"

Mr. Pendyce handed it to her without a word. She touched
his shoulder gratefully, for his unusual silence went to her heart.
Mr. Pendyce took no notice, staring at his pen as though surprised that, of its own accord, it did not write his answer; but
suddenly he flung it down and looked round, and his look
seemed to say: 'You brought this fellow into the world; now
see the result!'

He had had so many days to think and put his finger on the
doubtful spots of his son's character. All that week he had
become more and more certain of how, without his wife, George
would have been exactly like himself. Words sprang to his lips,
and kept on dying there. The doubt whether she would agree
with him, the feeling that she sympathised with her son, the
certainty that something even in himself responded to those
words: "You can tell Bellew I will see him d——d first!"—
all this, and the thought, never out of his mind, 'The name—
the estate!' kept him silent. He turned his head away, and
took up his pen again.

Mrs. Pendyce had read the letter now three times, and instinctively had put it in her bosom. It was not hers, but Horace must know it by heart, and in his anger he might tear it up. That letter, for which they had waited so long, told her nothing; she had known all there was to tell. Her hand had fallen from Mr. Pendyce's shoulder, and she did not put it back, but ran her fingers through and through each other, while the sunlight, traversing the narrow windows, caressed her from her hair down to her knees. Here and there that stream of sunlight formed little pools—in her eyes, giving them a touching, anxious brightness; in a curious heart-shaped locket of carved steel, worn by her mother and her grandmother before her, containing now, not locks of *their* son's hair, but a curl of George's; in her diamond rings and a bracelet of amethyst and pearl which she wore for the love of pretty things. And the warm sunlight disengaged from her a scent of lavender. Through the library door a scratching nose told that the dear dogs knew she was not in her bedroom. Mr. Pendyce, too, caught that scent of lavender, and in some vague way it augmented his discomfort. Her silence, too, distressed him. It did not occur to him that his silence was distressing her. He put down his pen.

"I can't write with you standing there, Margery!"

Mrs. Pendyce moved out of the sunlight.

"George says he is taking steps. What does that mean, Horace?"

This question, focussing his doubts, broke down the Squire's dumbness.

"I won't be treated like this!" he said. "I'll go up and see him myself!"

He went by the 10.20, saying that he would be down again by the 5.55.

Soon after seven the same evening a dogcart, driven by a young groom and drawn by a raking chestnut mare with a blaze face, swung into the railway-station at Worsted Skeynes, and drew up before the booking-office. Mr. Pendyce's brougham, behind a brown horse, coming a little later, was obliged to range itself behind. A minute before the train's arrival a wagonette and a pair of bays, belonging to Lord Quarryman, wheeled in, and, filing past the other two, took up its place in front. Outside this little row of vehicles the station fly and two farmers' gigs presented their backs to the station buildings. And in this arrangement there was something harmonious and fitting, as though Providence itself had guided them all and assigned to each its place. And Providence had only made one error—that of placing Captain Bellew's dogcart precisely opposite the booking-office, instead of Lord Quarryman's wagonette, with Mr. Pendyce's brougham next.

Mr. Pendyce came out first; he stared angrily at the dogcart, and moved to his own carriage. Lord Quarryman came out second. His massive sun-burned head—the back of which, sparsely adorned by hairs, ran perfectly straight into his neck—was crowned by a grey top-hat. The skirts of his grey coat were square-shaped, and so were the toes of his boots.

"Hallo, Pendyce!" he called out heartily; "didn't see you on the platform. How's your wife?"

Mr. Pendyce, turning to answer, met the little burning eyes of Captain Bellew, who came out third. They failed to salute each other, and Bellew, springing into his cart, wrenched his mare round, circled the farmers' gigs, and, sitting forward, drove off at a furious pace. His groom, running at full speed, clung to the cart and leaped on to the step behind. Lord Quarryman's wagonette backed itself into the place left vacant. And the mistake of Providence was rectified.

"Cracked chap, that fellow Bellew. D'you see anything of him?"

Mr. Pendyce answered:

"No; and I want to see less. I wish he'd take himself off!"

His lordship smiled.

"A huntin' country seems to breed fellows like that; there's always one of 'em to every pack of hounds. Where's his wife now? Good-lookin' woman; rather warm member, eh?"

It seemed to Mr. Pendyce that Lord Quarryman's eyes searched his own with a knowing look, and muttering "God knows!" he vanished into his brougham.

Lord Quarryman looked kindly at his horses. He was not a man who reflected on the whys, the wherefores, the becauses, of this life. The good God had made him Lord Quarryman, had made his eldest son Lord Quantock; the good God had made the Gaddesdon hounds—it was enough!

When Mr. Pendyce reached home he went to his dressing-room. In a corner by the bath the spaniel John lay surrounded by an assortment of his master's slippers, for it was thus alone that he could soothe in measure the bitterness of separation. His dark brown eye was fixed upon the door, and round it gleamed a crescent moon of white. He came to the Squire fluttering his tail, with a slipper in his mouth, and his eye said plainly: ' Oh, master, where have you been? Why have you been so long? I have been expecting you ever since half-past ten this morning!'

Mr. Pendyce's heart opened a moment and closed again. He said " John! " and began to dress for dinner.

Mrs. Pendyce found him tying his white tie. She had plucked the first rosebud from her garden; she had plucked it because she felt sorry for him, and because of the excuse it would give her to go to his dressing-room at once.

" I've brought you a buttonhole, Horace. Did you see him? "

" No."

Of all answers this was the one she dreaded most. She had not believed that anything would come of an interview; she had trembled all day long at the thought of their meeting; but now that they had not met she knew by the sinking in her heart that anything was better than uncertainty. She waited as long as she could, then burst out:

" Tell me something, Horace! "

Mr. Pendyce gave her an angry glance.

" How can I tell you, when there's nothing to tell? I went to his club. He's not living there now. He's got rooms, nobody knows where. I waited all the afternoon. Left a message at last for him to come down here to-morrow. I've sent for Paramor, and told him to come down too. I won't put up with this sort of thing."

Mrs. Pendyce looked out of the window, but there was nothing to see save the ha-ha, the coverts, the village spire, the cottage roofs, which for so long had been her world.

" George won't come down here," she said.

" George will do what I tell him."

Again Mrs. Pendyce shook her head, knowing by instinct that she was right.

Mr. Pendyce stopped putting on his waist-coat.

" George had better take care," he said; " he's entirely dependent on me."

And as if with those words he had summed up the situation, the philosophy of a system vital to his son, he no longer frowned. On Mrs. Pendyce those words had a strange effect. They stirred within her terror. It was like seeing her son's back bared to a lifted whip-lash; like seeing the door shut against him on a snowy night. But besides terror they stirred within her a more poignant feeling yet, as though someone had dared to show a whip to herself, had dared to defy that something more precious than life in her soul, that something which was of her blood, so utterly and secretly passed by the centuries into her fibre that no one had ever thought of defying it before. And there flashed before her with ridiculous concreteness the thought: 'I've got three hundred a year of my own!' Then the whole feeling left her, just as in dreams a mordant sensation grips and passes, leaving a dull ache, whose cause is forgotten, behind.

"There's the gong, Horace," she said. "Cecil Tharp is here to dinner. I asked the Barters, but poor Rose didn't feel up to it. Of course they are expecting it very soon now. They talk of the 15th of June."

Mr. Pendyce took from his wife his coat, passing his arms down the satin sleeves.

"If I could get the cottagers to have families like that," he said, "I shouldn't have much trouble about labour. They're a pig-headed lot—do nothing that they're told. Give me some eau-de-Cologne, Margery."

Mrs. Pendyce dabbed the wicker flask on her husband's handkerchief.

"Your eyes look tired," she said. "Have you a headache, dear?"

CHAPTER VIII

COUNCIL AT WORSTED SKEYNES

It was on the following evening—the evening on which he was expecting his son and Mr. Paramor—that the Squire leaned forward over the dining-table and asked:

"What do you say, Barter? I'm speaking to you as a man of the world."

The Rector bent over his glass of port and moistened his lower lip.

"There's no excuse for that woman," he answered. "I always thought she was a bad lot."

Mr. Pendyce went on:

"We've never had a scandal in my family. I find the thought of it hard to bear, Barter—I find it hard to bear——"

The Rector emitted a low sound. He had come from long usage to have a feeling like affection for his Squire.

Mr. Pendyce pursued his thoughts.

"We've gone on," he said, "father and son for hundreds of years. It's a blow to me, Barter."

Again the Rector emitted that low sound.

"What will the village think?" said Mr. Pendyce; "and the farmers—I mind that more than anything. Most of them knew my dear old father—not that he was popular. It's a bitter thing."

The Rector said:

"Well, well, Pendyce, perhaps it won't come to that."

He looked a little shamefaced, and his light eyes were full of something like contrition.

"How does Mrs. Pendyce take it?"

The Squire looked at him for the first time.

"Ah!" he said; "you never know anything about women. I'd as soon trust a woman to be just as I'd—I'd finish that magnum; it'd give me gout in no time."

The Rector emptied his glass.

"I've sent for George and my solicitor," pursued the Squire; "they'll be here directly."

Mr. Barker pushed his chair back, and raising his right ankle

123

on to his left leg, clasped his hands round his right knee; then, leaning forward, he stared up under his jutting brows at Mr. Pendyce. It was the attitude in which he thought best.

Mr. Pendyce ran on:

"I've nursed the estate ever since it came to me; I've carried on the tradition as best I could; I've not been as good a man, perhaps, as I should have wished, but I've always tried to remember my old father's words: 'I'm done for, Horry; the estate's in your hands now.'" He cleared his throat.

For a full minute there was no sound save the ticking of the clock. Then the spaniel John, coming silently from under the sideboard, fell heavily down against his master's leg with a lengthy snore of satisfaction. Mr. Pendyce looked down.

"This fellow of mine," he muttered, "is getting fat."

It was evident from the tone of his voice that he desired his emotion to be forgotten. Something very deep in Mr. Barter respected that desire.

"It's a first-rate magnum," he said.

Mr. Pendyce filled his Rector's glass.

"I forgot if you knew Paramor. He was before your time. He was at Harrow with me."

The Rector took a prolonged sip.

"I shall be in the way," he said. "I'll take myself off."

The Squire put out his hand affectionately.

"No, no, Barter, don't you go. It's all safe with you. I mean to act. I can't stand this uncertainty. My wife's cousin Vigil is coming too—he's her guardian. I wired for him. You know Vigil? He was about your time."

The Rector turned crimson, and set his underlip. Having scented his enemy, nothing would now persuade him to withdraw; and the conviction that he had only done his duty, a little shaken by the Squire's confidence, returned as though by magic.

"Yes, I know him."

"We'll have it all out here," muttered Mr. Pendyce, "over this port. There's the carriage. Get up, John."

The spaniel John rose heavily, looked sardonically at Mr. Barter, and again flopped down against his master's leg.

"Get up, John," said Mr. Pendyce again. The spaniel John snored.

'If I move, you'll move too, and uncertainty will begin for me again,' he seemed to say.

Mr. Pendyce disengaged his leg, rose, and went to the door. Before reaching it he turned and came back to the table.

"Barter," he said, "I'm not thinking of myself—I'm not thinking of myself—we've been here for generations—it's the principle." His face had the least twist to one side, as though conforming to a kink in his philosophy; his eyes looked sad and restless.

And the Rector, watching the door for the sight of his enemy, also thought:

'I'm not thinking of myself—I'm satisfied that I did right —I'm Rector of this parish—it's the principle.'

The spaniel John gave three short barks, one for each of the persons who entered the room. They were Mrs. Pendyce, Mr. Paramor, and Gregory Vigil.

"Where's George?" asked the Squire, but no one answered him.

The Rector, who had resumed his seat, stared at a little gold cross which he had taken out of his waistcoat pocket. Mr. Paramor lifted a vase and sniffed at the rose it contained; Gregory walked to the window.

When Mr. Pendyce realised that his son had not come, he went to the door and held it open.

"Be good enough to take John out, Margery," he said. "John!"

The spaniel John, seeing what lay before him, rolled over on his back.

Mrs. Pendyce fixed her eyes on her husband, and in those eyes she put all the words which the nature of a lady did not suffer her to speak.

'I claim to be here. Let me stay; it is my right. *Don't* send me away.' So her eyes spoke, and so those of the spaniel John, lying on his back, in which attitude he knew that he was hard to move.

Mr. Pendyce turned him over with his foot.

"Get up, John! Be good enough to take John out, Margery."

Mrs. Pendyce flushed, but did not move.

"John," said Mr. Pendyce, "go with your mistress." The spaniel John fluttered a drooping tail. Mr. Pendyce pressed his foot to it. "This is not a subject for women."

Mrs. Pendyce bent down.

"Come, John," she said. The spaniel John, showing the whites of his eyes, and trying to back through his collar, was assisted from the room. Mr. Pendyce closed the door behind them.

"Have a glass of port, Vigil; it's the '47. My father laid it down in '56, the year before he died. Can't drink it myself—I've had to put down two hogsheads of the Jubilee wine. Paramor, fill your glass. Take that chair next to Paramor, Vigil. You know Barter?"

Both Gregory's face and the Rector's were very red.

"We're all Harrow men here," went on Mr. Pendyce. And suddenly turning to Mr. Paramor, he said: "Well?"

Just as round the hereditary principle are grouped the State, the Church, Law, and Philanthropy, so round the dining-table at Worsted Skeynes sat the Squire, the Rector, Mr. Paramor, and Gregory Vigil, and none of them wished to be the first to speak. At last Mr. Paramor, taking from his pocket Bellew's note and George's answer, which were pinned in strange alliance, returned them to the Squire.

"I understand the position to be that George refuses to give her up; at the same time he is prepared to defend the suit and deny everything. Those are his instructions to me." Taking up the vase again, he sniffed long and deep at the rose.

Mr. Pendyce broke the silence.

"As a gentleman," he said in a voice sharpened by the bitterness of his feelings, "I suppose he's obliged——"

Gregory, smiling painfully, added:

"To tell lies."

Mr. Pendyce turned on him at once.

"I've nothing to say about that, Vigil. George has behaved abominably. I don't uphold him; but if the woman wishes the suit defended he can't play the cur—that's what *I* was brought up to believe."

Gregory leaned his forehead on his hand.

"The whole system is odious——" he was beginning.

Mr. Paramor chimed in.

"Let us keep to the facts; they are enough without the system."

The Rector spoke for the first time.

"I don't know what you mean about the system; both this man and this woman are guilty——"

Gregory said in a voice that quivered with rage:

"Be so kind as not to use the expression, ' this woman.' "

The Rector glowered.

"What expression then——"

Mr. Pendyce's voice, to which the intimate trouble of his thoughts lent a certain dignity, broke in:

"Gentlemen, this is a question concerning the honour of my house."

There was another and a longer silence, during which Mr. Paramor's eyes haunted from face to face, while beyond the rose a smile writhed on his lips.

"I suppose you have brought me down here, Pendyce, to give you my opinion," he said at last. "Well; don't let these matters come into court. If there is anything you can do to prevent it, do it. If your pride stands in the way, put it in your pocket. If your sense of truth stands in the way, forget it. Between personal delicacy and our law of divorce there is no relation; between absolute truth and our law of divorce there is no relation. I repeat, don't let these matters come into court. Innocent and guilty, you will all suffer; the innocent will suffer more than the guilty, and nobody will benefit. I have come to this conclusion deliberately. There are cases in which I should give the opposite opinion. But in *this* case, I repeat, there's nothing to be gained by it. Once more, then, don't let these matters come into court. Don't give people's tongues a chance. Take my advice, appeal to George again to give you that promise. If he refuses, well, we must try and bluff Bellew out of it."

Mr. Pendyce had listened, as he had formed the habit of listening to Edmund Paramor, in silence. He now looked up and said:

"It's all that red-haired ruffian's spite. I don't know what you were about to stir things up, Vigil. You must have put him on the scent." He looked moodily at Gregory. Mr. Barter, too, looked at Gregory with a sort of half-ashamed defiance.

Gregory, who had been staring at his untouched wineglass, turned his face, very flushed, and began speaking in a voice that emotion and anger caused to tremble. He avoided looking at the Rector, and addressed himself to Mr. Paramor.

"George can't give up the woman who has trusted herself to him; *that* would be playing the cur, if you like. Let them go and live together honestly until they can be married. Why do you all speak as if it were the man who mattered? It is the woman that we should protect!"

The Rector first recovered speech.

"You're talking rank immorality," he said almost good-humouredly.

Mr. Pendyce rose.

"Marry her!" he cried. "What on earth—that's worse than all—the very thing we're trying to prevent! We've been here, father and son—father and son—for generations!"

"All the more shame," burst out Gregory, "if you can't stand by a woman at the end of them!"

Mr. Paramor made a gesture of reproof.

"There's moderation in all things," he said. "Are you sure that Mrs. Bellew requires protection? If you are right, I agree; but are you right?"

"I will answer for it," said Gregory.

Mr. Paramore paused a full minute with his head resting on his hand.

"I am sorry," he said at last, "I must trust to my own judgment."

The Squire looked up.

"If the worst comes to the worst, can I cut the entail, Paramore?"

"No."

"What? But that's all wrong—that's——"

"You can't have it both ways," said Mr. Paramor.

The Squire looked at him dubiously, then blurted out:

"If I choose to leave him nothing but the estate, he'll soon find himself a beggar. I beg your pardon, gentlemen; fill your glasses! I'm forgetting everything!"

The Rector filled his glass.

"I've said nothing so far," he began; "I don't feel that it's my business. My conviction is that there's far too much divorce nowadays. Let this woman go back to her husband, and let him show her where she's to blame"—his voice and his eyes hardened—"then let them forgive each other like Christians. You talk," he said to Gregory, "about standing up for the woman. I've no patience with that; it's the way immorality's fostered in these days. I raise my voice against this sentimentalism. I always have, and I always shall!"

Gregory jumped to his feet.

"I've told you once before," he said, "that you were indelicate; I tell you so again."

Mr. Barter got up, and stood bending over the table, crimson in the face, staring at Gregory, and unable to speak.

"Either you or I," he said at last, stammering with passion, "must leave this room!"

Gregory tried to speak; then turning abruptly, he stepped out on to the terrace, and passed from the view of those within.

The Rector said:

"Good-night, Pendyce; I'm going, too!"

The Squire shook the hand held out to him with a face perplexed to sadness. There was silence when Mr. Barter had left the room.

The Squire broke it with a sigh.

"I wish we were back at Oxenham's, Paramor! This serves me right for deserting the old house! What on earth made me send George to Eton?"

Mr. Paramor buried his nose in the vase. In this saying of his old schoolfellow was the whole of the Squire's creed:

'I believe in my father, and his father, and his father's father, the makers and keepers of my estate; and I believe in myself and my son and my son's son. And I believe that we have made the country, and shall keep the country what it is. And I believe in the Public Schools, and especially the Public School that I was at. And I believe in my social equals and the country house, and in things as they are, for ever and ever. Amen.'

Mr. Pendyce went on:

"I'm not a Puritan, Paramor; I dare say there are allowances to be made for George. I don't even object to the woman herself; she may be too good for Bellew; she must be too good for a fellow like that! But for George to marry her would be ruination. Look at Lady Rose's case! Anyone but a stargazing fellow like Vigil must see that! It's taboo! It's sheer taboo! And think—think of my—my grandson! No, no, Paramor; no, no, by God!"

The Squire covered his eyes with his hand.

Mr. Paramor, who had no son himself, answered with feeling:

"Now, now, old fellow; it won't come to that!"

"God knows what it will come to, Paramor! My nerve's shaken! You know yourself that if there's a divorce he'll be bound to marry her!"

To this Mr. Paramor made no reply, but pressed his lips together.

"There's your poor dog whining," he said.

And without waiting for permission he opened the door. Mrs. Pendyce and the spaniel John came in. The Squire looked up and frowned. The spaniel John, panting with delight, rubbed against him. 'I have been through torment, master,' he seemed to say. 'A second separation at present is not possible for me!'

Mrs. Pendyce stood waiting silently, and Mr. Paramor addressed himself to her.

"*You* can do more than any of us, Mrs. Pendyce, both with George and with this man Bellew—and, if I am not mistaken, with his wife."

The Squire broke in:

"Don't think that I'll have any humble pie eaten to that fellow Bellew!"

The look Mr. Paramor gave him at those words was like that of a doctor diagnosing a disease. Yet there was nothing in the expression of the Squire's face with its thin grey whiskers and moustache, its twist to the left, its swan-like eyes, decided jaw, and sloping brow, different from what this idea might bring on the face of any country gentleman.

Mrs. Pendyce said eagerly:

"Oh, Mr. Paramor, if I could only see George!"

She longed so for a sight of her son that her thoughts carried her no further.

"See him!" cried the Squire. "You'll go on spoiling him till he's disgraced us all!"

Mrs. Pendyce turned from her husband to his solicitor. Excitement had fixed an unwonted colour in her cheeks; her lips twitched as if she wished to speak.

Mr. Paramor answered for her:

"No, Pendyce; if George is spoilt, the system is to blame."

"System!" said the Squire. "I've never had a system for him. I'm no believer in systems! I don't know what you're talking of. I have another son, thank God!"

Mrs. Pendyce took a step forward.

"Horace," she said, "you would never——"

Mr. Pendyce turned from his wife, and said sharply:

"Paramor, are you sure I can't cut the entail?"

"As sure," said Mr. Paramor, "as I sit here!"

CHAPTER IX

DEFINITION OF "PENDYCITIS"

GREGORY walked along in the Scotch garden with his eyes on the stars. One, larger than all the rest, over the larches, shone on him ironically, for it was the star of love. And on his beat between the yew-trees that, living before Pendyces came to Worsted Skeynes, would live when they were gone, he cooled his heart in the silver light of that big star. The irises restrained their perfume lest it should whip his senses; only the young larch-trees and the far fields sent him their fugitive sweetness through the dark. And the same brown owl that had hooted when Helen Bellew kissed George Pendyce in the conservatory hooted again now that Gregory walked grieving over the fruits of that kiss.

His thoughts were of Mr. Barter, and with the injustice natural to a man who took a warm and personal view of things, he painted the Rector in colours darker than his cloth.

'Indelicate, meddlesome,' he thought. 'How dare he speak of her like that!'

Mr. Paramor's voice broke in on his meditations.

"Still cooling your heels? Why did you play the deuce with us in there?"

"I hate a sham," said Gregory. "This marriage of my ward's is a sham. She had better live honestly with the man she really loves!"

"So you said just now," returned Mr. Paramor. "Would you apply that to everyone?"

"I would."

"Well," said Mr. Paramor with a laugh, "there is nothing like an idealist for making hay! You once told me, if I remember, that marriage was sacred to you!"

"Those are my own private feelings, Paramor. But here the mischief's done already. It is a sham, a hateful sham, and it ought to come to an end!"

"That's all very well," replied Mr. Paramor, "but when you come to put it into practice in that wholesale way it leads to goodness knows what. It means reconstructing marriage on a

131

basis entirely different from the present. It's marriage on the basis of the heart, and not on the basis of property. Are you prepared to go to that length?"

"I am."

"You're as much of an extremist one way as Barter is the other. It's you extremists who do all the harm. There's a golden mean, my friend. I agree that something ought to be done. But what you don't see is that laws must suit those they are intended to govern. You're too much in the stars, Vigil. Medicine must be graduated to the patient. Come, man, where's your sense of humour? Imagine your conception of marriage applied to Pendyce and his sons, or his Rector, or his tenants, and the labourers on his estate."

"No, no," said Gregory; "I refuse to believe——"

"The country classes," said Mr. Paramor quietly, "are especially backward in such matters. They have strong, meat-fed instincts, and what with the county Members, the Bishops, the Peers, all the hereditary force of the country, they still rule the roast. And there's a certain disease—to make a very poor joke, call it 'Pendycitis'—with which most of these people are infected. They're 'crass.' They do things, but they do them the wrong way! They muddle through with the greatest possible amount of unnecessary labour and suffering! It's part of the hereditary principle. I haven't had to do with them thirty-five years for nothing!"

Gregory turned his face away.

"Your joke *is* very poor," he said. "I don't believe they are like that! I won't admit it. If there is such a disease, it's our business to find a remedy."

"Nothing but an operation will cure it," said Mr. Paramor; "and before operating there's a preliminary process to be gone through. It was discovered by Lister."

Gregory answered:

"Paramor, I hate your pessimism!"

Mr. Paramor's eyes haunted Gregory's back.

"But I am not a pessimist," he said. "Far from it.

> "'When daisies pied and violets blue,
> And lady-smocks all silver-white,
> And cuckoo-buds of yellow hue
> Do paint the meadows with delight,
> The cuckoo then, on every tree——'"

Gregory turned on him.

"How can you quote poetry, and hold the views you do? We ought to construct——"

"You want to build before you've laid your foundations," said Mr. Paramor. "You let your feelings carry you away, Vigil. The state of the marriage laws is only a symptom. It's this disease, this grudging narrow spirit in men, that makes such laws necessary. Unlovely men, unlovely laws—what can you expect?"

"I will never believe that we shall be content to go on living in a slough of—of——"

"Provincialism!" said Mr. Paramor. "You should take to gardening; it makes one recognise what you idealists seem to pass over—that men, my dear friend, are, like plants, creatures of heredity and environment; their growth is slow. You can't get grapes from thorns, Vigil, or figs from thistles—at least, not in one generation—however busy and hungry you may be!"

"Your theory degrades us all to the level of thistles."

"Social laws depend for their strength on the harm they have it in their power to inflict, and that harm depends for its strength on the ideals held by the man on whom the harm falls. If you dispense with the marriage tie, or give up your property and take to Brotherhood, you'll have a very thistley time, but you won't mind that if you're a fig. And so on ad lib. It's odd, though, how soon the thistles that thought themselves figs get found out. There are many things I hate, Vigil. One is extravagance, and another humbug!"

But Gregory stood looking at the sky.

"We seem to have wandered from the point," said Mr. Paramor, "and I think we had better go in. It's nearly eleven."

Throughout the length of the low white house there were but three windows lighted, three eyes looking at the moon, a fairy shallop sailing the night sky. The cedar-trees stood black as pitch. The old brown owl had ceased his hooting. Mr. Paramor gripped Gregory by the arm.

"A nightingale! Did you hear him down in that spinney? It's a sweet place, this! I don't wonder Pendyce is fond of it. You're not a fisherman, I think? Did you ever watch a school of fishes coasting along a bank? How blind they are, and how they follow their leader! In our element we men know just about as much as the fishes do. A blind lot, Vigil! We take a mean view of things; we're damnably provincial!"

Gregory pressed his hands to his forehead.

"I'm trying to think," he said, "what will be the consequences to my ward of this divorce."

"My friend, listen to some plain speaking. Your ward and her husband and George Pendyce are just the sort of people for whom our law of divorce is framed. They've all three got courage, they're all reckless and obstinate, and—forgive me—thick-skinned. Their case, if fought, will take a week of hard swearing, a week of the public's money and time. It will give admirable opportunities to eminent counsel, excellent reading to the general public, first-rate sport all round. The papers will have a regular carnival. I repeat, they are the very people for whom our law of divorce is framed. There's a great deal to be said for publicity, but all the same it puts a premium on insensibility, and causes a vast amount of suffering to innocent people. I told you once before, to get a divorce, even if you deserve it, you mustn't be a sensitive person. Those three will go through it all splendidly, but every scrap of skin will be torn off you and our poor friends down here, and the result will be a drawn battle at the end! That's if it's fought, and if it comes on I don't see how we can let it go unfought; it's contrary to my instincts. If we let it go undefended, mark my words, your ward and George Pendyce will be sick of each other before the law allows them to marry, and George, as his father says, for the sake of 'morality,' will have to marry a woman who is tired of him, or of whom he is tired. Now you've got it straight from the shoulder, and I'm going up to bed. It's a heavy dew. Lock this door after you."

Mr. Paramor made his way into the conservatory. He stopped and came back.

"Pendyce," he said, "perfectly understands all I've been telling you. He'd give his eyes for the case not to come on, but you'll see he'll rub everything up the wrong way, and it'll be a miracle if we succeed. That's ' Pendycitis '! We've all got a touch of it. Good-night!"

Gregory was left alone outside the country house with his big star. And as his thoughts were seldom of an impersonal kind he did not reflect on "Pendycitis," but on Helen Bellew. And the longer he thought the more he thought of her as he desired to think, for this was natural to him; and ever more ironical grew the twinkling of his star above the spinney where the nightingale was singing.

CHAPTER X

GEORGE GOES FOR THE GLOVES

ON the Thursday of the Epsom Summer Meeting, George Pendyce sat in the corner of a first-class railway-carriage trying to make two and two into five. On a sheet of Stoics' Club note-paper his racing-debts were stated to a penny—one thousand and forty-five pounds overdue, and below, seven hundred and fifty lost at the current meeting. Below these again his private debts were indicated by the round figure of one thousand pounds. It was round by courtesy, for he had only calculated those bills which had been sent in, and Providence, which knows all things, preferred the rounder figure of fifteen hundred. In sum, therefore, he had against him a total of three thousand two hundred and ninety-five pounds. And since at Tattersalls and the Stock Exchange, where men are engaged in perpetual motion, an almost absurd, punctiliousness is required in the payment of those sums which have for the moment inadvertently been lost, seventeen hundred and ninety-five of this must infallibly be raised by Monday next. Indeed, only a certain liking for George, a good loser, and a good winner, and the fear of dropping a good customer, had induced the firm of bookmakers to let that debt of one thousand and forty-five stand over the Epsom Meeting.

To set against these sums (in which he had not counted his current trainer's bill, and the expenses, which he could not calculate, of the divorce suit), he had, first, a bank balance which he might still overdraw another twenty pounds; secondly, the Ambler and two bad selling platers; and thirdly (more considerable item), X, or that which he might, or indeed must, win over the Ambler's race this afternoon.

Whatever else, it was not pluck that was lacking in the character of George Pendyce. This quality was in his fibre, in the consistency of his blood, and confronted with a situation which, to some men, and especially to men not brought up on the hereditary plan, might have seemed desperate, he exhibited no sign of anxiety or distress. Into the consideration of his difficulties he imported certain principles: (1) He did not intend to be posted at Tattersalls. Sooner than that he would go to the Jews; the entail was all he could look to borrow on; the Hebrews would force him to pay through the nose. (2) He did not intend to show the white feather, and in backing his horse meant to "go for the gloves." (3) He did not intend to think of the future; the thought of the present was quite bad enough.

The train bounded and swung as though rushing onwards to a tune, and George sat quietly in his corner.

Amongst his fellows in the carriage was the Hon. Geoffrey Winlow, who, though not a racing-man, took a kindly interest in our breed of horses, which by attendance at the principal meetings he hoped to improve.

"Your horse going to run, George?"

George nodded.

"I shall have a fiver on him for luck. I can't afford to bet. Saw your mother at the Foxholme garden-party last week. You seen them lately?"

George shook his head and felt an odd squeeze at his heart.

"You know they had a fire at old Peacock's farm; I hear the Squire and Barter did wonders. He's as game as a pebble, the Squire."

Again George nodded, and again felt that squeeze at his heart.

"Aren't they coming to town this season?"

"Haven't heard," answered George. "Have a cigar?"

Winlow took the cigar, and cutting it with a small pen-knife, scrutinised George's square face with his leisurely eyes. It needed a physiognomist to penetrate its impassivity. Winlow thought to himself:

'I shouldn't be surprised if what they say about old George is true.' . . . "Had a good meeting so far?"

"So-so."

They parted on the racecourse. George went at once to see his trainer and thence into Tattersalls' ring. He took with him that equation with X, and sought the society of two gentlemen, quietly dressed, one of whom was making a note in a little book with a gold pencil. They greeted him respectfully, for it was to them that he owed the bulk of that seventeen hundred and ninety-five pounds.

"What price will you lay against my horse?"

" Evens, Mr. Pendyce," replied the gentleman with the gold pencil, " to a monkey."

George booked the bet. It was not his usual way of doing business, but to-day everything seemed different, and something stronger than custom was at work.

' I am going for the gloves,' he thought; ' if it doesn't come off, I'm done anyhow.'

He went to another quietly dressed gentleman with a diamond pin and a Jewish face. And as he went from one quietly dressed gentleman to another there preceded him some subtle messenger, who breathed the words, ' Mr. Pendyce is going for the gloves,' so that at each visit he found they had greater confidence than ever in his horse. Soon he had promised to pay two thousand pounds if the Ambler lost, and received the assurance of eminent gentlemen, quietly dressed, that they would pay him fifteen hundred if the Ambler won. The odds now stood at two to one on, and he had found it impossible to back the Ambler for " a place," in accordance with his custom.

' Made a fool of myself,' he thought; ' ought never to have gone into the ring at all; ought to have let Barney's work it quietly. It doesn't matter ! '

He still required to win three hundred pounds to settle on the Monday, and laid a final bet of seven hundred to three hundred and fifty pounds upon his horse. Thus, without spending a penny, simply by making a few promises, he had solved the equation with X.

On leaving the ring, he entered the bar and drank some whisky. He then went to the paddock. The starting-bell for the second race had rung; there was hardly anyone there, but in a far corner the Ambler was being led up and down by a boy. George glanced round to see that no acquaintances were near, and joined in this promenade. The Ambler turned his black, wild eye, crescented with white, threw up his head, and gazed far into the distance.

' If one could only make him understand ! ' thought George.

When his horse left the paddock for the starting-post George went back to the stand. At the bar he drank some more whisky, and heard someone say:

" I had to lay six to four. I want to find Pendyce; they say he's backed it heavily."

George put down his glass, and instead of going to his usual place, mounted slowly to the top of the stand.

' I don't want them buzzing round me,' he thought.

At the top of the stand—that national monument, visible for twenty miles around—he knew himself to be safe. Only " the many" came here, and amongst the many he thrust himself till at the very top he could rest his glasses on a rail and watch the colours. Besides his own peacock blue there was a straw, a blue with white stripes, a red with white stars.

They say that through the minds of drowning men troop ghosts of past experience. It was not so with George; his soul was fastened on that little daub of peacock blue. Below the glasses his lips were colourless from hard compression; he moistened them continually. The four little coloured daubs stole into line, the flag fell.

"They're off!" That roar, like the cry of a monster, sounded all around. George steadied his glasses on the rail. Blue with white stripes was leading, the Ambler lying last. Thus they came round the further bend. And Providence, as though determined that someone should benefit by his absorption, sent a hand sliding under George's elbows, to remove the pin from his tie and slide away. Round Tattenham Corner George saw his horse take the lead. So, with straw closing up, they came into the straight. The Ambler's jockey looked back and raised his whip; in that instant, as if by magic, straw drew level; down came the whip on the Ambler's flank; again as by magic straw was in front. The saying of his old jockey darted through George's mind: "Mark my words, sir, that 'orse knows what's what, and when they're like that they're best let alone."

" Sit still, you fool! " he muttered.

The whip came down again; straw was two lengths in front. Someone behind said:

"The favourite's beat! No, he's not, by Jove!"

For as though George's groan had found its way to the jockey's ears, he dropped his whip. The Ambler sprang forward. George saw that he was gaining. All his soul went out to his horse's struggle. In each of those fifteen seconds he died and was born again; with each stride all that was loyal and brave in his nature leaped into flame, all that was base sank, for he himself was racing with his horse, and the sweat poured down his brow. And his lips babbled broken sounds that no one heard, for all around were babbling too.

Locked together, the Ambler and straw ran home. Then

followed a hush, for no one knew which of the two had won. The numbers went up; "Seven—Two—Five."

"The favourite's second! Beaten by a nose!" said a voice.

George bowed his head, and his whole spirit felt numb. He closed his glasses and moved with the crowd to the stairs. A voice behind him said:

"He'd have won in another stride!"

Another answered:

"I hate that sort of horse. He curled up at the whip."

George ground his teeth.

"Curse you!" he muttered, "you little Cockney; what do you know about a horse?"

The crowd surged; the speakers were lost to sight.

The long descent from the stand gave him time. No trace of emotion showed on his face when he appeared in the paddock. Blacksmith the trainer stood by the Ambler's stall.

"That idiot Tipping lost us the race, sir," he began with quivering lips. "If he'd only left him alone, the horse would have won in a canter. What on earth made him use his whip? He deserves to lose his license. He——"

The gall and bitterness of defeat surged into George's brain.

"It's no good *your* talking, Blacksmith," he said; "you put him up. What the devil made you quarrel with Swells?"

The little man's chin dropped in sheer surprise.

George turned away, and went up to the jockey, but at the sick look on the poor youth's face the angry words died off his tongue.

"All right, Tipping; I'm not going to rag you." And with the ghost of a smile he passed into the Ambler's stall. The groom had just finished putting him to rights; the horse stood ready to be led from the field of his defeat. The groom moved out, and George went to the Ambler's head. There is no place, no corner, on a racecourse where a man may show his heart. George did but lay his forehead against the velvet of his horse's muzzle, and for one short second hold it there. The Ambler awaited the end of that brief caress, then with a snort threw up his head, and with his wild, soft eyes seemed saying, 'You fools! what do you know of me?'

George stepped to one side.

"Take him away," he said, and his eyes followed the Ambler's receding form.

A racing-man of a different race, whom he knew and did not like, came up to him as he left the paddock.

"I suppothe you won't thell your horse, Pendythe?" he said. "I'll give you five thou. for him. He ought never to have lotht; the beating won't help him with the handicappers a little bit."

'You carrion crow!' thought George.

"Thanks; he's not for sale," he answered.

He went back to the stand, but at every step and in each face, he seemed to see the equation which now he could only solve with $X2$. Thrice he went into the bar. It was on the last of these occasions that he said to himself: "The horse must go. I shall never have a horse like him again."

Over that green down which a hundred thousand feet had trodden brown, which a hundred thousand hands had strewn with bits of paper, cigar-ends, and the fragments of discarded food, over the great approaches to the battlefield where all was pathway leading to and from the fight, those who make livelihood in such a fashion, least and littlest followers, were bawling, hawking, whining to the warriors flushed with victory or wearied by defeat. Over that green down, between one-legged men and ragged acrobats, women with babies at the breast, thimble-riggers, touts, walked George Pendyce, his mouth hard set and his head bent down.

"Good luck, Captain, good luck to-morrow; good luck, good luck! . . . For the love of Gawd, your lordship! . . . Roll, bowl, or pitch!"

The sun, flaming out after long hiding, scorched the back of his neck; the free down wind, fouled by fœtid odours, brought to his ears the monster's last cry, "They're off!"

A voice hailed him.

George turned and saw Winlow, and with a curse and a smile he answered:

"Hallo!"

The Hon. Geoffrey ranged alongside, examining George's face at leisure.

"Afraid you had a bad race, old chap! I hear you've sold the Ambler to that fellow Guilderstein."

In George's heart something snapped.

'Already?' he thought. 'The brute's been crowing. And it's *that* little bounder that my horse—my horse——'

He answered calmly:

" Wanted the money."

Winlow, who was not lacking in cool discretion, changed the subject.

Late that evening George sat in the Stoics' window overlooking Piccadilly. Before his eyes, shaded by his hand, the hansoms passed, flying East and West, each with the single pale disc of face, or the twin discs of faces close together; and the gentle roar of the town came in, and the cool air refreshed by night. In the light of the lamps the trees of the Green Park stood burnished out of deep shadow where nothing moved; and high over all, the stars and purple sky seemed veiled with golden gauze. Figures without end filed by. Some glanced at the lighted windows and the man in the white shirt-front sitting there. And many thought: ' Wish I were that swell, with nothing to do but step into his father's shoes;' and to many no thought came. But now and then some passer murmured to himself: " Looks lonely sitting there."

And to those faces gazing up, George's lips were grim, and over them came and went a little bitter smile; but on his forehead he felt still the touch of his horse's muzzle, and his eyes, which none could see, were dark with pain.

CHAPTER XI

MR. BARTER TAKES A WALK

THE event at the Rectory was expected every moment. The Rector, who practically never suffered, disliked the thought and sight of others' suffering. Up to this day, indeed, there had been none to dislike, for in answer to inquiries his wife had always said: "No, dear, no; I'm all right—really, it's nothing." And she had always said it smiling, even when her smiling lips were white. But this morning in trying to say it she had failed to smile. Her eyes had lost their hopelessly hopeful shining, and sharply between her teeth she said: "Send for Dr. Wilson, Hussell."

The Rector kissed her, shutting his eyes, for he was afraid of her face with its lips drawn back, and its discoloured cheeks. In five minutes the groom was hastening to Cornmarket on the roan cob, and the Rector stood in his study, looking from one to another of his household gods, as though calling them to his assistance. At last he took down a bat and began oiling it. Sixteen years ago, when Hussell was born, he had been overtaken by sounds that he had never to this day forgotten; they had clung to the nerves of his memory, and for no reward would he hear them again. They had never been uttered since, for like most wives, his wife was a heroine; but, used as he was to this event, the Rector had ever since suffered from panic. It was as though Providence, storing all the anxiety which he might have felt throughout, let him have it with a rush at the last moment. He put the bat back into its case, corked the oil-bottle, and again stood looking at his household gods. None came to his aid. And his thoughts were as they had nine times been before. 'I ought not to go out. I ought to wait for Wilson. Suppose anything were to happen. Still, nurse is with her, and I can do nothing. Poor Rose—poor darling! It's my duty to—— What's that? I'm better out of the way.'

Softly, without knowing that it was softly, he opened the door; softly, without knowing it was softly, he stepped to the hat-rack and took his black straw hat; softly, without knowing it was softly, he went out, and, unfaltering, hurried down the drive.

Three minutes later he appeared again, approaching the house faster than he had set forth.   He passed the hall door, ran up the stairs, and entered his wife's room.

" Rose dear, Rose, can I do anything? "

Mrs. Barter put out her hand, a gleam of malice shot into her eyes.   Through her set lips came a vague murmur, and the words:

" No, dear, nothing. Better go for your walk."

Mr. Barter pressed his lips to her quivering hand, and backed from the room.   Outside the door he struck at the air with his fist, and, running downstairs, was once more lost to sight. Faster and faster he walked, leaving the village behind, and among the country sights and sounds and scents his nerves began to recover. He was able to think again of other things: of Cecil's school report—far from satisfactory; of old Hermon in the village, whom he suspected of overdoing his bronchitis with an eye to port; of the return match with Coldingham, and his belief that their left-hand bowler only wanted " hitting"; of the new edition of hymn-books, and the slackness of the upper village in attending church—five households less honest and ductile than the rest, a foreign look about them, dark people, un-English.   In thinking of these things he forgot what he wanted to forget; but hearing the sound of wheels, he entered a field as though to examine the crops until the vehicle had passed.   It was not Wilson, but it might have been, and at the next turning he unconsciously branched off the Cornmarket road.

It was noon when he came within sight of Coldingham, six miles from Worsted Skeynes. He would have enjoyed a glass of beer, but, unable to enter the public-house, he went into the churchyard instead. He sat down on a bench beneath a syca- more opposite the Winlow graves, for Coldingham was Lord Montrossor's seat, and it was here that all the Winlows lay. Bees were busy above them in the branches, and Mr. Barter thought:

' Beautiful site. We've nothing like this at Worsted Skeynes. . . .'

But suddenly he found that he could not sit there and think. Suppose his wife were to die! It happened sometimes; the wife of John Tharp of Blechingham had died in giving birth to her tenth child! His forehead was wet, and he wiped it. Casting an angry glance at the Winlow graves, he left the seat.

He went down by the further path, and came out on the green. A cricket-match was going on, and in spite of himself the Rector stopped. The Coldingham team were in the field. Mr. Barter watched. As he had thought, that left-hand bowler bowled a good pace, and " came in " from the off, but his length was poor, very poor! A determined batsman would soon knock him off! He moved into line with the wickets to see how much the fellow " came in," and he grew so absorbed that he did not at first notice the Hon. Geoffrey Winlow in pads and a blue and green blazer, smoking a cigarette astride of a camp-stool.

" Ah, Winlow, it's your team against the village. Afraid I can't stop to see you bat. I was just passing—matter I *had* to attend to—must get back! "

The real solemnity of his face excited Winlow's curiosity.

" Can't you stop and have lunch with us? "

" No, no; my wife—— Must get back! "

Winlow murmured:

" Ah yes, of course." His leisurely blue eyes, always in command of the situation, rested on the Rector's heated face. " By the way," he said, " I'm afraid George Pendyce is rather hard hit. Been obliged to sell his horse. I saw him at Epsom the week before last."

The Rector brightened.

" I made certain he'd come to grief over that betting," he said. " I'm very sorry—very sorry indeed."

" They say," went on Winlow, " that he dropped four thousand over the Thursday race. He was pretty well dipped before, I know. Poor old George! such an awfully good chap! "

" Ah," repeated Mr. Barter, " I'm very sorry—very sorry indeed. Things were bad enough as it was."

A ray of interest illumined the leisureliness of the Hon. Geoffrey's eyes.

" You mean about Mrs.—— H'm, yes? " he said. " People are talking; you can't stop that. I'm so sorry for the poor Squire, and Mrs. Pendyce. I hope something 'll be done."

The Rector frowned.

" I've done *my* best," he said. " Well hit, sir! I've always said that anyone with a little pluck can knock off that left-hand man you think so much of. He 'comes in ' a bit, but he bowls a shocking bad length. Here I am dawdling. I must get back ! ”

And once more that real solemnity came over Mr. Barter's face.

“ I suppose you'll be playing for Coldingham against us on Thursday? Good-bye ! ”

Nodding in response to Winlow's salute, he walked away.

He avoided the churchyard, and took a path across the fields. He was hungry and thirsty. In one of his sermons there occurred this passage: “ We should habituate ourselves to hold our appetites in check. By constantly accustoming ourselves to abstinence—little abstinences in our daily life—we alone can attain to that true spirituality without which we cannot hope to know God.” And it was well known throughout his household and the village that the Rector's temper was almost dangerously spiritual if anything detained him from his meals. For he was a man physiologically sane and healthy to the core, whose digestion and functions, strong, regular, and straightforward as the day, made calls upon him which would not be denied. After preaching that particular sermon, he frequently for a week or more denied himself a second glass of ale at lunch, or his after-dinner cigar, smoking a pipe instead. And he was perfectly honest in his belief that he attained a greater spirituality thereby, and perhaps indeed he did. But even if he did not, there was no one to notice this, for the majority of his flock accepted his spirituality as a matter of course, and of the insignificant minority there were few who did not make allowances for the fact that he was their pastor by virtue of necessity, by virtue of a system which had placed him there almost mechanically, whether he would or no. Indeed, they respected him the more that he was their Rector, and could not be removed, and were glad that theirs was no common Vicar like that of Coldingham, dependent on the caprices of others. For, with the exception of two bad characters and one atheist, the whole village, Conservatives or Liberals (there were Liberals now that they were beginning to believe that the ballot was really secret), were believers in the hereditary system.

Insensibly the Rector directed himself towards Bletchingham, where there was a temperance house. At heart he loathed lemonade and gingerbeer in the middle of the day, both of which made his economy cold and uneasy, but he felt he could go nowhere else. And his spirits rose at the site of Bletching-ham spire.

'Bread and cheese,' he thought. 'What's better than bread and cheese? And they shall make me a cup of coffee.'

In that cup of coffee there was something symbolic and fit-ting to his mental state. It was agitated and thick, and im-pregnated with the peculiar flavour of country coffee. He swal-lowed but little, and resumed his march. At the first turning he passed the village school, whence issued a rhythmic but dis-cordant hum, suggestive of some dull machine that had served its time. The Rector paused to listen. Leaning on the wall of the little play-yard, he tried to make out the words that, like a religious chant, were being intoned within. It sounded like, "Twice two's four, twice four's six, twice six's eight," and he passed on, thinking. 'A fine thing; but if we don't take care we shall go too far; we shall unfit them for their stations,' and he frowned. Crossing a stile, he took a footpath. The air was full of the singing of larks, and the bees were pulling down the clover-stalks. At the bottom of the field was a little pond overhung with willows. On a bare strip of pasture, within thirty yards, in the full sun, an old horse was tethered to a peg. It stood with its face towards the pond, baring its yellow teeth, and stretching out its head, all bone and hol-lows, to the water which it could not reach. The Rector stopped. He did not know the horse personally, for it was three fields short of his parish, but he saw that the poor beast wanted water. He went up, and finding that the knot of the halter hurt his fingers, stooped down and wrenched at the peg. While he was thus straining and tugging, crimson in the face, the old horse stood still, gazing at him out of his bleary eyes. Mr. Barter sprang upright with a jerk, the peg in his hand, and the old horse started back.

"So ho, boy!" said the Rector, and angrily he muttered: "A shame to tie the poor beast up here in the sun. I should like to give his owner a bit of my mind!"

He led the animal towards the water. The old horse followed tranquilly enough, but as he had done nothing to deserve his misfortune, neither did he feel any gratitude towards his de-liverer. He drank his fill, and fell to grazing. The Rector experienced a sense of disillusionment, and drove the peg again into the softer earth under the willows; then raising himself, he looked hard at the old horse.

The animal continued to graze. The Rector took out his handkerchief, wiped the perspiration from his brow, and frowned. He hated ingratitude in man or beast.

Suddenly he realised that he was very tired.

"It must be over by now," he said to himself, and hastened on in the heat across the fields.

The Rectory door was open. Passing into the study, he sat down a moment to collect his thoughts. People were moving above; he heard a long, moaning sound that filled his heart with terror.

He got up and rushed to the bell, but did not ring it, and ran upstairs instead. Outside his wife's room he met his children's old nurse. She was standing on the mat, with her hands to her ears, and the tears were rolling down her face.

"Oh, sir!" she said—"oh, sir!"

The Rector glared.

"Woman!" he cried—"woman!"

He covered his ears and rushed downstairs again. There was a lady in the hall. It was Mrs. Pendyce, and he ran to her, as a hurt child runs to its mother.

"My wife," he said—"my poor wife! God knows what they're doing to her up there, Mrs. Pendyce!" and he hid his face in his hands.

She, who had been a Totteridge, stood motionless; then, very gently putting her gloved hand on his thick arm, where the muscles stood out from the clenching of his hands, she said:

"Dear Mr. Barter, Dr. Wilson is so clever! Come into the drawing-room!"

The Rector, stumbling like a blind man, suffered himself to be led. He sat down on the sofa, and Mrs. Pendyce sat down beside him, her hand still on his arm; over her face passed little quivers, as though she were holding herself in. She repeated in her gentle voice:

"It will be all right—it will be all right. Come, come!"

In her concern and sympathy there was apparent, not aloofness, but a faint surprise that she should be sitting there stroking the Rector's arm.

Mr. Barter took his hands from before his face.

"If she dies," he said in a voice unlike his own, "I'll not bear it."

In answer to those words, forced from him by that which is deeper than habit, Mrs. Pendyce's hand slipped from his arm and rested on the shiny chintz covering of the sofa, patterned with green and crimson. Her soul shrank from the violence in his voice.

"Wait here," she said. "I will go up and see."

To command was foreign to her nature, but Mr. Barter, with a look such as a little rueful boy might give, obeyed.

When she was gone he stood listening at the door for some sound—for any sound, even the sound of her dress—but there was none, for her petticoat was of lawn, and the Rector was alone with a silence that he could not bear. He began to pace the room in his thick boots, his hands clenched behind him, his forehead butting the air, his lips folded; thus a bull, penned for the first time, turns and turns, showing the whites of its full eyes.

His thoughts drove here and there, fearful, angered, without guidance; he did not pray. The words he had spoken so many times left him as though of malice. "We are all in the hands of God!—we are all in the hands of God!" Instead of them, he could think of nothing but the old saying Mr. Paramor had used in the Squire's dining-room, "There is moderation in all things," and this with cruel irony kept humming in his ears. "Moderation in all things—moderation in all things!" and his wife lying there—his doing, and——

There was a sound. The Rector's face, so brown and red, could not grow pale, but his great fists relaxed. Mrs. Pendyce was standing in the doorway with a peculiar half-pitiful, half-excited smile.

"It's all right—a boy. The poor dear has had a dreadful time!"

The Rector looked at her, but did not speak; then abruptly he brushed past her in the doorway, hurried into his study and locked the door. Then, and then only, he knelt down, and remained there many minutes, thinking of nothing.

CHAPTER XII

THE SQUIRE MAKES UP HIS MIND

THAT same evening at nine o'clock, sitting over the last glass of a pint of port, Mr. Barter felt an irresistible longing for enjoyment, an impulse towards expansion and his fellow-men.

Taking his hat and buttoning his coat—for though the June evening was fine the easterly breeze was eager—he walked towards the village.

Like an emblem of that path to God of which he spoke on Sundays, the grey road between trim hedges threaded the shadow of the elm-trees where the rooks had long since gone to bed. A scent of wood-smoke clung in the air; the cottages appeared, the forge, the little shops facing the village green. Lights in the doors and windows deepened; a breeze, which hardly stirred the chestnut leaves, fled with a gentle rustling through the aspens. Houses and trees, houses and trees! Shelter through the past and through the days to come!

The Rector stopped the first man he saw.

"Fine weather for the hay, Aiken! How's your wife doing —a girl? Ah, ha! You want some boys! You heard of our event at the Rectory? I'm thankful to say——"

From man to man and house to house he soothed his thirst for fellowship, for the lost sense of dignity that should efface again the scar of suffering. And above him the chestnuts in their breathing stillness, the aspens with their tender rustling, seemed to watch and whisper: "Oh, little men! oh, little men!"

The moon, at the end of her first quarter, sailed out of the shadow of the churchyard—the same young moon that had sailed in her silver irony when the first Barter preached, the first Pendyce was Squire at Worsted Skeynes; the same young moon that, serene, ineffable, would come again when the last Barter slept, the last Pendyce was gone, and on their gravestones, through the amethystine air, let fall her gentle light.

The Rector thought:

'I shall set Stedman to work on that corner. We must have more room; the stones there are a hundred and fifty

149

years old if they're a day. You can't read a single word.
They'd better be the first to go.'

He passed on along the paddock footway leading to the
Squire's.

Day was gone, and only the moonbeams lighted the tall
grasses.

At the Hall the long French windows of the dining-room
were open; the Squire was sitting there alone, brooding sadly
above the remnants of the fruit he had been eating. Flanking
him on either wall hung a silent company, the effigies of past
Pendyces; and at the end, above the oak and silver of the
sideboard, the portrait of his wife was looking at them under
lifted brows, with her faint wonder.

He raised his head.

" Ah, Barter! How's your wife? "

" Doing as well as can be expected."

" Glad to hear that! A fine constitution—wonderful vitality.
Port or claret? "

" Thanks; just a glass of port."

" Very trying for your nerves. I know what it is. We're
different from the last generation; they thought nothing of it.
When Charles was born my dear old father was out hunting
all day. When my wife had George, it made *me* as nervous
as a cat!"

The Squire stopped, then hurriedly added:

" But you're so used to it."

Mr. Barter frowned.

" I was passing Coldingham to-day," he said. " I saw Winlow. He asked after you."

" Ah! Winlow! His wife's a very nice woman. They've
only the one child, I think? "

The Rector winced.

" Winlow tells me," he said abruptly, " that George has sold
his horse."

The Squire's face changed. He glanced suspiciously at Mr.
Barter, but the Rector was looking at his glass.

" Sold his horse! What's the meaning of that? He told
you why, I suppose? "

The Rector drank off his wine.

" I never ask for reasons," he said, " where racing-men are
concerned. It's my belief they know no more what they're about
than so many dumb animals."

"Ah! racing-men!" said Mr. Pendyce. "But George doesn't bet."

A gleam of humour shot into the Rector's eyes. He pressed his lips together.

The Squire rose.

"Come now, Barter!" he said.

The Rector blushed. He hated tale-bearing—that is, of course, in the case of a man; the case of a woman was different —and just as, when he went to Bellew he had been careful not to give George away, so now he was still more on his guard.

"No, no, Pendyce."

The Squire began to pace the room, and Mr. Barter felt something stir against his foot; the spaniel John emerging at the end, just where the moonlight shone, a symbol of all that was subservient to the Squire, gazed up at his master with tragic eyes. 'Here again,' they seemed to say, 'is something to disturb me!'

The Squire broke the silence.

"I've always counted on you, Barter; I count on you as I would on my own brother. Come, now, what's this about George?"

'After all,' thought the Rector, 'it's his father!' "I know nothing but what they say," he blurted forth; "they talk of his having lost a lot of money. I dare say it's all nonsense. I never set much store by rumour. And if he's sold the horse, well, so much the better. He won't be tempted to gamble again."

But Horace Pendyce made no answer. A single thought possessed his bewildered, angry mind:

'My son a gambler! Worsted Skeynes in the hands of a gambler!'

The Rector rose.

"It's all rumour. You shouldn't pay any attention. I should hardly think he's been such a fool. I only know that I must get back to my wife. Good-night."

And, nodding but confused, Mr. Barter went away through the French window by which he had come.

The Squire stood motionless.

A gambler!

To him, whose existence was bound up in Worsted Skeynes, whose every thought had some direct or indirect connection with it, whose son was but the occupier of that place he must at last vacate, whose religion was ancestor-worship, whose dread was change, no word could be so terrible. A gambler!

It did not occur to him that his system was in any way responsible for George's conduct. He had said to Mr. Paramor: "I never had a system; I'm no believer in systems." He had brought him up simply as a gentleman. He would have preferred that George should go into the Army, but George had failed; he would have preferred that George should devote himself to the estate, marry, and have a son, instead of idling away his time in town, but George had failed; and so, beyond furthering his desire to join the Yeomanry, and getting him proposed for the Stoics' Club, what was there he could have done to keep him out of mischief? And now he was a gambler!

Once a gambler always a gambler!

To his wife's face, looking down from the wall, he said: "He gets it from you!"

But for all answer the face stared gently.

Turning abruptly, he left the room, and the spaniel John, for whom he had been too quick, stood with his nose to the shut door, scenting for someone to come and open it.

Mr. Pendyce went to his study, took some papers from a locked drawer, and sat a long time looking at them. One was the draft of his will, another a list of the holdings at Worsted Skeynes, their acreage and rents, a third a fair copy of the settlement, re-settling the estate when he had married. It was at this piece of supreme irony that Mr. Pendyce looked longest. He did not read it, but he thought:

'And I can't cut it! Paramor says so! A gambler!'

That "crassness" common to all men in this strange world, and in the Squire intensified, was rather a process than a quality —obedience to an instinctive dread of what was foreign to himself, an instinctive fear of seeing another's point of view, an instinctive belief in precedent. And it was closely allied to his most deep and moral quality—the power of making a decision. Those decisions might be "crass" and stupid, conduce to unnecessary suffering, have no relation to morality or reason; but he could make them, and he could stick to them. By virtue of this power he was where he was, had been for centuries, and hoped to be for centuries to come. It was in his blood. By this alone he kept at bay the destroying forces that Time brought against him, his order, his inheritance; by this alone he could continue to hand down that inheritance to his son. And at the document which did hand it down he looked with angry and resentful eyes.

Men who conceive great resolutions do not always bring them forth with the ease and silence which they themselves desire. Mr. Pendyce went to his bedroom determined to say no word of what he had resolved to do. His wife was asleep. The Squire's entrance wakened her, but she remained motionless, with her eyes closed, and it was the site of that immobility, when he himself was so disturbed, which drew from him the words:

"Did you know that George was a gambler?"

By the light of the candle in his silver candlestick her dark eyes seemed suddenly alive.

"He's been betting; he's sold his horse. He'd never have sold that horse unless he were pushed. For all I know, he may be posted at Tattersalls!"

The sheets shivered as though she who lay within them were struggling. Then came her voice, cool and gentle:

"All young men bet, Horace; you must know that!"

The Squire at the foot of the bed held up the candle; the movement had a sinister significance.

"Do you defend him?" it seemed to say. "Do you defy me?"

Gripping the bed-rail, he cried:

"I'll have no gambler and profligate for my son! I'll not risk the estate!"

Mrs. Pendyce raised herself, and for many seconds stared at her husband. Her heart beat furiously. It had come! What she had been expecting all these days had come! Her pale lips answered:

"What do you mean? I don't understand you, Horace."

Mr. Pendyce's eyes searched here and there—for what, he did not know.

"This has decided me," he said. "I'll have no half-measures. Until he can show me he's done with that woman, until he can prove he's given up this betting, until—until the heaven's fallen, I'll have no more to do with him!"

To Margery Pendyce, with all her senses quivering, that saying, "Until the heaven's fallen," was frightening beyond the rest. On the lips of her husband, those lips which had never spoken in metaphors, never swerved from the direct and commonplace, nor deserted the shibboleth of his order, such words had an evil and malignant sound.

He went on:

"I've brought him up as I was brought up myself. I never thought to have had a scamp for my son!"

Mrs. Pendyce's heart stopped fluttering.

"How dare you, Horace!" she cried.

The Squire, letting go the bed-rail, paced to and fro. There was something savage in the sound of his footsteps through the utter silence.

"I've made up my mind," he said. "The estate——"

There broke from Mrs. Pendyce a torrent of words:

"You talk of the way you brought George up! You—you never understood him! You—you never did anything for him! He just grew up like you all grow up in this——" But no word followed, for she did not know herself what was that against which her soul had blindly fluttered its wings. "You never loved him as I do! What do I care about the estate? I wish it were sold! D'you think I like living here? D'you think I've ever liked it? D'you think I've ever——" But she did not finish that saying: D'you think I've ever loved you? "My boy a scamp! I've heard you laugh and shake your head and say a hundred times: 'Young men will be young men!' You think I don't know how you'd all go on if you dared! You think I don't know how you talk among yourselves! As for gambling, you'd gamble too, if you weren't afraid! And now George is in trouble——"

As suddenly as it had broken forth the torrent of her words dried up.

Mr. Pendyce had come back to the foot of the bed, and once more gripped the rail whereon the candle, still and bright, showed them each other's faces, very changed from the faces that they knew. In the Squire's lean brown throat, between the parted points of his stiff collar, a string seemed working. He stammered:

"You—you're talking like a madwoman! My father would have cut me off, his father would have cut him off! By God! do you think I'll stand quietly by and see it all played ducks and drakes with, and see that woman here, and see her son, a bastard, or as bad as a bastard, in my place? You don't know me!"

The last words came through his teeth like the growl of a

dog. Mrs. Pendyce made the crouching movement of one who gathers herself to spring.

"If you give him up, I shall go to him; I will never come back!"

The Squire's grip on the rail relaxed; in the light of the candle, still and steady and bright, his jaw could be seen to fall. He snapped his teeth together, and turning abruptly said:

"Don't talk such rubbish!"

Then, taking the candle, he went into his dressing-room.

And at first his feelings were simple enough; he had merely that sore sensation, that sense of raw offence, as at some gross and violent breach of taste.

'What madness,' he thought, 'gets into women! It would serve her right if I slept here!'

He looked around him. There was no place where he could sleep, not even a sofa, and taking up the candle, he moved towards the door. But a feeling of hesitation and forlornness rising, he knew not whence, made him pause irresolute before the window.

The young moon, riding low, shot her light upon his still, lean figure, and in that light it was strange to see how grey he looked—grey from head to foot, grey, and sad, and old, as though in summary of all the squires who in turn had looked upon that prospect frosted with young moonlight to the boundary of their lands. Out in the paddock he saw his old hunter Bob, with his head turned towards the house; and from the very bottom of his heart he sighed.

In answer to that sigh came a sound of something falling outside against the door. He opened it to see what might be there. The spaniel John, lying on a cushion of blue linen, with his head propped up against the wall, darkly turned his eyes.

'I am here, master,' he seemed to say; 'it is late—I was about to go to sleep; it has done me good, however, to see you;' and hiding his eyes from the light under a long black ear, he drew a stertorous breath. Mr. Pendyce shut-to the door. He had forgotten the existence of his dog. But, as though with the sight of that faithful creature he had regained belief in all that he was used to, in all that he was master of, in all that was—himself, he opened the bedroom door and took his place beside his wife.

And soon he was asleep.

PART III

CHAPTER I

MRS. PENDYCE'S ODYSSEY

But Mrs. Pendyce did not sleep. That blessed anodyne of the long day spent in his farmyards and fields was on her husband's eyes—no anodyne on hers; and through them, all that was deep, most hidden, sacred, was laid open to the darkness. If only those eyes could have been seen that night! But if the darkness had been light, nothing of all this so deep and sacred would have been there to see, for more deep, more sacred still, in Margery Pendyce, was the instinct of a lady. So elastic and so subtle, so interwoven of consideration for others and consideration for herself, so old, so very old, this instinct wrapped her from all eyes, like a suit of armour of the finest chain. The night must have been black indeed when she took that off and lay without it in the darkness.

With the first light she put it on again, and stealing from bed, bathed long and stealthily those eyes which felt as though they had been burned all night; thence went to the open window and leaned out. Dawn had passed, the birds were at morning music. Down there in the garden her flowers were meshed with the grey dew, and the trees were grey, spun with haze; dim and spectre-like, the old hunter, with his nose on the paddock rail, dozed in the summer mist.

And all that had been to her like prison out there, and all that she had loved, stole up on the breath of the unaired morning, and kept beating in her face, fluttering at the white linen above her heart like the wings of birds flying.

The first morning song ceased, and at the silence the sun smiled out in golden irony, and everything was shot with colour. A wan glow fell on Mrs. Pendyce's spirit, that for so many hours had been heavy and grey in lonely resolution. For to her gentle soul, unused to action, shrinking from violence, whose strength was the gift of the ages, passed into it against her very nature, the resolution she had formed was full of pain. Yet painful, even terrible in its demand for action, it

157

did not waver, but shone like a star behind the dark and heavy clouds. In Margery Pendyce (who had been a Totteridge) there was no irascible and acrid "people's blood," no fierce misgivings, no ill-digested beer and cider—it was pure claret in her veins—she had nothing thick and angry in her soul to help her; that which she had resolved she must carry out, by virtue of a thin, fine flame, breathing far down in her—so far that nothing could extinguish it, so far that it had little warmth. It was not "I will not be over-ridden" that her spirit felt, but "I must not be over-ridden, for if I am over-ridden, I, and in me something beyond me, more important than myself, is all undone." And though she was far from knowing this, that *something* was her country's civilisation, its very soul, the meaning of it all—gentleness, balance. Her spirit, of that quality so little gross that it would never set up a mean or petty quarrel, make mountains out of mole-hills, distort proportion, or get images awry, had taken its stand unconsciously, no sooner than it must, no later than it ought, and from that stand would not recede. The issue had passed beyond mother love to that self-love, deepest of all, which says: "Do this, or forfeit the essence of your soul."

And now that she stole to her bed again, she looked at her sleeping husband whom she had resolved to leave, with no anger, no reproach, but rather with a long, incurious look which told nothing even to herself.

So, when the morning came of age and it was time to rise, by no action, look, or sign, did she betray the presence of the unusual in her soul. If this which was before her must be done, it would be carried out as though it were of no import, as though it were a daily action; nor did she force herself to quietude, or pride herself thereon, but acted thus from instinct, the instinct for avoiding fuss and unnecessary suffering that was bred in her.

Mr. Pendyce went out at half-past ten accompanied by his bailiff and the spaniel John. He had not the least notion that his wife still meant the words she had spoken overnight. He had told her again while dressing that he would have no more to do with George, that he would cut him out of his will, that he would force him by sheer rigour to come to heel, that, in short, he meant to keep his word, and it would have been unreasonable in him to believe that a woman, still less his wife, meant to keep hers.

Mrs. Pendyce spent the early part of the morning in the usual way. Half an hour after the Squire went out she ordered the carriage round, had two small trunks, which she had packed herself, brought down, and leisurely, with her little green bag, got in. To her maid, to the butler Bester, to the coachman Benson, she said that she was going up to stay with Mr. George. Norah and Bee were at the Tharps', so that there was no one to take leave of but old Roy, the Skye; and lest that leave-taking should prove too much for her, she took him with her to the station.

For her husband she left a little note, placing it where she knew he must see it at once, and no one else see it at all.

"DEAR HORACE,

"I have gone up to London to be with George. My address will be Green's Hotel, Bond Street. You will remember what I said last night. Perhaps you did not quite realise that I meant it. Take care of poor old Roy, and don't let them give him too much meat this hot weather. Jackman knows better than Ellis how to manage the roses this year. I should like to be told how poor Rose Barter gets on. Please do not worry about me. I shall write to dear Gerald when necessary, but I don't feel like writing to him or the girls at present.

"Good-bye, dear Horace; I am sorry if I grieve you.
"Your wife,
"MARGERY PENDYCE."

Just as there was nothing violent in her manner of taking this step, so there was nothing violent in her conception of it. To her it was not running away, a setting of her husband at defiance; there was no concealment of address, no melodramatic "I cannot come back to you." Such methods, such pistol-holdings, would have seemed to her ridiculous. It is true that practical details, such as the financial consequences, escaped the grasp of her mind, but even in this, her view, or rather lack of view, was really the wide, the even one. Horace would not let her starve: the idea was inconceivable. There was, too, her own three hundred a year. She had, indeed, no idea how much this meant, or what it represented, neither was she concerned, for she said to herself, "I should be quite happy in a cottage with Roy and my flowers;" and though, of course, she had not the smallest experience to go by, it was quite possible that she was right. Things which to others came only by money, to a Totteridge came without, and even if they came not, could well be dispensed with—for to this quality of soul, this gentle self-sufficiency, had the ages worked to bring her.

Yet it was hastily and with her head bent that she stepped from the carriage at the station, and the old Skye, who from the brougham seat could just see out of the window, from the tears on his nose that were not his own, from something in his heart that was, knew this was no common parting and whined behind the glass.

Mrs. Pendyce told her cabman to drive to Green's Hotel, and it was only after she had arrived, arranged her things, washed, and had lunch, that the beginnings of confusion and home-sickness stirred within her. Up to then a simmering excitement had kept her from thinking of how she was to act, or of what she had hoped, expected, dreamed, would come of her proceedings. Taking her sunshade, she walked out into Bond Street.

A passing man took off his hat.

'Dear me,' she thought, 'who was that? I ought to know!'

She had a rather vague memory for faces, and though she could not recall his name, felt more at home at once, not so lonely and adrift. Soon a quaint brightness showed in her eyes, looking at the toilettes of the passers-by, and at each shop-front, more engrossing than the last. Pleasure, like that which touches the soul of a young girl at her first dance, the souls of men landing on strange shores, touched Margery Pendyce. A delicious sense of entering the unknown, of braving the unexpected, and of the power to go on doing this delightfully for ever, enveloped her with the gay London air of this bright June day. She passed a perfume shop, and thought she had never smelt anything so nice. And next door she lingered long looking at some lace; and though she said to herself, " I must not buy anything; I shall want all my money for poor George," it made no difference to that sensation of having all things to her hand.

A list of theatres, concerts, operas confronted her in the next window, together with the effigies of prominent artistes. She looked at them with an eagerness that might have seemed absurd to anyone who saw her standing there. Was there, indeed, all this going on all day and every day, to be seen and heard for so few shillings? Every year, religiously, she had visited the opera once, the theatre twice, and no concerts; her husband did not care for music that was "classical." While she was standing there a woman begged of her, looking very tired and hot, with a baby in her arms so shrivelled and so small that it could hardly be seen. Mrs. Pendyce took out her purse and gave her half a crown, and as she did so felt a gush of feeling which was almost rage.

'Poor little baby!' she thought. 'There must be thousands like that, and I know nothing of them!'

She smiled to the woman, who smiled back at her; and a fat Jewish youth in a shop doorway, seeing them smile, smiled too, as though he found them charming. Mrs. Pendyce had a feeling that the town was saying pretty things to her, and this was so strange and pleasant that she could hardly believe it, for Worsted Skeynes had omitted to say that sort of thing to her for over thirty years. She looked in the window of a hat shop, and found pleasure in the sight of herself. The window was kind to her grey linen with black velvet knots and guipure, though it was two years old; but, then, she had only been able to wear it once last summer, owing to poor Hubert's death. The window was kind, too, to her cheeks, and eyes, which had that touching brightness, and to the silver-powdered darkness of her hair. And she thought: 'I don't look so very old!' But her own hat reflected in the hat-shop window displeased her now; it turned down all round, and though she loved that shape, she was afraid it was not fashionable this year. And she looked long in the window of that shop, trying to persuade herself that the hats in there would suit her, and that she liked what she did not like. In other shop windows she looked, too. It was a year since she had seen any, and for thirty-four years past she had only seen them in company with the Squire or with her daughters, none of whom cared much for shops.

The people, too, were different from the people that she saw when she went about with Horace or her girls. Almost all seemed charming, having a new, strange life, in which she —Margery Pendyce—had unaccountably a little part; as though really she might come to know them, as though they might tell her something of themselves, of what they felt and thought, and even might stand listening, taking a kindly interest in what she said. This, too, was strange, and a friendly smile became fixed upon her face, and of those who saw it— shop-girls, women of fashion, coachmen, clubmen, po· licemen—most felt a little warmth about their hearts; it was pleasant to see on the lips of that faded lady with the silvered arching hair under a hat whose brim turned down all round.

So Mrs. Pendyce came to Piccadilly and turned westward towards George's club. She knew it well, for she never failed to look at the windows when she passed, and once—on the occasion of Queen Victoria's Jubilee—had spent a whole day there to see that royal show.

She began to tremble as she neared it, for though she did not, like the Squire, torture her mind with what might or might not come to pass, care had nested in her heart.

George was not in his club, and the porter could not tell her where he was. Mrs. Pendyce stood motionless. He was her son; how could she ask for his address? The porter waited, knowing a lady when he saw one. Mrs. Pendyce said gently:

" Is there a room where I could write a note, or would it be——"

"Certainly not, ma'am. I can show you to a room at once."

And though it was only a mother to a son, the porter preceded her with the quiet discretion of one who aids a mistress to her lover; and perhaps he was right in his view of the relative values of love, for he had great experience, having lived long in the best society.

On paper headed with the fat white " Stoics' Club," so well known on George's letters, Mrs. Pendyce wrote what she had to say. The little dark room where she sat was without sound, save for the buzzing of a largish fly in a streak of sunlight below the blind. It was dingy in colour; its furniture was old. At the Stoics' was found neither the new art nor the resplendent drapings of those larger clubs sacred to the middle classes. The little writing-room had an air of mourning: 'I am so seldom used; but be at home in me: you might find me tucked away in almost any country-house!"

Yet many a solitary Stoic had sat there and written many a note to many a woman. George, perhaps, had written to Helen

Bellew at that very table with that very pen, and Mrs. Pendyce's heart ached jealously.

"DEAREST GEORGE" (she wrote),

"I have something very particular to tell you. Do come to me at Green's Hotel. Come soon, my dear. I shall be lonely and unhappy till I see you.

"Your loving

"MARGERY PENDYCE."

And this note, which was just what she would have sent to a lover, took that form, perhaps unconsciously, because she had never had a lover thus to write to.

She slipped the note and half a crown diffidently into the porter's hand; refused his offer of some tea, and walked vaguely towards the Park.

It was five o'clock; the sun was brighter than ever. People in carriages and people on foot in one leisurely, unending stream were filing in at Hyde Park Corner. Mrs. Pendyce went, too, and timidly—she was unused to traffic—crossed to the further side and took a chair. Perhaps George was in the Park and she might see him; perhaps Helen Bellew was there, and she might see her; and the thought of this made her heart beat and her eyes under their uplifted brows stare gently at each figure—old men and young men, women of the world, fresh young girls. How charming they looked, how sweetly they were dressed! A feeling of envy mingled with the joy she ever felt at seeing pretty things; she was quite unconscious that she herself was pretty under that hat whose brim turned down all round. But as she sat a leaden feeling slowly closed her heart, varied by nervous flutterings, when she saw someone whom she ought to know. And whenever, in response to a salute, she was forced to bow her head, a blush rose in her cheeks, a wan smile seemed to make confession:

"I know I look a guy; I know it's odd for me to be sitting here alone!"

She felt old—older than she had ever felt before. In the midst of this gay crowd, of all this life and sunshine, a feeling of loneliness which was almost fear—a feeling of being utterly adrift, cut off from all the world—came over her; and she felt like one of her own plants, plucked up from its native earth, with all its poor roots hanging bare, as though groping for the earth to cling to. She knew now that she had lived too long in the soil that she had hated; and was too old to be transplanted. The custom of the country—that weighty, wingless creature borne of time and of the earth—had its limbs fast twined around her. It had made of her its mistress, and was not going to let her go.

CHAPTER II

THE SON AND THE MOTHER

HARDER than for a camel to pass through the eye of a needle is it for a man to become a member of the Stoics' Club, except by virtue of the hereditary principle; for unless he be nourished he cannot be elected, and since by the club's first rule he may have no occupation whatsoever, he must be nourished by the efforts of those who have gone before. And the longer they have gone before the more likely he is to receive no black-balls.

Yet without entering into the Stoics' Club it is difficult for a man to attain that supreme outward control which is necessary to conceal his lack of control within; and, indeed, the club is an admirable instance of how Nature places the remedy to hand for the disease. For, perceiving how George Pendyce and hundreds of other young men "to the manner born" had lived from their birth up in no connection whatever with the struggles and sufferings of life, and fearing lest, when Life in her careless and ironical fashion brought them into abrupt contact with ill-bred events they should make themselves a nuisance by their cries of dismay and wonder, Nature had devised a mask and shaped it to its highest form within the portals of the Stoics' Club. With this mask she clothed the faces of these young men whose souls she doubted, and called them—gentlemen. And when she, and she alone, heard their poor squeaks behind that mask, as Life placed clumsy feet on them, she pitied them, knowing that it was not they who were in fault, but the unpruned system which had made them what they were. And in her pity she endowed many of them with thick skins, steady feet, and complacent souls, so that, treading in well-worn paths their lives long, they might slumber to their deaths in those halls where their fathers had slumbered to their deaths before them. But sometimes Nature (who was not yet a Socialist) rustled her wings and heaved a sigh, lest the excesses and excrescences of their system should bring about excesses and excrescences of the opposite sort. For extravagance of all kinds was what she hated, and of that particular form

of extravagance which Mr. Paramor so vulgarly called " Pendycitis " she had a horror.

It may happen that for long years the likeness between father
and son will lie dormant, and only when disintegrating forces
threaten the links of the chain binding them together will that
likeness leap forth, and by a piece of Nature's irony become
the main factor in destroying the hereditary principle for which
it is the silent, the most worthy, excuse.

It is certain that neither George nor his father knew the
depth to which this " Pendycitis " was rooted in the other;
neither suspected, not even in themselves, the amount of essential bulldog at the bottom of their souls, the strength of their
determination to hold their own in the way that would cause
the greatest amount of unnecessary suffering.   They did not
deliberately desire to cause unnecessary suffering; they simply
could not help an instinct passed by time into their fibre, through
atrophy of the reasoning powers and the constant mating,
generation after generation, of those whose motto had been,
" Kings of our own dunghills."   And now George came forward,
defying his mother's belief that he was a Totteridge, as champion of the principle in tail male; for in the Totteridges, from
whom in this stress he diverged more and more towards his
father's line, there was some freer strain, something non-pro-
vincial, and this had been so ever since Hubert de Toterydge
had led his private crusade, from which he had neglected
to return.   With the Pendyces it had been otherwise;
from immemorial time " a county family," they had construed the phrase literally, had taken no poetical li-
cences.   Like innumerable other country families, they were
perforce what their tradition decreed—provincial in their
souls.

George, a man-about-town, would have stared at being called
provincial, but a man cannot stare away his nature.   He was
provincial enough to keep Mrs. Bellew bound when she herself
was tired of him, and consideration for her, and for his own
self-respect asked him to give her up.   He had been keeping
her bound for two months or more.   But there was much
excuse for him.   His heart was sore to breaking-point; he was
sick with longing, and deep, angry wonder that he, of all men,
should be cast aside like a worn-out glove.   Men tired of women
daily—that was the law.   But what was this?   His dogged
instinct had fought against the knowledge as long as he could,

and now that it was certain he fought against it still. George was a true Pendyce!

To the world, however, he behaved as usual. He came to the club about ten o'clock to eat his breakfast and read the sporting papers. Towards noon a hansom took him to the railway-station appropriate to whatever race-meeting was in progress, or, failing that, to the cricket-ground at Lord's, or Prince's Tennis Club. Half-past six saw him mounting the staircase at the Stoics to that card-room where his effigy still hung, with its look of "Hard work, hard work; but I must keep it going!" At eight he dined, a bottle of champagne screwed deep down into ice, his face flushed with the day's sun, his shirt-front and his hair shining with gloss. What happier man in all great London!

But with the dark the club's swing-doors opened for his passage into the lighted streets, and till next morning the world knew him no more. It was then that he took revenge for all the hours he wore a mask. He would walk the pavements for miles trying to wear himself out, or in the Park fling himself down on a chair in the deep shadow of the trees, and sit there with his arms folded and his head bowed down. On other nights he would go into some music-hall, and amongst the glaring lights, the vulgar laughter, the scent of painted women, try for a moment to forget the face, the laugh, the scent of that woman for whom he craved. And all the time he was jealous, with a dumb, vague jealousy of he knew not whom; it was not his nature to think impersonally, and he could not believe that a woman would drop him except for another man. Often he went to her Mansions, and walked round and round casting a stealthy stare at her windows. Twice he went up to her door, but came away without ringing the bell. One evening, seeing a light in her sitting-room, he rang, but there came no answer. Then an evil spirit leaped up in him, and he rang again and again. At last he went away to his room—a studio he had taken near—and began to write to her. He was long composing that letter, and many times tore it up; he despised the expression of feelings in writing. He only tried because his heart wanted relief so badly. And this, in the end, was all that he produced:

"I know you were in to-night. It's the only time I've come. Why couldn't you have let me in? You've no right

to treat me like this. You are leading me the life of a
dog. GEORGE."

The first light was silvering the gloom above the river, the
lamps were paling to the day, when George went out and
dropped this missive in the letter-box. He came back to the
river and lay down on an empty bench under the plane-trees
of the Embankment, and while he lay there one of those without
refuge or home, who lie there night after night, came up unseen and looked at him.

But morning comes, and with it that sense of the ridiculous,
so merciful to suffering men. George got up lest anyone
should see a Stoic lying there in his evening clothes; and when
it became time he put on his mask and sallied forth. At the
club he found his mother's note, and set out for her hotel.

Mrs. Pendyce was not yet down, but sent to ask him to come
up. George found her standing in her dressing-gown in the
middle of the room, as though she knew not where to place
herself for this, their meeting. Only when he was quite close
did she move and throw her arms round his neck. George
could not see her face, and his own was hidden from her, but
through the thin dressing-gown he felt her straining to him,
and her arms that had pulled his head down quivering; and
for a moment it seemed to him as if he were dropping a burden. But only for a moment, for at the clinging of those arms
his instinct took fright. And though she was smiling, the
tears were in her eyes, and this offended him.

"Don't, mother!"

Mrs. Pendyce's answer was a long look. George could not
bear it, and turned away.

" Well," he said gruffly, " when you can tell me what's brought
you up——"

Mrs. Pendyce sat down on the sofa. She had been brushing
her hair; though silvered, it was still thick and soft, and the
sight of it about her shoulders struck George. He had never
thought of her having hair that would hang down.

Sitting on the sofa beside her, he felt her fingers stroking
his, begging him not to take offence and leave her. He felt
her eyes trying to see his eyes, and saw her lips trembling; but
a stubborn, almost evil smile was fixed upon his face.

"And so, dear—and so," she stammered, "I told your father
that I couldn't see that done, and so I came up to you."

Many sons have found no hardship in accepting all that their mothers do for them as a matter of right, no difficulty in assuming their devotion a matter of course, no trouble in leaving their own affections to be understood; but most sons have found great difficulty in permitting their mothers to diverge one inch from the conventional, to swerve one hair's breadth from the standard of propriety appropriate to mothers of men of their importance.

It is decreed of mothers that their birth pangs shall not cease until they die.

And George was shocked to hear his mother say that she had left his father to come to him. It affected his self-esteem in a strange and subtle way. The thought that tongues might wag about her revolted his manhood and his sense of form. It seemed strange, incomprehensible, and wholly wrong; the thought, too, flashed through his mind: "She is trying to put pressure on me!"

"If you think I'll give her up, Mother——" he said.

Mrs. Pendyce's fingers tightened.

"No, dear," she answered painfully; "of course, if she loves you so much, I couldn't ask you. That's why I——"

George gave a grim little laugh.

"What on earth can you do, then? What's the good of your coming up like this? How are you to get on here all alone? I can fight my own battles. You'd much better go back."

Mrs. Pendyce broke in:

"Oh, George; I can't see you cast off from us! I must be with you!"

George felt her trembling all over. He got up and walked to the window. Mrs. Pendyce's voice followed:

"I won't try to separate you, George; I promise, dear. I couldn't, if she loves you, and you love her so!"

Again George laughed that grim little laugh. And the fact that he was deceiving her, meant to go on deceiving her, made him as hard as iron.

"Go back, Mother!" he said. "You'll only make things worse. This isn't a woman's business. Let father do what he likes; I can hold on!"

Mrs. Pendyce did not answer, and he was obliged to look round. She was sitting perfectly still with her hands in her lap, and his man's hatred of anything conspicuous happening to a woman, to his own mother of all people, took fierce fire.

"Go back!" he repeated, "before there's any fuss! What good can you possibly do? You can't leave father; that's absurd! You *must* go!"

Mrs. Pendyce answered:

"I can't do that, dear."

George made an angry sound, but she was so motionless and pale that he dimly perceived how she was suffering, and how little he knew of her who had borne him.

Mrs. Pendyce broke the silence:

"But you, George dear? What is going to happen? How are you going to manage?" And suddenly clasping her hands: "Oh! what is coming?"

Those words, embodying all that had been in his heart so long, were too much for George. He went abruptly to the door.

"I can't stop now," he said; "I'll come again this evening."

Mrs. Pendyce looked up.

"Oh, George——"

But as she had the habit of subordinating her feelings to the feelings of others, she said no more, but tried to smile.

That smile smote George to the heart.

"Don't worry, Mother; try and cheer up. We'll go to the theatre. You get the tickets!"

And trying to smile too, but turning lest he should lose his self-control, he went away.

In the hall he came on his uncle, General Pendyce. He came on him from behind, but knew him at once by that look of feeble activity about the back of his knees, by his sloping yet upright shoulders, and the sound of his voice, with its dry and querulous precision, as of a man whose occupation has been taken from him.

The General turned round.

"Ah, George," he said, "your mother's here, isn't she? Look at this that your father's sent me!"

He held out a telegram in a shaky hand.

"Margery up at Green's Hotel. Go and see her at once.
"HORACE."

And while George read the General looked at his nephew with eyes that were ringed by little circles of darker pigment, and had crow's-footed purses of skin beneath, earned by serving his country in tropical climes.

" What's the meaning of it ? " he said. " Go and see her ? Of course, I'll go and see her! Always glad to see your mother. But where's all the hurry ? "

George perceived well enough that his father's pride would not let him write to her, and though it was for himself that his mother had taken this step, he sympathised with his father. The General fortunately gave him little time to answer.

" She's up to get herself some dresses, I suppose ? I've seen nothing of you for a long time. When are you coming to dine with me ? I heard at Epsom that you'd sold your horse. What made you do that ? What's your father telegraphing to me like this for ? It's not like him. Your mother's not ill, is she ? "

George shook his head, and muttering something about " Sorry, an engagement—awful hurry," was gone.

Left thus abruptly to himself, General Pendyce summoned a page, slowly pencilled something on his card, and with his back to the only persons in the hall, waited, his hands folded on the handle of his cane. And while he waited he tried as far as possible to think of nothing. Having served his country, his time now was nearly all devoted to waiting, and to think fatigued and made him feel discontented, for he had had sunstroke once, and fever several times. In the perfect precision of his collar, his boots, his dress, his figure; in the way from time to time he cleared his throat, in the strange yellow driedness of his face between his carefully brushed whiskers, in the immobility of his white hands on his cane, he gave the impression of a man sucked dry by a system. Only his eyes, restless and opinionated, betrayed the essential Pendyce that was behind.

He went up to the ladies' drawing-room, clutching the telegram. It worried him. There was something odd about it, and he was not accustomed to pay calls in the morning. He found his sister-in-law seated at an open window, her face unusually pink, her eyes rather defiantly bright. She greeted him gently, and General Pendyce was not the man to discern what was not put under his nose. Fortunately for him, that had never been his practice.

" How are you, Margery ? " he said. " Glad to see you in town. How's Horace ? Look here what he's sent me! " He offered her the telegram, with the air of slightly avenging an offence; then added in surprise, as thought he had just thought of it: " Is there anything I can do for you? "

Mrs. Pendyce read the telegram, and she, too, like George, felt sorry for the sender.

" Nothing, thanks, dear Charles," she said slowly. " I'm all right. Horace gets so nervous ! "

General Pendyce looked at her; for a moment his eyes flickered, then, since the truth was so improbable and so utterly in any case beyond his philosophy, he accepted her statement.

" He shouldn't go sending telegrams like this," he said. " You might have been ill' for all I could tell. It spoiled my breakfast ! " For though, as a fact, it had not prevented his completing a hearty meal, he fancied that he felt hungry. " When I was quartered at Halifax there was a fellow who never sent anything but telegrams. Telegraph Jo they called him. He commanded the old Bluebottles. You know the old Bluebottles? If Horace is going to take to this sort of thing he'd better see a specialist; it's almost certain to mean a breakdown. You're up about dresses, I see. When do you come to town? The season's getting on."

Mrs. Pendyce was not afraid of her husband's brother, for though punctilious and accustomed to his own way with inferiors, he was hardly a man to inspire awe in his social equals. It was, therefore, not through fear that she did not tell him the truth, but through an instinct for avoiding all unnecessary suffering too strong for her, and because the truth was really untellable. Even to herself it seemed slightly ridiculous, and she knew the poor General would take it so dreadfully to heart.

" I don't know about coming up this season. The garden is looking so beautiful, and there's Bee's engagement. The dear child is so happy ! "

The General caressed a whisker with his white hand.

" Ah yes," he said—" young Tharp ! Let's see, he's not the eldest. His brother's in my old corps. What does this young fellow do with himself? "

Mrs. Pendyce answered:

" He's only farming. I'm afraid he'll have nothing to speak of, but he's a dear good boy. It'll be a long engagement. Of course, there's nothing in farming, and Horace insists on their having a thousand a year. It depends so much on Mr. Tharp. I think they could do perfectly well on seven hundred to start with, don't you, Charles? "

General Pendyce's answer was not more conspicuously to the

point than usual, for he was a man who loved to pursue his
own trains of thought.

"What about George?" he said. "I met him in the hall as
I was coming in, but he ran off in the very deuce of a hurry.
They told me at Epsom that he was hard hit."

His eyes, distracted by a fly for which he had taken a dislike,
failed to observe his sister-in-law's face.

"Hard hit?" she repeated.

"Lost a lot of money. That won't do, you know, Margery—
that won't do. A little mild gambling's one thing."

Mrs. Pendyce said nothing; her face was rigid. It was the
face of a woman on the point of saying: "Do not compel me
to hint that you are boring me!"

The General went on:

"A lot of new men have taken to racing that no one knows
anything about. That fellow who bought George's horse, for
instance; you'd never have seen *his* nose in Tattersalls when I
was a young man. I find when I go racing I don't know half
the colours. It spoils the pleasure. It's no longer the close
borough that it was. George had better take care what he's
about. I can't imagine what we're coming to!"

On Margery Pendyce's hearing, those words, "I can't imagine
what we're coming to," had fallen for four-and-thirty years, in
every sort of connection, from many persons. It had become
part of her life, indeed, to take it for granted that people could
imagine nothing; just as the solid food and solid comfort of
Worsted Skeynes and the misty mornings and the rain had
become part of her life. And it was only the fact that her
nerves were on edge and her heart bursting that made those
words seem intolerable that morning; but habit was even now
too strong, and she kept silence.

The General, to whom an answer was of no great moment,
pursued his thoughts.

"And you mark my words, Margery; the elections will go
against us. The country's in a dangerous state."

Mrs. Pendyce said:

"Oh, do you think the Liberals will really get in?"

From custom there was a shade of anxiety in her voice which
she did not feel.

"Think?" repeated General Pendyce. "I pray every night
to God they won't!"

Folding both hands on the silver knob of his Malacca cane,

he stared over them at the opposing wall; and there was something universal in that fixed stare, a sort of blank and not quite selfish apprehension. Behind his personal interests his ancestors had drilled into him the impossibility of imagining that he did not stand for the welfare of his country. Mrs. Pendyce, who had so often seen her husband look like that, leaned out of the window above the noisy street.

The General rose.

"Well," he said, "if I can't do anything for you, Margery, I'll take myself off; you're busy with your dressmakers. Give my love to Horace, and tell him not to send me another telegram like that."

And bending stiffly, he pressed her hand with a touch of real courtesy and kindness, took up his hat, and went away. Mrs. Pendyce, watching him descend the stairs, watching his stiff sloping shoulders, his head with its grey hair brushed carefully away from the centre parting, the backs of his feeble, active knees, put her hand to her breast and sighed, for with him she seemed to see descending all her past life, and that one cannot see unmoved.

CHAPTER III

MRS. BELLEW SQUARES HER ACCOUNTS

MRS. BELLEW sat on her bed smoothing out the halves of a letter; by her side was her jewel-case. Taking from it an amethyst necklet, an emerald pendant, and a diamond ring, she wrapped them in cottonwool, and put them in an envelope. The other jewels she dropped one by one into her lap, and sat looking at them. At last, putting two necklets and two rings back into the jewel-case, she placed the rest in a little green box, and taking that and the envelope, went out. She called a hansom, drove to a post-office, and sent a telegram:

" PENDYCE, STOICS' CLUB.
    " Be at studio six to seven.—H."

From the post-office she drove to her jeweller's, and many a man who saw her pass with the flush on her cheeks and the smouldering look in her eyes, as though a fire were alight within her, turned in his tracks and bitterly regretted that he knew not who she was, or whither going. The jeweller took the jewels from the green box, weighed them one by one, and slowly examined each through his lens. He was a little man with a yellow wrinkled face and a weak little beard, and having fixed in his mind the sum that he would give, he looked at his client prepared to mention less. She was sitting with her elbows on the counter, her chin resting in her hands, and her eyes were fixed on him. He decided somehow to mention the exact sum.

" Is that all ? "

" Yes, madam; that is the utmost."

" Very well, but I must have it now in cash ! "

The jeweller's eyes flickered.

" It's a large sum," he said—" most unusual. I haven't got such a sum in the place."

" Then please send out and get it, or I must go elsewhere."

The jeweller brought his hands together, and washed them nervously.

"Excuse me a moment; I'll consult my partner."

He went away, and from afar he and his partner spied her nervously. He came back with a forced smile. Mrs. Bellew was sitting as he had left her.

"It's a fortunate chance; I think we can just do it, madam."

"Give me notes, please, and a sheet of paper."

The jeweller brought them.

Mrs. Bellew wrote a letter, enclosed it with the bank notes in the bulky envelope she had brought, addressed it, and sealed the whole.

"Call a cab, please!"

The jeweller called a cab.

"Chelsea Embankment!"

The cab bore her away.

Again in the crowded streets so full of traffic, people turned to look after her. The cabman, who put her down at the Albert Bridge, gazed alternately at the coins in his hands and the figure of his fare, and wheeling his cab towards the stand, jerked his thumb in her direction.

Mrs. Bellew walked fast down a street till, turning a corner, she came suddenly on a small garden with three poplar-trees in a row. She opened its green gate without pausing, went down a path, and stopped at the first of three green doors. A young man with a beard, resembling an artist, who was standing behind the last of the three doors, watched her with a knowing smile on his face. She took out a latch-key, put it in the lock, opened the door, and passed in.

The sight of her face seemed to have given the artist an idea. Propping his door open, he brought an easel and canvas, and setting them so that he could see the corner where she had gone in, began to sketch.

An old stone fountain with three stone frogs stood in the garden near the corner, and beyond it was a flowering currant-bush, and beyond this again the green door on which a slanting gleam of sunlight fell. He worked for an hour, then put his easel back and went out to get his tea.

Mrs. Bellew came out soon after he was gone. She closed the door behind her, and stood still. Taking from her pocket the bulky envelope, she slipped it into the letter-box; then bending down, picked up a twig, and placed it in the slit, to prevent the lid falling with a rattle. Having done this, she swept her hands down her face and breast as though to brush something from her, and walked away. Beyond the outer gate she turned to the left, and took the same street back to the river. She walked slowly, luxuriously, looking about her. Once or twice she stopped, and drew a deep breath, as though she could not have enough of the air. She went as far as the Embankment, and stood leaning her elbows on the parapet. Between the finger and thumb of one hand she held a small object on which the sun was shining. It was a key. Slowly, luxuriously, she stretched her hand out over the water, parted her thumb and finger, and let it fall.

CHAPTER IV

MRS. PENDYCE'S INSPIRATION

But George did not come to take his mother to the theatre, and she whose day had been passed in looking forward to the evening, passed that evening in a drawing-room full of furniture whose history she did not know, and a dining-room full of people eating in twos and threes and fours, at whom she might look, but to whom she must not speak, to whom she did not even want to speak, so soon had the wheel of life rolled over her wonder and her expectation, leaving it lifeless in her breast. And all that night, with one short interval of sleep, she ate of bitter isolation and futility, and of the still more bitter knowledge: "George does not want me; I'm no good to him!"

Her heart, seeking consolation, went back again and again to the time when he *had* wanted her; but it was far to go, to the days of holland suits, when all those things that he desired —slices of pineapple, Benson's old carriage-whip, the daily reading out of "Tom Brown's School-days," the rub with Elliman when he sprained his little ankle, the tuck-up in bed—were in her power alone to give.

This night she saw with fatal clearness that since he went to school he had never wanted her at all. She had tried so many years to believe that he did, till it had become part of her life, as it was part of her life to say her prayers night and morning; and now she found it was all pretence. But, lying awake, she still tried to believe it, because to that she had been bound when she brought him, first-born, into the world. Her other son, her daughters, she loved them too, but it was not the same thing, quite; she had never wanted them to want her, because that part of her had been given once for all to George.

The street noises died down at last; she had slept two hours when they began again. She lay listening. And the noises and her thoughts became tangled in her exhausted brain—one great web of weariness, a feeling that it was all senseless and unnecessary, the emanation of cross-purposes and cross-grainedness, the negation of that gentle moderation, her own most sacred instinct. And an early wasp, attracted by the sweet

178

perfumes of her dressing-table, roused himself from the corner where he had spent the night, and began to hum and hover over the bed. Mrs. Pendyce was a little afraid of wasps, so, taking a moment when he was otherwise engaged, she stole out, and fanned him with her nightdress-case till, perceiving her to be a lady, he went away. Lying down again, she thought: 'People *will* worry them until they sting, and then kill them; it's so urreasonable,' not knowing that she was putting all her thoughts on suffering in a single nutshell.

She breakfasted upstairs, unsolaced by any news from George. Then with no definite hope, but a sort of inner certainty, she formed the resolution to call on Mrs. Bellew. She determined, however, first to visit Mr. Paramor, and, having but a hazy notion of the hour when men begin to work, she did not care to start till past eleven, and told her cabman to drive her slowly. He drove her, therefore, faster than his wont. In Leicester Square the passage of a Personage between two stations blocked the traffic, and on the footways were gathered a crowd of simple folk with much in their hearts and little in their stomachs, who raised a cheer as the Personage passed. Mrs. Pendyce looked eagerly from her cab, for she too loved a show.

The crowd dispersed, and the cab went on.

It was the first time she had ever found herself in the business apartment of any professional man less important than a dentist. From the little waiting-room, where they handed her the *Times,* which she could not read from excitement, she caught sight of rooms lined to the ceilings with leather books and black tin boxes, initialed in white to indicate the brand, and of young men seated behind lumps of paper that had been written on. She heard a perpetual clicking noise which roused her interest, and smelled a peculiar odour of leather and disinfectant which impressed her disagreeably. A youth with reddish hair and a pen in his hand passed through and looked at her with a curious stare immediately averted. She suddenly felt sorry for him and all those other young men behind the lumps of paper, and the thought went flashing through her mind, 'I suppose it's all because people can't agree.'

She was shown in to Mr. Paramor at last. In his large empty room, with its air of past grandeur, she sat gazing at three La France roses in a tumbler of water with the feeling that she would never be able to begin.

Mr. Paramor's eyebrows, which jutted from his clean, brown face like little clumps of pothooks, were iron-grey, and iron-grey his hair brushed back from his high forehead. Mrs. Pendyce wondered why he looked five years younger than Horace, who was his junior, and ten years younger than Charles, who, of course, was younger still. His eyes, which from iron-grey some inner process of spiritual manufacture had made into steel colour, looked young too, although they were grave, and the smile which twisted up the corners of his mouth looked very young.

"Well," he said, "it's a great pleasure to see you."

Mrs. Pendyce could only answer with a smile.

Mr. Paramor put the roses to his nose.

"Not so good as yours," he said, "are they? but the best I can do."

Mrs. Pendyce blushed with pleasure.

"My garden is looking so beautiful——" Then, remembering that she no longer had a garden, she stopped; but remembering also that, though she had lost her garden, Mr. Paramor still had his, she added quickly: "And yours, Mr. Paramor—I'm sure it must be looking lovely."

Mr. Paramor drew out a kind of dagger with which he had stabbed some papers to his desk, and took a letter from the bundle.

"Yes," he said, "it's looking very nice. You'd like to see this, I expect."

"Bellew v. Bellew and Pendyce" was written at the top. Mrs. Pendyce stared at those words as though fascinated by their beauty; it was long before she got beyond them. For the first time the full horror of these matters pierced the kindly armour that lies between mortals and what they do not like to think of. Two men and a woman wrangling, fighting, tearing each other before the eyes of all the world. A woman and two men stripped of charity and gentleness, of moderation and sympathy—stripped of all that made life decent and lovable, squabbling like savages before the eyes of all the world. Two men, and one of them her son, and between them a woman whom both of them had *loved!* "Bellew v. Bellew and Pendyce"! And this would go down to fame in company with the pitiful stories she had read from time to time with a sort of offended interest; in company with "Snooks v. Snooks and Stiles," "Horaday v. Horaday," "Bethany v. Bethany and

Sweetenham." In company with all those cases where everybody seemed so dreadful, yet where she had often and often felt
so sorry, as if these poor creatures had been fastened in the
stocks by some malignant, loutish spirit, for all that would
to come and jeer at. And horror filled her heart. It was all so
mean, and gross, and common.

The letter contained but a few words from a firm of solicitors
confirming an appointment. She looked up at Mr. Paramor. He stopped penciling on his blotting-paper, and said at
once:

"I shall be seeing these people myself to-morrow afternoon.
I shall do my best to make them see reason."

She felt from his eyes that he knew what she was suffering,
and was even suffering with her.

"And if—if they won't?"

"Then I shall go on a different tack altogether, and they
must look out for themselves."

Mrs. Pendyce sank back in her chair; she seemed to smell
again that smell of leather and disinfectant, and hear a sound
of incessant clicking. She felt faint, and to disguise that faintness asked at random, "What does 'without prejudice' in this
letter mean?"

Mr. Paramor smiled.

"That's an expression we always use," he said. "It means
that when we give a thing away, we reserve to ourselves the
right of taking it back again."

Mrs. Pendyce, who did not understand, murmured:

"I see. But what have they given away?"

Mr. Paramor put his elbows on the desk, and lightly pressed
his finger-tips together.

"Well," he said, "properly speaking, in a matter like this,
the other side and I are cat and dog. We are supposed to know
nothing about each other and to want to know less, so that
when we do each other a courtesy we are obliged to save our
faces by saying, 'We don't really do you one.' D'you understand?"

Again Mrs. Pendyce murmured:

"I see."

"It sounds a little provincial, but we lawyers exist by reason
of provincialism. If people were once to begin making allowances for each other, I don't know where we should be."

Mrs. Pendyce's eyes fell again on those words, "Bellew v.

Bellew and Pendyce," and again, as though fascinated by their beauty, rested there.

"But you wanted to see me about something else too, perhaps?" said Mr. Paramor.

A sudden panic came over her.

"Oh no, thank you. I just wanted to know what had been done. I've come up on purpose to see George. You told me that I——"

Mr. Paramor hastened to her aid.

"Yes, yes; quite right—quite right."

"Horace hasn't come with me."

"Good!"

"He and George sometimes don't quite——"

"Hit it off? They're too much alike."

"Do you think so? I never saw——"

"Not in face, not in face; but they've both got——"

Mr. Paramor's meaning was lost in a smile; and Mrs. Pendyce, who did not know that the word "Pendycitis" was on the tip of his tongue, smiled vaguely too.

"George is very determined," she said. "Do you think—oh, do you think, Mr. Paramor, that you will be able to persuade Captain Bellew's solicitors——"

Mr. Paramor threw himself back in his chair, and his hand covered what he had written on his blotting-paper.

"Yes," he said slowly—"oh yes, yes!"

But Mrs. Pendyce had had her answer. She had meant to speak of her visit to Helen Bellew, but now her thought was:

'He won't persuade them; I feel it. Let me get away!'

Again she seemed to hear the incessant clicking, to smell leather and disinfectant, to see those words, "Bellew v. Bellew and Pendyce."

She held out her hand.

Mr. Paramor took it in his own and looked at the floor.

"Good-bye," he said—"good-bye. What's your address— Green's Hotel? I'll come and tell you what I do. I know—I know!"

Mrs. Pendyce, on whom those words "I know—I know!" had a strange, emotionalising effect, as though no one had ever known before, went away with quivering lips. In her life no one *had* ever "known"—not indeed that she could or would complain of such a trifle, but the fact remained. And at this

moment, oddly, she thought of her husband, and wondered what
he was doing, and felt sorry for him.

But Mr. Paramor went back to his seat and stared at what
he had written on his blotting-paper. It ran thus:

> "We stand on our petty rights here,
>   And our potty dignity there;
>   We make no allowance for others,
>   They make no allowance for us;
>   We catch hold of them by the ear,
>   They grab hold of us by the hair—
>   The result is a bit of a muddle
>   That ends in a bit of a fuss."

He saw that it neither rhymed nor scanned, and with a grave
face he tore it up.

Again Mrs. Pendyce told her cabman to drive slowly, and
again he drove her faster than usual; yet that drive to Chelsea
seemed to last for ever, and interminable were the turnings
which the cabman took, each one shorter than the last, as if he
had resolved to see how much his horse's mouth could bear.

'Poor thing!' thought Mrs. Pendyce; 'its mouth must be so
sore, and it's quite unnecessary.' She put her hand up through
the trap. "Please take me in a straight line. I don't like
corners."

The cabman obeyed. It worried him terribly to take one
corner instead of the six he had purposed on his way; and when
she asked him his fare, he charged her a shilling extra for the
distance he had saved by going straight. Mrs. Pendyce paid
it, knowing no better, and gave him sixpence over, thinking it
might benefit the horse; and the cabman, touching his hat, said:

"Thank you, my lady," for to say "my lady" was his principle when he received eighteenpence above his fare.

Mrs. Pendyce stood quite a minute on the pavement, stroking the horse's nose and thinking:

'I *must* go in; it's silly to come all this way and not go
in!'

But her heart beat so that she could hardly swallow.

At last she rang.

Mrs. Bellew was seated on the sofa in her little drawing-room
whistling to a canary in the open window. In the affairs of men
there is an irony constant and deep, mingled with the very
springs of life. The expectations of Mrs. Pendyce, those timid

apprehensions of this meeting which had racked her all the way, were lamentably unfulfilled. She had rehearsed the scene ever since it came into her head; the reality seemed unfamiliar. She felt no nervousness and no hostility, only a sort of painful interest and admiration. And how could this or any other woman help falling in love with George?

The first uncertain minute over, Mrs. Bellew's eyes were as friendly as if she had been quite within her rights in all she had done; and Mrs. Pendyce could not help meeting friendliness half-way.

"Don't be angry with me for coming. George doesn't know. I felt I must come to see you. Do you think that you two quite know all you're doing? It seems so dreadful, and it's not only yourselves, is it?"

Mrs. Bellew's smile vanished.

"Please don't say ' you two,' " she said.

Mrs. Pendyce stammered:

"I don't understand."

Mrs. Bellew looked her in the face and smiled; and as she smiled she seemed to become a little coarser.

"Well, I think it's quite time you did! I don't love your son. I did once, but I don't now. I told him so yesterday, once for all."

Mrs. Pendyce heard those words, which made so vast, so wonderful a difference—words which should have been like water in a wilderness—with a sort of horror, and all her spirit flamed up into her eyes.

"You don't love him?" she cried.

She felt only a blind sense of insult and affront.

This woman tire of George? Tire of her son? She looked at Mrs. Bellew, on whose face was a kind of inquisitive compassion, with eyes that had never before held hatred.

"You have tired of him? You have given him up? Then the sooner I go to him the better! Give me the address of his rooms, please."

Helen Bellew knelt down at the bureau and wrote on an envelope, and the grace of the woman pierced Mrs. Pendyce to the heart.

She took the paper. She had never learned the art of abuse, and no words could express what was in her heart, so she turned and went out.

Mrs. Bellew's voice sounded quick and fierce behind her.

" How could I help getting tired? I am not you. Now go! "

Mrs. Pendyce wrenched open the outer door. Descending the stairs, she felt for the bannister. She had that awful sense of physical soreness and shrinking which violence, whether their own or others', brings to gentle souls.

CHAPTER V

THE MOTHER AND THE SON

To Mrs. Pendyce, Chelsea was an unknown land, and to find her way to George's rooms would have taken her long had she been by nature what she was by name, for Pendyces never asked their way to anything, or believed what they were told, but found out for themselves with much unnecessary trouble, of which they afterwards complained.

A policeman first, and then a young man with a beard, resembling an artist, guided her footsteps. The latter, who was leaning by a gate, opened it.

"In here," he said; "the door in the corner on the right."

Mrs. Pendyce walked down the little path, past the ruined fountain with its three stone frogs, and stood by the first green door and waited. And while she waited she struggled between fear and joy; for now that she was away from Mrs. Bellew she no longer felt a sense of insult. It was the actual sight of her that had aroused it, so personal is even the most gentle heart.

She found the rusty handle of a bell amongst the creeper-leaves, and pulled it. A cracked metallic tinkle answered her, but no one came; only a faint sound as of someone pacing to and fro. Then in the street beyond the outer gate a coster began calling to the sky, and in the music of his prayers the sound was lost. The young man with a beard, resembling an artist, came down the path.

"Perhaps you could tell me, sir, if my son is out?"

"I've not seen him go out, and I've been painting here all the morning."

Mrs. Pendyce looked with wonder at an easel which stood outside another door a little further on. It seemed to her strange that her son should live in such a place.

"Shall I knock for you?" said the artist. "All these knockers are stiff."

"If you would be so kind!"

The artist knocked.

"He must be in," he said. "I haven't taken my eyes off his door, because I've been painting it."

186

Mrs. Pendyce gazed at the door.

"I can't get it," said the artist. "It's worrying me to death."

Mrs. Pendyce looked at him doubtfully.

"Has he no servant?" she said.

"Oh no," said the artist; "it's a studio. The light's all wrong. I wonder if you would mind standing just as you are for one second; it would help me a lot!"

He moved back and curved his hand over his eyes, and through Mrs. Pendyce there passed a shiver.

'Why doesn't George open the door?' she thought. 'What—what is this man doing?'

The artist dropped his hand.

"Thanks so much!" he said. "I'll knock again. There! that would raise the dead!"

And he laughed.

An unreasoning terror seized on Mrs. Pendyce.

"Oh," she stammered, "I *must* get in—I *must* get in!"

She took the knocker herself, and fluttered it against the door.

"You see," said the artist, "they're all alike; these knockers are as stiff as pokers."

He again curved his hand over his eyes. Mrs. Pendyce leaned against the door; her knees were trembling violently.

'What is happening?' she thought. 'Perhaps he's only asleep, perhaps—— Oh God!'

She beat the knocker with all her force. The door yielded, and in the space stood George. Choking back a sob, Mrs. Pendyce went in. He banged the door behind her.

For a full minute she did not speak, possessed still by that strange terror and by a sort of shame. She did not even look at her son, but cast timid glances round his room. She saw a gallery at the far end, and a conical roof half made of glass. She saw curtains hanging all the gallery length, a table with tea-things and decanters, a round iron stove, rugs on the floor, and a large full-length mirror in the centre of the wall. A silver cup of flowers was reflected in that mirror. Mrs. Pendyce saw that they were dead, and the sense of their vague and nauseating odour was her first definite sensation.

"Your flowers are dead, my darling," she said. "I must get you some fresh!"

Not till then did she look at George. There were circles under his eyes; his face was yellow; it seemed to her that it had shrunk. This terrified her, and she thought:

'I must show nothing; I must keep my head!'

She was afraid—afraid of something desperate in his face, of something desperate and headlong, and she was afraid of his stubbornness, the dumb, unthinking stubbornness that holds to what has been because it has been, that holds to its own when its own is dead. She had so little of this quality herself that she could not divine where it might lead him; but she had lived in the midst of it all her married life, and it seemed natural that her son should be in danger from it now.

Her terror called up her self-possession. She drew George down on the sofa by her side, and the thought flashed through her: 'How many times has he not sat here with that woman in his arms!'

"You didn't come for me last night, dear! I got the tickets, such good ones!"

George smiled.

"No," he said; "I had something else to see to!"

At the sight of that smile Margery Pendyce's heart beat till she felt sick, but she, too, smiled.

"What a nice place you have here, darling!"

"There's room to walk about."

Mrs. Pendyce remembered the sound she had heard of pacing to and fro. From his not asking her how she had found out where he lived she knew he must have guessed where she had been, that there was nothing for either of them to tell the other. And though this was a relief, it added to her terror—the terror of that which is desperate. All sorts of images passed through her mind. She saw George back in her bedroom after his first run with the hounds, his chubby cheek scratched from forehead to jaw, and the blood-stained pad of a cub fox in his little gloved hand. She saw him sauntering into her room the last day of the 1880 match at Lord's, with a battered top-hat, a blackened eye, and a cane with a light-blue tassel. She saw him deadly pale with tightened lips that afternoon after he had escaped from her, half cured of laryngitis, and stolen out shooting by himself, and she remembered his words: "Well, Mother, I couldn't stand it any longer; it was too beastly slow!"

Suppose he could not stand it now! Suppose he should do something rash! She took out her handkerchief.

"It's very hot in here, dear; your forehead is quite wet!"

She saw his eyes turn on her suspiciously, and all her woman's wits stole into her own eyes, so that they did not flicker, but looked at him with matter-of-fact concern.

"That skylight is what does it," he said. "The sun gets full on there."

Mrs. Pendyce looked at the skylight.

"It seems odd to see you here, dear, but it's very nice—so unconventional. You must let me put away those poor flowers!" She went to the silver cup and bent over them. "My dear boy, they're quite nasty! Do throw them outside somewhere; it's so dreadful, the smell of old flowers!"

She held the cup out, covering her nose with her handkerchief.

George took the cup, and like a cat spying a mouse, Mrs. Pendyce watched him take it out into the garden. As the door closed, quicker, more noiseless than a cat, she slipped behind the curtains.

'I know he has a pistol,' she thought.

She was back in an instant, gliding round the room, hunting with her eyes and hands, but she saw nothing, and her heart lightened, for she was terrified of all such things.

'It's only these terrible first hours,' she thought.

When George came back she was standing where he had left her. They sat down in silence, and in that silence, the longest of her life, she seemed to feel all that was in his heart, all the blackness and bitter aching, the rage of defeat and starved possession, the lost delight, the sensation of ashes and disgust; and yet her heart was full enough already of relief and shame, compassion, jealousy, love, and deep longing. Only twice was the silence broken. Once when he asked her whether she had lunched, and she who had eaten nothing all day answered:

"Yes, dear—yes."

Once when he said:

"You shouldn't have come here, Mother; I'm a bit out of sorts!"

She watched his face, dearest to her in all the world, bent towards the floor, and she so yearned to hold it to her breast that, since she dared not, the tears stole up, and silently rolled down her cheeks. The stillness in that room, chose for remoteness, was like the stillness of a tomb, and, as in a tomb, there was no outlook on the world, for the glass of the skylight was opaque.

That deathly stillness settled round her heart; her eyes fixed themselves on the skylight, as though beseeching it to break and let in sound. A cat, making a pilgrimage from roof to roof, the four dark moving spots of its paws, the faint blur of its body, was all she saw. And suddenly, unable to bear it any longer, she cried:

"Oh, George, speak to me! Don't put me away from you like this!"

George answered:

"What do you want me to say, Mother?"

"Nothing—only——"

And falling on her knees beside her son, she pulled his head down against her breast, and stayed rocking herself to and fro, silently shifting closer till she could feel his head lie comfortably; so, she had his face against her heart, and she could not bear to let it go. Her knees hurt her on the boarded floor, her back and all her body ached; but not for worlds would she relax an inch, believing that she could comfort him with her pain, and her tears fell on his neck. When at last he drew his face away she sank down on the floor, and could not rise, but her fingers felt that the bosom of her dress was wet. He said hoarsely:

"It's all right, Mother; you needn't worry!"

For no reward would she have looked at him just then, but with a deeper certainty than reason she knew that he was safe.

Stealthily on the sloping skylight the cat retraced her steps, its four paws dark moving spots, its body a faint blur.

Mrs. Pendyce rose.

"I won't stay now, darling. May I use your glass?"

Standing before that mirror, smoothing back her hair, passing her handkerchief over her cheeks and eyes and lips, she thought:

'That woman has stood here! That woman has smoothed her hair, looking in this class, and wiped his kisses from her cheeks! May God give to her the pain that she has given to my son!'

But when she had wished that wish she shivered.

She turned to George at the door with a smile that seemed to say:

'It's no good to weep, or try and tell you what is in my heart, and so, you see, I'm smiling. Please smile, too, so as to comfort me a little.'

George put a small paper parcel in her hand and tried to smile.

Mrs. Pendyce went quickly out. Bewildered by the sunlight, she did not look at this parcel till she was beyond the outer gate. It contained an amethyst necklace, an emerald pendant, and a diamond ring. In the little grey street that led to this garden with its poplars, old fountain, and green gate, the jewels glowed and sparkled as though all light and life had settled there. Mrs. Pendyce, who loved colour and glowing things, saw that they were beautiful.

That woman had taken them, used their light and colour, and then flung them back! She wrapped them again in the paper, tied the string, and went towards the river. She did not hurry, but walked with her eyes steadily before her. She crossed the Embankment, and stood leaning on the parapet with her hands over the grey water. Her thumb and fingers unclosed; the white parcel dropped, floated a second, and then disappeared.

Mrs. Pendyce looked round her with a start. A young man with a beard, whose face was familiar, was raising his hat.

"So your son *was* in," he said. "I'm very glad. I must thank you again for standing to me just that minute; it made all the difference. It was the relation between the figure and the door that I wanted to get. Good-morning!"

Mrs. Pendyce murmured "Good-morning," following him with startled eyes, as though he had caught her in the commission of a crime. She had a vision of those jewels, buried, poor things! in the grey slime, a prey to gloom, and robbed for ever of their light and colour. And, as though she had sinned, wronged the gentle essence of her nature, she hurried away.

CHAPTER VI

GREGORY LOOKS AT THE SKY

WHEN Gregory Vigil called Mr. Paramor a pessimist it was because, like other people, he did not know the meaning of the term; for with a confusion common to the minds of many persons who have been conceived in misty moments, he thought that, to see things as they were, meant, to try and make them worse. Gregory had his own way of seeing things that was very dear to him—so dear that he would shut his eyes sooner than see them any other way. And since things to him were not the same as things to Mr. Paramor, it cannot, after all, be said that he did not see things as they were. But dirt upon a face that he wished to be clean he could not see—a fluid in his blue eyes dissolved that dirt while the image of the face was passing on to their retinæ. The process was unconscious, and has been called idealism. This was why the longer he reflected the more agonisedly certain he became that his ward was right to be faithful to the man she loved, right to join her life to his. And he went about pressing the blade of this thought into his soul.

About four o'clock on the day of Mrs. Pendyce's visit to the studio a letter was brought him by a page-boy.

> "GREEN'S HOTEL,
> "*Thursday.*
>
> " DEAR GRIG,
> "I have seen Helen Bellew, and have just come from George. We have all been living in a bad dream. She does not love him —perhaps has never loved him. I do not know; I do not wish to judge. *She has given him up.* I will not trust myself to say anything about that. From beginning to end it all seemed so unnecessary, such a needless, cross-grained muddle. I write this line to tell you how things really are, and to beg you, if you have a moment to spare, to look in at George's club this evening and let me know if he is there and how he seems. There is no one else that I could possibly ask to do this for me. Forgive me if this letter pains you.
> "Your affectionate cousin,
> "MARGERY PENDYCE."

To those with the single eye, the narrow personal view of all
things human, by whom the irony underlying the affairs of men
is unseen and unenjoyed, whose simple hearts afford that irony
its most precious smiles, who, vanquished by that irony, remain
invincible—to these no blow of Fate, no reversal of their ideas,
can long retain importance.   The darts stick, quaver, and fall
off like arrows from chain-armour, and the last dart, slipping
upwards under the harness, quivers into the heart to the cry of
"What—you! No, no; I don't believe you're here!"

Such as these have done much of what has had to be done in
this old world, and perhaps still more of what has had to be
undone.

When Gregory received this letter he was working on the case
of a woman with the morphia habit. He put it into his pocket
and went on working. It was all he was capable of doing.

"Here is the memorandum, Mrs. Shortman. Let them take
her for six weeks. She will come out a different woman."

Mrs. Shortman, supporting her thin face in her thin hand,
rested her glowing eyes on Gregory.

"I'm afraid she has lost all moral sense," she said.   "Do you
know, Mr. Vigil, I'm almost afraid she never had any!"

"What do you mean?"

Mrs. Shortman turned her eyes away.

"I'm sometimes tempted to think," she said, "that there are
such people. I wonder whether we allow enough for that. When
I was a girl in the country I remember the daughter of our vicar,
a very pretty creature. There were dreadful stories about her,
even before she was married, and then we heard she was divorced.
She came up to London and earned her own living by playing the
piano until she married again. I won't tell you her name,
but she is very well known, and nobody has ever seen her
show the slightest sign of being ashamed. If there is one
woman like that there may be dozens, and I sometimes think
we waste——"

Gregory said dryly:

"I have heard you say that before."

Mrs. Shortman bit her lips.

"I don't think," she said, "that I grudge my efforts or my
time."

Gregory went quickly up, and took her hand.

"I know that—oh, I know that," he said with feeling.

The sound of Miss Mallow furiously typing rose suddenly

from the corner.   Gregory removed his hat from the peg on which it hung.

"I must go now," he said.   "Good-night."

Without warning, as is the way with hearts, his heart had begun to bleed, and he felt that he must be in the open air.   He took no omnibus or cab, but strode along with all his might, trying to think, trying to understand.   But he could only feel— confused and battered feelings, with now and then odd throbs of pleasure of which he was ashamed.   Whether he knew it or not, he was making his way to Chelsea, for though a man's eyes may be fixed on the stars, his feet cannot take him there, and Chelsea seemed to them the best alternative.   He was not alone upon this journey, for many another man was going there, and many a man had been and was coming now away, and the streets were the one long streaming crowd of the summer afternoon.   And the men he met looked at Gregory, and Gregory looked at them, and neither saw the other, for so it is written of men, lest they pay attention to cares that are not their own.   The sun that scorched his face fell on their backs, the breeze that cooled his back blew on their cheeks.   For the careless world, too, was on its way, along the pavement of the universe, one of millions going to Chelsea, meeting millions coming away. . . .

"Mrs. Bellew at home?"

He went into a room fifteen feet square and perhaps ten high, with a sulky canary in a small gilt cage, an upright piano with an open operatic score, a sofa with piled-up cushions, and on it a woman with a flushed and sullen face, whose elbows were resting on her knees, whose chin was resting on her hand, whose gaze was fixed on nothing.   It was a room of that size, with all these things, but Gregory took into it with him something that made it all seem different to Gregory.   He sat down by the window with his eyes carefully averted, and spoke in soft tones broken by something that sounded like emotion.   He began by telling her of his woman with the morphia habit, and then he told her that he knew everything.   When he had said this he looked out of the window, where builders had left by inadvertence a narrow strip of sky.   And thus he avoided seeing the look on her face, contemptuous, impatient, as though she were thinking: 'You are a good fellow, Gregory, but for Heaven's sake do see things for once as they are!   I have had enough of it.'   And he avoided seeing her stretch her arms out and spread the fingers, as an angry cat will stretch and spread its toes. He told her that he did not want to worry her, but that when she wanted him for anything she must send for him—he was always there; and he looked at her feet, so that he did not see her lip curl. He told her that she would always be the same to him, and he asked her to believe that. He did not see the smile which never left her lips again while he was there—the smile he could not read, because it was the smile of life, and of a woman that he did not understand. But he did see on that sofa a beautiful creature for whom he had longed for years, and so he went away, and left her standing at the door with her teeth fastened on her lip. And since with him Gregory took his eyes, he did not see her reseated on the sofa, just as she had been before he came in, her elbows on her knees, her chin in her hand, her moody eyes like those of a gambler staring into the distance. . . .

In the streets of tall houses leading away from Chelsea were many men, some, like Gregory, hungry for love, and some hungry for bread—men in twos and threes, in crowds, or by themselves, some with their eyes on the ground, some with their eyes level, some with their eyes on the sky, but all with courage and loyalty of one poor kind or another in their hearts. For by courage and loyalty alone it is written that man shall live, whether he goes to Chelsea or whether he comes away. Of all these men, not one but would have smiled to hear Gregory saying to himself: "She will always be the same to me! She will always be the same to me!" And not one that would have grinned. . . .

It was getting on for the Stoics' dinner hour when Gregory found himself in Piccadilly, and, Stoic after Stoic, they were getting out of cabs and passing the club doors. The poor fellows had been working hard all day on the race-course, the cricket-ground, at Hurlingham, or in the Park; some had been to the Royal Academy, and on their faces was a pleasant look: " Ah, God is good—we can rest at last! " And many of them had had no lunch, hoping to keep their weights down, and many who had lunched had not done themselves as well as might be hoped, and some had done themselves too well; but in all their hearts the trust burned bright that they might do themselves better at dinner, for their God *was* good, and dwelt between the kitchen and the cellar of the Stoics' Club. And all—for all had poetry in their souls—looked forward to those hours in paradise when, with cigars between their lips, good wine below, they might dream the daily dream that comes to all true Stoics for about fifteen shillings or even less, all told.

From a little back slum, within two stones'-throw of the god of the Stoics' Club, there had come out two seamstresses to take the air; one was in consumption, having neglected to earn enough to feed herself properly for some years past, and the other looked as if she would be in consumption shortly, for the same reason. They stood on the pavement, watching the cabs drive up. Some of the Stoics saw them and thought: 'Poor girls! they look awfully bad.' Three or four said to themselves: "It oughtn't to be allowed. I mean, it's so painful to see; and it's not as if one could do anything. They're not beggars, don't you know, and so what *can* one do?"

But most of the Stoics did not look at them at all, feeling that their soft hearts could not stand these painful sights, and anxious not to spoil their dinners. Gregory did not see them either, for it so happened that he was looking at the sky, and just then the two girls crossed the road and were lost among the passers-by, for they were not dogs, who could smell out the kind of a man he was.

"Mr. Pendyce *is* in the club; I will send your name up, sir." And rolling a little, as though Gregory's name were heavy, the porter gave it to the boy, who went away with it.

Gregory stood by the empty hearth and waited, and while he waited, nothing struck him at all, for the Stoics seemed very natural, just mere men like himself, except that their clothes were better, which made him think: 'I shouldn't care to belong here and have to dress for dinner every night.'

"Mr. Pendyce is very sorry, sir, but he's engaged."

Gregory bit his lip, said "Thank you," and went away.

'That's all Margery wants,' he thought; 'the rest is nothing to me,' and, getting on a bus, he fixed his eyes once more on the sky.

But George was not engaged. Like a wounded animal taking its hurt for refuge to its lair, he sat in his favourite window overlooking Piccadilly. He sat there as though youth had left him, unmoving, never lifting his eyes. In his stubborn mind a wheel seemed turning, grinding out his memories to the last grain. And Stoics, who could not bear to see a man sit thus throughout that sacred hour, came up from time to time.

"Aren't you going to dine, Pendyce?"

Dumb brutes tell no one of their pains; the law is silence. So with George. And as each Stoic came up, he only set his teeth and said:

" Presently, old chap."

CHAPTER VII

TOUR WITH THE SPANIEL JOHN

Now the spaniel John—whose habit it was to smell of heather and baked biscuits when he rose from a night's sleep—was in disgrace that Thursday. Into his long and narrow head it took time for any new idea to enter, and not till forty hours after Mrs. Pendyce had gone did he recognise fully that something definite had happened to his master. During the agitated minutes that this conviction took in forming, he worked hard. Taking two and a half brace of his master's shoes and slippers, and placing them in unaccustomed spots, he lay on them one by one till they were warm, then left them for some bird or other to hatch out, and returned to Mr. Pendyce's door. It was for all this that the Squire said, " John! " several times, and threatened him with a razor-strop. And partly because he could not bear to leave his master for a single second —the scolding had made him love him so—and partly because of that new idea, which let him have no peace, he lay in the hall waiting.

Having once in his hot youth inadvertently followed the Squire's horse, he could never be induced to follow it again. He both personally disliked this needlessly large and swift form of animal, and suspected it of designs upon his master; for when the creature had taken his master up, there was not a smell of him left anywhere—not a whiff of that pleasant scent that so endeared him to the heart. As soon, therefore, as the horse appeared, the spaniel John would lie down on his stomach with his forepaws close to his nose, and his nose close to the ground; nor until the animal vanished could he be induced to abandon an attitude in which he resembled a couching Sphinx.

But this afternoon, with his tail down, his lips pouting, his shoulders making heavy work of it, his nose lifted in deprecation of that ridiculous and unnecessary plane on which his master sat, he followed at a measured distance. In such-wise, aforetime, the village had followed the Squire and Mr. Barter when they introduced into it its one and only drain.

Mr. Pendyce rode slowly; his feet, in their well-blacked boots, his nervous legs in Bedford cord and mahogany-coloured leggings, moved in rhyme to the horse's trot. A long-tailed coat fell clean and full over his thighs; his back and shoulders were a wee bit bent to lessen motion, and above his neat white stock under a grey bowler hat his lean, grey-whiskered and moustachioed face, with harassed eyes, was preoccupied and sad. His horse, a brown blood mare, ambled lazily, head raking forward, and bang tail floating outward from her hocks. And so, in the June sunshine, they went all three, along the leafy lane to Worsted Scotton. . . .

On Tuesday, the day that Mrs. Pendyce had left, the Squire had come in later than usual, for he felt that after their difference of the night before, a little coolness would do her no harm. The first hour of discovery had been as one confused and angry minute, ending in a burst of nerves and the telegram to General Pendyce. He took the telegram himself, returning from the village with his head down, a sudden prey to a feeling of shame—an odd and terrible feeling that he never remembered to have felt before, a sort of fear of his fellow-creatures. He would have chosen a secret way, but there was none, only the highroad, or the path across the village green, and through the churchyard to his paddocks. An old cottager was standing at the turnstile, and the Squire made for him with his head down, as a bull makes for a fence. He had meant to pass in silence, but between him and this old broken husbandman there was a bond forged by the ages. Had it meant death, Mr. Pendyce could not have passed one whose fathers had toiled for his fathers, eaten his fathers' bread, died with his fathers, without a word and a movement of his hand.

"Evenin', Squire; naice evenin'. Faine weather fur th' hay!"

The voice was warped and wavery.

'This is my Squire,' it seemed to say, 'whatever ther' be agin him!'

Mr. Pendyce's hand went up to his hat.

"Evenin', Hermon. Aye, fine weather for the hay! Mrs. Pendyce has gone up to London. We young bachelors, ha!"

He passed on.

Not until he had gone some way did he perceive why he had made that announcement. It was simply because he must tell everyone, everyone; then no one could be astonished.

He hurried on to the house to dress in time for dinner, and show all that nothing was amiss. Seven courses would have been served him had the sky fallen; but he ate little, and drank more claret than was his wont. After dinner he sat in his study with the windows open, and in the mingled day and lamp light read his wife's letter over again. As it was with the spaniel John, so with his master—a new idea penetrated but slowly into his long and narrow head.

She was cracked about George; she did not know what she was doing; would soon come to her senses. It was not for him to take any steps. What steps, indeed, could he take without confessing that Horace Pendyce had gone too far, that Horace Pendyce was in the wrong? That had never been his habit, and he could not alter now. If she and George chose to be stubborn, they must take the consequences, and fend for themselves.

In the silence and the lamplight, growing mellower each minute under the green silk shade, he sat confusedly thinking of the past. And in that dumb reverie, as though of fixed malice, there came to him no memories that were not pleasant, no images that were not fair. He tried to think of her unkindly, he tried to paint her black; but with the perversity born into the world when he was born, to die when he was dead, she came to him softly, like the ghost of gentleness, to haunt his fancy. She came to him smelling of sweet scents, with a slight rustling of silk, and the sound of her expectant voice, saying, "Yes, dear?" as though she were not bored. He remembered when he brought her first to Worsted Skeynes thirty-four years ago, "That timid, and like a rose, but a lady every hinch, the love!" as his old nurse had said.

He remembered her when George was born, like wax for whiteness and transparency, with eyes that were all pupils, and a hovering smile. So many other times he remembered her throughout those years, but never as a woman, faded, old; never as a woman of the past. Now that he had not got her, for the first time Mr. Pendyce realised that she had not grown old, that she was still to him "timid, and like a rose, but a lady every hinch, the love!" And he could not bear this thought; it made him feel so miserable and lonely in the lamplight, with the grey moths hovering round, and the spaniel John asleep upon his foot.

So, taking his candle, he went up to bed. The doors that barred away the servants' wing were closed. In all that great remaining space of house his was the only candle, the only sounding footstep. Slowly he mounted as he had mounted many thousand times, but never once like this, and behind him, like a shadow, mounted the spaniel John.

And She that knows the hearts of men and dogs, the Mother from whom all things come, to whom they all go home, was watching, and presently, when they were laid, the one in his deserted bed, the other on blue linen, propped against the door, She gathered them to sleep.

But Wednesday came, and with it Wednesday duties. They who have passed the windows of the Stoics' Club and seen the Stoics sitting there have haunting visions of the idle landed classes. These visions will not let them sleep, will not let their tongues to cease from bitterness, for they so long to lead that "idle" life themselves. But though in a misty land illusions be our cherished lot, that we may all think falsely of our neighbours and enjoy ourselves, the word "idle" is not at all the word.

Many and heavy tasks weighed on the Squire at Worsted Skeynes. There was the visit to the stables to decide as to firing Beldame's hock, or selling the new bay horse because he did not draw men fast enough, and the vexed question of Bruggan's oats or Beal's, talked out with Benson, in a leather belt and flannel shirt-sleeves, like a corpulent, white-whiskered boy. Then the long sitting in the study with memorandums and accounts, all needing care, lest So-and-so should give too little for too little, or too little for too much; and the smart walk across to Jarvis, the head keeper, to ask after the health of the new Hungarian bird, or discuss a scheme whereby in the last drive so many of those creatures he had nurtured from their youth up might be deterred from flying over to his friend Lord Quarryman. And this took long, for Jarvis's feelings forced him to say six times, "Well, Mr. Pendyce, sir, what I say is we didn't oughter lose s'many birds in that last drive;" and Mr. Pendyce to answer: "No, Jarvis, certainly not. Well, what do you suggest?" And that other grievous question—how to get plenty of pheasants and plenty of foxes to dwell together in perfect harmony—discussed with endless sympathy, for, as the Squire would say, "Jarvis is quite safe with foxes." He could not bear his covers to be drawn blank.

Then back to a sparing lunch, or perhaps no lunch at all, that he might keep fit and hard; and out again at once on horseback or on foot to the home farm or further, as need might take

him, and a long afternoon, with eyes fixed on the ribs of bullocks, the colour of swedes, the surfaces of walls or gates or
fences.

Then home again to tea and to the *Times*, which had as yet
received but fleeting glances, with close attention to all those
Parliamentary measures threatening, remotely, the existing state
of things, except, of course, that future tax on wheat so needful
to the betterment of Worsted Skeynes. There were occasions,
too, when they brought him tramps to deal with, to whom his
one remark would be, " Hold out your hands, my man," which,
being found unwarped by honest toil, were promptly sent to
gaol. When found so warped, Mr. Pendyce was at a loss, and
would walk up and down, earnestly trying to discover what
his duty was to them. There were days, too, almost entirely
occupied by sessions, when many classes of offenders came
before him, to whom he meted justice according to the heinousness of the offence, from poaching at the top down and down
to wife-beating at the bottom; for, though a humane man, tradition did not suffer him to look on this form of sport as really
criminal—at any rate, not in the country.

It was true that all these matters could have been settled in
a fraction of the time by a young and trained intelligence, but
this would have wronged tradition, disturbed the Squire's settled
conviction that he was doing his duty, and given cause for slanderous tongues to hint at idleness. And though, further, it was
true that all this daily labour was devoted directly or indirectly
to interests of his own, what was that but doing his duty to the
country and asserting the prerogative of every Englishman at
all costs to be provincial?

But on this Wednesday the flavour of the dish was gone. To
be alone amongst his acres, quite alone—to have no one to care
whether he did anything at all, no one to whom he might confide
that Beldame's hock was to be fired, that Peacock was asking
for more gates, was almost more than he could bear. He would
have wired to the girls to come home, but he could not bring
himself to face their questions. Gerald was at Gib! George—
George was no son of his!—and his pride forbade him to write
to her who had left him thus to solitude and shame. For deep
down below his stubborn anger it was shame that the Squire
felt—shame that he should have to shun his neighbours, lest
they should ask him questions which, for his own good name
and his own pride, he must answer with a lie; shame that he

should not be master in his own house—still more, shame that anyone should see that he was not. To be sure, he did not know that he felt shame, being unused to introspection, having always kept it at arm's length. For he always meditated concretely, as, for instance, when he looked up and did not see his wife at breakfast, but saw Bester making coffee, he thought, ' That fellow knows all about it, I shouldn't wonder!' and he felt angry for thinking that. When he saw Mr. Barter coming down the drive he thought, ' Confound it! I can't meet him,' and slipped out, and felt angry that he had thus avoided him. When in the Scotch garden he came on Jackman syringing the rose-trees, he said to him, " Your mistress has gone to London," and abruptly turned away, angry that he had been obliged by a mysterious impulse to tell him that.

So it was, all through that long, sad day, and the only thing that gave him comfort was to score through, in the draft of his will, bequests to his eldest son, and busy himself over drafting a clause to take their place:

" Forasmuch as my eldest son, George Hubert, has by conduct unbecoming to a gentleman and a Pendyce, proved himself unworthy of my confidence, and forasmuch as to my regret I am unable to cut the entail of my estate, I hereby declare that he shall in no way participate in any division of my other property or of my personal effects, conscientiously believing that it is my duty so to do in the interests of my family and of the country, and I make this declaration without anger."

For, all the anger that he was balked of feeling against his wife, because he missed her so, was added to that already felt against his son.

By the last post came a letter from General Pendyce. He opened it with fingers as shaky as his brother's writing.

" ARMY AND NAVY CLUB.

" DEAR HORACE,

" What the deuce and all made you send that telegram? It spoiled my breakfast, and sent me off in a tearing hurry, to find Margery perfectly well. If she'd been seedy or anything I should have been delighted, but there she was, busy about her dresses and what not, and I dare say she thought me a lunatic for coming at that time in the morning. You shouldn't get into the habit of sending telegrams. A telegram is a thing that means something—at least, I've always thought so. I met George coming away from her in a deuce of a hurry. I can't write any more now. I'm just going to have my lunch.

"Your affectionate brother,
"CHARLES PENDYCE."

She was well. She had been seeing George. With a hardened heart the Squire went up to bed.

And Wednesday came to an end. . . .

And so on the Thursday afternoon the brown blood mare carried Mr. Pendyce along the lane, followed by the spaniel John. They passed the Firs, where Bellow lived, and, bending sharply to the right, began to mount towards the Common; and with them mounted the image of that fellow who was at the bottom of it all—an image that ever haunted the Squire's mind nowadays; a ghost, high-shouldered, with little burning eyes, clipped red moustaches, thin bowed legs. A plague spot on that system which he loved, a whipping-post to heredity, a scourge like Attila the Hun; a sort of damnable caricature of all that a country gentleman should be—of his love of sport and open air, of his "hardness" and his pluck; of his powers of knowing his own mind, and taking his liquor like a man; of his creed, now out of date, of gallantry. Yes—a kind of cursed bogey of a man, a spectral follower of the hounds, a desperate character—a man that in old days someone would have shot; a drinking, white-faced devil who despised Horace Pendyce, whom Horace Pendyce hated, yet could not quite despise. "Always one like that in a hunting country!" A black dog on the shoulders of his order. *Post equitem sedet Jaspar Bellew!*

The Squire came out on the top of the rise, and all Worsted Scotton was in sight. It was a sandy stretch of broom and gorse and heather, with a few Scotch firs; it had no value at all, and he longed for it, as a boy might long for the bite someone else had snatched out of his apple. It distressed him lying there, his and yet not his, like a wife who was no wife—as though Fortune were enjoying her at his expense. Thus was he deprived of the fulness of his mental image; for as with all men, so with the Squire, that which he loved and owned took definite form—a something that he *saw*. Whenever the words "Worsted Skeynes" were in his mind—and that was almost always—there rose before him an image defined and concrete, however indescribable; and whatever this image was, he knew that Worsted Scotton spoiled it. It was true that he could not think of any use to which to put the Common, but he felt deeply that it was pure dog-in-the-mangerism of the cottagers, and this he could not stand. Not one beast in two years had fattened on its barrenness. Three old donkeys alone eked out the remnants of their days. A bundle of firewood or old bracken, a few peat sods from one especial corner, were all the selfish peasants gathered. But the cottagers were no great matter—he could soon have settled them; it was that fellow Peacock whom he could not settle, just because he happened to abut on the Common, and his fathers had been nasty before him. Mr. Pendyce rode round looking at the fence his father had put up, until he came to the portion that Peacock's father had pulled down; and here, by a strange fatality—such as will happen even in printed records—he came on Peacock himself standing in the gap, as though he had foreseen this visit of the Squire's. The mare stopped of her own accord, the spaniel John at a measured distance lay down to think, and all those yards away he could be heard doing it, and now and then swallowing his tongue.

Peacock stood with his hands in his breeches' pockets. An old straw hat was on his head, his little eyes were turned towards the ground; and his cob, which he had tied to what his father had left standing of the fence, had his eyes, too, turned towards the ground, for he was eating grass. Mr. Pendyce's fight with his burning stable had stuck in the farmer's "gizzard" ever since. He felt that he was forgetting it day by day—would soon forget it altogether. He felt the old sacred doubts inherited from his fathers rising every hour within him. And so he had come up to see what looking at the gap would do for his sense of gratitude. At sight of the Squire his little eyes turned here and there, as a pig's eyes turn when it receives a blow behind. That Mr. Pendyce should have chosen this moment to come up was as though Providence, that knoweth all things, knew the natural thing for Mr. Pendyce to do.

"Afternoon, Squire. Dry weather; rain's badly wanted. I'll get no feed if this goes on."

Mr. Pendyce answered:

"Afternoon, Peacock. Why, your fields are first-rate for grass."

They hastily turned their eyes away, for at that moment they could not bear to see each other.

There was a silence; then Peacock said:

"What about those gates of mine, Squire?" and his voice quavered, as though gratitude might yet get the better of him.

The Squire's irritable glance swept over the unfenced space to right and left, and the thought flashed through his mind:

'Suppose I were to give the beggar those gates, would he—would he let me enclose the Scotton again?'

He looked at that square, bearded man, and the infallible instinct, christened so wickedly by Mr. Paramor, guided him.

"What's wrong with *your* gates, man, I should like to know?"

Peacock looked at him full this time; there was no longer any quaver in his voice, but a sort of rough good-humour.

"Wy, the 'arf o' them's as rotten as matchwood!" he said; and he took a breath of relief, for he knew that gratitude was dead within his soul.

"Well, I wish mine at the home farm were half as good. Come, John!" and, touching the mare with his heel, Mr. Pendyce turned; but before he had gone a dozen paces he was back.

"Mrs. Peacock well, I hope? Mrs. Pendyce has gone up to London."

And touching his hat, without waiting for Peacock's answer, he rode away. He took the lane past Peacock's farm across the home paddocks, emerging on the cricket-ground, a field of his own which he had caused to be converted.

The return match with Coldingham was going on, and, motionless on his horse, the Squire stopped to watch. A tall figure in the "long field" came leisurely towards him. It was the Hon. Geoffrey Winlow. Mr. Pendyce subdued an impulse to turn the mare and ride away.

"We're going to give you a licking, Squire! How's Mrs. Pendyce? My wife sent her love."

On the Squire's face in the full sun was more than the sun's flush.

"Thanks," he said, "she's very well. She's gone up to London."

"And aren't you going up yourself this season?"

The Squire crossed those leisurely eyes with his own.

"I don't think so," he said slowly.

The Hon. Geoffrey returned to his duties.

"We got poor old Barter for a 'blob'!" he said over his shoulder.

The Squire became aware that Mr. Barter was approaching from behind.

"You see that left-hand fellow?" he said, pouting. "Just watch his foot. D'you mean to say that wasn't a no-ball? He bowled *me* with a no-ball. He's a rank no-baller. That fellow Locke's no more an umpire than——"

He stopped and looked earnestly at the bowler.

The Squire did not answer, sitting on his mare as though carved in stone. Suddenly his throat clicked.

"How's your wife?" he said. "Margery would have come to see her, but—but she's gone up to London."

The Rector did not turn his head.

"My wife? Oh, going on first-rate. There's another! I say, Winlow, this is too bad!"

The Hon. Geoffrey's pleasant voice was heard:

"Please not to speak to the man at the wheel!"

The Squire turned the mare and rode away; and the spaniel John, who had been watching from a measured distance, followed after, his tongue lolling from his mouth.

The Squire turned through a gate down the main aisle of the home covert, and the nose and the tail of the spaniel John, who scented creatures to the left and right, were in perpetual motion. It was cool in there. The June foliage made one long colonnade, broken by a winding river of sky. Among the oaks and hazels, the beeches and the elms, the ghostly body of a birch-tree shone here and there, captured by those grosser trees which seemed to cluster round her, proud of their prisoner, loth to let her go, that subtle spirit of their wood. They knew that, were she gone, their forest lady, wilder and yet gentler than themselves—they would lose credit, lose the grace and essence of their corporate being.

The Squire dismounted, tethered his horse, and sat under one of those birch trees, on the fallen body of an elm. The spaniel John also sat and loved him with his eyes. And sitting there they thought their thoughts, but their thoughts were different.

For under this birch-tree Horace Pendyce had stood and kissed his wife the very day he brought her home to Worsted Skeynes, and though he did not see the parallel between her and the birch-tree that some poor imaginative creature might have drawn, yet he was thinking of that long past afternoon. But the spaniel John was not thinking of it; his recollection was too dim, for he had been at that time twenty-eight years short of being born.

Mr. Pendyce sat there long with his horse and with his dog, and from out the blackness of the spaniel John, who was more than less asleep, there shone at times an eye turned on his master like some devoted star. The sun, shining too, gilded the stem of the birch-tree. The birds and beasts began their evening stir all through the undergrowth, and rabbits, popping out into the ride, looked with surprise at the spaniel John, and popped in back again. They knew that men with horses had no guns, but could not bring themselves to trust that black and hairy thing whose nose so twitched whenever they appeared. The gnats came out to dance, and at their dancing, every sound and scent and shape became the sounds and scents and shapes of evening; and there was evening in the Squire's heart.

Slowly and stiffly he got up from the log and mounted to ride home. It would be just as lonely when he got there, but a house is better than a wood, where the gnats dance, the birds and creatures stir and stir, and shadows lengthen; where the sun steals upwards on the tree-stems, and all is careless of its owner, Man.

It was past seven o'clock when he went to his study. There was a lady standing at the window, and Mr. Pendyce said:

" I beg your pardon? "

The lady turned; it was his wife. The Squire stopped with a hoarse sound, and stood silent, covering his eyes with his hand.

CHAPTER VIII

ACUTE ATTACK OF—" PENDYCITIS "

MRS. PENDYCE felt very faint when she hurried away from Chelsea. She had passed through hours of great emotion, and eaten nothing.

Like sunset clouds or the colours in mother-o'-pearl, so, it is written, shall be the moods of men—interwoven as the threads of an embroidery, less certain than an April day, yet with a rhythm of their own that never fails, and no one can squite scan.

A single cup of tea on her way home, and her spirit revived. It seemed suddenly as if there had been a great ado about nothing! As if someone had known how stupid men could be, and been playing a fantasia on that stupidity. But this gaiety of spirit soon died away, confronted by the problem of what she should do next.

She reached her hotel without making a decision. She sat down in the reading-room to write to Gregory, and while she sat there with her pen in her hand a dreadful temptation came over her to say bitter things to him, because by not seeing people as they were he had brought all this upon them. But she had so little practice in saying bitter things that she could not think of any that were nice enough, and in the end she was obliged to leave them out. After finishing and sending off the note she felt better. And it came to her suddenly that, if she packed at once, there was just time to catch the *5.55* to Worsted Skeynes.

As in leaving her home, so in returning, she followed her instinct, and her instinct told her to avoid unnecessary fuss and suffering.

The decrepit station fly, mouldy and smelling of stables, bore her almost lovingly towards the Hall. Its old driver, clean-faced, cheery, somewhat like a bird, drove her almost furiously, for, though he knew nothing, he felt that two whole days and half a day were quite long enough for her to be away. At the lodge gate old Roy, the Skye, was seated on his haunches, and the sight of him set Mrs. Pendyce trembling as though till then she had not realised that she was coming home.

Home! The long narrow lane without a turning, the mists

209

and stillness, the driving rain and hot bright afternoons; the scents of wood smoke and hay and the scent of her flowers; the Squire's voice, the dry rattle of grass-cutters, the barking of dogs, and distant hum of threshing; and Sunday sounds—church bells and rooks, and Mr. Barter's preaching; the tastes, too, of the very dishes! And all these scents and sounds and tastes, and the feel of the air to her cheeks, seemed to have been for ever in the past, and to be going on for ever in the time to come.

She turned red and white by turns, and felt neither joy nor sadness, for in a wave the old life came over her. She went at once to the study to wait for her husband to come in. At the hoarse sound he made, her heart beat fast, while old Roy and the spaniel John growled gently at each other.

" John," she murmured, " aren't you glad to see me, dear? "

The spaniel John, without moving, beat his tail against his master's foot.

The Squire raised his head at last.

" Well, Margery? " was all he said.

It shot through her mind that he looked older, and very tired!

The dinner-gong began to sound, and as though attracted by its long monotonous beating, a swallow flew in at one of the narrow windows and fluttered round the room. Mrs. Pendyce's eyes followed its flight.

The Squire stepped forward suddenly and took her hand.

" Don't run away from me again, Margery! " he said; and stooping down, he kissed it.

At this action, so unlike her husband, Mrs. Pendyce blushed like a girl. Her eyes above his grey and close-cropped head seemed grateful that he did not reproach her, glad of that caress.

" I have some news to tell you, Horace. Helen Bellew has given George up! "

The Squire dropped her hand.

" And quite time too," he said. " I dare say George has refused to take his dismissal. He's as obstinate as a mule."

" I found him in a dreadful state."

Mr. Pendyce asked uneasily:

" What? What's that? "

" He looked so desperate."

" Desperate? " said the Squire, with a sort of startled anger.

Mrs. Pendyce went on:

" It was dreadful to see his face. I was with him this after-noon——"

The Squire said suddenly:

"He's not ill, is he?"

"No, not ill. Oh, Horace, don't you understand? I was afraid he might do something rash. He was so—miserable."

The Squire began to walk up and down.

"Is he—is he safe now?" he burst out.

Mrs. Pendyce sat down rather suddenly in the nearest chair.

"Yes," she said with difficulty, "I—I think so."

"Think! What's the good of that? What—— Are you feeling faint, Margery?"

Mrs. Pendyce, who had closed her eyes, said:

"No dear, it's all right."

Mr. Pendyce came close, and since air and quiet were essential to her at that moment, he bent over and tried by every means in his power to rouse her; and she, who longed to be let alone, sympathised with him, for she knew that it was natural that he should do this. In spite of his efforts the feeling of faintness passed, and, taking his hand, she stroked it gratefully.

"What is to be done now, Horace?"

"Done!" cried the Squire. "Good God! how should I know? Here you are in this state, all because of that d——d fellow Bellew and his d——d wife! What you want is some dinner."

So saying, he put his arm around her, and half leading, half carrying, took her to her room.

They did not talk much at dinner, and of indifferent things, of Mrs. Barter, Peacock, the roses, and Beldame's hock. Only once they came too near to that which instinct told them to avoid, for the Squire said suddenly:

"I suppose you saw that woman?"

And Mrs. Pendyce murmured:

"Yes."

She soon went to her room, and had barely got into bed when he appeared, saying as though ashamed:

"I'm very early."

She lay awake, and every now and then the Squire would ask her, "Are you asleep, Margery?" hoping that she might have dropped off, for he himself could not sleep. And she knew that he meant to be nice to her, and she knew, too, that as he lay awake, turning from side to side, he was thinking like herself: 'What's to be done next?' And that his fancy, too, was haunted by a ghost, high-shouldered, with little burning eyes, red hair, and white freckled face. For, save that George was miserable, nothing was altered, and the cloud of vengeance still hung over Worsted Skeynes. Like some weary lesson she rehearsed her thoughts: ' Now Horace can answer that letter of Captain Bellew's, can tell him that George will not—indeed, cannot—see her again. He *must* answer it. But will he?'

She groped after the secret springs of her husband's character, turning and turning and trying to understand, that she might know the best way of approaching him. And she could not feel sure, for behind all the little outside points of his nature, that she thought so " funny," yet could comprehend, there was something which seemed to her as unknown, as impenetrable as the dark, a sort of thickness of soul, a sort of hardness, a sort of barbaric—what? And as when in working at her embroidery the point of her needle would often come to a stop against stiff buckram, so now was the point of her soul brought to a stop against the soul of her husband. ' Perhaps,' she thought, ' Horace feels like that with me.' She need not so have thought, for the Squire never worked embroideries, nor did the needle of his soul make voyages of discovery.

By lunch-time the next day she had not dared to say a word. ' If I say nothing,' she thought, ' he may write it of his own accord.'

Without attracting his attention, therefore, she watched every movement of his morning. She saw him sitting at his bureau with a creased and crumpled letter, and knew it was Bellew's; and she hovered about, coming softly in and out, doing little things here and there and in the hall, outside. But the Squire gave no sign, motionless as the spaniel John couched along the ground with his nose between his paws.

After lunch she could bear it no longer.

" What do you think ought to be done now, Horace?"

The Squire looked at her fixedly.

" If you imagine," he said at last, " that I'll have anything to do with that fellow Bellew, you're very much mistaken."

Mrs. Pendyce was arranging a vase of flowers, and her hand shook so that some of the water was spilled over the cloth. She took out her handkerchief and dabbed it up.

" You never answered his letter, dear," she said.

The Squire put his back against the sideboard; his stiff figure, with lean neck and angry eyes, whose pupils were mere pin-points, had a certain dignity.

" Nothing shall induce me ! " he said, and his voice was harsh and strong, as though he spoke for something bigger than himself. "I've thought it over all the morning, and I'm d——d if I do! The man is a ruffian. I won't knuckle under to him!"

Mrs. Pendyce clasped her hands.

"Oh, Horace," she said; "but for the sake of us all! Only just give him that assurance."

"And let him crow over me!" cried the Squire. "By Jove, no!"

"But, Horace, I thought that was what you wanted George to do. You wrote to him and asked him to promise."

The Squire answered:

"You know nothing about it, Margery; you know nothing about me. D'you think I'm going to tell him that his wife has thrown my son over—let him keep me gasping like a fish all this time, and then get the best of it in the end? Not if I have to leave the county—not if I——"

But, as though he had imagined the most bitter fate of all, he stopped.

Mrs. Pendyce, putting her hands on the lapels of his coat, stood with her head bent. The colour had flushed into her cheeks, her eyes were bright with tears. And there came from her in her emotion a warmth and fragrance, a charm, as though she were again young, like the portrait under which they stood.

"Not if *I* ask you, Horace?"

The Squire's face was suffused with dusky colour; he clenched his hands and seemed to sway and hesitate.

"No, Margery," he said hoarsely; "it's—it's—I can't!"

And, breaking away from her, he left the room.

Mrs. Pendyce looked after him; her fingers, from which he had torn his coat, began twining the one with the other.

CHAPTER IX

BELLEW BOWS TO A LADY

THERE was silence at the Firs, and in that silent house, where only five rooms were used, an old man-servant sat in his pantry on a wooden chair, reading from an article out of *Rural Life*. There was no one to disturb him, for the master was asleep, and the housekeeper had not yet come to cook the dinner. He read slowly, through spectacles, engraving the words for ever on the tablets of his mind. He read about the construction and habits of the owl: "In the tawny, or brown, owl there is a manubrial process; the furcula, far from being joined to the keel of the sternum, consists of two stylets, which do not even meet; while the posterior margin of the sternum presents two pairs of projections, with corresponding fissures between." The old manservant paused, resting his blinking eyes on the pale sunlight through the bars of his narrow window, so that a little bird on the window-sill looked at him and instantly flew away.

The old manservant read on again: "The pterylological characters of Photodilus seem not to have been investigated, but it has been found to want the tarsal loop, as well as the manubrial process, while its clavicles are not joined in a furcula, nor do they meet the keel, and the posterior margin of the sternum has processes and fissures like the tawny section." Again he paused, and his gaze was satisfied and bland.

Up in the little smoking-room in a leather chair his master sat asleep. In front of him were stretched his legs in dusty riding-boots. His lips were closed, but through a little hole at one corner came a tiny puffing sound. On the floor by his side was an empty glass, between his feet a Spanish bulldog. On a shelf above his head reposed some frayed and yellow novels with sporting titles, written by persons in their inattentive moments. Over the chimneypiece presided the portrait of Mr. Jorrocks persuading his horse to cross a stream.

And the face of Jaspar Bellew asleep was the face of a man who has ridden far, to get away from himself, and to-morrow will have to ride far again. His sandy eyebrows twitched with his dreams against the dead-white, freckled skin above high cheekbones, and two hard ridges were fixed between his brows; now and then over the sleeping face came the look of one riding at a gate.

In the stables behind the house she who had carried him on his ride, having rummaged out her last grains of corn, lifted her nose and poked it through the bars of her loose-box to see what he was doing who had not carried her master that swelter- ing afternoon, and seeing that he was awake, she snorted lightly, to tell him there was thunder in the air. All else in the stables was deadly quiet; the shrubberies around were still; and in the hushed house the master slept.

But on the edge of his wooden chair in the silence of his pantry the old manservant read, "This bird is a voracious feeder," and he paused, blinking his eyes and nervously pucker- ing his lips, for he had partially understood. . . .

Mrs. Pendyce was crossing the fields. She had on her prettiest frock, of smoky-grey crêpe, and she looked a little anxiously at the sky. Gathered in the west a coming storm was chasing the whitened sunlight. Against its purple the trees stood black- ish-green. Everything was very still, not even the poplars stirred, yet the purple grew with sinister, unmoving speed. Mrs. Pendyce hurried, grasping her skirts in both her hands, and she noticed that the cattle were all grouped under the hedge.

'What dreadful-looking clouds!' she thought. 'I wonder if I shall get to the Firs before it comes?' But though her frock made her hasten, her heart made her stand still, it fluttered so, and was so full. Suppose he were not sober! She remembered those little burning eyes, which had frightened her so the night he dined at Worsted Skeynes and fell out of his dogcart after- wards. A kind of legendary malevolence clung about his image.

'Suppose he is horrid to me!' she thought.

She could not go back now; but she wished—how she wished! —that it were over. A heat-drop splashed her glove. She crossed the lane and opened the Firs gate. Throwing frightened glances at the sky, she hastened down the drive. The purple was couched like a pall on the tree-tops, and these had begun to sway and moan as though struggling and weeping at their fate. Some splashes of warm rain were falling. A streak of lightning tore the firmament. Mrs. Pendyce rushed into the porch covering her ears with her hands.

'How long will it last?' she thought. 'I'm so fright- ened!' . . .

A very old manservant, whose face was all puckers, opened the door suddenly to peer out at the storm, but seeing Mrs. Pendyce, he peered at her instead.

"Is Captain Bellew at home?"

"Yes, ma'am. The Captain's in the study. We don't use the drawing-room now. Nasty storm coming on, ma'am—nasty storm. Will you please to sit down a minute, while I let the Captain know?"

The hall was low and dark; the whole house was low and dark, and smelled a little of woodrot. Mrs. Pendyce did not sit down, but stood under an arrangement of three foxes' heads, supporting two hunting-crops, with their lashes hanging down. And the heads of those animals suggested to her the thought: 'Poor man! He must be very lonely here.'

She started. Something was rubbing against her knees: it was only an enormous bulldog. She stooped down to pat it, and having once begun, found it impossible to leave off, for when she took her hand away the creature pressed against her, and she was afraid for her frock.

"Poor old boy—poor old boy!" she kept on murmuring. "Did he want a little attention?"

A voice behind her said:

"Get out, Sam! Sorry to have kept you waiting. Won't you come in here?"

Mrs. Pendyce, blushing and turning pale by turns, passed into a low, small, panelled room, smelling of cigars and spirits. Through the window, which was cut up into little panes, she could see the rain driving past, the shrubs bent and dripping from the downpour.

"Won't you sit down?"

Mrs. Pendyce sat down. She had clasped her hands together; she now raised her eyes and looked timidly at her host.

She saw a thin, high-shouldered figure, with bowed legs a little apart, rumpled sandy hair, a pale, freckled face, and a little dark blinking eyes.

"Sorry the room's in such a mess. Don't often have the pleasure of seeing a lady. I was asleep; generally am at this time of year!"

The bristly red moustache was contorted as though his lips were smiling.

Mrs. Pendyce murmured vaguely.

It seemed to her that nothing of this was real, but all

some horrid dream. A clap of thunder made her cover her ears.

Bellew walked to the window, glanced at the sky, and came back to the hearth. His little burning eyes seemed to look her through and through. ' If I don't speak at once,' she thought, ' I never shall speak at all.'

" I've come," she began, and with those words she lost her fright; her voice, that had been so uncertain hitherto, regained its trick of speech; her eyes, all pupil, stared dark and gentle at this man who had them all in his power—" I've come to tell you something, Captain Bellew ! "

The figure by the hearth bowed, and her fright, like some evil bird, came fluttering down on her again. It was dreadful, it was barbarous that she, that anyone, should have to speak of such things; it was barbarous that men and women should so misunderstand each other, and have so little sympathy and consideration; it was barbarous that she, Margery Pendyce, should have to talk on this subject that must give them both such pain. It was all so mean and gross and common ! She took out her handkerchief and passed it over her lips.

" Please forgive me for speaking. Your wife has given my son up, Captain Bellew ! "

Bellew did not move.

" She does not love him; she told me so herself ! He will never see her again ! "

How hateful, how horrible, how odious !

And still Bellew did not speak, but stood devouring her with his little eyes; and how long this went on she could not tell.

He turned his back suddenly, and leaned against the mantel-piece.

Mrs. Pendyce passed her hand over her brow to get rid of a feeling of unreality.

" That is all," she said.

Her voice sounded to herself unlike her own.

' If that is really all,' she thought, ' I suppose I must get up and go ! ' And it flashed through her mind: ' My poor dress will be ruined ! '

Bellew turned round.

" Will you have some tea ? "

Mrs. Pendyce smiled a pale little smile.

" No, thank you; I don't think I could drink any tea."

" I wrote a letter to your husband."

" Yes."

" He didn't answer it"

" No."

Mrs. Pendyce saw him staring at her, and a desperate struggle began within her. Should she not ask him to keep his promise, now that George——? Was not that what she had come for? Ought she not—ought she not for all their sakes?

Bellew went up to the table, poured out some whisky, and drank it off.

" You don't ask me to stop the proceedings," he said.

Mrs. Pendyce's lips were parted, but nothing came through those parted lips. Her eyes, black as sloes in her white face, never moved from his; she made no sound.

Bellew dashed his hand across his brow.

" Well, I will!" he said, " for your sake. There's my hand on it. You're the only lady I know!"

He gripped her gloved fingers, brushed past her, and she saw that she was alone.

She found her own way out, with the tears running down her face. Very gently she shut the hall door.

' My poor dress!' she thought. ' I wonder if I might stand here a little? The rain looks nearly over!'

The purple cloud had passed, and sunk behind the house, and a bright white sky was pouring down a sparkling rain; a patch of deep blue showed behind the fir-trees in the drive. The thrushes were out already after worms. A squirrel scampering along a branch stopped and looked at Mrs. Pendyce, and Mrs. Pendyce looked absently at the squirrel from behind the little handkerchief with which she was drying her eyes.

' That poor man!' she thought—' poor solitary creature! There's the sun!'

And it seemed to her that it was the first time the sun had shone all this fine hot year. Gathering her dress in both hands, she stepped into the drive, and soon was back again in the fields.

Every green thing glittered, and the air was so rain-sweet that all the summer scents were gone, before the crystal scent of nothing. Mrs. Pendyce's shoes were soon wet through.

' How happy I am!' she thought—' how glad and happy I am!'

And the feeling, which was not as definite as this possessed her to the exclusion of all other feelings in the rain-soaked fields.

The cloud that had hung over Worsted Skeynes so long had spent itself and gone. Every sound seemed to be music, every moving thing danced. She longed to get to her early roses, and see how the rain had treated them. She had a stile to cross, and when she was safely over she paused a minute to gather her skirts more firmly. It was a home-field she was in now, and right before her lay the country house. Long and low and white it stood in the glamourous evening haze, with two bright panes, where the sunlight fell, watching, like eyes, the confines of its acres; and behind it, to the left, broad, square, and grey among its elms, the village church. Around above, beyond, was peace—the sleepy, misty peace of the English afternoon.

Mrs. Pendyce walked towards her garden. When she was near it, away to the right, she saw the Squire and Mr. Barter. They were standing together looking at a tree and—symbol of a subservient under-world—the spaniel John was seated on his tail, and he, too, was looking at the tree. The faces of the Rector and Mr. Pendyce were turned up at the same angle, and different as those faces and figures were in their eternal rivalry of type, a sort of essential likeness struck her with a feeling of surprise. It was as though a single spirit seeking for a body had met with these two shapes, and becoming confused, decided to inhabit both.

Mrs. Pendyce did not wave to them, but passed quickly, between the yew-trees, through the wicket-gate.

In her garden bright drops were falling one by one from every rose-leaf, and in the petals of each rose were jewels of water. A little down the path a weed caught her eye; she looked closer, and saw that there were several.

'Oh,' she thought, 'how dreadfully they've let the weeds—— I must really speak to Jackman!'

A rose-tree, that she herself had planted, rustled close by, letting fall a shower of drops.

Mrs. Pendyce bent down, and took a white rose in her fingers With her smiling lips she kissed its face.

1907.

BOOK II

FRATERNITY

'Brother, brother, on some far shore
Hast thou a city, is there a door
That knows thy footfall, Wandering One?'

—Murray's Electra of Euripides.

TO

J. M. BARRIE

CHAPTER I

THE SHADOW

ON the afternoon of the last day of April, 190—, a billowy sea of little broken clouds crowned the thin air above High Street, Kensington. This soft tumult of vapours, covering nearly all the firmament, was in onslaught round a patch of blue sky, shaped somewhat like a star, which still gleamed—a single gentian flower amongst innumerable grass. Each of these small clouds seemed fitted with a pair of unseen wings, and, as insects flight on their too constant journeys, they were setting forth all ways round this starry blossom which burned so clear with the colour of its far fixity. On one side they were massed in fleecy congeries, so crowding each other that no edge or outline was preserved; on the other, higher, stronger, emergent from their fellow-clouds, they seemed leading the attack on that surviving gleam of the ineffable. Infinite was the variety of those million separate vapours, infinite the unchanging unity of that fixed blue star.

Down in the street beneath this eternal warring of the various, soft-winged clouds on the unmisted ether, men, women, children, and their familiars—horses, dogs, and cats—were pursuing their occupations with the sweet zest of the Spring. They streamed along, and the noise of their frequenting rose in an unbroken roar: "I, I—I, I!"

The crowd was perhaps thickest outside the premises of Messrs. Rose and Thorn. Every kind of being, from the highest to the lowest, passed in front of the hundred doors of this establishment; and before the costume window a rather tall, slight, graceful woman stood thinking: 'It really is gentian blue! But I don't know whether I ought to buy it, with all this distress about!'

Her eyes, which were greenish-grey, and often ironical lest they should reveal her soul, seemed probing a blue gown displayed in that window, to the very heart of its desirability.

'And suppose Stephen doesn't like me in it!' This doubt set her gloved fingers pleating the bosom of her frock. Into that little pleat she folded the essence of herself, the wish to have and the fear of having, the wish to be and the fear of being, and her veil, falling from the edge of her hat, three inches from her face, shrouded with its tissue her half-decided little features, her rather too high cheek-bones, her cheeks which were slightly hollowed, as though Time had kissed them just too much.

The old man, with a long face, eyes rimmed like a parrot's, and discoloured nose, who, so long as he did not sit down, was permitted to frequent the pavement just there and sell the *Westminster Gazette,* marked her, and took his empty pipe out of his mouth.

It was his business to know all the passers-by, and his pleasure too; his mind was thus distracted from the condition of his feet. He knew this particular lady with the delicate face, and found her puzzling; she sometimes bought the paper which Fate condemned him, against his politics, to sell. The Tory journals were undoubtedly those which her class of persons ought to purchase. He knew a lady when he saw one. In fact, before Life threw him into the streets, by giving him a disease in curing which his savings had disappeared, he had been a butler, and for the gentry had a respect as incurable as was his distrust of " all that class of people " who bought their things at " these 'ere large establishments," and attended " these 'ere subscription dances at the Town 'All over there." He watched her with special interest, not, indeed, attempting to attract attention, though conscious in every fibre that he had only sold five copies of his early issues. And he was sorry and surprised when she passed from his sight through one of the hundred doors.

The thought which spurred her into Messrs. Rose and Thorn's was this: ' I am thirty-eight; I have a daughter of seventeen. I cannot afford to lose my husband's admiration. The time is on me when I really must make myself look nice ! '

Before a long mirror, in whose bright pool there yearly bathed hundreds of women's bodies, divested of skirts and bodices, whose unruffled surface reflected daily a dozen women's souls divested of everything, her eyes became as bright as steel; but having ascertained the need of taking two inches off the chest of the gentian frock, one off its waist, three off its hips, and of adding one to its skirt, they clouded again with doubt, as though prepared to fly from the decision she had come to. Resuming her bodice, she asked:

" When could you let me have it? "

" At the end of the week, madam."

" Not till then ? "

" We are very pressed, madam."

" Oh, but you *must* let me have it by Thursday at the latest, please."

The fitter sighed: " I will do my best."

" I shall rely on you. Mrs. Stephen Dallison, 76, The Old Square."

Going downstairs she thought: ' That poor girl looked very tired; it's a shame they give them such long hours! ' and she passed into the street.

A voice said timidly behind her: " *Westminister*, marm ? "

' That's the poor old creature,' thought Cecilia Dallison, ' whose nose is so unpleasant. I don't really think I——' and she felt for a penny in her little bag. Standing beside the ' poor old creature ' was a woman clothed in worn but neat black clothes, and an ancient toque which had once known a better head. The wan remains of a little bit of fur lay round her throat. She had a thin face, not without refinement, mild, very clear brown eyes, and a twist of smooth black hair. Beside her was a skimpy little boy, and in her arms a baby. Mrs. Dallison held out two-pence for the paper, but it was at the woman that she looked.

" Oh, Mrs. Hughs," she said, " we've been expecting you to hem the curtains ! "

The woman slightly pressed the baby.

" I am very sorry, ma'am. I knew I was expected, but I've had such trouble."

Cecilia winced. " Oh, really ? "

" Yes, m'm; it's my husband."

" Oh, dear ! " Cecilia murmured. " But why didn't you come to us ? "

" I didn't feel up to it, ma'am; I didn't really——"

A tear ran down her cheek, and was caught in a furrow near the mouth.

Mrs. Dallison said hurriedly: " Yes, yes; I'm very sorry."

" This old gentleman, Mr. Creed, lives in the same house with us, and he is going to speak to my husband."

The old man wagged his head on its lean stalk of neck.

" He ought to know better than be'ave 'imself so disrespect-able," he said.

Cecilia looked at him, and murmured: " I hope he won't turn on *you!* "

The old man shuffled his feet.

"I likes to live at peace with everybody. I shall have the police to 'im if he misdemeans hisself with me! . . . *Westminister*, sir?" And, screening his mouth from Mrs. Dallison, he added in a loud whisper: "Execution of the Shoreditch murderer!"

Cecilia felt suddenly as though the world were listening to her conversation with these two rather seedy persons.

"I don't really know what I can do for you, Mrs. Hughs. I'll speak to Mr. Dallison, and to Mr. Hilary, too."

"Yes, ma'am; thank you, ma'am."

With a smile which seemed to deprecate its own appearance, Cecilia grasped her skirts and crossed the road. 'I hope I wasn't unsympathetic,' she thought, looking back at the three figures on the edge of the pavement—the old man with his papers, and his discoloured nose thrust upwards under iron-rimmed spectacles; the seamstress in her black dress; the skimpy little boy. Neither speaking nor moving, they were looking out before them at the traffic; and something in Cecilia revolted at this sight. It was lifeless, hopeless, unæsthetic.

'What can one do,' she thought, 'for women like Mrs. Hughs, who always look like that? And that poor old man! I suppose I oughtn't to have bought that dress, but Stephen *is* tired of this.'

She turned out of the main street into a road preserved from commoner forms of traffic, and stopped at a long low house half hidden behind the trees of its front garden.

It was the residence of Hilary Dallison, her husband's brother, and himself the husband of Bianca, her own sister.

The queer conceit came to Cecilia that it resembled Hilary. Its look was kindly and uncertain; its colour a palish tan; the eyebrows of its windows rather straight and arched, and those deep-set eyes, the windows, twinkled hospitably; it had, as it were, a sparse moustache and beard of creepers, and dark marks here and there, like the lines and shadows on the faces of those who think too much. Beside it, and apart, though connected by a passage, a studio stood, and about that studio—of white rough-cast, with a black oak door, and peacock-blue paint—was something a little hard and fugitive, well suited to Bianca, who used it, indeed, to paint in. It seemed to stand, with its eyes on the house, shrinking defiantly from too close company, as though it could not entirely give itself to anything. Cecilia, who often worried over the relations between her sister and her brother-in-law, suddenly felt how fitting and symbolical this was.

But, mistrusting inspirations, which, experience told her, committed one too much, she walked quickly up the stone-flagged pathway to the door. Lying in the porch was a little moonlight-coloured lady bulldog, of toy breed, who gazed up with eyes like agates, delicately waving her bell-rope tail, as it was her habit to do towards everyone, for she had been handed down clearer and paler with each generation, till she had at last lost all the peculiar virtues of dogs that bait the bull.

Speaking the word " Miranda ! " Mrs. Stephen Dallison tried to pat this daughter of the house. The little bulldog withdrew from her caress, being also unaccustomed to commit herself. . . .

Mondays were Bianca's " days," and Cecilia made her way towards the studio. It was a large high room, full of people.

Motionless, by himself, close to the door, stood an old man, very thin and rather bent, with silvery hair, and a thin silvery beard grasped in his transparent fingers. He was dressed in a suit of smoke-grey cottage tweed, which smelt of peat, and an Oxford shirt, whose collar, ceasing prematurely, exposed a lean brown neck; his trousers, too, ended very soon, and showed light socks. In his attitude there was something suggestive of the patience and determination of a mule. At Cecilia's approach he raised his eyes. It was at once apparent why, in so full a room, he was standing alone. Those blue eyes looked as if he were about to utter a prophetic statement.

" They have been speaking to me of an execution," he said.

Cecilia made a nervous movement.

" Yes, Father ? "

" To take life," went on the old man in a voice which, though charged with strong emotion, seemed to be speaking to itself, " was the chief mark of the insensate barbarism still prevailing in those days. It sprang from the most irreligious fetish, the belief in the permanence of the individual ego after death. From the worship of that fetish had come all the sorrows of the human race."

Cecilia, with an involuntary quiver of her little bag, said:

" Father, how can you ? "

" They did not stop to love each other in this life; they were so sure they had all eternity to do it in. The doctrine was an invention to enable men to act like dogs with clear consciences. Love could never come to full fruition till it was destroyed."

Cecilia looked hastily round; no one had heard. She moved a little sideways, and became merged in another group. Her father's lips continued moving. He had resumed the patient attitude which so slightly suggested mules. A voice behind her said: " I do think your father is such an interesting man, Mrs. Dallison."

Cecilia turned and saw a woman of middle height, with her hair done in the early Italian fashion, and very small, dark, lively eyes, which looked as though her love of living would keep her busy each minute of her day and all the minutes that she could occupy of everybody else's days.

" Mrs. Tallents Smallpeace? Oh! how do you do? I've been meaning to come and see you for quite a long time, but I know you're always so busy."

With doubting eyes, half friendly and half defensive, as though chaffing to prevent herself from being chaffed, Cecilia looked at Mrs. Tallents Smallpeace, whom she had met several times at Bianca's house. The widow of a somewhat famous connoisseur, she was now secretary of the League for Educating Orphans who have Lost both Parents, vice-president of the Forlorn Hope for Maids in Peril, and treasurer to Thursday Hops for Working Girls. She seemed to know every man and woman who was worth knowing, and some besides; to see all picture-shows; to hear every new musician; and attend the opening performance of every play. With regard to literature, she would say that authors bored her; but she was always doing them good turns, inviting them to meet their critics or editors, and sometimes—though this was not generally known—pulling them out of the holes they were prone to get into, by lending them a sum of money—after which, as she would plaintively remark, she rarely saw them more.

She had a peculiar spiritual significance to Mrs. Stephen Dallison, being just on the borderline between those of Bianca's friends whom Cecilia did not wish and those whom she did wish to come to her own house, for Stephen, a barrister in an official position, had a keen sense of the ridiculous. Since Hilary wrote books and was a poet, and Bianca painted, their friends would naturally be either interesting or queer; and though for Stephen's sake it was important to establish which was which, they were so very often both. Such people stimulated, taken in small doses, but neither on her husband's account nor on her daughter's did Cecilia desire that they should come to her in swarms. Her attitude of mind towards them was, in fact similar—a sort of pleasurable dread—to that in which she purchased the *Westminster Gazette* to feel the pulse of social progress.

Mrs. Tallents Smallpeace's dark little eyes twinkled.

" I hear that Mr. Stone—that *is* your father's name, I think— is writing a book which will create quite a sensation when it comes out."

Cecilia bit her lips. ' I hope it never will come out,' she was on the point of saying.

" What will it be called? " asked Mrs. Tallents Smallpeace. " I gather that it's a book of Universal Brotherhood. That's so nice ! "

Cecilia made a movement of annoyance. " Who told you? "

" Ah ! " said Mrs. Tallents Smallpeace, " I do think your sister gets such attractive people at her At Homes. They all take *such* an interest in things."

A little surprised at herself, Cecilia answered: " Too much for me ! "

Mrs. Tallents Smallpeace smiled. " I mean in art and social questions. Surely one can't be too interested in them? "

Cecilia said rather hastily:

" Oh, no, of course not." And both ladies looked around them. A buzz of conversation fell on Cecilia's ears.

" Have you seen the ' Aftermath '? It's really quite wonderful ! "

" Poor old chap ! He's so rococo. . . ."

" There's a new man. . . ."

" She's very sympathetic. . . ."

" But the condition of the poor. . . ."

" Is that Mr. Balladyce? Oh, really. . . ."

" It gives you such a feeling of life. . . ."

" Bourgeois ! . . ."

The voice of Mrs. Tallents Smallpeace broke through: " But do please tell me who is that young girl with the young man looking at the picture over there. She's quite charming ! "

Cecilia's cheeks went a very pretty pink.

" Oh, that's my little daughter."

" Really ! Have you a daughter as big as that? Why, she must be seventeen ! "

" Nearly eighteen ! "

"What is her name?"

"Thyme," said Cecilia, with a little smile. She felt that Mrs. Tallents Smallpeace was about to say: ' How charming!'

Mrs. Tallents Smallpeace saw her smile and paused. "Who is the young man with her?"

"My nephew, Martin Stone."

"The son of your brother who was killed with his wife in that dreadful Alpine accident? He looks a very decided sort of young man. He's got that new look. What is he?"

"He's very nearly a doctor. I never know whether he's quite finished or not."

"I thought perhaps he might have something to do with Art."

"Oh no, he despises Art."

"And does your daughter despise it, too?"

"No; she's studying it."

"Oh, really! How interesting! I do think the rising generation amusing, don't you? They're so independent."

Cecilia looked uneasily at the rising generation. They were standing side by side before the picture, curiously observant and detached, exchanging short remarks and glances. They seemed to watch all these circling, chatting, bending, smiling people with a sort of youthful, matter-of-fact, half-hostile curiosity. The young man had a pale face, clean-shaven, with a strong jaw, a long, straight nose, a rather bumpy forehead which did not recede, and clear grey eyes. His sarcastic lips were firm and quick, and he looked at people with disconcerting straightness. The young girl wore a blue-green frock. Her face was charming, with eager, hazel, grey eyes, a bright colour, and fluffy hair the colour of ripe nuts.

"That's your sister's picture, ' The Shadow,' they're looking at, isn't it?" asked Mrs. Tallents Smallpeace. "I remember seeing it on Christmas Day, and the little model who was sitting for it—an attractive type! Your brother-in-law told me how interested you all were in her. Quite a romantic story, wasn't it, about her fainting from want of food when she first came to sit?"

Cecilia murmured something. Her hands were moving nervously; she looked ill at ease.

These signs passed unperceived by Mrs. Tallents Smallpeace, whose eyes were busy.

"In the F.H.M.P., of course, I see a lot of young girls placed in delicate positions, just on the borders, don't you know? You should really join the F.H.M.P., Mrs. Dallison. It's a first-rate thing—most absorbing work."

The doubting deepened in Cecilia's eyes.

" Oh, it must be ! " she said. " I've so little time."

Mrs. Tallents Smallpeace went on at once.

" Don't you think that we live in the most interesting days? There are such a lot of movements going on. It's quite exciting. We all feel that we can't shut our eyes any longer to social questions. I mean the condition of the people alone is enough to give one nightmare ! "

" Yes, yes," said Cecilia; " it is dreadful, of course."

" Politicians and officials are so hopeless, one can't look for anything from them."

Cecilia drew herself up. " Oh, do you think so ?" she said. " I was just talking to Mr. Balladyce. He says that Art and Literature must be put on a new basis altogether."

" Yes," said Cecilia; " really? Is he that funny little man ? "

" I think he's so monstrously clever."

Cecilia answered quickly: " I know—I know. Of course, *something* must be done."

" Yes," said Mrs. Tallents Smallpeace absently, " I think we all feel that. Oh, do tell me! I've been talking to such a delightful person—just the type you see when you go into the City—thousands of them, all in such good black coats. It's so unusual to really meet one nowadays; and they're so refreshing, they have such nice simple views. There he is, standing just behind your sister."

Cecilia by a nervous gesture indicated that she recognized the personality alluded to. " Oh, yes," she said; " Mr. Purcey. I don't know why he comes to see us."

" I think he's so delicious ! " said Mrs. Tallents Smallpeace dreamily. Her little dark eyes, like bees, had flown to sip honey from the flower in question—a man of broad build and medium height, dressed with accuracy, who seemed just a little out of his proper bed. His mustachioed mouth wore a set smile; his cheerful face was rather red, with a forehead of no extravagant height or breadth, and a conspicuous jaw; his hair was thick and light in colour, and his eyes were small, grey, and shrewd. He was looking at a picture.

" He's so delightfully unconscious," murmured Mrs. Tallents Smallpeace. " He didn't even seem to know that there was a problem of the lower classes."

"Did he tell you that he had a picture?" asked Cecilia gloomily.

"Oh, yes, by Harpignies, with the accent on the 'pig.' It's worth three times what he gave for it. It's so nice to be made to feel that there is still all that mass of people just simply measuring everything by what they gave for it."

"And did he tell you my grandfather Carfax's dictum in the Banstock case?" muttered Cecilia.

"Oh yes: 'The man who does not know his own mind should be made an Irishman by Act of Parliament.' He said it was so awfully good."

"He would," replied Cecilia.

"He seems to depress you, rather!"

"Oh, no; I believe he's quite a nice sort of person. One can't be rude to him; he really did what he thought a very kind thing to my father. That's how we came to know him. Only it's rather trying when he will come to call regularly. He gets a little on one's nerves."

"Ah, that's just what I feel is so jolly about him; no one would ever get on his nerves. I do think we've got too many nerves, don't you? Here's your brother-in-law. He's such an uncommon-looking man; I want to have a talk with him about that little model. A country girl, wasn't she?"

She had turned her head towards a tall man with a very slight stoop and a brown, thin, bearded face, who was approaching from the door. She did not see that Cecilia had flushed, and was looking at her almost angrily. The tall thin man put his hand on Cecilia's arm, saying gently: "Hallo Cis! Stephen here yet?"

Cecilia shook her head.

"You know Mrs. Tallents Smallpeace, Hilary?"

The tall man bowed. His hazel-coloured eyes were shy, gentle, and deep-set; his eyebrows, hardly ever still, gave him a look of austere whimsicality. His dark brown hair was very lightly touched with grey, and a frequent kindly smile played on his lips. His unmannerismed manner was quiet to the point of extinction. He had long, thin, brown hands, and nothing peculiar about his dress.

"I'll leave you to talk to Mrs. Tallents Smallpeace," Cecilia said.

A knot of people round Mr. Balladyce prevented her from

moving far, however, and the voice of Mrs. Smallpeace travelled
to her ears.

"I was talking about that little model. It was so good of
you to take such an interest in the girl. I wondered whether
we could do anything for her."

Cecilia's hearing was too excellent to miss the tone of Hilary's
reply:

"Oh, thank you; I don't think so."

"I fancied perhaps you might feel that our Society—here is
an unsatisfactory profession for young girls."

Cecilia saw the back of Hilary's neck grow red. She turned
her head away.

"Of course, there are many very nice models indeed," said
the voice of Mrs. Tallents Smallpeace. "I don't mean that they
are necessarily at all—if they're girls of strong character; and
especially if they don't sit for the—the altogether."

Hilary's dry, stacatto answer came to Cecilia's ears: "Thank
you; it's very kind of you."

"Oh, of course, if it's not necessary. Your wife's picture was
so clever, Mr. Dallison—such an interesting type."

Without intention Cecilia found herself before that picture.
It stood with its face a little turned towards the wall, as though
somewhat in disgrace, portraying the full-length figure of a girl
standing in deep shadow, with her arms half outstretched, as if
asking for something. Her eyes were fixed on Cecilia, and
through her parted lips breath almost seemed to come. The only
colour in the picture was the pale blue of those eyes, the pallid
red of those parted lips, the still paler brown of the hair; the
rest was shadow. In the foreground light was falling as though
from a street-lamp.

Cecilia thought: 'That girl's eyes and mouth haunt me.
Whatever made Bianca choose such a subject? It is clever, of
course—for her.'

CHAPTER II

A FAMILY DISCUSSION

THE marriage of Sylvanus Stone, Professor of the Natural Sciences, to Anne, daughter of Mr. Justice Carfax of the well-known county family—the Carfaxes of Spring Deans, Hants —was recorded in the sixties. The baptisms of Martin, Cecilia, and Bianca, son and daughters of Sylvanus and Anne Stone, were to be discovered registered in Kensington in the three consecutive years following, as though some single-minded person had been connected with their births. After this the baptisms of no more offspring were to be found anywhere, as if that single mind had encountered opposition. But in the eighties there was noted in the register of the same church the burial of "Anne, *née* Carfax, wife of Sylvanis Stone." In that "*née* Carfax" there was, to those who knew, something more than met the eye. It summed up the mother of Cecilia and Bianca, and, in more subtle fashion, Cecilia and Bianca, too. It summed up that fugitive, barricading look in their bright eyes, which, though spoken of in the family as "the Carfax eyes," were in reality far from coming from old Mr. Justice Carfax. They had been his wife's in turn, and had much annoyed a man of his decided character. He himself had always known his mind, and had let others know it, too; reminding his wife that she was an impracticable woman, who knew not her own mind; and devoting his lawful gains to securing the future of his progeny. It would have disturbed him if he had lived to see his grand-daughters and their times. Like so many able men of his generation, far-seeing enough in practical affairs, he had never considered the possibility that the descendants of those who, like himself, had laid up treasure for their children's children might acquire the quality of taking time, balancing pros and cons, looking ahead, and not putting one foot down before picking the other up. He had not foreseen, indeed, that to wobble might become an art, in order that, before anything was done, people might know the full necessity for doing something, and how impossible it would be to do—indeed, foolish to attempt to do—that which would fully meet the case. He, who had been a man of action all his life, had not perceived how it would grow to be matter of common instinct that to act was to commit oneself, and that, while what one had was not precisely what one wanted, what one had not (if one had it) would be as bad. He had never been self-conscious—it was not the custom of his generation—and, having but little imagination, had never suspected that he was laying up that quality for his descendants, together with a competence which secured them a comfortable leisure.

Of all the persons in his grand-daughter's studio that afternoon, that stray sheep Mr. Purcey would have been, perhaps, the only one whose judgments he would have considered sound. No one had laid up a competence for Mr. Purcey, who had been in business from the age of twenty.

It is uncertain whether the mere fact that he was not in his own fold kept this visitor lingering in the studio when all other guests were gone; or whether it was simply the feeling that the longer he stayed in contact with really artistic people the more distinguished he was becoming. Probably the latter, for the possession of that Harpignies, a good specimen, which he had bought by accident, and subsequently by accident discovered to have a peculiar value, had become a factor in his life, marking him out from all his friends, who went in more for a neat type of Royal Academy landscape, together with reproductions of young ladies in eighteenth-century costumes seated on horseback, or in Scotch gardens. A junior partner in a banking-house of some importance, he lived at Wimbledon, whence he passed up and down daily in his car. To this he owed his acquaintance with the family of Dallison. For one day, after telling his chauffeur to meet him at the Albert Gate, he had set out to stroll down Rotten Row, as he often did on the way home, designing to nod to anybody that he knew. It had turned out a somewhat barren expedition. No one of any consequence had met his eye; and it was with a certain almost fretful longing for distraction that in Kensington Gardens he came on an old man feeding birds out of a paper bag. The birds having flown away on seeing him, he approached the feeder to apologize.

"I'm afraid I frightened your birds, sir," he began.

This old man, who was dressed in smoke-grey tweeds which exhaled a poignant scent of peat, looked at him without answering.

"I'm afraid your birds saw me coming," Mr. Pursey said again.

"In those days," said the aged stranger, "birds were afraid of men."

Mr. Purcey's shrewd grey eyes perceived at once that he had a character to deal with.

"Ah, yes!" he said; "I see—you allude to the present time. That's very nice. Ha, ha!"

The old man answered: "The emotion of fear is inseparably connected with a primitive state of fratricidal rivalry."

This sentence put Mr. Purcey on his guard.

'The old chap,' he thought, 'is touched. He evidently oughtn't to be out here by himself.' He debated, therefore, whether he should hasten away toward his car, or stand by in case his assistance should be needed. Being a kind-hearted man, who believed in his capacity for putting things to rights, and noticing a certain delicacy—a "sort of something rather distinguished," as he phrased it afterwards—in the old fellow's face and figure, he decided to see if he could be of any service. They walked along together, Mr. Purcey watching his new friend askance, and directing the march to where he had ordered his chauffeur to await him.

"You are very fond of birds, I suppose," he said cautiously.

"The birds are our brothers."

The answer was of a nature to determine Mr. Pursey in his diagnosis of the case.

"I've got my car here," he said. "Let me give you a lift home."

This new but aged acquaintance did not seem to hear; his lips moved as though he were following out some thought.

"In those days," Mr. Purcey heard him say, "the congeries of men were known as rookeries. The expression was hardly just towards that handsome bird."

Mr. Purcey touched him hastily on the arm.

"I've got my car here, sir," he said. "Do let me put you down!"

Telling the story afterwards, he had spoken thus:

"The old chap knew where he lived right enough; but dash me if I believe he noticed that I was taking him there in my car—I had the A.1. Damyer out. That's how I came to make the acquaintance of these Dallisons. He's the writer, you know, and she paints—rather the new school—she admires Harpignies.

Well, when I got there in the car I found Dallison in the garden. Of course I was careful not to put my foot into it. I told him: ' I found this old gentleman wandering about. I've just brought him back in my car.' Who should the old chap turn out to be but her father! They were awfully obliged to me. Charmin' people, but very what d'you call it—*fin de siècle*—like all these professors, these artistic pigs—seem to know rather a queer set, advanced people, and all that sort of cuckoo, always talkin' about the poor, and societies, and new religions, and that kind of thing."

Though he had since been to see them several times, the Dallisons had never robbed him of the virtuous feeling of that good action—they had never let him know that he had brought home, not, as he imagined, a lunatic, but merely a philosopher.

It had been somewhat of a quiet shock to him to find Mr. Stone close to the doorway when he entered Bianca's studio that afternoon; for though he had seen him since the encounter in Kensington Gardens, and knew that he was writing a book, he still felt that he was not quite the sort of old man that one ought to meet about. He had at once begun to tell him of the hanging of the Shoreditch murderer, as recorded in the evening papers. Mr. Stone's reception of that news had still further confirmed his original views. When all the guests were gone— with the exception of Mr. and Mrs. Stephen Dallison and Miss Dallison, " that awfully pretty girl," and the young man " who was always hangin' about her "—he had approached his hostess for some quiet talk. She stood listening to him, very well bred, with just that habitual spice of mockery in her smile, which to Mr. Purcey's eyes made her " a very strikin'-lookin' woman, but rather——" There he would stop, for it required a greater psychologist than he to describe a secret disharmony which a little marred her beauty. Due to some too violent cross of blood, to an environment too unsuited, to what not—it was branded on her. Those who knew Bianca Dallison better than Mr. Purcey were but too well aware of this fugitive, proud spirit permeating one whose beauty would otherwise have passed unquestioned.

She was a little taller than Cecilia, her figure rather fuller and more graceful, her hair darker, her eyes, too, darker and more deeply set, her cheek-bones higher, her colouring richer. That spirit of the age, Disharmony, must have presided when a child so vivid and dark-coloured was christened Bianca.

Mr. Purcey, however, was not a man who allowed the finest shades of feeling to interfere with his enjoyments. She was a "strikin'-lookin' woman," and there was, thanks to Harpignies, a link between them.

"Your father and I, Mrs. Dallison, can't quite understand each other," he began. "Our views of life don't seem to hit it off exactly."

"Really," murmured Bianca: "I should have thought that you'd have got on so well."

"He's a little bit too—er—scriptural for me, perhaps," said Mr. Purcey, with some delicacy.

"Did we never tell you," Bianca answered softly, "that my father was a rather well-known man of science before his illness?"

"Ah!" replied Mr. Purcey, a little puzzled; "that, of course. D'you know, of all your pictures, Mrs. Dallison, I think that one you call 'The Shadow' is the most rippin'. There's a something about it that gets hold of you. That was the original, wasn't it, at your Christmas party—attractive girl—it's an awf'ly good likeness."

Bianca's face had changed, but Mr. Purcey was not a man to notice a little thing like that.

"If ever you want to part with it," he said, "I hope you'll give me a chance. I mean it'd be a pleasure to me to have it. I think it'll be worth a lot of money some day."

Bianca did not answer, and Mr. Purcey, feeling suddenly a little awkward, said: "I've got my car waiting. I must be off—really." Shaking hands with all of them, he went away.

When the door had closed behind his back, a universal sigh went up. It was followed by a silence, which Hilary broke.

"We'll-smoke, Stevie, if Cis doesn't mind."

Stephen Dallison placed a cigarette between his moustacheless lips, always rather screwed up, and ready to nip with a smile anything that might make him feel ridiculous.

"Phew!" he said. "Our friend Purcey becomes a little tedious. He seems to take the whole of Philistia about with him."

"He's a very decent fellow," murmured Hilary.

"A bit heavy, surely!" Stephen Dallison's face, though also long and narrow, was not much like his brother's. His eyes, though not unkind, were far more scrutinising, inquisitive, and practical; his hair darker, smoother.

Letting a puff of smoke escape, he added:

"Now, that's the sort of man to give you a good sound opinion. You should have asked *him*, Cis."

Cecilia answered with a frown:

"Don't chaff, Stephen; I'm perfectly serious about Mrs. Hughs."

"Well, I don't see what I can do for the good woman, my dear. One can't interfere in these domestic matters."

"But it seems dreadful that we who employ her should be able to do nothing for her. Don't you think so, B.?"

"I suppose we could do something for her if we wanted to badly enough."

Bianca's voice, which had the self-distrustful ring of modern music, suited her personality.

A glance passed between Stephen and his wife.

"That's B. all over!" it seemed to say.

"Hound Street, where they live, is a horrid place."

It was Thyme who spoke, and everybody looked round at her.

"How do you know that?" asked Cecilia.

"I went to see."

"With whom?"

"Martin."

The lips of the young man whose name she mentioned curled sarcastically.

Hilary asked gently:

"Well, my dear, what *did* you see?"

"Most of the doors are open——"

Bianca murmured: "That doesn't tell us much."

"On the contrary," said Martin suddenly, in a deep bass voice, "it tells you everything. Go on."

"The Hughs live on the top floor at No. 1. It's the best house in the street. On the ground-floor are some people called Budgen; he's a labourer, and she's lame. They've got one son. The Hughs have let off the first-floor front-room to an old man named Creed——"

"Yes, I know," Cecilia muttered.

"He makes about one and tenpence a day by selling papers. The back-room on that floor they let, of course, to your little model, Aunt B."

"She is not my model now."

There was a silence such as falls when no one knows how far

the matter mentioned is safe to touch on. Thyme proceeded with her report.

"Her room's much the best in the house; it's airy, and it looks out over someone's garden. I suppose she stays there because it's so cheap. The Hughs' rooms are——" She stopped, wrinkling her straight nose.

"So that's the household," said Hilary. "Two married couples, one young man, one young girl"—his eyes travelled from one to another of the two married couples, the young man, and the young girl, collected in this room—"and one old man," he added softly.

"Not quite the sort of place for you to go poking about in, Thyme," Stephen said ironically. "Do you think so, Martin?"

"Why not?"

Stephen raised his brows, and glanced towards his wife. Her face was dubious, a little scared. There was a silence. Then Bianca spoke:

"Well?" That word, like nearly all her speeches, seemed rather to disconcert her hearers.

"So Hughs ill-treats her?" said Hilary.

"She says so," replied Cecilia—"at least, that's what I understood. Of course, I don't know any details."

"She had better get rid of him, I should think," Bianca murmured.

Out of the silence that followed Thyme's clear voice was heard saying:

"She can't get a divorce; she could get a separation."

Cecilia rose uneasily. These words concreted suddenly a wealth of half-acknowledged doubts about her little daughter. This came of letting her hear people talk, and go about with Martin! She might even have been listening to her grandfather —such a thought was most disturbing. And, afraid, on the one hand, of gainsaying the liberty of speech, and, on the other, of seeming to approve her daughter's knowledge of the world, she looked at her husband.

But Stephen did not speak, feeling, no doubt, that to pursue the subject would be either to court an ethical, even an abstract, disquisition, and this one did not do in anybody's presence, much less one's wife's or daughter's; or to touch on sordid facts of doubtful character, which was equally distasteful in the circumstances. He, too, however, was uneasy that Thyme should know so much.

The dusk was gathering outside; the fire threw a flickering light, fitfully outlining their figures, making those faces, so familiar to each other, a little mysterious.

At last Stephen broke the silence. "Of course, I'm very sorry for her, but you'd better let it alone—you can't tell with that sort of people; you never can make out what they want—it's safer not to meddle. At all events, it's a matter for a Society to look into first!"

Cecilia answered: "But she's on my conscience, Stephen."

"They're all on *my* conscience," muttered Hilary.

Bianca looked at him for the first time; then, turning to her nephew, said: "What do you say, Martin?"

The young man, whose face was stained by the firelight the colour of pale cheese, made no answer.

But suddenly through the stillness came a voice:

"I have thought of something."

Everyone turned round. Mr. Stone was seen emerging from behind "The Shadow"; his frail figure, in its grey tweeds, his silvery hair and beard, were outlined sharply against the wall.

"Why, Father," Cecilia said, "we didn't know that you were here!"

Mr. Stone looked round bewildered; it seemed as if he, too, had been ignorant of that fact.

"What is it that you've thought of?"

The firelight leaped suddenly on to Mr. Stone's thin yellow hand.

"Each of us," he said, "has a shadow in those places—in those streets."

There was a vague rustling, as of people not taking a remark too seriously, and the sound of a closing door.

CHAPTER III

HILARY'S BROWN STUDY

"WHAT do you really think, Uncle Hilary?"

Turning at his writing-table to look at the face of his young niece, Hilary Dallison answered:

"My dear, we have had the same state of affairs since the beginning of the world. There is no chemical process, so far as my knowledge goes, that does not make waste products. What your grandfather calls our 'shadows' are the waste products of the social process. That there is a submerged tenth is as certain as that there is an emerged fiftieth like ourselves; exactly who they are and how they come, whether they can ever be improved away, is, I think, as uncertain as anything can be."

The figure of the girl seated in the big armchair did not stir. Her lips pouted contemptuously, a frown wrinkled her forehead.

"Martin says that a thing is only impossible when we think it so."

"Faith and the mountain, I'm afraid."

Thyme's foot shot forth; it nearly came into contact with Miranda, the little bulldog.

"Oh, duckie!"

But the little moonlight bulldog backed away.

"I hate these slums, uncle; they're so disgusting!"

Hilary leaned his face on his thin hand; it was his characteristic attitude.

"They are hateful, disgusting, and heartrending. That does not make the problem any the less difficult, does it?"

"I believe we simply make the difficulties ourselves by seeing them."

Hilary smiled. "Does Martin say that too?"

"Of course he does."

"Speaking broadly," murmured Hilary, "I see only one difficulty—human nature."

Thyme rose. "I think it horrible to have a low opinion of human nature."

"My dear," said Hilary, "don't you think perhaps that people who have what is called a low opinion of human nature are really

242

more tolerant of it, more in love with it, in fact, than those who, looking to what human nature might be, are bound to hate what human nature is?'"

The look which Thyme directed at her uncle's amiable, attractive face, with its pointed beard, high forehead, and special little smile, seemed to alarm Hilary.

" I don't want you to have an unnecessarily low opinion of me, my dear. I'm not one of those people who tell you that everything's all right because the rich have their troubles as well as the poor. A certain modicum of decency and comfort is obviously necessary to man before we can begin to do anything but pity him; but that doesn't make it any easier to know how you're going to insure him that modicum of decency and comfort, does it?"

" We've got to do it," said Thyme; " it won't wait any longer."

" My dear," said Hilary, " think of Mr. Purcey! What proportion of the upper classes do you imagine is even conscious of that necessity? We, who have got what I call the social conscience, rise from the platform of Mr. Purcey; we're just a gang of a few thousands to Mr. Purcey's tens of thousands, and how many even of us are prepared, or, for the matter of that, fitted, to act on our consciousness? In spite of your grandfather's ideas, I'm afraid we're all too much divided into classes; man acts, and always has acted, in classes."

" Oh—classes!" answered Thyme—"that's the old superstition, uncle."

" Is it? I thought one's class, perhaps, was only oneself exaggerated—not to be shaken off. For instance, what are you and I, with our particular prejudices, going to do?"

Thyme gave him the cruel look of youth, which seemed to say: ' You are my very good uncle, and a dear; but you are more than twice my age. That, I think, is conclusive!'

" Has something been settled about Mrs. Hughs?" she asked abruptly.

" What does your father say this morning?"

Thyme picked up her portfolio of drawings, and moved towards the door.

" Father's hopeless. He hasn't an idea beyond referring her to the S.P.B."

She was gone; and Hilary, with a sigh, took his pen up, but he wrote nothing down. . . .

Hilary and Stephen Dallison were grandsons of that Canon Dallison, well known as a friend, and sometime adviser, of a certain Victorian novelist. The Canon, who came of an old Oxfordshire family, which for three hundred years at least had served the Church or State, was himself the author of two volumes of " Socratic Dialogues." He had bequeathed to his son —a permanent official in the Foreign Office—if not his literary talent, the tradition at all events of culture. This tradition had in turn been handed on to Hilary and Stephen.

Educated at a public school and Cambridge, blessed with competent, though not large, independent incomes, and brought up never to allude to money if it could possibly be helped, the two young men had been turned out of the mint with something of the same outward stamp on them. Both were kindly, both fond of open-air pursuits, and neither of them lazy. Both, too, were very civilised, with that bone-deep decency, that dislike of violence, nowhere so prevalent as in the upper classes of a country whose settled institutions are as old as its roads, or the walls which insulate its parks. But as time went on, the one great quality which heredity and education, environment and means, had bred in both of them—self-consciousness—acted in these two brothers very differently. To Stephen it was preservative, keeping him, as it were, in ice throughout hot-weather seasons, enabling him to know exactly when he was in danger of decomposition, so that he might nip the process in the bud; it was with him a healthy, perhaps slightly chemical, ingredient, binding his component parts, causing them to work together safely, homogeneously. In Hilary the effect seemed to have been otherwise; like some slow and subtle poison, this great quality, self-consciousness, had soaked his system through and through; permeated every cranny of his spirit, so that to think a definite thought, or do a definite deed, was obviously becoming difficult to him. It took in the main the form of a sort of gentle desiccating humour.

" It's a remarkable thing," he had one day said to Stephen, " that by the process of assimilating little bits of chopped-up cattle one should be able to form the speculation of how remarkable a thing it is."

Stephen had paused a second before answering—they were lunching off roast beef in the Law Courts—he had then said:

" You're surely not going to eschew the higher mammals, like our respected father-in-law ? "

"On the contrary," said Hilary, "to chew them; but it *is* remarkable, for all that; you missed my point."

It was clear that a man who could see anything remarkable in such a thing was far gone, and Stephen had murmured:

"My dear old chap, you're getting too introspective."

Hilary, having given his brother the special retiring smile, which seemed not only to say, "Don't let me bore you," but also, "Well, perhaps you *had* better wait outside," the conversation closed.

That smile of Hilary's, which jibbed away from things, though disconcerting and apt to put an end to intercourse, was natural enough. A sensitive man, who had passed his life amongst cultivated people in the making of books, guarded from real wants by modest, not vulgar, affluence, had not reached the age of forty-two without finding his delicacy sharpened to the point of fastidiousness. Even his dog could see the sort of man he was. She knew that he would take no liberties, either with her ears or with her tail. She knew that he would never hold her mouth ajar, and watch her teeth, as some men do; that when she was lying on her back he would gently rub her chest without giving her the feeling that she was doing wrong, as women will; and if she sat, as she was sitting now, with her eyes fixed on his study fire, he would never, she knew, even from afar, prevent her thinking of the nothing she loved to think on.

In his study, which smelt of a particular mild tobacco warranted to suit the nerves of any literary man, there was a bust of Socrates, which always seemed to have a strange attraction for its owner. He had once described to a fellow-writer the impression produced on him by that plaster face, so capaciously ugly, as though comprehending the whole of human life, sharing all man's gluttony and lust, his violence and rapacity, but sharing also his strivings toward love and reason and serenity.

"He's telling us," said Hilary, "to drink deep, to dive down and live with mermaids, to lie out on the hills under the sun, to sweat with helots, to know all things and all men. No seat, he says, among the Wise, unless we've been through it all before we climb! That's how he strikes me—not too cheering for people of our sort!"

Under the shadow of this bust Hilary rested his forehead on his hand. In front of him were three open books and a pile of manuscript, and pushed to one side a little sheaf of pieces of green-white paper, press-cuttings of his latest book.

The exact position occupied by his work in the life of such a man is not too easy to define. He earned an income by it, but he was not dependent on that income. As poet, critic, writer of essays, he had made himself a certain name—not a great name, but enough to swear by. Whether his fastidiousness could have stood the conditions of literary existence without private means was now and then debated by his friends; it could probably have done so better than was supposed, for he sometimes startled those who set him down as a dilettante by a horny way of retiring into his shell for the finish of a piece of work.

Try as he would that morning to keep his thoughts concentrated on his literary labour, they wandered to his conversation with his niece and to the discussion on Mrs. Hughs, the family seamstress, in his wife's studio the day before. Stephen had lingered behind Cecilia and Thyme when they went away after dinner, to deliver a last counsel to his brother at the garden gate.

"Never meddle between man and wife—you know what the lower classes are!"

And across the dark garden he had looked back towards the house. One room on the ground-floor alone was lighted. Through its open window the head and shoulders of Mr. Stone could be seen close to a small green reading-lamp. Stephen shook his head, murmuring:

"But, I say, our old friend, eh? 'In those places—in those streets!' It's worse than simple crankiness—the poor old chap is getting almost——" And, touching his forehead lightly with two fingers, he had hurried off with the ever-springy step of one whose regularity habitually controls his imagination.

Pausing a minute amongst the bushes, Hilary too had looked at the lighted window which broke the dark front of his house, and his little moonlight bulldog, peering round his legs, had gazed up also. Mr. Stone was still standing, pen in hand, presumably deep in thought. His silvered head and beard moved slightly to the efforts of his brain. He came over to the window, and, evidently not seeing his son-in-law, faced out into the night.

In that darkness were all the shapes and lights and shadows of a London night in spring: the trees in dark bloom; the wan yellow of the gas-lamps, pale emblems of the self-consciousness of towns; the clustered shades of the tiny leaves, spilled, purple, on the surface of the road, like bunches of black grapes squeezed down into the earth by the feet of the passers-by. There, too, were shapes of men and women hurrying home, and the great blocked shapes of the houses where they lived. A halo hovered above the City—a high haze of yellow light, dimming the stars. The black, slow figure of a policeman moved noiselessly along the railings opposite.

From then till eleven o'clock, when he would make himself some cocoa on a little spirit-lamp, the writer of the " Book of Universal Brotherhood " would alternate between his bent posture above his manuscript and his blank consideration of the night. . . .

With a jerk, Hilary came back to his reflections beneath the bust of Socrates.

" Each of us has a shadow in those places—in those streets! "

There certainly was a virus in that notion. One must either take it as a jest, like Stephen; or, what must one do? How far was it one's business to identify oneself with other people, especially the helpless—how far to preserve oneself intact—*integer vitæ?* Hilary was no young person, like his niece or Martin, to whom everything seemed simple; nor was he an old person like their grandfather, for whom life had lost its complications.

And, very conscious of his natural disabilities for a decision on a like, or indeed on any, subject except, perhaps, a point of literary technique, he got up from his writing-table, and, taking his little bulldog, went out. His intention was to visit Mrs. Hughs in Hound Street, and see with his own eyes the state of things. But he had another reason, too, for wishing to go there. . . .

CHAPTER IV

THE LITTLE MODEL

WHEN in the preceding autumn Bianca began her picture called
"The Shadow," nobody was more surprised than Hilary that she
asked him to find her a model for the figure. Not knowing the
nature of the picture, nor having been for many years—perhaps
never—admitted into the workings of his wife's spirit, he said:
"Why don't you ask Thyme to sit for you?"

Bianca answered: "She's not the type at all—too matter-of-
fact. Besides, I don't want a lady; the figure's to be half
draped."

Hilary smiled.

Bianca knew quite well that he was smiling at this distinction
between ladies and other women, and understood that he was
smiling, not so much at her, but at himself, for secretly agreeing
with the distinction she had made.

And suddenly she smiled too.

There was the whole history of their married life in those two
smiles. They meant so much: so many thousand hours of suppressed irritation, so many baffled longings and earnest efforts to
bring their natures together. They were the supreme, quiet
evidence of the divergence of two lives—that slow divergence
which had been far from being wilful, and was the more hopeless
in that it had been so gradual and so gentle. They had never
really had a quarrel, having enlightened views of marriage; but
they had smiled. They had smiled so often through so many
years that no two people in the world could very well be further
from each other. Their smiles had banned the revelation even
to themselves of the tragedy of their wedded state. It is certain
that neither could help those smiles, which were not intended to
wound, but came on their faces as naturally as moonlight falls
on water, out of their inimically constituted souls.

Hilary spent two afternoons among his artist friends, trying,
by means of the indications he had gathered, to find a model
for "The Shadow." He had found one at last. Her name,
Barton, and address had been given him by a painter of still
life, called French.

" She's never sat to me," he said; " my sister discovered her in the West Country somewhere. She's got a story of some sort. I don't know what. She came up about three months ago, I think."

" She's not sitting to your sister now?" Hilary asked.

" No," said the painter of still life; " my sister's married and gone out to India. I don't know whether she'd sit for the half-draped, but I should think so. She'll have to, sooner or later; she may as well begin, especially to a woman. There's something about her that's attractive—you might try her!" And with these words he resumed the painting of still life which he had broken off to talk to Hilary.

Hilary had written to this girl to come and see him. She had come just before dinner the same day.

He found her standing in the middle of his study, not daring, as it seemed, to go near the furniture, and as there was very little light, he could hardly see her face. She was resting a foot, very patient, very still, in an old brown skirt, an ill-shaped blouse, and a blue-green tam-o'-shanter cap. Hilary turned up the light. He saw a round little face with broad cheekbones, flower-blue eyes, short lamp-black lashes, and slightly parted lips. It was difficult to judge of her figure in those old clothes, but she was neither short nor tall; her neck was white and well set on, her hair pale brown and abundant. Hilary noted that her chin, though not receding, was too soft and small; but what he noted chiefly was her look of patient expectancy, as though beyond the present she were seeing something, not necessarily pleasant, which had to come. If he had not known from the painter of still life that she was from the country, he would have thought her a town-bred girl, she looked so pale. Her appearance, at all events, was not " too matter-of-fact." Her speech, however, with its slight West-Country burr, was matter-of-fact enough, concerned entirely with how long she would have to sit, and the pay she was to get for it. In the middle of their conversation she sank down on the floor, and Hilary was driven to restore her with biscuits and liqueur, which in his haste he took for brandy. It seemed she had not eaten since her breakfast the day before, which had consisted of a cup of tea. In answer to his remonstrance, she made this matter-of-fact remark:

" If you haven't money, you can't buy things. . . . There's no one I can ask up here; I'm a stranger."

" Then you haven't been getting work ? "

" No," the little model answered sullenly; " I don't want to sit as most of them want me to till I'm obliged." The blood rushed up in her face with startling vividness, then left it white again.

' Ah ! ' thought Hilary, ' she has had experience already.'

Both he and his wife were accessible to cases of distress, but the nature of their charity was different. Hilary was constitutionally unable to refuse his aid to anything that held out a hand for it. Bianca (whose sociology was sounder), while affirming that charity was wrong, since in a properly constituted State no one should need help, referred her cases, like Stephen, to the " Society for the Prevention of Begging," which took much time and many pains to ascertain the worst.

But in this case what was of importance was that the poor girl should have a meal, and after that to find out if she were living in a decent house; and since she appeared not to be, to recommend her somewhere better. And as in charity it is always well to kill two birds with one expenditure of force, it was found that Mrs. Hughs, the seamstress, had a single room to let unfurnished, and would be more than glad of four shillings, or even three and six, a week for it. Furniture was also found for her : a bed that creaked, a washstand, table, and chest of drawers; a carpet, two chairs, and certain things to cook with; some of those old photographs and prints that hide in cupboards, and a peculiar little clock, which frequently forgot the time of day. All these and some elementary articles of dress were sent round in a little van, with three ferns whose time had nearly come, and a piece of the plant called " honesty." Soon after this she came to " sit." She was a very quiet and passive little model, and was not required to pose half-draped, Bianca having decided that, after all, " The Shadow " was better represented fully clothed; for, though she discussed the nude, and looked on it with freedom, when it came to painting unclothed people, she felt a sort of physical aversion.

Hilary, who was curious, as a man naturally would be, about anyone who had fainted from hunger at his feet, came every now and then to see, and would sit watching this little half-starved girl with kindly and screwed-up eyes. About his personality there was all the evidence of that saying current among those who knew him: " Hilary would walk a mile sooner than tread on an ant." The little model, from the moment when he poured liqueur between her teeth, seemed to feel he had a claim on her, for she reserved her small, mattter-of-fact confessions for his ears. She made them in the garden, coming in or going out; or outside, and, now and then, inside his study, like a child who comes and shows you a sore finger. Thus, quite suddenly: " I've four shillings left over this week, Mr. Dallison," or "Old Mr. Creed's gone to the hospital to-day, Mr. Dallison."

Her face soon became less bloodless than on that first evening, but it was still pale, inclined to colour in the wrong places on cold days, with little blue veins about the temples and shadows under the eyes. The lips were still always a trifle parted, and she still seemed to be looking out for what was coming, like a little Madonna, or Venus, in a Botticelli picture. This look of hers, coupled with the matter-of-factness of her speech, gave its flavour to her personality. . . .

On Christmas Day the picture was on view to Mr. Purcey, who had changed to " give his car a run," and to other connoisseurs. Bianca had invited her model to be present at this function, intending to get her work. But, slipping at once into a corner, the girl had stood as far as possible behind a canvas. People, seeing her standing there, and noting her likeness to the picture, looked at her with curiosity, and passed on, murmuring that she was an interesting type. They did not talk to her, either because they were afraid she could not talk of the things they could talk of, or that they could not talk of the things she could talk of, or because they were anxious not to seem to patronise her. She talked to no one, therefore. This occasioned Hilary some distress. He kept coming up and smiling at her, or making tentative remarks or jests, to which she would reply: " Yes, Mr. Dallison," or " No, Mr. Dallison," as the case might be.

Seeing him return from one of these little visits, an Art Critic standing before the picture had smiled, and his round, clean-shaven, sensual face had assumed a greenish tint in eyes and cheeks, as of the fat in turtle soup.

The only two other people who had noticed her particularly were those old acquaintances, Mr. Purcey and Mr. Stone. Mr. Purcey had thought, ' Rather a good-lookin' girl,' and his eyes strayed somewhat continually in her direction. There was something piquant and, as it were, unlawfully enticing to him in the fact that she was a real artist's model.

Mr. Stone's way of noticing her had been different. He had

approached in his slightly inconvenient way, as though seeing but one thing in the whole world.

"You are living by yourself?" he had said. "I shall come and see you."

Made by the Art Critic or by Mr. Purcey, that somewhat strange remark would have had one meaning; made by Mr. Stone it obviously had another. Having finished what he had to say, the author of the book of "Universal Brotherhood" had bowed and turned to go. Perceiving that he saw before him the door and nothing else, everybody made way for him at once. The remarks that usually arose behind his back began to be heard—"Extraordinary old man!" "You know, he bathes in the Serpentine all the year round?" "And he cooks his food himself, and does his own room, they say; and all the rest of his time he writes a book!" "A perfect crank!"

CHAPTER V

THE COMEDY BEGINS

THE Art Critic who had smiled was—like all men—a subject for pity rather than for blame. An Irishman of real ability, he had started life with high ideals and a belief that he could live with them. He had hoped to serve Art, to keep his service pure; but, having one day let his acid temperament out of hand to revel in an orgy of personal retaliation, he had since never known when she would slip her chain and come home smothered in mire. Moreover, he no longer chastised her when she came. His ideals had left him, one by one; he now lived alone, immune from dignity and shame, soothing himself with whisky. A man of rancour, meet for pity, and, in his cups, contented.

He had lunched freely before coming to Bianca's Christmas function, but by four o'clock, the gases which had made him feel the world a pleasant place had nearly all evaporated, and he was suffering from a wish to drink again. Or it may have been that this girl, with her soft look, gave him the feeling that she ought to have belonged to him; and as she did not, he felt, perhaps, a natural irritation that she belonged, or might belong, to somebody else. Or, again, it was possibly his natural male distaste for the works of women painters which induced an awkward frame of mind.

Two days later in a daily paper over no signature, appeared this little paragraph: "We learn that ' The Shadow,' painted by Bianca Stone, who is not generally known to be the wife of the writer, Mr. Hilary Dallison, will soon be exhibited at the Bencox Gallery. This very *fin-de-siècle* creation, with its unpleasant subject, representing a woman (presumably of the streets) standing beneath a gas-lamp, is a somewhat anæmic piece of painting. If Mr. Dallison, who finds the type an interesting one, embodies her in one of his very charming poems, we trust the result will be less bloodless."

The little piece of green-white paper containing this information was handed to Hilary by his wife at breakfast. The blood mounted slowly in his cheeks. Bianca's eyes fastened themselves on that flush. Whether or no—as philosophers say—little things are all big with the past, of whose chain they are the latest links, they frequently produce what apparently are great results.

The marital relations of Hilary and his wife, which till then had been those of, at all events, formal conjugality, changed from that moment. After ten o'clock at night their lives became as separate as though they lived in different houses. And this change came about without expostulations, reproach, or explanation, just by the turning of a key; and even this was the merest symbol, employed once only, to save the ungracefulness of words. Such a hint was quite enough for a man like Hilary, whose delicacy, sense of the ridiculous, and peculiar faculty of starting back and retiring into himself, put the need of anything further out of the question. Both must have felt, too, that there was nothing that could be explained. An anonymous *double entendre* was not precisely evidence on which to found a rupture of the marital tie. The trouble was so much deeper than that—the throbbing of a woman's wounded self-esteem, of the feeling that she was no longer loved, which had long cried out for revenge.

One morning in the middle of the week after this incident the innocent author of it presented herself in Hilary's study, and, standing in her peculiar patient attitude, made her little statements. As usual, they were very little ones; as usual, she seemed helpless, and suggested a child with a sore finger. She had no other work; she owed the week's rent; she did not know what would happen to her; Mrs. Dallison did not want her any more; she could not tell what she had done! The picture was finished, she knew, but Mrs. Dallison had said she was going to paint her again in another picture. . . .

Hilary did not reply.

". . . That old gentleman, Mr.—Mr. Stone, had been to see her. He wanted her to come and copy out his book for two hours a day, from four to six, at a shilling an hour. Ought she to come, please? He said his book would take him years."

Before answering her Hilary stood for a full minute staring at the fire. The little model stole a look at him. He suddenly turned and faced her. His glance was evidently disconcerting to the girl. It was, indeed, a critical and dubious look, such as he might have bent on a folio of doubtful origin.

"Don't you think," he said at last, "that it would be much better for you to go back into the country?"

The little model shook her head vehemently.

"Oh no!"

"Well, but why not? This is a most unsatisfactory sort of life."

The girl stole another look at him, then said sullenly:

"I can't go back there."

"What is it? Aren't your people nice to you?"

She grew red.

"No; and I don't want to go"; then, evidently seeing from Hilary's face that his delicacy forbade his questioning her further, she brightened up, and murmured: "The old gentleman said it would make me independent."

"Well," replied Hilary, with a shrug, "you'd better take his offer."

She kept turning her face back as she went down the path, as though to show her gratitude. And presently, looking up from his manuscript, he saw her face still at the railings, peering through a lilac bush. Suddenly she skipped, like a child let out of school. Hilary got up, perturbed. The sight of that skipping was like the rays of a lantern turned on the dark street of another human being's life. It revealed, as in a flash, the loneliness of this child, without money and without friends, in the midst of this great town.

The months of January, February, March passed, and the little model came daily to copy the "Book of Universal Brotherhood."

Mr. Stone's room, for which he insisted on paying rent, was never entered by a servant. It was on the ground-floor, and anyone passing the door between the hours of four and six could hear him dictating slowly, pausing now and then to spell a word. In these two hours it appeared to be his custom to read out, for fair copying, the labours of the other seven.

At five o'clock there was invariably a sound of plates and cups, and out of it the little model's voice would rise, matter-of-fact, soft, monotoned, making little statements; and in turn Mr. Stone's, also making statements which clearly lacked cohesion with those of his young friend. On one occasion, the door being open, Hilary heard distinctly the following conversation:

The LITTLE MODEL: "Mr. Creed says he was a butler. He's got an ugly nose." (A pause.)

Mr. STONE: "In those days men were absorbed in thinking of their individualities. Their occupations seemed to them important——"

The LITTLE MODEL: "Mr. Creed says his savings were all swallowed up by illness."

Mr. STONE: "—it was not so."

The LITTLE MODEL: "Mr. Creed says he was always brought up to go to church."

Mr. STONE (suddenly): "There has been no church worth going to since A. D. 700."

The LITTLE MODEL: "But he doesn't go."

And with a flying glance through the just open door Hilary saw her holding bread-and-butter with inky fingers, her lips a little parted, expecting the next bite, and her eyes fixed curiously on Mr. Stone, whose transparent hand held a teacup, and whose eyes were immovably fixed on distance.

It was one day in April that Mr. Stone, heralded by the scent of Harris tweed and baked potatoes which habitually encircled him, appeared at five o'clock in Hilary's study doorway.

"She has not come," he said.

Hilary laid down his pen. It was the first real Spring day. "Will you come for a walk with me, sir, instead?" he asked.

"Yes," said Mr. Stone.

They walked out into Kensington Gardens, Hilary with his head rather bent towards the ground, and Mr. Stone, with eyes fixed on his far thoughts, slightly poking forward his silver beard.

In their favourite firmaments the stars of crocuses and daffodils were shining. Almost every tree had its pigeon cooing, every bush its blackbird in full song. And on the paths were babies in perambulators. These were their happy hunting-grounds, and here they came each day to watch from a safe distance the little dirty girls sitting on the grass nursing little dirty boys, to listen to the ceaseless chatter of these common urchins, and learn to deal with the great problem of the lowest classes. And babies sat in their perambulators, thinking and sucking indiarubber tubes. Dogs went before them, and nursemaids followed after.

The spirit of colour was flying in the distant trees, swathing them with brownish-purple haze; the sky was saffroned by dying sunlight. It was such a day as brings a longing to the heart, like that which the moon brings to the hearts of children.

Mr. Stone and Hilary sat down in the Broad Walk.

"Elm-trees!" said Mr. Stone. "It is not known when they assumed their present shape. They have one universal soul. It

is the same with man." He ceased, and Hilary looked round
uneasily. They were alone on the bench.

Mr. Stone's voice rose again. "Their form and balance is
their single soul; they have preserved it from century to century.
This is all they live for. In those days "—his voice sank; he
had plainly forgotten that he was not alone—" when men had
no universal conceptions, they would have done well to look
at the trees. Instead of fostering a number of little souls on
the pabulum of varying theories of future life, they should have
been concerned to improve their present shapes, and thus to
dignify man's single soul."

"Elms were always considered dangerous trees, I believe,"
said Hilary.

Mr. Stone turned, and, seeing his son-in-law beside him,
asked:

"You spoke to me, I think?"

"Yes, sir."

Mr. Stone said wistfully:

"Shall we walk?"

They rose from the bench and walked on. . . .

The explanation of the little model's absence was thus stated
by herself to Hilary: "I had an appointment."

"More work?"

"A friend of Mr. French."

"Yes—who?"

"Mr. Lennard. He's a sculptor; he's got a studio in Chelsea.
He wants me to pose to him."

"Ah!"

She stole a glance at Hilary, and hung her head.

Hilary turned to the window. "You know what posing to a
sculptor means, of course?"

The little model's voice sounded behind him, matter-of-fact
as ever: "He said I was just the figure he was looking for."

Hilary continued to stare through the window. "I thought
you didn't mean to begin standing for the nude."

"I don't want to stay poor always."

Hilary turned round at the strange tone of these unexpected
words.

The girl was in a streak of sunlight; her pale cheeks flushed;
her pale, half-opened lips red; her eyes, in their setting of short
black lashes, wide and mutinous; her young round bosom heaving as if she had been running.

"I don't want to go on copying books all my life."

"Oh, very well."

"Mr. Dallison! I didn't mean that—I didn't really! I want to do what you tell me to do—I do!"

Hilary stood contemplating her with the dubious, critical look, as though asking: "What is there behind you? Are you really a genuine edition, or what?" which had so disconcerted her before. At last he said: "You must do just as you like. I never advise anybody."

"But you don't want me to—I know you don't. Of course, if *you* don't want me to, then it'll be a pleasure not to!"

Hilary smiled.

"Don't you like copying for Mr. Stone?"

The little model made a face. "I like Mr. Stone—he's such a funny old gentleman."

"That *is* the general opinion," answered Hilary. "But Mr. Stone, you know, thinks that *we* are funny."

The little model smiled, too; the streak of sunlight had slanted past her, and, standing there behind its glamour and million floating specks of gold-dust, she looked for the moment like the young Shade of Spring, watching with expectancy for what the year would bring her.

With the words "I am ready," spoken from the doorway, Mr. Stone interrupted further colloquy. . . .

But though the girl's position in the household had, to all seeming, become established, now and then some little incident —straws blowing down the wind—showed feelings at work beneath the family's apparent friendliness, beneath that tentative and almost apologetic manner towards the poor or helpless, which marks out those who own what Hilary had called the "social conscience." Only three days, indeed, before he sat in his brown study, meditating beneath the bust of Socrates, Cecilia, coming to lunch, had let fall this remark:

"Of course, I know nobody can read his handwriting; but I can't think why father doesn't dictate to a typist, instead of to that little girl. She could go twice the pace!"

Bianca's answer, deferred for a few seconds, was:

"Hilary perhaps knows."

"Do you dislike her coming here?" asked Hilary.

"Not particularly. Why?"

"I thought from your tone you did."

"I don't dislike her coming here for that purpose."

" Does she come for any other? "

Cecilia, dropping her quick glance to her fork, said just a little hastily: " Father *is* extraordinary, of course."

But the next three days Hilary was out in the afternoon when the little model came.

This, then, was the other reason, on the morning of the first of May, which made him not averse to go and visit Mrs. Hughs in Hound Street, Kensington.

CHAPTER VI

FIRST PILGRIMAGE TO HOUND STREET

HILARY and his little bulldog entered Hound Street from its eastern end. It was a grey street of three-storied houses, all in one style of architecture. Nearly all their doors were open, and on the doorsteps babes and children were enjoying Easter holidays. They sat in apathy, varied by sudden little slaps and bursts of noise. Nearly all were dirty; some had whole boots, some half boots, and two or three had none. In the gutters more children were at play; their shrill tongues and febrile movements gave Hilary the feeling that their " caste " exacted of them a profession of this faith: " To-day we live; to-morrow —if there be one—will be like to-day."

He had unconsciously chosen the very centre of the street to walk in, and Miranda, who had never in her life demeaned herself to this extent, ran at his heels, turning up her eyes, as though to say: ' One thing I make a point of—no dog must speak to me!'

Fortunately, there were no dogs; but there were many cats, and these cats were thin.

Through the upper windows of the houses Hilary had glimpses of women in poor habiliments doing various kinds of work, but stopping now and then to gaze into the street. He walked to the end, where a wall stopped him, and, still in the centre of the road, he walked the whole length back. The children stared at his tall figure with indifference; they evidently felt that he was not of those who, like themselves, had no to-morrow.

No. 1, Hound Street, abutting on the garden of a house of better class, was distinctly the show building of the street. The door, however, was not closed, and pulling the remnant of a bell, Hilary walked in.

The first thing that he noticed was a smell; it was not precisely bad, but it might have been better. It was a smell of walls and washing, varied rather vaguely by red herrings. The second thing he noticed was his moonlight bulldog, who stood on the doorstep eyeing a tiny sandy cat. This very little cat, whose back was arched with fury, he was obliged to chase away

260

before his bulldog would come in. The third thing he noticed was a lame woman of short stature, standing in the doorway of a room. Her face, with big cheek-bones, and wide-open, light grey, dark-lashed eyes, was broad and patient; she rested her lame leg by holding to the handle of the door.

"I dunno if you'll find anyone upstairs. I'd go and ask, but my leg's lame."

"So I see," said Hilary; "I'm sorry."

The woman sighed: "Been like that these five years"; and turned back into her room.

"Is there nothing to be done for it?"

"Well, I did think so once," replied the woman, "but they say the bone's diseased; I neglected it at the start."

"Oh dear!"

"We hadn't the time to give to it," the woman said defensively, retiring into a room so full of china cups, photographs, coloured prints, wax-work fruits, and other ornaments, that there seemed no room for the enormous bed.

Wishing her good-morning, Hilary began to mount the stairs. On the first floor he paused. Here, in the back room, the little model lived.

He looked around him. The paper on the passage walls was of a dingy orange colour, the blind of the window torn, and still pursuing him, pervading everything, was the scent of walls and washing and red herrings. There came on him a sickness, a sort of spiritual revolt. To live here, to pass up these stairs, between these dingy, bilious walls, on this dirty carpet, with this—ugh! every day; twice, four times, six times, who knew how many times a day! And that sense, the first to be attracted or revolted, the first to become fastidious with the culture of the body, the last to be expelled from the temple of the pure-spirit; that sense to whose refinement all breeding and all education is devoted; that sense which, ever an inch at least in front of man, is able to retard the development of nations, and paralyse all social schemes—this Sense of Smell awakened within him the centuries of his gentility, the ghosts of all those Dallisons who, for three hundred years and more, had served Church or State. It revived the souls of scents he was accustomed to, and with them, subtly mingled, the whole live fabric of æstheticism, woven in fresh air and laid in lavender. It roused the simple, non-extravagant demand of perfect cleanliness. And though he knew that chemists would have certified the composition of his blood to be the same as that of the dwellers in this house, and that this smell, composed of walls and washing and red herrings, was really rather healthy, he stood frowning fixedly at the girl's door, and the memory of his young niece's delicately wrinkled nose as she described the house rose before him. He went on upstairs, followed by his moonlight bulldog.

Hilary's tall thin figure appearing in the open doorway of the top-floor front, his kind and worried face, and the pale agate eyes of the little bulldog peeping through his legs, were witnessed by nothing but a baby, who was sitting in a wooden box in the centre of the room. This baby, who was very like a piece of putty to which Nature had by some accident fitted two movable black eyes, was clothing in a woman's knitted undervest, spreading beyond his feet and hands, so that nothing but his head was visible. This vest divided him from the wooden shavings on which he sat, and, since he had not yet attained the art of rising to his feet, the box divided him from contacts of all other kinds. As completely isolated from his kingdom as a Czar of all the Russias, he was doing nothing. In this realm there was a dingy bed, two chairs, and a washstand, with one lame leg, supported by an aged footstool. Clothes and garments were hanging on nails, pans lay about the hearth, a sewing-machine stood on a bare deal table. Over the bed was hung an oleograph, from a Christmas supplement, of the birth of Jesus, and above it a bayonet, under which was printed in an illiterate hand on a rough scroll of paper: " Gave three of em what for at Elandslaagte. S. Hughs." Some photographs adorned the walls, and two drooping ferns stood on the window-ledge. The room withal had a sort of desperate tidiness; in a large cupboard, slightly open, could be seen stowed all that must not see the light of day. The window of the baby's kingdom was tightly closed; the scent was the scent of walls and washing and red herrings, and—of other things.

Hilary looked at the baby, and the baby looked at him. The eyes of that tiny scrap of grey humanity seemed saying:

' You are not my mother, I believe? '

He stooped down and touched its cheek. The baby blinked its black eyes once.

' No,' it seemed to say again, ' you are *not* my mother.'

A lump rose in Hilary's throat; he turned and went downstairs. Pausing outside the little model's door, he knocked, and, receiving no answer, turned the handle. The little square room was empty; it was neat and clean enough, with a pink-flowered paper of comparatively modern date. Through its open window could be seen a pear-tree in full bloom. Hilary shut the door again with care, ashamed of having opened it.

On the half-landing, staring up at him with black eyes like the baby's, was a man of medium height and active build, whose short face, with broad cheek-bones, cropped dark hair, straight nose, and little black moustache, was burnt a dark dun colour. He was dressed in the uniform of those who sweep the streets— a loose blue blouse, and trousers tucked into boots reaching half-way up his calves; he held a peaked cap in his hand.

After some seconds of mutual admiration, Hilary said:

" Mr. Hughs, I believe? "

" Yes."

" I've been up to see your wife."

" Have you? "

" You know me, I suppose? "

" Yes, I know you."

" Unfortunately, there's only your baby at home."

Hughs motioned with his cap towards the little model's room. " I thought perhaps you'd been to see *her*," he said. His black eyes smouldered; there was more than class resentment in the expression of his face.

Flushing slightly and giving him a keen look, Hilary passed down the stairs without replying. But Miranda had not followed. She stood, with one paw delicately held up above the topmost step.

' I don't know this man,' she seemed to say, ' and I don't like his looks.'

Hughs grinned. " I never hurt a dumb animal," he said; " come on, tykie ! "

Stimulated by a word she had never thought to hear, Miranda descended rapidly.

' He meant that for impudence,' thought Hilary as he walked away.

"Westminister, sir? Oh dear ! "

A skinny trembling hand was offering him a greenish news-paper.

" Terrible cold wind for the time o' year ! "

A very aged man in black-rimmed spectacles, with a distended nose and long upper lip and chin, was tentatively fumbling out change for sixpence.

" I seem to know your face," said Hilary.

" Oh dear, yes. You deals with this 'ere shop—the tobacco department. I've often seen you when you've a-been a-goin' in. Sometimes you has the *Pell Mell* off o' this man here." He jerked his head a trifle to the left, where a younger man was standing armed with a sheaf of whiter papers. In that gesture were years of envy, heart-burning, and sense of wrong. ' That's my paper,' it seemed to say, ' by all the rights of man; and that low-class fellow sellin' it, takin' away my profits ! '

" I sells this 'ere *Westminister*. I reads it on Sundays—it's a gentleman's paper, 'igh-class paper—notwithstandin' of its politics. But, Lor', sir, with this 'ere man a-sellin' the *Pell Mell* "—lowering his voice, he invited Hilary to confidence— " so many o' the gentry takes that; an' there ain't too many o' the gentry about 'ere—I mean, not o' the *real* gentry—that I can afford to 'ave 'em took away from me."

Hilary, who had stopped to listen out of delicacy, had a flash of recollection. " You live in Hound Street ? "

The old man answered eagerly: " Oh dear ! Yes, sir—No. 1, name of Creed. You're the gentleman where the young person goes for to copy of a book ! "

" It's not my book she copies."

" Oh no; it's an old gentleman; I know 'im. He come an' see me once. He come in one Sunday morning. ' Here's a pound o' tobacca for you ! ' 'e says. ' You was a butler,' 'e says. ' Butler ! ' 'e says, ' there'll be no butlers in fifty years.' An' out 'e goes. Not quite "—he put a shaky hand up to his head —" not quite—oh dear ! "

" Some people called Hughs live in your house, I think ? "

" I rents my room off o' them. A lady was a-speakin' to me yesterday about 'em; that's not your lady, I suppose, sir ? "

His eyes seemed to apostrophise Hilary's hat, which was of soft felt with a: ' Yes, yes—I've seen your sort a-stayin' about in the best houses. They has you down because of your learin'; and quite the manners of a gentleman you've got.'

" My wife's sister, I expect."

" Oh dear ! She often has a paper off o' me. A real lady— not one o' these "—again he invited Hilary to confidence—" you know what I mean, sir—that buys their things a' ready-made at these 'ere large establishments. Oh, I know her well."

" The old gentleman who visited you is her father."

"Is he? Oh dear!" The old butler was silent, evidently puzzled.

Hilary's eyebrows began to execute those intricate manœuvres which always indicated that he was about to tax his delicacy.

"How—how does Hughs treat the little girl who lives in the next room to you?"

The old butler replied in a rather gloomy tone:

"She takes my advice, and don't 'ave nothin' to say to 'im. Dreadful foreign-lookin' man 'e is. Wherever 'e was brought up I can't think!"

"A soldier, wasn't he?"

"So he says. He's one o' these that works for the Vestry; an' then 'e'll go an' get upon the drink, an' when that sets 'im off, it seems as if there wasn't no respect for nothing in 'im; he goes on against the gentry, and the Church, and every sort of institution. I never met no soldiers like *him*. Dreadful foreign —Welsh, they tell me."

"What do you think of the street you're living in?"

"I keeps myself to myself; low class o' street it is; dreadful low class o' person there—no self-respect about 'em."

"Ah!" said Hilary.

"These little 'ouses, they get into the hands o' little men, and *they* don't care so long as they makes their rent out o' them. They can't help themselves—low class o' man like that; 'e's got to do the best 'e can for 'imself. They say there's thousands o' these 'ouses all over London. There's some that's for pullin' of 'em down, but that's talkin' rubbish; where are you goin' to get the money for to do it? These 'ere little men, they can't afford not even to put a paper on the walls, and the big ground landlords—you can't expect *them* to know what's happenin' behind their backs. There's some ignorant fellers like this Hughs talks a lot o' wild nonsense about the duty o' ground landlords; but you can't expect the real gentry to look into these sort o' things. They've got their estates down in the country. I've lived with them, and of course I know."

The little bulldog, incommoded by the passersby, now took the opportunity of beating with her tail against the old butler's legs.

"Oh dear! what's this? He don't bite, do 'e? Good Sambo!"

Miranda sought her master's eye at once. 'You see what happens to her if a lady loiters in the streets,' she seemed to say.

"It must be hard standing about here all day, after the life you've led," said Hilary.

"I mustn't complain; it's been the salvation o' me."

"Do you get shelter?"

Again the old butler seemed to take him into confidence.

"Sometimes of a wet night they lets me stand up in the archway there; they know I'm respectable. 'Twouldn't never do for that man "—he nodded at his rival—" or any of them boys to get standin' there, obstructin' of the traffic."

".I wanted to ask you, Mr. Creed, is there anything to be done for Mrs. Hughs?"

The frail old body quivered with the vindictive force of his answer.

"Accordin' to what she says, if I'm a-to believe 'er, I'd have him up before the magistrate, sure as my name's Creed, an' get a separation, an' I wouldn't never live with 'im again: that's what she ought to do. An' if he come to go for her after that, I'd have 'im in prison, if 'e killed me first! I've no patience with a low class o' man like that! He insulted of me this morning."

"Prison's a dreadful remedy," murmured Hilary.

The old butler answered stoutly: "There ain't but one way o' treatin' them low fellers—ketch hold o' them until they holler!"

Hilary was about to reply when he found himself alone. At the edge of the pavement some yards away, Creed, his face upraised to heaven, was embracing with all his force the second edition of the *Westminster Gazette*, which had been thrown him from a cart.

'Well,' thought Hilary, walking on, '*you* know your own mind, anyway!'

And trotting by his side, with her jaw set very firm, his little bulldog looked up above her eyes, and seemed to say: 'It was time we left that man of action!'

CHAPTER VII

CECILIA'S SCATTERED THOUGHTS

In her morning room Mrs. Stephen Dallison sat at an old oak bureau collecting her scattered thoughts. They lay about on pieces of stamped notepaper, beginning " Dear Cecilia," or " Mrs. Tallents Smallpeace requests," or on bits of pasteboard headed by the names of theatres, galleries, or concert-halls; or, again, on paper of not quite so good a quality, commencing, " Dear Friend," and ending with a single well-known name like " Wessex," so that no suspicion should attach to the appeal contained between the two. She had before her also sheets of her own writing-paper, headed " 76, The Old Square, Kensington," and two little books. One of these was bound in marbleised paper, and on it written: " Please keep this book in safety "; across the other, cased in the skin of some small animal deceased, was inscribed the solitary word " Engagements."

Cecilia had on a Persian-green silk blouse with sleeves that would have hidden her slim hands, but for silver buttons made in the likeness of little roses at her wrists; on her brow was a faint frown, as though she were wondering what her thoughts were all about. She sat there every morning catching those thoughts, and placing them in one or other of her little books. Only by thus working hard could she keep herself, her husband, and daughter, in due touch with all the different movements going on. And that the touch might be as due as possible, she had a little headache nearly every day. For the dread of letting slip one movement, or of being too much taken with another, was very real to her; there were so many people who were interesting, so many sympathies of hers and Stephen's which she desired to cultivate, that it was a matter of the utmost import not to cultivate any single one too much. Then, too, the duty of remaining feminine with all this going forward taxed her constitution. She sometimes thought enviously of the splendid isolation now enjoyed by Bianca, of which some subtle instinct, rather than definite knowledge, had informed her; but not often, for she was a loyal little person, to whom Stephen and his comforts were of the first moment. And though she worried

267

somewhat because her thoughts *would* come by every post, she did not worry very much—hardly more than the Persian kitten on her lap, who also sat for hours trying to catch her tail, with a line between her eyes, and two small hollows in her cheeks.

When she had at last decided what concerts she would be obliged to miss, paid her subscription to the League for the Suppression of Tinned Milk, and accepted an invitation to watch a man fall from a balloon, she paused. Then, dipping her pen in ink, she wrote as follows:

"Mrs. Stephen Dallison would be glad to have the blue dress ordered by her yesterday sent home at once without alteration.—Messrs. Rose and Thorn, High Street, Kensington."

Ringing the bell, she thought: 'It will be a job for Mrs. Hughs, poor thing. I believe she'll do it quite as well as Rose and Thorn.'—"Would you please ask Mrs. Hughs to come to me?—Oh, is that you, Mrs. Hughs? Come in."

The seamstress, who had advanced into the middle of the room, stood with her worn hands against her sides, and no sign of life but the liquid patience in her large brown eyes. She was an enigmatic figure. Her presence always roused a sort of irritation in Cecilia, as if she had been suddenly confronted with what might possibly have been herself if certain little accidents had omitted to occur. She was so conscious that she ought to sympathise, so anxious to show that there was no barrier between them, so eager to be all she ought to be, that her voice almost purred.

"Are you getting on with the curtains, Mrs. Hughs?"

"Yes, m'm, thank you, m'm."

"I shall have another job for you to-morrow—altering a dress. Can you come?"

"Yes, m'm, thank you, m'm."

"Is the baby well?"

"Yes, m'm, thank you, m'm."

There was a silence.

'It's no good talking of her domestic matters,' thought Cecilia; 'not that I don't care!' But the silence getting on her nerves, she said quickly: "Is your husband behaving himself better?"

There was no answer; Cecilia saw a tear trickle slowly down the woman's cheek.

'Oh dear, oh dear,' she thought; 'poor thing! I'm in for it!'

Mrs. Hughs' whispering voice began: "He's behaving himself dreadful, m'm. I was going to speak to you. It's ever since that young girl "—her face hardened—" come to live down in my room there; he seem to—he seem to—just do nothing but neglect me."

Cecilia's heart gave the little pleasurable flutter which the heart must feel at the love dramas of other people, however painful.

"You mean the little model?" she said.

The seamstress answered in an agitated voice: "I don't want to speak against her, but she's put a spell on him, that's what she has; he don't seem able to do nothing but talk of her, and hang about her room. It was that troubling me when I saw you the other day. And ever since yesterday midday, when Mr. Hilary came—he's been talking that wild—and he pushed me—and—and——" Her lips ceased to form articulate words, but, since it was not etiquette to cry before her superiors, she used them to swallow down her tears, and something in her lean throat moved up and down.

At the mention of Hilary's name the pleasurable sensation in Cecilia had undergone a change. She felt curiosity, fear, offence.

"I don't quite understand you," she said.

The seamstress plaited at her frock. "Of course, I can't help the way he talks, m'm. I'm sure I don't like to repeat the wicked things he says about Mr. Hilary. It seems as if he were out of his mind when he gets talkin' about *that young girl.*"

The tone of those last three words was almost fierce.

Cecilia was on the point of saying: 'That will do, please; I want to hear no more.' But her curiosity and queer subtle fear forced her instead to repeat: "I don't understand. Do you mean he insinuates that Mr. Hilary has anything to do with—with this girl, or what?" And she thought: 'I'll stop that, at any rate.'

The seamstress's face was distorted by her efforts to control her voice.

"I tell him he's wicked to say such things, m'm, and Mr. Hilary such a kind gentleman. And what business is it of his, I say, that's got a wife and children of his own? I've seen him in the street, I've watched him hanging about Mrs. Hilary's house when I've been working there—waiting for that girl, and following her—home——" Again her lips refused to do service, except in the swallowing of her tears.

Cecilia thought: ' I must tell Stephen at once. That man is dangerous.' A spasm gripped her heart, usually so warm and snug; vague feelings she had already entertained presented themselves now with startling force; she seemed to see the face of sordid life staring at the family of Dallison. Mrs. Hughs' voice, which did not dare to break, resumed:

"I've said to him: 'Whatever are you thinking of? And after Mrs. Hilary's been so kind to me!' But he's like a mad-man when he's in liquor, and he says he'll go to Mrs. Hilary——"

" Go to my sister? What about? The ruffian! "

At hearing her husband called a ruffian by another woman the shadow of resentment passed across Mrs. Hughs' face, leaving it quivering and red. The conversation had already made a strange difference in the manner of these two women to each other. It was as though each now knew exactly how much sym-pathy and confidence could be expected of the other, as though life had suddenly sucked up the mist, and shown them standing one on either side of a deep trench. In Mrs. Hughs' eyes there was the look of those who have long discovered that they must not answer back for fear of losing what little ground they have to stand on; and Cecilia's eyes were cold and watchful. ' I sym-pathise,' they seemed to say, ' I sympathise; but you must please understand that you cannot expect sympathy if your affairs compromise the members of my family.' Her chief thought now was to be relieved of the company of this woman, who had been betrayed into showing what lay beneath her dumb, stub-born patience. It was not callousness, but the natural result of being fluttered. Her heart was like a bird agitated in its gilt-wire cage by the contemplation of a distant cat. She did not, however, lose her sense of what was practical, but said calmly: " Your husband was wounded in South Africa, you told me? It looks as if he wasn't quite . . . I think you should have a doctor ! "

The seamstress's answer, slow and matter-of-fact, was worse than her emotion.

" No, m'm, he isn't mad."

Crossing to the hearth—whose Persian-blue tiling had taken her so long to find—Cecilia stood beneath a reproduction of Botticelli's " Primavera," and looked doubtfully at Mrs. Hughs. The Persian kitten, sleepy and disturbed on the bosom of her blouse, gazed up into her face. ' Consider me,' it seemed to say; ' I am worth consideration; I am of a piece with you, and

everything round you. We are both elegant and rather slender;
we both love warmth and kittens; we both dislike interference
with our fur. You took a long time to buy me, so as to get me
perfect. You see that woman over there! I sat on her lap
this morning while she was sewing your curtains. She has no
right in here; she's not what she seems; she can bite and
scratch, I know; her lap is skinny; she drops water from her
eyes. She made me wet all down my back. Be careful what
you're doing, or she'll make you wet down yours!'

All that was like the little Persian kitten within Cecilia—
cosiness and love of pretty things, attachment to her own abode
with its high-art lining, love for her mate and her own kitten,
Thyme, dread of disturbance—all made her long to push this
woman from the room; this woman with the skimpy figure, and
eyes that, for all their patience, had in them something virago-
like; this woman who carried about with her an atmosphere
of sordid grief, of squalid menaces, and scandal. She longed
all the more because it could well be seen from the seamstress's
helpless attitude that she too would have liked an easy life.
To dwell on things like this was to feel more than thirty-
eight!

Cecilia had no pocket, Providence having removed it now for
some time past, but from her little bag she drew forth the two
essentials of gentility. Taking her nose, which she feared was
shining, gently within one, she fumbled in the other. And
again she looked doubtfully at Mrs. Hughs. Her heart said:
'Give the poor woman half a sovereign; it might comfort her!'
But her brain said: 'I owe her four-and-six; after what she's
just been saying about her husband and that girl and Hilary, it
mayn't be safe to give her more.' She held out two half-crowns,
and had an inspiration: "I shall mention to my sister what
you've said; you can tell your husband that!"

No sooner had she said this, however, than she saw, from a
little smile devoid of merriment and quickly extinguished, that
Mrs. Hughs did not believe she would do anything of the kind;
from which she concluded that the seamstress was convinced of
Hilary's interest in the little model. She said hastily:

"You can go now, Mrs. Hughs."

Mrs. Hughs went, making no noise or sign of any sort.

Cecilia returned to her scattered thoughts. They lay there
still, with a gleam of sun from the low window smearing their
importance; she felt somehow that it did not now matter very

much whether she and Stephen, in the interests of science, saw
that man fall from his balloon, or, in the interests of art, heard
Herr von Kraaffe sing his Polish songs; she experienced, too,
almost a revulsion in favour of tinned milk. After meditatively
tearing up her note to Messrs. Rose and Thorn, she lowered the
bureau lid and left the room.

Mounting the stairs, whose old oak banisters on either side
were a real joy, she felt she was stupid to let vague, sordid
rumours, which, after all, affected her but indirectly, disturb
her morning's work. And entering Stephen's dressing-room
she stood looking at his boots.

Inside each one of them was a wooden soul; none had any
creases, none had any holes. The moment they wore out, their
wooden souls were taken from them and their bodies given to
the poor, whilst—in accordance with that theory, to hear a
course of lectures on which a scattered thought was even now
inviting her—the wooden souls migrated instantly to other
leathern bodies.

Looking at that polished row of boots, Cecelia felt lonely
and unsatisfied. Stephen worked in the Law Courts, Thyme
worked at Art; both were doing something definite. She alone,
it seemed, had to wait at home, and order dinner, answer
letters, shop, pay calls, and do a dozen things that failed to
stop her thoughts from dwelling on that woman's tale. She
was not often conscious of the nature of her life, so like
the lives of many hundred women in this London, which she
said she could not stand, but which she stood very well.
As a rule, with practical good sense, she kept her doubting
eyes fixed friendily on every little phase in turn, enjoying
well enough fitting the Chinese puzzle of her scattered thoughts,
setting out on each small adventure with a certain cautious
zest, and taking Stephen with her as far as he allowed. This
last year or so, now that Thyme was a grown girl, she had
felt at once a loss of purpose and a gain of liberty. She
hardly knew whether to be glad or sorry. It freed her for
the tasting of more things, more people, and more Stephen;
but it left a little void in her heart, a little soreness round
it. What would Thyme think if she heard this story about
her uncle? The thought started a whole train of doubts
that had of late beset her. Was her little daughter going to
turn out like herself? If not, why not? Stephen joked about
his daughter's skirts, her hockey, her friendship with young

men. He joked about the way Thyme refused to let him joke about her art or about her interest in "the people." His joking was a source of irritation to Cecilia. For, by woman's instinct rather than by any reasoning process, she was conscious of a disconcerting change. Amongst the people she knew, young men were not now attracted by girls as they had been in her young days. There was a kind of cool and friendly matter-of-factness in the way they treated them, a sort of almost scientific playfulness. And Cecilia felt uneasy as to how far this was to go. She seemed left behind. If young people were really becoming serious, if youths no longer cared about the colour of Thyme's eyes, or dress, or hair, what would there be left to care for—that is, up to the point of definite relationship? Not that she wanted her daughter to be married. It would be time enough to think of that when she was twenty-five. But her own experiences had been so different. She had spent so many youthful hours in wondering about men, had seen so many men cast furtive looks at her; and now there did not seem in men or girls anything left worth the other's while to wonder or look furtive about. She was not of a philosophic turn of mind, and had attached no deep meaning to Stephen's jest—" If young people will reveal their ankles, they'll soon have no ankles to reveal."

To Cecilia the extinction of the race seemed threatened; in reality her species of the race alone was vanishing, which to her, of course, was very much the same disaster. With her eyes on Stephen's boots she thought: 'How shall I prevent what I've heard from coming to Bianca's ears? I know how she would take it! How shall I prevent Thyme's hearing? I'm sure I don't know what the effect would be on her! I must speak to Stephen. He's so fond of Hilary.'

And, turning away from Stephen's boots, she mused: ' Of course it's nonsense. Hilary's much too—too nice, too fastidious, to be more than just interested; but he's so kind he might easily put himself in a false position. And—it's ugly nonsense! B. can be so disagreeable; even now she's not—on terms with him!' And suddenly the thought of Mr. Purcey leaped into her mind—Mr. Purcey, who, as Mrs. Tallents Smallpeace had declared, was not even conscious that there was a problem of the poor. To think of him seemed somehow at that moment comforting, like rolling oneself in a blanket against a draught. Passing into her room, she opened her wardrobe door.

'Bother the woman!' she thought. 'I do want that gentian dress got ready, but now I simply *can't* give it to her to do.'

CHAPTER VIII

THE SINGLE MIND OF MR. STONE

SINCE in the flutter of her spirit caused by the words of Mrs. Hughs, Cecilia felt she must do something, she decided to change her dress.

The furniture of the pretty room she shared with Stephen had not been hastily assembled. Conscious, even fifteen years ago, when they moved into this house, of the grave Philistinism of the upper classes, she and Stephen had ever kept their duty to æstheticism green; and, in the matter of their bed, had lain for two years on two little white affairs, comfortable, but purely temporary, that they might give themselves a chance. The chance had come at last—a bed in real keeping with the period they had settled on, and going for twelve pounds. They had not let it go, and now slept in it—not quite so comfortable, perhaps, but comfortable enough, and conscious of duty done.

For fifteen years Cecilia had been furnishing her house; the process approached completion. The only things remaining on her mind—apart, that is, from Thyme's development and the condition of the people—were: item, a copper lantern that would allow some light to pass its framework; item, an old oak washstand not going back to Cromwell's time. And now this third anxiety had come!

She was rather touching, as she stood before the wardrobe glass divested of her bodice, with dimples of exertion in her thin white arms while she hooked her skirt behind, and her greenish eyes troubled, so anxious to do their best for every-one, and save risk of any sort. Having put on a bramble-coloured frock, which laced across her breast with silver lattice-work, and a hat (without feathers, so as to encourage birds) fastened to her head with pins (bought to aid a novel school of metal-work), she went to see what sort of day it was.

The window looked out at the back over some dreary streets, where the wind was flinging light drifts of smoke athwart the sunlight. They had chosen this room, not indeed for its view over the condition of the people, but because of the sky effects at sunset, which were extremely fine. For the first

275

time, perhaps, Cecilia was conscious that a sample of the class she was so interested in was exposed to view beneath her nose. 'The Hughses live somewhere there,' she thought. 'After all I think B. ought to know about that man. She might speak to father, and get him to give up having the girl to copy for him—the whole thing's so worrying.'

In pursuance of this thought, she lunched hastily, and went out, making her way to Hilary's. With every step she became more uncertain. The fear of meddling too much, of not meddling enough, of seeming meddlesome; timidity at touching anything so awkward; distrust, even ignorance, of her sister's character, which was like, yet so very unlike, her own; a real itch to get the matter settled, so that nothing whatever should come of it—all this she felt. She hurried, dawdled, finished the adventure almost at a run, then told the servant not to announce her. The vision of Bianca's eyes, while she listened to this tale, was suddenly too much for Cecilia. She decided to pay a visit to her father first.

Mr. Stone was writing, attired in his working dress—a thick brown woollen gown, revealing his thin neck above the line of a blue shirt, and tightly gathered round the waist with tasselled cord; the lower portions of grey trousers were visible above the woollen-slippered feet. His hair straggled over his thin long ears. The window, wide open, admitted an east wind; there was no fire. Cecilia shivered.

"Come in quickly," said Mr. Stone. Turning to a big high desk of stained deal which occupied the middle of one wall, he began methodically to place the inkstand, a heavy paper-knife, a book, and stones of several sizes, on his fluttering sheets of manuscript.

Cecilia looked about her; she had not been inside her father's room for several months. There was nothing in it but that desk, a camp bed in the far corner (with blankets, but no sheets), a folding washstand, and a narrow bookcase, the books in which Cecilia unconsciously told off on the fingers of her memory. They never varied. On the top shelf the Bible and the works of Plautus and Diderot; on the second from the top the plays of Shakespeare in a blue edition; on the third from the bottom Don Quixote, in four volumes, covered with brown paper; a green Milton; the "Comedies of Aristophanes"; a leather book, partially burned, comparing the philosophy of Epicurus with the philosophy of Spinoza; and in a yellow

binding Mark Twain's "Huckleberry Finn." On the second
from the bottom was lighter literature: "The Iliad"; a "Life
of Francis of Assisi"; Speke's "Discovery of the Sources of
the Nile"; the "Pickwick Papers"; "Mr. Midshipman Easy";
The Verses of Theocritus, in a very old translation; Renan's
"Life of Christ"; and the "Autobiography of Benvenuto Cel-
lini." The bottom shelf of all was full of books on natural
science.

The walls were whitewashed, and, as Cecilia knew, came
off on anybody who leaned against them. The floor was stained,
and had no carpet. There was a little gas cooking-stove, with
cooking things ranged on it; a small bare table; and one large
cupboard. No draperies, no pictures, no ornaments of any
kind; but by the window an ancient golden leather chair.
Cecilia could never bear to sit in that oasis; its colour in
this wilderness was too precious to her spirit.

"It's an east wind, father; aren't you terribly cold without
a fire?"

Mr. Stone came from his writing-desk, and stood so that
light might fall on a sheet of paper in his hand. Cecilia noted
the scent that went about with him of peat and baked potatoes. He spoke:

"Listen to this: 'In the condition of society, dignified in
those days with the name of civilisation, the only source of
hope was the persistence of the quality called courage. Amongst
a thousand nerve-destroying habits, amongst the dram-shops,
patent medicines, the undigested chaos of inventions and discoveries, while hundreds were prating in their pulpits of things
believed in by a negligible fraction of the population, and
thousands writing down to-day what nobody would want to
read in two days' time; while men shut animals in cages, and
made bears jig to please their children, and all were striving
one against the other; while, in a word, like gnats above a
stagnant pool on a summer's evening, man danced up and down
without the faintest notion why—in this condition of affairs
the quality of courage was alive. It was the only fire within
that gloomy valley.'" He stopped, though evidently anxious
to go on, because he had read the last word on that sheet of
paper. He moved towards the writing-desk. Cecilia said
hastily:

"Do you mind if I shut the window, father?"

Mr. Stone made a movement of his head, and Cecilia saw

that he held a second sheet of paper in his hand. She rose, and, going towards him, said:

"I want to talk to you, Dad!" Taking up the cord of his dressing-gown, she pulled it by its tassel.

"Don't!" said Mr. Stone; "it secures my trousers."

Cecilia dropped the cord. 'Father is really terrible!' she thought.

Mr. Stone, lifting the second sheet of paper, began again:

"'The reason, however, was not far to seek——'"

Cecilia said desperately:

"It's about that girl who comes to copy for you."

Mr. Stone lowered the sheet of paper, and stood, slightly curved from head to foot; his ears moved as though he were about to lay them back; his blue eyes, with little white spots of light alongside the tiny black pupils, stared at his daughter.

Cecilia thought: 'He's listening now.'

She made haste. "*Must* you have her here? Can't you do without her?"

"Without whom?" said Mr. Stone.

"Without the girl who comes to copy for you."

"Why?"

"For this very good reason——"

Mr. Stone dropped his eyes, and Cecilia saw that he had moved the sheet of paper up as far as his waist.

"Does she copy better than any other girl could?" she asked hastily.

"No," said Mr. Stone.

"Then, Father, I do wish, to please me, you'd get someone else. I know what I'm talking about, and I——" Cecilia stopped; her father's lips and eyes were moving; he was obviously reading to himself. 'I've no patience with him,' she thought; 'he thinks of nothing but his wretched book.'

Aware of his daughter's silence, Mr. Stone let the sheet of paper sink, and waited patiently again.

"What do you want, my dear?" he said.

"Oh, Father, do listen just a minute!"

"Yes, yes."

"It's about that girl who comes to copy for you. Is there any reason why she should come instead of any other girl?"

"Yes," said Mr. Stone.

"What reason?"

"Because she has no friends."

So awkward a reply was not expected by Cecilia; she looked at the floor, forced to search within her soul. Silence lasted several seconds; then Mr. Stone's voice rose above a whisper:

" ' The reason was not far to seek. Man, differentiated from the other apes by his desire to *know,* was from the first obliged to steel himself against the penalties of knowledge. Like animals subjected to the rigours of an Arctic climate, and putting forth more fur with each reduction in the temperature, man's hide of courage thickened automatically to resist the spear-thrusts dealt him by his own insatiate curiosity. In those days of which we speak, when undigested knowledge, in a great invading horde, had swarmed all his defences, man, suffering from a foul dyspepsia, with a nervous system in the latest stages of exhaustion, and a reeling brain, survived by reason of his power to go on making courage. Little heroic as (in the then general state of petty competition) his deeds appeared to be, there never had yet been a time when man in bulk was more courageous, for there never had yet been a time when he had more need to be. Signs were not wanting that this desperate state of things had caught the eyes of the community. A little sect——' " Mr. Stone stopped; his eyes had again tumbled over the bottom edge; he moved hurriedly towards the desk. Just as his hand removed a stone and took up a third sheet, Cecilia cried out:

"Father!"

Mr. Stone stopped, and turned towards her. His daughter saw that he had gone quite pink; her annoyance vanished.

"Father! About that girl——"

Mr. Stone seemed to reflect. "Yes, yes," he said.

"I don't think Bianca likes her coming here."

Mr. Stone passed his hand across his brow.

"Forgive me for reading to you, my dear," he said; "it's a great relief to me at times."

Cecilia went close to him, and refrained with difficulty from taking up the tasselled cord.

"Of course, dear," she said: "I quite understand that."

Mr. Stone looked her full in her face, and before a gaze which seemed to go through her and see things the other side, Cecilia dropped her eyes.

"It is strange," he said, "how you came to be my daughter!"

To Cecilia, too, this had often seemed a problem.

"There is a great deal in atavism," said Mr. Stone, "that we know nothing of at present."

Cecilia cried with heat, "I do wish you would attend a minute, Father; it's really an important matter," and she turned towards the window, tears being very near her eyes.

The voice of Mr. Stone said humbly: "I will try, my dear."

But Cecilia thought: 'I must give him a good lesson. He really is too self-absorbed'; and she did not move, conveying by the posture of her shoulders how gravely she was vexed.

She could see nursemaids wheeling babies towards the Gardens, and noted their faces gazing, not at the babies, but, uppishly, at other nursemaids, or with a sort of cautious longing, at men who passed. How selfish they looked! She felt a little glow of satisfaction that she was making this thin and bent old man behind her conscious of his egoism.

'He will know better another time,' she thought. Suddenly she heard a whistling, squeaking sound—it was Mr. Stone whispering the third page of his manuscript:

"'—animated by some admirable sentiments, but whose doctrines—riddled by the fact that life is but the change of form to form—were too constricted for the evils they designed to remedy; this little sect, who had as yet to learn the meaning of universal love, were making the most strenuous efforts, in advance of the community at large, to understand themselves. The necessary movement which they voiced—reaction against the high-tide of the fratricidal system then prevailing—was young, and had the freshness and honesty of youth. . . .'"

Without a word Cecilia turned round and hurried to the door. She saw her father drop the sheet of paper; she saw his face, all pink and silver, stooping after it; and remorse visited her anger.

In the corridor outside she was arrested by a noise. The uncertain light of London halls fell there; on close inspection the sufferer was seen to be Miranda, who, unable to decide whether she wanted to be in the garden or the house, was seated beneath the hatrack snuffling to herself. On seeing Cecilia she came out.

"What do you want, you little beast?"

Peering at her over the tops of her eyes, Miranda vaguely lifted a white foot. 'Why ask me that?' she seemed to say. 'How am I to know? Are we not all like this?'

Her conduct, coming at that moment, overtried Cecilia's nerves. She threw open Hilary's study-door, saying sharply: "Go in and find your master!"

Miranda did not move, but Hilary came out instead. He had been correcting proofs to catch the post, and wore the look of a man abstracted, faintly contemptuous of other forms of life.

Cecilia, once more saved from the necessity of approaching her sister, the mistress of the house, so fugitive, haunting, and unseen, yet so much the centre of this situation, said:

"Can I speak to you a minute, Hilary?"

They went into his study, and Miranda came creeping in behind.

To Cecilia her brother-in-law always seemed an amiable and more or less pathetic figure. In his literary preoccupations he allowed people to impose on him. He looked unsubstantial beside the bust of Socrates, which moved Cecilia strangely—it was so very massive and so very ugly! She decided not to beat about the bush.

"I've been hearing some odd things from Mrs. Hughs about that little model, Hilary."

Hilary's smile faded from his eyes, but remained clinging to his lips.

"Indeed!"

Cecilia went on nervously: "Mrs. Hughs says it's because of her that Hughs behaves so badly. I don't want to say anything against the girl, but she seems—she seems to have——"

"Yes?" said Hilary.

"To have cast a spell on Hughs, as the woman puts it."

"On Hughs!" repeated Hilary.

Cecilia found her eyes resting on the bust of Socrates, and hastily proceeded:

"She says he follows her about, and comes down here to lie in wait for her. It's a most strange business altogether. You went to see them, didn't you?"

Hilary nodded.

"I've been speaking to Father," Cecilia murmured; "but he's hopeless—I couldn't get him to pay the least attention."

Hilary seemed thinking deeply.

"I wanted him," she went on, "to get some other girl instead to come and copy for him."

"Why?"

Under the seeming impossibility of ever getting any farther, without saying what she had come to say, Cecilia blurted out:

"Mrs. Hughs says that Hughs has threatened *you*."

Hilary's face became ironical.

"Really!" he said. "That's good of him! What for?"

The frightful indelicacy of her situation at this moment, the feeling of unfairness that she should be placed in it, almost overwhelmed Cecilia. "Goodness knows I don't want to meddle. I never meddle in anything—it's horrible!"

Hilary took her hand.

"My dear Cis," he said, "of course! But we'd better have this out!"

Grateful for the pressure of his hand, she gave it a convulsive squeeze.

"It's so sordid, Hilary!"

"Sordid! H'm! Let's get it over, then."

Cecilia had grown crimson. "Do you want me to tell you everything?"

"Certainly."

"Well, Hughs evidently thinks you're interested in the girl. You can't keep anything from servants and people who work about your house; they always think the worst of everything—and, of course, they know that you and B. don't— aren't——"

Hilary nodded.

"Mrs. Hughs actually said the man meant to go to B.!"

Again the vision of her sister seemed to float into the room, and she went on desperately: "And, Hilary, I can see Mrs. Hughs really thinks you *are* interested. Of course, she wants to, for if you were, it would mean that a man like her husband could have no chance."

Astonished at this flash of cynical inspiration, and ashamed of such plain speaking, she checked herself. Hilary had turned away.

Cecilia touched his arm. "Hilary, dear," she said, "isn't there any chance of you and B——?"

Hilary's lips twitched. "I should say not."

Cecilia looked sadly at the floor. Not since Stephen was bad with pleurisy had she felt so worried. The sight of Hilary's face brought back her doubts with all their force. It might, of course, be only anger at the man's impudence, but it might be—she hardly liked to frame her thought—a more personal feeling.

"Don't you think," she said, "that, anyway, she had better not come here again?"

Hilary paced the room.

"It's her only safe and certain piece of work; it keeps her independent. It's much more satisfactory than this sitting. I can't have any hand in taking it away from her."

Cecilia had never seen him moved like this. Was it possible that he was not incorrigibly gentle, but had in him some of that animality which she, in a sense, admired? This uncertainty terribly increased the difficulties of the situation.

"But, Hilary," she said at last, "are you satisfied about the girl—I mean, are you satisfied that she really is worth helping?"

"I don't understand."

"I mean," murmured Cecilia, "that we don't know anything about her past." And, seeing from the movement of his eyebrows that she was touching on what had evidently been a doubt with him, she went on with great courage: "Where are her friends and relations? I mean, she may have had a—adventures."

Hilary withdrew into himself.

"You can hardly expect me," he said, "to go into that with her."

His reply made Cecilia feel ridiculous.

"Well," she said in a hard little voice, "if this is what comes of helping the poor, I don't see the use of it."

The outburst evoked no reply from Hilary; she felt more tremulous than ever. The whole thing was so confused, so unnatural. What with the dark, malignant Hughs and that haunting vision of Bianca, the matter seemed almost Italian. That a man of Hughs' class might be affected by the passion of love had somehow never come into her head. She thought of the back streets she had looked out on from her bedroom window. Could anything like passion spring up in those dismal alleys? The people who lived there, poor downtrodden things, had enough to do to keep themselves alive. She knew all about them; they were in the air; their condition was deplorable! Could a person whose condition was deplorable find time or strength for any sort of lurid exhibition such as this? It was incredible.

She became aware that Hilary was speaking.

" I daresay the man is dangerous ! "

Hearing her fears confirmed, and in accordance with the secret vein of hardness which kept her living, amid all her sympathies and hesitations, Cecilia felt suddenly that she had gone as far as it was in her to go.

" I shall have no more to do with them," she said; " I've tried my best for Mrs. Hughs. I know quite as good a needle-woman, who'll be only too glad to come instead. Any other girl will do as well to copy father's book. If you take my advice, Hilary, you'll give up trying to help them too."

Hilary's smile puzzled and annoyed her. If she had known, this was the smile that stood between him and her sister.

" You may be right," he said, and shrugged his shoulders.

" Very well," said Cecilia, " I've done all I can. I must go now. Good-bye."

During her progress to the door she gave one look behind. Hilary was standing by the bust of Socrates. Her heart smote her to leave him thus embarrassed. But again the vision of Bianca—fugitive in her own house, and with something tragic in her mocking immobility—came to her, and she hastened away.

A voice said: " How are you, Mrs. Dallison? Your sister at home ? "

Cecilia saw before her Mr. Purcey, rising and falling a little with the oscillation of his A.1. Damyer.

A sense as of having just left a house visited by sickness or misfortune made Cecilia murmur:

" I'm afraid she's not."

" Bad luck ! " said Mr. Purcey. His face fell as far as so red and square a face could fall. " I was hoping perhaps I might be allowed to take them for a run. She's wanting exercise." Mr. Purcey laid his hand on the flank of his palpitating car. " Know these A.1. Damyers, Mrs. Dallison? Best value you can get, simply rippin' little cars. Wish you'd try her."

The A.1. Damyer, diffusing an aroma of the finest petrol, leaped and trembled, as though conscious of her master's praise. Cecilia looked at her.

" Yes," she said, " she's very sweet."

" Now do ! " said Mr. Purcey. " Let me give you a run— just to please me, I mean. I'm sure you'll like her."

A little compunction, a little curiosity, a sudden revolt against all the discomfiture and sordid doubts she had been suffering from, made Cecilia glance softly at Mr. Purcey's figure; almost before she knew it, she was seated in the A.1. Damyer. It trembled, emitted two small sounds, one large scent, and glided forward. Mr. Purcey said:

"That's rippin' of you!"

A postman, dog, and baker's cart, all hurrying at top speed, seemed to stand still; Cecilia felt the wind beating her cheeks. She gave a little laugh.

"You must just take me home, please."

Mr. Purcey touched the chauffeur's elbow.

"Round the park," he said. "Let her have it."

The A.1. Damyer uttered a tiny shriek. Cecilia, leaning back in her padded corner, glanced askance at Mr. Purcey leaning back in his; an unholy, astonished little smile played on her lips.

'What am I doing?' it seemed to say. 'The way he got me here—really! And now I am here I'm just going to enjoy it!'

There were no Hughses, no little model—all that sordid life had vanished; there was nothing but the wind beating her cheeks and the A.1. Damyer leaping under her.

Mr. Purcey said: "It just makes all the difference to me; keeps my nerves in order."

"Oh," Cecilia murmured, "have *you* got nerves?"

Mr. Purcey smiled. When he smiled his cheeks formed two hard red blocks, his trim moustache stood out, and many little wrinkles ran from his light eyes.

"Chock full of them," he said; "least thing upsets me. Can't bear to see a hungry-lookin' child, or anything."

A strange feeling of admiration for this man had come upon Cecilia. Why could not she, and Thyme, and Hilary and Stephen, and all the people they knew and mixed with be like him, so sound and healthy, so unravaged by disturbing sympathies, so innocent of "social conscience," so content?

As though jealous of these thoughts about her master, the A.1. Damyer stopped of her own accord.

"Hallo," said Mr. Purcey, "hallo, I say! Don't you get out; she'll be all right directly."

"Oh," said Cecilia, "thanks; but I must go in here anyhow; I think I'll say good-bye. Thank you so much. I *have* enjoyed it."

From the threshold of a shop she looked back. Mr. Purcey, on foot, was leaning forward from the waist, staring at his A.1. Damyer with profound concentration.

CHAPTER IX

HILARY GIVES CHASE

THE ethics of a man like Hilary were not those of the million pure-bred Purceys of this life, founded on a sense of property in this world and the next; nor were they precisely the morals and religion of the aristocracy, who, though æstheticised in parts, quietly used, in bulk, their fortified position to graft on Mr. Purcey's ethics the principle of ' You be damned!' In the eyes of the majority he was probably an immoral and irreligious man; but in fact his morals and religion were those of his special section of society—the cultivated classes, " the professors, the artistic pigs, advanced people, and all that sort of cuckoo," as Mr. Purcey called them—a section of society supplemented by persons, placed beyond the realms of want, who speculated in ideas.

Had he been required to make confession of his creed he would probably have framed it in some such way as this: " I disbelieve in all Church dogmas, and do not go to church; I have no definite ideas about a future state, and do not want to have; but in a private way I try to identify myself as much as possible with what I see about me, feeling that if I could ever really be at one with the world I live in I should be happy. I think it foolish not to trust my senses and my reason; as for what my senses and my reason will not tell me, I assume that all is as it had to be, for if one could get to know the why of everything, one would be the Universe. I do not believe that chastity is a virtue in itself, but only so far as it ministers to the health and happiness of the community. I do not believe that marriage confers the rights of ownership, and I loathe all public wrangling on such matters; but I am temperamentally averse to the harming of my neighbours, if in reason it can be avoided. As to manners, I think that to repeat a bit of scandal, and circulate backbiting stories, are worse offences than the actions that give rise to them. If I mentally condemn a person, I feel guilty of moral lapse. I hate self-assertion; I am ashamed of self-advertisement. I dislike loudness of any kind. Probably I have too much tendency to negation of all sorts. Small-talk bores me to extinction, but I will discuss a point of ethics or psychology half the night. To make capital out of a person's weakness is repugnant to me. I want to be a decent man, but—I really can't take myself too seriously."

Though he had preserved his politeness towards Cecilia, he was in truth angry, and grew angrier every minute. He was angry with her, himself, and the man Hughs; and suffered from this anger as only they can who are not accustomed to the rough-and-tumble of things.

Such a retiring man as Hilary was seldom given the opportunity for an obvious display of chivalry. The tenor of his life removed him from those situations. Such chivalry as he displayed was of a negative order. And confronted suddenly with the conduct of Hughs, who, it seemed, knocked his wife about, and dogged the footsteps of a helpless girl, he took it seriously to heart.

When the little model came walking up the garden on her usual visit, he fancied her face looked scared. Quieting the growling of Miranda, who from the first had stubbornly refused to know this girl, he sat down with a book to wait for her to go away. After sitting an hour or more, turning over pages, and knowing little of their sense, he saw a man peer over his garden gate. He was there for half a minute, then lounged across the road, and stood hidden by some railings.

'So?' thought Hilary. 'Shall I go out and warn the fellow to clear off, or shall I wait to see what happens when she goes away?'

He determined on the latter course. Presently she came out, walking with her peculiar gait, youthful and pretty, but too matter-of-fact, and yet, as it were, too purposeless to be a lady's. She looked back at Hilary's window, and turned uphill.

Hilary took his hat and stick and waited. In half a minute Hughs came out from under cover of the railings and followed. Then Hilary, too, set forth.

There is left in every man something of the primeval love of stalking. The delicate Hilary, in cooler blood, would have revolted at the notion of dogging people's footsteps. He now experienced the holy pleasures of the chase. Certain that Hughs was really following the girl, he had but to keep him in sight and remain unseen. This was not hard for a man given to mountain-climbing, almost the only sport left to one who thought it immoral to hurt anybody but himself.

Taking advantage of shop-windows, omnibuses, passers-by, and other bits of cover, he prosecuted the chase up the steepy heights of Campden Hill. But soon a nearly fatal check occurred; for, chancing to take his eyes off Hughs, he saw the little model returning on her tracks. Ready enough in physical emergencies, Hilary sprang into a passing omnibus. He saw her stopping before the window of a picture-shop. From the expression of her face and figure, she evidently had no idea that she was being followed, but stood with a sort of slack-lipped wonder, lost in admiration of a well-known print. Hilary had often wondered who could possibly admire that picture— he now knew. It was obvious that the girl's æsthetic sense was deeply touched.

While this was passing through his mind, he caught sight of Hughs lurking outside a public-house. The dark man's face was sullen and dejected, and looked as if he suffered. Hilary felt a sort of pity for him.

The omnibus leaped forward, and he sat down smartly almost on a lady's lap. This was the lap of Mrs. Tallents Smallpeace, who greeted him with a warm, quiet smile, and made a little room.

"Your sister-in-law has just been to see me, Mr. Dallison. She's such a dear—so interested in everything. I tried to get her to come on to my meeting with me."

Raising his hat, Hilary frowned. For once his delicacy was at fault. He said:

"Ah, yes! Excuse me!" and got out.

Mrs. Tallents Smallpeace looked after him, and then glanced round the omnibus. His conduct was very like the conduct of a man who had got in to keep an assignation with a lady, and found that lady sitting next his aunt. She was unable to see a soul who seemed to foster this view, and sat thinking that he was "rather attractive." Suddenly her dark busy eyes lighted on the figure of the little model strolling along again.

'Oh!' she thought. 'Ah! Yes, really! How very interesting!'

Hilary, to avoid meeting the girl point-blank, had turned up a by-street, and, finding a convenient corner, waited. He was puzzled. If this man were persecuting her with his attentions, why had he not gone across when she was standing at the picture-shop?

She passed across the opening of the by-street, still walking in the slack way of one who takes the pleasures of the streets. She passed from view; Hilary strained his eyes to see if Hughs were following. He waited several minutes. The man did not appear. The chase was over! And suddenly it flashed across him that Hughs had merely dogged her to see that she had no assignation with anybody. They had both been playing the same game! He flushed up in that shady little street, in which he was the only person to be seen. Cecilia was right! It was a sordid business. A man more in touch with facts than Hilary would have had some mental pigeon-hole into which to put an incident like this; but, being by profession concerned mainly with ideas and thoughts, he did not quite know where he was. The habit of his mind precluded him from thinking very definitely on any subject except his literary work—precluded him especially in a matter of this sort, so inextricably entwined with that delicate, dim question, the impact of class on class.

Pondering deeply, he ascended the leafy lane that leads between high railings from Notting Hill to Kensington.

It was so far from traffic that every tree on either side was loud with the Spring songs of birds; the scent of running sap came forth shyly as the sun sank low. Strange peace, strange feeling of old Mother Earth up there above the town; wild tunes, and the quiet sight of clouds. Man in this lane might rest his troubled thoughts, and for a while trust the goodness of the Scheme that gave him birth, the beauty of each day, that laughs or broods itself into night. Some budding lilacs exhaled a scent of lemons; a sandy cat on the coping of a garden wall was basking in the setting sun.

In the centre of the lane a row of elm-trees displayed their gnarled, knotted roots. Human beings were seated there, whose matted hair clung round their tired faces. Their gaunt limbs were clothed in rags; each had a stick, and some sort of dirty bundle tied to it. They were asleep. On a bench beyond, two toothless old women sat, moving their eyes from side to side, and a crimson-faced woman was snoring. Under the next tree a Cockney youth and his girl were sitting side by side—pale young things, with loose mouths, and hollow cheeks, and restless eyes. Their arms were enlaced; they were silent. A little farther on two young men in working clothes were looking straight before them, with desperately tired faces. They, too, were silent.

On the last bench of all Hilary came on the little model, seated slackly by herself.

CHAPTER X

THE TROUSSEAU

This, the first time these two had met each other at large, was clearly not a comfortable event for either of them. The girl blushed, and hastily got off her seat. Hilary, who raised his hat and frowned, sat down on it.

"Don't get up," he said; "I want to talk to you."

The little model obediently resumed her seat. A silence followed. She had on the old brown skirt and knitted jersey, the old blue-green tam-o'-shanter cap, and there were marks of weariness beneath her eyes.

At last Hilary remarked: "How are you getting on?"

The little model looked at her feet.

"Pretty well, thank you, Mr. Dallison."

"I came to see you yesterday."

She slid a look at him which might have meant nothing or meant much, so perfect its shy stolidity.

"I was out," she said, "sitting to Miss Boyle."

"So you have some work?'

"It's finished now."

"Then you're only getting the two shillings a day from Mr. Stone?"

She nodded.

"H'm!"

The unexpected fervour of this grunt seemed to animate the little model.

"Three and sixpence for my rent, and breakfast costs three-pence nearly—only bread-and-butter—that's five and two; and washing's always at least tenpence—that's six; and little things last week was a shilling—even when I don't take buses—seven; that leaves five shillings for my dinners. Mr. Stone always gives me tea. It's my clothes worries me." She tucked her feet farther beneath the seat, and Hilary refrained from looking down. "My hat is awful, and I do want some——" She looked Hilary in the face for the first time. "I do wish I was rich."

"I don't wonder."

The little model gritted her teeth, and, twisting at her dirty

gloves, said: " Mr. Dallison, d'you know the first thing I'd buy
if I was rich? "

" No."

" I'd buy everything new on me from top to toe, and I
wouldn't ever wear any of these old things again."

Hilary got up: " Come with me now, and buy everything
new from top to toe."

" Oh! "

Hilary had already perceived that he had made an awkward,
even dangerous, proposal; short, however, of giving her money,
the idea of which offended his sense of delicacy, there was no
way out of it. He said brusquely: " Come along! "

The little model rose obediently. Hilary noticed that her
boots were split, and this—as though he had seen someone strike
a child—so moved his indignation that he felt no more qualms,
but rather a sort of pleasant glow, such as will come to the
most studious man when he levels a blow at the conventions.

He looked down at his companion—her eyes were lowered;
he could not tell at all what she was thinking of.

" This is what I was going to speak to you about," he said:
" I don't like that house you're in; I think you ought to be somewhere else. What do you say? "

" Yes, Mr. Dallison."

" You'd better make a change, I think; you could find another
room, couldn't you? "

The little model answered as before: " Yes, Mr. Dallison."

" I'm afraid that Hughs is—a dangerous sort of fellow."

" He's a funny man."

" Does he annoy you? "

Her expression baffled Hilary; there seemed a sort of slow
enjoyment in it. She looked up knowingly.

" I don't mind him—he won't hurt me. Mr. Dallison, do
you think blue or green? "

Hilary answered shortly: " Bluey-green."

She clasped her hands, changed her feet with a hop, and went
on walking as before.

" Listen to me," said Hilary; " has Mrs. Hughs been talking
to you about her husband? "

The little model smiled again.

" She goes on," she said.

Hilary bit his lips.

" Mr. Dallison, please—about my hat? "

" What about your hat? "

" Would you like me to get a large one or a small one? "

" For God's sake," answered Hilary, " a small one—no feathers."

" Oh! "

" Can you attend to me a minute? Have either Hughs or Mrs. Hughs spoken to you about—coming to my house, about—me? "

The little model's face remained impassive, but by the movement of her fingers Hilary saw that she was attending now.

" I don't care what they say."

Hilary looked away; an angry flush slowly mounted in his face.

With surprising suddenness the little model said:

" Of course, if I was a lady, I might mind! "

" Don't talk like that! " said Hilary; " every woman is a lady."

The stolidity of the girl's face, more mocking far than any smile, warned him of the cheapness of this verbiage.

" If I was a lady," she repeated simply, " I shouldn't be livin' there, should I? "

" No," said Hilary; " and you had better not go on living there, anyway."

The little model making no answer, Hilary did not quite know what to say. It was becoming apparent to him that she viewed the situation with a very different outlook from himself, and that he did not understand that outlook.

He felt thoroughly at sea, conscious that this girl's life contained a thousand things he did not know, a thousand points of view he did not share.

Their two figures attracted some attention in the crowded street, for Hilary—tall and slight, with his thin, bearded face and soft felt hat—was what is known as " a distinguished-looking man "; and the little model, though not " distinguished-looking " in her old brown skirt and tam-o'-shanter cap, had the sort of face which made men and even women turn to look at her. To men she was a little bit of strangely interesting, not too usual, flesh and blood; to women, she was that which made men turn to look at her. Yet now and again there would rise in some passer-by a feeling more impersonal, as though the God of Pity had shaken wings overhead, and dropped a tiny feather.

So walking, and exciting vague interest, they reached the first of the hundred doors of Messrs. Rose and Thorn.

Hilary had determined on this end door, for, as the adventure grew warmer, he was more alive to its dangers. To take this child into the very shop frequented by his wife and friends seemed a little mad; but that same reason which caused them to frequent it—the fact that there was no other shop of the sort half so handy—was the reason which caused Hilary to go there now. He had acted on impulse; he knew that if he let his impulse cool he would not act at all. The bold course was the wise one; this was why he chose the end door round the corner. Standing aside for her to go in first, he noticed the girl's brightened eyes and cheeks; she had never looked so pretty. He glanced hastily round; the department was barren for their purposes, filled entirely with pyjamas. He felt a touch on his arm. The little model, rather pink, was looking up at him.

"Mr. Dallison, am I to get more than one set of—under-things?"

"Three—three," muttered Hilary; and suddenly he saw that they were on the threshold of that sanctuary. "Buy them," he said, "and bring me the bill."

He waited close beside a man with a pink face, a moustache, and an almost perfect figure, who was standing very still, dressed from head to foot in blue-and-white stripes. He seemed the apotheosis of what a man should be, his face composed in a deathless simper: 'Long, long have been the struggles of man, but civilization has produced me at last. Further than this it cannot go. Nothing shall make me continue my line. In me the end is reached. See my back: "The Amateur. This perfect style, 8s. 11d. Great reduction."'

He would not talk to Hilary, and the latter was compelled to watch the shopmen. It was but half an hour to closing time; the youths were moving languidly, bickering a little, in the absence of their customers—like flies on a pane unable to get out into the sun. Two of them came and asked him what they might serve him with; they were so refined and pleasant that Hilary was on the point of buying what he did not want. The reappearance of the little model saved him.

"It's thirty shillings; five and eleven was the cheapest, and stockings, and I bought some sta——"

Hilary produced the money hastily.

"This is a very dear shop," she said.

When she had paid the bill, and Hilary had taken from her a large brown-paper parcel, they journeyed on together. He had armoured his face now in a slightly startled quizzicality, as though, himself detached, he were watching the adventure from a distance.

On the central velvet seat of the boot and shoe department, a lady, with an egret in her hat, was stretching out a slim silk-stockinged foot, waiting for a boot. She looked with negligent amusement at this common little girl and her singular companion. This look of hers seemed to affect the women serving, for none came near the little model. Hilary saw them eyeing her boots, and, suddenly forgetting his rôle of looker-on, he became very angry. Taking out his watch, he went up to the eldest woman.

"If somebody," he said, "does not attend this young lady within a minute, I shall make a personal complaint to Mr. Thorn."

The hand of the watch, however, had not completed its round before a woman was at the little model's side. Hilary saw her taking off her boot, and by a sudden impulse he placed himself between her and the lady. In doing this, he so far forgot his delicacy as to fix his eyes on the little model's foot. The sense of physical discomfort which first attacked him became a sort of aching in his heart. That brown, dingy stocking was darned till no stocking, only darning, and one toe and two little white bits of foot were seen, where the threads refused to hold together any longer.

The little model wagged the toe uneasily—she had hoped, no doubt, that it would not protrude, then concealed it with her skirt. Hilary moved hastily away; when he looked again, it was not at her, but at the lady.

Her face had changed; it was no longer amused and negligent, but stamped with an expression of offence. 'Intolerable,' it seemed to say, 'to bring a girl like that into a shop like this! I shall never come here again!' The expression was but the outward sign of that inner physical discomfort Hilary himself had felt when he first saw the little model's stocking. This naturally did not serve to lessen his anger, especially as he saw her animus mechanically reproduced on the faces of the serving women.

He went back to the little model, and sat down by her side.

"Does it fit? You'd better walk in it and see."

The little model walked.

" It squeezes me," she said.

" Try another, then," said Hilary.

The lady rose, stood for a second with her eyebrows raised and her nostrils slightly distended, then went away, and left a peculiarly pleasant scent of violets behind.

The second pair of boots not " squeezing " her, the little model was soon ready to go down. She had all her trousseau now, except the dress—selected and, indeed, paid for, but which, as she told Hilary, she was coming back to try on to-morrow, when—when—— She had obviously meant to say when she was all new underneath. She was laden with one large and two small parcels, and in her eyes there was a holy look.

Outside the shop she gazed up in his face.

" Well, you are happy now ? " asked Hilary.

Between the short black lashes were seen two very bright, wet shining eyes; her parted lips began to quiver.

" Good-night, then," he said abruptly, and walked away.

But looking round, he saw her still standing there, half buried in parcels, gazing after him. Raising his hat, he turned into the High Street towards home. . . .

The old man, known to that low class of fellow with whom he was now condemned to associate as " *Westminister*," was taking a whiff or two out of his old clay pipe, and trying to forget his feet. He saw Hilary coming, and carefully extended a copy of the last edition.

" Good-evenin', sir! Quite seasonable to-day for the time of year! Ho yes! *Westminister!* "

His eyes followed Hilary's retreat. He thought:

" Oh dear! He's a-given me an 'arf-a-crown. He does look well—I like to see 'im look as well as that—quite young! Oh dear! "

The sun—that smoky, flaring ball, which in its time had seen so many last editions of the *Westminster Gazette*—was dropping down to pass the night in Shepherd's Bush. It made the old butler's eyelids blink when he turned to see if the coin really was a half-crown, or too good to be true.

And all the spires and house-roofs, and the spaces up above and underneath them, glittered and swam, and men and horses looked as if they had been powdered with golden dust.

CHAPTER XI

PEAR BLOSSOM

WEIGHED down by her three parcels, the little model pursued her way to Hound Street. At the door of No. 1 the son of the lame woman, a tall weedy youth with a white face, was resting his legs alternately, and smoking a cigarette. Closing one eye, he addressed her thus:

" 'Allo, miss! Kerry your parcels for you?"

The little model gave him a look. 'Mind your own business!' it said; but there was that in the flicker of her eyelashes which more than nullified this snub.

Entering her room, she deposited the parcels on her bed, and untied the strings with quick, pink fingers. When she had freed the garments from wrappings and spread them out, she knelt down, and began to touch them, putting her nose down once or twice to sniff the linen and feel its texture. There were little frills attached here and there, and to these she paid particular attention, ruffling their edges with the palms of her hands, while the holy look came back to her face. Rising at length, she locked the door, drew down the blind, undressed from head to foot, and put on the new garments. Letting her hair down, she turned herself luxuriously round and round before the too-small looking-glass. There was utter satisfaction in each gesture of that whole operation, as if her spirit, long starved, were having a good meal. In this rapt contemplation of herself, all childish vanity and expectancy, and all that wonderful quality found in simple unspiritual natures of delighting in the present moment, were perfectly displayed. So, motionless, with her hair loose on her neck, she was like one of those half-hours of Spring that have lost their restlessness and are content just to *be*.

Presently, however, as though suddenly remembering that her happiness was not utterly complete, she went to a drawer, took out a packet of pear-drops, and put one in her mouth.

The sun, near to setting, had found its way through a hole in the blind, and touched her neck. She turned as though she had received a kiss, and, raising a corner of the blind, peered out.

The pear-tree, which, to the annoyance of its proprietor, was placed so close to the back court of this low-class house as almost to seem to belong to it, was bathed in slanting sunlight. No tree in all the world could have looked more fair than it did just then in its garb of gilded bloom. With her hand up to her bare neck, and her cheeks indrawn from sucking the sweet, the little model fixed her eyes on the tree. Her expression did not change; she showed no signs of admiration. Her gaze passed on to the back windows of the house that really owned the pear-tree, spying out whether anyone could see her—hoping, perhaps, someone *would* see her while she was feeling so nice and new. Then, dropping the blind, she went back to the glass and began to pin her hair up. When this was done she stood for a long minute looking at her old brown skirt and blouse, hesitating to defile her new-found purity. At last she put them on and drew up the blind. The sunlight had passed off the pear-tree; its bloom was now white, and almost as still as snow. The little model put another sweet into her mouth, and producing from her pocket an ancient leather purse, counted out her money. Evidently discovering that it was no more than she expected, she sighed, and rummaged out of a top drawer an old illustrated magazine.

She sat down on the bed, and, turning the leaves rapidly till she reached a certain page, rested the paper in her lap. Her eyes were fixed on a photograph in the left-hand corner— one of those effigies of writers that appear occasionally in the public press. Under it were printed the words: " Mr. Hilary Dallison." And suddenly she heaved a sigh.

The room grew darker; the wind, getting up as the sun went down, blew a few dropped petals of the pear-tree against the window-pane.

CHAPTER XII

SHIPS IN SAIL

In due accord with the old butler's comment on his looks, Hilary had felt so young that, instead of going home, he mounted an omnibus, and went down to his club—the "Pen and Ink," so called because the man who founded it could not think at the moment of any other words. This literary person had left the club soon after its initiation, having conceived for it a sudden dislike. It had indeed a certain reputation for bad cooking, and all its members complained bitterly at times that you never could go in without meeting someone you knew. It stood in Dover Street. Unlike other clubs, it was mainly used to talk in, and had special arrangements for the safety of umbrellas and such books as had not yet vanished from the library; not, of course, owing to any peculative tendency among its members, but because, after interchanging their ideas, those members would depart, in a long row, each grasping some material object in his hand. Its maroon-coloured curtains, too, were never drawn, because, in the heat of their discussions, the members were always drawing them. On the whole, those members did not like each other much; wondering a little, one by one, why the others wrote; and when the printed reasons were detailed to them, reading them with irritation. If really compelled to hazard an opinion about each other's merits, they used to say that, no doubt " So-and-so " was " very good," but they had never read him! For it had early been established as the principle underlying membership not to read the writings of another man, unless you could be certain he was dead, lest you might have to tell him to his face that you disliked his work. For they were very jealous of the purity of their literary consciences. Exception was made, however, in the case of those who lived by written criticism, the opinions of such persons being read by all, with a varying smile, and a certain cerebral excitement. Now and then, however, some member, violating every sense of decency, would take a violent liking for another member's books. This he would express in words, to the discomfort of his fellows, who, with a sudden chilly feeling in

300

the stomach, would wonder why it was not their books that he was praising.

Almost every year, and generally in March, certain aspirations would pass into the club; members would ask each other why there was no Academy of British Letters; why there was no concerted movement to limit the production of other authors' books; why there was no prize given for the best work of the year. For a little time it almost seemed as if their individualism were in danger; but, the windows maving been opened wider than usual some morning, the aspirations would pass out, and all would feel secretly as a man feels when he has swallowed the mosquito that has been worrying him all night—relieved, but just a little bit embarrassed. Socially sympathetic in their dealings with each other—they were mostly quite nice fellows— each kept a little fame-machine, on which he might be seen sitting every morning about the time the papers and his correspondence came, wondering if his fame were going up.

Hilary stayed in the club till half-past nine; then, avoiding a discussion which was just setting in, he took his own umbrella, and bent his steps towards home.

It was the moment of suspense in Piccadilly; the tide had flowed up to the theatres, and had not yet begun to ebb. The tranquil trees, still feathery, draped their branches along the farther bank of that broad river, resting from their watch over the tragi-comedies played on its surface by men, their small companions. The gentle sighs which distilled from their plume-like boughs seemed utterances of the softest wisdom. Not far beyond their trunks it was all dark velvet, into which separate shapes, adventuring, were lost, as wild birds vanishing in space, or the souls of men received into their Mother's heart.

Hilary walked, hearing no sighs of wisdom, noting no smooth darkness, wrapped in thought. The mere fact of having given pleasure was enough to produce a warm sensation in a man so naturally kind. But, as with all self-conscious, self-distrustful, natures, that sensation had not lasted. He was left with a feeling of emptiness and disillusionment, as of having given himself a good mark without reason.

While walking, he was a target for the eyes of many women, who passed him rapidly, like ships in sail. The special fastidious shyness of his face attracted those accustomed to another kind of face. And though he did not precisely look at them, they in turn inspired in him the compassionate, morbid curiosity which persons who live desperate lives necessarily inspire in the leisured, speculative mind. One of them deliberately approached him from a side-street. Though taller and fuller, with heightened colour, frizzy hair, and a hat with feathers, she was the image of the little model—the same shape of face, broad cheekbones, mouth a little open; the same flower-coloured eyes and short black lashes, all coarsened and accentuated as Art coarsens and accentuates the lines of life. Looking boldly into Hilary's startled face, she laughed. Hilary winced and walked on quickly.

He reached home at half-past ten. The lamp was burning in Mr. Stone's room, and his window was, as usual, open; that which was not usual, however, was a light in Hilary's own bedroom. He went gently up. Through the door—ajar—he saw, to his surprise, the figure of his wife. She was reclining in a chair, her elbows on its arms, the tips of her fingers pressed together. Her face, with its dark hair, vivid colouring, and sharp lines, was touched with shadows, her head turned as though towards somebody beside her; her neck gleamed white. So—motionless, dimly seen—she was like a woman sitting alongside her own life, scrutinising, criticising, watching it live, taking no part in it. Hilary wondered whether to go in or slip away from his strange visitor.

"Ah! it's you," she said.

Hilary approached her. For all her mocking of her own charms, this wife of his was strangely graceful. After nineteen years in which to learn every line of her face and body, every secret of her nature, she still eluded him; that elusiveness, which had begun by being such a charm, had got on his nerves, and extinguished the flame it had once lighted. He had so often tried to see, and never seen, the essence of her soul. Why was she made like this? Why was she for ever mocking herself, himself, and every other thing? Why was she so hard to her own life, so bitter a foe to her own happiness? Leonardo da Vinci might have painted her, less sensual and cruel than his women, more restless and disharmonic, but physically, spiritually enticing, and, by her refusals to surrender either to her spirit or her senses, baffling her own enticements.

"I don't know why I came," she said.

Hilary found no better answer than: "I am sorry I was out to dinner."

"Has the wind gone round? My room is cold."

"Yes, north-east. Stay here."

Her hand touched his; that warm and restless clasp was agitating.

"It's good of you to ask me; but we'd better not begin what we can't keep up."

"Stay here," said Hilary again, kneeling down beside her chair.

And suddenly he began to kiss her face and neck. He felt her answering kisses; for a moment they were clasped together in a fierce embrace. Then, as though by mutual consent, their arms relaxed; their eyes grew furtive, like the eyes of children who have egged each other on to steal; and on their lips appeared the faintest of faint smiles. It was as though those lips were saying: 'Yes, but we are not quite animals!'

Hilary got up and sat down on his bed. Bianca stayed in the chair, looking straight before her, utterly inert, her head thrown back, her white throat gleaming, on her lips and in her eyes that flickering smile. Not a word more, nor a look, passed between them.

Then rising, without noise, she passed behind him and went out.

Hilary had a feeling in his mouth as though he had been chewing ashes. And a phrase—as phrases sometimes fill the spirit of a man without rhyme or reason—kept forming on his lips: "The house of harmony!"

Presently he went to her door, and stood there listening. He could hear no sound whatever. If she had been crying—if she had been laughing—it would have been better than this silence. He put his hands up to his ears and ran downstairs.

CHAPTER XIII

SOUND IN THE NIGHT

PASSING his study door, he halted at Mr. Stone's; the thought of the old man, so steady and absorbed in the face of all external things, refreshed him.

Still in his brown woollen gown, Mr. Stone was sitting with his eyes fixed on something in the corner, whence a little perfumed steam was rising.

"Shut the door," he said; "I am making cocoa; will you have a cup?"

"Am I disturbing you?" asked Hilary.

Mr. Stone looked at him steadily before answering:

"If I work after cocoa, I find it clogs the liver."

"Then, if you'll let me, sir, I'll stay a little."

"It is boiling," said Mr. Stone. He took the saucepan off the flame, and, distending his frail cheeks, blew. Then, while the steam mingled with his frosty beard, he brought two cups from a cupboard, filled one of them, and looked at Hilary.

"I should like you," he said, "to hear three or four pages I have just completed; you may perhaps be able to suggest a word or two."

He placed the saucepan back on the stove, and grasped the cup he had filled.

"I will drink my cocoa, and read them to you."

Going to the desk, he stood, blowing at the cup.

Hilary turned up the collar of his coat against the night wind which was visiting the room, and glanced at the empty cup, for he was rather hungry. He heard a curious sound: Mr. Stone was blowing his own tongue. In his haste to read, he had drunk too soon and deeply of the cocoa.

"I have burnt my mouth," he said.

Hilary moved hastily towards him: "Badly? Try cold milk, sir."

Mr. Stone lifted the cup.

"There is none," he said, and drank again.

'What would I not give,' thought Hilary, 'to have his singleness of heart!'

There was the sharp sound of a cup set down. Then, out of a rustling of papers, a sort of droning rose:

" ' The Proletariat—with a cynicism natural to those who really are in want, and even amongst their leaders only veiled when these attained a certain position in the public eyes—desired indeed the wealth and leisure of their richer neighbors, but in their long night of struggle with existence they had only found the energy to formulate their pressing needs from day to day. They were a heaving, surging sea of creatures, slowly, without consciousness or real guidance, rising in long tidal movements to set the limits of the shore a little farther back, and cast afresh the form of social life; and on its peagreen bosom——' " Mr. Stone paused. " She has copied it wrong," he said; " the word is ' sea-green.' ' And on its sea-green bosom sailed a fleet of silver cockle-shells, wafted by the breath of those not in themselves driven by the wind of need. The voyage of these silver cockle-shells, all heading across each other's bows, was, in fact, the advanced movement of that time. In the stern of each of these little craft, blowing at the sails, was seated a by-product of the accepted system. These by-products we should now examine.' "

Mr. Stone paused, and looked into his cup. There were some grounds in it. He drank them, and went on:

" ' The fratricidal principle of the survival of the fittest, which in those days was England's moral teaching, had made the country one huge butcher's shop. Amongst the carcasses of countless victims there had fattened and grown purple many butchers, physically strengthened by the smell of blood and sawdust. These had begotten many children. Following out the laws of Nature providing against surfeit, a proportion of these children were born with a feeling of distaste for blood and sawdust; many of them, compelled for the purpose of making money to follow in their fathers' practices, did so unwillingly; some, thanks to their fathers' butchery, were in a position to abstain from practising; but whether in practice or at leisure, distaste for the scent of blood and sawdust was the common feature that distinguished them. Qualities hitherto but little known, and generally despised—not, as we shall see, without some reason—were developed in them. Self-consciousness, æstheticism, a dislike for waste, a hatred of injustice; these—or some one of these, when coupled with that desire natural to men throughout all ages to accomplish something—constituted the motive forces which enabled them to work their bellows. In practical affairs those who were under the necessity of labouring were driven, under the then machinery of social life, to the humaner and less exacting kinds of butchery, such as the Arts, Education, the practice of Religions and Medicine, and the paid representation of their fellow-creatures. Those not so driven occupied themselves in observing and complaining of the existing state of things. Each year saw more of their silver cockle-shells putting out from port, and the cheeks of those who blew the sails more violently distended. Looking back on that pretty voyage, we see the reason why those ships were doomed never to move, but, seated on the sea-green bosom of that sea, to heave up and down, heading across each other's bows in the self-same place for ever. That reason, in few words, was this: "The man who blew should have been in the sea, not on the ship." ' "

The droning ceased. Hilary saw that Mr. Stone was staring fixedly at his sheet of paper, as though the merits of this last sentence were surprising him. The droning instantly began again: " 'In social effort, as in the physical processes of Nature, there had ever been a single fertilising agent—the mysterious and wonderful attraction known as Love. To this— that merging of one being in another—had been due all the progressive variance of form, known by man under the name of Life. It was this merger, this mysterious, unconscious Love, which was lacking to the windy efforts of those who tried to sail that fleet. They were full of reason, conscience, horror, full of impatience, contempt, revolt; but they did not *love* the masses of their fellow-men. They could not fling themselves into the sea. Their hearts were glowing; but the wind which made them glow was not the salt and universal zephyr; it was the desert wind of scorn. As with the flowering of the aloe-tree—so long awaited, so strange and swift when once it comes—man had yet to wait for his delirious impulse to Universal Brotherhood, and the forgetfulness of Self.' "

Mr. Stone had finished, and stood gazing at his visitor with eyes that clearly saw beyond him. Hilary could not meet those eyes; he kept his own fixed on the empty cocoa cup. It was not, in fact, usual for those who heard Mr. Stone read his manuscript to look him in the face. He stood thus absorbed so long that Hilary rose at last, and glanced into the saucepan. There was no cocoa in it. Mr. Stone had only made enough for one. He

had meant it for his visitor, but self-forgetfulness had super-
vened.

"You know what happens to the aloe, sir, when it has flowered?" asked Hilary with malice.

Mr. Stone moved, but did not answer.

"It dies," said Hilary.

"No," said Mr. Stone; "it is at peace."

"When is self at peace, sir? The individual is surely as
immortal as the universal. That is the eternal comedy of life."

"What is?" said Mr. Stone.

"The fight or game between the two."

Mr. Stone stood a moment looking wistfully at his son-in-law.
He laid down the sheet of manuscript. "It is time for me to
do my exercises." So saying, he undid the tasselled cord tied
round the middle of his gown.

Hilary hastened to the door. From that point of vantage he
looked back.

Divested of his gown and turned towards the window, Mr.
Stone was already rising on his toes, his arms were extended,
his palms pressed hard together in the attitude of prayer, his
trousers slowly slipping down.

"One, two, three, four, five!" There was a sudden sound
of breath escaping. . . .

In the corridor upstairs, flooded with moonlight from a window at the end, Hilary stood listening again. The only sound
that came to him was the light snoring of Miranda, who slept
in the bathroom, not caring to lie too near to anyone. He went
to his room, and for a long time sat buried in thought; then,
opening the side window, he leaned out. On the trees of the
next garden, and the sloping roofs of stables and outhouses, the
moonlight had come down like a flight of milk-white pigeons;
with outspread wings, vibrating faintly as though yet in motion, they covered everything. Nothing stirred. A clock was
striking two. Past that flight of milk-white pigeons were black
walls as yet unvisited. Then, in the stillness, Hilary seemed to
hear, deep and very faint, the sound as of some monster breathing, or the far beating of muffled drums. From every side of the
pale sleeping town it seemed to come, under the moon's cold
glamour. It rose, and fell, and rose, with a weird, creepy
rhythm, like a groaning of the hopeless and hungry. A hansom
cab rattled down the High Street; Hilary strained his ears after
the failing clatter of hoofs and bell. They died; there was

silence. Creeping nearer, drumming, throbbing, he heard again the beating of that vast heart. It grew and grew. His own heart began thumping. Then, emerging from that sinister dumb groan, he distinguished a crunching sound, and knew that it was no muttering echo of men's struggles, but only the waggons journeying to Covent Garden Market.

CHAPTER XIV

A WALK ABROAD

THYME DALLISON, in the midst of her busy life, found leisure to record her recollections and ideas in the pages of old school notebooks. She had no definite purpose in so doing, nor did she desire the solace of luxuriating in her private feelings—this she would have scorned as out of date and silly. It was done from the fulness of youthful energy, and from the desire to express oneself that was "in the air." It was everywhere, that desire: among her fellow-students, among her young men friends, in her mother's drawing-room, and her aunt's studio. Like sentiment and marriage to the Victorian miss, so was this duty to express herself to Thyme; and, going hand-in-hand with it, the duty to have a good and jolly youth. She never read again the thoughts which she recorded, she took no care to lock them up, knowing that her liberty, development, and pleasure were sacred things which no one would dream of touching—she kept them stuffed down in a drawer among her handkerchiefs and ties and blouses, together with the indelible fragment of a pencil.

This journal, naïve and slipshod, recorded without order the current impression of things on her mind.

In the early morning of the 4th of May she sat, night-gowned, on the foot of her white bed, with chestnut hair all fluffy about her neck, eyes bright and cheeks still rosy with sleep, scribbling away and rubbing one bare foot against the other in the ecstasy of self-expression. Now and then, in the middle of a sentence, she would stop and look out of the window, or stretch herself deliciously, as though life were too full of joy for her to finish anything.

"I went into grandfather's room yesterday, and stayed while he was dictating to the little model. I do think grandfather's so splendid. Martin says an enthusiast is worse than useless; people, he says, can't afford to dabble in ideas or dreams. He calls grandfather's idea palæolithic. I hate him to be laughed at. Martin's so cocksure. I don't think he'd find many men of eighty who'd bathe in the Serpentine all the year round, and do his own room, cook his own food, and live on about ninety pounds a year out of his pension of three hundred, and give all the rest away. Martin says that's unsound, and the 'Book of Universal Brotherhood' rot. I don't care if it is; it's fine to go on writing it as he does all day. Martin admits that. That's the worst of him: he's so cool, you can't score him off; he seems to be always criticising you; it makes me wild. . . . That little model is a hopeless duffer. I could have taken it all down in half the time. She kept stopping and looking up with that mouth of hers half open, as if she had all day before her. Grandfather's so absorbed he doesn't notice; he likes to read the thing over and over, to hear how the words sound. That girl would be no good at any sort of work, except 'sitting,' I suppose. Aunt B. used to say she sat well. There's something queer about her face; it reminds me a little of that Botticelli Madonna in the National Gallery, the full-face one; not so much in the shape as in the expression—almost stupid, and yet as if things were going to happen to her. Her hands and arms are pretty, and her feet are smaller than mine. She's two years older than me. I asked her why she went in for being a model, which is beastly work. She said she was glad to get anything! I asked her why she didn't go into a shop or into service. She didn't answer at once, and then said she hadn't had any recommendations—didn't know where to try; then, all of a sudden, she grew quite sulky, and said she didn't want to. . . ."

Thyme paused to pencil in a sketch of the little model's profile. . . .

"She had on a really pretty frock, quite simple and well made—it must have cost three or four pounds. She can't be so very badly off, or somebody gave it her. . . ."

And again Thyme paused.

"She looked ever so much prettier in it than she used to in her old brown skirt, I thought. . . . Uncle Hilary came to dinner last night. We talked of social questions; we always discuss things when he comes. I can't help liking Uncle Hilary; he has such kind eyes, and he's so gentle that you never lose your temper with him. Martin calls him weak and unsatisfactory because he's not in touch with life. I should say it was more as if he couldn't bear to force anyone to do anything; he seems to see both sides of every question, and he's not good at making up his mind, of course. He's rather like Hamlet might have been, only nobody seems to know now what Hamlet was really like. I told him what I thought about the lower classes. One can talk to him. I hate father's way of making feeble little jokes, as if nothing were serious. I said I didn't think it was any use to dabble; we ought to go to the root of everything. I said that money and class distinctions are two bogeys we have got to lay. Martin says, when it comes to real dealing with social questions and the poor, all the people we know are amateurs. He says that we have got to shake ourselves free of all the old sentimental notions, and just work at putting everything to the test of Health. Father calls Martin a 'Sanitist'; and Uncle Hilary says that if you wash people by *law* they'll all be as dirty again to-morrow. . . ."

Thyme paused again. A blackbird in the garden of the Square was uttering a long, low, chuckling trill. She ran to the window and peeped out. The bird was on a plane-tree, and, with throat uplifted, was letting through his yellow beak that delicious piece of self-expression. All things seemed to praise—the sky, the sun, the trees, the dewy grass, himself!

'You darling!' thought Thyme. With a shudder of delight she dropped her notebook back into the drawer, flung off her nightgown, and flew into her bath.

That same morning she slipped out quietly at ten o'clock. Her Saturdays were free of classes, but she had to run the gauntlet of her mother's liking for her company and her father's wish for her to go with him to Richmond and play golf. For on Saturdays Stephen almost always left the precincts of the Courts before three o'clock. Then, if he could induce his wife or daughter to accompany him, he liked to get a round or two in preparation for Sunday, when he always started off at half-past ten and played all day. If Cecilia and Thyme failed him, he would go to his club, and keep himself in touch with every kind of social movement by reading the reviews.

Thyme walked along with her head up and a wrinkle in her brow, as though she were absorbed in serious reflection; if admiring glances were flung at her, she did not seem aware of them. Passing not far from Hilary's, she entered the Broad Walk, and crossed it to the farther end.

On a railing, stretching out his long legs and observing the passers-by, sat her cousin, Martin Stone. He got down as she came up.

"Late again," he said. "Come on!"

" Where are we going first? " Thyme asked.

" The Notting Hill district's all we can do to-day if we're to go again to Mrs. Hughs'. I must be down at the hospital this afternoon."

Thyme frowned. " I do envy you living by yourself, Martin. It's silly having to live at home."

Martin did not answer, but one nostril of his long nose was seen to curve, and Thyme acquiesced in this without remark. They walked for some minutes between tall houses, looking about them calmly. Then Martin said: " All Purceys round here."

Thyme nodded. Again there was silence; but in these pauses there was no embarrassment, no consciousness apparently that it was silence, and their eyes—those young, impatient, interested eyes—were for ever busy observing.

" Boundary line. We shall be in a patch directly."

" Black? " asked Thyme.

" Dark blue—black farther on."

They were passing down a long, grey, curving road, whose narrow houses, hopelessly unpainted, showed marks of grinding poverty. The Spring wind was ruffling straw and little bits of paper in the gutters; under the bright sunlight a bleak and bitter struggle seemed raging. Thyme said:

" This street gives me a hollow feeling."

Martin nodded. " Worse than the real article. There's half a mile of this. Here it's all grim fighting. Farther on they've given it up."

And still they went on up the curving street, with its few pinched shops and its unending narrow grimness.

At the corner of a by-street Martin said: " We'll go down here."

Thyme stood still, wrinkling her nose. Martin eyed her.

" Don't funk! "

" I'm not funking, Martin, only I can't stand the smells."

" You'll have to get used to them."

" Yes, I know; but—but I forgot my eucalyptus."

The young man took out a handkerchief which had not yet been unfolded.

" Here, take mine."

" They do make me feel so—it's a shame to take yours," and she took the handkerchief.

" That's all right," said Martin. " Come on! "

The houses of this narrow street, inside and out, seemed full of women. Many of them had babies in their arms; they were working or looking out of windows or gossiping on doorsteps. And all stopped to stare as the young couple passed. Thyme stole a look at her companion. His long stride had not varied; there was the usual pale, observant, sarcastic expression on his face. Clenching the handkerchief in readiness, and trying to imitate his callous air, she looked at a group of five women on the nearest doorstep. Three were seated and two were standing. One of these, a young woman with a round, open face, was clearly very soon to have a child; the other, with a short, dark face and iron-grey, straggling hair, was smoking a clay pipe. Of the three seated, one, quite young, had a face as grey-white as a dirty sheet, and a blackened eye; the second, with her ragged dress disarranged, was nursing a baby; the third, in the centre, on the top step, with red arms akimbo, her face scored with drink, was shouting friendly obscenities to a neighbour in the window opposite. In Thyme's heart rose the passionate feeling, 'How disgusting! how *disgusting!*' and since she did not dare to give expression to it, she bit her lips and turned her head from them, resenting, with all a young girl's horror, that her sex had given her away. The women stared at her, and in those faces, according to their different temperaments, could be seen first the same vague, hard interest that had been Thyme's when she first looked at them, then the same secret hostility and criticism, as though they too felt that by this young girl's untouched modesty, by her flushed cheeks and un-soiled clothes, their sex had given *them* away. With contemptu-ous movements of their lips and bodies, on that doorstep they proclaimed their emphatic belief in the virtue and reality of their own existences and in the vice and unreality of her in-truding presence

" Give the doll to Bill; 'e'd make 'er work for once, the——"
In a burst of laughter the epithet was lost.

Martin's lips curled.

" Purple just here," he said.

Thyme's cheeks were crimson.

At the end of the little street he stopped before a shop.

" Come on," he said, " you'll see the sort of place where they buy their grub."

In the doorway were standing a thin brown spaniel, a small fair woman with a high, bald forehead, from which the hair was gleaned into curl-papers, and a little girl with some affection of the skin.

Nodding coolly, Martin motioned them aside. The shop was ten feet square; its counters, running parallel to two of the walls, were covered with plates of cake, sausages, old ham-bones, peppermint sweets, and household soap; there was also bread, margarine, suet in bowls, sugar, bloaters—many bloaters—Captain's biscuits, and other things besides. Two or three dead rabbits hung against the wall. All was uncovered, so that what flies there were sat feeding socialistically. Behind the counter a girl of seventeen was serving a thin-faced woman with portions of a cheese which she was holding down with her strong, dirty hand, while she sawed it with a knife. On the counter, next the cheese, sat a quiet-looking cat.

They all glanced round at the two young people, who stood and waited.

" Finish what you're at," said Martin, " then give me three pennyworth of bull's-eyes."

The girl, with a violent effort, finished severing the cheese. The thin-faced woman took it, and, coughing above it, went away. The girl, who could not take her eyes off Thyme, now served them with three pennyworth of bull's-eyes, which she took out with her fingers, for they had stuck. Putting them in a screw of newspaper, she handed them to Martin. The young man, who had been observing negligently, touched Thyme's elbow. She, who had stood with eyes cast down, now turned. They went out, Martin handing the bull's-eyes to the little girl with an affection of the skin.

The street now ended in a wide road formed of little low houses.

" Black," said Martin, " here; all down this road—casual labour, criminals, loafers, drunkards, consumps. Look at the faces ! "

Thyme raised her eyes obediently. In this main thoroughfare it was not as in the by-street, and only dull or sullen glances, or none at all, were bent on her. Some of the houses had ragged plants on the window-sills; in one window a canary was singing. Then, at a bend, they came into a blacker reach of human river. Here were outbuildings, houses with broken windows, houses with windows boarded up, fried-fish shops, low public-houses, houses without doors. There were more men here than women, and those men were wheeling barrows full of rags and bottles, or not even full of rags and bottles; or they were standing by the public-houses gossiping or quarreling in groups of three or four; or very slowly walking in the gutters, or on the pavements, as though trying to remember if they were alive. Then suddenly some young man with gaunt violence in his face would pass, pushing his barrow desperately, striding fiercely by. And every now and then, from a fried-fish or hardware shop, would come out a man in a dirty apron to take the sun and contemplate the scene, not finding in it, seemingly, anything that in any way depressed his spirit. Amongst the constant, crawling, shifting stream of passengers were seen women carrying food wrapped up in newspaper, or with bundles beneath their shawls. The faces of these women were generally either very red and coarse or of a sort of bluish-white; they wore the expression of such as know themselves to be existing in the way that Providence has arranged they should exist. No surprise, revolt, dismay, or shame was ever to be seen on those faces; in place of these emotions a drab and brutish acquiescence or mechanical coarse jocularity. To pass like this about their business was their occupation each morning of the year; it was needful to accept it. Not having any hope of ever being different, not being able to imagine any other life, they were not so wasteful of their strength as to attempt either to hope or to imagine. Here and there, too, very slowly passed old men and women, crawling along, like winter bees who, in some strange and evil moment, had forgotten to die in the sunlight of their toil, and, too old to be of use, had been chivied forth from their hive to perish slowly in the cold twilight of their days.

Down the centre of the street Thyme saw a brewer's dray creeping its way due south under the sun. Three horses drew it, with braided tails and beribboned manes, the brass glittering on their harness. High up, like a god, sat the drayman, his little slits of eyes above huge red cheeks fixed immovably on his horses' crests. Behind him, with slow, unceasing crunch, the dray rolled, piled up with hogsheads, whereon the drayman's mate lay sleeping. Like the slumbrous image of some mighty unrelenting Power, it passed, proud that its monstrous bulk contained all the joy and blessing those shadows on the pavement had ever known.

The two young people emerged on to the high road running east and west.

"Cross here," said Martin, "and cut down into Kensington.

Nothing more of interest now till we get to Hound Street. Purceys and Purceys all round about this part."

Thyme shook herself.

"O Martin, let's go down a road where there's some air. I feel so dirty." She put her hand up to her chest.

"There's one here," said Martin.

They turned to the left into a road that had many trees. Now that she could breathe and look about her, Thyme once more held her head erect and began to swing her arms.

"Martin, something must be done!"

The young doctor did not reply; his face still wore its pale, sarcastic, observant look. He gave her arm a squeeze with a half-contemptuous smile.

CHAPTER XV

SECOND PILGRIMAGE TO HOUND STREET

ARRIVING in Hound Street, Martin Stone and his companion went straight up to Mrs. Hughs' front room. They found her doing the week's washing, and hanging out before a scanty fire part of the little that the week had been suffered to soil. Her arms were bare, her face and eyes red; the steam of soapsuds had congealed on them.

Attached to the bolster by a towel, under his father's bayonet and the oleograph depicting the Nativity, sat the baby. In the air there was the scent of him, of walls, and washing, and red herrings. The two young people took their seats on the window-sill.

"May we open the window, Mrs. Hughs?" said Thyme. "Or will it hurt the baby?"

"No, miss."

"What's the matter with your wrists?" asked Martin.

The seamstress, muffling her arms with the garment she was dipping in soapy water, did not answer.

"Don't do that. Let me have a look."

Mrs. Hughs held out her arms; the wrists were swollen and discoloured.

"The brute!" cried Thyme.

The young doctor muttered: "Done last night. Got any arnica?"

"No, sir."

"Of course not." He laid a sixpence on the sill. "Get some and rub it in. Mind you don't break the skin."

Thyme suddenly burst out: "Why don't you leave him, Mrs. Hughs? Why do you live with a brute like that?"

Martin frowned.

"Any particular row," he said, "or only just the ordinary?"

Mrs. Hughs turned her face to the scanty fire. Her shoulders heaved spasmodically.

Thus passed three minutes, then she again began rubbing the soapy garment.

"If you don't mind, I'll smoke," said Martin. "What's your

317

baby's name? Bill? Here, Bill!" He placed his little finger in the baby's hand. "Feeding him yourself?"

"Yes, sir."

"What's his number?"

"I've lost three, sir; there's only his brother Stanley now."

"One a year?"

"No, sir. I missed two years in the war, of course."

"Hughs wounded out there?"

"Yes, sir—in the head."

"Ah! And fever?"

"Yes, sir."

Martin tapped his pipe against his forehead. "Least drop of liquor goes to it, I suppose?"

Mrs. Hughs paused in the dipping of a cloth; her tear-stained face expressed resentment, as though she had detected an attempt to find excuses for her husband.

"He didn't ought to treat me as he does," she said.

All three now stood round the bed, over which the baby presided with solemn gaze.

Thyme said: "I wouldn't care what he did, Mrs. Hughs; I wouldn't stay another day if I were you. It's your duty as a woman."

To hear her duty as a woman Mrs. Hughs turned; slow vindictiveness gathered on her thin face.

"Yes, miss?" she said. "I don't know what to do."

"Take the children and go. What's the good of waiting? We'll give you money if you haven't got enough."

But Mrs. Hughs did not answer.

"Well?" said Martin, blowing out a cloud of smoke.

Thyme burst out again: "Just go, the very minute your little boy comes back from school. Hughs 'll never find you. It'll serve him right. No woman ought to put up with what you have; it's simply weakness, Mrs. Hughs."

As though that word had forced its way into her very heart and set the blood free suddenly, Mrs. Hughs' face turned the colour of tomatoes. She poured forth words:

"And leave him to that young· girl—and leave him to his wickedness! After I've been his wife eight years and borne him five! after I've done what I have for him! I never want no better husband that what he used to be, till *she* came with her pale face and her prinky manners, and—and her mouth that you can tell she's bad by. Let her keep to her profession—sitting naked's

what she's fit for—coming here to decent folk——" And holding out her wrists to Thyme, who had shrunk back, she cried:
" He's never struck me before. I got these all because of her
new clothes ! "

Hearing his mother speak with such strange passion, the
baby howled. Mrs. Hughs stopped, and took him up. Pressing
him close to her thin bosom, she looked above his little dingy
head at the two young people.

" I got my wrists like this last night, wrestling with him.
He swore he'd go and leave me, but I held him, I did. And
don't you ever think that I'll let him go to that young girl—
not if he kills me first ! "

With those words the passion in her face died down. She
was again a meek, mute woman.

During this outbreak, Thyme, shrinking, stood by the doorway with lowered eyes. She now looked up at Martin, clearly
asking him to come away. The latter had kept his gaze fixed
on Mrs. Hughs, smoking silently. He took his pipe out of his
mouth, and pointed with it at the baby.

" This gentleman," he said, " can't stand too much of that."

In silence all three bent their eyes on the baby. His little
fists, and nose, and forehead, even his little naked, crinkled feet,
were thrust with all his feeble strength against his mother's
bosom, as though he were striving to creep into some hole away
from life. There was a sort of dumb despair in that tiny pushing of his way back to the place whence he had come. His
head, covered with dingy down, quivered with his effort to
escape. He had been alive so little; that little had sufficed.
Martin put his pipe back into his mouth.

" This won't do, you know," he said. " He can't stand it.
And look here ! If you stop feeding him, I wouldn't give that
for him to-morrow ! " He held up the circle of his thumb and
finger. " You're the best judge of what sort of chance you've
got of going on in your present state of mind ! " Then, motioning to Thyme, he went down the stairs.

CHAPTER XVI

BENEATH THE ELMS

SPRING was in the hearts of men, and their tall companions, trees. Their troubles, the stiflings of each other's growth, and all such things, seemed of little moment. Spring had them by the throat. It turned old men round, and made them stare at women younger than themselves. It made young men and women walking side by side touch each other, and every bird on the branches tune his pipe. Flying sunlight speckled the fluttered leaves, and flushed the cheeks of crippled boys who limped into the Gardens, till their pale Cockney faces shone with a strange glow.

In the Broad Walk, beneath those dangerous trees, the elms, people sat and took the sun—cheek by jowl, generals and nurse-maids, parsons and the unemployed. Above, in that Spring wind, the elm-tree boughs were swaying, rustling, creaking ever so gently, carrying on the innumerable talk of trees—their sapient, wordless conversation over the affairs of men. It was pleasant, too, to see and hear the myriad movement of the million little separate leaves, each shaped differently, flighting never twice alike, yet all obedient to the single spirit of their tree.

Thyme and Martin were sitting on a seat beneath the largest of all the elms. Their manner lacked the unconcern and dignity of the moment, when, two hours before, they had started forth on their discovery from the other end of the Broad Walk. Martin spoke:

"It's given you the hump! First sight of blood, and you're like all the rest of them!"

"I'm not, Martin. How perfectly beastly of you!"

"Oh yes, you are. There's plenty of æstheticism about you and your people—plenty of good intentions—but not an ounce of real business!"

"Don't abuse my people; they're just as kind as you!"

"Oh, they're kind enough, and they can see what's wrong. It's not that which stops them. But your dad's a regular

320

official. He's got so much sense of what he ought not to do
that he never does anything; just as Hilary's got so much consciousness of what he *ought* to do that *he* never does anything.
You went to that woman's this morning with your ideas of
helping her all cut and dried, and now that you find the facts
aren't what you thought, you're stumped! "

" One can't believe anything they say. That's what I hate.
I thought Hughs simply knocked her about. I didn't know it
was her jealousy——"

" Of course you didn't. Do you imagine those people give
anything away to our sort unless they're forced? They know
better."

" Well, I hate the whole thing—it's all so sordid! "

" O Lord! "

" Well, it is! I don't feel that I want to help a woman who
can say and feel such horrid things, or the girl, or any of
them."

" Who cares what they say or feel? that's not the point. It's
simply a case of common sense. Your people put that girl
there, and they must get her to clear out again sharp. It's just
a question of what's healthy."

" Well, I know it's not healthy for me to have anything to
do with, and I won't! I don't believe you can help people unless
they want to be helped."

Martin whistled.

" You're rather a brute, I think," said Thyme.

" A brute, not rather a brute. That's all the difference."

" For the worse! "

" I don't think so, Thyme! "

There was no answer.

" Look at me."

Very slowly Thyme turned her eyes.

" Well? "

" Are you one of us, or are you not? "

" Of course I am."

" You're not! "

" I am."

" Well, don't let's fight about it. Give me your hand."

He dropped his hand on hers. Her face had flushed rose
colour. Suddenly she freed herself. " Here's Uncle Hilary! "

It was indeed Hilary, with Miranda, trotting in advance.
His hands were crossed behind him, his face bent towards the

ground. The two young people on the bench sat looking at him.

"Buried in self-contemplation," murmured Martin; "that's the way he always walks. I shall tell him about this!"

The colour of Thyme's face deepened from rose to crimson.

"No!"

"Why not?"

"Well—those new——" She could not bring out that word "clothes." It would have given her thoughts away.

Hilary seemed making for their seat, but Miranda, aware of Martin, stopped. "A man of action!" she appeared to say. "The one who pulls my ears." And turning, as though unconscious, she endeavoured to lead Hilary away. Her master, however, had already seen his niece. He came and sat down on the bench beside her.

"We wanted *you!*" said Martin, eyeing him slowly, as a young dog will eye another of a different age and breed. "Thyme and I have been to see the Hughs in Hound Street. Things are blowing up for a mess. You, or whoever put the girl there, ought to get her away again as quickly as possible."

Hilary seemed at once to withdraw into himself.

"Well," he said, "let us hear all about it."

"The woman's jealous of her: that's all the trouble!"

"Oh!" said Hilary; "that's all the trouble?"

Thyme murmured: "I don't see a bit why Uncle Hilary should bother. If they will be so horrid—I didn't think the poor were like that. I didn't think they had it in them. I'm sure the girl isn't worth it, or the woman either!"

"I didn't say they were," growled Martin. "It's a question of what's healthy."

Hilary looked from one of his young companions to the other.

"I see," he said. "I thought perhaps the matter was more delicate."

Martin's lip curled.

"Ah, your precious delicacy! What's the good of that? What did it ever do? It's the curse that you're all suffering from. Why don't you act? You could think about it afterwards."

A flush came into Hilary's sallow cheeks.

"Do you never think before you act, Martin?"

Martin got up and stood looking down on Hilary.

" Look here ! " he said ; " I don't go in for your subtleties.
I use my eyes and nose. I can see that the woman will never
be able to go on feeding the baby in the neurotic state she's in.
It's a matter of health for both of them."

" Is everything a matter of health with you ? "

" It is. Take any subject that you like. Take the poor
themselves—what's wanted? Health. Nothing on earth but
health ! The discoveries and inventions of the last century
have knocked the floor out of the old order ; we've got to put
a new one in, and we're going to put it in, too—the floor of
health. The crowd doesn't yet see what it wants, but *they're
looking for it,* and when we show it them they'll catch on fast
enough."

" But who are ' you ' ? " murmured Hilary.

" Who are we? I'll tell you one thing. While all the re-
formers are pecking at each other we shall quietly come along
and swallow up the lot. We've simply grasped this elementary
fact, that theories are no basis for reform. We go on the evidence of our eyes and noses ; what we see and smell is wrong we
correct by practical and scientific means."

" Will you apply that to human nature ? "

" It's human nature to want health."

" I wonder ! It doesn't look much like it at present."

" Take the case of this woman."

" Yes," said Hilary, " take her case. You can't make this
too clear to me, Martin."

" She's no use—poor sort altogether. The man's no use. A
man who's been wounded in the head, and isn't a teetotaller,
is done for. The girl's no use—regular pleasure-loving type ! "

Thyme flushed crimson, and, seeing that flood of colour in
his niece's face, Hilary bit his lips.

" The only things worth considering are the children. There's
this baby—well, as I said, the important thing is that the mother
should be able to look after it properly. Get hold of that, and
let the other facts go hang."

" Forgive me, but my difficulty is to isolate this question of the
baby's health from all the other circumstances of the case."

Martin grinned.

" And you'll make that an excuse, I'm certain, for doing
nothing."

Thyme slipped her hand into Hilary's.

" You *are* a brute, Martin," she murmured.

The young man turned on her a look that said: ' It's no use calling me a brute; I'm proud of being one. Besides, you know you don't dislike it.'

"It's better to be a brute than an amateur," he said.

Thyme, pressing close to Hilary, as though he needed her protection, cried out:

"Martin, you really are a Goth!"

Hilary was still smiling, but his face quivered.

"Not at all," he said. "Martin's powers of diagnosis do him credit." And, raising his hat, he walked away.

The two young people, both on their feet now, looked after him. Martin's face was a queer study of contemptuous compunction; Thyme's was startled, softened, almost tearful.

"It won't do him any harm," muttered the young man. "It'll shake him up."

Thyme flashed a vicious look at him.

"I hate you sometimes," she said. "You're so coarse-grained —your skin's just like leather."

Martin's hand descended on her wrist.

"And yours," he said, "is tissue-paper. You're all the same, you amateurs."

"I'd rather be an amateur than a—than a bounder!"

Martin made a queer movement of his jaw, then smiled. That smile seemed to madden Thyme. She wrenched her wrist away and darted after Hilary.

Martin impassively looked after her. Taking out his pipe, he filled it with tobacco, slowly pressing the golden threads down into the bowl with his little finger.

CHAPTER XVII

TWO BROTHERS

It has been said that Stephen Dallison, when unable to get his golf on Saturdays, went to his club, and read reviews. The two forms of exercise, in fact, were very similar: in playing golf you went round and round; in reading reviews you did the same, for in course of time you were assured of coming to articles that nullified articles already read. In both forms of sport the balance was preserved which keeps a man both sound and young.

And to be both sound and young was to Stephen an everyday necessity. He was essentially a Cambridge man, springy and undemonstrative, with just that air of taking a continual pinch of really perfect snuff. Underneath this manner he was a good worker, a good husband, a good father, and nothing could be urged against him except his regularity and the fact that he was never in the wrong. Where he worked, and indeed in other places, many men were like him. In one respect he resembled them, perhaps, too much—he disliked leaving the ground unless he knew precisely where he was coming down again.

He and Cecilia had "got on" from the first. They had both desired to have one child—no more; they had both desired to keep up with the times—no more; they now both considered Hilary's position awkward—no more; and when Cecilia, in the special Jacobean bed, and taking care to let him have his sleep out first, had told him of this matter of the Hughses, they had both turned it over very carefully, lying on their backs, and speaking in grave tones. Stephen was of opinion that poor old Hilary must look out what he was doing. Beyond this he did not go, keeping even from his wife the more unpleasant of what seemed to him the possibilities.

Then, in the words she had used to Hilary, Cecilia spoke:

"It's so sordid, Stephen."

He looked at her, and almost with one accord they both said:

"But it's all nonsense!"

These speeches, so simultaneous, stimulated them to a robuster view. What was this affair, if real, but the sort of episode that they read of in their papers? What was it, if true, but a duplicate of some bit of fiction or drama which they daily saw described by that word " sordid "? Cecilia, indeed, had used this word instinctively. It had come into her mind at once. The whole affair disturbed her ideals of virtue and good taste—that particular mental atmosphere mysteriously, inevitably woven round the soul by the conditions of special breeding and special life. If, then, this affair were real it was sordid, and if it were sordid it was repellent to suppose that her family could be mixed up in it; but her people *were* mixed up in it, therefore it must be—nonsense!

So the matter rested until Thyme came back from her visit to her grandfather, and told them of the little model's new and pretty clothes. When she detailed this news they were all sitting at dinner, over the ordering of which Cecilia's loyalty had been taxed till her little headache came, so that there might be nothing too conventional to overnourish Stephen or so essentially æsthetic as not to nourish him at all. The manservant being in the room, they neither of them raised their eyes. But when he was gone to fetch the bird, each found the other looking furtively across the table. By some queer misfortune the word " sordid " had leaped into their minds again. Who had given her those clothes? But feeling that it was sordid to pursue this thought, they looked away, and, eating hastily, began pursuing it. Being man and woman, they naturally took a different line of chase, Cecilia hunting in one grove and Stephen in another.

Thus ran Stephen's pack of meditations:

'If old Hilary has been giving her money and clothes and that sort of thing, he's either a greater duffer than I took him for, or there's something in it. B.'s got herself to thank, but that won't help to keep Hughs quiet. He wants money, I expect. Oh, damn!'

Cecilia's pack ran other ways:

'I know the girl can't have bought those things out of her proper earnings. I believe she's a really bad lot. I don't like to think it, but it must be so. Hilary can't have been so stupid after what I said to him. If she really *is* bad, it simplifies things very much; but Hilary is just the sort of man who will never believe it. Oh dear!'

It was, to be quite fair, immensely difficult for Stephen and his wife—or any of their class and circle—in spite of genuinely good intentions, to really feel the existence of their " shadows," except in so far as they saw them on the pavements. They knew that these people lived, because they saw them, but they did not *feel* it—with such extraordinary care had the web of social life been spun. They were, and were bound to be, as utterly divorced from understanding of, or faith in, all that shadowy life, as those " shadows " in their by-streets were from knowledge or belief that gentlefolk really existed except in so far as they had money from them.

Stephen and Cecilia, and their thousands, knew these " shadows " as " the people," knew them as slums, as districts, as sweated industries, of different sorts of workers, knew them in the capacity of persons performing odd jobs for them; but as human beings possessing the same faculties and passions with themselves, they did not, could not, know them. The reason, the long reason, extending back through generations, was so plain, so very simple, that it was never mentioned—in their heart of hearts, where there was no room for cant, they knew it to be just a little matter of the senses. They knew that, whatever they might say, whatever money they might give, or time devote, their hearts could never open, unless—unless they closed their ears, and eyes, and noses. This little fact, more potent than all the teaching of philosophers, than every Act of Parliament, and all the sermons ever preached, reigned paramount, supreme. It divided class from class, man from his shadow—as the Great Underlying Law had set dark apart from light.

On this little fact, too gross to mention, they and their kind had in secret built and built, till it was not too much to say that laws, worship, trade, and every art were based on it, if not in theory, then in fact. For it must not be thought that those eyes were dull or that nose plain—no, no, those eyes could put two and two together; that nose, of myriad fancy, could imagine countless things unsmelled which must lie behind a state of life not quite its own. It could create, as from the scent of an old slipper dogs create their masters.

So Stephen and Cecilia sat, and their butler brought in the bird. It was a nice one, nourished down in Surrey, and as he cut it into portions the butler's soul turned sick within him—not because he wanted some himself, or was a vegetarian, or for any sort of principle, but because he was by natural gifts an engineer, and deadly tired of cutting up and handing birds to other people and watching while they ate them. Without a glimmer of expression on his face he put the portions down before the persons who, having paid him to do so, could not tell his thoughts.

That same night, after working at a Report on the present Laws of Bankruptcy, which he was then drawing up, Stephen entered the joint apartment with excessive caution, having first made all his dispositions, and, stealing to the bed, slipped into it. He lay there, offering himself congratulations that he had not awakened Cecilia, and Cecilia, who was wide awake, knew by his unwonted carefulness that he had come to some conclusion which he did not wish to impart to her. Devoured, therefore, by disquiet, she lay sleepless til the clock struck two.

The conclusion to which Stephen had come was this: Having twice gone through the facts—Hilary's corporeal separation from Bianca (communicated to him by Cecilia), cause unknowable; Hilary's interest in the little model, cause unknown; her known poverty; her employment by Mr. Stone; her tenancy of Mrs. Hughs' room; the latter's outburst to Cecilia; Hughs' threat; and, finally, the girl's pretty clothes—he had summed it up as just a common " plant," to which his brother's possibly innocent, but in any case imprudent, conduct had laid him open. It was a man's affair. He resolutely tried to look on the whole thing as unworthy of attention, to feel that nothing would occur. He failed dismally, for three reasons. First, his inherent love of regularity, of having everything in proper order; secondly, his ingrained mistrust of and aversion from Bianca; thirdly, his unavowed conviction, for all his wish to be sympathetic to them, that the lower classes always wanted something out of you. It was a question of how much they would want, and whether it were wise to give them anything. He decided that it would not be wise at all. What then? Impossible to say. It worried him. He had a natural horror of any sort of scandal, and he was very fond of Hilary. If only he knew the attitude Bianca would take up! He could not even guess it.

Thus, on that Saturday afternoon, the 4th of May, he felt for once such a positive aversion from the reading of reviews, as men will feel from their usual occupations when their nerves have been disturbed. He stayed late at Chambers, and came straight home outside an omnibus.

The tide of life was flowing in the town. The streets were awash with wave on wave of humanity, sucked into a thousand crossing currents. Here men and women were streaming out

from the meeting of a religious congress, there streaming in at
the gates of some social function; like bright water confined
within long shelves of rock and dyed with myriad scales of shifting colour, they thronged Rotten Row, and along the closed
shop-fronts were woven into an inextricable network of little
human runlets. And everywhere amongst this sea of men and
women could be seen their shadows, meandering like streaks of
grey slime stirred up from the lower depths by some huge,
never-ceasing finger. The innumerable roar of that human sea
climbed out above the roofs and trees, and somewhere in illimitable space blended, and slowly reached the meeting-point of
sound and silence—that Heart where Life, leaving its little
forms and barriers, clasps Death, and from that clasp springs
forth new-formed, within new barriers.

Above this crowd of his fellow-creatures, Stephen drove, and
the same Spring wind which had made the elm-trees talk,
whispered to him, and tried to tell him of the million flowers
it had fertilised, the million leaves uncurled, the million ripples
it had awakened on the sea, of the million flying shadows flung
by it across the Downs, and how into men's hearts its scent had
driven a million longings and sweet pains.

It was but moderately successful, for Stephen, like all men of
culture and neat habits, took Nature only at those moments when
he had gone out to take her, and of her wild heart he had a
secret fear.

On his own doorstep he encountered Hilary coming out.

"I ran across Thyme and Martin in the Gardens," the latter
said. "Thyme brought me back to lunch, and here I've been
ever since." .

"Did she bring our young Sanitist in too?" asked Stephen
dubiously.

"No," said Hilary.

"Good! That young man gets on my nerves."

Taking his elder brother by the arm, he added: "Will you
come in again, old boy, or shall we go for a stroll?"

"A stroll," said Hilary.

Though different enough, perhaps because they were so different, these two brothers had the real affection for each other
which depends on something deeper and more elementary than
a similarity of sentiments, and is permanent because uncon-
nected with the reasoning powers. It depended on the countless
times they had kissed and wrestled as tiny boys, slept in small

beds alongside, refused to "tell" about each other, and even now and then taken up the burden of each other's peccadilloes. They might get irritated or tired of being in each other's company, but it would have been impossible for either to have been disloyal to the other in any circumstances, because of that traditional loyalty which went back to their cribs.

Preceded by Miranda, they walked along the flower walk towards the Park, talking of indifferent things, though in his heart each knew well enough what was in the other's.

Stephen broke through the hedge.

"Cis has been telling me," he said, "that this man Hughs is making trouble of some sort."

Hilary nodded.

Stephen glanced a little anxiously at his brother's face; it struck him as looking different, neither so gentle nor so impersonal as usual.

"He's a ruffian, isn't he?"

"I can't tell you," Hilary answered. "Probably not."

"He must be, old chap," murmured Stephen. Then, with a friendly pressure of his brother's arm, he added: "Look here, old boy, can I be of any use?"

"In what?" asked Hilary.

Stephen took a hasty mental view of his position; he had been in danger of letting Hilary see that he suspected him. Frowning slightly, and with some colour in his clean-shaven face, he said:

"Of course, there's nothing in it."

"In what?" said Hilary again.

"In what this ruffian says."

"No," said Hilary, "there's nothing in it, though what there may be if people give me credit for what there isn't, is another thing."

Stephen digested this remark, which hurt him. He saw that his suspicions had been fathomed, and this injured his opinion of his own diplomacy.

"You mustn't lose your head, old man," he said at last.

They were crossing the bridge over the Serpentine. On the bright waters, below, young clerks were sculling their inamoratas up and down; the ripples set free by their oars gleamed beneath the sun, and ducks swam lazily along the banks. Hilary leaned over.

"Look here, Stephen, I take an interest in this child—she's

a helpless sort of little creature, and she seems to have put herself under my protection. I can't help that. But that's all. Do you understand?"

This speech produced a queer turmoil in Stephen, as though his brother had accused him of a petty view of things. Feeling that he must justify himself somehow, he began:

"Oh, of course I understand, old boy! But don't think, any-way, that I should care a damn—I mean as far as I'm concerned—even if you had gone as far as ever you liked, considering what you have to put up with. What I'm thinking of is the general situation."

By this clear statement of his point of view Stephen felt he had put things back on a broad basis, and recovered his position as a man of liberal thought. He too leaned over, looking at the ducks. There was a silence. Then Hilary said:

"If Bianca won't get that child into some fresh place, I shall."

Stephen looked at his brother in surprise, amounting almost to dismay; he had spoken with such unwonted resolution.

"My dear old chap," he said, "I wouldn't go to B. Women are so funny."

Hilary smiled. Stephen took this for a sign of restored impersonality.

"I'll tell you exactly how the thing appeals to me. It'll be much better for you to chuck it altogether. Let Cis see to it!"

Hilary's eyes became bright with angry humour.

"Many thanks," he said, "but this is entirely our affair."

Stephen answered hastily:

"That's exactly what makes it difficult for you to look at it all round. That fellow Hughs could make himself quite nasty. I wouldn't give him any sort of chance. I mean to say—giving the girl clothes and that kind of thing——"

"I see," said Hilary.

"You know, old man," Stephen went on hastily, "I don't think you'll get Bianca to look at things in your light. If you were on—on terms, of course it would be different. I mean the girl, you know, is rather attractive in her way."

Hilary roused himself from contemplation of the ducks, and they moved on towards the Powder Magazine. Stephen carefully abstained from looking at his brother; the respect he had for Hilary—result, perhaps, of the latter's seniority, perhaps of the feeling that Hilary knew more of him than he of Hilary—was beginning to assert itself in a way he did not like. With every word, too, of this talk, the ground, instead of growing firmer, felt less and less secure. Hilary spoke:

"You mistrust my powers of action?"

"No, no," said Stephen. "I don't want you to act at all."

Hilary laughed. Hearing that rather bitter laugh, Stephen felt a little ache about his heart.

"Come, old boy," he said, "we can trust each other, anyway."

Hilary gave his brother's arm a squeeze.

Moved by that pressure, Stephen spoke:

"I hate you to be worried over such a rotten business."

The whizz of a motor-car rapidly approaching them became a sort of roar, and out of it a voice shouted: "How are you?" A hand was seen to rise in salute. It was Mr. Purcey driving his A.1. Damyer back to Wimbledon. Before him in the sunlight a little shadow fled; behind him the reek of petrol seemed to darken the road.

"There's a symbol for you," muttered Hilary.

"How do you mean?" said Stephen dryly. The word "symbol" was distasteful to him.

"The machine in the middle moving on its business; shadows like you and me skipping in front; oil and used-up stuff dropping behind. Society—body, beak, and bones."

Stephen took time to answer. "That's rather far-fetched," he said. "You mean these Hughses and people are the droppings?"

"Quite so," was Hilary's sardonic answer. "There's the body of that fellow and his car between our sort and them—and no getting over it, Stevie."

"Well, who wants to? If you're thinking of our old friend's Fraternity, I'm not taking any." And Stephen suddenly added: "Look here, I believe this affair is all 'a plant.'"

"You see that Powder Magazine?" said Hilary. "Well, this business that you call a 'plant' is more like that. I don't want to alarm you, but I think you as well as our young friend Martin, are inclined to underrate the emotional capacity of human nature."

Disquietude broke up the customary mask on Stephen's face. "I don't understand," he stammered.

"Well, we're none of us machines, not even amateurs like me —not even under-dogs like Hughs. I fancy you may find a certain warmth, not to say violence, about this business. I tell

you frankly that I don't live in married celibacy quite with
impunity. I can't answer for anything, in fact. You had
better stand clear, Stephen—that's all."

Stephen marked his thin hands quivering, and this alarmed
him as nothing else had done.

They walked on beside the water. Stephen spoke quietly,
looking at the ground. " How can I stand clear, old man, if
you are going to get into a mess? That's impossible."

He saw at once that this shot, which indeed was from his
heart, had gone right home to Hilary's. He sought within him
how to deepen the impression.

" You mean a lot to us," he said. " Cis and Thyme would
feel it awfully if you and B——." He stopped.

Hilary was looking at him; that faintly smiling glance, searching him through and through, suddenly made Stephen feel
inferior. He had been detected trying to extract capital from
the effect of his little piece of brotherly love. He was irritated
at his brother's insight.

" I have no right to give advice, I suppose," he said; " but in
my opinion you should drop it—drop it dead. The girl is not
worth your looking after. Turn her over to that Society—Mrs.
Tallents Smallpeace's thing—whatever it's called."

At a sound as of mirth Stephen, who was not accustomed to
hear his brother laugh, looked round.

" Martin," said Hilary, " also wants the case to be treated on
strictly hygienic grounds."

Nettled by this, Stephen answered:

" Don't confound me with our young Sanitist, please; I simply
think there are probably a hundred things you don't know about
the girl which ought to be cleared up? "

" And then? "

" Then," said Stephen, " they could—er—deal with her
accordingly."

Hilary shrank so palpably at this remark that he added rather
hastily:

" You call that cold-blooded, I suppose; but I think, you
know, old chap, that you're too sensitive."

Hilary stopped rather abruptly.

" If you don't mind, Stevie," he said, " we'll part here. I
want to think it over." So saying, he turned back, and sat down
on a seat that faced the sun.

CHAPTER XVIII

THE PERFECT DOG

HILARY sat long in the sun, watching the pale bright waters and many well-bred ducks circling about the shrubs, searching with their round bright eyes for worms. Between the bench where he was sitting and the spiked iron railings people passed continually—men, women, children of all kinds. Every now and then a duck would stop and cast her knowing glance at these creatures, as though comparing the condition of their forms and plumage with her own. 'If I had had the breeding of you,' she seemed to say, 'I could have made a better fist of it than that. A worse-looking lot of ducks, take you all round, I never wish to see!' And with a quick but heavy movement of her shoulders, she would turn away and join her fellows.

Hilary, however, got small distraction from the ducks. The situation gradually developing was something of a dilemma to a man better acquainted with ideas than facts, with the trimming of words than with the shaping of events. He turned a queer, perplexed, almost quizzical eye on it. Stephen had irritated him profoundly. He had such a way of pettifying things! Yet, in truth, the affair would seem ridiculous enough to an ordinary observer. What would a man of sound common sense, like Mr. Purcey, think of it? Why not, as Stephen had suggested, drop it? Here, however, Hilary approached the marshy ground of feeling.

To give up befriending a helpless girl the moment he found himself personally menaced was exceedingly distasteful. But would she be friendless? Were there not, in Stephen's words, a hundred things he did not know about her? Had she not other resources? Had she not a story? But here, too, he was hampered by his delicacy: one did not pry into the private lives of others!

The matter, too, was hopelessly complicated by the domestic troubles of the Hughs family. No conscientious man—and whatever Hilary lacked, no one ever accused him of a lack of conscience—could put aside that aspect of the case.

Wandering among these reflections were his thoughts about

334

Bianca. She was his wife. However he might feel towards her now, whatever their relations, he must not put her in a false position. Far from wishing to hurt her, he desired to preserve her, and everyone, from trouble and annoyance. He had told Stephen that his interest in the girl was purely protective. But since the night when, leaning out into the moonlight, he heard the waggons coming in to Covent Garden Market, a strange feeling had possessed him—the sensation of a man who lies, with a touch of fever on him, listening to the thrum of distant music—sensuous, not unpleasurable.

Those who saw him sitting there so quietly, with his face resting on his hand, imagined, no doubt, that he was wrestling with some deep, abstract proposition, some great thought to be given to mankind; for there was that about Hilary which forced everyone to connect him instantly with the humaner arts.

The sun began to leave the long pale waters.

A nursemaid and two children came and sat down beside him. Then it was that, underneath his seat, Miranda found what she had been looking for all her life. It had no smell, made no movement, was pale-grey in colour, like herself. It had no hair that she could find; its tail was like her own; it took no liberties, was silent, had no passions, committed her to nothing. Standing a few inches from its head, closer than she had ever been of her free will to any dog, she smelt its smell-lessness with a long, delicious snuffling, wrinkling up the skin on her forehead, and through her upturned eyes her little moonlight soul looked forth. ' How unlike you are,' she seemed to say, ' to all the other dogs I know! I would love to live with you. Shall I ever find a dog like you again? " The latest—sterilized cloth—see white label underneath: 4s. 3d. ! " ' Suddenly she slithered out her slender grey-pink tongue and licked its nose. The creature moved a little way and stopped. Miranda saw that it had wheels. She lay down close to it, for she knew it was the perfect dog.

Hilary watched the little moonlight lady lying vigilant, affectionate, beside this perfect dog, who could not hurt her. She panted slightly, and her tongue showed between her lips.

Presently behind his seat he saw another idyll. A thin white spaniel had come running up. She lay down in the grass quite close, and three other dogs who followed, sat and looked at her. A poor, dirty little thing she was, who seemed as if she had not seen a home for days. Her tongue lolled out, she panted piteously, and had no collar. Every now and then she turned her eyes, but though they were so tired and desperate, there was a gleam in them. 'For all its thirst and hunger and exhaustion, this is life!' they seemed to say. The three dogs, panting too, and watching till it should be her pleasure to begin to run again, seemed with their moist, loving eyes to echo: 'This is life!'

Because of this idyll, people near were moving on.

And suddenly the thin white spaniel rose, and, like a little harried ghost, slipped on amongst the trees, and the three dogs followed her.

CHAPTER XIX

BIANCA

In her studio that afternoon Bianca stood before her picture of the little model—the figure with parted pale-red lips and haunting, pale-blue eyes, gazing out of shadow into lamplight.

She was frowning, as though resentful of a piece of work which had the power to kill her other pictures. What force had moved her to paint like that? What had she felt while the girl was standing before her, still as some pale flower placed in a cup of water? Not love—there was no love in the presentment of that twilight figure; not hate—there was no hate in the painting of her dim appeal. Yet in the picture of this shadow girl, between the gloom and glimmer, was visible a spirit, driving the artist on to create that which had the power to haunt the mind.

Bianca turned away and went up to a portrait of her husband, painted ten years before. She looked from one picture to the other, with eyes as hard and stabbing as the points of daggers.

In the more poignant relationships of human life there is a point beyond which men and women do not quite truthfully analyse their feelings—they *feel* too much. It was Bianca's fortune, too, to be endowed to excess with that quality which, of all others, most obscures the real significance of human issues. Her pride had kept her back from Hilary, till she had felt herself a failure. Her pride had so revolted at that failure that she had led the way to utter estrangement. Her pride had forced her to the attitude of one who says: " Live your own life; I should be ashamed to let you see that I care what happens between us." Her pride had concealed from her the fact that beneath her veil of mocking liberality there was an essential woman tenacious of her dues, avid of affection and esteem. Her pride prevented the world from guessing that there was anything amiss. Her pride even prevented Hilary from really knowing what had spoiled his married life—this ungovernable itch to be appreciated, governed by ungovernable pride. Hundreds of times he had been baffled by the hedge round that disharmonic nature. With each failure something had shrivelled in him, till

337

the very roots of his affection had dried up. She had worn out a man who, to judge from his actions and appearance, was naturally long-suffering to a fault. Beneath all manner of kindness and consideration for each other—for their good taste, at all events, had never given way—this tragedy of a woman, who wanted to be loved, slowly killing the power of loving her in the man, had gone on year after year. It had ceased to be tragedy, as far as Hilary was concerned; the nerve of his love for her was quite dead, slowly frozen out of him. It was still active tragedy with Bianca, the nerve of whose jealous desire for his appreciation was not dead. Her instinct, too, ironically, informed her that, had he been a man with some brutality, a man who had set himself to ride and master her, instead of one too delicate, he might have trampled down the hedge. This gave her a secret grudge against him, a feeling that it was not she who was to blame.

Pride was Bianca's fate, her flavour, and her charm. Like a shadowy hill-side behind glamorous bars of waning sunlight, she was enveloped in smiling pride—mysterious, one thinks, even to herself. This pride of hers took part even in her many generous impulses, kind actions which she did rather secretly and scoffed at herself for doing. She scoffed at herself continually, even for putting on dresses of colours which Hilary was fond of. She would not admit her longing to attract him.

Standing between those two pictures, pressing her mahlstick against her bosom, she suggested somewhat the image of an Italian saint forcing the dagger of martyrdom into her heart.

That other person, who had once brought the thought of Italy into Cecilia's mind—the man Hughs—had been for the last eight hours or so walking the streets, placing in a cart the refuses of Life; nor had he at all suggested the aspect of one tortured by the passions of love and hate. For the first two hours he had led the horse without expression of any sort on his dark face, his neat soldier's figure garbed in the costume which had made "Westminister" describe him as a "dreadful foreign-lookin' man." Now and then he had spoken to the horse; save for those speeches, of no great importance, he had been silent. For the next two hours, following the cart, he had used a shovel, and still his square, short face, with little black moustache and still blacker eyes, had given no sign of conflict in his breast. So he had passed the day. Apart from the fact, indeed, that men of any kind are not too given to expose private passions to public gaze, the circumstances of a life devoted from the age of twenty onwards to the service of his country, first as a soldier, now in the more defensive part of Vestry scavenger, had given him a kind of gravity. Life had cloaked him with passivity—the normal look of men whose bread and cheese depends on their not caring much for anything. Had Hughs allowed his inclinations to play, or sought to express himself, he could hardly have been a private soldier; still less, on his retirement from that office with an honourable wound, would he have been selected out of many others as a Vestry scavenger. For such an occupation as the lifting from the streets of the refuses of Life—a calling greatly sought after, and, indeed, one of the few open to a man who had served his country—charm of manner, individuality, or the engaging quality of self-expression, were perhaps out of place.

He had never been trained in the voicing of his thoughts, and, ever since he had been wounded, felt at times a kind of desperate looseness in his head. It was not, therefore, remarkable that he should be liable to misconstruction, more especially by those who had nothing in common with them, except that somewhat negligible factor, common humanity. The Dallisons had misconstrued him as much as, but no more than, he had misconstrued them when, as "Westminister" had informed Hilary, he "went on against the gentry." He was, in fact, a ragged screen, a broken vessel, that let light through its holes. A glass or two of beer, the fumes of which his wounded head no longer dominated, and he at once became "dreadful foreign." Unfortunately, it was his custom, on finishing his work, to call at the "Green Glory." On this particular afternoon the glass had become three, and in sallying forth he had felt a confused sense of duty urging him to visit the house where this girl for whom he had conceived his strange infatuation "carried on her games." The "no-tale-bearing" tradition of a soldier fought hard with this sense of duty; his feelings were mixed when he rang the bell and asked for Mrs. Dallison. Habit, however, masked his face, and he stood before her at "attention," his black eyes lowered, clutching his peaked cap.

Bianca noted curiously the scar on the left side of his cropped black head.

Whatever Hughs had to say was not said easily.

"I've come," he began at last in a dogged voice, "to let you know. I never wanted to come into this house. I never wanted to see no one."

Bianca could see his lips and eyelids quivering in a way strangely out of keeping with his general stolidity.

"My wife has told you tales of me, I suppose. She's told you I knock her about, I daresay. I don't care what she tells you or any o' the people that she works for. But this I'll say: I never touched her but she touched me first. Look here! that's marks of hers!" and, drawing up his sleeve he showed a scratch on his sinewy tattooed forearm. "I've not come here about her; that's no business of anyone's."

Bianca turned towards her pictures. "Well?" she said, "but what *have* you come about, please? You see I'm busy."

Hughs' face changed. Its stolidity vanished, the eyes became as quick, passionate, and leaping as a dark torrent. He was more violently alive than she had ever seen a man. Had it been a woman she would have felt—as Cecilia had felt with Mrs. Hughs—the indecency, the impudence of this exhibition; but from that male violence the feminine in her derived a certain satisfaction. So in Spring, when all seems lowering and grey, the hedges and trees suddenly flare out against the purple clouds, their twigs all in flame. The next moment that white glare is gone, the clouds are no longer purple, fiery light no longer quivers and leaps along the hedgerows. The passion in Hughs' face was gone as soon. Bianca felt a sense of disappointment, as though she could have wished her life held a little more of that. He stole a glance at her out of his dark eyes, which, when narrowed, had a velvety look, like the body of a wild bee, then jerked his thumb at the picture of the little model.

"It's about *her* I come to speak."

Bianca faced him frigidly.

"I have not the slightest wish to hear."

Hughs looked round, as though to find something that would help him to proceed; his eyes lighted on Hilary's portrait.

"Ah! I'd put the two together if I was you," he said.

Bianca walked past him to the door.

"Either you or I must leave the room."

The man's face was neither sullen now nor passionate, but simply miserable.

"Look here, lady," he said, "don't take it hard o' me coming here. I'm not out to do you a harm. I've got a wife of my own, and Gawd knows I've enough to put up with from her about this girl. I'll be going in the water one of these days. It's him giving her them clothes that set me coming here."

Bianca opened the door. "Please go," she said.

"I'll go quiet enough," he muttered, and, hanging his head, walked out.

Having seen him through the side door out into the street, Bianca went back to where she had been standing before he came. She found some difficulty in swallowing; for once there was no armour on her face. She stood there a long time without moving, then put the pictures back into their places and went down the little passage to the house. Listening outside her father's door, she turned the handle quietly and went in.

Mr. Stone, holding some sheets of paper out before him, was dictating to the little model, who was writing laboriously with her face close above her arm. She stopped at Bianca's entrance. Mr. Stone did not stop, but, holding up his other hand, said:

"I will take you through the last three pages again. Follow!"

Bianca sat down at the window.

Her father's voice, so thin and slow, with each syllable disjointed from the other, rose like monotony itself.

"'There were tra-cea-able indeed, in those days, certain rudi-men-tary at-tempts to f-u-s-e the classes . . .'"

It went on unwaveringly, neither rising high nor falling low, as though the reader knew he had yet far to go, like a runner that brings great news across mountains, plains, and rivers.

To Bianca that thin voice might have been the customary sighing of the wind, her attention was so fast fixed on the girl, who sat following the words down the pages with her pen's point.

Mr. Stone paused.

"Have you got the word 'insane'?" he asked.

The little model raised her face. "Yes, Mr. Stone."

"Strike it out."

With his eyes fixed on the trees he stood breathing audibly. The little model moved her fingers, freeing them from cramp. Bianca's curious, smiling scrutiny never left her, as though trying to fix an indelible image on her mind. There was something terrifying in that stare, cruel to herself, cruel to the girl.

"The precise word," said Mr. Stone, "eludes me. Leave a blank. Follow! . . . 'Neither that sweet fraternal interest of man in man, nor a curiosity in phenomena merely as phenomena . . .'" His voice pursued its tenuous path through spaces, frozen by the calm eternal presence of his beloved idea, which, like a golden moon, far and cold, presided glamorously above the thin track of words. And still the girl's pen-point traced his utterance across the pages. Mr. Stone paused again, and looking at his daughter as though surprised to see her sitting there, asked:

"Do you wish to speak to me, my dear?"

Bianca shook her head.

"Follow!" said Mr. Stone.

But the little model's glance had stolen round to meet the scrutiny fixed on her.

A look passed across her face which seemed to say: 'What have I done to you, that you should stare at me like this?'

Furtive and fascinated, her eyes remained fixed on Bianca, while her hand moved, mechanically ticking the paragraphs. That silent duel of eyes went on—the woman's fixed, cruel, smiling; the girl's uncertain, resentful. Neither of them heard a word that Mr. Stone was reading. They treated it as, from the beginning, Life has treated Philosophy—and to the end will treat it.

Mr. Stone paused again, seeming to weigh his last sentences.

"That, I think," he murmured to himself, "is true." And suddenly he addressed his daughter. "Do you agree with me, my dear?"

He was evidently waiting with anxiety for her answer, and the little silver hairs that straggled on his lean throat beneath his beard were clearly visible.

"Yes, Father, I agree."

"Ah!" said Mr. Stone. "I am glad that you confirm me. I was anxious. Follow!"

Bianca rose. Burning spots of colour had settled in her cheeks. She went towards the door, and the little model pursued her figure with a long look, cringing, mutinous, and wistful.

CHAPTER XX

THE HUSBAND AND THE WIFE

IT was past six o'clock when Hilary at length reached home, preceded a little by Miranda, who almost felt within her the desire to eat. The lilac bushes, not yet in flower, were giving forth spicy fragrance. The sun still netted their top boughs, as with golden silk and a blackbird, seated on a low branch of the acacia-tree, was summoning the evening. Mr. Stone, accompanied by the little model, dressed in her new clothes, was coming down the path. They were evidently going for a walk, for Mr. Stone wore his hat, old and soft and black, with a strong green tinge, and carried a paper parcel, which leaked crumbs of bread at every step.

The girl grew very red. She held her head down, as though afraid of Hilary's inspection of her new clothes. At the gate she suddenly looked up. His face said: 'Yes, you look very nice!' And into her eyes a look leaped such as one may see in dogs' eyes lifted in adoration to their masters' faces. Manifestly disconcerted, Hilary turned to Mr. Stone. The old man was standing very still; a thought had evidently struck him.

"I have not, I think," he said, "given enough consideration to the question whether force is absolutely, or only relatively, evil. If I saw a man ill-treat a cat, should I be justified in striking him?"

Accustomed to such divagations, Hilary answered: "I don't know whether you would be justified, but I believe that you would strike him."

"I am not sure," said Mr. Stone. "We are going to feed the birds."

The little model took the paper bag. "It's all dropping out," she said. From across the road she turned her head.

'Won't you come, too?' she seemed to say.

But Hilary passed rather hastily into the garden and shut the gate behind him. He sat in his study, with Miranda near him, for fully an hour, without doing anything whatever, sunk in a strange, half-pleasurable torpor. At this hour he should have been working at his book; and the fact that his idleness did not trouble him might well have given him uneasiness. Many thoughts passed through his mind, imaginings of things he had thought left behind for ever—sensations and longings which to the normal eye of middle age are but dried forms hung in the museum of memory. They started up at the whip of the still-living youth, the lost wildness at the heart of every man. Like the reviving flame of half-spent fires, longing for discovery leaped and flickered in Hilary—to find out once again what things were like before he went down the hill of age.

No trivial ghost was beckoning him; it was the ghost, with unseen face and rosy finger, which comes to men when youth has gone.

Miranda, hearing him so silent, rose. At this hour it was her master's habit to scratch paper. She, who seldom scratched anything, because it was not delicate, felt dimly that this was what he should be doing. She held up a slim foot and touched his knee. Receiving no discouragement, she delicately sprang into his lap, and, forgetting for once her modesty, placed her arms on his chest, and licked his face all over.

It was while receiving this embrace that Hilary saw Mr. Stone and the little model returning across the garden. The old man was walking very rapidly, holding out the fragment of a broken stick. He was extremely pink.

Hilary went to meet them.

"What's the matter, sir?" he said.

"I cut him over the legs," said Mr. Stone. "I do not regret it"; and he walked on to his room.

Hilary turned to the little model.

"It was a little dog. The man kicked it, and Mr. Stone hit him. He broke his stick. There were several men; they threatened us." She looked up at Hilary. "I—I was frightened. Oh! Mr. Dallison, isn't he—funny?"

"All heroes are funny," murmured Hilary.

"He wanted to hit them again, after his stick was broken. Then a policeman came, and they all ran away."

"That was quite as it should be," said Hilary. "And what did *you* do?"

Perceiving that she had not as yet made much effect, the little model cast down her eyes.

"I shouldn't have been frightened if *you* had been there!"

"Heavens!" muttered Hilary. "Mr. Stone is far more valiant than I."

"I don't think he is," she replied stubbornly, and again looked up at him.

"Well, good-night!" said Hilary hastily. "You must run off. . . ."

That same evening, driving with his wife back from a long, dull dinner, Hilary began:

"I've something to say to you."

An ironic "Yes?" came from the other corner of the cab.

"There is some trouble with the little model."

"Really!"

"This man Hughs has become infatuated with her. He has even said, I believe, that he was coming to see you."

"What about?"

"Me."

"And what is he going to say about you?"

"I don't know; some vulgar gossip—nothing true."

There was a silence, and in the darkness Hilary moistened his dry lips.

Bianca spoke: "May I ask how you knew of this?"

"Cecilia told me."

A curious noise, like a little strangled laugh, fell on Hilary's ears.

"I am very sorry," he muttered:

Presently Bianca said:

"It was good of you to tell me, considering that we go our own ways. What made you?"

"I thought it right."

"And—of course, the man might have come to me!"

"That you need not have said."

"One does not always say what one ought."

"I have made the child a present of some clothes which she badly needed. So far as I know, that's all I've done!"

"Of course!"

This wonderful "of course" acted on Hilary like a tonic. He said dryly:

"What do you wish me to do?"

"I?" No gust of the east wind, making the young leaves curl and shiver, the gas jets flare and die down in their lamps, could so have nipped the flower of amity. Through Hilary's mind flashed Stephen's almost imploring words: "Oh, I wouldn't go to her! Women are so funny!"

He looked round. A blue gauze scarf was wrapped over his wife's dark head. There, in her corner, as far away from him as she could get, she was smiling. For a moment Hilary had the sensation of being stifled by fold on fold of that blue gauze scarf, as if he were doomed to drive for ever, suffocated, by the side of this woman who had killed his love for her.

"You will do what you like, of course," she said suddenly.

A desire to laugh seized Hilary. "What do you wish me to do?" "You will do what you like, of course!" Could civilised restraint and tolerance go further?

"B.," he said, with an effort, "the wife is jealous. We put the girl into that house—we ought to get her out."

Bianca's reply came slowly.

"From the first," she said, "the girl has been your property; do what you like with her. I shall not meddle."

"I am not in the habit of regarding people as my property."

"No need to tell me that—I have known you twenty years."

Doors sometimes slam in the minds of the mildest and most restrained of men.

"Oh, very well! I have told you; you can see Hughs when he comes—or not, as you like."

"I *have* seen him."

Hilary smiled.

"Well, was his story very terrible?"

"He told me no story."

"How was that?"

Bianca suddenly sat forward, and threw back the blue scarf, as though she, too, were stifling. In her flushed face her eyes were bright as stars; her lips quivered.

"Is it likely," she said, "that I should listen? That's enough, please, of these people."

Hilary bowed. The cab, bearing them fast home, turned into the last short cut. This narrow street was full of men and women circling round barrows and lighted booths. The sound of course talk and laughter floated out into air thick with the reek of paraffin and the scent of frying fish. In every couple of those men and women Hilary seemed to see the Hughses, that other married couple, going home to wedded happiness above the little model's head. The cab turned out of the gay alley.

"Enough, please, of these people!"

That same night, past one o'clock, he was roused from sleep by hearing bolts drawn back. He got up, hastened to the window, and looked out. At first he could distinguish nothing. The moonless night, like a dark bird, had nested in the garden; the sighing of the lilac bushes was the only sound. Then, dimly, just below him, on the steps of the front door, he saw a figure standing.

"Who is that?" he called.

The figure did not move.

"Who are you?" said Hilary again.

The figure raised its face, and by the gleam of his white beard Hilary knew that it was Mr. Stone.

"What is it, sir?" he said. "Can I do anything?"

"No," answered Mr. Stone. "I am listening to the wind. It has visited everyone to-night." And lifting his hand, he pointed out into the darkness.

CHAPTER XXI

A DAY OF REST

CECILIA's house in the Old Square was steeped from roof to basement in the appropriate atmosphere on Sunday to houses whose inmates have no need of religion or of rest.

Neither she nor Stephen had been to church since Thyme was christened; they did not expect to go again till she was married, and they felt that even to go on these occasions was against their principles; but for the sake of other people's feelings they had made the sacrifice, and they meant to make it once more, when the time came. Each Sunday, therefore, everything tried to happen exactly as it happened on every other day, with indifferent success. This was because, for all Cecilia's resolutions, a joint of beef and Yorkshire pudding would appear on the luncheon-table, notwithstanding the fact that Mr. Stone—who came when he remembered that it was Sunday—did not devour the higher mammals. Every week, when it appeared, Cecilia, who for some reason carved on Sundays, regarded it with a frown. Next week she would really discontinue it; but when next week came, there it was, with its complexion that reminded her so uncomfortably of cabmen. And she would partake of it with unexpected heartiness. Something very old and deep, some horrible whole-hearted appetite, derived, no doubt, from Mr. Justice Carfax, rose at that hour precisely every week to master her. Having given Thyme the second helping which she invariably took, Cecilia, who detested carving, would look over the fearful joint at a piece of glass procured by her in Venice, and at the daffodils standing upright in it, apparently without support. Had it not been for this joint of beef, which had made itself smelt all the morning, and would make itself felt all the afternoon, it need never have come into her mind at all that it was Sunday—and she would cut herself another slice.

To have told Cecilia that there was still a strain of the Puritan in her would have been to occasion her some uneasiness, and provoked a strenuous denial; yet her way of observing Sunday furnished indubitable evidence of this singular fact. She did more that day than any other. For, in the morning she invariably "cleared off" her correspondence; at lunch she carved the beef; after lunch she cleared off the novel or book on social questions she was reading; went to a concert, clearing off a call on the way back; and on first Sundays—a great bore—stayed at home to clear off the friends who came to visit her. In the evening she went to some play or other, produced by Societies for the benefit of persons compelled, like her, to keep a Sunday with which they felt no sympathy.

On this particular "first Sunday," having made the circuit of her drawing-room, which extended the whole breadth of her house, and through long, low windows cut into leaded panes, looked out both back and front, she took up Mr. Balladyce's latest book. She sat, with her paper-knife pressed against the tiny hollow in her flushed cheek, and pretty little bits of lace and real old jewellery nestling close to her. And while she turned the pages of Mr. Balladyce's book Thyme sat opposite in a bright blue frock, and turned the pages of Darwin's work on earthworms.

Regarding her "little daughter," who was so much more solid than herself, Cecilia's face wore a very sweet, faintly surprised expression.

'My kitten is a bonny thing,' it seemed to say. 'It is queer that I should have a thing so large.'

Outside in the Square Gardens a shower, the sunlight, and blossoms, were entangled. It was the time of year when all the world had kittens; young things were everywhere—soft, sweet, uncouth. Cecilia felt this in her heart. It brought depth into her bright, quick eyes. What a secret satisfaction it was that she had once so far committed herself as to have borne a child! What a queer vague feeling she sometimes experienced in the Spring—almost amounting to a desire to bear another! So one may mark the warm eye of a staid mare, following with her gaze the first strayings of her foal. 'I must get used to it,' she seems to say. 'I certainly do miss the little creature, though I used to threaten her with my hoofs, to show I couldn't be bullied by anything of that age. And there she goes! Ah, well!'

Remembering suddenly, however, that she was sitting there to clear off Mr. Balladyce, because it was so necessary to keep up with what he wrote, Cecilia dropped her gaze to the page before her; and instantly, by uncomfortable chance, not the choice pastures of Mr. Balladyce appeared, where women might browse at leisure, but a vision of the little model. She had not thought of her for quite an hour; she had tired herself out with thinking—not, indeed, of her, but of all that hinged on her, ever since Stephen had spoken of his talk with Hilary. Things Hilary had said seemed to Cecilia's delicate and rather timid soul so ominous, so unlike himself. Was there really going to be complete disruption between him and Bianca—worse, an ugly scandal? She, who knew her sister better, perhaps, than anyone, remembered from schoolroom days Bianca's moody violence when anything had occurred to wound her—remembered, too, the long fits of brooding that followed. This affair, which she had tried to persuade herself was exaggerated, loomed up larger than ever. It was not an isolated squib; it was a lighted match held to a train of gunpowder. This girl of the people, coming from who knew where, destined for who knew what—this young, not very beautiful, not even clever child, with nothing but a sort of queer haunting naïveté to give her charm—might even be a finger used by Fate! Cecilia sat very still before that sudden vision of the girl. There was no staid mare to guard *that* foal with the dark devotion of her eye. There was no wise whinnying to answer back those tiny whinnies; no long look round to watch the little creature nodding to sleep on its thin trembling legs in the hot sunlight; no ears to prick up and hoofs to stamp at the approach of other living things. These thoughts passed through Cecilia's mind and were gone, being too far and pale to stay. Turning the page which she had not been reading, she heaved a sigh. Thyme sighed also.

"These worms are fearfully interesting," she said. "Is anybody coming in this afternoon?"

"Mrs. Tallents Smallpeace was going to bring a young man in, a Signor Pozzi—Egregio Pozzi, or some such name. She says he is the coming pianist." Cecilia's face was spiced with faint amusement. Some strain of her breeding (the Carfax strain, no doubt) still heard such names and greeted such proclivities with an inclination to derision.

Thyme snatched up her book. "Well," she said, "I shall be in the attic. If anyone interesting comes you might send up to me."

She stood, luxuriously stretching, and turning slowly round

in a streak of sunlight so as to bathe her body in it. Then, with a long soft yawn, she flung up her chin till the sun streamed on her face. Her eyelashes rested on cheeks already faintly browned; her lips were parted; little shivers of delight ran down her; her chestnut hair glowed, burnished by the kisses of the sun.

'Ah!' Cecilia thought, 'if that other girl were like this, now, I could understand well enough!'

"Oh, Lord!" said Thyme, "there they are!" She flew towards the door.

"My dear," murmured Cecilia, "if you *must* go, do please tell Father."

A minute later Mrs. Tallents Smallpeace came in, followed by a young man with an interesting, pale face and a crop of dusky hair.

Let us consider for a minute the not infrequent case of a youth cursed with an Italian mother and a father of the name of Potts, who had baptised him William. Had he emanated from the lower classes, he might with impunity have ground an organ under the name of Bill; but springing from the bourgeoisie, and playing Chopin at the age of four, his friends had been confronted with a problem of no mean difficulty. Heaven, on the threshold of his career, had intervened to solve it. Hovering, as it were, with one leg raised before the gladiatorial arena of musical London, where all were waiting to turn their thumbs down on the figure of the native Potts, he had received a letter from his mother's birthplace. It was inscribed: "Egregio Signor Pozzi." He was saved. By the simple inversion of the first two words, the substitution of z's for t's, without so fortunately making any difference in the sound, and the retention of that i, all London knew him now to be the rising pianist.

He was a quiet, well-mannered youth, invaluable just then to Mrs. Tallents Smallpeace, a woman never happy unless slightly leading a genius in strings.

Cecilia, while engaging them to right and left in her half-sympathetic, faintly mocking way—as if doubting whether they really wanted to see her or she them—heard a word of fear.

"Mr. Purcey."

'Oh Heaven!' she thought.

Mr. Purcey, whose A.1 Damyer could be heard outside, advanced in his direct and simple way.

"I thought I'd give my car a run," he said. "How's your sister?" And seeing Mrs. Tallents Smallpeace, he added: "How do you do? We met the other day."

"We did," said Mrs. Tallents Smallpeace, whose little eyes were sparkling. "We talked about the poor, do you remember?"

Mr. Purcey, a sensitive man if you could get through his skin, gave her a shrewd look. 'I don't quite cotton to this woman,' he seemed saying; 'there's a laugh about her I don't like.'

"Ah! yes—you were tellin' me about them."

"Oh, Mr. Purcey, but you had heard of them, you remember!"

Mr. Purcey made a movement of his face which caused it to seem all jaw. It was a sort of unconscious declaration of a somewhat formidable character. So one may see bulldogs, those amiable animals, suddenly disclose their tenacity.

"It's rather a blue subject," he said bluntly.

Something in Cecilia fluttered at those words. It was like the saying of a healthy man looking at a box of pills which he did not mean to open. Why could not she and Stephen keep that lid on, too? And at this moment, to her deep astonishment, Stephen entered. She had sent for him, it is true, but had never expected he would come.

His entrance, indeed, requires explanation.

Feeling, as he said, a little "off colour," Stephen had not gone to Richmond to play golf. He had spent the day instead in the company of his pipe and those ancient coins, of which he had the best collection of any man he had ever met. His thoughts had wandered from them, more than he thought proper, to Hilary and that girl. He had felt from the beginning that he was so much more the man to deal with an affair like this than poor old Hilary. When, therefore, Thyme put her head into his study and said, "Father, Mrs. Tallents Smallpeace!" he had first thought, 'That busybody!' and then, 'I wonder—perhaps I'd better go and see if I can get anything out of her.'

In considering Stephen's attitude towards a woman so firmly embedded in the various social movements of the day, it must be remembered that he represented that large class of men who, unhappily too cultivated to put aside, like Mr. Purcey, all blue subjects, or deny the need for movements to make them less blue, still could not move, for fear of being out of order. He was also temperamentally distrustful of anything too feminine; and Mrs. Tallents Smallpeace was undoubtedly extremely feminine. Her merit, in his eyes, consisted of her attachment to Societies. So long as mankind worked through Societies, Stephen, who knew the power of rules and minute books, did not despair of too little progress being made. He sat down beside her, and turned the conversation on her chief work—"the Maids in Peril."

Searching his face with those eyes so like little black bees sipping honey from all the flowers that grew, Mrs. Tallents Smallpeace said:

"Why don't you get your wife to take an interest in our work?"

To Stephen this question was naturally both unexpected and annoying, one's wife being the last person he wished to interest in other people's movements. He kept his head.

"Ah well!" he said, "we haven't all got a talent for that sort of thing."

The voice of Mr. Purcey travelled suddenly across the room.

"Do tell me! How do you go to work to worm things out of them?"

Mrs. Tallents Smallpeace, prone to laughter, bubbled.

"Oh, that is such a delicious expression, Mr. Purcey! I almost think we ought to use it in our Report. Thank you!"

Mr. Purcey bowed. "Not at all!" he said.

Mrs. Tallents Smallpeace turned again to Stephen.

"We have our trained inquirers. That is the advantage of Societies such as ours; so that we don't personally have the unpleasantness. Some cases do baffle everybody. It's such very delicate work."

"You sometimes find you let in a rotter?" said Mr. Purcey—"or, I should say, a rotter lets you in! Ha, ha!"

Mrs. Tallents Smallpeace's eyes flew deliciously down his figure.

"Not often," she said; and turning rather markedly once more to Stephen: "Have you any special case that you are interested in, Mr. Dallison?"

Stephen consulted Cecilia with one of those masculine half-glances so discreet that Mrs. Tallents Smallpeace intercepted it without looking up. She found it rather harder to catch

Cecilia's reply, but she caught it before Stephen did. It was, 'You'd better wait, perhaps,' conveyed by a tiny raising of the left eyebrow and a slight movement to the right of the lower lip. Putting two and two together, she felt within her bones that they were thinking of the little model. And she remembered the interesting moment in the omnibus when that attractive-looking man had got out so hastily.

There was no danger whatever from Mrs. Tallents Small-peace feeling anything. The circle in which she moved did not now talk scandal, or, indeed, allude to matters of that sort without deep sympathy; and in the second place she was really far too good a fellow, with far too dear a love of life, to interfere with anybody else's love of it. At the same time it was interesting.

"That little model, now," she said, "what about her?"

"Is that the girl I saw?" broke in Mr. Purcey, with his accustomed shrewdness.

Stephen gave him the look with which he was accustomed to curdle the blood of persons who gave evidence before Commissions.

'This fellow is impossible,' he thought.

The little black bees flying below Mrs. Tallents Smallpeace's dark hair, done in the Early Italian fashion, tranquilly sucked honey from Stephen's face.

"She seemed to me," she answered, "such a very likely type."

"Ah!" murmured Stephen, "there would be, I suppose, a danger——" And he looked angrily at Cecilia.

Without ceasing to converse with Mr. Purcey and Signor Egregio Pozzi, she moved her left eye upwards. Mrs. Tallents Smallpeace understood this to mean: 'Be frank, and guarded!' Stephen, however, interpreted it otherwise. To him it signified: 'What the deuce do you look at me for?' And he felt justly hurt. He therefore said abruptly:

"What would you do in a case like that?"

Mrs. Tallents Smallpeace, sliding her face sideways, with a really charming little smile, asked softly:

"In a case like what?"

And her little eyes fled to Thyme, who had slipped into the room, and was whispering to her mother.

Cecilia rose.

"You know my daughter," she said. "Will you excuse me

just a minute? I'm so very sorry." She glided towards the door, and drew a flying look back. It was one of those social moments precious to those who are escaping them.

Mrs. Tallents Smallpeace was smiling, Stephen frowning at his boots; Mr. Purcey stared admiringly at Thyme, and Thyme, sitting very upright, was calmly regarding the unfortunate Egregio Pozzi, who apparently could not bring himself to speak.

When Cecilia found herself outside, she stood still a moment to compose her nerves. Thyme had told her that Hilary was in the dining-room, and wanted specially to see her.

As in most women of her class and bringing-up, Cecilia's qualities of reticence and subtlety, the delicate treading of her spirit, were seen to advantage in a situation such as this. Unlike Stephen, who had shown at once that he had something on his mind, she received Hilary with that exact shade of friendly, intimate, yet cool affection long established by her as the proper manner towards her husband's brother. It was not quite sisterly, but it was very nearly so. It seemed to say: 'We understand each other as far as it is right and fitting that we should; we even sympathise with the difficulties we have each of us experienced in marrying the other's sister or brother, as the case may be. We know the worst. And we like to see each other, too, because there are bars between us, which make it almost piquant.'

Giving him her soft little hand, she began at once to talk of things farthest from her heart. She saw that she was deceiving Hilary, and this feather in the cap of her subtlety gave her pleasure. But her nerves fluttered at once when he said: "I want to speak to you, Cis. You know that Stephen and I had a talk yesterday, I suppose?"

Cecilia nodded.

"I have spoken to B.!"

"Oh!" Cecilia murmured. She longed to ask what Bianca had said, but did not dare, for Hilary had his armour on, the retired, ironical look he always wore when any subject was broached for which he was too sensitive.

She waited.

"The whole thing is distasteful to me," he said; "but I must do something for this child. I can't leave her completely in the lurch."

Cecilia had an inspiration.

"Hilary," she said softly, "Mrs. Tallents Smallpeace is in the drawing-room. She was just speaking of the girl to Stephen. Won't you come in, and arrange with her quietly?"

Hilary looked at his sister-in-law for a moment without speaking, then said:

"I draw the line there. No, thank you. I'll see this through myself."

Cecilia fluttered out:

"Oh, but, Hilary, what do you mean?"

"I am going to put an end to it."

It needed all Cecilia's subtlety to hide her consternation. End to what? Did he mean that he and B. were going to separate?

"I won't have all this vulgar gossip about the poor girl. I shall go and find another room for her."

Cecilia sighed with relief.

"Would you—would you like me to come too, Hilary?"

"It's very good of you," said Hilary dryly. "My actions appear to rouse suspicions."

Cecilia blushed.

"Oh, that's absurd! Still, no one could think *anything* if I come with you. Hilary, have you thought that if she continues coming to Father——"

"I shall tell her that she mustn't!"

Cecilia's heart gave two thumps, the first with pleasure, the second with sympathy.

"It will be horrid for you," she said. "You hate doing anything of that sort."

Hilary nodded.

"But I'm afraid it's the only way," went on Cecilia, rather hastily. "And, of course, it will be no good saying anything to Father; one must simply let him suppose that she has got tired of it."

Again Hilary nodded.

"He will think it very funny," murmured Cecilia pensively. "Oh, and have you thought that taking her away from where she is will only make those people talk the more?"

Hilary shrugged his shoulders.

"It may make that man furious," Cecilia added.

"It will."

"Oh, but then, of course, if you don't see her afterwards, they will have no—no excuse at all."

" I shall not see her afterwards," said Hilary, " if I can avoid it."

Cecilia looked at him.

" It's very sweet of you, Hilary."

" What is sweet? " asked Hilary stonily.

" Why, to take all this trouble. Is it really necessary for you to do anything? " But looking in his face, she went on hastily: " Yes, yes, it's best. Let's go at once. Oh, those people in the drawing-room! Do wait ten minutes."

A little later, running up to put her hat on, she wondered why it was that Hilary always made her want to comfort him. Stephen never affected her like this.

Having little or no notion where to go, they walked in the direction of Bayswater. To place the Park between Hound Street and the little model was the first essential. On arriving at the other side of the Broad Walk, they made instinctively away from every sight of green. In a long, grey street of dismally respectable appearance they found what they were looking for, a bed-sitting room furnished, advertised on a card in the window. The door was opened by the landlady, a tall woman of narrow build, with a West-Country accent, and a rather hungry sweetness running through her hardness. They stood talking with her in a passage, whose oilcloth of variegated pattern emitted a faint odour. The staircase could be seen climbing steeply up past walls covered with a shining paper cut by narrow red lines into small yellow squares. An almanack, of so floral a design that nobody would surely want to steal it, hung on the wall; below it was an umbrella stand without umbrellas. The dim little passage led past two grimly closed doors painted rusty red to two half-open doors with dull glass in their panels. Outside, in the street from which they had mounted by stone steps, a shower of sleet had begun to fall. Hilary shut the door, but the cold spirit of that shower had already slipped into the bleak, narrow house.

" This is the apartment, m'm," said the landlady, opening the first of the rusty-coloured doors. The room, which had a paper of blue roses on a yellow ground, was separated from another room by double doors.

" I let the rooms together sometimes, but just now that room's taken—a young gentleman in the City; that's why I'm able to let this cheap."

Cecilia looked at Hilary. " I hardly think——"

The landlady quickly turned the handles of the doors, showing that they would not open.

"*I* keep the key," she said. " There's a bolt on both sides."

Reassurèd, Cecilia walked round the room as far as this
was possible, for it was practically all furniture.   There was
the same little wrinkle across her nose as across Thyme's nose
when she spoke of Hound Street.   Suddenly she caught sight
of Hilary.   He was standing with his back against the door.
On his face was a strange and bitter look, such as a man might
have on seeing the face of Ugliness herself, feeling that she
was not only without him, but within—a universal spirit; the
look of a man who had thought that he was chivalrous, and
found that he was not; of a leader about to give an order
that he would not himself have executed.

Seeing that look, Cecilia said with some haste:

" It's all very nice and clean; it will do very well, I think.
Seven shillings a week, I believe you said.   We will take it
for a fortnight, at all events."

The first glimmer of a smile appeared on the landlady's grim
face, with its hungry eyes, sweetened by patience.

" When would she be coming in? " she asked.

" When do you think, Hilary? "

" I don't know," muttered Hilary.   " The sooner the better
—if it must be.   To-morrow, or the day after."

And with one look at the bed, covered by a piece of cheap
red-and-yellow tasselled tapestry, he went out into the street.
The shower was over, but the house faced north, and no sun
was shining on it.

CHAPTER XXII

HILARY PUTS AN END TO IT

LIKE flies caught among the impalpable and smoky threads of cobwebs, so men struggle in the webs of their own natures, giving here a start, there a pitiful small jerking, long sustained, and failing into stillness. Enmeshed they were born, enmeshed they die, fighting according to their strength to the end; to fight in the hope of freedom, their joy; to die, not knowing they are beaten, their reward. Nothing, too, is more to be remarked than the manner in which Life devises for each man the particular dilemmas most suited to his nature; that which to the man of gross, decided, or fanatic turn of mind appears a simple sum, to the man of delicate and speculative temper seems to have no answer.

So it was with Hilary in that special web wherein his spirit struggled, sunrise unto sunset, and by moonlight afterward. Inclination, and the circumstances of a life which had never forced him to grips with either men or women, had detached him from the necessity for giving or taking orders. He had almost lost the faculty. Life had been a picture with blurred outlines melting into a softly shaded whole. Not for years had anything seemed to him quite a case for " Yes " or " No." It had been his creed, his delight, his business, too, to try and put himself in everybody's place, so that now there were but few places where he did not, speculatively speaking, feel at home.

Putting himself into the little model's place gave him but small delight. Making due allowance for the sentiment men naturally import into their appreciation of the lives of women, his conception of her place was doubtless not so very wrong.

Here was a child, barely twenty years of age, country bred, neither a lady nor quite a working-girl, without a home or relatives, according to her own accounts—at all events, without those who were disposed to help her—without apparently any sort of friend; helpless by nature, and whose profession required a more than common wariness—this girl he was proposing to set quite adrift again by cutting through the single slender rope which tethered her. It was like digging up a little rose-tree planted with one's own hands in some poor shelter, just when it had taken root, and setting it where the full winds would beat against it. To do so brusque and, as it seemed to Hilary, so inhumane a thing was foreign to his nature. There was also the little matter of that touch of fever —the distant music he had been hearing since the waggons came in to Covent Garden.

With a feeling that was almost misery, therefore, he waited for her on Monday afternoon, walking to and fro in his study, where all the walls were white, and all the woodwork coloured like the leaf of a cigar; where the books were that colour too, in Hilary's special deerskin binding; where there were no flowers nor any sunlight coming through the windows, but plenty of sheets of paper—a room which youth seemed to have left for ever, the room of middle age!

He called her in with the intention of at once saying what he had to say, and getting it over in the fewest words. But he had not reckoned fully either with his own nature or with woman's instinct. Nor had he allowed—being, for all his learning, perhaps because of it, singularly unable to gauge the effects of simple actions—for the proprietary relations he had established in the girl's mind by giving her those clothes.

As a dog whose master has it in his mind to go away from him, stands gazing up with tragic inquiry in his eyes, scenting to his soul that coming cruelty—as a dog thus soon to be bereaved, so stood the little model.

By the pose of every limb, and a fixed gaze bright as if tears were behind it, and by a sort of trembling, she seemed to say: 'I know why you have sent for me.'

When Hilary saw her stand like that he felt as a man might when told to flog his fellow-creature. To gain time he asked her what she did with herself all day. The little model evidently tried to tell herself that her foreboding had been needless.

Now that the mornings were nice, she said with some animation—she got up much earlier, and did her needlework first thing; she then " did out " the room. There were mouse-holes in her room, and she had bought a trap. She had caught a mouse last night. She hadn't liked to kill it; she had put it in a tin box, and let it go when she went out. Quick to see that Hilary was interested in this, as well he might be, she told him that she could not bear to see cats hungry or lost dogs, especially

lost dogs, and she described to him one that she had seen. She
had not liked to tell a policeman; they stared so hard. Those
words were of strange omen, and Hilary turned his head away.
The little model, perceiving that she had made an effect of some
sort, tried to deepen it. She had heard they did all sorts of
things to people—but, seeing at once from Hilary's face that
she was not improving her effect, she broke off suddenly, and
hastily began to tell him of her breakfast, of how comfortable
she was now she had got her clothes; how she liked her room;
how old Mr. Creed was very funny, never taking any notice of
her when he met her in the morning. Then followed a minute
account of where she had been trying to get work; of an engagement promised; Mr. Lennard, too, still wanted her to pose to
him. At this she flashed a look at Hilary, then cast down her
eyes. She could get plenty of work if she began that way. But
she hadn't, because he had told her not, and, of course, she didn't
want to; she liked coming to Mr. Stone so much. And she got
on very well, and she liked London, and she liked the shops.
She mentioned neither Hughs nor Mrs. Hughs. In all this rig-
marole, told with such obvious purpose, stolidity was strangely
mingled with almost cunning quickness to see the effect made;
but the dog-like devotion was never quite out of her eyes when
they were fixed on Hilary.

This look got through the weakest places in what little armour
Nature had bestowed on him. It touched one of the least conceited and most amiable of men profoundly. He felt it an
honour that anything so young as this should regard him in
that way. He had always tried to keep out of his mind that
which might have given him the key to her special feeling for
himself—those words of the painter of still life: "She's got
a story of some sort." But it flashed across him suddenly like an
inspiration: If her story were the simplest of all stories—the
direct, rather brutal, love affair of a village boy and girl—
would not she, naturally given to surrender, be forced this time
to the very antithesis of that young animal amour which had
brought on her such sharp consequences?

But, wherever her devotion came from, it seemed to Hilary the
grossest violation of the feelings of a gentleman to treat it un-
gratefully. Yet it was as if for the purpose of saying, "You are
a nuisance to me, or worse!" that he had asked her to his study.
Her presence had hitherto chiefly roused in him the half-amused,
half-tender feelings of one who strokes a foal or calf, watching

its soft uncouthness; now, about to say good-bye to her, there was the question of whether that was the only feeling.

Miranda, stealing out between her master and his visitor, growled.

The little model, who was stroking a china ash-tray with her ungloved, inky fingers, muttered, with a smile, half pathetic, half cynical: "She doesn't like me! She knows I don't belong here. She hates me to come. She's jealous!"

Hilary said abruptly:

"Tell me! Have you made any friends since you've been in London?"

The girl flashed a look at him that said:

'Could I make *you* jealous?'

Then, as though guilty of a far too daring thought, drooped her head, and answered:

"No."

"Not one?"

The little model repeated almost passionately: "No, I don't want any friends; I only want to be let alone."

Hilary began speaking rapidly.

"But these Hughses have not left you alone. I told you, I thought you ought to move; I've taken another room for you quite away from them. Leave your furniture with a week's rent, and take your trunk quietly away to-morrow in a cab without saying a word to anyone. This is the new address, and here's the money for your expenses. They're dangerous for you, those people."

The little model muttered desperately: "But I don't care what they do!"

Hilary went on: "Listen! You mustn't come here again, or the man will trace you. We will take care you have what's necessary till you can get other work."

The little model looked up at him without a word. Now that the thin link which bound her to some sort of household gods had snapped, all the patience and submission bred in her by village life, by the hard facts of her story, and by these last months in London, served her well enough. She made no fuss. Hilary saw a tear roll down her cheek.

He turned his head away, and said: "Don't cry, my child!"

Quite obediently the little model swallowed the tear. A thought seemed to strike her:

"But I could see you, Mr. Dallison, couldn't I, sometimes?"

Seeing from his face that this was not in the programme, she stood silent again, looking up at him.

It was a little difficult for Hilary to say: "I can't see you because my wife is jealous!" It was cruel to tell her: "I don't want to see you!"—besides, it was not true.

"You'll soon be making friends," he said at last, "and you can always write to me"; and with a queer smile he added: "You're only just beginning life; you mustn't take these things to heart; you'll find plenty of people better able to advise and help you than ever I shall be!"

The little model answered this by seizing his hand with both of hers. She dropped it again at once, as if guilty of presumption, and stood with her head bent. Hilary, looking down on the little hat which, by his special wish, contained no feathers, felt a lump rise in his throat.

"It's funny," he said; "I don't know your Christian name."

"Ivy," muttered the little model.

"Ivy! Well, I'll write to you. But you must promise me to do exactly as I said."

The girl looked up; her face was almost ugly—like a child's in whom a storm of feeling is repressed.

"Promise!" repeated Hilary.

With a bitter droop of her lower lip, she nodded, and suddenly put her hand to her heart. That action, of which she was clearly unconscious, so naïvely, so almost automatically was it done, nearly put an end to Hilary's determination.

"Now you must go," he said.

The little model choked, grew very red, and then quite white.

"Aren't I even to say good-bye to Mr. Stone?"

Hilary shook his head.

"He'll miss me," she said desperately. "He will. I know he will!"

"So shall I," said Hilary. "We can't help that."

The little model drew herself up to her full height; her breast heaved beneath the clothes which had made her Hilary's. She was very like "The Shadow" at that moment, as though whatever Hilary might do there she would be—a little ghost, the spirit of the helpless submerged world, for ever haunting with its dumb appeal the minds of men.

"Give me your hand," said Hilary.

The little model put out her not too white, small hand. It was soft, clinging, and as hot as fire.

" Good-bye, my dear, and bless you ! "

The little model gave him a look with who-knows-what of re-proach in it, and, faithful to her training, went submissively away.

Hilary did not look after her, but, standing by the lofty mantelpiece above the ashes of the fire, rested his forehead on his arm. Not even a fly's buzzing broke the stillness. There was sound for all that—not of distant music, but of blood beating in his ears and temples.

CHAPTER XXIII

THE "BOOK OF UNIVERSAL BROTHERHOOD"

It is fitting that a few words should be said about the writer of the "Book of Universal Brotherhood."

Sylvanus Stone, having graduated very highly at the London University, had been appointed at an early age lecturer to more than one Public Institution. He had soon received the professorial robes due to a man of his profound learning in the natural sciences, and from that time till he was seventy his life had flowed on in one continual round of lectures, addresses, disquisitions, and arguments on the subjects in which he was a specialist. At the age of seventy, long after his wife's death and the marriages of his three children, he had for some time been living by himself, when a very serious illness—the result of liberties taken with an iron constitution by a single mind —prostrated him.

During the long convalescence following this illness the power of contemplation, which the Professor had up to then given to natural science, began to fix itself on life at large. But the mind which had made of natural science an idea, a passion, was not content with vague reflections on life. Slowly, subtly, with irresistible centrifugal force—with a force which perhaps it would not have acquired but for that illness—the idea, the passion of Universal Brotherhood had sucked into itself all his errant wonderings on the riddle of existence. The single mind of this old man, divorced by illness from his previous existence, pensioned and permanently shelved, began to worship a new star, that with every week and month and year grew brighter, till all other stars had lost their glimmer and died out.

At the age of seventy-four he had begun his book. Under the spell of his subject and of advancing age, his extreme inattention to passing matters became rapidly accentuated. His figure had become almost too publicly conspicuous before Bianca, finding him one day seated on the roof of his lonely little top-story flat, the better to contemplate his darling Universe, had inveigled him home with her, and installed him in a room in her own house. After the first day or two he had not noticed any change to speak of.

His habits in his new home were soon formed, and once formed, they varied not at all; for he admitted into his life nothing which took him from the writing of his book.

On the afternoon following Hilary's dismissal of the little model, being disappointed of his amanuensis, Mr. Stone had waited for an hour, reading his pages over and over to himself. He had then done his exercises. At the usual time for tea he had sat down, and, with his cup and brown bread-and-butter alternately at his lips, had looked long and fixedly at the place where the girl was wont to sit. Having finished, he left the room and went about the house. He found no one but Miranda, who, seated in the passage leading to the studio, was trying to keep one eye on the absence of her master and the other on the absence of her mistress. She joined Mr. Stone, maintaining a respect-compelling interval behind him when he went before, and before him when he went behind. When they had finished hunting, Mr. Stone went down to the garden gate. Here Bianca found him presently motionless, without a hat, in the full sun, craning his white head in the direction from which he knew the little model habitually came.

The mistress of the house was herself returning from her annual visit to the Royal Academy, where she still went, as dogs, from some perverted sense, will go and sniff round other dogs to whom they have long taken a dislike. A loose-hanging veil depended from her mushroom-shaped and coloured hat. Her eyes were brightened by her visit.

Mr. Stone soon seemed to take in who she was, and stood regarding her a minute without speaking. His attitude towards his daughters was rather like that of an old drake towards two swans whom he has inadvertently begotten—there was inquiry in it, disapproval, admiration, and faint surprise.

" Why has she not come? " he said.

Bianca winced behind her veil. " Have you asked Hilary? "

" I cannot find him," answered Mr. Stone. Something about his patient stooping figure and white head, on which the sunlight was falling, made Bianca slip her hand through his arm.

" Come in, Dad. I'll do your copying."

Mr. Stone looked at her intently, and shook his head.

" It would be against my principles; I cannot take an unpaid service. But if you would come, my dear, I should like to read to you. It is stimulating."

At that request Bianca's eyes grew dim. Pressing Mr. Stone's shaggy arm against her breast, she moved with him towards the house.

"I think I may have written something that will interest you," Mr. Stone said, as they went along.

"I am sure you have," Bianca murmured.

"It is universal," said Mr. Stone; "it concerns birth. Sit at the table. I will begin, as usual, where I left off yesterday."

Bianca took the little model's seat, resting her chin on her hand, as motionless as any of the statues she had just been viewing.

It almost seemed as if Mr. Stone were feeling nervous. He twice arranged his papers; cleared his throat; then, lifting a sheet suddenly, took three steps, turned his back on her, and began to read.

"'In that slow, incessant change of form to form, called Life, men, made spasmodic by perpetual action, had seized on a certain moment, no more intrinsically notable than any other moment, and had called it Birth. This habit of honouring one single instant of the universal process to the disadvantage of all the other instants had done more, perhaps, than anything to obfuscate the crystal clearness of the fundamental flux. As well might such as watch the process of the green, unfolding earth, emerging from the brumous arms of winter, isolate a single day and call it Spring. In the tides of rhythm by which the change of form to form was governed'"—Mr. Stone's voice, which had till then been but a thin, husky murmur, gradually grew louder and louder, as though he were addressing a great concourse—"'the golden universal haze in which men should have flown like bright wing-beats round the sun gave place to the parasitic halo which every man derived from the glorifying of his own nativity. To this primary mistake could be traced his intensely personal philosophy. Slowly but surely there had dried up in his heart the wish to be his brother.'"

He stopped reading suddenly.

"I see him coming in," he said.

The next minute the door opened, and Hilary entered.

"She has not come," said Mr. Stone; and Bianca murmured: "We miss her!"

"Her eyes," said Mr. Stone, "have a peculiar look; they help me to see into the future. I have noticed the same look in the eyes of female dogs."

With a little laugh, Bianca murmured again:

" That is good ! "

" There is one virtue in dogs," said Hilary, " which human beings lack—they are incapable of mockery."

But Bianca's lips, parted, indrawn, seemed saying: ' You ask too much ! I no longer attract you. Am I to sympathise in the attraction this common little girl has for you ? '

Mr. Stone's gaze was fixed intently on the wall.

" The dog," he said, " has lost much of its primordial character."

And, moving to his desk, he took up his quill pen.

Hilary and Bianca made no sound, nor did they look at one another; and in this silence, so much more full of meaning than any talk, the scratching of the quill went on. Mr. Stone put it down at last, and, seeing two persons in the room, read:

" ' Looking back ·at those days when the doctrine of evolution had reached its pinnacle, one sees how the human mind, by its habit of continual crystallisations, had destroyed all the meaning of the process. Witness, for example, that sterile phenomenon, the pagoda of ' caste ' ! Like this Chinese building, so was Society then formed. Men were living there in layers, as divided from each other, class from class——' " He took up the quill, and again began to write.

" You understand, I suppose," said Hilary in a low voice, " that she has been told not to come ? "

Bianca moved her shoulders.

With a most unwonted look of anger, he added:

" Is it within the scope of your generosity to credit me with the desire to meet your wishes ? "

Bianca's answer was a laugh so strangely hard, so cruelly bitter, that Hilary involuntarily turned, as though to retrieve the sound before it reached the old man's ears.

Mr. Stone had laid down his pen. " I shall write no more to-day," he said; " I have lost my feeling—I am not myself." He spoke in a voice unlike his own.

Very tired and worn his old figure looked; as some lean horse, whose sun has set, stands with drooped head, the hollows in his neck showing under his straggling mane. And suddenly, evidently quite oblivious that he had any audience, he spoke:

" O Great Universe, I am an old man of a faint spirit, with

no singleness of purpose. Help me to write on—help me to write a book such as the world has never seen!"

A dead silence followed that strange prayer; then Bianca, with tears rolling down her face, got up and rushed out of the room.

Mr. Stone came to himself. His mute, white face had suddenly grown scared and pink. He looked at Hilary.

"I fear that I forgot myself. Have I said anything peculiar?"

Not feeling certain of his voice, Hilary shook his head, and he, too, moved towards the door.

CHAPTER XXIV

SHADOWLAND

" EACH of us has a shadow in those places—in those streets."

That saying of Mr. Stone's, which—like so many of his sayings—had travelled forth to beat the air, might have seemed, even " in those days," not altogether without meaning to anyone who looked into the room of Mr. Joshua Creed in Hound Street.

This aged butler lay in bed waiting for the inevitable striking of a small alarum clock placed in the very centre of his mantelpiece. Flanking that round and ruthless arbiter, which drove him day by day to stand up on feet whose time had come to rest, were the effigies of his past triumphs. On the one hand, in a papier-mâché frame, slightly tinged with smuts, stood a portrait of the " Honorable Bateson," in the uniform of his Yeomanry. Creed's former master's face wore that dare-devil look with which he had been wont to say: " D——n it, Creed! lend me a pound. I've got no money ! " On the other hand, in a green frame which had once been plush, and covered by a glass with a crack in the left-hand corner, was a portrait of the Dowager Countess of Glengower, as this former mistress of his appeared, conceived by the local photographer, laying the foundation-stone of the local almshouse. During the wreck of Creed's career, which, following on a lengthy illness, had preceded his salvation by the *Westminster Gazette,* these two household gods had lain at the bottom of an old tin trunk, in the possession of the keeper of a lodging-house, waiting to be bailed out. The " Honorable Bateson " was now dead, nor had he paid as yet the pounds he had borrowed. Lady Glengower, too, was in heaven, remembering that she had forgotten all her servants in her will. He who had served them was still alive, and his first thought, when he had secured his post on the " *Westminster,*" was to save enough to rescue them from a dishonourable confinement. It had taken him six months. He had found them keeping company with three pairs of woollen drawers; an old but respectable black tail-coat; a plaid cravat; a Bible; four socks, two of which had toes and two of which had heels; some darning-cotton and a needle; a pair of elastic-

sided boots; a comb and a sprig of white heather, wrapped up
with a little piece of shaving-soap and two pipe-cleaners in a
bit of the *Globe* newspaper; also two collars, whose lofty points,
separated by gaps of quite two inches, had been wont to reach
their master's gills; the small alarum clock aforesaid; and a tie-
pin formed in the likeness of Queen Victoria at the date of her
first Jubilee. How many times had he not gone in thought over
those stores of treasure while he was parted from them! How
many times since they had come back to him had he not pondered with a slow but deathless anger on the absence of a certain shirt, which he could have sworn had been amongst them!

But now he lay in bed waiting. to hear the clock go off, with
his old bristly chin beneath the bedclothes, and his old discoloured nose above. He was thinking the thoughts which
usually came into his mind about this hour—that Mrs. Hughs
ought not to scrape the butter off his bread for breakfast in the
way she did; that she ought to take that sixpence off his rent;
that the man who brought his late editions in the cart ought to
be earlier, letting 'that man' get his *Pell Mells* off before him,
when he himself would be having the one chance of his day;
that, sooner than pay the ninepence which the bootmaker had
proposed to charge for resoling him, he would wait until the
summer came—'low-class o' feller' as he was, he'd be glad
enough to sole him then for sixpence!

And the high-souled critic, finding these reflections sordid,
would have thought otherwise, perhaps, had he been standing on
those feet (now twitching all by themselves beneath the bedclothes) up to eleven o'clock the night before, because there were
still twelve numbers of the late edition that nobody would buy.
No one knew more surely than Joshua Creed himself that, if
he suffered himself to entertain any large and lofty views of
life, he would infallibly find himself in that building to keep
out of which he was in the habit of addressing to God his only
prayer to speak of. Fortunately, from a boy up, together with
a lengthy, oblong, square-jawed face, he had been given by
Nature a single-minded view of life. In fact, the mysterious,
stout tenacity of a soul born in the neighbourhood of Newmarket could not have been done justice to had he constitutionally seen—any more than Mr. Stone himself—two things at
a time. The one thing he had seen, for the five years that he
had now stood outside Messrs. Rose and Thorn's, was the workhouse; and, as he was not going there so long as he was living,

he attended carefully to all little matters of expense in this somewhat sordid way.

While attending thus, he heard a scream. Having by temperament considerable caution, but little fear, he waited till he heard another, and then got out of bed. Taking the poker in his hand, and putting on his spectacles, he hurried to the door. Many a time and oft in old days had he risen in this fashion to defend the plate of the "Honorable Bateson" and the Dowager Countess of Glengower from the periodical attacks of his imagination. He stood with his ancient nightgown flapping round his still more ancient legs, slightly shivering; then, pulling the door open, he looked forth. On the stairs just above him Mrs. Hughs, clasping her baby with one arm, was holding the other out at full length between herself and Hughs. He heard the latter say: "You've drove me to it; I'll do a swing for you!" Mrs. Hughs' thin body brushed past into his room; blood was dripping from her wrist. Creed saw that Hughs had his bayonet in his hand. With all his might he called out: "Ye ought to be ashamed of yourself!" raising the poker to a position of defence. At this moment—more really dangerous than any he had ever known—it was remarkable that he instinctively opposed to it his most ordinary turns of speech. It was as though the extravagance of this un-English violence had roused in him the full measure of a native moderation. The sight of the naked steel deeply disgusted him; he uttered a long sentence. What did Hughs call this—disgracin' of the house at this time in the mornin'? Where was he brought up? Call 'imself a soldier, attackin' of old men and women in this way? He ought to be ashamed!

While these words were issuing between the yellow stumps of teeth in that withered mouth, Hughs stood silent, the back of his arm covering his eyes. Voices and a heavy tread were heard. Distinguishing in that tread the advancing footsteps of the Law, Creed said: "You attack me if you dare!"

Hughs dropped his arm. His short, dark face had a desperate look, as of a caged rat; his eyes were everywhere at once.

"All right, daddy," he said; "I won't hurt *you*. She's drove my head all wrong again. Catch hold o' this; I can't trust myself." He held out the bayonet.

"Westminister" took it gingerly in his shaking hand.

"To use a thing like that!" he said. "An' call yourself an Englishman! I'll ketch me death standin' here, I will."

Hughs made no answer leaning against the wall. The old butler regarded him severely. He did not take a wide or philosophic view of him, as a tortured human being, driven by the whips of passion in his dark blood; a creature whose moral nature was the warp, stunted tree his life had made it; a poor devil half destroyed by drink and by his wound. The old butler took a more single-minded and old-fashioned line. 'Ketch 'old of 'im!' he thought. 'With these low fellers there's nothin' else to be done. Ketch 'old of 'im until he squeals.'

Nodding his ancient head, he said:

"Here's an orficer. I shan't speak for yer; you deserves all you'll get, and more."

Later, dressed in an old Newmarket coat, given him by some client, and walking towards the police-station alongside Mrs. Hughs, he was particularly silent, presenting a front of some austerity, as became a man mixed up in a low class of incident like this. And the seamstress, very thin and scared, with her wounded wrist slung in a muffler of her husband's and carrying the baby on her other arm, because the morning's incident had upset the little thing, slipped along beside him, glancing now and then into his face.

Only once did he speak, and to himself:

"I don't know what they'll say to me down at the orfice, when I go again—missin' my day like this! Oh dear, what a misfortune! What put it into him to go on like that?"

At this, which was far from being intended as encouragement, the waters of speech broke up and flowed from Mrs. Hughs. She had only told Hughs how that young girl had gone, and left a week's rent, with a bit of writing to say she wasn't coming back; it wasn't *her* fault that she was gone—that ought never to have come there at all, a creature that knew no better than to come between husband and wife. She couldn't tell no more than he could where that young girl had gone!

The tears, stealing forth, chased each other down the seamstress's thin cheeks. Her face had now but little likeness to the face with which she had stood confronting Hughs when she informed him of the little model's flight. None of the triumph which had leaped out of her bruised heart, none of the strident malice with which her voice, whether she would or no, strove to avenge her wounded sense of property; none of that unconscious abnegation, so very near to heroism, with which she had rushed and caught up her baby from beneath the bayonet, when, goaded by her malice and triumph, Hughs had rushed to seize that weapon. None of all that, but, instead, a pitiable terror of the ordeal before her—a pitiful, mute, quivering distress, that this man, against whom, two hours before, she had felt such a store of bitter rancour, whose almost murderous assault she had so narrowly escaped, should now be in this plight.

The sight of her emotion penetrated through his spectacles to something lying deep in the old butler.

"Don't you take on," he said; "I'll stand by yer. He shan't treat yer with impuniness."

To his uncomplicated nature the affair was still one of tit for tat. Mrs. Hughs became mute again. Her torn heart yearned to cancel the penalty that would fall on all of them, to deliver Hughs from the common enemy—the Law; but a queer feeling of pride and bewilderment, and a knowledge, that, to demand an eye for an eye was expected of all self-respecting persons, kept her silent.

Thus, then, they reached the great consoler, the grey resolver of all human tangles, haven of men and angels, the police court. It was situated in a back street. Like trails of ooze, when the tide, neither ebb nor flow, is leaving and making for some estuary, trails of human beings were moving to and from it. The faces of these shuffling "shadows" wore a look as though masked with some hard but threadbare stuff—the look of those whom Life has squeezed into a last resort. Within the porches lay a stagnant marsh of suppliants, through whose centre trickled to and fro that stream of ooze. An old policeman, too, like some grey lighthouse, marked the entrance to the port of refuge. Close to that lighthouse the old butler edged his way. The love of regularity, and of an established order of affairs, born in him and fostered by a life passed in the service of the "Honorable Bateson" and the other gentry, made him cling instinctively to the only person in this crowd whom he could tell for certain to be on the side of law and order. Something in his oblong face and lank, scanty hair parted precisely in the middle, something in that high collar supporting his lean gills, not subservient exactly, but as it were suggesting that he was in league against all this low-class of fellow, made the policeman say to him:

"What's your business, daddy?"

"Oh!" the old butler answered. "This poor woman. I'm a witness to her battery."

The policeman cast his not unkindly look over the figure of the seamstress. " You stand here," he said; " I'll pass you in directly."

And soon by his offices the two were passed into the port of refuge.

They sat down side by side on the edge of a long, hard, wooden bench; Creed fixing his eyes, whose colour had run into a brownish rim round their centres, on the magistrate, as in old days sun-worshippers would sit blinking devoutly at the sun; and Mrs. Hughs fixing her eyes on her lap, while tears of agony trickled down her face. On her unwounded arm the baby slept. In front of them, and unregarded, filed one by one those shadows who had drunk the day before too deeply of the waters of forgetfulness. To-day, instead, they were to drink the water of remembrance, poured out for them with no uncertain hand. And somewhere very far away, it may have been that Justice sat with her ironic smile watching men judge their shadows. She had watched them so long about that business. With her elementary idea that hares and tortoises should not be made to start from the same mark she had a little given up expecting to be asked to come and lend a hand; they had gone so far beyond her. Perhaps she knew, too, that men no longer punished, but now only reformed, their erring brothers, and this made her heart as light as the hearts of those who had been in the prisons where they were no longer punished.

The old butler, however, was not thinking of her; he had thoughts of a simpler order in his mind. He was reflecting that he had once valeted the nephew of the late Lord Justice Hawthorn, and in the midst of this low-class business the reminiscence brought him refreshment. Over and over to himself he conned these words: " I interpylated in between them, and I says, ' You ought to be ashamed of yourself; call yourself an Englishman, I says, attackin' of old men and women with cold steel, I says!' " And suddenly he saw that Hughs was in the dock.

The dark man stood with his hands pressed to his sides, as though at attention on parade. A pale profile, broken by a line of black moustache, was all " Westminister " could see of that impassive face, whose eyes, fixed on the magistrate, alone betrayed the fires within. The violent trembling of the seamstress roused in Joshua Creed a certain irritation, and seeing the baby open his black eyes, he nudged her, whispering: " Ye've woke the baby! "

Responding to words, which alone perhaps could have moved her at such a moment, Mrs. Hughs rocked the dumb spectator of the drama. Again the old butler nudged her.

" They want yer in the box," he said.

Mrs. Hughs rose, and took her place.

He who wished to read the hearts of this husband and wife who stood at right angles, to have their wounds healed by Law, would have needed to have watched the hundred thousand hours of their wedded life, known and heard the million thoughts and words, which had passed in the dim spaces of their world, to have been cognisant of the million reasons why they neither of them felt that they could have done other than they had done. Reading their hearts by the light of knowledge such as this, he would not have been surprised that, brought into this place of remedy, they seemed to enter into a sudden league. A look passed between them. It was not friendly, it had no appeal; but it sufficed. There seemed to be expressed in it the knowledge bred by immemorial experience and immemorial time: This Law before which we stand was not made by us! As dogs, when they hear the crack of a far whip, will shrink, and in their whole bearing show wary quietude, so Hughs and Mrs. Hughs, confronted by the questionings of Law, made only such answers as could be dragged from them. In a voice hardly above a whisper Mrs. Hughs told her tale. They had fallen out. What about? She did not know. Had he attacked her? He had had it in his hand. What then? She had slipped, and hurt her wrist against the point. At this statement Hughs turned his eyes on her, and seemed to say: " You drove me to it; I've got to suffer, for all your trying to get me out of what I've done. I gave you one, and I don't want your help. But I'm glad you stick to me against this —— Law ! " Then, lowering his eyes, he stood motionless during her breathless little outburst. He was her husband; she had borne him five; he had been wounded in the war. She had never wanted him brought here.

No mention of the little model. . . .

The old butler dwelt on this reticence of Mrs. Hughs, when, two hours afterwards, in pursuance of his instinctive reliance on the gentry, he called on Hilary.

The latter, surrounded by books and papers—for, since his dismissal of the girl, he had worked with great activity—was partaking of lunch, served to him in his study on a tray.

"There's an old gentleman to see you, sir; he says you know him; his name is Creed."

"Show him in," said Hilary.

Appearing suddenly from behind the servant in the doorway, the old butler came in at a stealthy amble; he looked round, and, seeing a chair, placed his hat beneath it, then advanced, with nose and spectacles upturned, to Hilary. Catching sight of the tray, he stopped, checked in an evident desire to communicate his soul.

"Oh dear," he said, "I'm intrudin' on your luncheon. I can wait; I'll go and sit in the passage."

Hilary, however, shook his hand, faded now to skin and bone, and motioned him to a chair.

He sat down on the edge of it, and again said:

"I'm intrudin' on yer."

"Not at all. Is there anything I can do?"

Creed took off his spectacles, wiped them to help himself to see more clearly what he had to say, and put them on again.

"It's a-concerning of these domestic matters," he said. "I come up to tell yer, knowing as you're interested in this family."

"Well," said Hilary. "What has happened?"

"It's along of the young girl's having left them, as you may know."

"Ah!"

"It's brought things to a crisax," explained Creed.

"Indeed, how's that?"

The old butler related the facts of the assault. "I took 'is bayonet away from him," he ended; "he didn't frighten *me*."

"Is he out of his mind?" asked Hilary.

"I've no conscience of it," replied Creed. "His wife, she's gone the wrong way to work with him, in my opinion, but that's particular to women. She's a-goaded of him respecting a certain party. I don't say but what that young girl's no better than what she ought to be; look at her profession, and her a country girl, too! She must be what she oughtn't to. But he ain't the sort o' man you can treat like that. You can't get thorns from figs; you can't expect it from the lower orders. They only give him a month, considerin' of him bein' wounded in the war. It'd been more if they'd a-known he was a-hankerin' after that young girl—a married man like him; don't ye think so, sir?"

Hilary's face had assumed its retired expression. 'I cannot go into that with you,' it seemed to say.

Quick to see the change, Creed rose. "But I'm intrudin' on your dinner," he said—"your luncheon, I should say. The woman goes on irritatin' of him, but he must expect of that, she bein' his wife. But what a misfortune! He'll be back again in no time, and what'll happen then? It won't improve him, shut up in one of them low prisons!" Then, raising his old face to Hilary: "Oh dear! It's like a-walkin' on a black night, when ye can't see your 'and before yer."

Hilary was unable to find a suitable answer to this simile.

The impression made on him by the old butler's recital was queerly twofold; his more fastidious side felt distinct relief that he had severed connection with an episode capable of developments so sordid and conspicuous. But all the side of him —and Hilary was a complicated product—which felt compassion for the helpless, his suppressed chivalry, in fact, had also received its fillip. The old butler's references to the girl showed clearly how the hands of all men and women were against her. She was that pariah, a young girl without property or friends, spiritually soft, physically alluring.

To recompense "Westminister" for the loss of his day's work, to make a dubious statement that nights were never so black as they appeared to be, was all that he could venture to do. Creed hesitated in the doorway.

"Oh dear," he said, "there's a-one thing that the woman was a-saying that I've forgot to tell you. It's a-concernin' of what this 'ere man was boastin' in his rage. 'Let them,' he says, 'as is responsive for the movin' of her look out,' he says; 'I ain't done with them!' That's conspiracy, I should think!"

Smiling away this diagnosis of Hughs' words, Hilary shook the old man's withered hand, and closed the door. Sitting down again at his writing-table, he buried himself almost angrily in his work. But the queer, half-pleasurable, fevered feeling, which had been his, since the night he walked down Piccadilly, and met the image of the little model, was unfavourable to the austere process of his thoughts.

CHAPTER XXV

MR. STONE IN WAITING

THAT same afternoon, while Mr. Stone was writing, he heard a voice saying:

"Dad, stop writing just a minute, and talk to me."

Recognition came into his eyes. It was his younger daughter.

"My dear," he said, "are you unwell?"

Keeping his hand, fragile and veined and chill, under her own warm grasp, Bianca answered: "Lonely."

Mr. Stone looked straight before him.

"Loneliness," he said, "is man's chief fault"; and seeing his pen lying on the desk, he tried to lift his hand. Bianca held it down. At that hot clasp something seemed to stir in Mr. Stone. His cheeks grew pink.

"Kiss me, Dad."

Mr. Stone hesitated. Then his lips resolutely touched her eye. "It is wet," he said. He seemed for a moment struggling to grasp the meaning of moisture in connection with the human eye. Soon his face again became serene. "The heart," he said, "is a dark well; its depth unknown. I have lived eighty years. I am still drawing water."

"Draw a little for me, Dad."

This time Mr. Stone looked at his daughter anxiously, and suddenly spoke, as if afraid that if he waited he might forget.

"You are unhappy!"

Bianca put her face down to his tweed sleeve. "How nice your coat smells!" she murmured.

"You are unhappy," repeated Mr. Stone.

Bianca dropped his hand, and moved away.

Mr. Stone followed her. "Why?" he said. Then, grasping his brow, he added: "If it would do you any good, my dear, to hear a page or two, I could read to you."

Biance shook her head.

"No; talk to me!"

Mr. Stone answered simply: "I have forgotten."

"You talk to that little girl," murmured Bianca.

Mr. Stone seemed to lose himself in reverie.

"If that is true," he said, following out his thoughts, "it must be due to the sex instinct not yet quite extinct. It is stated that the blackcock will dance before his females to a great age, though I have never seen it."

"If you dance before *her*," said Bianca, with her face averted, "can't you even talk to me?"

"I do not dance, my dear," said Mr. Stone; "I will do my best to talk to you."

There was a silence, and he began to pace the room. Bianca, by the empty fireplace, watched a shower of rain driving past the open window.

"This is the time of year," said Mr. Stone suddenly, "when lambs leap off the ground with all four legs at a time." He paused as though for an answer; then, out of the silence, his voice rose again—it sounded different: "There is nothing in Nature more symptomatic of that principle which should underlie all life. Live in the future; regret nothing; leap! A lamb which has left earth with all four legs at once is the symbol of true life. That she must come down again is but an inevitable accident. 'In those days men were living on their pasts. They leaped with one, or, at the most, two legs at a time; they never left the ground, or in leaving, they wished to know the reason why. It was this paralysis'"—Mr. Stone did not pause, but, finding himself close beside his desk, took up his pen—"'it was this paralysis of the leaping nerve which undermined their progress. Instead of millions of leaping lambs, ignorant of why they leaped, they were a flock of sheep lifting up one leg and asking whether it was or was not worth their while to lift another.'"

The words were followed by a silence, broken only by the scratching of the quill with which Mr. Stone was writing.

Having finished, he again began to pace the room, and coming suddenly on his daughter, stopped short. Touching her shoulder timidly, he said: "I was talking to you, I think, my dear; where were we?"

Bianca rubbed her cheek against his hand.

"In the air, I think."

"Yes, yes," said Mr. Stone, "I remember. You must not let me wander from the point again."

"No, dear."

"Lambs," said Mr. Stone, "remind me at times of that young girl who comes to copy for me. I make her skip to promote her circulation before tea. I myself do this exercise." Leaning against the wall, with his feet twelve inches from it, he rose slowly on his toes. "Do you know that exercise? It is excellent for the calves of the legs, and for the lumbar regions." So saying, Mr. Stone left the wall, and began again to pace the room; the whitewash had also left the wall, and clung in a large square patch on his shaggy coat.

"I have seen sheep in Spring," he said, "actually imitate their lambs in rising from the ground with all four legs at once." He stood still. A thought had evidently struck him.

"If Life is not all Spring, it is of no value whatsoever; better to die, and to begin again. Life is a tree putting on a new green gown; it is a young moon rising—no, that is not so, we do not see the young moon rising—it is a young moon setting, never younger than when we are about to die——"

Bianca cried out sharply: "Don't, Father! Don't talk like that; it's so untrue! Life is all autumn, it seems to me!"

Mr. Stone's eyes grew very blue.

"That is a foul heresy," he stammered; "I cannot listen to it. Life is the cuckoo's song; it is a hill-side bursting into leaf; it is the wind; I feel it in me every day!"

He was trembling like a leaf in the wind he spoke of, and Bianca moved hastily towards him, holding out her arms. Suddenly his lips began to move; she heard him mutter: "I have lost force; I will boil some milk. I must be ready when she comes." And at those words her heart felt like a lump of ice.

Always that girl! And without again attracting his attention she went away. As she passed out through the garden she saw him at the window holding a cup of milk, from which the steam was rising.

CHAPTER XXVI

THIRD PILGRIMAGE TO HOUND STREET

LIKE water, human character will find its level; and Nature, with her way of fitting men to their environment, had made young Martin Stone what Stephen called a " Sanitis." There had been nothing else for her to do with him.

This young man had come into the social scheme at a moment when the conception of existence as a present life corrected by a life to come, was tottering; and the conception of the world as an upper-class preserve somewhat seriously disturbed.

Losing his father and mother at an early age, and brought up till he was fourteen by Mr. Stone, he had formed the habit of thinking for himself. This had rendered him unpopular, and added force to the essential single-heartedness transmitted to him through his grandfather. A particular aversion to the sights and scenes of suffering, which had caused him as a child to object to killing flies, and to watching rabbits caught in traps, had been regulated by his training as a doctor. His fleshly horror of pain and ugliness was now disciplined, his spiritual dislike of them forced into a philosophy. The peculiar chaos surrounding all young men who live in large towns and think at all, had made him gradually reject all abstract speculation; but a certain fire of aspiration coming, we may suppose, through Mr. Stone, had nevertheless impelled him to embrace something with all his might. He had therefore embraced health. And living, as he did, in the Euston Road, to be in touch with things, he had every need of the health which he embraced.

Late in the afternoon of the day when Hughs had committed his assault, having three hours of respite from his hospital, Martin dipped his face and head into cold water, rubbed them with a corrugated towel, put on a hard bowler hat, took a thick stick in his hand, and went by Underground to Kensington.

With his usual cool, high-handed air he entered his aunt's house, and asked for Thyme. Faithful to his definite, if somewhat crude theory, that Stephen and Cecilia and all their sort

382

were amateurs, he never inquired for them, though not unfrequently he would, while waiting, stroll into Cecilia's drawing-room, and let his sarcastic glance sweep over the pretty things she had collected, or, lounging in some luxurious chair, cross his long legs, and fix his eyes on the ceiling.

Thyme soon came down. She wore a blouse of some blue stuff bought by Cecilia for the relief of people in the Balkan States, a skirt of purplish tweed woven by Irish gentlewomen in distress, and held in her hand an open envelope addressed in Cecilia's writing to Mrs. Tallents Smallpeace.

" Hallo! " she said.

Martin answered by a look that took her in from head to foot.

" Get on a hat! I haven't got much time. That blue thing's new."

" It's pure flax. Mother bought it."

" It's rather decent. Hurry up! "

Thyme raised her chin; that lazy movement showed her round, creamy neck in all its beauty.

" I feel rather slack," she said; " besides, I must get back to dinner, Martin."

" Dinner! "

Thyme turned quickly to the door. " Oh, well, I'll come," and ran upstairs.

When they had purchased a postal order for ten shillings, placed it in the envelope addressed to Mrs. Tallents Smallpeace, and passed the hundred doors of Messrs. Rose and Thorn, Martin said : " I'm going to see what that precious amateur has done about the baby. If he hasn't moved the girl, I expect to find things in a pretty mess."

Thyme's face changed at once.

" Just remember," she said, " that I don't want to go there. I don't see the good, when there's such a tremendous lot waiting to be done."

" Every other case, except the one in hand! "

" It's not my case. You're so disgustingly unfair, Martin. I don't like those people."

" Oh, you amateur! "

Thyme flushed crimson. " Look here! " she said, speaking with dignity, " I don't care what you call me, but I won't have you call Uncle Hilary an amateur."

" What is he, then ? "

"I like him."

"That's conclusive."

"Yes, it is."

Martin did not reply, looking sideways at Thyme with his queer, protective smile. They were passing through a street superior to Hound Street in its pretensions to be called a slum.

"Look here!" he said suddenly; "a man like Hilary's interest in all this sort of thing is simply sentimental. It's on his nerves. He takes philanthropy just as he'd take sulphonal for sleeplessness."

Thyme looked shrewdly up at him.

"Well," she said, "it's just as much on your nerves. You see it from the point of view of health; he sees it from the point of view of sentiment, that's all."

"Oh! you think so?"

"You just treat all these people as if they were in hospital."

The young man's nostrils quivered. "Well, and how should they be treated?"

"How would you like to be looked at as a 'case'?" muttered Thyme.

Martin moved his hand in a slow half-circle.

"These houses and these people," he said, "are in the way —in the way of you and me, and everyone."

Thyme's eyes followed that slow, sweeping movement of her cousin's hand. It seemed to fascinate her.

"Yes, of course; I know," she murmured. "Something must be done!"

And she reared her head up, looking from side to side, as if to show him that she, too, could sweep away things. Very straight, and solid, fair, and fresh, she looked just then.

Thus, in the hypnotic silence of high thoughts, the two young "Sanitists" arrived in Hound Street.

In the doorway of No. 1 the son of the lame woman, Mrs. Budgen—the thin, white youth as tall as Martin, but not so broad—stood, smoking a dubious-looking cigarette. He turned his lack-lustre, jeering gaze on the visitors.

"Who d'you want?" he said. "If it's the girl, she's gone away, and left no address."

"I want Mrs. Hughs," said Martin.

The young man coughed. "Right-o! You'll find *her;* but for *him,* apply Wormwood Scrubs."

"Prison! What for?"

" Stickin' her through the wrist with his bayonet "; and the young man let a long, luxurious fume of smoke trickle through his nose.

" How horrible! " said Thyme.

Martin regarded the young man, unmoved. " That stuff you're smoking's rank," he said. " Have some of mine; I'll show you how to make them. It'll save you one and three per pound of baccy, and won't rot your lungs."

Taking out his pouch, he rolled a cigarette. The white young man bent his dull wink on Thyme, who, wrinkling her nose, was pretending to be far away.

Mounting the narrow stairs that smelt of walls and washing and red herrings, Thyme spoke: " Now, you see, it wasn't so simple as you thought. I don't want to go up; I don't want to see her. I shall wait for you here." She took her stand in the open doorway of the little model's empty room. Martin ascended to the second floor.

There, in the front room, Mrs. Hughs was seen standing with the baby in her arms beside the bed. She had a frightened and uncertain air. After examining her wrist, and pronouncing it a scratch, Martin looked long at the baby. The little creature's toes were stiffened against its mother's waist, its eyes closed, its tiny fingers crisped against her breast. While Mrs. Hughs poured forth her tale, Martin stood with his eyes still fixed on the baby. It could not be gathered from his face what he was thinking, but now and then he moved his jaw, as though he were suffering from toothache. In truth, by the look of Mrs. Hughs and her baby, his recipe did not seem to have achieved conspicuous success. He turned away at last from the trembling, nerveless figure of the seamstress, and went to the window. Two pale hyacinth plants stood on the inner edge; their perfume penetrated through the other savours of the room—and very strange they looked, those twin, starved children of the light and air.

" These are new," he said.

" Yes, sir," murmured Mrs. Hughs. " I brought them upstairs. I didn't like to see the poor things left to die."

From the bitter accent of these words Martin understood that they had been the little model's.

" Put them outside," he said; " they'll never live in here. They want watering, too. Where are your saucers? "

Mrs. Hughs laid the baby down, and, going to the cupboard

where all the household gods were kept, brought out two old, dirty saucers. Martin raised the plants, and as he held them, from one close, yellow petal there rose up a tiny caterpillar. It reared a green, transparent body, feeling its way to a new resting-place. The little writhing shape seemed, like the wonder and the mystery of life, to mock the young doctor, who watched it with eyebrows raised, having no hand at liberty to remove it from the plant.

"*She* came from the country. There's plenty of men there for her!"

Martin put the plants down, and turned round to the seamstress.

"Look here!" he said, "it's no good crying over spilt milk. What you've got to do is to set to and get some work."

"Yes, sir."

"Don't say it in that sort of way," said Martin; "you must rise to the occasion."

"Yes, sir."

"You want a tonic. Take this half-crown, and get in a dozen pints of stout, and drink one every day."

And again Mrs. Hughs said, "Yes, sir."

"And about that baby."

Motionless, where it had been placed against the foot-rail of the bed, the baby sat with its black eyes closed. The small grey face was curled down on the bundle of its garments.

"It's a silent gentleman," Martin muttered.

"It never was a one to cry," said Mrs. Hughs.

"That's lucky, anyway. When did you feed it last?"

Mrs. Hughs did not reply at first. "About half-past six last evening, sir."

"What?"

"It slept all night; but to-day, of course, I've been all torn to pieces; my milk's gone. I've tried it with the bottle, but it wouldn't take it."

Martin bent down to the baby's face, and put his finger on its chin; bending lower yet, he raised the eyelid of the tiny eye.

"It's dead," he said.

At the word "dead" Mrs. Hughs, stooping behind him, snatched the baby to her throat. With its drooping head close to her face, she clutched and rocked it without sound. Full five minutes this desperate mute struggle with eternal silence lasted —the feeling, and warming, and breathing on the little limbs.

Then, sitting down, bent almost double over her baby, she moaned. That single sound was followed by utter silence. The tread of footsteps on the creaking stairs broke it. Martin, rising from his crouching posture by the bed, went towards the door.

His grandfather was standing there, with Thyme behind him. "She has left her room," said Mr. Stone. "Where has she gone?"

Martin, understanding that he meant the little model, put his finger to his lips, and, pointing to Mrs. Hughs, whispered: "This woman's baby has just died."

Mr. Stone's face underwent the queer discoloration which marked the sudden summoning of his far thoughts. He stepped past Martin, and went up to Mrs. Hughs.

He stood there a long time gazing at the baby, and at the dark head bending over it with such despair. At last he spoke. "Poor woman! He is at peace."

Mrs. Hughs looked up, and, seeing that old face, with its hollows and thin silver hair, she spoke: "He's dead, sir."

Mr. Stone put out his veined and fragile hand, and touched the baby's toes. "He is flying; he is everywhere; he is close to the sun—Little brother!" And turning on his heel, he went out.

Thyme followed him as he walked on tiptoe down stairs which seemed to creak the louder for his caution. Tears were rolling down her cheeks.

Martin sat on, with the mother and her baby, in the close, still room, where, like strange visiting spirits, came stealing whiffs of the perfume of hyacinths.

CHAPTER XXVII

STEPHEN'S PRIVATE LIFE

MR. STONE and Thyme, going out, again passed the tall, white young man. He had thrown away the hand-made cigarette, finding that it had not enough saltpetre to make it draw, and was smoking one more suited to the action of his lungs. He directed towards them the same lack-lustre, jeering stare.

Unconscious, seemingly, of where he went, Mr. Stone walked with his eyes fixed on space. His head jerked now and then, as a dried flower will shiver in a draught.

Scared at these movements, Thyme took his arm. The touch of that soft young arm squeezing his own brought speech back to Mr. Stone.

" In those places . . ." he said, " in those streets ! . . . I shall not see the flowering of the aloe—I shall not see the living peace ! ' As with dogs, each couched over his proper bone, so men were living then ! ' "

Thyme, watching him askance, pressed still closer to his side, as though to try and warm him back to every day.

' Oh ! ' went her fluttered thoughts. ' I do wish grandfather would say something one could understand. I wish he would lose that dreadful stare.'

Mr. Stone spoke in answer to his granddaughter's thoughts.

" I have seen a vision of fraternity. A barren hillside in the sun, and on it a man of stone talking to the wind. I have heard an owl hooting in the daytime; a cuckoo singing in the night."

" Grandfather, grandfather ! "

To that appeal Mr. Stone responded: " Yes, what is it ? "

But Thyme, thus challenged, knew not what to say, having spoken out of terror.

" If the poor baby had lived," she stammered out, " it would have grown up. . . . It's all for the best, isn't it ? "

" Everything is for the best," said Mr. Stone. " ' In those days men, possessed by thoughts of individual life, made moan at death, careless of the great truth that the world was one unending song.' "

Thyme thought : ' I have never seen him as bad as this ! ' She

388

drew him on more quickly. With deep relief she saw her father, latchkey in hand, turning into the Old Square.

Stephen, who was still walking with his springy step, though he had come on foot the whole way from the Temple, hailed them with his hat. It was tall and black, and very shiny, neither quite oval nor positively round, and had a little curly brim. In this and his black coat, cut so as to show the front of him and cover the behind, he looked his best. The costume suited his long, rather narrow face, corrugated by two short parallel lines slanting downwards from his eyes and nostrils on either cheek; suited his neat, thin figure and the close-lipped corners of his mouth. His permanent appointment in the world of Law had ousted from his life (together with all uncertainty of income) the need for putting on a wig and taking his moustache off; but he still preferred to go clean-shaved.

"Where have you two sprung from?" he inquired, admitting them into the hall.

Mr. Stone gave him no answer, but passed into the drawing-room, and sat down on the verge of the first chair he came across, leaning forward with his hands between his knees.

Stephen, after one dry glance at him, turned to his daughter.

"My child," he said softly, "what have you brought the old boy here for? If there happens to be anything of the high mammalian order for dinner, your mother will have a fit."

Thyme answered: "Don't chaff, Father!"

Stephen, who was very fond of her, saw that for some reason she was not herself. He examined her with unwonted gravity. Thyme turned away from him. He heard, to his alarm, a little gulping sound.

"My dear!" he said.

Conscious of her sentimental weakness, Thyme made a violent effort.

"I've seen a baby dead," she cried in a quick, hard voice; and, without another word, she ran upstairs.

In Stephen there was a horror of emotion amounting almost to disease. It would have been difficult to say when he had last shown emotion; perhaps not since Thyme was born, and even then not to anyone except himself, having first locked the door, and then walked up and down, with his teeth almost meeting in the mouthpiece of his favourite pipe. He was unaccustomed, too, to witness this weakness on the part of other people. His looks and speech unconsciously discouraged it, so that if Cecilia had been at all that way inclined, she must long ago have been healed. Fortunately, she never had been, having too much distrust of her own feelings to give way to them completely. And Thyme, that healthy product of them both, at once younger for her age, and older, than they had ever been, with her incapacity for nonsense, her love for open air and facts—that fresh, rising plant, so elastic and so sane—she had never given them a single moment of uneasiness.

Stephen, close to his hat-rack, felt soreness in his heart. Such blows as Fortune had dealt, and meant to deal him, he had borne, and he could bear, so long as there was nothing in his own manner, or in that of others, to show him they *were* blows.

Hurriedly depositing his hat, he ran to Cecilia. He still preserved the habit of knocking on her door before he entered, though she had never, so far, answered, "Don't come in!" because she knew his knock. The custom gave, in fact, the measure of his idealism. What he feared, or what he thought he feared, after nineteen years of unchecked entrance, could never have been ascertained; but there it was, that flower of something formal and precise, of something reticent, within his soul.

This time, for once, he did not knock, and found Cecilia hooking up her tea-gown and looking very sweet. She glanced at him with mild surprise.

"What's this, Cis," he said, "about a baby dead? Thyme's quite upset about it; and your dad's in the drawing-room!"

With the quick instinct that was woven into all her gentle treading, Cecilia's thoughts flew—she could not have told why —first to the little model, then to Mrs. Hughs.

"Dead?" she said. "Oh, poor woman!"

"What woman?" Stephen asked.

"It must be Mrs. Hughs."

The thought passed darkly through Stephen's mind: 'Those people again! What now?' He did not express it, being neither brutal nor lacking in good taste.

A short silence followed, then Cecilia said suddenly: "Did you say that father was in the drawing-room? There's fillet of beef, Stephen!"

Stephen turned away. "Go and see Thyme!" he said.

Outside Thyme's door Cecilia paused, and, hearing no sound, tapped gently. Her knock not being answered, she slipped in. On the bed of that white room, with her face pressed into the pillow, her little daughter lay. Cecilia stood aghast. Thyme's whole body was quivering with suppressed sobs.

"My *darling!*" said Cecilia, "what is it?"

Thyme's answer was inarticulate.

Cecilia sat down on the bed and waited, drawing her fingers through the girl's hair, which had fallen loose; and while she sat there she experienced all that sore, strange feeling—as of being skinned—which comes to one who watches the emotion of someone near and dear without knowing the exact cause.

'This is dreadful,' she thought. 'What am I to do?'

To see one's child cry was bad enough, but to see her cry when that child's whole creed of honour and conduct for years past had precluded this relief as unfeminine, was worse than disconcerting.

Thyme raised herself on her elbow, turning her face carefully away.

"I don't know what's the matter with me," she said, choking. "It's—it's purely physical."

"Yes, darling," murmured Cecilia; "I know."

"Oh, Mother!" said Thyme suddenly, "it looked so tiny."

"Yes, yes, my sweet."

Thyme faced round; there was a sort of passion in her darkened eyes, rimmed pink with grief, and in all her flushed, wet face.

"Why should it have been choked out like that? It's—it's so brutal!"

Cecilia slid an arm round her.

"I'm so distressed you saw it, dear," she said.

"And grandfather *was* so——" A long sobbing quiver choked her utterance.

"Yes, yes," said Cecilia; "I'm sure he was."

Clasping her hands together in her lap, Thyme muttered: "He called him 'Little brother.'"

A tear trickled down Cecilia's cheek, and dropped on her daughter's wrist. Feeling that it was not her own tear, Thyme started up.

"It's weak and ridiculous," she said. "I don't! Oh, go away, Mother, please. I'm only making you feel bad, too. You'd better go and see to grandfather."

Cecilia saw that she would cry no more, and since it was the sight of tears which had so disturbed her, she gave the girl a little hesitating stroke, and went away. Outside she thought:

'How dreadfully unlucky and pathetic; and there's father in the drawing-room!' Then she hurried down to Mr. Stone.

He was sitting where he had first placed himself, motionless. It struck her suddenly how frail and white he looked. In the shadowy light of her drawing-room, he was almost like a spirit sitting there in his grey tweed—silvery from head to foot. Her conscience smote her. It is written of the very old that they shall pass, by virtue of their long travel, out of the country of the understanding of the young, till the natural affections are blurred by creeping mists such as steal across the moors when the sun is going down. Cecilia's heart ached with a little ache for all the times she had thought: 'If father were only not quite so——'; for all the times she had shunned asking him to come to them, because he was so——; for all the silences she and Stephen had maintained after he had spoken; for all the little smiles she had smiled. She longed to go and kiss his brow, and make him feel that she was aching. But she did not dare; he seemed so far away; it would be ridiculous.

Coming down the room, and putting her slim foot on the fender with a noise, so that if possible he might both see and hear her, she turned her anxious face towards him, and said: "Father!"

Mr. Stone looked up, and seeing somebody who seemed to be his elder daughter, answered: "Yes, my dear?"

"Are you sure you're feeling quite the thing? Thyme said she thought seeing that poor baby had upset you."

Mr. Stone felt his body with his hand.

"I am not conscious of any pain," he said.

"Then you'll stay to dinner, dear, won't you?"

Mr. Stone's brow contracted as though he were trying to recall his past.

"I have had no tea," he said. Then, with a sudden, anxious look at his daughter: "The little girl has not come to me. I miss her. Where is she?"

The ache within Cecilia became more poignant.

"It is now two days," said Mr. Stone, "and she has left her room in that house—in that street."

Cecilia, at her wits' end, answered: "Do you really miss her, Father?"

"Yes," said Mr. Stone. "She is like——" His eyes wandered round the room as though seeking something which would help him to express himself. They fixed themselves on the far wall. Cecilia, following their gaze, saw a little solitary patch of sunlight dancing and trembling there. It had escaped the screen of trees and houses, and, creeping through some chink, had quivered in. " She is like that," said Mr. Stone, pointing with his finger. " It is gone! " His finger dropped; he uttered a deep sigh.

'How dreadful this is!' Cecilia thought. 'I never expected him to feel it, and yet I can do nothing!' Hastily she asked: " Would it do if you had Thmye to copy for you? I'm sure she'd love to come."

" She is my grand-daughter," Mr. Stone said simply. " It would not be the same."

Cecilia could think of nothing now to say but: " Would you like to wash your hands, dear? "

" Yes," said Mr. Stone.

"Then will you go up to Stephen's dressing-room for hot water, or will you wash them in the lavatory? "

" In the lavatory," said Mr. Stone. " I shall be freer there."

When he had gone Cecilia thought: 'Oh dear, how shall I get through the evening? Poor darling, he is so single-minded!'

At the sounding of the dinner-gong they all assembled— Thmye from her bedroom with cheeks and eyes still pink, Stephen with veiled inquiry in his glance, Mr. Stone from freedom in the lavatory—and sat down, screened, but so very little, from each other by sprays of white lilac. Looking round her table, Cecilia felt rather like one watching a dew-belled cobweb, most delicate of all things in the world, menaced by the tongue of a browsing cow.

Both soup and fish had been achieved, however, before a word was spoken. It was Stephen who, after taking a mouthful of dry sherry, broke the silence.

" How are you getting on with your book, sir? "

Cecilia heard that question with something like dismay. It was so bald; for, however inconvenient Mr. Stone's absorption in his manuscript might be, her delicacy told her how precious beyond life itself that book was to him. To her relief, however, her father was eating spinach.

" You must be getting near the end, I should think," proceeded Stephen.

Cecilia spoke hastily: " Isn't this white lilac lovely, Dad? "

Mr. Stone looked up.

"It is not white; it is really pink. The test is simple." He paused with his eyes fixed on the lilac.

'Ah!' thought Cecilia, 'now, if I can only keep him on natural science—he used to be so interesting.'

"All flowers are one!" said Mr. Stone. His voice had changed.

'Oh!' thought Cecilia, 'he is gone!'

"They have but a single soul. In those days men divided, and subdivided them, oblivious of the one pale spirit which underlay those seemingly separate forms."

Cecilia's glance passed swiftly from the man-servant to Stephen.

She saw one of her husband's eyes rise visibly. Stephen did so hate one thing to be confounded with another.

"Oh, come, sir," she heard him say; "you don't surely tell us that dandelions and roses have the same pale spirit!"

Mr. Stone looked at him wistfully.

"Did I say that?" he said. "I had no wish to be dogmatic."

"Not at all, sir, not at all," murmured Stephen.

Thyme, leaning over to her mother, whispered: "Oh, Mother, don't let grandfather be queer; I can't bear it to-night!"

Cecilia, at her wits' end, said hurriedly:

"Dad, will you tell us what sort of character you think that little girl who comes to you has?"

Mr. Stone paused in the act of drinking water; his attention had evidently been riveted; he did not, however, speak. And Cecilia, seeing that the butler, out of the perversity which she found so conspicuous in her servants, was about to hand him beef, made a desperate movement with her lips. "No, Charles, not there, not there!"

The butler, tightening his lips, passed on. Mr. Stone spoke:

"I had not considered that. She is rather of a Celtic than an Anglo-Saxon type; the cheek-bones are prominent; the jaw is not massive; the head is broad—if I can remember I will measure it; the eyes are of a peculiar blue, resembling chicory flowers; the mouth——" Mr. Stone paused.

Cecilia thought: 'What a lucky find! Now perhaps he will go on all right!'

"I do not know," Mr. Stone resumed, speaking in a far-off voice, "whether she would be virtuous."

Cecilia heard Stephen drinking sherry; Thyme, too, was

drinking something; she herself drank nothing, but, pink and quiet, for she was a well-bred woman, said:

"You have no new potatoes, dear. Charles, give Mr. Stone some new potatoes."

By the almost vindictive expression on Stephen's face she saw, however, that her failure had decided him to resume command of the situation. "Talking of brotherhood, sir," he said dryly, "would you go so far as to say that a new potato is the brother of a bean?"

Mr. Stone, on whose plate these two vegetables reposed, looked almost painfully confused.

"I do not perceive," he stammered, "any difference between them."

"It's true," said Stephen; "the same pale spirit can be extracted from them both."

Mr. Stone looked up at him.

"You laugh at me," he said. "I cannot help it; but you must not laugh at life—that is blasphemy."

Before the piercing wistfulness of that sudden gaze Stephen was abashed. Cecilia saw him bite his lower lip.

"We're talking too much," he said; "we really must let your father eat!" And the rest of the dinner was achieved in silence.

When Mr. Stone, refusing to be accompanied, had taken his departure, and Thyme had gone to bed, Stephen withdrew to his study. This room, which had a different air from any other portion of the house, was sacred to his private life. Here, in specially designed compartments, he kept his golf clubs, pipes, and papers. Nothing was touched by anyone except himself, and twice a week by one particular housemaid. Here was no bust of Socrates, no books in deerskin bindings, but a bookcase filled with treatises on law, Blue Books, reviews, and the novels of Sir Walter Scott; two black oak cabinets stood side by side against the wall filled with small drawers. When these cabinets were opened and the drawers drawn forward there emerged a scent of metal polish. If the green-baize covers of the drawers were lifted, there were seen coins, carefully arranged with labels —as one may see plants growing in rows, each with its little name tied on. To these tidy rows of shining metal discs Stephen turned in moments when his spirit was fatigued. To add to them, touch them, read their names, gave him the sweet, secret feeling which comes to a man who rubs one hand against the other. Like a dram-drinker, Stephen drank—in little doses—

of the feeling these coins gave him. They were his creative work, his history of the world. To them he gave that side of him which refused to find its full expression in summarising law, playing golf, or reading the reviews; that side of a man which aches, he knows not wherefore, to construct something ere he die. From Rameses to George IV, the coins lay within those drawers—links of the long unbroken chain of authority.

Putting on an old black velvet jacket laid out for him across a chair, and lighting the pipe that he could never bring himself to smoke in his formal dinner clothes, he went to the right-hand cabinet, and opened it. He stood with a smile, taking up coins one by one. In this particular drawer they were of the best Byzantine dynasty, very rare. He did not see that Cecilia had stolen in, and was silently regarding him. Her eyes seemed doubting at that moment whether or no she loved him who stood there touching that other mistress of his thoughts—that other mistress with whom he spent so many evening hours. The little green-baize cover fell. Cecilia said suddenly:

" Stephen, I feel as if I must tell Father where that girl is ! "

Stephen turned.

" My dear child," he answered in his special voice, which, like champagne, seemed to have been dried by artifice, " you don't want to reopen the whole thing ? "

" But I can see he really is upset about it; he's looking so awfully white and thin."

" He ought to give up that bathing in the Serpentine. At his age it's monstrous. And surely any other girl will do just as well ? "

" He seems to set store by reading to her specially."

Stephen shrugged his shoulders. It had happened to him on one occasion to be present when Mr. Stone was declaiming some pages of his manuscript. He had never forgotten the discomfort of the experience. " That crazy stuff," as he had called it to Cecilia afterwards, had remained on his mind, heavy and damp, like a cold linseed poultice. His wife's father was a crank, and perhaps even a little more than a crank, a wee bit " touched "— that *she* couldn't help, poor girl; but any illusion to his cranky produce gave Stephen pain. Nor had he forgotten his experience at dinner.

" He seems to have grown fond of her," murmured Cecilia.

" But it's absurd at his time of life ! "

"Perhaps that makes him feel it more; people do miss things when they are old!"

Stephen slid the drawer back into its socket. There was dry decision in that gesture.

"Look here! Let's exercise a little common sense; it's been sacrificed to sentiment all through this wretched business. One wants to be kind, of course; but one's got to draw the line."

"Ah!" said Cecilia; "where?"

"The thing," went on Stephen, "has been a mistake from first to last. It's all very well up to a certain point, but after that it becomes destructive of all comfort. It doesn't do to let those people come into personal contact with you. There are the proper channels for that sort of thing."

Cecilia's eyes were lowered, as though she did not dare to let him see her thoughts.

"It seems so horrid," she said; "and father is not like other people."

"He is not," said Stephen dryly; "we had a pretty good instance of that this evening. But Hilary and your sister are. There's something most distasteful to me, too, about Thyme's going about slumming. You see what she's been let in for this afternoon. The notion of that baby being killed through the man's treatment of his wife, and that, no doubt, arising from the girl's leaving them, is most repulsive!"

To these words Cecilia answered with a sound almost like a gasp. "I hadn't thought of that. Then we're responsible; it was we who advised Hilary to make her change her lodging."

Stephen stared; he regretted sincerely that his legal habit of mind had made him put the case so clearly.

"I can't imagine," he said, almost violently, "what possesses everybody! We—responsible! Good gracious! Because we gave Hilary some sound advice! What next?"

Cecilia turned to the empty hearth.

"Thyme has been telling me about that poor little thing. It seems so dreadful, and I can't get rid of the feeling that we're —we're all mixed up with it!"

"Mixed up with what?"

"I don't know; it's just a feeling like—like being haunted."

Stephen took her quietly by the arm.

"My dear old girl," he said. "I'd no idea that you were run down like this. To-morrow's Thursday, and I can get away at three. We'll motor down to Richmond, and have a round or two!"

Cecilia quivered; for a moment it seemed that she was about to burst out crying. Stephen stroked her shoulder steadily. Cecilia must have felt his dread; she struggled loyally with her emotion.

"That will be very jolly," she said at last.

Stephen drew a deep breath.

"And don't you worry, dear," he said, "about your dad; he'll have forgotten the whole thing in a day or two; he's far too wrapped up in his book. Now trot along to bed; I'll be up directly."

Before going out Cecilia looked back at him. How wonderful was that look, which Stephen did not—perhaps intentionally— see. Mocking, almost hating, and yet thanking him for having refused to let her be emotional and yield herself up for once to what she felt, showing him too how clearly she saw through his own masculine refusal to be made to feel, and how she half-admired it—all this was in that look, and more. Then she went out.

Stephen glanced quickly at the door, and, pursing up his lips, frowned. He threw the window open, and inhaled the night air.

'If I don't look out,' he thought, 'I shall be having her mixed up with this. I was an ass ever to have spoken to old Hilary. I ought to have ignored the matter altogether. It's a lesson not to meddle with people in those places. I hope to God she'll be herself to-morrow!'

Outside, under the soft black foliage of the Square, beneath the slim sickle of the moon, two cats were hunting after happiness; their savage cries of passion rang in the blossom-scented air like a cry of dark humanity in the jungle of dim streets. Stephen, with a shiver of disgust, for his nerves were on edge, shut the window with a slam.

CHAPTER XXVIII

HILARY HEARS THE CUCKOO SING

IT was not left to Cecilia alone to remark how very white Mr. Stone looked in these days.

The wild force which every year visits the world, driving with its soft violence snowy clouds and their dark shadows, breaking through all crusts and sheaths, covering the earth in a fierce embrace; the wild force which turns form to form, and with its million leapings, swift as the flight of swallows and the arrow-darts of the rain, hurries everything on to sweet mingling—this great, wild force of universal life, so-called the Spring, had come to Mr. Stone, like new wine to some old bottle. And Hilary, to whom it had come, too, watching him every morning setting forth with a rough towel across his arm, wondered whether the old man would not this time leave his spirit swimming in the chill waters of the Serpentine—so near that spirit seemed to breaking through its fragile shell.

Four days had gone by since the interview at which he had sent away the little model, and life in his household—that quiet backwater choked with lilies—seemed to have resumed the tranquillity enjoyed before this intrusion of rude life. The paper whiteness of Mr. Stone was the only patent evidence that anything disturbing had occurred—that and certain feelings about which the strictest silence was preserved.

On the morning of the fifth day, seeing the old man stumble on the level flagstones of the garden, Hilary finished dressing hastily, and followed. He overtook him walking forward feebly beneath the candelabra of flowering chestnut-trees, with a hail-shower striking white on his high shoulders; and, placing himself alongside, without greeting—for forms were all one to Mr. Stone—he said:

"Surely you don't mean to bathe during a hail-storm, sir! Make an exception this once. You're not looking quite yourself."

Mr. Stone shook his head; then, evidently following out a thought which Hilary had interrupted, he remarked:

"The sentiment that men call honour is of doubtful value.

I have not as yet succeeded in relating it to universal brother-hood."

"How is that, sir?"

"In so far," said Mr. Stone, "as it consists in fidelity to principle, one might assume it worthy of conjunction. The difficulty arises when we consider the nature of the principle. . . . There is a family of young thrushes in the garden. If one of them finds a worm, I notice that his devotion to that principle of self-preservation which prevails in all low forms of life forbids his sharing it with any of the other little thrushes."

Mr. Stone had fixed his eyes on distance.

"So it is, I fear," he said, "with 'honour.' In those days men looked on women as thrushes look on worms——"

He paused, evidently searching for a word; and Hilary, with a faint smile, said:

"And how did women look on men, sir?"

Mr. Stone observed him with surprise. "I did not perceive that it was you," he said. "I have to avoid brain action before bathing."

They had crossed the road dividing the Gardens from the Park, and, seeing that Mr. Stone had already seen the water where he was about to bathe, and would now see nothing else, Hilary stopped beside a little lonely birch-tree. This wild, small, graceful visitor, who had long bathed in winter, was already draping her bare limbs in a scarf of green. Hilary leaned against her cool, pearly body. Below were the chilly waters, now grey, now starch-blue, and the pale forms of fifteen or twenty bathers. While he stood shivering in the frozen wind, the sun, bursting through the hail-clouds, burned his cheeks and hands. And suddenly he heard, clear, but far off, the sound which, of all others, stirs the hearts of men: "Cuckoo, cuckoo!"

Four times over came the unexpected call. When had that ill-advised, indelicate grey bird flown into this great haunt of men and shadows? Why had it come with its arrowy flight and mocking cry to pierce the heart and set it aching? There were trees enough outside the town, cloud-swept hollows, tangled brakes of furze just coming into bloom, where it could preside over the process of Spring. What solemn freak was this which made it come and sing to one who had no longer any business with the Spring?

With a real spasm in his heart Hilary turned away from that distant bird, and went down to the water's edge. Mr. Stone was swimming, slower than man had ever swum before. His silver head and lean arms alone were visible, parting the water feebly; suddenly he disappeared. He was but a dozen yards from the shore; and Hilary, alarmed at not seeing him reappear, ran in. The water was not deep. Mr. Stone, seated at the bottom, was doing all he could to rise. Hilary took him by his bathing-dress, raised him to the surface, and supported him towards the land. By the time they reached the shore he could just stand on his legs. With the assistance of a policeman, Hilary enveloped him in garments and got him to a cab. He had regained some of his vitality, but did not seem aware of what had happened.

"I was not in as long as usual," he mused, as they passed out into the high road.

"Oh, I think so, sir."

Mr. Stone looked troubled.

"It is odd," he said. "I do not recollect leaving the water."

He did not speak again till he was being assisted from the cab.

"I wish to recompense the man. I have half a crown indoors."

"I will get it, sir," said Hilary.

Mr. Stone, who shivered violently now that he was on his feet, turned his face up to the cabman.

"Nothing is nobler than the horse," he said; "take care of him."

The cabman removed his hat. "I will, sir," he answered.

Walking by himself, but closely watched by Hilary, Mr. Stone reached his room. He groped about him as though not distinguishing objects too well through the crystal clearness of the fundamental flux.

"If I might advise you," said Hilary, "I would get back into bed for a few minutes. You seem a little chilly."

Mr. Stone, who was indeed shaking so that he could hardly stand, allowed Hilary to assist him into bed and tuck the blankets round him.

"I must be at work by ten o'clock," he said.

Hilary, who was also shivering, hastened to Bianca's room. She was just coming down, and exclaimed at seeing him all wet. When he had told her of the episode she touched his shoulder.

"What about you?"

"A hot bath and drink will set me right. You'd better go to *him*."

He turned towards the bathroom, where Miranda stood, lifting a white foot. Compressing her lips, Bianca ran downstairs. Startled by his tale, she would have taken his wet body in her arms, if the ghosts of innumerable moments had not stood between. So this moment passed, too, and itself became a ghost.

Mr. Stone, greatly to his disgust, had not succeeded in resuming work at ten o'clock. Failing simply because he could not stand on his legs, he had announced his intention of waiting until half-past three, when he should get up, in preparation for the coming of the little girl. Having refused to see a doctor, or have his temperature taken, it was impossible to tell precisely what degree of fever he was in. In his cheeks, just visible over the blankets, there was more colour than there should have been; and his eyes, fixed on the ceiling, shone with suspicious brilliancy. To the dismay of Bianca—who sat as far out of sight as possible, lest he should see her, and fancy that she was doing him a service—he pursued his thoughts aloud:

"Words—words—they have taken away brotherhood!" Bianca shuddered, listening to that uncanny sound. "'In those days of words they called it death—pale death—*mors pallida*. They saw that word like a gigantic granite block suspended over them, and slowly coming down. Some, turning up their faces at the sight, trembled painfully, awaiting their obliteration. Others, unable, while they still lived, to face the thought of nothingness, inflated by some spiritual wind, and thinking always of their individual forms, called out unceasingly that those selves of theirs would and must survive this word—that in some fashion, which no man could understand, each self-conscious entity reaccumulated after distribution. Drunk with this thought, these, too, passed away. Some waited for it with grim, dry eyes, remarking that the process was molecular, and thus they also met their so-called death.'"

His voice ceased, and in place of it rose the sound of his tongue moistening his palate. Bianca, from behind, placed a glass of barley-water to his lips. He drank it with a slow, clucking noise; then, seeing that a hand held the glass, said: "Is that you? Are you ready for me? Follow. 'In those days no one leaped up to meet pale riding Death; no one saw in her face that she was brotherhood incarnate; no one with a heart as light as gossamer kissed her feet, and, smiling, passed into the Universe.'" His voice died away, and when next he spoke it was in a quick, husky whisper: "I must—I must—I must——" There was silence; then he added: "Give me my trousers."

Bianca placed them by his bed. The sight seemed to reassure him. He was once more silent.

For more than an hour after this he was so absolutely still that Bianca rose continually to look at him. Each time, his eyes, wide open, were fixed on a little dark mark across the ceiling; his face had a look of the most singular determination, as though his spirit were slowly, relentlessly, regaining mastery over his fevered body. He spoke suddenly:

"Who is there?"

"Bianca."

"Help me out of bed!"

The flush had left his face, the brilliance had faded from his eyes; he looked just like a ghost. With a sort of terror Bianca helped him out of bed. This weird display of mute white will-power was unearthly.

When he was dressed in his woollen gown and seated before the fire, she gave him a cup of strong beef-tea, with brandy. He swallowed it with great avidity.

"I should like some more of that," he said, and fell asleep.

While he was asleep Cecilia came, and the two sisters watched his slumber, and, watching it, felt nearer to each other than they had for many years. Before she went away Cecilia whispered:

"B., if he seems to want that little girl while he's like this, don't you think she ought to come?"

Bianca answered: "I don't know where she is."

"I do."

"Ah!" said Bianca; "of course!" And she turned her head away.

Disconcerted by that sarcastic little speech, Cecilia was silent; then, summoning all her courage, she said:

"Here's the address, B. I've written it down for you;" and, with puckers of anxiety in her face, she left the room.

Bianca sat on in the old golden chair, watching the deep hollows beneath the sleeper's temples, the puffs of breath stirring the silver round his mouth. Her ears burned crimson. Carried out of herself by the sight of that old form, dearer to her than she had thought, fighting its great battle for the sake of its idea, her spirit grew all tremulous and soft within her. With eagerness she embraced the thought of self-effacement. It did not seem to matter whether she were first with Hilary. Her spirit should so manifest its capacity for sacrifice that she would be first with him through sheer nobility. At this moment she could almost have taken that common little girl into her arms and kissed her. So would all disquiet end! Some harmonious messenger had fluttered to her for a second—the gold-winged bird of peace. In this sensuous exaltation her nerves vibrated like the strings of a violin.

When Mr. Stone woke it was past three o'clock and Bianca at once handed him another cup of strong beef-tea.

He swallowed it, and said: "What is this?"

"Beef-tea."

Mr. Stone looked at the empty cup.

"I must not drink it. The cow and the sheep are on the same plane as man."

"But how do you feel, dear?"

"I feel," said Mr. Stone, "able to dictate what I have already written—not more. Has she come?"

"Not yet; but I will go and find her if you like."

Mr. Stone looked at his daughter wistfully.

"That will be taking up your time," he said.

Bianca answered: "My time is of no consequence."

Mr. Stone stretched his hands out to the fire.

"I will not consent," he said, evidently to himself, "to be a drag on anyone. If that has come, then I must go!"

Bianca, placing herself beside him on her knees, pressed her hot cheek against his temple.

"But it has *not* come, Dad."

"I hope not," said Mr. Stone. "I wish to end my book first."

The sudden grim coherence of his last two sayings terrified Bianca more than all his feverish utterances.

"I rely on your sitting quite still," she said, "while I go and find her." And with a feeling in her heart as though two hands had seized and were pulling it asunder, she went out.

Some half-hour later Hilary slipped quietly in, and stood watching at the door. Mr. Stone, seated on the very verge of his armchair, with his hands on its arms, was slowly rising to his feet, and slowly falling back again, not once, but many times, practising a standing posture. As Hilary came into his line of sight, he said:

"I have succeeded twice."

"I am very glad," said Hilary. "Won't you rest now, sir?"

"It is my knees," said Mr. Stone. "She has gone to find her."

Hilary heard those words with bewilderment, and, sitting down on the other chair, waited.

"I have fancied," said Mr. Stone, looking at him wistfully, "that when we pass away from life we may become the wind. Is that your opinion?"

"It is a new thought to me," said Hilary.

"It is not tenable," said Mr. Stone. "But it is restful. The wind is everywhere and nowhere, and nothing can be hidden from it. When I have missed that little girl, I have tried, in a sense, to become the wind; but I have found it difficult."

His eyes left Hilary's face, whose mournful smile he had not noticed, and fixed themselves on the bright fire. "'In those days,'" he said, "'men's relation to the eternal airs was the relation of a billion little separate draughts blowing against the south-west wind. They did not wish to merge themselves in that soft, moon-uttered sigh, but blew in its face through crevices, and cracks, and keyholes, and were borne away on the pellucid journey, whistling out their protests.'"

He again tried to stand, evidently wishing to get to his desk to record this thought, but, failing, looked painfully at Hilary. He seemed about to ask for something, but checked himself.

"If I practise hard," he murmured, "I shall master it."

Hilary rose and brought him paper and a pencil. In bending, he saw that Mr. Stone's eyes were dim with moisture. This sight affected him so that he was glad to turn away and fetch a book to form a writing-pad.

When Mr. Stone had finished, he sat back in his chair with closed eyes. A supreme silence reigned in the bare room above those two men of different generations and of such strange dissimilarity of character. Hilary broke that silence.

"I heard the cuckoo sing to-day," he said, almost in a whisper, lest Mr. Stone should be asleep.

"The cuckoo," replied Mr. Stone, "has no sense of brotherhood."

"I forgive him—for his song," murmured Hilary.

"His song," said Mr. Stone, "is alluring; it excites the sexual instinct."

Then to himself he added:

" She has not come, as yet ! "

Even as he spoke there was heard by Hilary a faint tapping on the door. He rose and opened it. The little model stood outside.

CHAPTER XXIX

RETURN OF THE LITTLE MODEL

THAT same afternoon in High Street, Kensington, " Westminis-ter," with his coat-collar raised against the inclement wind, his old hat spotted with rain, was drawing at a clay pipe and fixing his iron-rimmed gaze on those who passed him by. It had been a day when singularly few as yet had bought from him his faintly green-tinged journal, and the low class of fellow who sold the other evening prints had especially exasperated him. His single mind, always torn to some extent between an ingrained loyalty to his employers and those politics of his which differed from his paper's, had vented itself twice since coming on his stand; once in these words to the seller of " Pell Mells ": " I stupulated with you not to come beyond the lamp-post. Don't you never speak to me again—a-crowdin' of me off my stand "; and once to the younger vendors of the less expensive journals, thus: " Oh, you boys! I'll make you regret of it —a-snappin' up my customers under my very nose! Wait until ye're old! " To which the boys had answered: " All right, daddy; don't you have a fit. You'll be a deader soon enough without that, y'know! "

It was now his time for tea, but " Pell Mell " having gone to partake of this refreshment, he waited on, hoping against hope to get a customer or two of that low fellow's. And while in black insulation he stood there a timid voice said at his elbow:

" Mr. Creed! "

The aged butler turned, and saw the little model.

" Oh," he said dryly, " it's you, is it? " His mind, with its incessant love of rank, knowing that she earned her living as a handmaid to that disorderly establishment, the House of Art, had from the first classed her as lower than a lady's-maid. Recent events had made him think of her unkindly. Her new clothes, which he had not been privileged to see before, while giving him a sense of Sunday, deepened his moral doubts.

" And where are you living now? " he said in tones incorpo-rating these feelings.

" I'm not to tell you."

"Oh, very well. Keep yourself to yourself."

The little model's lower lip drooped more than ever. There were dark marks beneath her eyes; her face was altogether rather pinched and pitiful.

"Won't you tell me any news?" she said in her matter-of-fact voice.

The old butler gave a strange grunt.

"Ho!" he said. "The baby's dead, and buried to-morrer."

"Dead!" repeated the little model.

"I'm a-goin' to the funeral—Brompton Cemetery. Half-past nine I leave the door. And that's a-beginnin' at the end. The man's in prison, and the woman's gone a shadder of herself."

The little model rubbed her hands against her skirt.

"What did he go to prison for?"

"For assaultin' of her; I was witness to his battery."

"Why did he assault her?"

Creed looked at her, and, wagging his head, answered:

"That's best known to them as caused of it."

The little model's face went the colour of carnations.

"I can't help what he does," she said. "What should *I* want him for—a man like that? It wouldn't be *him* I'd want!" The genuine contempt in that sharp burst of anger impressed the aged butler.

"I'm not a-sayin' anything," he said; "it's all a-one to me. I never mixes up with no other people's business. But it's very ill-convenient. I don't get my proper breakfast. That poor woman—she's half off her head. When the baby's buried I'll have to go and look out for another room before he gets a-comin' out."

"I hope they'll keep him there," muttered the little model suddenly.

"They give him a month," said Creed.

"Only a month!"

The old butler looked at her. 'There's more stuff in you,' he seemed to say, 'than ever I had thought.'

"Because of his servin' of his country," he remarked aloud.

"I'm sorry about the poor little baby," said the little model in her stolid voice.

"Westminister" shook his head. "I never suspected *him* of goin' to live," he said.

The girl, biting the finger-tip of her white cotton glove, was staring out at the traffic. Like a pale ray of light entering the now dim cavern of the old man's mind, the thought came to Creed that he did not quite understand her. He had in his time had occasion to class many young persons, and the feeling that he did not quite know her class of person was like the sensation a bat might have, surprised by daylight.

Suddenly, without saying good-bye to him, she walked away.

'Well,' he thought, looking after her, 'your manners ain't improved by where you're living, nor your appearance neither, for all your new clothes.' And for some time he stood thinking of the stare in her eyes and that abrupt departure.

Through the crystal clearness of the fundamental flux the mind could see at that same moment Bianca leaving her front gate.

Her sensuous exaltation, her tremulous longing after harmony, had passed away; in her heart, strangely mingled, were these two thoughts: 'If only she were a lady!' and, 'I am glad she is not a lady!'

Of all the dark and tortuous places of this life the human heart is the most dark and tortuous; and of all human hearts none are less clear, more intricate than the hearts of all that class of people among whom Bianca had her being. Pride was a simple quality when joined with a simple view of life, based on the plain philosophy of property; pride was no simple quality when the hundred paralysing doubts and aspirations of a social conscience also hedged it round. In thus going forth with the full intention of restoring the little model to her position in the household, her pride fought against her pride, and her woman's sense of ownership in the man whom she had married wrestled with the acquired sentiments of freedom, liberality, equality, good taste. With her spirit thus confused, and her mind so at variance with itself, she was really acting on the simple instinct of compassion.

She had run upstairs from Mr. Stone's room, and now walked fast, lest that instinct, the most physical, perhaps, of all—awakened by sights and sounds, and requiring constant nourishment—should lose its force.

Rapidly, then, she made her way to the grey street in Bayswater where Cecilia had told her that the girl now lived.

The tall, gaunt landlady admitted her.

"Have you a Miss Barton lodging here?" Bianca asked.

"Yes," said the landlady, "but I think she's out."

She looked into the little model's room.

"Yes," she said, "she's out; but if you'd like to leave a note you could write in here. If you're looking for a model, she wants work, I believe."

That modern faculty of pressing on an aching nerve was assuredly not lacking to Bianca. To enter the girl's room was jabbing at the nerve indeed.

She looked round her. The mental vacuity of that little room! There was not one single thing—with the exception of a torn copy of *Tit-Bits*—which suggested that a mind of any sort lived there. For all that, perhaps because of that, it was neat enough.

"Yes," said the landlady, "she keeps her room tidy. Of course, she's a country girl—comes from down my way." She said this with a dry twist of her grim, but not unkindly, features. "If it weren't for that," she went on, "I don't think I should care to let to one of her profession."

Her hungry eyes, gazing at Bianca, had in them the aspirations of all Nonconformity.

Bianca pencilled on her card:

"If you can come to my father to-day or to-morrow, please do."

"Will you give her this, please? It will be quite enough."

"I'll give it her," the landlady said; "she'll be glad of it, I daresay. I see her sitting here. Girls like that, if they've got nothing to do—see, she's been moping on her bed. . . ."

The impress of a form was, indeed, clearly visible on the red and yellow tasselled tapestry of the bed.

Bianca cast a look at it.

"Thank you," she said; "good day."

With the jabbed nerve aching badly she came slowly homewards.

Before the garden gate the little model herself was gazing at the house, as if she had been there some time. Approaching from across the road, Bianca had an admirable view of that young figure, now very trim and neat, yet with something in its lines —more supple, perhaps, but less refined—which proclaimed her not a lady; a something fundamentally undisciplined or disciplined by the material facts of life alone, rather than by a secret creed of voluntary rules. It showed here and there in ways women alone could understand; above all, in the way her eyes looked out on that house which she was clearly longing to enter. Not 'Shall I go in?' was in that look, but 'Dare I go in?'

Suddenly she saw Bianca. The meeting of these two was very like the ordinary meeting of a mistress and her maid. Bianca's face had no expression, except the faint, distant curiosity which seems to say: 'You are a sealed book to me; I have always found you so. What you really think and do I shall never know.'

The little model's face wore a half-caught-out, half-stolid look.

"Please go in," Bianca said; "my father will be glad to see you."

She held the garden gate open for the girl to pass through. Her feeling at that moment was one of slight amusement at the futility of her journey. Not even this small piece of generosity was permitted her, it seemed.

"How are you getting on?"

The little model made an impulsive movement at such an unexpected question. Checking it at once, she answered:

"Very well, thank you; that is, not very——"

"You will find my father tired to-day; he has caught a chill. Don't let him read too much, please."

The little model seemed to try and nerve herself to make some statement, but, failing, passed into the house.

Bianca did not follow, but stole back into the garden, where the sun was still falling on a bed of wallflowers at the far end. She bent down over these flowers till her veil touched them. Two wild bees were busy there, buzzing with smoky wings, clutching with their black, tiny legs at the orange petals, plunging their black, tiny tongues far down into the honey centres. The flowers quivered beneath the weight of their small dark bodies. Bianca's face quivered too, bending close to them, nor making the slightest difference to their hunt.

Hilary, who, it has been seen, lived in thoughts about events rather than in events themselves, and to whom crude acts and words had little meaning save in relation to what philosophy could make of them, greeted with a startled movement the girl's appearance in the corridor outside Mr. Stone's apartment. But the little model, who mentally lived very much from hand to mouth, and had only the philosophy of wants, acted differently. She knew that for the last five days, like a spaniel dog shut away from where it feels it ought to be, she had wanted to be where she was now standing; she knew that, in her new room with its rust-red doors, she had bitten her lips and fingers till blood came, and, as newly caged birds will flutter, had beaten her wings against those walls with blue roses on a yellow ground. She remembered how she had lain, brooding, on that piece of red and yellow tapestry, twisting its tassels, staring through half-closed eyes at nothing.

There was something different in her look at Hilary. It had lost some of its childish devotion; it was bolder, as if she had lived and felt, and brushed a good deal more down off her wings during those few days.

"Mrs. Dallison told me to come," she said. "I thought I might. Mr. Creed told me about *him* being in prison."

Hilary made way for her, and, following her into Mr. Stone's presence, shut the door.

"The truant has returned," he said.

Hearing herself called so unjustly by that name, the little model flushed deeply, and tried to speak. She stopped at the smile on Hilary's face, and gazed from him to Mr. Stone and back again, the victim of mingled feelings.

Mr. Stone was seen to have risen to his feet, and to be very slowly moving towards his desk. He leaned both arms on his papers for support, and, seeming to gather strength, began sorting out his manuscript.

Through the open window the distant music of a barrel-organ came drifting in. Faint, and much too slow, was the sound of the waltz it played, but there was invitation, allurement, in that tune. The little model turned towards it, and Hilary looked hard at her. The girl and that sound together—there, quite plain, was the music he had heard for many days, like a man lying with the touch of fever on him.

"Are you ready?" said Mr. Stone.

The little model dipped her pen in ink. Her eyes crept towards the door, where Hilary was still standing with the same expression on his face. He avoided her eyes, and went up to Mr. Stone.

"Must you read to-day, sir?"

Mr. Stone looked at him with anger.

"Why not?" he said.

"You are hardly strong enough."

Mr. Stone raised his manuscript.

"We are three days behind"; and very slowly he began dictating: "'Bar-be-rous ha-bits in those days, such as the custom known as War——'" His voice died away; it was apparent that his elbows, leaning on the desk, alone prevented his collapse.

Hilary moved the chair, and, taking him beneath the arms, lowered him gently into it.

Noticing that he was seated, Mr. Stone raised his manuscript and read on: "'—were pursued regardless of fraternity. It was as though a herd of horn-èd cattle driven through green pastures to that Gate, where they must meet with certain dissolution, had set about to prematurely gore and disembowel each other, out of a passionate devotion to those individual shapes which they were so soon to lose. So men—tribe against tribe, and country against country—glared across the valleys with their ensanguined eyes; they could not see the moonlit wings, or feel the embalming airs of brotherhood.'"

Slower and slower came his sentences, and as the last word died away he was heard to be asleep, breathing through a tiny hole left beneath the eave of his moustache. Hilary, who had waited for that moment, gently put the manuscript on the desk, and beckoned to the girl. He did not ask her to his study, but spoke to her in the hall.

"While Mr. Stone is like this he misses you. You will come, then, at present, please, so long as Hughs is in prison. How do you like your room?"

The little model answered simply: "Not very much."

"Why not?"

"It's lonely there. I shan't mind, now I'm coming here again."

"Only for the present," was all Hilary could find to say.

The little model's eyes were lowered.

"Mrs. Hughs' baby's to be buried to-morrow," she said suddenly.

"Where?"

"In Brompton Cemetery. Mr. Creed's going."

"What time is the funeral?"

The girl looked up stealthily.

"Mr. Creed's going to start at half-past nine."

"I should like to go myself," said Hilary.

A gleam of pleasure passing across her face was instantly obscured behind the cloud of her stolidity. Then, as she saw Hilary move nearer to the door, her lip began to droop.

"Well, good-bye," he said.

The little model flushed and quivered. 'You don't even look at me,' she seemed to say; 'you haven't spoken kindly to me once.' And suddenly she said in a hard voice:

"Now I shan't go to Mr. Lennard's any more."

"Oh, then you have been to him!"

Triumph at attracting his attention, fear of what she had admitted, supplication, and a half-defiant shame—all this was in her face.

"Yes," she said.

Hilary did not speak.

"I didn't care any more when you told me I wasn't to come here."

Still Hilary did not speak.

"I haven't done anything wrong," she said, with tears in her voice.

"No, no," said Hilary; "of course not!"

The little model choked.

"It's my profession."

"Yes, yes," said Hilary; "it's all right."

"I don't care what he thinks; I won't go again so long as I can come here."

Hilary touched her shoulder.

"Well, well," he said, and opened the front door.

The little model, tremulous, like a flower kissed by the sun after rain, went out with a light in her eyes.

The master of the house returned to Mr. Stone. Long he sat looking at the old man's slumber. "A thinker meditating upon action!" So might Hilary's figure, with its thin face resting on its hand, a furrow between the brows, and that painful smile, have been entitled in any catalogue of statues.

CHAPTER XXX

FUNERAL OF A BABY

FOLLOWING out the instinct planted so deeply in human nature for treating with the utmost care and at great expense when dead those, who, when alive, have been served with careless parsimony, there started from the door of No. 1 in Hound Street a funeral procession of three four-wheeled cabs.

The first bore the little coffin, on which lay a great white wreath (gift of Cecilia and Thyme). The second bore Mrs. Hughs, her son Stanley, and Joshua Creed. The third bore Martin Stone.

In the first cab Silence was presiding with the scent of lilies over him who in his short life had made so little noise, the small grey shadow which had crept so quietly into being, and, taking his chance when he was not noticed, had crept so quietly out again. Never had he felt so restful, so much at home, as in that little common coffin, washed as he was to an unnatural whiteness, and wrapped in his mother's only spare sheet. Away from all the strife of men he was journeying to a greater peace. His little aloe-plant had flowered; and, between the open windows of the only carriage he had ever been inside, the wind—which, who knows? he had perhaps become —stirred the fronds of fern and the flowers of his funeral wreath. Thus he was going from that world where all men were his brothers.

From the second cab the same wind was rigidly excluded, and there was silence, broken by the aged butler's breathing. Dressed in his Newmarket coat, he was recalling with a certain sense of luxury past journeys in four-wheeled cabs—occasions when, seated beside a box corded and secured with sealing-wax, he had taken his master's plate for safety to the bank; occasions when, under a roof piled up with guns and boxes, he had sat holding the " Honorable Bateson's " dog; occasions when, with some young person by his side, he had driven at the tail of a baptismal, nuptial, or funeral cortège. These memories of past grandeur came back to him with curious poignancy, and for some reason the words kept rising in his mind: ' For richer or poorer, for better or worser, in health and in sick places, till death do us part.' But in the midst of the exaltation of these recollections the old heart beneath his old red flannel chest-protector—that companion of his exile—twittering faintly at short intervals, made him look at the woman by his side. He longed to convey to her some little of the satisfaction he felt in the fact that this was by no means the low class of funeral it might have been. He doubted whether, with her woman's mind, she was getting all the comfort she could out of three four-wheeled cabs and a wreath of lilies. The seamstress's thin face, with its pinched, passive look, was indeed thinner, quieter, than ever. What she was thinking of he could not tell. There were so many things she might be thinking of. She, too, no doubt, had seen her grandeur, if but in the solitary drive away from the church where, eight years ago, she and Hughs had listened to the words now haunting Creed. Was she thinking of that; of her lost youth and comeliness, and her man's dead love; of the long descent to shadowland; of the other children she had buried; of Hughs in prison; of the girl that had " put a spell on him "; or only of the last precious tugs the tiny lips at rest in the first four-wheeled cab had given at her breast? Or was she, with a nicer feeling for proportion, reflecting that, had not people been so kind, she might have had to walk behind a funeral provided by the parish?

The old butler could not tell, but he—whose one desire now, coupled with the wish to die outside a workhouse, was to save enough to bury his own body without the interference of other people—was inclined to think she must be dwelling on the brighter side of things; and, designing to encourage her, he said: " Wonderful improvement in these 'ere four-wheel cabs! Oh dear, yes! I remember of them when they were the shadders of what they are at the present time of speakin'."

The seamstress answered in her quiet voice: " Very comfortable this is. Sit still, Stanley! " Her little son, whose feet did not reach the floor, was drumming his heels against the seat. He stopped and looked at her, and the old butler addressed him.

" You'll a-remember of this occasion," he said, " when you gets older."

The little boy turned his black eyes from his mother to him who had spoken last.

" It's a beautiful wreath," continued Creed. " I could smell

of it all the way up the stairs. There's been no expense spared;
there's white laylock in it—that's a class of flower that's very
extravagant."

A train of thought having been roused too strong for his
discretion, he added: "I saw that young girl yesterday. She
came interrogatin' of me in the street."

On Mrs. Hughs' face, where till now expression had been
buried, came such a look as one may see on the face of an owl
—hard, watchful, cruel; harder, more cruel, for the softness
of the big dark eyes.

"She'd show a better feeling," she said, "to keep a quiet
tongue. Sit still, Stanley!"

Once more the little boy stopped drumming his heels, and
shifted his stare from the old butler back to her who spoke.
The cab, which had seemed to hestitate and start, as though
jibbing at something in the road, resumed its ambling pace.
Creed looked through the well-closed window. There before
him, so long that it seemed to have no end, like a building in
a nightmare, stretched that place where he did not mean to end
his days. He faced towards the horse again. The colour had
deepened in his nose. He spoke:

"If they'd a-give me my last edition earlier, 'stead of sending
of it down after that low-class feller's taken all my customers,
that'd make a difference to me o' two shillin's at the utmost in
the week, and all clear savin's." To these words, dark with
hidden meaning, he received no answer save the drumming of
the small boy's heels; and, reverting to the subject he had been
distracted from, he murmured: "She was a-wearin' of new
clothes."

He was startled by the fierce tone of a voice he hardly knew.
"I don't want to hear about her; she's not for decent folk
to talk of."

The old butler looked round askance. The seamstress was
trembling violently. Her fierceness at such a moment shocked
him. '"Dust to dust,"' he thought.

"Don't you be considerate of it," he said at last, summoning
all his knowledge of the world; "she'll come to her own place."
And at the sight of a slow tear trickling over her burning
cheek, he added hurriedly: "Think of your baby—I'll see yer
through. Sit still, little boy—sit still! Ye're disturbin' of your
mother."

Once more the little boy stayed the drumming of his heels

to look at him who spoke; and the closed cab rolled on with its slow, jingling sound.

In the third four-wheeled cab, where the windows again were wide open, Martin Stone, with his hands thrust deep into the pockets of his coat, and his long legs crossed, sat staring at the roof, with a sort of twisted scorn on his pale face.

Just inside the gate, through which had passed in their time so many dead and living shadows, Hilary stood waiting. He could probably not have explained why he had come to see this tiny shade committed to the earth—in memory, perhaps, of those two minutes when the baby's eyes had held parley with his own, or in the wish to pay a mute respect to her on whom life had weighed so hard of late. For whatever reason he had come, he was keeping quietly to one side. And unobserved, he, too, had his watcher—the little model, sheltering behind a tall grave.

Two men in rusty black bore the little coffin; then came the white-robed chaplain; then Mrs. Hughs and her little son; close behind, his head thrust forward with trembling movements from side to side, old Creed; and, last of all, young Martin Stone. Hilary joined the young doctor. So the five mourners walked.

Before a small dark hole in a corner of the cemetery they stopped. On this forest of unflowered graves the sun was falling; the east wind, with its faint reek, touched the old butler's plastered hair, and brought moisture to the corners of his eyes, fixed with absorption on the chaplain. Words and thoughts hunted in his mind.

'He's gettin' Christian burial. Who gives this woman away? I do. Ashes to ashes. I never suspected him of livin'.' The conning of the burial service, shortened to fit the passing of that tiny shade, gave him pleasurable sensation; films came down on his eyes; he listened like some old parrot on its perch, his head a little to one side.

'Them as dies young,' he thought, 'goes straight to heaven. We trusts in God—all mortial men; his godfathers and his godmothers in his baptism. Well, so it is! *I'm* not afeared o' death!'

Seeing the little coffin tremble above the hole, he craned his head still further forward. It sank; a smothered sobbing rose. The old butler touched the arm in front of him with shaking fingers.

" Don't 'e," he whispered; " he's a-gone to glory."

But, hearing the dry rattle of the earth, he took out his own handkerchief and put it to his nose.

' Yes, he's a-gone,' he thought; ' another little baby. Old men an' maidens, young men an' little children; it's a-goin' on all the time. Where 'e is now there'll be no marryin', no, nor givin' out in marriage; till death do us part.'

The wind, sweeping across the filled-in hole, carried the rustle of his husky breathing, the dry, smothered sobbing of the seamstress, out across the shadows' graves, to those places, to those streets. . . .

From the baby's funeral Hilary and Martin walked away together, and far behind them, across the road, the little model followed. For some time neither spoke; then Hilary, stretching out his hand towards a squalid alley, said:

" They haunt us and drag us down. A long dark passage. Is there a light at the far end, Martin?"

" Yes," said Martin gruffly.

" I don't see it."

Martin looked at him.

" Hamlet!"

Hilary did not reply.

The young man watched him sideways. " It's a disease to smile like that!"

Hilary ceased to smile. " Cure me, then," he said, with sudden anger, " you man of health!"

The young " Sanitist's " sallow cheeks flushed. " Atrophy of the nerve of action," he muttered; " there's no cure for that!"

" Ah!" said Hilary: " All kinds of us want social progress in our different ways. You, your grandfather, my brother, myself; there are four types for you. Will you tell me any one of us is the right man for the job? For instance, action's not natural to me."

" Any act," answered Martin, " is better than no act."

" And myopia is natural to you, Martin. Your prescription in this case has not been too successful, has it?"

" I can't help it if people will be d—d fools."

" There you hit it. But answer me this question: Isn't a social conscience, broadly speaking, the result of comfort and security?"

Martin shrugged his shoulders.

"And doesn't comfort also destroy the power of action?"

Again Martin shrugged.

"Then, if those who have the social conscience and can see what is wrong have lost their power of action, how can you say there is any light at the end of this dark passage?"

Martin took his pipe out, filled it, and pressed the filling with his thumb.

"There *is* light," he said at last, "in spite of all invertebrates. Good-bye! I've wasted enough time," and he abruptly strode away.

"And in spite of myopia?" muttered Hilary.

A few minutes later, coming out from Messrs. Rose and Thorn's, where he had gone to buy tobacco, he came suddenly on the little model, evidently waiting.

"I was at the funeral," she said; and her face added plainly: 'I've followed you.' Uninvited, she walked on at his side.

'This is not the same girl,' he thought, 'that I sent away five days ago. She has lost something, gained something. I don't know her.'

There seemed such a stubborn purpose in her face and manner. It was like the look in a dog's eyes that says: 'Master, you thought to shut me up away from you; I know now what that is like. Do' what you will, I mean in future to be near you.'

This look, by its simplicity, frightened one to whom the primitive was strange. Desiring to free himself of his companion, yet not knowing how, Hilary sat down in Kensington Gardens on the first bench they came to. The little model sat down beside him. The quiet siege laid to him by this girl was quite uncanny. It was as though someone were binding him with toy threads, swelling slowly into rope before his eyes. In this fear of Hilary's there was at first much irritation. His fastidiousness and sense of the ridiculous were roused. What did this little creature with whom he had no thoughts and no ideas in common, whose spirit and his could never hope to meet, think that she could get from him? Was she trying to weave a spell over him too, with her mute, stubborn adoration? Was she trying to change his protective weakness for her to another sort of weakness? He turned and looked; she dropped her eyes at once, and sat still as a stone figure.

As in her spirit, so in her body, she was different; her limbs looked freer, rounder; her breath seemed stirring her more deeply; like a flower of early June she was opening before his very eyes. This, though it gave him pleasure, also added to his fear. The strange silence, in its utter naturalness—for what could he talk about with her?—brought home to him more vividly than anything before, the barriers of class. All he thought of was how not to be ridiculous! She was inviting him in some strange, unconscious, subtle way to treat her as a woman, as though in spirit she had linked her round young arms about his neck, and through her half-closed lips were whispering the eternal call of sex to sex. And he, a middle-aged and cultivated man, conscious of everything, could not even speak for fear of breaking through his shell of delicacy. He hardly breathed, disturbed to his very depths by the young figure sitting by his side, and by the dread of showing that disturbance.

Beside the cultivated plant the self-sown poppy rears itself; round the stem of a smooth tree the honeysuckle twines; to a trim wall the ivy clings.

In her new-found form and purpose this girl had gained a strange, still power; she no longer felt it mattered whether he spoke or looked at her; her instinct, piercing through his shell, was certain of the throbbing of his pulses, the sweet poison in his blood.

The perception of this still power, more than all else, brought fear to Hilary. He need not speak; she would not care! He need not even look at her; she had but to sit there silent, motionless, with the breath of youth coming through her parted lips, and the light of youth stealing through her half-closed eyes.

And abruptly he got up and walked away.

CHAPTER XXXI

SWAN SONG

THE new wine, if it does not break the old bottle, after fierce effervescence seethes and bubbles quietly.

It was so in Mr. Stone's old bottle, hour by hour and day by day, throughout the month. A pinker, robuster look came back to his cheeks; his blue eyes, fixed on distance, had in them more light; his knees regained their powers; he bathed, and, all unknown to him, for he only saw the waters he cleaved with his ineffably slow stroke, Hilary and Martin, on alternate weeks, and keeping at a proper distance, for fear he should see them doing him a service, attended at that function in case Mr. Stone should again remain too long seated at the bottom of the Serpentine. Each morning after his cocoa and porridge he could be heard sweeping out his room with extraordinary vigour, and as ten o'clock came near anyone who listened would remark a sound of air escaping, as he moved up and down on his toes in preparation for the labours of the day. No letters, of course, nor any newspapers disturbed the supreme and perfect self-containment of this life devoted to Fraternity—no letters, partly because he lacked a known address, partly because for years he had not answered them; and with regard to newspapers, once a month he went to a Public Library, and could be seen with the last four numbers of two weekly reviews before him, making himself acquainted with the habits of those days, and moving his lips as though in prayer. At ten each morning anyone in the corridor outside his room was startled by the whirr of an alarum clock; perfect silence followed; then rose a sound of shuffling, whistling, rustling, broken by sharply muttered words; soon from this turbid lake of sound the articulate, thin fluting of an old man's voice streamed forth. This, alternating with the squeak of a quill pen, went on till the alarum clock once more went off. Then he who stood outside could smell that Mr. Stone would shortly eat; if, stimulated by that scent, he entered, he might see the author of the " Book of Universal Brotherhood " with a baked potato in one hand and a cup of hot milk in the other; on the table, too, the ruined forms of eggs, tomatoes, oranges, bananas, figs, prunes, cheese, and honeycomb, which had passed into other forms already, together with a loaf of wholemeal bread. Mr. Stone would presently emerge in his cottage-woven tweeds, and old hat of green-black felt; or, if wet, in a long coat of yellow gaberdine, and sou'-wester cap of the same material; but always with a little osier fruit-bag in his hand. Thus equipped, he walked down to Rose and Thorn's, entered, and to the first man he saw handed the osier fruit-bag, some coins, and a little book containing seven leaves, headed " Food: Monday, Tuesday, Wednesday," and so forth. He then stood looking through the pickles in some jar or other at things beyond, with one hand held out, fingers upwards, awaiting the return of his little osier fruit-bag. Feeling presently that it had been restored to him, he would turn and walk out of the shop. Behind his back, on the face of the department, the same protecting smile always rose. Long habit had perfected it. All now felt that, though so very different from themselves, this aged customer was dependent on them. By not one single farthing or one pale slip of cheese would they have defrauded him for all the treasures of the moon, and any new salesman who laughed at that old client was promptly told to " shut his head."

Mr. Stone's frail form, bent somewhat to one side by the increased gravamen of the osier bag, was now seen moving homewards. He arrived perhaps ten minutes before the three o'clock alarum, and soon passing through preliminary chaos, the articulate, thin fluting of his voice streamed forth again, broken by the squeaking and spluttering of his quill.

But towards four o'clock signs of cerebral excitement became visible; his lips would cease to utter sounds, his pen to squeak. His face, with a flushed forehead, would appear at the open window. As soon as the little model came in sight—her eyes fixed, not on his window, but on Hilary's—he turned his back, evidently waiting for her to enter by the door. His first words were uttered in a tranquil voice: " I have several pages. I have placed your chair. Are you ready? Follow! "

Except for that strange tranquillity of voice and the disappearance of the flush on his brow, there was no sign of the rejuvenescence that she brought, of such refreshment as steals on the traveller who sits down beneath a lime-tree toward the end of a long day's journey; no sign of the mysterious comfort distilled into his veins by the sight of her moody young face,

her young, soft limbs. So from some stimulant men very near
their end will draw energy, watching, as it were, a shape beckoning them forward, till suddenly it disappears in darkness.

In the quarter of an hour sacred to their tea and conversation he never noticed that she was always listening for sounds
beyond; it was enough that in her presence he felt singleness
of purpose strong within him.

When she had gone, moving languidly, moodily away, her
eyes darting about for signs of Hilary, Mr. Stone would sit
down rather suddenly and fall asleep, to dream, perhaps, of
Youth—Youth with its scent of sap, its close beckonings;
Youth with its hopes and fears; Youth that hovers round us
so long after it is dead! His spirit would smile behind its
covering—that thin china of his face; and, as dogs hunting in
their sleep work their feet, so he worked the fingers resting on
his woollen knees.

The seven o'clock alarum woke him to the preparation of
the evening meal. This eaten, he began once more to pace up
and down, to pour words out into the silence, and to drive his
squeaking quill.

So was being written a book such as the world had never
seen!

But the girl who came so moodily to bring him refreshment,
and went so moodily away, never in these days caught a glimpse
of that which she was seeking.

Since the morning when he had left her abruptly, Hilary
had made a point of being out in the afternoons and not returning till past six o'clock. By this device he put off facing
her and himself, for he could no longer refuse to see that he
had himself to face. In the few minutes of utter silence
when the girl sat beside him, magnetic, quivering with awakening force, he had found that the male in him was far from
dead. It was no longer vague, sensuous feeling; it was warm,
definite desire. The more she was in his thoughts, the less
spiritual his feeling for this girl of the people had become.

In those days he seemed much changed to such as knew
him well. Instead of the delicate, detached, slightly humorous
suavity which he had accustomed people to expect from him,
the dry kindliness which seemed at once to check confidence
and yet to say, 'If you choose to tell me anything, I should
never think of passing judgment on you, whatever you have
done'—instead of that rather abstracted, faintly quizzical air,

his manner had become absorbed and gloomy. He seemed to jib away from his friends. His manner at the " Pen and Ink " was wholly unsatisfactory to men who liked to talk. He was known to be writing a new book; they suspected him of having " got into a hat "—this Victorian expression, found by Mr. Balladyce in some chronicle of post-Thackerayan manners, and revived by him in his incomparable way, as who should say, ' What delicious expressions those good bourgeois had!' and now flourished in second childhood.

In truth, Hilary's difficulty with his new book was merely the one of not being able to work at it at all. Even the house-maid who " did " his study noticed that day after day she was confronted by Chapter XXIV., in spite of her employer's staying in, as usual, every morning.

The change in his manner and face, which had grown strained and harassed, had been noticed by Bianca, though she would have died sooner than admit she had noticed any-thing about him. It was one of those periods in the lives of households like an hour of a late summer's day—brooding, electric, as yet quiescent, but charged with the currents of coming storms.

Twice only in those weeks while Hughs was in prison did Hilary see the girl. Once he met her when he was driving home; she blushed crimson and her eyes lighted up. And one morning, too, he passed her on the bench where they had sat together. She was staring straight before her, the cor-ners of her mouth drooping discontentedly. She did not see him.

To a man like Hilary—for whom running after women had been about the last occupation in the world, who had, in fact, always fought shy of them and imagined that they would always fight shy of him—there was an unusual enticement and dismay in the feeling that a young girl really was pursuing him. It was at once too good, too unlikely, and too embarras-sing to be true. His sudden feeling for her was the painful sensation of one who sees a ripe nectarine hanging within reach. He dreamed continually of stretching out his hand, and so he did not dare, or thought he did not dare, to pass that way. All this did not favour the tenor of a studious, introspective life; it also brought a sense of unreality which made him avoid his best friends.

This, partly, was why Stephen came to see him one Sunday, his other reason for the visit being the calculation that Hughs would be released on the following Wednesday.

'This girl,' he thought, 'is going to the house still, and Hilary will let things drift till he can't stop them, and there'll be a real mess.'

The fact of the man's having been in prison gave a sinister turn to an affair regarded hitherto as merely sordid by Stephen's orderly and careful mind.

Crossing the garden, he heard Mr. Stone's voice issuing through the open window.

'Can't the old crank stop even on Sundays?' he thought.

He found Hilary in his study, reading a book on the civilisation of the Maccabees, in preparation for a review. He gave Stephen but a dubious welcome.

Stephen broke ground gently.

"We haven't seen you for an age. I hear our old friend at it. Is he working double tides to finish his *magnum opus?* I thought he observed the day of rest."

"He does as a rule," said Hilary.

"Well, he's got the girl there now dictating."

Hilary winced. Stephen continued with greater circumspection:

"You couldn't get the old boy to finish by Wednesday, I suppose? He must be quite near the end by now."

The notion of Mr. Stone's finishing his book by Wednesday procured a pale smile from Hilary.

"Could you get your Law Courts," he said, "to settle up the affairs of mankind for good and all by Wednesday?"

"By Jove! Is it as bad as that? I thought, at any rate, he must be meaning to finish some day."

"When men are brothers," said Hilary, "he will finish."

Stephen whistled.

"Look here, dear boy!" he said, "that ruffian comes out on Wednesday. The whole thing will begin over again."

Hilary rose and paced the room. "I refuse," he said, "to consider Hughs a ruffian. What do we know about him, or any of them?"

"Precisely! What do we know of this girl?"

"I am not going to discuss that," Hilary said shortly.

For a moment the faces of the two brothers wore a hard, hostile look, as though the deep difference between their char-

acters had at last got the better of their loyalty. They both
seemed to recognise this, for they turned their heads away.

"I just wanted to remind you," Stephen said, "though you
know your own business best, of course." And at Hilary's nod
he thought: 'That's just exactly what he doesn't!'

He soon left, conscious of an unwonted awkwardness in his
brother's presence. Hilary watched him out through the wicket
gate, then sat down on the solitary garden bench.

Stephen's visit had merely awakened perverse desires in
him.

Strong sunlight was falling on that little London garden, disclosing its native shadowiness; streaks, and smudges such as
Life smears over the faces of those who live too consciously.
Hilary, beneath the acacia-tree not yet in bloom, marked an
early butterfly flitting over the geraniums blossoming round an
old sundial. Blackbirds were holding evensong; the late perfume of the lilac came stealing forth into air faintly smeeched
with chimney smoke. There was brightness, but no glory, in
that little garden; scent, but no strong air blown across golden
lakes of buttercups, from seas of springing clover, or the wind-
silver of young wheat; music, but no full choir of sound, no
hum. Like the face and figure of its master, so was this little
garden, whose sundial the sun seldom reached—refined, self-
conscious, introspective, obviously a creature of the town. At
that moment, however, Hilary was not looking quite himself; his
face was flushed, his eyes angry, almost as if he had been a man
of action.

The voice of Mr. Stone was still audible, fitfully quavering
out into the air, and the old man himself could now and then be
seen holding up his manuscript, his profile clear-cut against the
darkness of the room. A sentence travelled out across the
garden:

"'Amidst the tur-bu-lent dis-cov-eries of those days, which,
like cross-currented and multi-billowed seas, lapped and hollowed every rock——' "

A motor-car dashing past drowned the rest, and when the
voice rose again it was evidently dictating another paragraph.

"'In those places, in those streets, the shadows swarmed,
whispering and droning like a hive of dying bees, who, their
honey eaten, wandered through the winter day seeking flowers
that are frozen and dead.' "

A great bee which had been busy with the lilac began to circle,

booming, round his hair. Suddenly Hilary saw Mr. Stone raise
both his arms.

"'In huge congeries, crowded, devoid of light and air, they
were assembled, these bloodless imprints from forms of higher
caste. They lay, like the reflection of leaves which, fluttering
free in the sweet winds, let fall to the earth wan resemblances.
Imponderous, dark ghosts, wandering ones chained to the
ground, they had no hope of any Lovely City, nor knew whence
they had come. Men cast them on the pavements and marched
on. They did not in Universal Brotherhood clasp their shadows
to sleep within their hearts—for the sun was not then at noon,
when no man has a shadow.'"

As those words of swan song died away he swayed and trembled, and suddenly disappeared below the sight-line, as if he had
sat down. The little model took his place in the open window.
She started at seeing Hilary; then, motionless, stood gazing at
him. Out of the gloom of the opening her eyes were all pupil,
two spots of the surrounding darkness imprisoned in a face as
pale as any flower. Rigid as the girl herself, Hilary looked up
at her.

A voice behind him said: "How are you? I thought I'd give
my car a run." Mr. Purcey was coming from the gate, his eyes
fixed on the window where the girl stood. "How is your wife?"
he added.

The bathos of this visit roused an acid fury in Hilary. He
surveyed Mr. Purcey's figure from his cloth-topped boots to his
tall hat, and said: "Shall we go in and find her?"

As they went along Mr. Pursey said: "That's the young—the
—er—model I met in your wife's studio, isn't it? Pretty girl!"

Hilary compressed his lips.

"Now, what sort of living do those girls make?" pursued
Mr. Purcey. "I suppose they've most of them other resources.
Eh, what?"

"They make the living God will let them, I suppose, as other
people do."

Mr. Purcey gave him a sharp look. It was almost as if
Dallison had meant to snub him.

"Oh, exactly! I should think this girl would have no difficulty." And suddenly he saw a curious change come over
"that writing fellow," as he always afterwards described Hilary.
Instead of a mild, pleasant-looking chap enough, he had become
a regular cold devil.

"My wife appears to be out," Hilary said. "I also have an engagement."

In his surprise and anger Mr. Purcey said with great simplicity, "Sorry I'm *de trop!*" and soon his car could be heard bearing him away with some unnecessary noise.

CHAPTER XXXII

BEHIND BIANCA'S VEIL

BUT Bianca was not out. She had been a witness of Hilary's long look at the little model. Coming from her studio through the glass passage to the house, she could not, of course, see what he was gazing at, but she knew as well as if the girl had stood before her in the dark opening of the window. Hating herself for having seen, she went to her room, and lay on her bed with her hands pressed to her eyes. She was used to loneliness—that necessary lot of natures such as hers; but the bitter isolation of this hour was such as to drive even her lonely nature to despair.

She rose at last, and repaired the ravages made in her face and dress, lest anyone should see that she was suffering. Then, first making sure that Hilary had left the garden, she stole out.

She wandered towards Hyde Park. It was Whitsuntide, a time of fear to the cultivated Londoner. The town seemed all arid jollity and paper bags whirled on a dusty wind. People swarmed everywhere in clothes which did not suit them; desultory, dead-tired creatures who, in these few green hours of leisure out of the sandy eternity of their toil, were not suffered to rest, but were whipped on by starved instincts to hunt pleasures which they longed for too dreadfully to overtake.

Bianca passed an old tramp asleep beneath a tree. His clothes had clung to him so long and lovingly that they were falling off, but his face was calm as though masked with the finest wax. Forgotten were his sores and sorrows; he was in the blessed fields of sleep.

Bianca hastened away from the sight of such utter peace. She wandered into a grove of trees which had almost eluded the notice of the crowd. They were limes, guarding still within them their honey bloom. Their branches of light, broad leaves, near heart-shaped, were spread out like wide skirts. The tallest of these trees, a beautiful, gay creature, stood tremulous, like a mistress waiting for her tardy lover. What joy she seemed to promise, what delicate enticement, with every veined quivering leaf! And suddenly the sun caught hold of her, raised her up to him, kissed her all over; she gave forth a sigh of happiness, as though her very spirit had travelled through her lips up to her lover's heart.

A woman in a lilac frock came stealing through the trees towards Bianca, and sitting down not far off, kept looking quickly round under her sunshade.

Presently Bianca saw what she was looking for. A young man in black coat and shining hat came swiftly up and touched her shoulder. Half hidden by the foliage they sat, leaning forward, prodding gently at the ground with stick and parasol; the stealthy murmur of their talk, so soft and intimate that no word was audible, stole across the grass; and secretly he touched her hand and arm. They were not of the holiday crowd, and had evidently chosen out this vulgar afternoon for a stolen meeting.

Bianca rose and hurried on amongst the trees. She left the Park. In the streets many couples, not so careful to conceal their intimacy, were parading arm-in-arm. The sight of them did not sting her like the sight of those lovers in the Park; they were not of her own order. But presently she saw a little boy and girl asleep on the doorstep of a mansion, with their cheeks pressed close together and their arms round each other, and again she hurried on. In the course of that long wandering she passed the building which " Westminister " was so anxious to avoid. In its gateway an old couple were just about to separate, one to the men's, the other to the women's quarters. Their toothless mouths were close together. "Well, good-night, Mother!" "Good-night, Father, good-night—take care o' yourself!"

Once more Bianca hurried on.

It was past nine when she turned into the Old Square, and rang the bell of her sister's house with the sheer physical desire to rest—somewhere that was not her home.

At one end of the long, low drawing-room Stephen, in evening dress, was reading aloud from a review. Cecilia was looking dubiously at his sock, where she seemed to see a tiny speck of white that might be Stephen. In the window at the far end Thyme and Martin were exchanging speeches at short intervals; they made no move at Bianca's entrance; and their faces said: " We have no use for that handshaking nonsense!"

Receiving Cecilia's little, warm, doubting kiss and Stephen's polite, dry handshake, Bianca motioned to him not to stop reading. He resumed. Cecilia, too, resumed her scrutiny of Stephen's sock.

'Oh dear!' she thought. 'I know B.'s come here because she's unhappy. Poor thing! Poor Hilary! It's that wretched business again, I suppose.'

Skilled in every tone of Stephen's voice, she knew that Bianca's entry had provoked the same train of thought in him; to her he seemed reading out these words: 'I disapprove—I disapprove. She's Cis's sister. But if it wasn't for old Hilary I wouldn't have the subject in the house!'

Bianca, whose subtlety recorded every shade of feeling, could see that she was not welcome. Leaning back with veil raised, she seemed listening to Stephen's reading, but in fact she was quivering at the sight of those two couples.

Couples, couples—for all but her! What crime had she committed? Why was the china of her cup flawed so that no one could drink from it? Why had she been made so that nobody could love her? This, the most bitter of all thoughts, the most tragic of all questionings, haunted her.

The article which Stephen read—explaining exactly how to deal with people so that from one sort of human being they might become another, and going on to prove that if, after this conversion, they showed signs of a reversion, it would then be necessary to know the reason why—fell dryly on ears listening to that eternal question: Why is it with me as it is? It is not fair!—listening to the constant murmuring of her pride: I am not wanted here or anywhere. Better to efface myself!

From their end of the room Thyme and Martin scarcely looked at her. To them she was Aunt B., an amateur, the mockery of whose eyes sometimes penetrated their youthful armour; they were besides too interested in their conversation to perceive that she was suffering. The skirmish of that conversation had lasted now for many days—ever since the death of the Hughses' baby.

"Well," Martin was saying, "what are you going to do? It's no good to base it on the baby; you must know your own mind all round. You can't go rushing into real work on mere sentiment."

"*You* went to the funeral, Martin. It's bosh to say you didn't feel it too!"

Martin deigned no answer to this insinuation.

"We've gone past the need for sentiment," he said; "it's exploded; so is Justice, administered by an upper class with a patch over one eye and a squint in the other. When you see a dying donkey in a field, you don't want to refer the case to a society, as your dad would; you don't want an essay of Hilary's, full of sympathy with everybody, on 'Walking in a field: with reflections on the end of donkeys'—you want to put a bullet in the donkey."

"You're always down on Uncle Hilary," said Thyme.

"I don't mind Hilary himself; I object to his type."

"Well, he objects to yours," said Thyme.

"I'm not so sure of that," said Martin slowly; "he hasn't got character enough."

Thyme raised her chin, and, looking at him through half-closed eyes, said: "Well, I do think, of all the conceited persons I ever met you're the worst."

Martin's nostril curled.

"Are you prepared," he said, "to put a bullet in the donkey, or are you not?"

"I only see one donkey, and not a dying one!"

Martin stretched out his hand and gripped her arm below the elbow. Retaining it luxuriously, he said: "Don't wander!"

Thyme tried to free her arm. "Let go!"

Martin was looking straight into her eyes. A flush had risen in his cheeks.

Thyme, too, went the colour of the old-rose curtain behind which she sat.

"Let go!"

"I won't! I'll *make* you know your mind. What do you mean to do? Are you coming in a fit of sentiment, or do you mean business?"

Suddenly, half-hypnotised, the young girl ceased to struggle. Her face had the strangest expression of submission and defiance —a sort of pain, a sort of delight. So they sat full half a minute staring at each other's eyes. Hearing a rustling sound, they looked, and saw Bianca moving to the door. Cecilia, too, had risen.

"What is it, B.?"

Bianca, opening the door, went out. Cecilia followed swiftly, too late to catch even a glimpse of her sister's face behind the veil. . . .

In Mr. Stone's room the green lamp burned dimly, and he

who worked by it was sitting on the edge of his camp-bed, attired in his old brown woollen gown and slippers.

And suddenly it seemed to him that he was not alone.

"I have finished for to-night," he said. "I am waiting for the moon to rise. She is nearly full; I shall see her face from here."

A form sat down by him on the bed, and a voice said softly: "Like a woman's."

Mr. Stone saw his younger daughter. "You have your hat on. Are you going out, my dear?"

"I saw your light as I came in."

"The moon," said Mr. Stone, "is an arid desert. Love is unknown there."

"How can you bear to look at her, then?" Bianca whispered.

Mr. Stone raised his finger. "She has risen."

The wan moon had slipped out into the darkness. Her light stole across the garden and through the open window to the bed where they were sitting.

"Where there is no love, Dad," Bianca said, "there can be no life, can there?"

Mr. Stone's eyes seemed to drink the moonlight.

"That," he said, "is the great truth. The bed is shaking!"

With her arms pressed tight across her breast, Bianca was struggling with violent, noiseless sobbing. That desperate struggle seemed to be tearing her to death before his eyes, and Mr. Stone sat silent, trembling. He knew not what to do. From his frosted heart years of Universal Brotherhood had taken all knowledge of how to help his daughter. He could only sit touching her tremulously with thin fingers.

The form beside him, whose warmth he felt against his arm, grew stiller, as though, in spite of its own loneliness, his helplessness had made it feel that he, too, was lonely. It pressed a little closer to him. The moonlight, gaining pale mastery over the flickering lamp, filled the whole room.

Mr. Stone said: "I want her mother!"

The form beside him ceased to struggle.

Finding out an old, forgotten way, Mr. Stone's arm slid round that quivering body.

"I do not know what to say to her," he muttered, and slowly he began to rock himself.

"Motion," he said, "is soothing."

The moon passed on. The form beside him sat so still that Mr. Stone ceased moving. His daughter was no longer sobbing. Suddenly her lips seared his forehead.

Trembling from that desperate caress, he raised his fingers to the spot and looked round.

She was gone.

CHAPTER XXXIII

HILARY DEALS WITH THE SITUATION

To understand the conduct of Hilary and Bianca at what "Westminister" would have called this "crisax," not only their feelings as sentient human beings, but their matrimonial philosophy, must be taken into account. By education and environment they belonged to a section of society which had "in those days" abandoned the more old-fashioned views of marriage. Such as composed this section, finding themselves in opposition, not only to the orthodox proprietary creed, but even to their own legal rights, had been driven to an attitude of almost blatant freedom. Like all folk in opposition, they were bound, as a simple matter of principle, to disagree with those in power, to view with a contemptuous resentment that majority which said, "I believe the thing is mine, and mine it shall remain"—a majority which by force of numbers made this creed the law. Unable legally to be other than the proprietors of wife or husband, as the case might be, they were obliged, even in the most happy unions, to be very careful not to become disgusted with their own position. Their legal status was, as it were, a goad, spurring them on to show their horror of it. They were like children sent to school with trousers that barely reached their knees, aware that they could neither reduce their stature to the proportions of their breeches nor make their breeches grow. They were furnishing an instance of that immemorial "change of form to form" to which Mr. Stone had given the name of Life. In a past age thinkers and dreamers and "artistic pigs" rejecting the forms they found, had given unconscious shape to this marriage law, which, after they had become the wind, had formed itself out of their exiled pictures and thoughts and dreams. And now this particular law in turn was the dried rind, devoid of pips or speculation; and the thinkers and dreamers and "artistic pigs" were again rejecting it, and again themselves in exile.

This exiled faith, this honour amongst thieves, animated a little conversation between Hilary and Bianca on the Tuesday following the night when Mr. Stone sat on his bed to watch the rising moon.

Quietly Bianca said: " I think I shall be going away for a time."

" Wouldn't you rather that I went instead ? "

" You are wanted; I am not."

That ice-cold, ice-clear remark contained the pith of the whole matter; and Hilary said:

" You are not going at once ? "

" At the end of the week, I think."

Noting his eyes fixed on her, she added:

" Yes; we're neither of us looking quite our best."

" I am sorry."

" I know you are."

This had been all. It had been sufficient to bring Hilary once more face to face with the situation.

Its constituent elements remained the same; relative values had much changed. The temptations of St. Anthony were becoming more poignant every hour. He had no " principles " to pit again them: he had merely the inveterate distaste for hurting anybody, and a feeling that if he yielded to this inclination he would be faced ultimately with a worse situation than ever. It was not possible for him to look at the position as Mr. Purcey might have done, if *his* wife had withdrawn from him and a girl had put herself in his way. Neither hesitation because of the defenceless position of the girl, nor hesitation because of his own future with her, would have troubled Mr. Purcey. He—good man—in his straightforward way, would have only thought about the present—not, indeed, intending to have a future with a young person of that class. Consideration for a wife who had withdrawn from the society of Mr. Purcey would also naturally have been absent from the equation. That Hilary worried over all these questions was the mark of his " fin de sièclism." And in the meantime the facts demanded a decision.

He had not spoken to this girl since the day of the baby's funeral, but in that long look from the garden he had in effect said: ' You are drawing me to the only sort of union possible to us!' And she in effect had answered: ' Do what you like with me!'

There were other facts, too, to be reckoned with. Hughs would be released to-morrow; the little model would not stop her visits unless forced to; Mr. Stone could not well do without her; Bianca had in effect declared that she was being driven out of her own house. It was this situation which Hilary, seated beneath the bust of Socrates, turned over and over in his mind. Long and painful reflection brought him back continually to the thought that he himself, and not Bianca, had better go away. He was extremely bitter and contemptuous towards himself that he had not done so long ago. He made use of the names Martin had given him. "Hamlet," "Amateur," "Invertebrate." They gave him, unfortunately, little comfort.

In the afternoon he received a visit. Mr. Stone came in with his osier fruit-bag in his hand. He remained standing, and spoke at once.

"Is my daughter happy?"

At this unexpected question Hilary walked over to the fireplace.

"No," he said at last; "I am afraid she is not."

"Why?"

Hilary was silent; then, facing the old man, he said:

"I think she will be glad, for certain reasons, if I go away for a time."

"When are you going?" asked Mr. Stone.

"As soon as I can."

Mr. Stone's eyes, wistfully bright, seemed trying to see through heavy fog.

"She came to me, I think," he said; "I seem to recollect her crying. You are good to her?"

"I have tried to be," said Hilary.

Mr. Stone's face was discoloured by a flush. "You have no children," he said painfully; "do you live together?"

Hilary shook his head.

"You are estranged?" said Mr. Stone.

Hilary bowed. There was a long silence. Mr. Stone's eyes had travelled to the window.

"Without love there cannot be life," he said at last; and fixing his wistful gaze on Hilary, asked: "Does she love another?"

Again Hilary shook his head.

When Mr. Stone next spoke it was clearly to himself.

"I do not know why I am glad. Do you love another?"

At this question Hilary's eyebrows settled in a frown. "What do you mean by love?" he said.

Mr. Stone did not reply; it was evident that he was reflecting deeply. His lips began to move: "By love I mean the forgetfulness of self. Unions are frequent in which only the sexual instincts, or the remembrance of self, are roused——"

"That is true," muttered Hilary.

Mr. Stone looked up; painful traces of confusion showed in his face. "We were discussing something."

"I was telling you," said Hilary, "that it would be better for your daughter if I go away for a time."

"Yes," said Mr. Stone; "you are estranged."

Hilary went back to his stand before the empty fireplace.

"There is one thing, sir," he said, "on my conscience to say before I go, and I must leave it to you to decide. The little girl who comes to you no longer lives where she used to live."

"In that street . . ." said Mr. Stone.

Hilary went on quickly. "She was obliged to leave because the husband of the woman with whom she used to lodge became infatuated with her. He has been in prison, and comes out to-morrow. If she continues to come here he will, of course, be able to find her. I'm afraid he will pursue her again. Have I made it clear to you?"

"No," said Mr. Stone.

"The man," resumed Hilary patiently, "is a poor, violent creature, who has been wounded in the head; he is not quite responsible. He may do the girl an injury."

"What injury?"

"He has stabbed his wife already."

"I will speak to him," said Mr. Stone.

Hilary smiled. "I am afraid that words will hardly meet the case. She ought to disappear."

There was silence.

"My book!" said Mr. Stone.

It smote Hilary to see how white his face had become. 'It's better,' he thought, 'to bring his will-power into play; she will never come here, anyway, after I'm gone.'

But, unable to bear the tragedy in the old man's eyes, he touched him on the arm.

"Perhaps she will take the risk, sir, if you ask her."

Mr. Stone did not answer, and, not knowing what more to say, Hilary went back to the window. Miranda was slumbering lightly out there in the speckled shade, where it was not too warm and not too cold, her cheek resting on her paw and white teeth showing.

Mr. Stone's voice rose again. "You are right; I cannot ask her to run a risk like that!"

"She is just coming up the garden," Hilary said huskily. "Shall I tell her to come in?"

"Yes," said Mr. Stone.

Hilary beckoned.

The girl came in, carrying a tiny bunch of lilies of the valley; her face fell at sight of Mr. Stone; she stood still, raising the lilies to her breast. Nothing could have been more striking than the change from her look of fluttered expectancy to a sort of hard dismay. A spot of red came into both her cheeks. She gazed from Mr. Stone to Hilary and back again. Both were staring at her. No one spoke. The little model's bosom began heaving as though she had been running; she said faintly: "Look; I brought you this, Mr. Stone!" and held out to him the bunch of lilies. But Mr. Stone made no sign. "Don't you like them?"

Mr. Stone's eyes remained fastened on her face.

To Hilary this suspense was, evidently, most distressing. "Come, will you tell her, sir," he said, "or shall I?"

Mr. Stone spoke.

"I shall try and write my book without you. You must not run this risk. I cannot allow it."

The little model turned her eyes from side to side. "But I *like* to copy out your book," she said.

"The man will injure you," said Mr. Stone.

The little model looked at Hilary.

"I don't care if he does; I'm not afraid of him. I can look after myself; I'm used to it."

"*I* am going away," said Hilary quietly.

After a desperate look, that seemed to ask, 'Am I going, too?' the little model stood as though frozen.

Wishing to end the painful scene, Hilary went up to Mr. Stone.

"Do you want to dictate to her this afternoon, sir?"

"No," said Mr. Stone.

"Nor to-morrow?"

"Will you come a little walk with me?"

Mr. Stone bowed.

Hilary turned to the little model. "It is good-bye then," he said.

She did not take his hand. Her eyes, turned sideways, glinted; her teeth were fastened on her lower lip. She dropped the lilies, suddenly looked up at him, gulped, and slunk away. In passing she had smeared the lilies with her foot.

Hilary picked up the fragments of the flowers, and dropped them into the grate. The fragrance of the bruised blossoms remained clinging to the air.

"Shall we get ready for our walk?" he said.

Mr. Stone moved feebly to the door, and very soon they were walking silently towards the Gardens.

CHAPTER XXXIV

THYME'S ADVENTURE

THIS same afternoon Thyme, wheeling a bicycle and carrying a light valise, was slipping into a back street out of the Old Square. Putting her burden down at the pavement's edge, she blew a whistle. A hansom-cab appeared, and a man in ragged clothes, who seemed to spring out of the pavement, took hold of her valise. His lean, unshaven face was full of wolfish misery.

"Get off with you!" the cabman said.

"Let him do it!" murmured Thyme.

The cab-runner hoisted up the trunk, then waited motionless beside the cab.

Thyme handed him two coppers. He looked at them in silence, and went away.

'Poor man,' she thought; 'that's one of the things we've got to do away with!'

The cab now proceeded in the direction of the Park, Thyme following on her bicycle, and trying to stare about her calmly.

'This,' she thought, 'is the end of the old life. I won't be romantic, and imagine I'm doing anything special; I must take it all as a matter of course.' She thought of Mr. Purcey's face—'that person!'—if he could have seen her at this moment turning her back on comfort. 'The moment I get there,' she mused, 'I shall let mother know; she can come out to-morrow, and see for herself. I can't have hysterics about my disappearance, and all that. They must get used to the idea that I mean to be in touch with things. I can't be stopped by what anybody thinks!'

An approaching motor-car brought a startled frown across her brow. Was it 'that person'? But though it was not Mr. Purcey and his A. 1. Damyer, it was somebody so like him as made no difference. Thyme uttered a little laugh.

In the Park a cool light danced and glittered on the trees and water, and the same cool, dancing glitter seemed lighting the girl's eyes.

442

The cabman, unseen, took an admiring look at her. 'Nice little bit, this!' it said.

'Grandfather bathes here,' thought Thyme. 'Poor darling! I pity everyone that's old.'

The cab passed on under the shade of trees out into the road.

'I wonder if we have only one self in us,' thought Thyme. 'I sometimes feel that I have two—Uncle Hilary would understand what I mean. The pavements are beginning to smell horrid already, and it's only June to-morrow. Will mother feel my going very much? How glorious if one didn't feel!'

The cab turned into a narrow street of little shops.

'It must be dreadful to have to serve in a small shop. What millions of people there are in the world! Can anything be of any use? Martin says what matters is to do one's job; but what *is* one's job?'

The cab emerged into a broad, quiet square.

'But I'm not going to think of anything,' thought Thyme; 'that's fatal. Suppose father stops my allowance; I should have to earn my living as a typist, or something of that sort; but he won't, when he sees I mean it. Besides, mother wouldn't let him.'

The cab entered the Euston Road, and again the cabman's broad face was turned towards Thyme with an inquiring stare.

'What a hateful road!' Thyme thought. 'What dull, ugly, common-looking faces all the people seem to have in London! as if they didn't care for anything but just to get through their day somehow. I've only seen two really pretty faces!'

The cab stopped before a small tobacconist's on the south side of the road.

'Have I got to live here?' thought Thyme.

Through the open door a narrow passage led to a narrow staircase covered with oilcloth. She raised her bicycle and wheeled it in. A Jewish-looking youth emerging from the shop accosted her.

"Your gentleman friend says you are to stay in your rooms, please, until he comes."

His warm red-brown eyes dwelt on her lovingly. "Shall I take your luggage up, miss?"

"Thank you; I can manage."

"It's the first floor," said the young man.

The little rooms which Thyme entered were stuffy, clean, and neat. Putting her trunk down in her bedroom, which looked out on a bare yard, she went into the sitting-room and threw the window up. Down below the cabman and tobacconist were engaged in conversation. Thyme caught the expression on their faces—a sort of leering curiosity.

'How disgusting and horrible men are!' she thought, moodily staring at the traffic. All seemed so grim, so inextricable, and vast, out there in the grey heat and hurry, as though some monstrous devil were sporting with a monstrous ant-heap. The reek of petrol and of dung rose to her nostrils. It was so terribly big and hopeless; it was so *ugly!* 'I shall never do anything,' thought Thyme—'never—never! Why doesn't Martin come?'

She went into her bedroom and opened her valise. With the scent of lavender that came from it, there sprang up a vision of her white bedroom at home, and the trees of the green garden and the blackbirds on the grass.

The sound of footsteps on the stairs brought her back into the sitting-room. Martin was standing in the doorway.

Thyme ran towards him, but stopped abruptly. "I've come, you see. What made you choose this place?"

"I'm next door but two; and there's a girl here—one of us. She'll show you the ropes."

"Is she a lady?"

Martin raised his shoulders. "She *is* what is called a lady," he said; "but she's the right sort, all the same. Nothing will stop her."

At this proclamation of supreme virtue, the look on Thyme's face was very queer. 'You don't trust me,' it seemed to say, 'and you trust that girl. You put me here for her to watch over me! . . .'

"I want to send this telegram," she said aloud.

Martin read the telegram. "You oughtn't to have funked telling your mother what you meant to do."

Thyme crimsoned. "I'm not cold-blooded, like you."

"This is a big matter," said Martin. "I told you that you had no business to come at all if you couldn't look it squarely in the face."

"If you want me to stay you had better be more decent to me, Martin."

"It must be your own affair," said Martin.

Thyme stood at the window, biting her lips to keep the tears

back from her eyes. A very pleasant voice behind her said:
" I do think it's so splendid of you to come ! "

A girl in grey was standing there—thin, delicate, rather
plain, with a nose ever so little to one side, lips faintly smiling,
and large, shining, greenish eyes.

" I am Mary Daunt. I live above you. Have you had some
tea ? "

In the gentle question of this girl with the faintly smiling
lips and shining eyes Thyme fancied that she detected mockery.

" Yes, thanks. I want to be shown what my work's to be, at
once, please."

The grey girl looked at Martin.

" Oh! Won't to-morrow do for all that sort of thing? I'm
sure you must be tired. Mr. Stone, do make her rest ! "

Martin's glance seemed to say: ' Please leave your femi-
ninities ! '

" If you mean business, your work will be the same as hers,"
he said; " you're not qualified. All you can do will be visiting,
noting the state of the houses and the condition of the children."

The girl in grey said gently: " You see, we only deal with
sanitation and the children. It seems hard on the grown people
and the old to leave them out; but there's sure to be so much
less money than we want, so that it *must* all go towards the
future."

There was a silence. The girl with the shining eyes added
softly: " 1950 ! "

" 1950 ! " repeated Martin. It seemed to be some formula of
faith.

" I must send this telegram ! " muttered Thyme.

Martin took it from her and went out.

Left alone in the little room, the two girls did not at first
speak. The girl in grey was watching Thyme half timidly, as
if she could not tell what to make of this young creature who
looked so charming, and kept shooting such distrustful glances.

" I think it's so awfully sweet of you to come," she said at
last. " I know what a good time you have at home; your cousin's often told me. Don't you think he's splendid? "

To that question Thyme made no answer.

" Isn't this work horrid," she said—" prying into people's
houses? "

The grey girl smiled. "It *is* rather awful sometimes. I've been at it six months now. You get used to it. I've had all the worst things said to me by now, I should think."

Thyme shuddered.

"You see," said the grey girl's faintly smiling lips, "you soon get the feeling of having to go through with it. We all realise it's got to be done, of course. Your cousin's one of the best of us; nothing seems to put him out. He has such a nice sort of scornful kindness. I'd rather work with him than anyone."

She looked past her new associate into that world outside, where the sky seemed all wires and yellow heat-dust. She did not notice Thyme appraising her from head to foot, with a stare hostile and jealous, but pathetic, too, as though confessing that this girl was her superior.

"I'm sure I can't do that work!" she said suddenly.

The grey girl smiled. "Oh, *I* thought that at first." Then, with an admiring look: "But I do think it's rather a shame for you, you're so pretty. Perhaps they'd put you on to tabulation work, though that's awfully dull. We'll ask your cousin."

"No; I'll do the whole or nothing."

"Well," said the grey girl, "I've got one house left to-day. Would you like to come and see the sort of thing?"

She took a small notebook from a side pocket in her skirt.

"I can't get on without a pocket. You must have something that you can't leave behind. I left four little bags and two dozen handkerchiefs in five weeks before I came back to pockets. It's rather a horrid house, I'm afraid!"

"*I* shall be all right," said Thyme shortly.

In the shop doorway the young tobacconist was taking the evening air. He greeted them with his polite but constitutionally leering smile.

"Good-evening, mith," he said; "nithe evening!"

"He's rather an awful little man," the grey girl said when they had achieved the crossing of the street; "but he's got quite a nice sense of humour."

"Ah!" said Thyme.

They had turned into a by-street, and stopped before a house which had obviously seen better days. Its windows were cracked, its doors unpainted, and down in the basement could be seen a pile of rags, an evil-looking man seated by it, and a blazing fire. Thyme felt a little gulping sensation. There was a putrid scent as of burning refuse. She looked at her companion. The grey girl was consulting her notebook, with a faint smile on her lips. And in Thyme's heart rose a feeling almost of hatred for this girl, who was so business-like in the presence of such sights and scents.

The door was opened by a young red-faced woman, who looked as if she had been asleep.

The grey girl screwed up her shining eyes. " Oh, do you mind if we come in a minute? " she said. " It would be so good of you. We're making a report."

" There's nothing to report here," the young woman answered. But the grey girl had slipped as gently past as though she had been the very spirit of adventure.

" Of course, I see that, but just as a matter of form, you know."

" I've parted with most of my things," the young woman said defensively, " since my husband died. It's a hard life."

" Yes, yes, but not worse than mine—always poking my nose into other people's houses."

The young woman was silent, evidently surprised.

" The landlord ought to keep you in better repair," said the grey girl. " He owns next door, too, doesn't he? "

The young woman nodded. " He's a bad landlord. All down the street 'ere it's the same. Can't get nothing done."

The grey girl had gone over to a dirty bassinette where a half-naked child sprawled. An ugly little girl with fat red cheeks was sitting on a stool beside it, close to an open locker wherein could be seen a number of old meat bones.

" Your chickabiddies? " said the grey girl. "Aren't they sweet? "

The young woman's face became illumined by a smile.

" They're healthy," she said.

" That's more than can be said for all the children in the house, I expect," murmured the grey girl.

The young woman replied emphatically, as though voicing an old grievance: " The three on the first floor's not so bad, but I don't let 'em 'ave anything to do with that lot at the top."

Thyme saw her new friend's hand hover over the child's head like some pale dove. In answer to that gesture, the mother nodded. " Just that; you've got to clean 'em every time they go near them children at the top."

The grey girl looked at Thyme. ' That's where we've got to go, evidently,' she seemed to say.

"A dirty lot!" muttered the young woman.

"It's very hard on you." •

"It is. I'm workin' at the laundry all day when I can get it. I can't look after the children—they get everywhere."

"Very hard," murmured the grey girl. "I'll make a note of that."

Together with the little book, in which she was writing furiously, she had pulled out her handkerchief, and the sight of this handkerchief reposing on the floor gave Thyme a queer satisfaction, such as comes when one remarks in superior people the absence of a virtue existing in oneself.

"Well, we mustn't keep you, Mrs.—Mrs.——?"

"Cleary."

"Cleary. How old's this little one? Four? And the other? Two? They *are* ducks. Good-bye!"

In the corridor outside the grey girl whispered: "I do like the way we all pride ourselves on being better than someone else. I think it's so hopeful and jolly. Shall we go up and see the abyss at the top?"

CHAPTER XXXV

A YOUNG GIRL'S MIND

A YOUNG girl's mind is like a wood in Spring—now a rising mist of bluebells and flakes of dappled sunlight; now a world of still, wan, tender saplings, weeping they know not why. Through the curling twigs of boughs just green, its wings fly towards the stars; but the next moment they have drooped to mope beneath the damp bushes. It is ever yearning for and trembling at the future; in its secret places all the countless shapes of things that are to be are taking stealthy counsel of how to grow up without letting their gown of mystery fall. They rustle, whisper, shriek suddenly, and as suddenly fall into a delicious silence. From the first hazel-bush to the last may-tree it is an unending meeting-place of young solemn things eager to find out what they are, eager to rush forth to greet the kisses of the wind and sun, and for ever trembling back and hiding their faces. The spirit of that wood seems to lie with her ear close to the ground, a pale petal of a hand curved like a shell behind it, listening for the whisper of her own life. There she lies, white and supple, with dewy, wistful eyes, sighing: 'What is my meaning? Ah, I am everything! Is there in all the world a thing so wonderful as I? . . . Oh, I am nothing—my wings are heavy; I faint, I die!'

When Thyme, attended by the grey girl, emerged from the abyss at the top, her cheeks were flushed and her hands clenched. She said nothing. The grey girl, too, was silent, with a look such as a spirit divested of its body by long bathing in the river of reality might bend on one who has just come to dip her head. Thyme's quick eyes saw that look, and her colour deepened. She saw, too, the glance of the Jewish youth when Martin joined them in the doorway.

'Two girls now,' he seemed to say. 'He goes it, this young man!'

Supper was laid in her new friend's room—pressed beef, potato salad, stewed prunes, and ginger ale. Martin and the grey girl talked. Thyme ate in silence, but though her eyes seemed fastened on her plate, she saw every glance that passed between

449

them, heard every word they said. Those glances were not re-markable, nor were those words particularly important, but they were spoken in tones that seemed important to Thyme. 'He never talks to me like that,' she thought.

When supper was over they went out into the streets to walk, but at the door the grey girl gave Thyme's arm a squeeze, her cheek a swift kiss, and turned back up the stairs.

" Aren't you coming? " shouted Martin.

Her voice was heard answering from above: " No, not to-night."

With the back of her hand Thyme rubbed off the kiss. The two cousins walked out amongst the traffic.

The evening was very warm and close; no breeze fanned the reeking town. Speaking little, they wandered among endless darkening streets, whence to return to the light and traffic of the Euston Road seemed like coming back to Heaven. At last, close again to her new home, Thyme said: " Why should one bother? It's all a horrible great machine, trying to blot us out; people are like insects when you put your thumb on them and smear them on a book. I hate—I loathe it! "

" They might as well be healthy insects while they last," an-swered Martin.

Thyme faced round at him. " I shan't sleep to-night, Martin; get out my bicycle for me."

Martin scrutinised her by the light of the street lamp. " All right," he said; " I'll come too."

There are, say moralists, roads that lead to Hell, but it was on a road that leads to Hampstead that the two young cyclists set forth towards eleven o'clock. The difference between the character of the two destinations was soon apparent, for whereas man taken in bulk had perhaps made Hell, Hampstead had ob-viously been made by the upper classes. There were trees and gardens, and instead of dark canals of sky banked by the roofs of houses and hazed with the yellow scum of London lights, the heavens spread out in a wide trembling pool. From that ram-part of the town, the Spaniard's Road, two plains lay exposed to left and right; the scent of may-tree blossom had stolen up the hill; the rising moon clung to a fir-tree bough. Over the country the far stars presided, and sleep's dark wings were spread above the fields—silent, scarce breathing, lay the body of the land. But to the south, where the town, that restless head, was lying, the stars seemed to have fallen and were sown in the thousand furrows of its great grey marsh, and from the dark miasma of those streets there travelled up a rustle, a whisper, the far allurement of some deathless dancer, dragging men to watch the swirl of her black, spangled drapery, the gleam of her writhing limbs. Like the song of the sea in a shell was the murmur of that witch of motion, clasping to her the souls of men, drawing them down into a soul whom none had ever known to rest.

Above the two young cousins, scudding along that ridge between the country and the town, three thin white clouds trailed slowly towards the west—like tired sea-birds drifting exhausted far out from land on a sea blue to blackness with unfathomable depth.

For an hour those two rode silently into the country.

"Have we come far enough?" Martin said at last.

Thyme shook her head. A long, steep hill beyond a little sleeping village had brought them to a standstill. Across the shadowy fields a pale sheet of water gleamed out in moonlight. Thyme turned down towards it.

"I'm hot," she said; "I want to bathe my face. Stay here. Don't come with me."

She left her bicycle, and, passing through a gate, vanished among the trees.

Martin stayed leaning against the gate. The village clock struck one. The distant call of a hunting owl, "Qu-wheek, qu-wheek!" sounded through the grave stillness of this last night of May. The moon at her curve's summit floated at peace on the blue surface of the sky, a great closed water-lily. And Martin saw through the trees scimitar-shaped reeds clustering black along the pool's shore. All about him the mayflowers were alight. It was such a night as makes dreams real and turns reality to dreams.

'All moonlit nonsense!' thought the young man, for the night had disturbed his heart.

But Thyme did not come back. He called to her, and in the death-like silence following his shouts he could hear his own heart beat. He passed in through the gate. She was nowhere to be seen. Why was she playing him this trick?

He turned up from the water among the trees, where the incense of the may-flowers hung heavy in the air.

'Never look for a thing!' he thought, and stopped to listen. It was so breathless that the leaves of a low bough against his

cheek did not stir while he stood there. Presently he heard
faint sounds, and stole towards them. Under a beech-tree he
almost stumbled over Thyme, lying with her face pressed to
the ground. The young doctor's heart gave a sickening leap; he
quickly knelt down beside her. The girl's body, pressed close
to the dry beech-mat, was being shaken by long sobs. From
head to foot it quivered; her hat had been torn off, and the
fragrance of her hair mingled with the fragrance of the night.
In Martin's heart something seemed to turn over and over, as
when a boy he had watched a rabbit caught in a snare. He
touched her. She sat up, and dashing her hand across her eyes,
cried: " Go away! Oh, go away! "

He put his arm round her and waited. Five minutes passed.
The air was trembling with a sort of pale vibration, for the
moonlight had found a hole in the dark foliage and flooded
on to the ground beside them, whitening the black beech-husks.
Some tiny bird, disturbed by these unwonted visitors, began
chirruping and fluttering, but was soon still again. To Martin,
so strangely close to this young creature in the night, there came
a sense of utter disturbance.

' Poor little thing! ' he thought; ' be careful of her, comfort
her! ' Hardness seemed so broken out of her, and the night so
wonderful! And there came into the young man's heart a throb
of the knowledge—very rare with him, for he was not, like
Hilary, a philosophising person—that she was as real as himself—suffering, hoping, feeling, not his hopes and feelings, but
her own. His fingers kept pressing her shoulder through her
thin blouse. And the touch of those fingers was worth more
than any words, as this night, all moonlit dreams, was worth
more than a thousand nights of sane reality.

Thyme twisted herself away from him at last.

" I can't," she sobbed. " I'm not what you thought me—I'm
not made for it! "

A scornful little smile curled Martin's lip. So that was it!
But the smile soon died away. One did not hit what was already
down!

Thyme's voice wailed through the silence. " I thought I
could—but I want beautiful things. I can't bear it all so grey
and horrible. I'm not like *that girl*. I'm—an—amateur! "

' If I kissed her——' Martin thought.

She sank down again, burying her face in the dark beech-
mat. The moonlight had passed on. Her voice came faint and

stifled, as out of the tomb of faith. "I'm no good. I never shall be. I'm as bad as mother!"

But to Martin there was only the scent of her hair.

"No," murmured Thyme's voice, "I'm only fit for miserable Art. . . . I'm only fit for—nothing!"

They were so close together on the dark beech-mat that their bodies touched, and a longing to clasp her in his arms came over him.

"I'm a selfish beast!" moaned the smothered voice. "I don't really care for all these people—I only care because they're ugly for me to see!"

Martin reached his hand out to her hair. If she had shrunk away he would have seized her, but as though by instinct she let it rest there. And at her sudden stillness, strange and touching, Martin's quick passion left him. He slipped his arm round her and raised her up, as if she had been a child, and for a long time sat listening with a queer twisted smile to the moanings of her lost illusions.

The dawn found them still sitting there against the bole of the beech-tree. Her lips were parted; the tears had dried on her sleeping face, pillowed against his shoulder, while he still watched her sideways with the ghost of that twisted smile.

And beyond the grey water, like some tired wanton, the moon in an orange hood was stealing down to her rest between the trees.

CHAPTER XXXVI

STEPHEN SIGNS CHEQUES

WHEN Cecilia received the mystic document containing these words: "Am quite all right. Address, 598, Euston Road, three doors off Martin. Letter follows explaining.—Thyme," she had not even realised her little daughter's departure. She went up to Thyme's room at once, and opening all the drawers and cupboards, stared into them one by one. The many things she saw there allayed the first pangs of her disquiet.

'She has only taken one little trunk,' she thought, 'and left all her evening frocks.'

This act of independence alarmed rather than surprised her, such had been her sense of the unrest in the domestic atmosphere during the last month. Since the evening when she had found Thyme in floods of tears because of the Hughs' baby, her maternal eyes had not failed to notice something new in the child's demeanour—a moodiness, an air almost of conspiracy, together with an emphatic increase of youthful sarcasm. Fearful of probing deep, she had sought no confidence, nor had she divulged her doubts to Stephen.

Amongst the blouses a sheet of blue ruled paper, which had evidently escaped from a note-book, caught her eye. Sentences were scrawled on it in pencil. Cecilia read: "That poor little dead thing was so grey and pinched, and I seemed to realise all of a sudden how awful it is for them. I must—I must—I *will* do something!"

Cecilia dropped the sheet of paper; her hand was trembling. There was no mystery in that departure now, and Stephen's words came into her mind: "It's all very well up to a certain point, and nobody sympathises with them more than I do; but after that it becomes destructive of all comfort, and that does no good to anyone."

The sound sense of those words had made her feel queer when they were spoken; they were even more sensible than she had thought. Did her little daughter, so young and pretty, seriously mean to plunge into the rescue work of dismal slums, to cut herself adrift from sweet sounds and scents and colours, from music and art, from dancing, flowers, and all that made life beautiful? The secret forces of fastidiousness, an inborn dread of the fanatical, and all her real ignorance of what such a life was like, rose in Cecilia with a force which made her feel quite sick. Better that she herself should do this thing than that her own child should be deprived of air and light and all the just environment of her youth and beauty. 'She must come back— she must listen to me!' she thought. 'We will begin together; we will start a nice little *crèche* of our own, or perhaps Mrs. Tallents Smallpeace could find us some regular work on one of her committees.'

Then suddenly she conceived a thought which made her blood run positively cold. What if it were a matter of heredity? What if Thyme had inherited her grandfather's single-mindedness? Martin was giving proof of it. Things, she knew, often skipped a generation and then set in again. Surely, surely, it could not have done that! With longing, yet with dread, she waited for the sound of Stephen's latchkey. It came at its appointed time.

Even in her agitation Cecilia did not forget to spare him, all she could. She began by giving him a kiss, and then said casually: "Thyme has got a whim into her head."

"What whim?"

"It's rather what you might expect," faltered Cecilia, "from her going about so much with Martin."

Stephen's face assumed at once an air of dry derision; there was no love lost between him and his young nephew-in-law.

"The Sanitist?" he said; "ah! Well?"

"She has gone off to do work—some place in the Euston Road. I've had a telegram. Oh, and I found this, Stephen."

She held out to him half-heartedly the two bits of paper, one pinkish-brown, the other blue. Stephen saw that she was trembling. He took them from her, read them, and looked at her again. He had a real affection for his wife, and the tradition of consideration for other people's feelings was bred in him, so that at this moment, so vitally disturbing, the first thing he did was to put his hand on her shoulder and give it a reassuring squeeze. But there was also in Stephen a certain primitive virility, pickled, it is true, at Cambridge, and in the Law Courts dried, but still preserving something of its possessive and assertive quality, and the second thing he did was to say, "No, I'm damned!"

In that little sentence lay the whole psychology of his attitude towards this situation and all the difference between two classes of the population. Mr. Purcey would undoubtedly have said: " *Well,* I'm damned! " Stephen, by saying " *No,* I'm damned! " betrayed that before he could be damned he had been obliged to wrestle and contend with something, and Cecilia, who was always wrestling too, knew this something to be that queer new thing, a Social Conscience, the dim bogey stalking pale about the houses of those who, through the accidents of leisure or of culture, had once left the door open to the suspicion: Is it possible that there is a class of people besides my own, or am I dreaming? Happy the millions, poor or rich, not yet condemned to watch the wistful visiting or hear the husky mutter of that ghost, happy in their homes, blessed by a less disquieting god. Such were Cecilia's inner feelings.

Even now she did not quite plumb the depths of Stephen's; she felt his struggle with the ghost, she felt and admired his victory. What she did not, could not, perhaps, realise, was the precise nature of the outrage inflicted on him by Thyme's action. With her—being a woman—the matter was more practical; she did not grasp, had never grasped, the architectural nature of Stephen's mind—how really hurt he was by what did not seem to him in due and proper order.

He spoke: " Why on earth, if she felt like that, couldn't she have gone to work in the ordinary way? She could have put herself in connection with some proper charitable society—I should never have objected to that. It's all that young Sanitary idiot! "

" I believe," Cecilia faltered, " that Martin's *is* a society. It's a kind of medical Socialism, or something of that sort. He has tremendous faith in it."

Stephen's lip curled.

" He may have as much faith as he likes," he said, with the restraint that was one of his best qualities, " so long as he doesn't infect my daughter with it."

Cecilia said suddenly: " Oh! what are we to do, Stephen? Shall I go over there to-night? "

As one may see a shadow pass down on a cornfield, so came the cloud on Stephen's face. It was as though he had not realised till then the full extent of what this meant. For a minute he was silent.

" Better wait for her letter," he said at last. " He's her

cousin, after all, and Mrs. Grundy's dead—in the Euston Road, at all events."

So, trying to spare each other all they could of anxiety, and careful to abstain from any hint of trouble before the servants, they dined and went to bed.

At that hour between the night and morning, when man's vitality is lowest, and the tremors of his spirit, like birds of ill omen, fly round and round him, beating their long plumes against his cheeks, Stephen woke.

It was very still. A bar of pearly-grey dawn showed between the filmy curtains, which stirred with a regular, faint movement, like the puffing of a sleeper's lips. The tide of the wind, woven in Mr. Stone's fancy of the souls of men, was at low ebb. Feebly it fanned the houses and hovels where the myriad forms of men lay sleeping, unconscious of its breath; so faint life's pulse, that men and shadows seemed for that brief moment mingled in the town's sleep. Over the million varied roofs, over the hundred million little different shapes of men and things, the wind's quiet, visiting wand had stilled all into the wonder state of nothingness, when life is passing into death, death into new life, and self is at its feeblest.

And Stephen's self, feeling the magnetic currents of that ebb-tide drawing it down into murmurous slumber, out beyond the sand-bars of individuality and class, threw up its little hands and began to cry for help. The purple sea of self-forgetfulness, under the dim, impersonal sky, seemed to him so cold and terrible. It had no limit that he could see, no rules but such as hung too far away, written in the hieroglyphics of paling stars. He could feel no order in the lift and lap of the wan waters round his limbs. Where would those waters carry him? To what depth of still green silence? Was his own little daughter to go down into this sea that knew no creed but that of self-forgetfulness, that respected neither class nor person—this sea where a few wandering streaks seemed all the evidence of the precious differences between mankind? God forbid it!

And, turning on his elbow, he looked at her who had given him this daughter. In the mystery of his wife's sleeping face—the face of her most near and dear to him—he tried hard not to see a likeness to Mr. Stone. He fell back somewhat comforted with the thought: 'That old chap has his one idea—his Universal Brotherhood. He's absolutely absorbed in it. I don't see it in Cis's face a bit. Quite the contrary.'

But suddenly a flash of clear, hard cynicism amounting to inspiration utterly disturbed him: The old chap, indeed, was so wrapped up in himself and his precious book as to be quite unconscious that anyone else was alive. Could one be everybody's brother if one were blind to their existence? But this freak of Thyme's was an actual try to be everybody's sister. For that, he supposed, one *must* forget oneself. Why, it was really even a worse case than that of Mr. Stone! And to Stephen there was something awful in this thought.

The first small bird of morning, close to the open window, uttered a feeble chirrup. Into Stephen's mind there leaped without reason recollection of the morning after his first term at school, when, awakened by the birds, he had started up and fished out from under his pillow his catapult and the box of shot he had brought home and taken to sleep with him. He seemed to see again those leaden shot with their bluish sheen, and to feel them, round, and soft, and heavy, rolling about his palm. He seemed to hear Hilary's surprised voice saying: "Hallo, Stevie! you awake?"

No one had ever had a better brother than old Hilary. His only fault was that he had always been too kind. It was his kindness that had done for him, and made his married life a failure. He had never asserted himself enough with that woman, his wife. Stephen turned over on his other side. 'All this confounded business,' he thought, 'comes from over-sympathizing. That's what's the matter with Thyme, too.' Long he lay thus, while the light grew stronger, listening to Cecilia's gentle breathing, disturbed to his very marrow by these thoughts.

The first post brought no letter from Thyme, and the announcement soon after, that Mr. Hilary had come to breakfast, was received by both Stephen and Cecilia with a welcome such as the anxious give to anything which shows promise of distracting them.

Stephen made haste down. Hilary, with a very grave and harassed face, was in the dining-room. It was he, however, who, after one look at Stephen, said:

"What's the matter, Stevie?"

Stephen took up the *Standard*. In spite of his self-control, his hand shook a little.

"It's a ridiculous business," he said. "That precious young Sanitist has so worked his confounded theories into Thyme that she has gone off to the Euston Road to put them into practice, of all things!"

At the half-concerned amusement on Hilary's face his quick and rather narrow eyes glinted.

"It's not exactly for you to laugh, Hilary," he said. "It's all of a piece with your cursed sentimentality about those Hughs, and that girl. I knew it would end in a mess."

Hilary answered this unjust and unexpected outburst by a look, and Stephen, with the strange feeling of inferiority which would come to him in Hilary's presence against his better judgment, lowered his own glance.

"My dear boy," said Hilary, "if any bit of my character has crept into Thyme, I'm truly sorry." ·

Stephen took his brother's hand and gave it a good grip; and, Cecilia coming in, they all sat down.

Cecilia at once noted what Stephen in his preoccupation had not—that Hilary had come to tell them something. But she did not like to ask him what it was, though she knew that in the presence of their trouble Hilary was too delicate to obtrude his own. She did not like, either, to talk of her trouble in the presence of his. They all talked, therefore, of indifferent things —what music they had heard, what plays they had seen—eating but little, and drinking tea. In the middle of a remark about the opera, Stephen, looking up, saw Martin himself standing in the doorway. The young Sanitist looked pale, dusty, and dishevelled. He advanced towards Cecilia, and said with his usual cool determination:

"I've brought her back, Aunt Cis."

At that moment, fraught with such relief, such pure joy, such desire to say a thousand things, Cecilia could only murmur: "Oh, Martin!"

Stephen, who had jumped up, asked: "Where is she?"

"Gone to her room."

"Then perhaps," said Stephen, regaining at once his dry composure, "you will give us some explanation of this folly."

"She's no use to us at present."

"Indeed!"

"None."

"Then," said Stephen, "kindly understand that we have no use for *you* in future, or any of your sort."

Martin looked round the table, resting his eyes on each in turn.

"You're right," he said. "Good-bye!"

Hilary and Cecilia had risen, too. There was silence. Stephen crossed to the door.

"You seem to me," he said suddenly, in his driest voice, "with your new manners and ideas, quite a pernicious youth."

Cecilia stretched her hands out towards Martin, and there was a faint tinkling as of chains.

"You must know, dear," she said, "how anxious we've all been. Of course, your uncle doesn't mean that."

The same scornful tenderness with which he was wont to look at Thyme passed into Martin's face.

"All right, Aunt Cis," he said; "if Stephen doesn't mean it, he ought to. To mean things is what matters." He stooped and kissed her forehead. "Give that to Thyme for me," he said. "I shan't see her for a bit."

"You'll never see her, sir," said Stephen dryly, "if I can help it! The liquor of your Sanitism is too bright and effervescent."

Martin's smile broadened. "For old bottles," he said, and with another slow look round went out.

Stephen's mouth assumed its driest twist. "Bumptious young devil!" he said. "If that is the new young man, defend us!"

Over the cool dining-room, with its faint scent of pinks, of melon, and of ham, came silence. Suddenly Cecilia glided from the room. Her light footsteps were heard hurrying, now that she was not visible, up to Thyme.

Hilary, too, had moved towards the door. In spite of his preoccupation, Stephen could not help noticing how very worn his brother looked.

"You look quite seedy, old boy," he said. "Will you have some brandy?"

Hilary shook his head.

"Now that you've got Thyme back," he said, "I'd better let you know my news. I'm going abroad to-morrow. I don't know whether I shall come back again to live with B."

Stephen gave a low whistle; then, pressing Hilary's arm, he said: "Anything you decide, old man, I'll always back you in, but——"

"I'm going alone."

In his relief Stephen violated the laws of reticence.

"Thank Heaven for that! I was afraid you were beginning to lose your head about that girl."

"I'm not quite fool enough," said Hilary, "to imagine that

such a liaison would be anything but misery in the long-run. If I took the child I should have to stick to her; but I'm not proud of leaving her in the lurch, Stevie."

The tone of his voice was so bitter that Stephen seized his hand.

"My dear old man, you're too kind. Why, she's no hold on you—not the smallest in the world!"

"Except the hold of this devotion I've roused in her, God knows how, and her destitution."

"You let these people haunt you," said Stephen. "It's quite a mistake—it really is."

"I had forgotten to mention that I am not an iceberg," muttered Hilary.

Stephen looked into his face without speaking, then with the utmost earnestness he said:

"However much you may be attracted, it's simply unthinkable for a man like you to go outside his class."

"Class! Yes!" muttered Hilary: "Good-bye!" And with a long grip of his brother's hand he went away.

Stephen turned to the window. For all the care and contrivance bestowed on the view, far away to the left the back courts of an alley could be seen; and as though some gadfly had planted in him its small poisonous sting, he moved back from the sight at once.

'Confusion!' he thought. 'Are we never to get rid of these infernal people?'

His eyes lighted on the melon. A single slice lay by itself on a blue-green dish. Leaning over a plate, with a desperation quite unlike himself, he took an enormous bite. Again and again he bit the slice, then almost threw it from him, and dipped his fingers in a bowl.

'Thank God!' he thought, 'that's over! What an escape!'

Whether he meant Hilary's escape or Thyme's was doubtful, but there came on him a longing to rush up to his little daughter's room, and hug her. He suppressed it, and sat down at the bureau; he was suddenly experiencing a sensation such as he had sometimes felt on a perfect day, or after physical danger, of too much benefit, of something that he would like to return thanks for, yet knew not how. His hand stole to the inner pocket of his black coat. It stole out again; there was a cheque-book in it. Before his mind's eye, starting up one after the other, he saw the names of the societies he supported, or meant sometime, if he could afford it, to support. He reached his hand out for a pen. The still, small noise of the nib travelling across the cheques mingled with the buzzing of a single fly.

These sounds Cecilia heard, when, from the open door, she saw the thin back of her husband's neck, with its softly graduated hair, bent forward above the bureau. She stole over to him, and pressed herself against his arm.

Stephen, staying the progress of his pen, looked up at her. Their eyes met, and, bending down, Cecilia put her cheek to his.

CHAPTER XXXVII

THE FLOWERING OF THE ALOE

THIS same day, returning through Kensington Gardens, from his preparations for departure, Hilary came suddenly on Bianca standing by the shores of the Round Pond.

To the eyes of the frequenters of these Elysian fields, where so many men and shadows daily steal recreation, to the eyes of all drinking in those green gardens their honeyed draught of peace, this husband and wife appeared merely a distinguished-looking couple, animated by a leisured harmony. For the time was not yet when men were one, and could tell by instinct what was passing in each other's hearts.

In truth, there were not too many people in London who, in their situation, would have behaved with such seemliness—not too many so civilised as they!

Estranged, and soon to part, they retained the manner of accord up to the last. Not for them the matrimonial brawl, the solemn accusation and recrimination, the pathetic protestations of proprietary rights. For them no sacred view that at all costs they must make each other miserable—not even the belief that they had the right to do so. No, there was no relief for their sore hearts. They walked side by side, treating each other's feelings with respect, as if there had been no terrible heart-burnings throughout the eighteen years in which they had first loved, then, through mysterious disharmony, drifted apart; as if there were now between them no question of this girl.

Presently Hilary said:

"I've been into town and made my preparations; I'm starting to-morrow for the mountains. There will be no necessity for you to leave your father."

"Are you taking her?"

It was beautifully uttered, without a trace of bias or curiosity, with an unforced accent, neither indifferent nor too interested—no one could have told whether it was meant for generosity or malice. Hilary took it for the former.

"Thank you," he said; "but that comedy is finished."

Close to the edge of the Round Pond a swan-like cutter was

putting out to sea; in the wake of this fair creature a tiny scooped-out bit of wood, with three feathers for masts, bobbed and trembled; and the two small ragged boys who owned that little galley were stretching bits of branch out towards her over the bright waters.

Bianca looked, without seeing, at this proof of man's pride in his own property. A thin gold chain hung round her neck; suddenly she thrust it into the bosom of her dress. It had broken into two, between her fingers.

They reached home without another word.

At the door of Hilary's study sat Miranda. The little person answered his caress by a shiver of her sleek skin, then curled herself down again on the spot she had already warmed.

"Aren't you coming in with me?" he said.

Miranda did not move.

The reason for her refusal was apparent when Hilary had entered. Close to the long bookcase, behind the bust of Socrates, stood the little model. Very still, as if fearing to betray itself by sound or movement, was her figure in its blue-green frock, and a brimless toque of brown straw, with two purplish roses squashed together into a band of darker velvet. Beside those roses a tiny peacock's feather had been slipped in—unholy little visitor, slanting backward, trying, as it were, to draw all eyes, yet to escape notice. And, wedged between the grim white bust and the dark bookcase, the girl herself was like some unlawful spirit which had slid in there, and stood trembling and vibrating, ready to be shuttered out.

Before this apparition Hilary recoiled towards the door, hesitated, and returned.

"You should not have come here," he muttered, "after what we said to you yesterday."

The little model answered quickly: "But I've seen Hughs, Mr. Dallison. He's found out where I live. Oh, he does look dreadful; he frightens me. I can't ever stay there now."

She had come a little out of her hiding-place, and stood fidgeting her hands and looking down.

'She's not speaking the truth,' thought Hilary.

The little model gave him a furtive glance. "I *did* see him," she said. "I must go right away now; it wouldn't be safe, would it?" Again she gave him that swift look.

Hilary thought suddenly: 'She is using my own weapon against me. If she *has* seen the man, he didn't frighten her. It serves me right!' With a dry laugh, he turned his back.

There was a rustling round. The little model had moved out of her retreat, and stood between him and the door. At this stealthy action, Hilary felt once more the tremor which had come over him when he sat beside her in the Broad Walk after the baby's funeral. Outside in the garden a pigeon was pouring forth a continuous love-song; Hilary heard nothing of it, conscious only of the figure of the girl behind him—that young figure which had twined itself about his senses.

" Well, what is it you want? " he said at last.

The little model answered by another question. " Are you really going away, Mr. Dallison? "

" I am."

She raised her hands to the level of her breast, as though she meant to clasp them together; without doing so, however, she dropped them to her sides. They were cased in very worn suède gloves, and in this dire movement of embarrassment Hilary's eyes fastened themselves on those slim hands moving against her skirt.

The little model tried at once to slip them away behind her. Suddenly she said in her matter-of-fact voice: " I only wanted to ask—Can't I come too? "

At this question, whose simplicity might have made an angel smile, Hilary experienced a sensation as if his bones had been turned to water. It was strange—delicious—as though he had been suddenly offered all that he wanted of her, without all those things that he did not want. He stood regarding her silently. Her cheeks and neck were red; there was a red tinge, too, in her eye-lids, deepening the " chicory-flower " colour of her eyes. She began to speak, repeating a lesson evidently learned by heart.

" I wouldn't be in your way. I wouldn't cost much. I could do everything you wanted. I could learn typewriting. I needn't live too near, or that, if you didn't want me, because of people talking; I'm used to being alone. Oh, Mr. Dallison, I could do everything for you. I wouldn't mind *anything,* and I'm not like some girls; I do know what I'm talking about."

" Do you? "

The little model put her hands up, and, covering her face, said:

" If you'd try and see! "

Hilary's sensuous feeling almost vanished; a lump rose in his throat instead.

"My child," he said, "you are too generous!"

The little model seemed to know instinctively that by touching his spirit she had lost ground. Uncovering her face, she spoke breathlessly, growing very pale:

"Oh no, I'm not. I *want* to be let come; I don't want to stay here. I know I'll get into mischief if you don't take me—oh, I know I will!"

"If I were to let you come with me," said Hilary, "what then? What sort of companion should I be to you, or you to me? You know very well. Only one sort. It's no use pretending, child, that we've any interests in common."

The little model came closer.

"I know what I am," she said, "and I don't want to be anything else. I can do what you tell me to, and I shan't ever complain. I'm not worth any more!"

"You're worth more," muttered Hilary, "than I can ever give you, and I'm worth more than you can ever give me."

The little model tried to answer, but her words would not pass her throat; she threw her head back trying to free them, and stood, swaying. Seeing her like this before him, white as a sheet, with her eyes closed and her lips parted, as though about to faint, Hilary seized her by the shoulders. At the touch of those soft shoulders, his face became suffused with blood, his lips trembled. Suddenly her eyes opened ever so little between their lids, and looked at him. And the perception that she was not really going to faint, that it was a little desperate wile of this child Delilah, made him wrench away his hands. The moment she felt that grasp relax she sank down and clasped his knees, pressing them to her bosom so that he could not stir. Closer and closer she pressed them to her, till it seemed as though she must be bruising her flesh. Her breath came in sobs; her eyes were closed; her lips quivered upwards. In the clutch of her clinging body there seemed suddenly the whole of woman's power of self-abandonment. It was just that, which, at this moment, so horribly painful to him, prevented Hilary from seizing her in his arms—just that queer seeming self-effacement, as though she were lost to knowledge of what she did. It seemed too brutal, too like taking advantage of a child.

From calm is born the wind, the ripple from the still pool, self out of nothingness—so all passes inperceptibly, no man knows how. The little model's moment of self-oblivion passed, and into her wet eyes her plain, twisting spirit suddenly writhed up again, for all the world as if she had said: 'I won't let you go; I'll keep you—I'll keep you.'

Hilary broke away from her, and she fell forward on her face.

"Get up, child," he said—"get up; for God's sake, don't lie there!"

She rose obediently, choking down her sobs, mopping her face with a small, dirty handkerchief. Suddenly, taking a step, towards him, she clenched both her hands and struck them downwards.

"I'll go to the bad," she said—"I *will*—if you don't take me!" And, her breast heaving, her hair all loose, she stared straight into his face with her red-rimmed eyes. Hilary turned suddenly, took a book up from the writing-table, and opened it. His face was again suffused with blood; his hands and lips trembled; his eyes had a queer fixed stare.

"Not now, not now," he muttered; "go away now. I'll come to you to-morrow."

The little model gave him the look a dog gives you when it asks if you are deceiving him. She made a sign on her breast, as a Catholic might make the sign of his religion, drawing her fingers together, and clutching at herself with them, then passed her little dirty handkerchief once more over her eyes, and, turning round, went out.

Hilary remained standing where he was, reading the open book without apprehending what it was.

There was a wistful sound, as of breath escaping hurriedly. Mr. Stone was standing in the open doorway.

"She has been here," he said. "I saw her go away."

Hilary dropped the book; his nerves were utterly unstrung. Then, pointing to a chair, he said: "Won't you sit down, sir?"

Mr. Stone came close up to his son-in-law.

"Is she in trouble?"

"Yes," murmured Hilary.

"She is too young to be in trouble. Did you tell her that?"

Hilary shook his head.

"Has the man hurt her?"

Again Hilary shook his head.

"What is her trouble, then?" said Mr. Stone.

The closeness of this catechism, the intent stare of the old man's eyes, were more than Hilary could bear. He turned away.

"You ask me something that I cannot answer."

"Why?"

"It is a private matter."

With the blood still beating in his temples, his lips still quivering, and the feeling of the girl's clasp round his knees, he almost hated this old man who stood there putting such blind questions.

Then suddenly in Mr. Stone's eyes he saw a startling change, as in the face of a man who regains consciousness after days of vacancy. His whole countenance had become alive with a sort of jealous understanding. The warmth which the little model brought to his old spirit had licked up the fog of his Idea, and made him see what was going on before his eyes.

At that look Hilary braced himself against the wall.

A flush spread slowly over Mr. Stone's face. He spoke with rare hesitation. In this sudden coming back to the world of men and things he seemed astray.

"I am not going," he stammered, "to ask you any more. I could not pry into a private matter. That would not be——" His voice failed; he looked down.

Hilary bowed, touched to the quick by the return to life of this old man, so long lost to facts, and by the delicacy in that old face.

"I will not intrude further on your trouble," said Mr. Stone, "whatever it may be. I am sorry that you are unhappy, too."

Very slowly, and without again looking up at his son-in-law, he went out.

Hilary remained standing where he had been left against the wall.

CHAPTER XXXVIII

THE HOME-COMING OF HUGHS

HILARY had evidently been right in thinking the little model was not speaking the truth when she said she had seen Hughs, for it was not until early on the following morning that three persons traversed the long winding road leading from Wormwood Scrubs to Kensington. They preserved silence, not because there was nothing in their hearts to be expressed, but because there was too much; and they walked in the giraffe-like formation peculiar to the lower classes—Hughs in front; Mrs. Hughs to the left, a foot or two behind; and a yard behind her, to the left again, her son Stanley. They made no sign of noticing anyone in the road besides themselves, and no one in the road gave sign of noticing that they were there; but in their three minds, so differently fashioned, a verb was dumbly, and with varying emotion, being conjugated:

"I've been in prison."
"You've been in prison."
"He's been in prison."

Beneath the seeming acquiescence of a man subject to domination from his birth up, those four words covered in Hughs such a whirlpool of surging sensation, such ferocity of bitterness, and madness, and defiance, that no outpouring could have appreciably relieved its course. The same four words summed up in Mrs. Hughs so strange a mingling of fear, commiseration, loyalty, shame, and trembling curiosity at the new factor which had come into the life of all this little family walking giraffe-like back to Kensington that to have gone beyond them would have been like plunging into a wintry river. To their son the four words were as a legend of romance, conjuring up no definite image, lighting merely the glow of wonder.

"Don't lag, Stanley. Keep up with your father."

The little boy took three steps at an increased pace, then fell behind again. His black eyes seemed to answer: 'You

469

say that because you don't know what else to say.' And without alteration in their giraffe-like formation, but again in silence, the three proceeded.

In the heart of the seamstress doubt and fear were being slowly knit into dread of the first sound to pass her husband's lips. What would he ask? How should she answer? Would he talk wild, or would he talk sensible? Would he have forgotten that young girl, or had he nursed and nourished his wicked fancy in the house of grief and silence? Would he ask where the baby was? Would he speak a kind word to her? But alongside her dread there was fluttering within her the undying resolution not to 'let him go from her, if it were ever so, to that young girl.'

" Don't lag, Stanley ! "

At the reiteration of those words Hughs spoke.

" Let the boy alone ! You'll be nagging at the baby next ! "

Hoarse and grating, like sounds issuing from a damp vault, was this first speech.

The seamstress's eyes brimmed over.

" I won't get the chance," she stammered out. " He's gone ! "

Hughs' teeth gleamed like those of a dog at bay.

" Who's taken him? You let me know the name."

Tears rolled down the seamstress's cheeks; she could not answer. Her little son's thin voice rose instead:

" Baby's dead. We buried him in the ground. I saw it. Mr. Creed came in the cab with me."

White flecks appeared suddenly at the corners of Hughs' lips. He wiped the back of his hand across his mouth, and once more, giraffe-like, the little family marched on. . . .

" Westminister," in his threadbare summer jacket—for the day was warm—had been standing for some little time in Mrs. Budgen's doorway on the ground floor at Hound Street. Knowing that Hughs was to be released that morning early, he had, with the circumspection and foresight of his character, reasoned thus: ' I shan't lie easy in my bed, I shan't have no peace until I know that low feller's not a-goin' to misdemean himself with me. It's no good to go a-puttin' of it off. I don't want him comin' to my room attackin' of old men. I'll be previous with him in the passage. The lame woman 'll let me. I shan't trouble her. She'll be palliable between me and him, in case he goes for to attack me. I ain't afraid of him.'

But, as the minutes of waiting went by, his old tongue, like

that of a dog expecting chastisement, appeared ever more frequently to moisten his twisted, discoloured lips. 'This comes
of mixin' up with soldiers,' he thought, 'and a low-class o'
man like that. I ought to ha' changed my lodgin's. He'll be
askin' me where that young girl is, I shouldn't wonder, an' him
lost his character and his job, and everything, and all because o'
women!'

He watched the broad-faced woman, Mrs. Budgen, in whose
grey eyes the fighting light so fortunately never died, painfully
doing out her rooms, and propping herself against the chest
of drawers whereon clustered china cups and dogs as thick as
toadstools on a bank.

"I've told my Charlie," she said, "to keep clear of Hughs
a bit. They comes out as prickly as hedgehogs. Pick a quarrel
as soon as look at you, they will."

'Oh, dear,' thought Creed, 'she's full o' cold comfort.' But,
careful of his dignity, he answered, "I'm a-waitin' here to
engage the situation. You don't think he'll attack of me with
definition at this time in the mornin'?"

The lame woman shrugged her shoulders. "He'll have had a
drop of something," she said, "before he comes home. They
gets a cold feelin' in the stomach in them places, poor creatures!"

The old butler's heart quavered up into his mouth. He lifted
his shaking hand, and put it to his lips, as though to readjust
himself.

"Oh, yes," he said: "I ought to ha' given notice, and took
my things away; but there, poor woman, it seemed a-hittin' of
her when she was down. And I don't *want* to make no move.
I ain't got no one else that's interested in me. This woman's
very good about mendin' of my clothes. Oh dear, yes; she
don't grudge a little thing like that!"

The lame woman hobbled from her post of rest, and began
to make the bed with the frown that always accompanied a task
which strained the contracted muscles of her leg. "If you
don't help your neighbour, your neighbour don't help you," she
said sententiously.

Creed fixed his iron-rimmed gaze on her in silence. He
was considering perhaps how he stood with regard to Hughs
in the light of that remark.

"I attended of his baby's funeral," he said. "Oh dear, he's
here a'ready!"

The family of Hughs, indeed, stood in the doorway. The spiritual process by which "Westminister" had gone through life was displayed completely in the next few seconds. 'It's so important for me to keep alive and well,' his eyes seemed saying. 'I know the class of man you are, but now you're here it's not a bit o' use my bein' frightened. I'm bound to get up-sides with you. Ho! yes; keep yourself to yourself, and don't you let me hev any o' your nonsense, 'cause I won't stand it. Oh dear, no!'

Beads of perspiration stood thick on his patchily coloured forehead; with lips stiffening, and intently staring eyes, he waited for what the released prisoner would say.

Hughs, whose face had blanched in the prison to a sallow grey-white hue, and whose black eyes seemed to have sunk back into his head, slowly looked the old man up and down. At last he took his cap off, showing his cropped hair.

"*You* got me that, daddy," he said, "but I don't bear you malice. Come up and have a cup o' tea with us."

And, turning on his heel, he began to mount the stairs, followed by his wife and child. Breathing hard, the old butler mounted too.

In the room on the second floor, where the baby no longer lived, a haddock on the table was endeavouring to be fresh; round it were slices of bread on plates, a piece of butter in a pie-dish, a teapot, brown sugar in a basin, and, side by side a little jug of cold blue milk and a half-empty bottle of red vinegar. Close to one plate a bunch of stocks and gilly flowers reposed on the dirty tablecloth, as though dropped and forgotten by the God of Love. Their faint perfume stole through the other odours. The old butler fixed his eyes on it.

'The poor woman bought that,' he thought, 'hopin' to remind him of old days. She had them flowers on her weddin'-day, I shouldn't wonder!' This poetical conception surprising him, he turned towards the little boy, and said: "This'll be a memorial to you, as you gets older." And without another word all sat down.

They ate in silence, and the old butler thought: 'That addick ain't what it was; but a beautiful cup o' tea. He don't eat nothing; he's more ameniable to reason than I expected. There's no one won't be too pleased to see him now!'

His eyes, travelling to the spot from which the bayonet had been removed, rested on the print of the Nativity. '"Suffer little children to come unto *Me*," ' he thought, ' " and forbid them not." He'll be glad to hear there was two carriages followed him home.'

And, taking his time, he cleared his throat in preparation for speech. But before the singular muteness of this family sounds would not come. Finishing his tea, he tremblingly arose. Things that he might have said jostled in his mind. 'Very pleased to 'a seen you. Hope you're in good health at the present time of speaking. Don't let me intrude on you. We've all a-got to die some time or other!' They remained unuttered. Making a vague movement of his skinny hand, he walked feebly but quickly to the door. When he stood but half-way within the room, he made his final effort.

"I'm not a-goin' to say nothing," he said;—"*that'd* be superlative! I wish you a good-morning."

Outside he waited a second, then grasped the banister.

'For all he sets so quiet, they've done him no good in that place,' he thought. 'Them eyes of his!' And slowly he descended, full of a sort of very deep surprise. 'I misjudged of him,' he was thinking; 'he never was nothing but a 'armless human being. We all has our predijuices—I misjudged of him. They've broke his 'eart between 'em—that they have.'

The silence in the room continued after his departure. But when the little boy had gone to school, Hughs rose and lay down on the bed. He rested there, unmoving, with his face towards the wall, his arms clasped round his head to comfort it. The seamstress, stealing about her avocations, paused now and then to look at him. If he had raged at her, if he had raged at everything, it would not have been so terrifying as this utter silence, which passed her comprehension—this silence as of a man flung by the sea against a rock, and pinned there with the life crushed out of him. All her inarticulate longing, now that her baby was gone, to be close to something in her grey life, to pass the unfranchisable barrier dividing her from the world, seemed to well up, to flow against this wall of silence and to recoil.

Twice or three times she addressed him timidly by name, or made some trivial remark. He did not answer, as though in very truth he had been the shadow of a man lying there. And the injustice of this silence seemed to her so terrible. Was she not his wife? Had she not borne him five, and toiled to keep him from that girl? Was it her fault if she had made his life a hell with her jealousy, as he had cried out that morning before he went for her, and was "put away"? He was her "man." It had been her right—nay, more, her duty!

And still he lay there silent. From the narrow street where no traffic passed, the cries of a coster and distant whistlings mounted through the unwholesome air. Some sparrows in the eave were chirruping incessantly. The little sandy housecat had stolen in, and, crouched against the door-post, was fastening her eyes on the plate which held the remnants of the fish. The seamstress bowed her forehead to the flowers on the table; unable any longer to bear the mystery of this silence, she wept. But the dark figure on the bed only pressed his arms closer round his head, as though there were within him a living death passing the speech of men.

The little sandy cat, creeping across the floor, fixed its claws in the backbone of the fish, and drew it beneath the bed.

CHAPTER XXXIX

THE DUEL

BIANCA did not see her husband after their return together from the Round Pond. She dined out that evening, and in the morning avoided any interview. When Hilary's luggage was brought down and the cab summoned, she slipped up to take shelter in her room. Presently the sound of his footsteps coming along the passage stopped outside her door. He tapped. She did not answer.

Good-bye would be a mockery! Let him go with the words unsaid! And as though the thought had found its way through the closed door, she heard his footsteps recede again. She saw him presently go out to the cab with his head bent down, saw him stoop and pat Miranda. Hot tears sprang into her eyes. She heard the cab-wheels roll away.

The heart is like the face of an Eastern woman—warm and glowing, behind swathe on swathe of fabric. At each fresh touch from the fingers of Life, some new corner, some hidden curve or angle, comes into view, to be seen last of all—perhaps never to be seen by the one who owns them.

When the cab had driven away there came into Bianca's heart a sense of the irreparable, and, mysteriously entwined with that arid ache, a sort of bitter pity. What would happen to this wretched girl now that he was gone? Would she go completely to the bad—till she became one of those poor creatures like the figure in "The Shadow," who stood beneath lampposts in the streets? Out of this speculation, which was bitter as the taste of aloes, there came to her a craving for some palliative, some sweetness, some expression of that instinct of fellow-feeling deep in each human breast, however disharmonic. But even with that craving was mingled the itch to justify herself, and prove that she could rise above jealousy.

She made her way to the little model's lodging.

A child admitted her into the bleak passage that served for hall. The strange medley of emotions passing through Bianca's breast while she stood outside the girl's door did not show in

475

her face, which wore its customary restrained, half-mocking look.

The little model's voice faintly said: " Come in."

The room was in disorder, as though soon to be deserted. A closed and corded trunk stood in the centre of the floor; the bed stripped of clothing, lay disclosed in all the barrenness of discoloured ticking. The china utensils of the washstand were turned head downwards. Beside that washstand the little model, with her hat on—the hat with the purplish-pink roses and the little peacock's feather—stood in the struck, shrinking attitude of one who, coming forward in the expectation of a kiss, has received a blow.

" You are leaving here, then? " Bianca said quietly.

" Yes," the girl murmured.

" Don't you like this part? Is it too far from your work? "

Again the little model whispered: " Yes."

Bianca's eyes travelled slowly over the blue beflowered walls and rust-red doors; through the dusty closeness of this dismantled room a rank scent of musk and violets rose, as though a cheap essence had been scattered as libation. A small empty scent-bottle stood on the shabby looking-glass.

" Have you found new lodgings? "

The little model edged closer to the window. A stealthy watchfulness was creeping into her shrinking, dazed face.

She shook her head.

" I don't know where I'm going."

Obeying a sudden impulse to see more clearly, Bianca lifted her veil. " I came to tell you," she said, " that I shall always be ready to help you."

The girl did not answer, but suddenly through her black lashes she stole a look upward at her visitor. ' Can *you*,' it seemed to say, ' *you*—help me? Oh no; I think not! ' And, as though she had been stung by that glance, Bianca said with deadly slowness:

" It is my business, of course, entirely, now that Mr. Dallison has gone abroad."

The little model received this saying with a quivering jerk. It might have been an arrow transfixing her white throat. For a moment she seemed almost about to fall, but, gripping the window-sill, held herself erect. Her eyes, like an animal's in pain, darted here, there, everywhere, then rested on her visitor's breast, quite motionless. This stare, which seemed to

see nothing, but to be doing, as it were, some fateful calculation, was uncanny. Colour came gradually back into her
lips and eyes and cheeks; she seemed to have succeeded in her
calculation, to be reviving from that stab.

And suddenly Bianca understood. This was the meaning
of the packed trunk, the dismantled room. He was going to
take her, after all!

In the turmoil of this discovery two words alone escaped
her:

"I see!"

They were enough. The girl's face at once lost all trace of
its look of desperate calculation, brightened, became guilty,
and from guilty sullen.

The antagonism of all the long past months was now declared
between these two—Bianca's pride could no longer conceal,
the girl's submissiveness no longer obscure it. They stood
like duellists, one on each side of the trunk—that common,
brown-japanned, tin trunk, corded with rope. Bianca looked
at it.

"You," she said, "and he? Ha, ha; ha, ha! Ha, ha, ha!"

Against that cruel laughter—more poignant than a hundred
homilies on caste, a thousand scornful words—the little model
literally could not stand; she sat down in the low chair where
she had evidently been sitting to watch the street. But as
a taste of blood will infuriate a hound, so her own laughter
seemed to bereave Bianca of all restraint.

"What do you imagine he's taking you for, girl? Only
out of pity! It's not exactly the emotion to live on in exile.
In exile—but that you do not understand!"

The little model staggered to her feet again. Her face
had grown painfully red.

"He wants me!" she said.

"Wants you? As he wants his dinner. And when he's
eaten it—what then? No, of course he'll never abandon you;
his conscience is too tender. But you'll be round his neck
—like this!" Bianca raised her arms, looped, and dragged
them slowly down, as a mermaid's arms drag at a drowning
sailor.

The little model stammered: "I'll do what he tells me!
I'll do what he tells me!"

Bianca stood silent, looking at the girl, whose heaving breast
and little peacock's feather, whose small round hands twisting

in front of her, and scent about her clothes, all seemed an offence.

"And do you suppose that he'll tell you what he wants? Do you imagine *he'll* have the necessary brutality to get rid of you? He'll think himself bound to keep you till you leave him, as I suppose you will some day!"

The girl dropped her hands. "I'll never leave him—never!" she cried out passionately.

"Then Heaven help him!" said Bianca.

The little model's eyes seemed to lose all pupil, like two chicory flowers that have no dark centres. Through them, all that she was feeling struggled to find an outlet; but, too deep for words, those feelings would not pass her lips, utterly unused to express emotion. She could only stammer:

"I'm not—I'm not—I will——" and press her hands again to her breast.

Bianca's lip curled.

"I see; you imagine yourself capable of sacrifice. Well, you have your chance. Take it!" She pointed to the corded trunk. "Now's your time; you have only to disappear!"

The little model shrank back against the window-sill. "He wants me!" she muttered. "I *know* he wants me."

Bianca bit her lips till the blood came.

"Your idea of sacrifice," she said, "is perfect! If you went now, in a month's time he'd never think of you again."

The girl gulped. There was something so pitiful in the movements of her hands that Bianca turned away. She stood for several seconds staring at the door, then, turning round again, said:

"Well?"

But the girl's whole face had changed. All tear-stained, indeed, she had already masked it with a sort of immovable stolidity.

Bianca went swiftly up to the trunk.

"You *shall!*" she said. "Take that thing and go!"

The little model did not move.

"So you won't?"

The girl trembled violently all over. She moistened her lips, tried to speak, failed, again moistened them, and this time murmured: "I'll only—I'll only—if *he* tells me!"

"So you still imagine he will tell you!"

The little model merely repeated: "I won't—I won't do anything without *he* tells me!"

Bianca laughed. "Why, it's like a dog!" she said.

But the girl had turned abruptly to the window. Her lips were parted. She was shrinking, fluttering, trembling at what she saw. She was indeed like a spaniel dog who sees her master coming. Bianca had no need of being told that Hilary was outside. She went into the passage and opened the front door.

He was coming up the steps, his face worn like that of a man in fever, and at the sight of his wife he stood quite still, looking into her face.

Without the quiver of an eyelid, without the faintest trace of emotion, or the slightest sign that she knew him to be there, Bianca passed and slowly walked away.

CHAPTER XL

FINISH OF THE COMEDY

THOSE who may have seen Hilary driving towards the little model's lodgings saw one who, by a fixed red spot on either cheek, and the over-compression of his quivering lips, betrayed the presence of that animality which underlies even the most cultivated men.

After eighteen hours of the purgatory of indecision, he had not so much decided to pay that promised visit on which hung the future of two lives, as allowed himself to be borne towards the girl.

There was no one in the passage to see him after he had passed Bianca in the doorway, but it was with a face darkened by the peculiar stabbing look of wounded egoism that he entered the little model's room.

The site of it coming so closely on the struggle she had just been through was too much for the girl's self-control.

Instead of going up to him, she sat down on the corded trunk and began to sob. It was the sobbing of a child whose school-treat has been cancelled, of a girl whose ball-dress has not come home in time. It only irritated Hilary, whose nerves had already borne all they could bear. He stood literally trembling, as though each one of these common little sobs were a blow falling on the drumskin of his spirit; and through every fiber he took in the features of the dusty, scent-besprinkled room—the brown tin trunk, the dismantled bed, the rust-red doors.

And he realised that she had burned her boats to make it impossible for a man of sensibility to disappoint her!

The little model raised her face and looked at him. What she saw must have been less reassuring even than the first sight had been, for it stopped her sobbing. She rose and turned to the window, evidently trying with handkerchief and powder-puff to repair the ravages caused by her tears; and when she had finished she still stood there with her back to him. Her deep breathing made her young form quiver from her waist up to the little peacock's feather in her hat;

and with each supple movement it seemed offering itself to Hilary.

In the street a barrel-organ had begun to play the very waltz it had played the afternoon when Mr. Stone had been so ill. Those two were neither of them conscious of that tune, too absorbed in their emotions; and yet, quietly, it was bringing something to the girl's figure—like the dowering of scent that the sun brings to a flower. It was bringing the compression back to Hilary's lips, the flush to his ears and cheeks, as a draught of wind will blow to redness a fire that has been choked. Without knowing it, without sound, inch by inch he moved nearer to her; and as though, for all there was no sign of his advance, she knew of it, she stayed utterly unmoving except for the deep breathing that so stirred the warm youth in her. In that stealthy progress was the history of life and the mystery of sex. Inch by inch he neared her; and she swayed, mesmerising his arms to fold round her thus poised, as if she must fall backward; mesmerising him to forget that there was anything there, anything in all the world, but just her young form waiting for him—nothing but that!

The barrel-organ stopped; the spell had broken! She turned round to him. As a wind obscures with grey wrinkles the still green waters of enchantment into which some mortal has been gazing, so Hilary's reason suddenly swept across the situation, and showed it once more as it was. Quick to mark every shade that passed across his face, the girl made as though she would again burst into tears; then, since tears had been so useless, she pressed her hand over her eyes.

Hilary looked at that round, not too cleanly hand. He could see her watching him between her fingers. It was uncanny, almost horrible, like the sight of a cat watching a bird; and he stood appalled at the terrible reality of his position, at the sight of his own future with this girl, with her traditions, customs, life, the thousand and one things that he did not know about her, that he would have to live with if he once took her. A minute passed, which seemed eternity, for into it was condensed every force of her long pursuit, her instinctive clutching at something that she felt to be security, her reaching upwards, her twining round him.

Conscious of all this, held back by that vision of his future, yet whipped towards her by his senses, Hilary swayed like a drunken man. And suddenly she sprang at him, wreathed her arms round his neck, and fastened her mouth to his. The touch of her lips was moist and hot. The scent of stale violet powder came from her, warmed by her humanity. It penetrated to Hilary's heart. He started back in sheer physical revolt.

Thus repulsed, the girl stood rigid, her breast heaving, her eyes unnaturally dilated, her mouth still loosened by the kiss. Snatching from his pocket a roll of notes, Hilary flung them on the bed.

"I can't take you!" he almost groaned. "It's madness! It's impossible!" And he went out into the passage. He ran down the steps and got into his cab. An immense time seemed to pass before it began to move. It started at last, and Hilary sat back in it, his hands clenched, still as a dead man.

His mortified face was recognised by the landlady, returning from her morning's visit to the shops. The gentleman looked, she thought, as if he had received bad news! She not unnaturally connected his appearance with her lodger. Tapping on the girl's door, and receiving no answer, she went in.

The little model was lying on the dismantled bed, pressing her face into the blue and white ticking of the bolster. Her shoulders shook, and a sound of smothered sobbing came from her. The landlady stood staring silently.

Coming of Cornish chapel-going stock, she had never liked this girl, her instinct telling her that she was one for whom life had already been too much. Those for whom life had so early been too much, she knew, were always "ones for pleasure!" Her experience of village life had enabled her to construct the little model's story—that very simple, very frequent little story. Sometimes, indeed, trouble of that sort was soon over and forgotten; but sometimes, if the young man didn't do the right thing by her, and the girl's folk took it hardly, well, then——! So had run the reasoning of this good woman. Being of the same class, she had looked at her lodger from the first without obliquity of vision.

But seeing her now apparently so overwhelmed, and having something soft and warm down beneath her granitic face and hungry eyes, she touched her on the back.

"Come, now!" she said; "you mustn't take on! What is it?"

The little model shook off the hand as a passionate child shakes itself free of consolation. "Let me alone!" she muttered.

The landlady drew back. "Has anyone done you a harm?" she said.

The little model shook her head.

Baffled by this dumb grief, the landlady was silent; then, with the stolidity of those whose lives are one long wrestling with fortune, she muttered:

"I don't like to see *anyone* cry like that!"

And finding that the girl remained obstinately withdrawn from sight or sympathy, she moved towards the door.

"Well," she said, with ironical compassion, "if you want me, I'll be in the kitchen."

The little model remained lying on her bed. Every now and then she gulped, like a child flung down on the grass apart from its comrades, trying to swallow down its rage, trying to bury in the earth its little black moment of despair. Slowly those gulps grew fewer, feebler, and at last died away. She sat up, sweeping Hilary's bundle of notes, on which she had been lying, to the floor.

At sight of that bundle she broke out afresh, flinging herself down sideways with her cheek on the wet bolster; and, for some time after her sobs had ceased again, still lay there. At last she rose and dragged herself over to the looking-glass, scrutinising her streaked, discoloured face, the stains in the cheeks, the swollen eyelids, the marks beneath her eyes; and listlessly she tidied herself. Then, sitting down on the brown tin trunk, she picked the bundle of notes off the floor. They gave forth a dry peculiar crackle. Fifteen ten-pound notes—all Hilary's travelling money. Her eyes opened wider and wider as she counted; and tears, quite suddenly, rolled down on to those thin slips of paper.

Then slowly she undid her dress, and forced them down till they rested, with nothing but her vest between them and the quivering warm flesh which hid her heart.

CHAPTER XLI

THE HOUSE OF HARMONY

At half-past ten that evening Stephen walked up the stone-flagged pathway of his brother's house.

"Can I see Mrs. Hilary?"

"Mr. Hilary went abroad this morning, sir, and Mrs. Hilary has not yet come in."

"Will you give her this letter? No, I'll wait. I suppose I can wait for her in the garden?"

"Oh yes, sir!"

"Very well."

"I'll leave the door open, sir, in case you want to come in."

Stephen walked across to the rustic bench and sat down. He stared gloomily through the dusk at his patent-leather boots, and every now and then he flicked his evening trousers with the letter. Across the dark garden, where the boughs hung soft, unmoved by wind, the light from Mr. Stone's open window flowed out in a pale river; moths, born of the sudden heat, were fluttering up this river to its source.

Stephen looked irritably at the figure of Mr. Stone, which could be seen, bowed, and utterly still, beside his desk; so, by lifting the spy-hole thatch, one may see a convict in his cell stand gazing at his work, without movement, numb with solitude.

'He's getting awfully broken up,' thought Stephen. 'Poor old chap! His ideas are killing him. They're not human nature, never will be.' Again he flicked his trousers with the letter, as though that document emphasised the fact. 'I can't help being sorry for the sublime old idiot!'

He rose, the better to see his father-in-law's unconscious figure. It looked as lifeless and as cold as though Mr. Stone had followed some thought below the ground, and left his body standing there to await his return. Its appearance oppressed Stephen.

'You might set the house on fire,' he thought; 'he'd never notice.'

Mr. Stone's figure moved; the sound of a long sigh came

484

out to Stephen in the windless garden. He turned his eyes away, with the sudden feeling that it was not the thing to watch the old chap like this; then, getting up, he went indoors. In his brother's study he stood turning over the knick-knacks on the writing-table.

'I warned Hilary that he was burning his fingers,' he thought.

At the sound of the latch-key he went back to the hall.

However much he had secretly disapproved of her from the beginning, because she had always seemed to him such an uncomfortable and tantalising person, Stephen was impressed that night by the haunting unhappiness of Bianca's face; as if it had been suddenly disclosed to him that she could not help herself. This was disconcerting, being, in a sense, a disorderly way of seeing things.

"You look tired, B.," he said. "I'm sorry, but I thought it better to bring this round to-night."

Bianca glanced at the letter.

"It is to you," she said. "I don't wish to read it, thank you."

Stephen compressed his lips.

"But I wish you to hear it, please," he said. "I'll read it out, if you'll allow me.

"'CHARING CROSS STATION.

"'DEAR STEVIE,

"'I told you yesterday morning that I was going abroad alone. Afterwards I changed my mind—I meant to take her. I went to her lodgings for the purpose. I have lived too long amongst sentiments for such a piece of reality as that. Class has saved me; it has triumphed over my most primitive instincts.

"'I am going alone—back to my sentiments. No slight has been placed on Bianca—but my married life having become a mockery, I shall not return to it. The following address will find me, and I shall ask you presently to send on my household gods.

"'Please let Bianca know the substance of this letter.

"'Ever your affectionate brother,

"'HILARY DALLISON.'"

With a frown Stephen folded up the letter, and restored it to his breast pocket.

'It's more bitter than I thought,' he reflected, 'and yet he's done the only possible thing!'

Bianca was leaning her elbow on the mantelpiece with her face turned to the wall. Her silence irritated Stephen, whose loyalty to his brother longed to find a vent.

"I'm very much relieved, of course," he said at last. "It would have been fatal."

She did not move, and Stephen became increasingly aware that this was a most awkward matter to touch on.

"Of course," he began again. "But, B., I do think you—rather—I mean——" And again he stopped before her utter silence, her utter immobility. Then, unable to go away without having in some sort expressed his loyalty to Hilary, he tried once more: "Hilary is the kindest man I know. It's not his fault if he's out of touch with life—if he's not fit to deal with things. He's *negative!*"

And having thus in a single word, somewhat to his own astonishment, described his brother, he held out his hand.

The hand which Bianca placed in it was feverishly hot. Stephen felt suddenly compunctious.

"I'm awfully sorry," he stammered, "about the whole thing. I'm awfully sorry for you——"

Bianca drew back her hand.

With a little shrug Stephen turned away.

'What are you to do with women like that?' was his thought, and saying dryly, "Good-night, B.," he went.

For some time Bianca sat in Hilary's chair. Then, by the faint glimmer coming through the half-open door, she began to wander round the room, touching the walls, the books, the prints, all the familiar things among which he had lived so many years.

In that dim continual journey she was like a disharmonic spirit traversing the air above where its body lies.

The door creaked behind her. A voice said sharply:

"What are you doing in this house?"

Mr. Stone was standing beside the bust of Socrates. Bianca went up to him.

"Father!"

Mr. Stone stared. "Is it you! I thought it was a thief! Where is Hilary?"

"Gone away."

"Alone?"

Bianca bowed her head. "It is very late, Dad," she whispered.

Mr. Stone's hand moved as though he would have stroked her.

"The human heart," he murmured, "is the tomb of many feelings."

Bianca put her arm round him.

"You must go to bed, Dad," she said, trying to get him to the door, for in her heart something seemed giving way.

Mr. Stone stumbled; the door swung to; the room was plunged in darkness. A hand, cold as ice, brushed her cheek. With all her force she stifled a scream.

"I am here," Mr. Stone said.

His hand, wandering downwards, touched her shoulder, and she seized it with her own burning hand. Thus linked, they groped their way out into the passage towards his room.

"Good-night, dear," Bianca murmured.

By the light of his now open door Mr. Stone seemed to try and see her face, but she would not show it him. Closing the door gently, she stole upstairs.

Sitting down in her bedroom by the open window, it seemed to her that the room was full of people—her nerves were so unstrung. It was as if walls had not the power this night to exclude human presences. Moving, or motionless, now distinct, then covered suddenly by the thick veil of some material object, they circled round her quiet figure, lying back in the chair with shut eyes. These disharmonic shadows flitting in the room made a stir like the rubbing of dry straw or the hum of bees among clover stalks. When she sat up they vanished, and the sounds became the distant din of homing traffic; but the moment she closed her eyes, her visitors again began to steal round her with that dry, mysterious hum.

She fell asleep presently, and woke with a start. There, in a glimmer of pale light, stood the little model, as in the fatal picture Bianca had painted of her. Her face was powder white, with shadows beneath the eyes. Breath seemed coming through her parted lips, just touched with colour. In her hat lay the tiny peacock's feather beside the two purplish-pink roses. A scent came from her, too—but faint, as ever was the scent of chicory flower. How long had she been standing there? Bianca started to her feet, and as she rose the vision vanished.

She went towards the spot. There was nothing in that corner but moonlight; the scent she had perceived was merely that of the trees drifting in.

But so vivid had that vision been that she stood at the window, panting for air, passing her hand again and again across her eyes.

Outside, over the dark gardens, the moon hung full and almost golden. Its honey-pale light filtered down on every little shape of tree, and leaf, and sleeping flower. That soft, vibrating radiance seemed to have woven all into one mysterious whole, stilling disharmony, so that each little separate shape had no meaning to itself.

Bianca looked long at the rain of moonlight falling on the earth's carpet, like a covering shower of blossom which bees have sucked and spilled. Then, below her, out through candescent space, she saw a shadow dart forth along the grass, and to her fright a voice rose, tremulous and clear, seeming to seek enfranchisement beyond the barrier of the dark trees: "My brain is clouded. Great Universe! I cannot write! I can no longer discover to my brothers that they are one. I am not worthy to stay here. Let me pass into You, and die!"

Bianca saw her father's fragile arms stretch out into the night through the sleeves of his white garment, as though expecting to be received at once into the Universal Brotherhood of the thin air.

There ensued a moment, when, by magic, every little dissonance in all the town seemed blended into a harmony of silence, as it might be the very death of self upon the earth.

Then, breaking that trance, Mr. Stone's voice rose again, trembling out into the night, as though blown through a reed.

"Brothers!" he said.

Behind the screen of lilac bushes at the gate Bianca saw the dark helmet of a policeman. He stood there staring steadily in the direction of that voice. Raising his lantern, he flashed it into every corner of the garden, searching for those who had been addressed. Satisfied, apparently, that no one was there, he moved it to right and left, lowered it to the level of his breast, and walked slowly on.

1907.

THE END

BOOK III

THE PATRICIAN

"ἦθου ἀνθρώπῳ δαίμων"

TO

GILBERT MURRAY

PART I

CHAPTER I

LIGHT, entering the vast room—a room so high that its carved ceiling refused itself to exact scrutiny—travelled, with the wistful, cold curiosity of the dawn, over a fantastic storehouse of time. Light, unaccompanied by the prejudice of human eyes, made strange revelation of incongruities, as though illuminating the dispassionate march of history.

For in this dining hall—one of the finest in England—the Carádoc family had for centuries assembled the trophies and records of their existence. Round about this dining hall they had built and pulled down and restored, until the rest of Monkland Court presented some aspect of homogeneity. Here alone they had left virgin the work of the old quasi-monastic builders, and within it unconsciously deposited their souls. For there were here, meeting the eyes of light, all those rather touching evidences of man's desire to persist for ever, those shells of his former bodies, the fetiches and queer proofs of his faiths, together with the remorseless demonstration of their treatment at the hands of Time.

The annalist might here have found all his needed confirmations; the analyst from this material formed the due equation of high birth; the philosopher traced the course of aristocracy, from its primeval rise in crude strength of subtlety, through centuries of power, to picturesque decadence, and the beginnings of its last stand. Even the artist might here, perchance, have seized on the dry ineffable pervading spirit, as one visiting an old cathedral seems to scent out the constriction of its heart.

From the legendary sword of that Welsh chieftain who by an act of high, rewarded treachery had passed into the favour of the conquering William, and received, with the widow of a Norman, many lands in Devenescire, to the Cup purchased for Geoffrey Carádoc, present Earl of Valleys, by subscription of his Devonshire tenants on the occasion of his marriage with the Lady Gertrude Semmering—no insignia were absent, save the family portraits in the gallery of Valleys House in London. There was even an ancient duplicate of that yellow tattered scroll royally reconfirming lands and title to John, the most distinguished of all the Carádocs, who had unfortunately neglected to be born in wedlock, by one of those humorous omissions to be found in the genealogies of most old families. Yes, it was there, almost cynically hung in a corner; for this incident, though no doubt a burning question in the fifteenth century, was now but staple for an ironical little tale, in view of the fact that descendants of John's " own " brother Edmund were undoubtedly to be found among the cottagers of a parish not far distant.

Light, glancing from the suits of armour to the tiger skins beneath them, brought from India but a year ago by Bertie Carádoc, the youngest son, seemed recording, how those, who had once been foremost by virtue of that simple law of Nature which crowns the adventuring and strong, now being almost washed aside out of the main stream of national life, were compelled to devise adventure, lest they should lose belief in their own strength.

The unsparing light of that first half-hour of summer morning recorded many other changes, wandering from austere tapestries to the velvety carpets, and dragging from the contrast sure proof of a common sense which denied to the present Earl and Countess the asceticisms of the past. And then it seemed to lose interest in this critical journey, as though longing to clothe all in witchery. For the sun had risen, and through the Eastern windows came pouring its level and mysterious joy. And with it, passing in at an open lattice, came a wild bee to settle among the flowers on the table athwart the Eastern end, used when there was only a small party in the house. The hours fled on silent, till the sun was high, and the first visitors came—three maids, rosy, not silent, bringing brushes. They passed, and were followed by two footmen—scouts of the breakfast brigade, who stood for a moment professionally doing nothing, then soberly commenced to set the table. Then came a little girl of six, to see if there were anything exciting—little Ann Shropton, child of Sir William Shropton by his marriage with Lady Agatha, eldest daughter of the house, the only one of the four young Carádocs as yet wedded. She came on tiptoe, thinking to surprise whatever was there. She had a broad little face, and wide frank hazel eyes over a little nose which came out straight and sudden. Encircled by a loose belt placed far below the waist of her holland frock, as if to symbolise freedom, she seemed to think everything in life good fun. And soon she found the exciting thing.

"Here's a bumble bee, William. Do you think I could tame it in my little glass box?"

"No, I don't, Miss Ann; and look out, you'll be stung!"

"It wouldn't sting *me.*"

"Why not?"

"Because it wouldn't."

"Of course—if you say so——"

"What time is the motor ordered?"

"Nine o'clock."

"I'm going with Grandpapa as far as the gate."

"Suppose he says you're not?"

"Well, then I shall go all the same."

"I see."

"I might go all the way with him to London! Is Auntie Babs going?"

"No, I don't think anybody is going with his lordship."

"I *would,* if she were. William!"

"Yes."

"Is Uncle Eustace sure to be elected?"

"Of course he is."

"Do you think he'll be a good Member of Parliament?"

"Lord Miltoun is very clever, Miss Ann."

"Is he?"

"Well, don't you think so?"

"Does Charles think so?"

"Ask him."

"William!"

"Yes."

"I don't like London. I like here, and I like Catton, and I like home pretty well, and I love Pendridny—and—I like Ravensham."

"His lordship is going to Ravensham to-day on his way up, I heard say."

"Oh! then he'll see great-granny. William——"

"Here's Miss Wallace."

From the doorway a lady with a broad pale patient face said:

"Come, Ann."

" All right! Hallo, Simmons! "

The entering butler replied:

" Hallo, Miss Ann! "

" I've got to go."

" I'm sure we're very sorry."

" Yes."

The door banged faintly, and in the great room rose the busy silence of those minutes which precede repasts. Suddenly the four men by the breakfast table stood back. Lord Valleys had come in.

He approached slowly, reading a blue paper, with his level grey eyes divided by a little uncharacteristic frown. He had a tanned yet ruddy, decisively shaped face, with crisp hair and moustache beginning to go iron-grey—the face of a man who knows his own mind and is contented with that knowledge. His figure too, well-braced and upright, with the back of the head carried like a soldier's, confirmed the impression, not so much of self-sufficiency, as of the sufficiency of his habits of life and thought. And there was apparent about all his movements that peculiar unconsciousness of his surroundings which comes to those who live a great deal in the public eye, have the material machinery of existence placed exactly to their hands, and never need to consider what others think of them. Taking his seat, and still perusing the paper, he at once began to eat what was put before him; then noticing that his eldest daughter had come in and was sitting down beside him, he said:

" Bore having to go up in such weather! "

" Is it a Cabinet meeting? "

" Yes. This confounded business of the balloons."

But the rather anxious dark eyes of Agatha's delicate narrow face were taking in the details of a tray for keeping dishes warm on a sideboard, and she was thinking: ' I believe that would be better than those I've got, after all. If William would only say whether he really likes these large trays better than single hot-water dishes! ' She contrived however to ask in her gentle voice—for all her words and movements were gentle, even a little timid, till anything appeared to threaten the welfare of her husband or children:

" Do you think this war scare good for Eustace's prospects, Father? "

But her father did not answer; he was greeting a new-

comer, a tall, fine-looking young man, with dark hair and a
fair moustache, between whom and himself there was no relationship, yet a certain negative resemblance. Claud Fresnay,
Viscount Harbinger, was indeed also a little of what is called
the "Norman" type—having a certain firm regularity of
feature, and a slight aquilinity of nose high up on the bridge
—but that which in the elder man seemed to indicate only
an unconscious acceptance of self as a standard, in the younger
man gave an impression at once more assertive and more
uneasy, as though he were a little afraid of not chaffing something all the time.

Behind him had come in a tall woman, of full figure and
fine presence, with hair still brown—Lady Valleys herself.
Though her eldest son was thirty, she was, herself, still little
more than fifty. From her voice, manner, and whole personality, one might suspect that she had been an acknowledged
beauty; but there was now more than a suspicion of maturity
about her almost jovial face, with its full grey-blue eyes, and
coarsened complexion. Good comrade, and essentially "woman
of the world," was written on every line of her, and in every
tone of her voice. She was indeed a figure suggestive of open
air and generous living, endowed with abundant energy, and
not devoid of humour. It was she who answered Agatha's
remark.

"Of course, my dear, the very best thing possible."

Lord Harbinger chimed in:

"By the way, Brabrook's going to speak on it. Did you
ever hear him, Lady Agatha? 'Mr. Speaker, Sir, I rise—
and with me rises the democratic principle——' "

But Agatha only smiled, for she was thinking:

'If I let Ann go as far as the gate, she'll only make it a
stepping-stone to something else to-morrow.' Taking no interest
in public affairs, her inherited craving for command had resorted for expression to a meticulous ordering of household
matters. It was indeed a cult with her, a passion—as though
she felt herself a sort of figurehead to national domesticity;
the leader of a patriotic movement.

Lord Valleys, having finished what seemed necessary, arose.

"Any message to your mother, Gertrude?"

"No, I wrote last night."

"Tell Miltoun to keep an eye on that Mr. Courtier. I heard
him speak one day—he's rather good."

Lady Valleys, who had not yet sat down, accompanied her husband to the door.

"By the way, I've told Mother about this woman, Geoff."

"Was it necessary?"

"Well, I think so; I'm uneasy—after all, Mother has some influence with Miltoun."

Lord Valleys shrugged his shoulders, and slightly squeezing his wife's arm, went out.

Though himself vaguely uneasy on that very subject, he was a man who did not go to meet disturbance. He had the nerves which seem to be no nerves at all—especially found in those of his class who have much to do with horses. He temperamentally regarded the evil of the day as quite sufficient to it. Moreover, his eldest son was a riddle that he had long given up, so far as women were concerned.

Emerging into the outer hall, he lingered a moment, remembering that he had not seen his younger and favourite daughter.

"Lady Barbara down yet?" Hearing that she was not, he slipped into the motor coat held for him by Simmons, and stepped out under the white portico, decorated by the Carádoc hawks in stone.

The voice of little Ann reached him, clear and high above the smoother whirring of the car.

"Come on, Grandpapa!"

Lord Valleys grimaced beneath his crisp moustache—the word grandpapa always fell queerly on the ears of one who was but fifty-six, and by no means felt it—and jerking his gloved hand towards Ann, he said:

"Send down to the lodge gate for *this*."

The voice of little Ann answered loudly:

"No; I'm coming back by myself."

The car starting, drowned discussion.

Lord Valleys, motoring, somewhat pathetically illustrated the invasion of institutions by their destroyer, Science. A supporter of the turf, and not long since Master of Foxhounds, most of whose soul (outside politics) was in horses, he had been, as it were, compelled by common sense, not only to tolerate, but to take up and even press forward the cause of their supplanters. His instinct of self-preservation was secretly at work, hurrying him to his own destruction; forcing him to persuade himself that science and her successive victories over brute nature could be wooed into the service of a prestige which rested on a crystallised and stationary base. All this keeping pace with the times, this immersion in the results of modern discoveries, this speeding-up of existence so that it was all surface and little root—the increasing volatility, cosmopolitanism, and even commercialism of his life, on which he rather prided himself as a man of the world—was, with a secrecy too deep for his perception, cutting at the aloofness logically demanded of one in his position. Stubborn, and not spiritually subtle, though by no means dull in practical matters, he was resolutely letting the waters bear him on, holding the tiller firmly, without perceiving that he was in the vortex of a whirlpool. Indeed, his common sense continually impelled him, against the sort of reactionaryism of which his son Miltoun had so much, to that easier reactionaryism, which, living on its spiritual capital, makes what material capital it can out of its enemy, Progress.

He drove the car himself, shrewd and self-contained, sitting easily, with his cap well drawn over those steady eyes; and though this unexpected meeting of the Cabinet in the Whitsuntide recess was not only a nuisance, but gave food for anxiety, he was fully able to enjoy the swift smooth movement through the summer air, which met him with such friendly sweetness under the great trees of the long avenue. Beside him, little Ann was silent, with her legs stuck out rather wide apart. Motoring was a new excitement, for at home it was forbidden; and a meditative rapture shone in her wide eyes above her sudden little nose. Only once she spoke, when close to the lodge the car slowed down, and they passed the lodge-keeper's little daughter.

"Hallo, Susie!"

There was no answer, but the look on Susie's small pale face was so humble and adoring that Lord Valleys, not a very observant man, noticed it with a sort of satisfaction. 'Yes,' he thought, somewhat irrelevantly, 'the country is sound at heart!'

CHAPTER II

At Ravensham House on the borders of Richmond Park, suburban seat of the Casterley family, ever since it became usual to have a residence within easy driving distance of Westminster—in a large conservatory adjoining the hall, Lady Casterley stood in front of some Japanese lilies. She was a slender, short old woman, with an ivory-coloured face, a thin nose, and keen eyes half-veiled by delicate wrinkled lids. Very still, in her grey dress, and with grey hair, she gave the impression of a little figure carved out of fine, worn steel. Her firm, spidery hand held a letter written in free somewhat sprawling style:

"Monkland Court,"
"Devon.

"My dear Mother,

"Geoffrey is motoring up to-morrow. He'll look in on you on the way if he can. This new war scare has taken him up. I shan't be in Town myself till Miltoun's election is over. The fact is, I daren't leave him down here alone. He sees his 'Anonyma' every day. That Mr. Courtier, who wrote the book against War—rather cool for a man who's been a soldier of fortune, don't you think?—is staying at the inn, working for the Radical. He knows her, too—and, one can only hope, for Miltoun's sake, too well—an attractive person, with red moustaches, rather nice and mad. Bertie has just come down; I must get him to have a talk with Miltoun, and see if he can find out how the land lies. One can trust Bertie—he's really very astute. I must say, that she's quite a sweet-looking woman; but absolutely nothing's known of her here except that she divorced her husband. How does one find out about people? Miltoun's being so extraordinarily straight-laced makes it all the more awkward. The earnestness of this rising generation is most remarkable. I don't remember taking such a serious view of life in my youth."

Lady Casterley lowered the coronetted sheet of paper. The ghost of a grimace haunted her face—she had not forgotten her daughter's youth. Raising the letter again, she read on:

498

"I'm sure Geoffrey and I feel years younger than either Miltoun or Agatha, though we did produce them. One doesn't feel it with Bertie or Babs, luckily. The war scare is having an excellent effect on Miltoun's candidature. Claud Harbinger is with us, too, working for Miltoun; but, as a matter of fact, I think he's after Babs. It's rather melancholy, when you think that Babs isn't quite twenty—still, one can't expect anything else, I suppose, with her looks; and Claud *is* rather a fine specimen. They talk of him a lot now; he's quite coming to the fore among the young Tories."

Lady Casterley again lowered the letter, and stood listening. A prolonged, muffled sound as of distant cheering and groans had penetrated the great conservatory, vibrating among the pale petals of the lilies and setting free their scent in short waves of perfume. She passed into the hall; where stood an old man with sallow face and long white whiskers.

"What was that noise, Clifton?"

"A posse of Socialists, my lady, on their way to Putney to hold a demonstration; the people are hooting them. They've got blocked just outside the gates."

"Are they making speeches?"

"They *are* talking some kind of rant, my lady."

"I'll go and hear them. Give me my black stick."

Above the velvet-dark, flat-boughed cedar trees, which rose like pagodas of ebony on either side of the drive, the sky hung lowering in one great purple cloud, endowed with sinister life by a single white beam striking up into it from the horizon. Beneath this canopy of cloud a small phalanx of dusty, dishevelled-looking men and women were drawn up in the road, guarding, and encouraging with cheers, a tall black-coated orator. Before and behind this phalanx, a little mob of men and boys kept up an accompaniment of groans and jeering.

Lady Casterley and her "major-domo" stood six paces inside the scrolled iron gates, and watched. The slight, steel-coloured figure with steel-coloured hair, was more arresting in its immobility than all the vociferations and gestures of the mob. Her eyes alone moved under their half-drooped lids; her right hand clutched tightly the handle of her stick. The speaker's voice rose in shrill protest against the exploitation of "the people"; it sank in ironical comment on Christianity; it demanded passionately to be free from the continuous burden of " this insensate militarist taxation " ; it threatened that the people would take things into their own hands.

Lady Casterley turned her head:

" He is talking nonsense, Clifton. It is going to rain. I shall go in."

Under the stone porch she paused. The purple cloud had broken; a blind fury of rain was deluging the fast-scattering crowd. A faint smile came on Lady Casterley's lips.

" It will do them good to have their ardour damped a little. You will get wet, Clifton—hurry! I expect Lord Valleys to dinner. Have a room got ready for him to dress. He's motoring from Monkland."

CHAPTER III

In a very high, white-panelled room, with but little furniture, Lord Valleys greeted his mother-in-law respectfully.

"Motored up in nine hours, Ma'am—not bad going."

"I am glad you came. When is Miltoun's election?"

"On the twenty-ninth."

"Pity! He should be away from Monkland, with that—anonymous woman living there."

"Ah! you've heard of her!"

Lady Casterley replied sharply:

"You're too easy-going, Geoffrey."

Lord Valleys smiled.

"These war scares," he said, "are getting a bore. Can't quite make out what the feeling of the country is about them."

Lady Casterley rose:

"It has none. When war comes, the feeling will be all right. It always is. Give me your arm. Are you hungry?" . . .

When Lord Valleys spoke of war, he spoke as one who, since he arrived at years of discretion, had lived within the circle of those who direct the destinies of States. It was for him —as for the lilies in the great glass house—impossible to see with the eyes, or feel with the feelings of a flower of the garden outside. Soaked in the best prejudices and manners of his class, he lived a life no more shut off from the general than was to be expected. Indeed, in some sort, as a man of facts and common sense, he was fairly in touch with the opinion of the average citizen. He was quite genuine when he said that he believed he knew what the people wanted better than those who prated on the subject; and no doubt he was right, for temperamentally he was nearer to them than their own leaders, though he would not perhaps have liked to be told so. His man-of-the-world, political shrewdness had been superimposed by life on a nature whose prime strength was its practicality and lack of imagination. It was his business to be efficient, but not strenuous, or desirous of pushing ideas to their logical conclusions; to be neither narrow nor puritanical, so long as the shell of "good form" was preserved intact; to be a liberal landlord up to the point of not seriously damaging his interests; to be will-disposed towards the arts until those arts revealed that which he had not before perceived; it was his business to have light hands, steady eyes, iron nerves, and those excellent manners that have no mannerisms. It was his nature to be easy-going as a husband; indulgent as a father; careful and straightforward as a politician; and as a man, addicted to pleasure, to work, and to fresh air. He admired, and was fond of his wife, and had never regretted his marriage. He had never perhaps regretted anything, unless it were that he had not yet won the Derby, or quite succeeded in getting his special strain of blue-ticked pointers to breed absolutely true to type. His mother-in-law he respected, as one might respect a principle.

There was indeed in the personality of that little old lady the tremendous force of accumulated decision—the inherited assurance of one whose prestige had never been questioned; who, from long immunity, and a certain clear-cut matter-of-factness, bred by the habit of command, had indeed lost the power of perceiving that her prestige ever could be questioned. Her knowledge of her own mind was no ordinary piece of learning, had not, in fact, been learned at all, but sprang full-fledged from an active dominating temperament. Fortified by the necessity, common to her class, of knowing thoroughly the more patent side of public affairs; armoured by the tradition of a culture demanded by leadership; inspired by ideas, but always the same ideas; owning no master, but in servitude to her own custom of leading, she had a mind, formidable as the two-edged swords wielded by her ancestors the Fitz-Harolds, at Agincourt or Poitiers—a mind which had ever instinctively rejected that inner knowledge of herself or of the selves of others, produced by those foolish practices of introspection, contemplation, and understanding, so deleterious to authority. If Lord Valleys was the body of the aristocratic machine, Lady Casterley was the steel spring inside it. All her life studiously unaffected and simple in attire; of plain and frugal habit; an early riser; working at something or other from morning till night, and as little worn-out at seventy-eight as most women of fifty, she had only one weak spot—and that was her strength —blindness as to the nature and size of her place in the scheme of things. She was a type, a force.

Wonderfully well she went with the room in which they

were dining, whose grey walls, surmounted by a deep frieze painted somewhat in the style of Fragonard, contained many nymphs and roses now rather dim; with the furniture, too, which had a look of having survived into times not its own. On the tables were no flowers, save five lilies in an old silver chalice; and on the wall over the great sideboard a portrait of the late Lord Casterley.

She spoke:

"I hope Miltoun is taking his own line?"

"That's the trouble. He suffers from swollen principles— only wish he could keep them out of his speeches."

"Let him be; and get him away from that woman as soon as his election's over. What is her real name?"

"Mrs. something Lees Noel."

"How long has she been there?"

"About a year, I think."

"And you don't know anything about her?"

Lord Valleys raised his shoulders.

"Ah!" said Lady Casterley; "exactly! You're letting the thing drift. I shall go down myself. I suppose Gertrude can have me? What has that Mr. Courtier to do with this good lady?"

Lord Valleys smiled. In this smile was the whole of his polite and easy-going philosophy. 'I am no meddler,' it seemed to say; and at sight of that smile Lady Casterley tightened her lips.

"He is a firebrand," she said. "I read that book of his against War—most inflammatory. Aimed at Grant—and Rosenstern, chiefly. I've just seen one of the results, outside my own gates. A mob of anti-War agitators."

Lord Valleys controlled a yawn.

"Really? I'd no idea Courtier had any influence."

"He is dangerous. Most idealists are negligible—his book was clever."

"I wish to goodness we could see the last of these scares, they only make both countries look foolish," muttered Lord Valleys.

Lady Casterley raised her glass, full of a blood-red wine. "The war would save us," she said.

"War is no joke."

"It would be the beginning of a better state of things."

"You think so?"

"We should get the lead again as a nation, and Democracy would be put back fifty years."

Lord Valleys made three little heaps of salt, and paused to count them; then, with a slight uplifting of his eyebrows, which seemed to doubt what he was going to say, he murmured: "I should have said that we were all democrats nowadays. . . . What is it, Clifton?"

"Your chauffeur would like to know, what time you will have the car?"

"Directly after dinner."

Twenty minutes later, he was turning through the scrolled iron gates into the road for London. It was falling dark; and in the tremulous sky clouds drifted here and there with a sort of endless lack of purpose. No direction seemed to have been decreed unto their wings. They had met together in the firmament like a flock of giant magpies crossing and re-crossing each other's flight. The smell of rain was in the air. The car raised no dust, but bored swiftly on, searching out the road with its lamps. On Putney Bridge its march was stayed by a string of waggons. Lord Valleys looked to right and left. The river reflected the thousand lights of buildings piled along her sides, lamps of the embankments, lanterns of moored barges. The sinuous pallid body of this great Creature, forever gliding down to the sea, roused in his mind no symbolic image. He had had to do with her, years back, at the Board of Trade, and knew her for what she was, extremely dirty, and getting abominably thin just where he would have liked her plump. Yet, as he lighted a cigar, there came to him a queer feeling —as if he were in the presence of a woman he was fond of.

'I hope to God,' he thought, 'nothing'll come of these scares!' The car glided on into the long road, swarming with traffic, towards the fashionable heart of London. Outside stationers' shops, however, the posters of evening papers were of no reassuring order.

"THE PLOT THICKENS."
"MORE REVELATIONS."
"GRAVE SITUATION THREATENED."

And before each poster could be seen a little eddy in the stream of the passers-by—formed by persons glancing at the news, and disengaging themselves, to press on again. The Earl

of Valleys caught himself wondering what they thought of it!
What was passing behind those pale rounds of flesh turned
towards the posters?

Did they think at all, these men and women in the street?
What was their attitude towards this vaguely threatened cata-
clysm? Face after face, stolid and apathetic, expressed nothing, no active desire, certainly no enthusiasm, hardly any dread.
Poor devils! The thing, after all, was no more within their
control than it was within the power of ants to stop the ruination of their ant-heap by some passing boy! It was no doubt
quite true, that the people had never had much voice in the
making of war. And the words of a Radical weekly, which
as an impartial man he always forced himself to read, recurred
to him. "Ignorant of the facts, hypnotised by the words
'Country' and 'Patriotism'; in the grip of mob-instinct and
inborn prejudice against the foreigner; helpless by reason of
his patience, stoicism, good faith, and confidence in those above
him; helpless by reason of his snobbery, mutual distrust, care-
lessness for the morrow, and lack of public spirit—in the face
of War how impotent and to be pitied is the man in the street!"
That paper, though clever, always seemed to him intolerably
hi-falutin'!

It was doubtful whether he would get to Ascot this year.
And his mind flew for a moment to his promising two-year-old
Casetta; then dashed almost violently, as though in shame,
to the Admiralty and the doubt whether they were fully alive
to possibilities. He himself occupied a softer spot of Government, one of those almost nominal offices necessary to qualify
into the Cabinet certain tried minds, for whom no more strenuous post can for the moment be found. From the Admiralty
again his thoughts leaped to his mother-in-law. Wonderful
old woman! What a statesman she would have made! Too
reactionary! Deuce of a straight line she had taken about
Mrs. Lees Noel! And with a connoisseur's twinge of pleasure
he recollected that lady's face and figure seen this morning as
he passed her cottage. Mysterious or not, the woman was
certainly attractive! Very graceful head with its dark hair
waved back from the middle over either temple—very charming
figure, no lumber of any sort! Bouquet about her! Some
story or other, no doubt, no affair of his! Always sorry for
that sort of woman!

A regiment of Territorials returning from a march stayed

the progress of his car. He leaned forward watching them with much the same contained, shrewd, critical look he would have bent on a pack of hounds. All the mistiness and speculation in his mind was gone now. Good stamp of man, would give a capital account of themselves! Their faces, flushed by a day in the open, were masked with passivity, or with a half-aggressive, half-jocular self-consciousness; *they* were clearly not troubled by abstract doubts, or any visions of the horrors of war.

Someone raised a cheer " for the Terriers! " Lord Valleys saw round him a little sea of hats, rising and falling, and heard a sound, rather shrill and tentative, swell into hoarse, high clamour, and suddenly die out. ' Seem keen enough! ' he thought. ' Very little does it! Plenty of fighting spirit in the country.' And again a thrill of pleasure shot through him.

Then, as the last soldier passed, his car slowly forged its way through the straggling crowd, pressing on behind the regiment— men of all ages, youths, a few women, young girls, who turned their eyes on him with a negligent stare as if their lives were too remote to permit them to take interest in this passing man at ease.

CHAPTER IV

At Monkland, that same hour, in the little white-washed "with-drawing-room" of a thatched, white-washed cottage, two men sat talking, one on either side of the hearth; and in a low chair between them a dark-eyed woman leaned back, watching, the tips of her delicate thin fingers pressed together, or held out transparent towards the fire. A log, dropping now and then, turned up its glowing underside; and the firelight and the lamplight seemed so to have soaked into the white walls that a wan warmth exuded. Silvery dun moths, fluttering in from the dark garden, kept vibrating like spun shillings, over a jade-green bowl of crimson roses; and there was a scent, as ever in that old thatched cottage, of wood-smoke, flowers, and sweetbriar.

The man on the left was perhaps forty, rather above middle height, vigorous, active, straight, with blue eyes and a sanguine face which glowed on small provocation. His hair was very bright, almost red, and his fiery moustaches descending to the level of his chin, like Don Quixote's, seemed bristling and charging.

The man on the right was nearer thirty, evidently tall, wiry, and very thin. He sat rather crumpled, in his low armchair, with hands clasped round a knee; and a little crucified smile haunted the lips of his lean face, which, in its parchmenty, tanned, shaven cheeks, and deep-set, very living eyes, had a certain beauty.

These two men, so extravagantly unlike, looked at each other like neighbouring dogs, who, having long decided that they are better apart, suddenly find that they have met at some spot where they cannot possibly have a fight. And the woman watched; the owner, as it were, of one, but who, from sheer love of dogs, had always stroked and patted the other.

"So, Mr. Courtier," said the younger man, whose dry, ironic voice, like his smile, seemed defending the fervid spirit in his eyes; "all you say only amounts, you see, to a defence of the so-called Liberal spirit; and, forgive my candour, that spirit, being an importation from the realms of philosophy and art, withers the moment it touches practical affairs."

The man with the red moustaches laughed; the sound was queer—at once so genial and so sardonic.

"Well put!" he said: "And far be it from me to gainsay. But since compromise is the very essence of politics, high-priests of caste and authority, like you, Lord Miltoun, are every bit as much out of it as any Liberal professor."

"I don't agree!"

"Agree or not, your position towards public affairs is very like the Church's attitude towards marriage and divorce; as remote from the realities of life as the attitude of the believer in Free Love, and not more likely to catch on. The death of your point of view lies in itself—it's too dried-up and far from things ever to understand them. If you don't understand you can never rule. You might just as well keep your hands in your pockets, as go into politics with your notions!"

"I fear we must continue to agree to differ."

"Well, perhaps I do pay you too high a compliment. After all, you *are* a patrician."

"You speak in riddles, Mr. Courtier."

The dark-eyed woman stirred; her hands gave a sort of flutter, as though in deprecation of acerbity.

Rising at once, and speaking in a deferential voice, the elder man said:

"We're tiring Mrs. Noel. Good-night, Audrey. It's high time I was off." Against the darkness of the open French window, he turned round to fire a parting shot.

"What I meant, Lord Miltoun, was that your class is the driest and most practical in the State—it's odd if it doesn't save you from a poet's dreams. Good-night!" He passed out on to the lawn, and vanished.

The young man sat unmoving; the glow of the fire had caught his face, so that a spirit seemed clinging round his lips, gleaming out of his eyes. Suddenly he said:

"Do you believe that, Mrs. Noel?"

For answer Audrey Noel smiled, then rose and went over to the window.

"Look at my dear toad! It comes here every evening!"

On a flagstone of the verandah, in the centre of the stream of lamplight, sat a little golden toad. As Miltoun came to look, it waddled to one side, and vanished.

"How peaceful your garden is!" he said; then taking her

hand, he very gently raised it to his lips, and followed his opponent out into the darkness.

Truly peace brooded over that garden. The Night seemed listening—all lights out, all hearts at rest. It watched, with a little white star for every tree, and roof, and slumbering tired flower, as a mother watches her sleeping child, leaning above him and counting with her love every hair of his head, and all his tiny tremors.

Argument seemed child's babble indeed under the smile of Night. And the face of the woman, left alone at her window, was a little like the face of this warm, sweet night. It was sensitive, harmonious; and its harmony was not, as in some faces, cold—but seemed to tremble and glow and flutter, as though it were a spirit which had found its place of resting.

In her garden, all velvety grey, with black shadows beneath the yew-trees, the white flowers alone seemed to be awake, and to look at her wistfully. The trees stood dark and still. Not even the night birds stirred. Alone, the little stream down in the bottom raised its voice, privileged when day voices were hushed.

It was not in Audrey Noel to deny herself to any spirit that was abroad; to repel was an art she did not practise. But this night she did not seem to know that the Spirit of Peace hovered so near. Her hands trembled, her cheeks were burning; her breast heaved, and sighs fluttered from her lips, just parted.

CHAPTER V

EUSTACE CARÁDOC, Viscount Miltoun, had lived a very lonely life, since he first began to understand the peculiarities of existence. With the exception of Clifton, his grandmother's "majordomo," he made, as a small child, no intimate friend. His nurses, governesses, tutors, by their own confession did not understand him, finding that he took himself with unnecessary seriousness; a little afraid, too, of one whom they discovered to be capable of pushing things to the point of enduring pain in silence. Much of that early time was passed at Ravensham, for he had always been Lady Casterley's favourite grandchild. She recognised in him the purposeful austerity which had somehow been omitted from the composition of her daughter. But only to Clifton, then a man of fifty with a great gravity and long black whiskers, did Eustace relieve his soul. "I tell you this, Clifton," he would say, sitting on the sideboard, or the arm of the big chair in Clifton's room, or wandering amongst the raspberries, "because you are my friend."

And Clifton, with his head a little on one side, and a sort of wise concern at his "friend's" confidences, whch were sometimes of an embarrassing description, would answer now and then: "Of course, my lord," but more often: "Of course, my dear."

There was in this friendship something fine and suitable, neither of these "friends" taking or suffering liberties, and both being interested in pigeons, which they would stand watching with a remarkable attention.

In course of time, following the tradition of his family, Eustace went to Harrow. He was there five years—always one of those boys a little out at wrists and ankles, who may be seen slouching, solitary, along the pavement to their own haunts, rather dusty, and with one shoulder slightly raised above the other, from the habit of carrying something beneath one arm. Saved from being thought a "smug," by his title, his lack of any conspicuous scholastic ability, his obvious independence of what was thought of him, and a sarcastic tongue, which no one was eager to encounter, he remained the ugly duckling who refused to paddle properly in the green ponds of Public School tradition.

He played games so badly that in sheer self-defence his fellows permitted him to play without them. Of " fives " they made an exception, for in this he attained much proficiency, owing to a certain windmill-like quality of limb. He was noted too for daring chemical experiments, of which he usually had one or two brewing, surreptitiously at first, and afterwards by special permission of his housemaster, on the principle that if a room must smell, it had better smell openly. He made few friendships, but these were lasting. His Latin verse was so poor, and his Greek verse so vile, that all had been surprised when towards the finish of his career he showed a very considerable power of writing and speaking his own language. He left school without a pang. But when in the train he saw the old Hill and the old spire on the top of it fading away from him, a lump rose in his throat, he swallowed violently two or three times, and, thrusting himself far back into the carriage corner, appeared to sleep.

At Oxford, he was happier, but still comparatively lonely; remaining, so long as custom permitted, in lodgings outside his College, and clinging thereafter to remote, panelled rooms high up, overlooking the gardens and a portion of the city wall. It was at Oxford that he first developed that passion for self-discipline which afterwards distinguished him. He took up rowing; and, though thoroughly unsuited by nature to this pastime, secured himself a place in his College " torpid." At the end of a race he was usually supported from his stretcher in a state of extreme extenuation, due to having pulled the last quarter of the course entirely with his spirit. The same craving for self-discipline guided him in the choice of Schools; he went out in " Greats," for which, owing to his indifferent mastery of Greek and Latin, he was the least fitted. With enormous labour he took a very fair degree. He carried off besides, the highest distinctions of the University for English Essays. The ordinary circles of College life knew nothing of him. Not once in the whole course of his University career, was he the better for wine. He did not hunt; he never talked of women, and none talked of women in his presence. But now and then he was visited by those gusts which come to the ascetic, when all life seemed suddenly caught up and devoured by a flame burning night and day, and going out mercifully, he knew not why, like a blown candle. However unsocial in the proper sense of the word, he by no means lacked company in these Oxford days. He knew many, both dons and undergraduates. His long stride, and determined absence of direction, had severely tried all those who could stomach so slow a pastime as walking for the sake of talking. The country knew him—though he never knew the country—from Abingdon to Bablock Hythe. His name stood high, too, at the Union, where he made his mark during his first term in a debate on a " Censorship of Literature," which he advocated with gloom, pertinacity, and a certain youthful brilliance which might well have carried the day, had not an Irishman got up and pointed out the danger hanging over the Old Testament. To that he had retorted: " Better, sir, it should run a risk than have no risk to run." From which moment he was notable.

He stayed up four years, and went down with a sense of bewilderment and loss. The matured verdict of Oxford on this child of hers, was " Eustace Miltoun! Ah! Queer bird! Will make his mark! "

He had about this time an interview with his father which confirmed the impression each had formed of the other. It took place in the library at Monkland Court, on a late November afternoon.

The light of eight candles in thin silver candlesticks, four on either side of the carved stone hearth, illumined that room. Their gentle radiance penetrated but a little way into the great dark space lined with books, panelled and floored with black oak, where the acrid fragrance of leather and dried rose-leaves seemed to drench the very soul with the aroma of the past. Above the huge fireplace, with light falling on one side of his shaven face, hung a portrait—painter unknown—of that Cardinal Carádoc who suffered for his faith in the sixteenth century. Ascetic, crucified, with a little smile clinging to the lips and deep-set eyes, he presided, above the blueish flames of a log fire.

Father and son found some difficulty in beginning.

Each of those two felt as though he were in the presence of someone else's very near relation. They had, in fact, seen extremely little of each other, and not seen that little long.

Lord Valleys uttered the first remark:

" Well, my dear fellow, what are you going to do now? I think we can make certain of this seat down here, if you like to stand."

Miltoun had answered: " Thanks very much; I don't think so at present."

Through the thin fume of his cigar Lord Valleys watched that long figure sunk deep in the chair opposite.

" Why not? " he said. " You can't begin too soon; unless you think you ought to go round the world."

" Before I can become a man of it? "

Lord Valleys gave a rather disconcerted laugh.

" There's nothing in politics you can't pick up as you go along," he said. " How old are you? "

" Twenty-four."

" You look older." A faint line, as of contemplation, rose between his eyes. Was it fancy that a little smile was hovering about Miltoun's lips?

" I've got a foolish theory," came from those lips, " that one must know the conditions first. I want to give at least five years to that."

Lord Valleys raised his eyebrows. " Waste of time," he said. " You'd know more at the end of it, if you went into the House at once. You take the matter too seriously."

" No doubt."

For fully a minute Lord Valleys made no answer; he felt almost ruffled. Waiting till the sensation had passed, he said: " Well, my dear fellow, as you please."

Miltoun's apprenticeship to the profession of politics was served in a slum settlement; on his father's estates; in Chambers at the Temple; in expeditions to Germany, America, and the British Colonies; in work at elections; and in two forlorn hopes to capture a constituency which could be trusted not to change its principles. He read much, slowly, but with conscientious tenacity, poetry, history, and works on philosophy, religion, and social matters. Fiction, and especially foreign fiction, he did not care for. With the utmost desire to be wide and impartial, he sucked in what ministered to the wants of his nature, rejecting unconsciously all that by its unsuitability endangered the flame of his private spirit. What he read, in fact, served only to strengthen those profounder convictions which arose from his temperament. With a contempt of the vulgar gewgaws of wealth and rank he combined a humble but intense and growing conviction of his capacity for leadership, of a spiritual superiority to those whom he desired to benefit. There was no trace, indeed, of the common Pharisee in Miltoun, he was simple and direct; but his eyes, his gestures, the whole man, proclaimed the presence of some secret spring of certainty, some fundamental well into which no disturbing glimmers penetrated. He was not devoid of wit, but he was devoid of that kind of wit which turns its eyes inward, and sees something of the fun that lies in being what you are. Miltoun saw the world and all the things thereof shaped like spires—even when they were circles. He seemed to have no sense that the Universe was equally compounded of those two symbols, whose point of reconciliation had not yet been discovered.

Such was he, then, when the Member for his native division was made a peer.

He had reached the age of thirty without ever having been in love, leading a life of almost savage purity, with one solitary breakdown. Women were afraid of him. And he was perhaps a little afraid of woman. She was in theory too lovely and desirable—the half-moon in a summer sky; in practice too cloying, or too harsh. He had an affection for Barbara, his younger sister; but to his mother, his grandmother, or his eldest sister Agatha, he had never felt close. It was indeed amusing to see Lady Valleys with her first-born. Her fine figure, the blown roses of her face, her grey-blue eyes which had a slight tendency to roll, as though amusement just touched with naughtiness bubbled behind them, were reduced to a queer, satirical decorum in Miltoun's presence. Thoughts and sayings verging on the risky were characteristic of her robust physique, of her soul which could afford to express almost all that occurred to it. Miltoun had never, not even as a child, given her his confidence. She bore him no resentment, being of that large, generous build in body and mind, rarely—never in her class—associated with the capacity for feeling aggrieved or lowered in any estimation, even its own. He was, and always had been, an odd boy, and there was an end of it! Nothing had perhaps so disconcerted Lady Valleys as his want of behaviour in regard to women. She felt it abnormal, just as she recognised the essential if duly veiled normality of her husband and younger son. It was this feeling which made her realise almost more vividly than she had time for, in the whirl of politics and fashion, the danger of his friendship with this lady to whom she alluded so discreetly as " Anonyma."

Pure chance had been responsible for the inception of that friendship. Going one December afternoon to the farmhouse of a tenant, just killed by a fall from his horse, Miltoun had found the widow in a state of bewildered grief, thinly cloaked in the manner of one who had almost lost the power to express her feelings, and had quite lost it in the presence of "the gentry." Having assured the poor soul that she need have no fear about her tenancy, he was just leaving, when he met, in the stone-flagged entrance, a lady in a fur cap and jacket, carrying in her arms a little crying boy, bleeding from a cut on the forehead. Taking him from her and placing him on a table in the parlour, Miltoun looked at this lady, and saw that she was extremely grave, and soft, and charming. He inquired of her whether the mother should be told.

She shook her head.

"Poor thing, not just now: let's wash it, and bind it up first."

Together therefore they washed and bound up the cut. Having finished, she looked at Miltoun, and seemed to say: 'You would do the telling so much better than I.'

He, therefore, told the mother and was rewarded by a little smile from the grave lady.

From that meeting he took away the knowledge of her name, Audrey Lees Noel, and the remembrance of a face, whose beauty, under a cap of squirrel's fur, pursued him. Some days later passing by the village green, he saw her entering a garden gate. On this occasion he had asked her whether she would like her cottage re-thatched; an inspection of the roof had followed; he had stayed talking a long time. Accustomed to women—over the best of whom, for all their grace and lack of affectation, high-caste life had wrapped the manner which seems to take all things for granted—there was a peculiar charm for Miltoun in this soft, dark-eyed lady who evidently lived quite out of the world, and had so poignant, and shy, a flavour. Thus from a chance seed had blossomed swiftly one of those rare friendships between lonely people, which can in short time fill great spaces of two lives.

One day she asked him: "You know about me, I suppose?" Miltoun made a motion of his head, signifying that he did. His informant had been the vicar.

"Yes, I am told, her story is a sad one—a divorce."

"Do you mean that she has been divorced, or——"

For the fraction of a second the vicar perhaps had hesitated.

"Oh! no—no. Sinned against, I am sure. A nice woman, so far as I have seen; though I'm afraid not one of my congregation."

With this, Miltoun, in whom chivalry had already been awakened, was content. When she asked if he knew her story, he would not for the world have had her rake up what was painful. Whatever that story, she could not have been to blame. She had begun already to be shaped by his own spirit; had become not a human being, as it was, but an expression of his aspiration. . . .

On the third evening after his passage of arms with Courtier, he was again at her little white cottage sheltering within its high garden walls. Smothered in roses, and with a black-brown thatch overhanging the old-fashioned leaded panes of the upper windows, it had an air of hiding from the world. Behind, as though on guard, two pine trees spread their dark boughs over the outhouses, and in any south-west wind could be heard speaking gravely about the weather. Tall lilac bushes flanked the garden, and a large lime-tree in the adjoining field sighed and rustled, or on still days let forth the drowsy hum of countless small dusky bees who frequented that green hostelry.

He found her altering a dress, sitting over it in her specially delicate fashion—as if all objects whatsoever, dresses, flowers, books, music, required from her the same sympathy.

He had come from a long day's electioneering, had been heckled at two meetings, and was still sore from the experience. To watch her, to be soothed, and ministered to by her had never been so restful; and stretched out in a long chair he listened to her playing.

Over the hill a Pierrot moon was slowly moving up in a sky the colour of grey irises. And in a sort of trance Miltoun stared at the burnt-out star, travelling in bright pallor.

Across the moor a sea of shallow mist was rolling; and the trees in the valley, like browsing cattle, stood knee-deep in whiteness, with all the air above them wan from an innumerable rain as of moon-dust, falling into that white sea. Then the moon passed behind the lime-tree, so that a great lighted Chinese lantern seemed to hang blue-black from the sky.

Suddenly, jarring and shivering the music, came a sound of hooting. It swelled, died away, and swelled again.

Miltoun rose.

"That has spoiled my vision," he said. "Mrs. Noel, I have something I want to say." But looking down at her, sitting so still, with her hands resting on the keys, he was silent in sheer adoration.

A voice from the door ejaculated:

"Oh! ma'am—oh! my lord! They're devilling a gentleman on the green!"

CHAPTER VI

WHEN the immortal Don set out to ring all the bells of merriment, he was followed by one clown. Charles Courtier on the other hand had always been accompanied by thousands, who really could not understand the conduct of this man with no commercial sense. But though he puzzled his contemporaries, they did not exactly laugh at him, because it was reported that he had really killed some men, and loved some women. They found such a combination irresistible, when coupled with an appearance both vigorous and gallant. The son of an Oxfordshire clergyman, and mounted on a lost cause, he had been riding through the world ever since he was eighteen, without once getting out of the saddle. The secret of this endurance lay perhaps in his unconsciousness that he was in the saddle at all. It was as much his natural seat as office stools to other mortals. He made no capital out of errantry, his temperament being far too like his red-gold hair, which people compared to flames, consuming all before them. His vices were patent; too incurable an optimism; an admiration for beauty such as must sometimes have caused him to forget which woman he was most in love with; too thin a skin; too hot a heart; hatred of humbug, and habitual neglect of his own interest. Unmarried, with many friends, and many enemies, he kept his body like a sword-blade, his soul always at white heat. \

That one who admitted to having taken part in five wars should be mixing in a by-election in the cause of Peace, was not so inconsistent as might be supposed; for he had always fought on the losing side, and there seemed to him at the moment no side so losing as that of Peace. No great politician, he was not an orator, nor even a glib talker; yet a quiet mordancy of tongue, and the white-hot look in his eyes, never failed to make an impression of some kind on an audience.

There was, however, hardly a corner of England where orations on behalf of Peace had a poorer chance than the Bucklandbury division. To say that Courtier had made himself unpopular with its matter-of-fact, independent, stolid, yet quick-tempered population, would be inadequate. He had outraged their beliefs, and roused the most profound suspicions. They could not, for the life of them, make out what he was at. Though by his adventures and his book, " Peace—a lost Cause," he was, in London, a conspicuous figure, they had naturally never heard of him; and his adventure to these parts seemed to them an almost ludicrous example of pure idea poking its nose into plain facts—the idea that nations ought to, and could live in peace being so very pure; and the fact that they never had, so very plain!

At Monkland, which was all Court estate, there were naturally but few supporters of Miltoun's opponent, Mr. Humphrey Chilcox, and the reception accorded to the champion of Peace soon passed from curiosity to derision, from derision to menace, till Courtier's attitude became so defiant, and his sentences so heated that he was only saved from a rough handling by the influential interposition of the vicar.

Yet when he began to address them he had felt irresistibly attracted. They looked such capital, independent fellows. Waiting for his turn to speak, he had marked them down as men after his own heart. For though Courtier knew that against an unpopular idea there must always be a majority, he never thought so ill of any individual as to suppose him capable of belonging to that ill-omened body.

Surely these fine, independent fellows were not to be hood-winked by the Jingoes! It had been one more disillusion. He had not taken it lying down; neither had his audience. They dispersed without forgiving; they came together again without having forgotten.

The village Inn, a little white building whose small windows were overgrown with creepers, had a single guest's bedroom on the upper floor, and a little sitting-room where Courtier took his meals. The rest of the house was but stone-floored bar with a long wooden bench against the back wall, whence nightly a stream of talk would issue, all harsh *a's*, and sudden soft *u's;* whence too a figure, a little unsteady, would now and again emerge, to a chorus of " Gude naights," stand still under the ash-trees to light his pipe, and then move slowly home.

But on that evening, when the trees, like cattle, stood knee-deep in the moon-dust, those who came out from the bar-room did not go away; they hung about in the shadows, and were joined by other figures creeping furtively through the bright moonlight, from behind the Inn. Presently more figures moved up from the lanes and the churchyard path, till thirty or more were huddled there, and their stealthy murmur of talk distilled a rare savour of illicit joy. Unholy hilarity, indeed, seemed lurking in the deep tree-shadow, before the wan Inn, whence from a single lighted window came forth the half-chanting sound of a man's voice reading out loud. Laughter was smothered, talk whispered.

"He'm a-practisin' his spaches." "Smoke the cunnin' old vox out!" "Red pepper's the proper stuff." "See mun sneeze! We've a-scrüed up the door."

Then, as a face showed at the lighted window, a burst of harsh laughter broke the hush.

He at the window was seen struggling violently to wrench away a bar. The laughter swelled to hooting. The prisoner forced his way through, dropped to the ground, rose, staggered, and fell.

A voice said sharply:

"What's this?"

Out of the sounds of scuffling and scattering came the whisper: "His lordship!" And the shade under the ash-trees became deserted, save by the tall dark figure of a man, and a woman's white shape.

"Is that you, Mr. Courtier? Are you hurt?"

A chuckle rose from the recumbent figure.

"Only my knee. The beggars! They precious nearly choked me, though!"

CHAPTER VII

BERTIE CARÁDOC, leaving the smoking-room at Monkland Court that same evening, on his way to bed, went to the Georgian corridor, where his pet barometer was hanging. To look at the glass had become the nightly habit of one who gave all the time he could spare from his profession to hunting in the winter and to racing in the summer.

The Hon. Hubert Carádoc, an apprentice to the calling of diplomacy, more completely than any living Carádoc embodied the characteristic strength and weaknesses of that family. He was of fair height, and wiry build. His weathered face, under sleek, dark hair, had regular, rather small features, and wore an expression of alert resolution, masked by impassivity. Over his inquiring, hazel-grey eyes the lids were almost religiously kept half drawn. He had been born reticent, and great, indeed, was the emotion under which he suffered when the whole of his eyes were visible. His nose was finely chiselled, and had little flesh. His lips, covered by a small, dark moustache, scarcely opened to emit his speeches, which were uttered in a voice singularly muffled, yet unexpectedly quick. The whole personality was that of a man practical, spirited, guarded, resourceful, with great power of self-control, who looked at life as if she were a horse under him, to whom he must give way just so far as was necessary to keep mastery of her. A man to whom ideas were of no value, except when wedded to immediate action; essentially neat; demanding to be " done well," but capable of stoicism if necessary; urbane, yet always in readiness to thrust; able only to condone the failings and to compassionate the kinds of distress which his own experience had taught him to understand. Such was Miltoun's younger brother at the age of twenty-six.

Having noted that the glass was steady, he was about to seek the stairway, when he saw at the farther end of the entrance-hall three figures advancing arm-in-arm. Habitually both curious and wary, he waited till they came within the radius of a lamp; then, seeing them to be those of Miltoun and a footman, supporting between them a lame man, he at once hastened forward.

" Have you put your knee out, sir? Hold on a minute! Get a chair, Charles."

Seating the stranger in this chair, Bertie rolled up the trouser, and passed his fingers round the knee. There was a sort of loving-kindness in that movement, as of a hand which had in its time felt the joints and sinews of innumerable horses.

" H'm! " he said; " can you stand a bit of a jerk? Catch hold of him behind, Eustace. Sit down on the floor, Charles, and hold the legs of the chair. Now then! " And taking up the foot, he pulled. There was a click, a little noise of teeth ground together; and Bertie said: " Good man—shan't have to have the vet. to you, this time."

Having conducted their lame guest to a room in the Georgian corridor hastily converted to a bedroom, the two brothers presently left him to the attentions of the footman.

" Well, old man," said Bertie, as they sought their rooms; " that's put paid to *his* name—won't do you any more harm this journey. Good plucked one, though! "

The report that Courtier was harboured beneath their roof went the round of the family before breakfast, through the agency of one whose practice it was to know all things, and to see that others partook of that knowledge. Little Ann, paying her customary morning visit to her mother's room, took her stand with face turned up and hands clasping her belt, and began at once.

" Uncle Eustace brought a man last night with a wounded leg, and Uncle Bertie pulled it out straight. William says that Charles says he only made a noise like this "—there was a faint sound of small chumping teeth: " And he's the man that's staying at the Inn, and the stairs were too narrow to carry him up, William says; and if his knee was put out he won't be able to walk without a stick for a long time. Can I go to Father? "

Agatha, who was having her hair brushed, thought:

' I'm not sure whether belts so low as that are wholesome '; and murmured: " Wait a minute! "

But little Ann was gone; and her voice could be heard in the dressing-room climbing up towards Sir William, who from the sound of his replies, was manifestly shaving. When Agatha, who never could resist a legitimate opportunity of approaching her husband, looked in, he was alone, and rather thoughtful—a tall man with a solid, steady face and cautious eyes, not in truth remarkable except to his own wife.

"That fellow Courtier's caught by the leg," he said. "Don't know what your Mother will say to an enemy in the camp."

"Isn't he a freethinker, and rather——"

Sir William, following his own thoughts, interrupted:

"Just as well, of course, so far as Miltoun's concerned, to have got him here."

Agatha sighed: "Well, I suppose we shall have to be nice to him. I'll tell Mother."

Sir William smiled.

"Ann will see to that," he said.

Ann was seeing to that.

Seated in the embrasure of the window behind the looking-glass, where Lady Valleys was still occupied, she was saying:

"He fell out of the window because of the red pepper. Miss Wallace says he is a hostage—what does hostage mean, Granny?"

When six years ago that word had first fallen on Lady Valleys' ears, she had thought: 'Oh! dear! Am I really Granny?' It had been a shock, had seemed the end of so much; but the matter-of-fact heroism of women, so much quicker to accept the inevitable than men, had soon come to her aid, and now, unlike her husband, she did not care a bit. For all that she answered nothing, partly because it was not necessary to speak in order to sustain a conversation with little Ann, and partly because she was deep in thought.

The man was injured! Hospitality, of course—especially since their own tenants had committed the outrage! Still, to welcome a man who had gone out of his way to come down here and stump the country against her own son, was rather a tall order. It might have been worse, no doubt. If, for instance, he had been some "impossible" Nonconformist Radical! This Mr. Courtier was a free lance—rather a well-known man, an interesting creature. She must see that he felt "at home" and comfortable. If he were pumped judiciously, no doubt one could find out about this woman. Moreover, the acceptance of their "salt" would silence him politically, if she knew anything of that type of man, who always had something in him of the Arab's creed. Her mind, that of a capable administrator, took in all the practical significance of this incident, which, although untoward, was not without its comic side to one disposed to find zest and humour in everything which did not absolutely run counter to her interests and philosophy.

The voice of little Ann broke in on her reflections.

" I'm going to Auntie Babs now."

" Very well; give me a kiss first."

Little Ann thrust up her face, so that its sudden little nose penetrated Lady Valleys' soft curving lips. . . .

When early that same afternoon Courtier, leaning on a stick, passed from his room out on to the terrace, he was confronted by three sunlit peacocks marching slowly across a lawn towards a statue of Diana. With incredible dignity those birds moved, as if never in their lives had they been hurried. They seemed indeed to know that when they got there, there would be nothing for them to do but to come back again. Beyond them, through the tall trees, over some wooded foot-hills of the moorland and a promised land of pinkish fields, pasture, and orchards, the prospect stretched to the far sea. Heat clothed this view with a kind of opalescence, a fairy garment, transmuting all values, so that the four square walls and tall chimneys of the pottery-works a few miles down the valley seemed to Courtier like a vision of some old fortified Italian town. His sensations, finding himself in this galley, were peculiar. For his feeling towards Miltoun, whom he had twice met at Mrs. Noel's, was, in spite of disagreements, by no means unfriendly, while his feeling towards Miltoun's family was not yet in existence. Having lived from hand to mouth, and in many countries, since he left Westminster School, he had now practically no class feelings. An attitude of hostility to aristocracy because it was aristocracy, was as incomprehensible to him as an attitude of deference. His sensations habitually shaped themselves in accordance with those two permanent requirements of his nature, liking for adventure, and hatred of tyranny. The labourer who beat his wife, the shopman who sweated his " hands," the parson who consigned his parishioners to hell, the peer who rode rough-shod—all were equally odious to him. He thought of people as individuals, and it was, as it were, by accident that he had conceived the class generalisation which he had fired back at Miltoun from Mrs. Noel's window. Sanguine, accustomed to queer environments, and always catching at the moment as it flew, he had not to fight with the timidities and irritations of a nervous temperament. His cheery courtesy was only disturbed when he became conscious of some sentiment which appeared to him mean or cowardly. On such occasions, not perhaps infrequent, his face looked as if his heart were phys-

ically fuming, and since his shell of stoicism was never quite
melted by this heat, a very peculiar expression was the result,
a sort of calm, sardonic, desperate, jolly look.

His chief feeling, then, at the outrage which had laid him
captive in the enemy's camp, was one of vague amusement, and
curiosity. People round about spoke fairly well of this Carádoc
family. There did not seem to be any lack of kindly feeling
between them and their tenants; there was said to be no griping
destitution, nor any particular ill-housing on their estate. And
if the inhabitants were not encouraged to improve themselves,
they were at all events maintained at a certain level, by steady
and not ungenerous supervision. When a roof required thatch-
ing it was thatched; when a man became too old to work, he
was not suffered to lapse into the Workhouse. In bad years for
wool, or beasts, or crops, the farmers received a graduated re-
mission of rent. The pottery-works were run on a liberal if
autocratic basis. It was true that though Lord Valleys was
said to be a staunch supporter of a " back to the land " policy,
no disposition was shown to encourage people to settle on these
particular lands, no doubt from a feeling that such settlers
would not do them so much justice as their present owner. Indeed so firmly did this conviction seemingly obtain, that Lord
Valleys' agent was not unfrequently observed to be buying a
little bit more.

But, since in this life one notices only what interests him, all
this gossip, half complimentary, half not, had fallen but lightly
on the ears of the champion of Peace during his campaign, for
he was, as has been said, but a poor politician, and rode his own
horse very much his own way.

While he stood there enjoying the view, he heard a small high
voice, and became conscious of a little girl in a very shady hat
so far back on her brown hair that it did not shade her; and
of a small hand put out in front. He took the hand, and
answered:

" Thank you, I am well—and you? " perceiving the while
that a pair of wide frank eyes were examining his leg.

" Does it hurt? "

" Not to speak of."

" My pony's leg was blistered. Granny is coming to look at
it."

" I see."

" I have to go now. I hope you'll soon be better. Good-bye! "

Then, instead of the little girl, Courtier saw a tall and rather florid woman regarding him with a sort of quizzical dignity. She wore a stiffish fawn-coloured dress which seemed to be cut a little too tight round her substantial hips, for it quite neglected to embrace her knees. She had on no hat, no gloves, no ornaments, except the rings on her fingers, and a little jewelled watch in a leather bracelet on her wrist. There was, indeed, about her whole figure an air of almost professional escape from finery.

Stretching out a well-shaped but not small hand, she said:
"I most heartily apologise to you, Mr. Courtier."

"Not at all."

"I do hope you're comfortable. Have they given you everything you want?"

"More than everything."

"It really was disgraceful! However it's brought us the pleasure of making your acquaintance. I've read your book, of course."

To Courtier it seemed that on this lady's face had come a look which seemed to say: 'Yes, very clever and amusing, quite enjoyable! But the ideas? What? You know very well they won't do—in fact they *mustn't* do!'

"That's very nice of you."

But into Lady Valleys' answer, "I don't agree with it a bit, you know!" there had crept a touch of asperity, as though she knew that he had smiled inside. "What we want preached in these days are the warlike virtues—especially by a warrior."

"Believe me, Lady Valleys, the warlike virtues are best left to men of more virgin imagination."

He received a quick look, and the words: "Anyway, I'm sure you don't care a rap for politics. You know Mrs. Lees Noel, don't you? What a pretty woman she is!"

But as she spoke Courtier saw a young girl coming along the terrace. She had evidently been riding, for she wore high boots and a skirt which had enabled her to sit astride. Her eyes were blue, and her hair—the colour of beech-leaves in autumn with the sun shining through—was coiled up tight under a small soft hat. She was tall, and moved towards them like one endowed with great length from the hip joint to the knee. Joy of life, serene, unconscious vigour, seemed to radiate from her whole face and figure.

At Lady Valleys' words:

" Ah, Babs! My daughter Barbara—Mr. Courtier," he put out his hand, received within it some gauntleted fingers held out with a smile, and heard her say:

" Miltoun's gone up to Town, Mother; I was going to motor in to Bucklandbury with a message he gave me; so I can fetch Granny out from the station."

" You had better take Ann, or she'll make our lives a burden; and perhaps Mr. Courtier would like an airing. Is your knee fit, do you think? "

Glancing at the apparition, Courtier replied:

" It is."

Never since the age of seven had he been able to look on feminine beauty without a sense of warmth and faint excitement; and seeing now perhaps the most beautiful girl he had ever beheld, he desired to be with her wherever she might be going. There was too something very fascinating in the way she smiled, as if she had a little seen through his sentiments.

" Well then," she said, " we'd better look for Ann."

After short but vigorous search little Ann was found—in the car, instinct having told her of a forward movement in which it was her duty to take part. And soon they had started, Ann between them in that state of silence to which she became liable when really interested.

From the Monkland estate, flowered, lawned, and timbered, to the open moor, was like passing to another world; for no sooner was the last lodge of the Western drive left behind, than there came into sudden view the most pagan bit of landscape in all England. In this wild parliament-house, clouds, rocks, sun, and winds met and consulted. The " old " men, too, had left their spirits among the great stones, which lay couched like lions on the hill-tops, under the white clouds, and their brethren, the hunting buzzard hawks. Here the very rocks were restless, changing form, and sense, and colour from day to day, as though worshipping the unexpected, and refusing themselves to law. The winds too in their passage revolted against their courses, and came tearing down wherever there were combes or crannies, so that men in their shelters might still learn the power of the wild gods.

The wonders of this prospect were entirely lost on little Ann, and somewhat so on Courtier, deeply engaged in reconciling those two alien principles, courtesy, and the love of looking at a pretty face. He was wondering too what this girl of twenty, who had the self-possession of a woman of forty, might be thinking. It was little Ann who broke the silence.

"Auntie Babs, it wasn't a very strong house, was it?"

Courtier looked in the direction of her small finger. There was the wreck of a little house, which stood close to a stone man who had obviously possessed that hill before there were men of flesh. Over one corner of the sorry ruin, a single patch of roof still clung, but the rest was open.

"He was a silly man to build it, wasn't he, Ann? That's why they call it Ashman's Folly."

"Is he alive?"

"Not quite—it's just a hundred years ago."

"What made him build it here?"

"He hated women, and—the roof fell in on him."

"Why did he hate women?"

"He was a crank."

"What is a crank?"

"Ask Mr. Courtier."

Under this girl's calm quizzical glance, Courtier endeavoured to find an answer to that question.

"A crank," he said slowly, "is a man like me."

He heard a little laugh, and became acutely conscious of Ann's dispassionate examining eyes.

"Is Uncle Eustace a crank?"

"You know now, Mr. Courtier, what Ann thinks of you. You think a good deal of Uncle Eustace, don't you, Ann?"

"Yes," said Ann, and fixed her eyes before her. But Courtier gazed sideways over her hatless head.

His exhilaration was increasing every moment. This girl reminded him of a two-year-old filly he had once seen, stepping out of Ascot paddock for her first race, with the sun glistening on her satin chestnut skin, her neck held high, her eyes all fire —as sure to win, as that grass was green. It was difficult to believe her Miltoun's sister. It was difficult to believe any of those four young Carádocs related. The grave ascetic Miltoun, wrapped in the garment of his spirit; mild, domestic, strait-laced Agatha; Bertie, muffled, shrewd, and steely; and this frank, joyful conquering Barbara—the range was wide.

But the car had left the moor, and, down a steep hill, was passing the small villas and little grey workmen's houses outside the town of Bucklandbury.

" Ann and I have to go on to Miltoun's headquarters. Shall I drop you at the enemy's, Mr. Courtier? Stop, please, Firth."

And before Courtier could assent, they had pulled up at a house on which was inscribed with extraordinary vigour: " Chilcox for Bucklandbury."

Hobbling into the Committee-room of Mr. Humphrey Chilcox, which smelled of paint, Courtier took with him the scented memory of youth, and ambergris, and Harris tweed.

In that room three men were assembled round a table; the eldest of whom, endowed with little grey eyes, a stubbly beard, and that mysterious something only found in those who have been mayors, rose at once and came towards him.

" Mr. Courtier, I believe," he said bluffly. " Glad to see you, sir. Most distressed to hear of this outrage. Though in a way, it's done us good. Yes, really. Grossly against fair play. Shouldn't be surprised if it turned a couple of hundred votes. You carry the effects of it about with you, I see."

A thin, refined man, with wiry hair, also came up, holding a newspaper in his hand.

" It has had one rather embarrassing effect," he said. " Read this:

" 'OUTRAGE ON A DISTINGUISHED VISITOR.
" 'LORD MILTOUN'S EVENING ADVENTURE.' "

Courtier read a paragraph.

The man with the little eyes broke the ominous silence which ensued.

" One of our side must have seen the whole thing, jumped on his bicycle and brought in the account before they went to press. They make no imputation on the lady—simply state the facts. Quite enough," he added with impersonal grimness; " I think he's done for himself, sir."

The man with the refined face added nervously:

" We couldn't help it, Mr. Courtier; I really don't know what we can do. I don't like it a bit."

" Has your candidate seen this? " Courtier asked.

" Can't have," struck in the third Committeeman; " we hadn't seen it ourselves until an hour ago."

" I should never have permitted it," said the man with the refined face; " I blame the editor greatly."

" Come to that——" said the little-eyed man, " it's a plain

piece of news. If it makes a stir, that's not our fault. The paper imputes nothing, it states. Position of the lady happens to do the rest. Can't help it, and moreover, sir, speaking for self, don't want to. We'll have no loose morals in public life down here, please God!" There was real feeling in his words; then, catching sight of Courtier's face, he added: "Do you know this lady?"

"Ever since she was a child. Anyone who speaks evil of her, has to reckon with me."

The man with the refined face said earnestly:

"Believe me, Mr. Courtier, I entirely sympathise. We had nothing to do with the paragraph. It's one of those incidents where one benefits against one's will. Most unfortunate that she came out on to the green with Lord Miltoun; you know what people are."

"It's the head-line that does it," said the third Committeeman; "they've put what will attract the public."

"I don't know, I don't know," said the little-eyed man stubbornly; "if Lord Miltoun will spend his evenings with lonely ladies, he can't blame anybody but himself."

Courtier looked from face to face.

"This closes my connection with the campaign," he said: "What's the address of this paper?" And without waiting for an answer, he took up the journal and hobbled from the room. He stood a minute outside finding the address, then made his way down the street.

CHAPTER VIII

By the side of little Ann, Barbara sat leaning back amongst the cushions of the car. In spite of being already launched into high-caste life which brings with it an early knowledge of the world, she had still some of the eagerness in her face which makes children lovable. Yet she looked negligently enough at the citizens of Bucklandbury, being already a little conscious of the strange mixture of sentiment peculiar to her countrymen in presence of herself—that curious expression on their faces resulting from the continual attempt to look down their noses while slanting their eyes upwards. Yes, she was already alive to that mysterious glance which had built the national house and insured it afterwards—foe to cynicism, pessimism, and anything French or Russian; parent of all the national virtues, and all the national vices of idealism and muddleheadedness, of independence and servility; fosterer of conduct, murderer of speculation; looking up and looking down, but never straight at anything; most high, most deep, most queer; and ever bubbling-up from the essential Well of Emulation.

Surrounded by that glance, waiting for Courtier, Barbara, not less British than her neighbours, was secretly slanting her own eyes up and down over the absent figure of her new acquaintance. She too wanted something she could look up to, and at the same time see damned first. And in this knight-errant it seemed to her that she had got it.

He was a creature from another world. She had met many men, but not as yet one quite of this sort. It was rather nice to be with a clever man, who had none the less done so many outdoor things, been through so many bodily adventures. The mere writers, or even the "Bohemians," whom she occasionally met, were after all only "chaplains to the Court," necessary to keep aristocracy in touch with the latest development of literature and art. But this Mr. Courtier was a man of action; he could not be looked on with the amused, admiring toleration suited to men remarkable only for ideas, and the way they put them into paint or ink. He had used, and could use, the sword, even in the cause of Peace. He could love, had loved, or so they said. If Barbara had been a girl of twenty in another

531

class, she would probably never have heard of this, and if she
had heard, it might very well have dismayed or shocked her.
But she had heard, and without shock, because she had already
learned that men were like that, and women too sometimes.

It was with quite a little pang of concern that she saw him
hobbling down the street towards her; and when he was once
more seated, she told the chauffeur: "To the station, Frith.
Quick, please!" and began,

"You are not to be trusted a bit. What were you doing?"

But Courtier smiled grimly over the head of Ann, in silence.

At this, almost the first time she had ever yet encountered a
distinct rebuff, Barbara quivered, as though she had been
touched lightly with a whip. Her lips closed firmly, her eyes
began to dance. 'Very well, my dear,' she thought. But presently stealing a look at him, she became aware of such a queer
expression on his face, that she forgot she was offended.

"Is anything wrong, Mr. Courtier?"

"Yes, Lady Barbara, something is very wrong—that miserable mean thing, the human tongue."

Barbara had an intuitive knowledge of how to handle things,
a kind of moral sangfroid, drawn in from the faces she had
watched, the talk she had heard, from her youth up. She
trusted those intuitions, and letting her eyes conspire with his
over Ann's brown hair, she said:

"Anything to do with Mrs. N——?" Seeing "Yes" in his
eyes, she added quickly: "And M——?"

Courtier nodded.

"I thought that was coming. Let them babble! Who cares?"

She caught an approving glance, and the word, "Good!"

But the car had drawn up at Bucklandbury Station.

The little grey figure of Lady Casterley, coming out of the
station doorway, showed but slight sign of her long travel.
She stopped to take the car in, from chauffeur to Courtier.

"Well, Frith!—Mr. Courtier, is it? I know your book, and
I don't approve of you; you're a dangerous man—How do you
do? I must have those two bags. The cart can bring the
rest. . . . Randle, get up in front, and don't get dusty. Ann!"
But Ann was already beside the chauffeur, having long planned
this improvement. "H'm! So you've hurt your leg, sir?
Keep still! We can sit three. . . . Now, my dear, I can kiss
you! You've grown!"

Lady Casterley's kiss, once received, was never forgotten;

neither perhaps was Barbara's. Yet they were different. For, in the case of Lady Casterley, the old eyes, bright and investigating, could be seen deciding the exact spot for the lips to touch; then the face with its firm chin was darted forward; the lips paused a second, as though to make quite certain, then suddenly dug hard and dry into the middle of the cheek, quavered for the fraction of a second as if trying to remember to be soft, and were relaxed like the elastic of a catapult. And in the case of Barbara, first a sort of light came into her eyes, then her chin tilted a little, then her lips pouted a little, her body quivered, as if it were getting a size larger, her hair breathed, there was a small sweet sound; it was over.

Thus kissing her grandmother, Barbara resumed her seat, and looked at Courtier. "Sitting three" as they were, he was touching her, and it seemed to her somehow that he did not mind.

The wind had risen, blowing from the West, and sunshine was flying on it. The call of the cuckoos—a little sharpened —followed the swift-travelling car. And that essential sweetness of the moor, born of the heather roots and the South-West wind, was stealing out from under the young ferns.

With her thin nostrils distended to this scent, Lady Casterley bore a distinct resemblance to a small, fine game-bird.

"You smell nice down here," she said. "Now, Mr. Courtier, before I forget—who is this Mrs. Lees Noel that I hear so much of?"

At that question, Barbara could not help sliding her eyes round. How would he stand up to Granny? It was the moment to see what he was made of. Granny was terrific!

"A very charming woman, Lady Casterley."

"No doubt; but I am tired of hearing that. What is her story?"

"Has she one?"

"Ha!" said Lady Casterley.

Ever so slightly Barbara let her arm press against Courtier's. It was so delicious to hear Granny getting no forwarder.

"I may take it she *has* a past, then?"

"Not from me, Lady Casterley."

Again Barbara gave him that imperceptible and flattering touch.

"Well, this is all very mysterious. I shall find out for myself. You know her, my dear. You must take me to see her."

"Dear Granny! If people hadn't pasts, they wouldn't have futures."

Lady Casterley let her little claw-like hand descend on her granddaughter's thigh.

"Don't talk nonsense, and don't stretch like that!" she said; "you're too large already. . . ."

At dinner that night they were all in possession of the news. Sir William had been informed by the local agent at Staverton, where Lord Harbinger's speech had suffered from some rude interruptions. The Hon. Geoffrey Winlow, having sent his wife on, had flown over in his biplane from Winkleigh, and brought a copy of "the rag" with him. The one member of the small house-party who had not heard the report before dinner was Lord Dennis Fitz-Harold, Lady Casterley's brother.

Little, of course, was said. But after the ladies had withdrawn, Harbinger, with that plain-spoken spontaneity which was so unexpected, perhaps a little intentionally so, in connection with his almost classically formed face, uttered words to the effect that, if they did not fundamentally kick that rumour, it was all up with Miltoun. Really this was serious! And the beggars knew it, and they were going to work it. And Miltoun had gone up to Town, no one knew what for. It was the devil of a mess!

In all the conversation of this young man there was that peculiar brand of voice which seems ever rebutting an accusation of being serious—a brand of voice and manner warranted against anything save ridicule; and in the face of ridicule apt to disappear. The words, just a little satirically spoken: "What is, my dear young man?" stopped him at once.

Looking for the complement and counterpart of Lady Casterley, one would perhaps have singled out her brother. All her abrupt decision was negated in his profound, ironical urbanity. His voice and look and manner were like his velvet coat, which had here and there a whitish sheen, as if it had been touched by moonlight. His hair too had that sheen. His very delicate features were framed in a white beard and moustache of Elizabethan shape. His eyes, hazel and still clear, looked out very straight, with a certain dry kindliness. His face, though unweathered and unseamed, and much too fine and thin in texture, had a curious affinity to the faces of old sailors or fishermen who have lived a simple, practical life in the light of an overmastering tradition. It was the face of a man with a very set creed, and inclined to be satiric towards innovations, examined by him and rejected full fifty years ago. One felt that a brain not devoid either of subtlety or æsthetic quality had long given up all attempts to interfere with conduct; that all shrewdness of speculation had given place to shrewdness of practical judgment based on very definite experience. Owing to lack of advertising power, natural to one so conscious of his dignity as to have lost all care for it, and to his devotion to a certain lady, only closed by death, his life had been lived, as it were, in shadow. Still, he possessed a peculiar influence in Society, because it was known to be impossible to get him to look at things in a complicated way. He was regarded rather as a last resort, however. "Bad as that? Well, there's old Fitz-Harold! Try him! He won't advise you, but he'll say something."

And in the heart of that irreverent young man, Harbinger, there stirred a sort of misgiving. Had he expressed himself too freely? Had he said anything too thick? He had forgotten the old boy! Stirring Bertie up with his foot, he murmured: "Forgot you didn't know, sir. Bertie will explain."

Thus called on, Bertie, opening his lips a very little way, and fixing his half-closed eyes on his great-uncle, explained. There was a lady at the cottage—a nice woman—Mr. Courtier knew her—old Miltoun went there sometimes—rather late the other evening—these devils were making the most of it—suggesting—lose him the election, if they didn't look out. Perfect rot, of course!

In his opinion, old Miltoun, though as steady as Time, had been a flat to let the woman come out with him on to the Green, showing clearly where he had been, when he ran to Courtier's rescue. You couldn't play about with women who had no form that anyone knew anything of, however promising they might look.

Then, out of a silence Winlow asked: What was to be done? Should Miltoun be wired for? A thing like this spread like wildfire! Sir William—a man not accustomed to underrate difficulties—was afraid it was going to be troublesome. Harbinger expressed the opinion that the editor ought to be kicked. Did anybody know what Courtier had done when he heard of it? Where was he—dining in his room? Bertie suggested that if Miltoun was at Valleys House, it mightn't be too late to wire to him. The thing ought to be stemmed at once! And in all this concern about the situation there kept cropping out quaint little outbursts of desire to disregard the whole thing as infernal insolence, and metaphorically to punch the beggars' heads, natural to young men of breeding.

Then, out of another silence came the voice of Lord Dennis:

"I am thinking of this poor lady."

Turning a little abruptly towards that dry suave voice, and recovering the self-possession which seldom deserted him, Harbinger murmured:

"Quite so, sir; of course!"

CHAPTER IX

In the lesser withdrawing room, used when there was so small a party, Mrs. Winlow had gone to the piano and was playing to herself, for Lady Casterley, Lady Valleys, and her two daughters had drawn together as though united to face this invading rumour.

It was curious testimony to Miltoun's character that, no more here than in the dining-hall, was there any doubt of the integrity of his relations with Mrs. Noel. But whereas, there the matter was confined to its electioneering aspect, here that aspect was already perceived to be only the fringe of its importance. Those feminine minds, going with intuitive swiftness to the core of anything which affected their own males, had already grasped the fact that the rumour would, as it were, chain a man of Miltoun's temper to this woman.

But they were walking on such a thin crust of facts, and there was so deep a quagmire of supposition beneath, that talk was almost painfully difficult. Never before perhaps had each of these four women realised so clearly how much Miltoun—that rather strange and unknown grandson, son, and brother —counted in the scheme of existence. Their suppressed agitation was manifested in very different ways. Lady Casterley, upright in her chair, showed it only by an added decision of speech, a continual restless movement of one hand, a thin line between her usually smooth brows. Lady Valleys wore a puzzled look, as if a little surprised that she felt serious. Agatha looked frankly anxious. She was in her quiet way a woman of much character, endowed with that natural piety, which accepts without questioning the established order in life and religion. The world to her being home and family, she had a real, if gently expressed, horror of all that she instinctively felt to be subversive of this ideal. People judged her a little quiet, dull, and narrow; they compared her to a hen for ever clucking round her chicks. The streak of heroism in her nature was not perhaps patent. Her feeling about her brother's situation however was sincere and not to be changed or comforted. She saw him in danger of being damaged in the only sense in which she

537

could conceive of a man—as a husband and a father. This went
to her heart, though her piety proclaimed to her also the peril
of his soul; for she shared the High Church view of the indis-
solubility of marriage.

As to Barbara, she stood by the hearth, leaning her white
shoulders against the carved marble, her hands behind her,
looking down. Now and then her lips curled, her level brows
twitched, a faint sigh came from her; then a little smile would
break out, and be instantly suppressed. She alone was silent—
Youth criticising Life; her judgment voiced itself only in the
untroubled rise and fall of her young bosom, the impatience
of her brows, the downward look of her blue eyes, full of a lazy,
inextinguishable light.

Lady Valleys sighed.

"If only he weren't such a queer boy! He's quite capable
of marrying her from sheer perversity."

"What!" said Lady Casterley.

"You haven't seen her, my dear. A most unfortunately attractive creature—quite a charming face."

Agatha said quietly:

"Mother, if she *was* divorced, I don't think Eustace would."

"There's *that*, certainly," murmured Lady Valleys; "hope
for the best!"

"Don't you even know which way it was?" said Lady Casterley.

"Well, the vicar says *she* did the divorcing. But he's very
charitable; it may be as Agatha hopes."

"I detest vagueness. Why doesn't someone ask the woman?"

"You shall come with me, Granny dear, and ask her yourself; you will do it so nicely."

Lady Casterley looked up.

"We shall see," she said. Something struggled with the
autocratic criticism in her eyes. No more than the rest of the
world could she help indulging Barbara. As one who believed
in the divinity of her order, she liked this splendid child. She
even admired—though admiration was not what she excelled in
—that warm joy in life, as of some great nymph, parting the
waves with bare limbs, tossing from her the foam of breakers.
She felt that in this granddaughter, rather than in the good
Agatha, the patrician spirit was housed. There were points to
Agatha, earnestness and high principle; but something morally
narrow and over-Anglican slightly offended the practical and

worldly temper of Lady Casterley. It was a weakness, and she disliked weakness. Barbara would never be squeamish over moral questions or matters such as were not really essential to aristocracy. She might, indeed, err too much the other way from sheer high spirits. As the impudent child had said: "If people had no pasts, they would have no futures." And Lady Casterley could not bear people without futures. She was ambitious; not with the low ambition of one who had risen from nothing, but with the high passion of one on the top, who meant to stay there.

"And where have *you* been meeting this—er—anonymous creature?" she asked.

Barbara came from the hearth, and bending down beside Lady Casterley's chair, seemed to envelop her completely.

"I'm all right, Granny; she couldn't corrupt me."

Lady Casterley's face peered out doubtfully from that warmth, wearing a look of disapproving pleasure.

"I know your wiles!" she said. "Come, now!"

"I see her about. She's nice to look at. We talk."

Again with that hurried quietness Agatha said:

"My dear Babs, I do think you ought to wait."

"My dear Angel, why? What is it to me if she's had four husbands?"

Agatha bit her lips, and Lady Valleys murmured with a laugh:

"You really are a terror, Babs."

But the sound of Mrs. Winlow's music had ceased—the men had come in. And the faces of the four women hardened, as if they had slipped on masks; for though this was almost or quite a family party, the Winlows being second cousins, still the subject was one which each of these four in their very different ways felt to be beyond general discussion. Talk, now, began glancing from the war scare—Winlow had it very specially that this would be over in a week—to Brabrook's speech, in progress at that very moment, of which Harbinger provided an imitation. It sped to Winlow's flight—to Andrew Grant's articles in the *Parthenon*—to the caricature of Harbinger in the *Cackler,* inscribed "The New Tory. L-rd H-rb-ng-r brings Social Reform beneath the notice of his friends," which depicted him introducing a naked baby to a number of coroneted old ladies. Thence to a dancer. Thence to the Bill for Universal Assurance. Then back to the war scare; to the last book of a great French writer; and once more to Winlow's flight. It was all straightforward and outspoken, each seeming to say exactly what came into the head. For all that, there was a curious avoidance of the spiritual significances of these things; or was it perhaps that such significances were not seen?

Lord Dennis, at the far end of the room, studying a portfolio of engravings, felt a touch on his cheek; and conscious of a certain fragrance, said without turning his head:

"Nice things, these, Babs!"

Receiving no answer he looked up.

There indeed stood Barbara.

"I do hate sneering behind people's backs!"

There had always been good comradeship between these two, since the days when Barbara, a golden-haired child, astride of a grey pony, had been his morning companion in the Row all through the season. His riding days were past; he had now no outdoor pursuit save fishing, which he followed with the ironic persistence of a self-contained, high-spirited nature, which refuses to admit that the mysterious finger of old age is laid across it. But though she was no longer his companion, he still had a habit of expecting her confidences; and he looked after her, moving away from him to a window, with surprised concern.

It was one of those nights, dark yet gleaming, when there seems a flying malice in the heavens; when the stars, from under and above the black clouds, are like eyes frowning and flashing down at men with purposed malevolence. The great sighing trees even had caught this spirit, save one, a dark, spire-like cypress, planted three hundred and fifty years before, whose tall form incarnated the very spirit of tradition, and neither swayed nor soughed like the others. From her, too close-fibred, too resisting, to admit the breath of Nature, only a dry rustle came. Still almost exotic, in spite of her centuries of sojourn, and now brought to life by the eyes of night, she seemed almost terrifying, in her narrow, spear-like austerity, as though something had dried and died within her soul. Barbara came back from the window.

"We can't do anything in our lives, it seems to me," she said, "but *play* at taking risks!"

Lord Dennis replied dryly:

"I don't think I understand, my dear."

"Look at Mr. Courtier!" muttered Barbara. "His life's so

much more risky altogether than any of our men folk lead.
And yet they sneer at him."

" Let's see, what has he done ? "

" Oh! I dare say not very much; but it's all neck or nothing.
But what does anything matter to Harbinger, for instance? If
his Social Reform comes to nothing, he'll still be Harbinger,
with fifty thousand a year."

Lord Dennis looked up a little queerly.

" What! Is it possible you don't take the young man seriously, Babs ? "

Barbara shrugged; a strap slipped a little off one white
shoulder.

" It's all play really; and he knows it—you can tell that from
his voice. He can't help its not mattering, of course; and he
knows that too."

" I have heard that he's after you, Babs; is that true ? "

" He hasn't caught me yet."

" Will he ? "

Barbara's answer was another shrug; and, for all their
statuesque beauty, the movement of her shoulders was like the
shrug of a little girl in her pinafore.

" And this Mr. Courtier," said Lord Dennis dryly: " Are you
after him ? "

" I'm after everything; didn't you know that, dear ? "

" In reason, my child."

" In reason, of course—like poor Eusty!" She stopped.
Harbinger himself was standing there close by, with an air
as nearly approaching reverence as was ever to be seen on him.
In truth, the way in which he was looking at her was almost
timorous.

" Will you sing that song I like so much, Lady Babs ? "

They moved away together; and Lord Dennis, gazing after
that magnificent young couple, stroked his beard gravely.

CHAPTER X

MILTOUN'S sudden journey to London had been undertaken in pursuance of a resolve slowly forming from the moment he met Mrs. Noel in the stone-flagged passage of Burracombe Farm. If she would have him—and since last evening he believed she would—he intended to marry her.

It has been said that except for one lapse his life had been austere, but this is not to assert that he had no capacity for passion. The contrary was the case. That flame which had been so jealously guarded smouldered deep within him—a smothered fire with but little air to feed on. The moment his spirit was touched by the spirit of this woman, it had flared up. She was the incarnation of all that he desired. Her hair, her eyes, her form; the tiny tuck or dimple at the corner of her mouth just where a child places its finger; her way of moving, a sort of unconscious swaying or yielding to the air; the tone in her voice, which seemed to come not so much from happiness of her own as from an innate wish to make others happy; and that natural, if not robust, intelligence, which belongs to the very sympathetic, and is rarely found in women of great ambitions or enthusiasms—all these things had twined themselves round his heart. He not only dreamed of her, and wanted her; he believed in her. She filled his thoughts as one who could never do wrong; as one who, though a wife, would remain a mistress, and, though a mistress, would always be the companion of his spirit.

It has been said that no one spoke or gossipped about women in Miltoun's presence, and the tale of her divorce was present to his mind simply in the form of a conviction that she was an injured woman. After his interview with the vicar, he had only once again alluded to it, and that in answer to the speech of a lady staying at the Court: " Oh! yes, I remember her case perfectly. She was the poor woman who——" " Did *not*, I am certain, Lady Bonington." The tone of his voice had made someone laugh uneasily; the subject was changed.

All divorce was against his convictions, but in a blurred way he admitted that there were cases where release was unavoidable. He was not a man to ask for confidences, or expect them to be given him. He himself had never confided his spiritual struggles to any living creature; and the unspiritual struggle had little interest for Miltoun. He was ready at any moment to stake his life on the perfection of the idol he had set up within his soul, as simply and straightforwardly as he would have placed his body in front of her to shield her from harm.

The same fanaticism, which looked on his passion as a flower by itself, entirely apart from its suitability to the social garden, was also the driving force which sent him up to London to declare his intention to his father before he spoke to Mrs. Noel. The thing should be done simply, and in right order. For he had the kind of moral courage found in those who live retired within the shell of their own aspirations. Yet it was not perhaps so much active moral courage as indifference to what others thought or did, coming from his inbred resistance to the appreciation of what they felt.

That peculiar smile of the old Tudor Cardinal—which had in it invincible self-reliance, and a sort of spiritual sneer—played over his face when he speculated on his father's reception of the coming news; and very soon he ceased to think of it at all, burying himself in the work he had brought with him for the journey. For he had in high degree the faculty, so essential to public life, of switching off his whole attention from one subject to another.

On arriving at Paddington he drove straight to Valleys House.

This large dwelling with its pillared portico, seemed to wear an air of faint surprise that, at the height of the season, it was not more inhabited. Three servants relieved Miltoun of his little luggage; and, having washed, and learned that his father would be dining in, he went for a walk, taking his way towards his rooms in the Temple. His long figure, somewhat carelessly garbed, attracted the usual attention, of which he was as usual unaware. Strolling along, he meditated deeply on a London, an England, different from this flatulent hurly-burly, this omnium gatherum, this great discordant symphony of sharps and flats. A London, an England, kempt and self-respecting; swept and garnished of slums, and plutocrats, advertisement, and jerry-building, of sensationalism, vulgarity, vice, and unemployment. An England where each man should know his place, and never change it, but serve in it loyally in his own caste. Where every man, from nobleman to labourer, should be an oligarch by faith, and a gentleman by practice. An England so steel-bright and efficient that the very sight should suffice to impose peace. An England whose soul should be stoical and fine with the stoicism and fineness of each soul amongst her many million souls; where the town should have its creed and the country its creed, and there should be contentment and no complaining in her streets.

And as he walked down the Strand, a little ragged boy cheeped out between his legs:

"Bloodee discoveree in a Bank—Grite sensytion! Pi—er!"

Miltoun paid no heed to that saying; yet, with it, the wind blowing where man lives, the careless, wonderful, unordered wind, had dispersed his austere and formal vision. Great was that wind—the myriad aspiration of men and women, the praying of the uncounted multitude to the goddess of Sensation —of Chance, and Change. A flowing from heart to heart, from lip to lip, as in Spring the wistful air wanders through a wood, imparting to every bush and tree the secrets of fresh life, the passionate resolve to grow, and *become*—no matter what! A sighing, as eternal as the old murmuring of the sea, as little to be hushed, as prone to swell into sudden roaring!

Miltoun held on through the traffic, not looking overmuch at the present forms of the thousands he passed, but seeing with the eyes of faith the forms he desired to see. Near St. Paul's he stopped in front of an old book-shop. His grave, pallid, not unhandsome face, was well-known to William Rimall, its small proprietor, who at once brought out his latest acquisition—a More's "Utopia." That particular edition (he assured Miltoun) was quite unprocurable—he had never sold but one other copy, which had been literally crumbling away. This copy was in even better condition. It could hardly last another twenty years—a genuine book, a bargain. There wasn't so much movement in More as there had been a little time back.

Miltoun opened the tome, and a small booklouse who had been sleeping on the word "Tranibore," began to make its way slowly towards the very centre of the volume.

"I see it's genuine," said Miltoun.

"It's not to read, my lord," the little man warned him: "Hardly safe to turn the pages. As I was saying—I've not had a better piece this year. I haven't really!"

"Shrewd old dreamer," muttered Miltoun; "the Socialists haven't got beyond him, even now."

The little man's eyes blinked, as though apologising for the views of Thomas More.

"Well," he said, "I suppose he *was* one of them. I forget if your lordship's very strong on politics?"

Miltoun smiled.

"I want to see an England, Rimall, something like the England of More's dream. But my machinery will be different. I shall begin at the top."

The little man nodded.

"Quite so, quite so," he said; "we shall come to that, I dare say."

"We must, Rimall." And Miltoun turned the page.

The little man's face quivered.

"I don't think," he said, "that book's quite strong enough for you, my lord, with your taste for reading. Now I've a most curious old volume here—on Chinese temples. It's rare—but not too old. You can peruse it thoroughly. It's what I call a book to browse on—just suit your palate. Funny principle they built those things on," he added, opening the volume at an engraving, "in layers. We don't build like that in England."

Miltoun looked up sharply; the little man's face wore no signs of understanding.

"Unfortunately we don't, Rimall," he said; "we ought to, and we shall. I'll take this book."

Placing his finger on the print of the pagoda, he added: "A good symbol."

The little bookseller's eyes strayed down the temple to the secret price mark.

"Exactly, my lord," he said; "I thought it'd be your fancy. The price to *you* will be twenty-seven and six."

Miltoun, pocketing the bargain, walked out. He made his way into the Temple, left the book at his Chambers, and passed on down to the bank of Mother Thames. The Sun was loving her passionately that afternoon; he had kissed her into warmth and light and colour. And all the buildings along her banks, as far as the towers at Westminster, seemed to be smiling. It was a great sight for the eyes of a lover. And another vision came haunting Miltoun, of a soft-eyed woman with a low voice, bending amongst her flowers. Nothing would be complete without her; no work bear fruit; no scheme could have full meaning.

Lord Valleys greeted his son at dinner with good-fellowship and a faint surprise.

"Day off, my dear fellow? Or have you come up to hear Brabrook pitch into us? He's rather late this time—we've got rid of that balloon business—no trouble after all."

And he eyed Miltoun with that clear grey stare of his, so cool, level, and curious. 'Now, what sort of bird *is* this?' it seemed saying. 'Certainly not the partridge I should have expected from its breeding!'"

Miltoun's answer: "I came up to tell you something, sir," riveted his father's stare for a second longer than was quite urbane.

It would not be true to say that Lord Valleys was afraid of his son. Fear was not one of his emotions, but he certainly regarded him with a respectful curiosity bordering on uneasiness. The oligarchic temper of Miltoun's mind and political convictions almost shocked one who knew both by temperament and experience how to wait in front. This instruction he had frequently had occasion to give his jockeys when he believed his horses could best get home first in that way. And it was an instruction he now longed to give his son. He himself had "waited in front" for over fifty years, and he knew it to be the finest way of insuring that he would never be compelled to alter this desirable policy—for something in Lord Valleys' character made him fear, that, in real emergency, he would exert himself to the point of the gravest discomfort sooner than be left to wait behind. A fellow like young Harbinger, of course, he understood—versatile, 'full of beans,' as he expressed it to himself in his more confidential moments, who had imbibed the new wine (very intoxicating it was) of desire for social reform. He would have to be given his head a little—but there would be no difficulty with him, he would never "run out"—light handy build of horse that only required steadying at the corners. He would want to hear himself talk, and be let feel that he was doing something. All very well, and quite intelligible. But with Miltoun (and Lord Valleys felt this to be no mere paternal fancy) it was a very different business. His son had a way of forcing things to their conclusions which was dangerous, and reminded him of his mother-in-law. He was a baby in public affairs, of course, as yet; but as soon as he once got going, the intensity of his convictions, together with his position, and real gift—not of the gab, like Harbinger's—but of restrained, biting oratory, was sure to bring him to the front with a bound in the present state of parties. And what were those convictions?

Lord Valleys had tried to understand them, but up to the present he had failed. And this did not surprise him exactly, since,
as he often said, political convictions were not, as they appeared
on the surface, the outcome of reason, but merely symptoms of
temperament. And he could not comprehend, because he could
not sympathise with, any attitude towards public affairs which
was not essentially level, attached to the plain, common-sense
factors of the case as they appeared to himself. Not that he
could fairly be called a temporiser, for deep down in him there
was undoubtedly a vein of obstinate, fundamental loyalty to the
traditions of a caste which prized high spirit beyond all things.
Still he did feel that Miltoun was altogether too much the
" pukka " aristocrat—no better than a Socialist, with his confounded way of seeing things all cut and dried; his ideas of
forcing reforms down people's throats and holding them there
with the iron hand! With his way too of acting on his principles! Why! He even admitted that he acted on his principles! This thought always struck a very discordant note in
Lord Valleys' breast. It was almost indecent; worse—ridiculous! The fact was, the dear fellow had unfortunately a deeper
habit of thought than was wanted in politics—dangerous—very!
Experience might do something for him! And out of his own
long experience the Earl of Valleys tried hard to recollect any
politician whom the practice of politics had left where he was
when he started. He could not think of one. But this gave him
little comfort; and, above a piece of late asparagus, his steady
eyes sought his son's. What had he come up to tell him?
   The phrase had been ominous; he could not recollect Miltoun's
ever having told him anything. For though a really kind and
indulgent father, he had—like so many men occupied with public
and other lives—a little acquired towards his offspring the look
and manner: Is this mine? Of his four children, Barbara
alone he claimed with conviction. He admired her; and, being
a man who savoured life, he was unable to love much except
where he admired. But, the last person in the world to hustle
any man or force a confidence, he waited to hear his son's news,
betraying no uneasiness.
   Miltoun seemed in no hurry. He described Courtier's adventure, which tickled Lord Valleys a good deal.
   " Ordeal by red pepper! Shouldn't have thought them equal
to that," he said. " So you've got him at Monkland now.
Harbinger still with you? "

"Yes. I don't think Harbinger has much stamina."

"Politically?"

Miltoun nodded.

"I rather resent his being on our side—I don't think he does us any good. You've seen that cartoon, I suppose; it cuts pretty deep. I couldn't recognise you amongst the old women, sir."

Lord Valleys smiled impersonally.

"Very clever thing. By the way, I shall win the Eclipse, I think."

And thus, spasmodically, the conversation ran till the last servant had left the room.

Then Miltoun, without preparation, looked straight at his father and said:

"I want to marry Mrs. Noel, sir."

Lord Valleys received the shot with exactly the same expression as that with which he was accustomed to watch his horses beaten. Then he raised his wineglass to his lips; and set it down again untouched. This was the only sign he gave of interest or discomfiture.

"Isn't this rather sudden?"

Miltoun answered: "I've wanted to from the moment I first saw her."

Lord Valleys, almost as good a judge of a man and a situation as of a horse or a pointer dog, leaned back in his chair, and said with faint sarcasm:

"My dear fellow, it's good of you to have told me this; though, to be quite frank, it's a piece of news I would rather not have heard."

A dusky flush burned slowly up in Miltoun's cheeks. He had underrated his father; the man had coolness and courage in a crisis.

"What is your objection, sir?" And suddenly he noticed that a wafer in Lord Valleys' hand was quivering. This brought into his eyes no look of compunction, but such a smouldering gaze as the old Tudor Churchman might have bent on an adversary who showed a sign of weakness. Lord Valleys, too, noticed the quivering of that wafer, and ate it.

"We are men of the world," he said.

Miltoun answered: "I am not."

Showing his first real symptom of impatience Lord Valleys rapped out:

"So be it! I am."

" Yes ? " said Miltoun.

" Eustace ! "

Nursing one knee, Miltoun faced that appeal without the faintest movement. His eyes continued to burn into his father's face. A tremor passed over Lord Valleys' heart. What intensity of feeling there was in the fellow, that he could look like this at the first breath of opposition !

He reached out and took up the cigar-box; held it absently towards his son, and drew it quickly back.

" I forgot," he said; " you don't."

And lighting a cigar, he smoked gravely, looking straight before him, a furrow between his brows. He spoke at last:

" She looks like a lady. I know nothing else about her."

The smile deepened round Miltoun's mouth.

" Why should you want to know anything else ? "

Lord Valleys shrugged. His philosophy had hardened.

" I understand for one thing," he said coldly, " that there is a matter of a divorce. I thought you took the Church's view on that subject."

" She has not done wrong."

" You know her story, then ? "

" No."

Lord Valleys raised his brows, in irony and a sort of admiration.

" Chivalry the better part of discretion ? "

Miltoun answered:

" You don't, I think, understand the kind of feeling I have for Mrs. Noel. It does not come into your scheme of things. It is the only feeling, however, with which I should care to marry, and I am not likely to feel it for anyone again."

Lord Valleys felt once more that uncanny sense of insecurity. Was this true? And suddenly he felt: Yes, it is true! The face before him was the face of one who would burn in his own fire sooner than depart from his standards. And a sudden sense of the utter seriousness of this dilemma dumbed him.

" I can say no more at the moment," he muttered, and got up from the table.

CHAPTER XI

LADY CASTERLEY was that inconvenient thing—an early riser. No woman in the kingdom was a better judge of a dew carpet. Nature had in her time displayed before her thousands of those pretty fabrics, where all the stars of the past night, dropped to the dark earth, were waiting to glide up to heaven again on the rays of the sun. At Ravensham she walked regularly in her gardens between half-past seven and eight, and when she paid a visit, was careful to subordinate whatever might be the local custom to this habit.

When therefore her maid Randle came to Barbara's maid at seven o'clock, and said: "My old lady wants Lady Babs to get up," there was no particular pain in the breast of Barbara's maid, who was doing up her corsets. She merely answered: "I'll see to it. Lady Babs won't be too pleased!" And ten minutes later she entered that white-walled room which smelled of pinks—a temple of drowsy sweetness, where the summer light was vaguely stealing through flowered chintz curtains.

Barbara was sleeping with her cheek on her hand, and her tawny hair, gathered back, streaming over the pillow. Her lips were parted; and the maid thought: 'I'd like to have hair and a mouth like that!' She could not help smiling to herself with pleasure; Lady Babs looked so pretty—prettier asleep even than awake! And at sight of that beautiful creature, sleeping and smiling in her sleep, the earthy, hothouse fumes steeping the mind of one perpetually serving in an atmosphere unsuited to her natural growth, dispersed. Beauty, with its queer touching power of freeing the spirit from all barriers and thoughts of self, sweetened the maid's eyes, and kept her standing, holding her breath. For Barbara asleep was a symbol of that Golden Age in which she so desperately believed. She opened her eyes, and seeing the maid, said:

"Is it eight o'clock, Stacey?"

"No, but Lady Casterley wants you to walk with her."

"Oh! bother! I was having such a dream!"

"Yes; you were smiling."

"I was dreaming that I could fly."

"Fancy!"

550

"I could see everything spread out below me, as close as I see you; I was hovering like a buzzard hawk. I felt that I could come down exactly where I wanted. It was fascinating. I had perfect power, Stacey."

And throwing her neck back, she closed her eyes again. The sunlight streamed in on her between the half-drawn curtains.

The queerest impulse to put out a hand and stroke that full white throat shot through the maid's mind.

"These flying machines are stupid," murmured Barbara; "the pleasure's in one's body—wings!"

"I can see Lady Casterley in the garden."

Barbara sprang out of bed. Close by the statue of Diana Lady Casterley was standing, gazing down at some flowers, a tiny, grey figure. Barbara sighed. With her, in her dream, had been another buzzard hawk, and she was filled with a sort of surprise, and queer pleasure which ran down her in little shivers while she bathed and dressed.

In her haste she took no hat; and still busy with the fastening of her linen frock, hurried down the stairs and Georgian corridor, towards the garden. At the end of it she almost ran into the arms of Courtier.

Awakening early this morning, he had begun first thinking of Audrey Noel, threatened by scandal; then of his yesterday's companion, that glorious young creature, whose image had so gripped and taken possession of him. In the pleasure of this memory he had steeped himself. She was youth itself! That perfect thing, a young girl without callowness.

And his words, when she nearly ran into him, were: "The Wingèd Victory!"

Barbara's answer was equally symbolic: "A buzzard hawk! Do you know, I dreamed we were flying, Mr. Courtier."

Courtier gravely answered:

"If the gods give *me* that dream——"

From the garden door Barbara turned her head, smiled, and passed through.

Lady Casterley, in the company of little Ann, who had perceived that it was novel to be in the garden at this hour, had been scrutinizing some newly founded colonies of a flower with which she was not familiar. On seeing her granddaughter approach, she said at once:

"What is this thing?"

"Nemesia."

"Never heard of it."

"It's rather the fashion, Granny."

"Nemesia?" repeated Lady Casterley. "What has Nemesis to do with flowers? I have no patience with gardeners, and these idiotic names. Where is your hat? I like that duck's egg colour in your frock. There's a button undone." And reaching up her little spidery hand, wonderfully steady considering its age, she buttoned the top button but one of Barbara's bodice.

"You look very blooming, my dear," she said. "How far is it to this woman's cottage? We'll go there now."

"She wouldn't be up."

Lady Casterley's eyes gleamed maliciously.

"You tell me she's so nice," she said. "No nice unencumbered woman lies in bed after half-past seven. Which is the very shortest way? No, Ann, we can't take you."

Little Ann, after regarding her great-grandmother rather too intently, replied:

"Well, I can't come you see, because I've got to go."

"Very well," said Lady Casterley, "then trot along."

Little Ann, tightening her lips, walked to the next colony of Nemesia, and bent over the colonists with concentration, showing clearly that she had found something more interesting than had yet been encountered.

"Ha!" said Lady Casterley, and led on at her brisk pace towards the avenue.

All the way down the drive she discoursed on woodcraft, glancing sharply at the trees. Forestry—she said—like building, and all other pursuits which required faith and patient industry, was a lost art in this second-hand age. She had made Barbara's grandfather practise it, so that at Catton (her country place) and even at Ravensham, the trees were worth looking at. Here, at Monkland, they were monstrously neglected. To have the finest Italian cypress in the country, for example, and not take more care of it, was a downright scandal!

Barbara listened, smiling lazily. Granny was so amusing in her energy and precision, and her turns of speech, so deliberately homespun, as if she—than whom none could better use a stiff and polished phrase, or the refinements of the French language —were determined to take what liberties she liked. To the girl, haunted still by the feeling that she could fly, almost drunk on the sweet air of that summer morning, it seemed funny that anyone should be like that. Then for a second she saw her

grandmother's face in repose, off guard, grim with anxious purpose, as if questioning its hold on life; and in one of those flashes
of intuition which come to women—even when young and conquering like Barbara—she felt suddenly sorry, as though she
had caught sight of the pale spectre never yet seen by her. 'Poor
old dear,' she thought; 'what a pity to be old!'

But they had entered the footpath crossing three long meadows
which climbed up towards Mrs. Noel's. It was so golden-sweet
here amongst the million tiny saffron cups frosted with lingering
dewshine; there was such flying glory in the limes and ash-trees;
so delicate a scent from the late whins and may-flowers; and on
every tree a grey bird calling—to be sorry was not possible!

In the far corner of the first field a chestnut mare was standing, with ears pricked at some distant sound whose charm she
alone perceived. On viewing the intruders, she laid those ears
back, and a little vicious star gleamed out at the corner of her
eye. They passed her and entered the second field. Half way
across, Barbara said quietly:

"Granny, there's a bull!"

It was indeed an enormous bull, who had been standing behind
a clump of bushes. He was moving slowly towards them, still
distant about two hundred yards; a great red beast, with the
huge development of neck and front which makes the bull, of all
living creatures, the symbol of brute force.

Lady Casterley envisaged him severely.

"I dislike bulls," she said; "I think I must walk backward."

"You can't; it's too uphill."

"I am not going to turn back," said Lady Casterley. "The
bull ought not to be here. Whose fault is it? I shall speak to
someone. Stand still and look at him. We must prevent his
coming nearer."

They stood still and looked at the bull, who continued to
approach.

"It doesn't stop him," said Lady Casterley. "We must take
no notice. Give me your arm, my dear; my legs feel rather
funny."

Barbara put her arm round the little figure. They walked
on.

"I have not been used to bulls lately," said Lady Casterley.
The bull came nearer.

"Granny," said Barbara, "you must go quietly on to the stile.
When you're over I'll come too."

"Certainly not," said Lady Casterley, "we will go together. Take no notice of him; I have great faith in that."

"Granny darling, you must do as I say, please; I remember this bull, he is one of ours."

At those rather ominous words Lady Casterley gave her a sharp glance.

"I shall not go," she said. "My legs feel quite strong now. We can run, if necessary."

"So can the bull," said Barbara.

"I'm not going to leave you," muttered Lady Casterley. "If he turns vicious I shall talk to him. He won't touch *me*. You can run faster than I; so that's settled."

"Don't be absurd, dear," answered Barbara; "I am not afraid of bulls."

Lady Casterley flashed a look at her which had a gleam of amusement.

"I can feel you," she said; "you're just as trembly as I am."

The bull was now distant some eighty yards, and they were still quite a hundred yards from the stile.

"Granny," said Barbara, "if you don't go on as I tell you, I shall just leave you, and go and meet him! You mustn't be obstinate!"

Lady Casterley's answer was to grip her granddaughter round the waist; the nervous force of that thin arm was surprising.

"You will do nothing of the sort," she said. "I refuse to have anything more to do with this bull; I shall simply pay no attention."

The bull now began very slowly ambling towards them.

"Take no notice," said Lady Casterley, who was walking faster than she had ever walked before.

"The ground is level now," said Barbara; "can you run?"

"I think so," gasped Lady Casterley; and suddenly she found herself half-lifted from the ground, and, as it were, flying towards the stile. She heard a noise behind; then Barbara's voice:

"We must stop. He's on us. Get behind me."

She felt herself caught and pinioned by two arms which seemed set on the wrong way. Instinct, and a general softness told her that she was back to back with her granddaughter.

"Let me go!" she gasped; "let me go!"

And suddenly she felt herself being propelled by that softness forward towards the stile.

"Shoo!" she said; "shoo!"

"Granny," Barbara's voice came, calm and breathless, "don't! You only excite him! Are we near the stile?"

"Ten yards," panted Lady Casterley.

"Look out, then!" There was a sort of warm flurry round her, a rush, a heave, a scramble; she was beyond the style. The bull and Barbara, a yard or two apart, were just the other side. Lady Casterley raised her handkerchief and fluttered it. The bull looked up; Barbara, all legs and arms, came slipping down beside her.

Without wasting a moment Lady Casterley leaned forward and addressed the bull:

"You awful brute!" she said; "I will have you well flogged."

Gently pawing the ground, the bull snuffled.

"Are you any the worse, child?"

"Not a scrap," said Barbara's serene, still breathless voice.

Lady Casterley put up her hands, and took the girl's face between them.

"What legs you have!" she said. "Give me a kiss!"

Having received a hot, rather quivering kiss, she walked on, holding somewhat firmly to Barbara's arm.

"As for that bull," she murmured, "the brute—to attack women!"

Barbara looked down at her.

"Granny, are you quite sure you're not shaken?"

Lady Casterley, whose lips were quivering, pressed them together very hard.

"Not a b-b-bit."

"Don't you think," said Barbara, "that we had better go back, at once—the other way?"

"Certainly not. There are no more bulls, I suppose, between us and this woman?"

"But are you fit to see her?"

Lady Casterley passed her handkerchief over her lips, to remove their quivering.

"Perfectly," she answered.

"Then, dear," said Barbara, "stand still a minute, while I dust you behind."

This having been accomplished, they proceeded in the direction of Mrs. Noel's cottage.

At sight of it, Lady Casterley said:

"I shall put my foot down. It's out of the question for a

man of Miltoun's prospects. I look forward to seeing him Prime Minister some day." Hearing Barbara's voice murmuring above her, she paused: " What's that you say? "

" I said: What is the use of our being what we are, if we can't love whom we like? "

" Love! " said Lady Casterley; " I was talking of marriage."

" I'm glad you admit the distinction, Granny dear."

" You are pleased to be sarcastic," said Lady Casterley. " Listen to me! It's the greatest nonsense to suppose that people in our caste are free to do as they please. The sooner you realise that, the better, Babs. I am talking to you seriously. The preservation of our position as a class depends on our observing certain decencies. What do you imagine would happen to the Royal Family if they were allowed to marry as they liked? All this marrying with Gaiety girls, and American money, and people with pasts, and writers, and so forth, is most damaging. There's far too much of it, and it ought to be stopped. It may be tolerated for a few cranks, or silly young men, and these new women, but for Eustace——" Lady Casterley paused again, and her fingers pinched Barbara's arm, "or for you—there's only one sort of marriage possible. As for Eustace, I shall speak to this good lady, and see that he doesn't get entangled further."

Absorbed in the intensity of her purpose, she did not observe a peculiar little smile playing round Barbara's lips.

" You had better speak to Nature, too, Granny! "

Lady Casterley stopped short, and looked up in her granddaughter's face.

" Now what do you mean by that? " she said: " Tell me! "

But noticing that Barbara's lips had closed tightly, she gave her arm a hard—if unintentional—pinch, and walked on.

CHAPTER XII

LADY CASTERLEY's rather malicious diagnosis of Audrey Noel was correct. The unencumbered woman was up and in her garden when Barbara and her grandmother appeared at the wicket gate; but being near the lime-tree at the far end she did not hear the rapid colloquy which passed between them.

"You are going to be good, Granny?"

"As to that—it will depend."

"You promised."

"H'm!"

Lady Casterley could not possibly have provided herself with a better introduction than Barbara, whom Mrs. Noel never met without the sheer pleasure felt by a sympathetic woman when she sees embodied in someone else that "joy in life" which Fate has not permitted to herself.

She came forward with her head a little on one side, a trick of hers not at all affected, and stood waiting.

The unembarrassed Barbara began at once:

"We've just had an encounter with a bull. This is my grandmother, Lady Casterley."

The little old lady's demeanour, confronted with this very pretty face and figure, was a thought less autocratic and abrupt than usual. Her shrewd eyes saw at once that she had no common adventuress to deal with. She was woman of the world enough, too, to know that "birth" was not what it had been in her young days, that even money was rather rococo, and that good looks, manners, and a knowledge of literature, art, and music (and this woman looked like one of that sort), were often considered socially more valuable. She was therefore both wary and affable.

"How do you do?" she said. "I have heard of you. May we sit down for a minute in your garden? The bull was a wretch!"

But even in speaking, she was uneasily conscious that Mrs. Noel's clear eyes were seeing very well what she had come for. The look in them indeed was almost cynical; and in spite of her sympathetic murmurs, she did not somehow seem to believe in the bull. This was disconcerting. Why had Barbara condescended to mention the wretched brute? And she decided to take him by the horns.

"Babs," she said, "go to the Inn and order me a ' fly.' I shall drive back, I feel very shaky," and, as Mrs. Noel offered to send her maid, she added: " No, no, my granddaughter will go."

Barbara having departed with a quizzical look, Lady Casterley patted the rustic seat, and said: " Do come and sit down, I want to talk to you."

Mrs. Noel obeyed. And at once Lady Casterley perceived that she had a most difficult task before her. She had not expected a woman with whom one could take no liberties. Those clear dark eyes, and that soft, perfectly graceful manner—to a person so "sympathetic" one should be able to say anything, and—one couldn't. It was awkward. And suddenly she noticed that Mrs. Noel was sitting perfectly upright, as upright—more upright, than she was herself. A bad sign—a very bad sign! Taking out her handkerchief, she put it to her lips.

" I suppose you think," she said, " that we were not chased by a bull."

" I am sure you were."

" Indeed! But you're quite right—I've something else to talk to you about."

Mrs. Noel's face quivered back, as a flower might when it was going to be plucked; and again Lady Casterley put her handkerchief to her lips. This time she rubbed them hard. There was nothing to come off; to do so, therefore, was a satisfaction.

" I am an old woman," she said, " and you mustn't mind what I say."

Mrs. Noel did not answer, but looked straight at her visitor; to whom it seemed suddenly that this was another person. What was it about that face, staring at her! In a weird way it reminded her of a child whom one had hurt—with those great eyes and that soft hair, and the mouth thin, in a line, all of a sudden. And as if it had been jerked out of her, she said:

" I don't want to hurt you, my dear. It's about my grandson, of course."

But Mrs. Noel made neither sign nor motion; and the feeling of irritation which so rapidly attacks the old when confronted by the unexpected, came to Lady Casterley's aid.

" His name," she said, " is being coupled with yours in a way that's doing him a great deal of harm. You don't wish to injure him, I'm sure."

Mrs. Noel shook her head, and Lady Casterley went on:

"I don't know what they're not saying since the evening your friend Mr. Courtier hurt his knee. Miltoun has been most unwise. You had not perhaps realised that."

Mrs. Noel's answer was bitterly distinct:

"I didn't know anyone was sufficiently interested in my doings."

Lady Casterley suffered a gesture of exasperation to escape her.

"Good heavens!" she said; "every common person is interested in a woman whose position is anomalous. Living alone as you do, and not a widow, you're fair game for everybody, especially in the country."

Mrs. Noel's sidelong glance, very clear and cynical, seemed to say: 'Even for you.'

"I am not entitled to ask your story," Lady Casterley went on, "but if you make mysteries you must expect the worst interpretation put on them. My grandson is a man of the highest principle; he does not see things with the eyes of the world, and that should have made you doubly careful not to compromise him, especially at a time like this."

Mrs. Noel smiled. This smile startled Lady Casterley; it seemed, by concealing everything, to reveal depths of strength and subtlety. Would the woman never show her hand? And she said abruptly:

"Anything serious, of course, is out of the question."

"Quite."

That word, which of all others seemed the right one, was spoken so that Lady Casterley did not know in the least what it meant. Though occasionally employing irony, she detested it in others. No woman should be allowed to use it as a weapon! But in these days, when they were so foolish as to want votes, one never knew what women would be at. This particular woman, however, did not look like one of that sort. She was feminine—very feminine—the sort of creature that spoiled men by being too nice to them. And though she had come determined to find out all about everything and put an end to it, she saw Barbara re-entering the wicket gate with considerable relief.

"I am ready to walk home now," she said. And getting up from the rustic seat, she made Mrs. Noel a satirical little bow.

"Thank you for letting me rest. Give me your arm, child."

Barbara gave her arm, and over her shoulder threw a swift smile at Mrs. Noel, who did not answer it, but stood looking quietly after them, her eyes very dark.

Out in the lane Lady Casterley walked on, silent, digesting her emotions.

"What about the 'fly,' Granny?"

"What 'fly'?"

"The one you told me to order."

"You don't mean to say that you took me seriously?"

"No," said Barbara.

"Ha!"

They proceeded some little way farther before Lady Casterley said suddenly:

"She is deep."

"And dark," said Barbara. "I am afraid you were not good!"

Lady Casterley glanced upwards.

"I detest this habit," she said, "amongst you young people, of taking nothing seriously. Not even bulls," she added, with a grim smile.

Barbara threw back her head and sighed.

"Nor 'flys,'" she said.

Lady Casterley saw that she had closed her eyes and opened her lips. And she thought:

'She's a very beautiful girl. I had no idea she was so beautiful—but too big!' And she added aloud:

"Shut your mouth! You will get one down!"

They spoke no more till they had entered the avenue; then Lady Casterley said sharply:

"Who is this coming down the drive?"

"Mr. Courtier, I think."

"What does he mean by it, with that leg?"

"He is coming to talk to you, Granny."

Lady Casterley stopped short.

"You are a cat," she said; "a sly cat. Now mind, Babs, I won't have it!"

"No, darling," murmured Barbara; "you shan't have it— I'll take him off your hands."

"What does your mother mean," stammered Lady Casterley, "letting you grow up like this! You're as bad as she was at your age!"

" Worse ! " said Barbara. " I dreamed last night that I could fly ! "

" If you try that," said Lady Casterley grimly, " you'll soon come to grief. Good morning, sir; you ought to be in bed ! "

Courtier raised his hat.

" Surely it is not for me to be where you are not ! " And he added gloomily : " The war scare's dead ! "

" Ah ! " said Lady Casterley : " your occupation's gone then. You'll go back to London now, I suppose." Looking suddenly at Barbara she saw that the girl's eyes were half-closed, and that she was smiling; it seemed to Lady Casterley too—or was it fancy?—that she shook her head.

CHAPTER XIII

THANKS to Lady Valleys, a patroness of birds, no owl was ever shot on the Monkland Court estate, and these soft-flying spirits of the dusk hooted and hunted, to the great benefit of all except the creeping voles. By every farm, cottage, and field, they passed invisible, quartering the dark air. Their voyages of discovery stretched up on to the moor as far as the wild stone man, whose origin their wisdom perhaps knew. Round Audrey Noel's cottage they were thick as thieves, for they had just there two habitations in a long, old, holly-grown wall, and almost seemed to be guarding the mistress of that thatched dwelling—so numerous were their fluttering rushes, so tenderly prolonged their soft sentinel callings. Now that the weather was really warm, so that joy of life was in the voles, they found those succulent creatures of an extraordinarily pleasant flavour, and on them each pair was bringing up a family of exceptionally fine little owls, very solemn, with big heads, bright large eyes, and wings as yet only able to fly downwards. There was scarcely any hour from noon of the day (for some of them had horns) to the small sweet hours when no one heard them, that they forgot to salute the very large, quiet, wingless owl whom they could espy moving about by day above their mouse-runs, or preening her white and sometimes blue and sometimes grey feathers morning and evening in a large square hole high up in the front wall. And they could not understand at all why no swift depredating graces nor any habit of long soft hooting belonged to that lady-bird.

On the evening of the day when she received that early morning call, as soon as dusk had fallen, wrapped in a long thin cloak, with black lace over her dark hair, Audrey Noel herself fluttered out into the lanes, as if to join the grave winged hunters of the invisible night. Those far, continual sounds, not still in the country till long after the sun dies, had but just ceased from haunting the air, where the late May-scent clung as close as fragrance clings to a woman's robe. There was just the barking of a dog, the boom of migrating chafers, the song of the stream, and of the owls, to proclaim the beating in the heart of this dark Night. Nor was there any light by which

562

Night's face could be seen; it was hidden, anonymous; so that when a lamp in a cottage threw a blink over the opposite bank, it was as if some wandering painter had wrought a picture of stones and leaves on the black air, framed it in purple, and left it hanging. Yet, if it could only have been come at, the Night was as full of emotion as this woman who wandered, shrinking away against the banks if anyone passed, stopping to cool her hot face with the dew on the ferns, walking swiftly to console her warm heart. Anonymous Night seeking for a symbol could have found none better than this errant figure, to express its hidden longings, the fluttering, unseen rushes of its dark wings, and all its secret passion of revolt against its own anonymity. . . .

At Monkland Court, save for little Ann, the morning passed but dumbly, everyone feeling that something must be done, and no one knowing what. At lunch, the only allusion to the situation had been Harbinger's inquiry:

"When does Miltoun return?"

He had wired, it seemed, to say that he was motoring down that night.

"The sooner the better," Sir William murmured: "we've still a fortnight."

But all had felt from the tone in which he spoke these words, how serious was the position in the eyes of that experienced campaigner.

What with the collapse of the war scare, and this canard about Mrs. Noel, there was indeed cause for alarm.

The afternoon post brought a letter from Lord Valleys marked *Express*.

Lady Valleys opened it with a slight grimace, which deepened as she read. Her handsome, florid face wore an expression of sadness seldom seen there. There was, in fact, more than a touch of dignity in her reception of the unpalatable news.

"Eustace declares his intention of marrying this Mrs. Noel" —so ran her husband's letter—"I know, unfortunately, of no way in which I can prevent him. If you can discover legitimate means of dissuasion, it would be well to use them. My dear, it's the very devil."

It *was* the very devil! For, if Miltoun had already made up his mind to marry her, without knowledge of the malicious rumour, what would not be his determination now? And the woman of the world rose up in Lady Valleys. This marriage must not come off. It was contrary to almost every instinct of one who was practical not only by character, but by habit of life and training. Her warm and full-blooded nature had a sneaking sympathy with love and pleasure, and had she not been practical, she might have found this side of her a serious drawback to the main tenor of a life so much in view of the public eye. Her consciousness of this danger in her own case made her extremely alive to the risks of an undesirable connection—especially if it were a marriage—to any public man. At the same time the mother-heart in her was stirred. Eustace had never been so deep in her affection as Bertie, still he was her first-born; and in face of news which meant that he was lost to her—for this must indeed be "the marriage of two minds" (or whatever that quotation was)—she felt strangely jealous of a woman, who had won her son's love, when she herself had never won it. The aching of the jealousy gave her face for a moment almost a spiritual expression, then passed away into impatience. Why should he marry her? Things could be arranged. People spoke of it already as an illicit relationship; well then, let people have what they had invented. If the worst came to the worst, this was not the only constituency in England; and a dissolution could not be far off. Better anything than a marriage which would handicap him all his life! But would it be so great a handicap? After all, beauty counted for much! If only her story were not too conspicuous! But what *was* her story? Not to know it was absurd! That was the worst of people who were not in Society, it was so difficult to find out! And there rose in her that almost brutal resentment, which ferments very rapidly in those who from their youth up have been hedged round with the belief that they and they alone are the whole of the world. In this mood Lady Valleys passed the letter to her daughters. They read, and in turn handed it to Bertie, who in silence returned it to his mother.

But that evening, in the billiard-room, having manœuvred to get him to herself, Barbara said to Courtier:

"I wonder if you will answer me a question, Mr. Courtier?"

"If I may, and can."

Her low-cut dress was of yew-green, with little threads of flame-colour, matching her hair, so that there was about her a splendour of darkness and whiteness and gold, almost dazzling; and she stood very still, leaning back against the lighter green of the billiard table, grasping its edge so tightly that the smooth strong backs of her hands quivered.

"We have just heard that Miltoun is going to ask Mrs. Noel to marry him. People are never mysterious, are they, without good reason? I wanted you to tell me—who is she?"

"I don't think I quite grasp the situation," murmured Courtier. "You said—to *marry* him?"

Seeing that she had put out her hand, as if begging for the truth, he added: "How can your brother marry her—she's married!"

"Oh!"

"I'd no idea you didn't know that much."

"We thought there was a divorce."

The expression of which mention has been made—that peculiar white-hot sardonically jolly look—visited Courtier's face at once. "Hoist with their own petard! The usual thing. Let a pretty woman live alone—the tongues of men will do the rest."

"It was not so bad as that," said Barbara dryly; "they said she had divorced her husband."

Caught out thus characteristically riding past the hounds Courtier bit his lips.

"You had better hear the story now. Her father was a country parson, and a friend of my father's; so that I've known her from a child. Stephen Lees Noel was his curate. It was a ' snap ' marriage—she was only twenty, and had met hardly any men. Her father was ill and wanted to see her settled before he died. Well, she found out almost directly, like a good many other people, that she'd made an utter mistake."

Barbara came a little closer.

"What was the man like?"

"Not bad in his way, but one of those narrow, conscientious pig-headed fellows who make the most trying kind of husband—tone egoistic. A parson of that type has no chance at all. Every mortal thing he has to do or say helps him to develop his worst points. The wife of a man like that's no better than a slave. She began to show the strain of it at last; though she's the sort who goes on till she snaps. It took him four years to realise. Then, the question was, what were they to do? He's very High Churchman, with all their feeling about marriage; but luckily his pride was wounded. Anyway, they separated two years ago; and there she is, left high and dry. People say it was her fault. She ought to have known her own mind—at twenty! She ought to have held on and hidden it up somehow. Confound their thick-skinned charitable souls, what do they know of how a sensitive woman suffers? Forgive me, Lady Barbara—I get hot over this." He was silent; then seeing her eyes fixed on him, went on: " Her mother died when she was born, her father soon after her marriage. She's enough money of her own, luckily, to live on quietly. As for him, he changed his parish and runs one somewhere in the Midlands. One's sorry for the poor devil, too, of course! They never see each other; and, so far as I know, they don't correspond. That, Lady Barbara, is the simple history."

Barbara said, " Thank you," and turned away; and he heard her mutter: " What a shame! "

But he could not tell whether it was Mrs. Noel's fate, or the husband's fate, or the thought of Miltoun that had moved her to those words.

She puzzled him by her self-possession, so almost hard, her way of refusing to show feeling. Yet what a woman she would make if the drying curse of high-caste life were not allowed to stereotype and shrivel her! If enthusiasm were suffered to penetrate and fertilise her soul! She reminded him of a great tawny lily. He had a vision of her, as that flower, floating, freed of roots and the mould of its cultivated soil, in the liberty of the impartial air. What a passionate and noble thing she might become! What radiance and perfume she would exhale! A spirit Fleur-de-Lys! Sister to all the noble flowers of light that inhabited the wind!

Leaning in the deep embrasure of his window, he looked at anonymous Night. He could hear the owls hoot, and feel a heart beating out there somewhere in the darkness, but there came no answer to his wondering. Would she—this great tawny lily of a girl—ever become unconscious of her environment, not in manner merely, but in the very soul, so that she might be just a woman, breathing, suffering, loving, and rejoicing with the poet soul of all mankind? Would she ever be capable of riding out with the little company of big hearts, naked of advantage? Courtier had not been inside a church for twenty years, having long felt that he must not enter the mosques of his country without putting off the shoes of freedom, but he read the Bible, considering it a very great poem. And the old words came haunting him: " Verily I say unto you, It is easier for a camel to pass through the eye of a needle than for a rich man to enter the kingdom of Heaven." And now, looking into the Night, whose darkness seemed to hold the answer to all secrets, he tried to read the riddle of this girl's future, with which there seemed so interwoven that larger enigma, how far the spirit can free itself, in this life, from the matter that encompasseth.

The night whispered suddenly, and low down, as if rising from the sea, came the moon, dropping a wan robe of light till she gleamed out nude against the sky-curtain. Night was no longer anonymous. There in the dusky garden the statue of Diana formed slowly before his eyes, and behind her—as it were, her temple—rose the tall spire of the cypress-tree.

CHAPTER XIV

A COPY of the *Bucklandbury News* containing an account of his evening adventure, did not reach Miltoun till he was just starting on his return journey. It came marked with blue pencil together with a note.

" MY DEAR EUSTACE,
    " The enclosed—however unwarranted and impudent—requires attention. But we shall do nothing till you come back.
            " Yours ever,
                    " WILLIAM SHROPTON."

The effect on Miltoun might perhaps have been different had he not been so conscious of his intention to ask Audrey Noel to be his wife; but in any circumstances it is doubtful whether he would have done more than smile, and tear the paper up. Truly that sort of thing had so little power to hurt or disturb him personally, that he was incapable of seeing how it could hurt or disturb others. If those who read it were affected, so much the worse for them. He had a real, if unobtrusive, contempt for groundlings, of whatever class; and it never entered his head to step an inch out of his course in deference to their vagaries. Nor did it come home to him that Mrs. Noel, wrapped in the glamour which he cast about her, could possibly suffer from the meanness of vulgar minds. Shropton's note, indeed, caused him the more annoyance of those two documents. It was like his brother-in-law to make much of little!

He hardly dozed at all during his swift journey through the sleeping country; nor when he reached his room at Monkland did he go to bed. He had the wonderful, upborne feeling of man on the verge of achievement. His spirit and senses were both on fire—for that was the quality of this woman, she suffered no part of him to sleep, and he was glad of her exactions.

He drank some tea, went out, and took a path up to the moor. It was not yet eight o'clock when he reached the top of the nearest tor. And there, below him, around, and above, was a land and sky transcending even his exaltation. It was like a symphony of great music; or the nobility of a stupendous mind laid bare; it was God up there, in His many moods. Serenity was spread in the middle heavens, blue, illimitable; and along to the East, three huge clouds, like thoughts brooding over the destinies below, moved slowly toward the sea, so that great shadows filled the valleys. And the land that lay under all the other sky was gleaming and quivering with every colour, as it were, clothed with the divine smile. The wind, from the North, whereon floated the white birds of the smaller clouds, had no voice, for it was above barriers, utterly free. Before Miltoun, turning to this wind, lay the maze of the lower lands, the misty greens, rose pinks, and browns of the fields, and white and grey dots and strokes of cottages and church towers, fading into the blue veil of distance, confined by a far range of hills. Behind him there was nothing but the restless surface of the moor, coloured purplish-brown. On that untamed sea of graven wildness could be seen no ship of man, save one, on the far horizon —the grim hulk, Dartmoor Prison. There was no sound, no scent, and it seemed to Miltoun as if his spirit had left his body, and become part of the solemnity of God. Yet, while he stood there, with his head bared, the strange smile which haunted him in moments of deep feeling, showed that he had not surrendered to the Universal, that his own spirit was but being fortified, and that this was the true and secret source of his delight. He lay down in a scoop of the stones. The sun entered there, but no wind, so that a dry sweet scent exuded from the young shoots of heather. That warmth and perfume crept through the shield of his spirit, and stole into his blood; ardent images rose before him, the vision of an unending embrace. Out of an embrace sprang Life, out of that the World was made, this World, with its innumerable forms, and natures—no two alike! And from him and her would spring forms to take their place in the great pattern! This seemed wonderful, and right—for they would be worthy forms, who would hand on those traditions which seemed to him so necessary and great. And then there broke on him one of those delirious waves of natural desire, against which he had so often fought, so often with great pain conquered. He got up, and ran downhill, leaping over the stones, and the thicker clumps of heather.

Audrey Noel, too, had been early astir, though she had gone late enough to bed. She dressed languidly, but very carefully, being one of those women who put on armour against Fate, because they are proud, and dislike the thought that their sufferings should make others suffer; because, too, their bodies are to them as it were sacred, having been given them in trust, to cause delight. When she had finished, she looked at herself in the glass rather more distrustfully than usual. She felt that her sort of woman was at a discount in these days, and being sensitive, she was never content either with her appearance, or her habits. But, for all that, she went on behaving in unsatisfactory ways, because she incorrigibly loved to look as charming as she could; and even if no one were going to see her, she never felt that she looked charming enough. She was—as Lady Casterley had shrewdly guessed—the kind of woman who spoils men by being too nice to them; of no use to those who wish women to assert themselves; yet having a certain passive stoicism, very disconcerting. With little or no power of initiative, she would do what she was set to do with a thoroughness that would shame an initiator; temperamentally unable to beg anything of anybody, she required love as a plant requires water; she could give herself completely, yet remain oddly incorruptible; in a word, hopeless, and usually beloved of those who thought her so. With all this, however, she was not quite what is called a "sweet woman"—a phrase she detested—for there was in her a queer vein of gentle cynicism. She "saw" with extraordinary clearness, as if she had been born in Italy and still carried that clear dry atmosphere about her soul. She loved glow and warmth and colour; such mysticism as she felt was pagan; and she had few aspirations—sufficient to her were things as they showed themselves to be.

This morning, when she had made herself smell of geraniums, and fastened all the small contrivances that hold even the best of women together, she went downstairs to her little dining-room, set the spirit lamp going, and taking up her newspaper, stood waiting to make tea.

It was the hour of the day most dear to her. If the dew had been brushed off her life, it was still out there every morning on the face of Nature, and on the faces of her flowers; there was before her all the pleasure of seeing how each of those little creatures in the garden had slept; how many children had been born since the Dawn; who was ailing, and needed attention. There was also the feeling, which renews itself every morning in people who live lonely lives, that they are not lonely, until, the day wearing on, assures them of the fact. Not that she was idle, for she had obtained through Courtier the work of reviewing music in a woman's paper, for which she was intuitively fitted. This, her flowers, her own music, and the affairs of certain families of cottagers, filled nearly all her time. And she asked no better fate than to have every minute occupied, having that passion for work requiring no initiation, which is natural to the owners of lazy minds.

Suddenly she dropped her newspaper, went to the bowl of flowers on the breakfast-table, and plucked forth two stalks of lavender; holding them away from her, she went out into the garden, and flung them over the wall.

This strange immolation of those two poor sprigs, born so early, gathered and placed before her with such kind intention by her maid, seemed of all acts the least to be expected of one who hated to hurt people's feelings, and whose eyes always shone at the sight of flowers. But in truth the smell of lavender— that scent carried on her husband's handkerchief and clothes— still affected her so strongly that she could not bear to be in a room with it. As nothing else did, it brought before her one, to live with whom had slowly become torture. And freed by that scent, the whole flood of memory broke in on her. The memory of three years when her teeth had been set doggedly on her discovery that she was chained to unhappiness for life; the memory of the abrupt end, and of her creeping away to let her scorched nerves recover. Of how during the first year of this release which was not freedom, she had twice changed her abode, to get away from her own story—not because she was ashamed of it, but because it reminded her of wretchedness. Of how she had then come to Monkland, where the quiet life had slowly given her elasticity again. And then of her meeting with Miltoun; the unexpected delight of that companionship; the frank enjoyment of the first four months. And she remembered all her secret rejoicing, her silent identification of another life with her own, before she acknowledged or even suspected love. And just three weeks ago now, helping to tie up her roses, he had touched her, and she had known. But even then, until the night of Courtier's accident, she had not dared to realise. More concerned now for him than for herself, she asked herself a thousand times if she had been to blame. She had let him grow fond of her, a woman out of court, a dead woman! An unpardonable sin! Yet surely that depended on what she was prepared to give! And she was frankly ready to give everything, and ask for nothing. He knew her position, he had told her that he knew. In her love for him she gloried, would continue to glory; would suffer for it without regret. Miltoun was right in believing that newspaper gossip was incapable of hurting her, though her reasons for being so impervious were not what he supposed. She was not, like him, secured from pain because such insinuations about the private affairs of others were mean and vulgar and beneath notice; it had not as yet occurred to her to look at the matter in so lofty and general a light; she simply was not hurt, because she was already so deeply Miltoun's property in spirit, that she was almost glad that they should assign him all the rest of her. But for Miltoun's sake she was disturbed to the soul. She had tarnished his shield in the eyes of men; and (for she was oddly practical, and saw things in very clear proportion) perhaps put back his career, who knew for how many years!

She sat down to drink her tea. Not being a crying woman, she suffered quietly. She felt that Miltoun would be coming to her. She did not know at all what she should say when he did come. He could not care for her so much as she cared for him! He was a man; men soon forget! Ah! but he was not like most men. One could not look at his eyes without feeling that he could suffer terribly! In all this her own reputation concerned her not at all. Life, and her clear way of looking at things, had rooted in her the conviction that to a woman the preciousness of her reputation was a fiction invented by men entirely for man's benefit; a second-hand fetish insidiously, inevitably set up by men for worship, in novels, plays, and law-courts. Her instinct told her that men could not feel secure in the possession of their women unless they could believe that women set tremendous store by sexual reputation. What they wanted to believe, that they did believe! But she knew otherwise. Such great-minded women as she had met or read of had always left on her the impression that reputation for them was a matter of the spirit, having little to do with sex. From her own feelings she knew that reputation, for a simple woman, meant to stand well in the eyes of him or her whom she loved best. For worldly women—and there were so many kinds of those, besides the merely fashionable—she had always noted that its value was not intrinsic, but commercial; not a crown of dignity, but just a marketable asset. She did not dread in the least what people might say of her friendship with Miltoun;

nor did she feel at all that her indissoluble marriage forbade her loving him. She had secretly felt free as soon as she had discovered that she had never really loved her husband; she had only gone on dutifully, until the separation, from sheer passivity and because it was against her nature to cause pain to anyone. The man who was still her husband was now as dead to her as if he had never been born. She could not marry again, it was true; but she could and did love. If that love was to be starved and die away, it would not be because of any moral scruples.

She opened her paper languidly; and almost the first words she read, under the heading of Election News, were these:

"Apropos of the outrage on Mr. Courtier, we are requested to state that the lady who accompanied Lord Miltoun to the rescue of that gentleman was Mrs. Lees Noel, wife of the Rev. Stephen Lees Noel, vicar of Clathampton, Warwickshire."

This dubious little daub of whitewash only brought a rather sad smile to her lips. She left her tea, and went out into the air. There at the gate was Miltoun coming in. Her heart leaped. But she went forward quietly, and greeted him with cast-down eyes, as if nothing were out of the ordinary.

CHAPTER XV

EXALTATION had not left Miltoun. His sallow face was flushed, his eyes glowed with a sort of beauty; and Audrey Noel who, better than most women, could read what was passing behind a face, saw those eyes with the delight of a moth fluttering towards a lamp. But in a very unemotional voice she said:

"So you have come to breakfast. How nice of you!"

It was not in Miltoun to observe the formalities of attack. Had he been going to fight a duel there would have been no preliminary, just a look, a bow, and the swords crossed. So in this first engagement of his with the soul of a woman!

He neither sat down nor suffered her to sit, but stood looking intently into her face, and said:

"I love you."

Now that it had come, with this disconcerting swiftness, she was strangely calm, and unashamed. The elation of knowing for sure that she was loved was like a wand waving away all tremors, stilling them to sweetness. Since nothing could take away that knowledge, it seemed that she could never again be utterly unhappy. Then, too, in her nature, so deeply, unreasoningly incapable of perceiving the importance of any principle but love, there was a secret feeling of assurance, of triumph. He *did* love her! And she, him! Well! And suddenly panic-stricken, lest he should take back those words, she put her hand up to his breast, and said:

"And I love you."

The feel of his arms round her, the strength and passion of that moment, were so terribly sweet, that she died to thought, just looking up at him, with lips parted and eyes darker with the depth of her love than he had ever dreamed that eyes could be. The madness of his own feeling kept him silent. And they stood there, so merged in one another that they knew and cared nothing for any other mortal thing. It was very still in the room; the roses and carnations in the lustre bowl, seeming to know that their mistress was caught up into heaven, had let their perfume steal forth and occupy every cranny of the abandoned air; a hovering bee, too, circled round the lovers' heads, scenting, it seemed, the honey in their hearts.

It has been said that Miltoun's face was not unhandsome; for Audrey Noel at this moment when his eyes were so near hers, and his lips touching her, he was transfigured, and had become the spirit of all beauty. And she, with heart beating fast against him, her eyes, half closing from delight, and her hair asking to be praised with its fragrance, her cheeks fainting pale with emotion, and her arms too languid with happiness to embrace him—she, to him, was the incarnation of the woman who visits dreams.

So passed that moment.

The bee ended it; impatient with flowers that hid their honey so deep, he was entangled in Audrey's hair. Then, seeing that words, those dreaded things, were on his lips, she tried to kiss them back.

"When will you marry me?"

It all swayed a little. And with marvellous rapidity the whole position started up before her. She saw, with preternatural insight, into its nooks and corners. Something he had said one day, when they were talking of the Church view of marriage and divorce, lighted all up. So he had really never known about her! At this moment of utter sickness, she was saved from fainting by her sense of humour—her cynicism. Not content to let her be, people's tongues had divorced her; he had believed them! And the crown of irony was that he should want to marry her, when she felt so utterly, so sacredly his, to do what he liked with *sans* forms or ceremonies. A surge of bitter feeling against the man who stood between her and Miltoun almost made her cry out. That man had captured her before she knew the world or her own soul, and she was tied to him, till by some beneficent chance he drew his last breath—when her hair was grey, and her eyes had no love light, and her cheeks no longer grew pale when they were kissed; when twilight had fallen, and the flowers, and bees no longer cared for her.

It was that feeling, the sudden revolt of the desperate prisoner, which steeled her to put out her hand, take up the paper, and give it to Miltoun.

When he had read the little paragraph, there followed one of those eternities which last perhaps two minutes.

He said, then:

"It's true, I suppose?" And, at her silence, added: "I am sorry."

This queer dry saying was so much more terrible than any outcry, that she remained, deprived even of the power of breathing, with her eyes still fixed on Miltoun's face.

The smile of the old Cardinal had come up there, and was to her like a living accusation. It seemed strange that the hum of the bees and flies and the gentle swishing of the lime-tree should still go on outside, insisting that there was a world moving and breathing apart from her, and careless of her misery. Then some of her courage came back, and with it her woman's mute power. It came haunting about her face, perfectly still, about her lips, sensitive and drawn, about her eyes, dark, almost mutinous under their arched brows. She stood, drawing him with silence and beauty.

At last he spoke:

" I have made a foolish mistake, it seems. I believed you were free."

Her lips just moved for the words to pass: " I thought you knew. I never dreamed you would want to marry me."

It seemed to her natural that he should be thinking only of himself, but with the subtlest defensive instinct, she put forward her own tragedy:

" I suppose I had got too used to knowing I was dead."

" Is there no release? "

" None. We have neither of us done wrong; besides with *him,* marriage is—for ever."

" My God ! "

She had broken his smile, which had been cruel without meaning to be cruel; and with a smile of her own that was cruel too, she said:

" I didn't know that *you* believed in release either."

Then, as though she had stabbed herself in stabbing him, her face quivered.

He looked at her now, conscious at last that she was suffering. And she felt that he was holding himself in with all his might from taking her again into his arms. Seeing this, the warmth crept back to her lips, and a little light into her eyes, which she kept hidden from him. Though she stood so proudly still, some wistful force was coming from her, as from a magnet, and Miltoun's hands and arms and face twitched as though palsied. This struggle, dumb and pitiful, seemed never to be coming to an end in the little white room, darkened by the thatch of the verandah, and sweet with the scent of pinks and of a wood fire just lighted somewhere out at the back. Then, without a word, he turned and went out. She heard the wicket gate swing to. He was gone.

CHAPTER XVI

LORD DENNIS was fly-fishing—the weather just too bright to allow the little trout of that shallow, never silent stream to accept with avidity the small enticements which he threw in their direction. Nevertheless he continued to invite them, exploring every nook of their watery pathway with his soft-swishing line. In a rough suit and battered hat adorned with those artificial and other flies, which infest Harris tweed, he crept along among the hazel bushes and thorn-trees, perfectly happy. Like an old spaniel, who has once gloried in the fetching of hares, rabbits, and all manner of fowl, and is now glad if you will but throw a stick for him, so one, who had been a famous fisher before the Lord, who had harried the waters of Scotland and Norway, Florida and Iceland, now pursued trout no bigger than sardines. The glamour of a thousand memories hallowed the hours he thus spent by that brown water. He fished unhasting, religious, like some good Catholic adding one more to the row of beads already told, as though he would fish himself, gravely, without complaint, into the other world. With each fish caught he experienced a solemn satisfaction.

Though he would have liked Barbara with him that morning, he had only looked at her once after breakfast in such a way that she could not see him, and with a dry smile gone off by himself. Down by the stream it was dappled, both cool and warm, windless; the trees met over the river, and there were many stones, forming little basins which held up the ripple, so that the casting of a fly required much cunning. This long dingle ran for miles through the foot-growth of folding hills. It was beloved of jays; but of human beings there were none, except a chicken-farmer's widow, who lived in a house thatched almost to the ground, and made her livelihood by directing tourists, with such cunning that they soon came back to her for tea.

It was while throwing a rather longer line than usual to reach a little dark piece of crisp water that Lord Dennis heard the swishing and crackling of someone advancing at full speed. He frowned slightly, feeling for the nerves of his fishes, whom he did not wish startled. The invader was Miltoun, hot, pale, dishevelled, with a queer, hunted look on his face. He stopped on seeing his great-uncle, and instantly assumed the mask of his smile.

Lord Dennis was not the man to see what was not intended for him, and he merely said:

"Well, Eustace!" as he might have spoken, meeting his nephew in the hall of one of his London Clubs.

Miltoun, no less polite, murmured:

"Hope I haven't lost you anything."

Lord Dennis shook his head, and laying his rod on the bank, said:

"Sit down and have a chat, old fellow. You don't fish, I think?"

He had not, in the least, missed the suffering behind Miltoun's mask; his eyes were still good, and there was a little matter of some twenty years' suffering of his own on account of a woman—ancient history now—which had left him quaintly sensitive, for an old man, to signs of suffering in others.

Miltoun would not have obeyed that invitation from anyone else, but there was something about Lord Dennis which people did not resist; his power lay in a dry ironic suavity which could not but persuade people that impoliteness was altogether too new and raw a thing to be indulged in.

The two sat side by side on the roots of trees. At first they talked a little of birds, and then were dumb, so dumb that the invisible creatures of the woods consulted together audibly. Lord Dennis broke that silence.

"This place," he said, "always reminds me of Mark Twain's writings—can't tell why, unless it's the evergreenness. I like the evergreen philosophers, Twain and Meredith. There's no salvation except through courage, though I never could stomach the 'strong man'—captain of his soul, Henley and Nietzsche and that sort—goes against the grain with me. What do you say, Eustace?"

"They meant well," answered Miltoun, "but they protested too much."

Lord Dennis moved his head in assent.

"To be captain of your soul!" continued Miltoun in a bitter voice; "it's a pretty phrase!"

"Pretty enough," murmured Lord Dennis.

Miltoun looked at him.

"And suitable to you," he said.

"No, my dear," Lord Dennis answered dryly, "a long way off that, thank God!"

His eyes were fixed intently on the place where a large trout had risen in the stillest coffee-coloured pool. He knew that fellow, a half-pounder at least, and his thoughts began flighting round the top of his head, hovering over the various merits of the flies. His fingers itched too, but he made no movement, and the ash-tree under which he sat let its leaves tremble, as though in sympathy.

"See that hawk?" said Miltoun.

At a height more than level with the tops of the hills a buzzard hawk was stationary in the blue directly over them. Inspired by curiosity at their stillness, he was looking down to see whether they were edible; the upcurved ends of his great wings flirted just once to show that he was part of the living glory of the air—a symbol of freedom to men and fishes.

Lord Dennis looked at his great-nephew. The boy—for what else was thirty to seventy-six?—was taking it hard, whatever it might be, taking it very hard! He was that sort—ran till he dropped. The worst kind to help—the sort that made for trouble —that let things gnaw at them! And there flashed before the old man's mind the image of Prometheus devoured by the eagle. It was his favourite tragedy, which he still read periodically, in the Greek, helping himself now and then out of his old lexicon to the meaning of some word which had flown to Erebus. Yes, Eustace was a fellow for the heights and depths!

He said quietly:

"You don't care to talk about it, I suppose?"

Miltoun shook his head, and again there was silence.

The buzzard hawk having seen them move, quivered his wings like a moth's, and deserted that plane of air. A robin from the dappled warmth of a mossy stone, was regarding them instead. There was another splash in the pool.

Lord Dennis said gently:

"That fellow's risen twice; I believe he'd take a ' Wistman's treasure.' " Extracting from his hat its latest fly, and binding it on, he began softly to swish his line.

"I shall have him yet!" he muttered. But Miltoun had stolen away. . . .

The further piece of information about Mrs. Noel, already known by Barbara, and diffused by the *Bucklandbury News,* had not become common knowledge at the Court till after Lord

Dennis had started out to fish. In combination with the report
that Miltoun had arrived and gone out without breakfast, it
had been received with mingled feelings. Bertie, Harbinger,
and Shropton, in a short conclave, after agreeing that from
the point of view of the election it was perhaps better than if
she had been a *divorcée,* were still inclined to the belief that no
time was to be lost—in doing what, however, they were unable
to determine. Apart from the impossibility of knowing how a
fellow like Miltoun would take the matter, they were faced with
the devilish subtlety of all situations to which the proverb
" Least said, soonest mended " applies. They were in the presence of that awe-inspiring thing, the power of scandal. Simple
statements of simple facts, without moral drawn (to which no
legal exception could be taken) laid before the public as pieces
of interesting information, or at the worst exposed in perfect
good faith, lest the public should blindly elect as their repre-
sentative one whose private life might not stand the inspection
of daylight—what could be more justifiable! And yet Miltoun's
supporters knew that this simple statement of where he spent
his evenings had a poisonous potency, through its power of
stimulating that side of the human imagination the most easily
excited. They recognised only too well, how strong was a certain
primitive desire, especially in rural districts, by yielding to
which the world was made to go, and how remarkably hard it
was not to yield to it, and how interesting and exciting to see or
hear of others yielding to it, and how (though here, of course,
men might differ secretly) reprehensible of them to do so! They
recognised, too well, how a certain kind of conscience would
appreciate this rumour; and how the puritans would lick their
lengthened chops. They knew, too, how irresistible to people
of any imagination at all, was the mere combination of a member of a class, traditionally supposed to be inclined to having
what it wanted, with a lady who lived alone! As Harbinger
said: It was really devilish awkward! For, to take any notice
of it would be to make more people than ever believe it true.
And yet, that it was working mischief, they felt by the secret
voice in their own souls, telling them that they would have believed it if they had not known better. They hung about, waiting for Miltoun to come in.

The news was received by Lady Valleys with a sigh of intense
relief, and the remark that it was probably another lie. When
Barbara confirmed it, she only said: " Poor Eustace ! " and

at once wrote off to her husband to say that "Anonyma" was still married, so that the worst fortunately could not happen.

Miltoun came in to lunch, but from his face and manner nothing could be guessed. He was a thought more talkative than usual, and spoke of Brabrook's speech—some of which he had heard. He looked at Courtier meaningly, and after lunch said to him:

"Will you come round to my den?"

In that room, the old withdrawing-room of the Elizabethan wing—where once had been the embroideries, tapestries, and missals of beruffled dames—were now books, pamphlets, oak-panels, pipes, fencing gear, and along one wall a collection of Red Indian weapons and ornaments brought back by Miltoun from the United States. High on the wall above these reigned the bronze death-mask of a famous Apache Chief, cast from a plaster taken of the face by a professor of Yale College, who had declared it to be a perfect specimen of the vanishing race. That visage, which had a certain weird resemblance to Dante's, presided over the room with cruel, tragic stoicism. No one could look on it without feeling that, there, the human will had been pushed to its farthest limits of endurance.

Seeing it for the first time, Courtier said:

"Fine thing—that! Only wants a soul."

Miltoun nodded.

"Sit down," he said.

Courtier sat down.

There followed one of those silences in which men—whose spirits, though different, have a certain bigness in common—can say so much to one another.

At last Miltoun spoke:

"I have been living in the clouds, it seems. You are her oldest friend. The immediate question is how to make it easiest for her in face of this miserable rumour!"

Not even Courtier himself could have put such whip-lash sting into the word "miserable."

He answered:

"Oh! take no notice of that. Let them stew in their own juice. She won't care."

Miltoun listened, not moving a muscle of his face.

"Your friends here," went on Courtier with a touch of contempt, "seem in a flutter. Don't let them do anything, don't let them say a word. Treat the thing as it deserves to be treated. It'll die."

Miltoun, however, smiled.

" I'm not sure," he said, " that the consequences will be what you think, but I shall do as you say."

" As for your candidature, any man with a spark of generosity in his soul will rally to you because of it."

" Possibly," said Miltoun. " It will lose me the election, for all that."

Then, dimly conscious that their last words had revealed the difference of their temperaments and creeds, they stared at one another.

" No," said Courtier, " I never believe people can be mean——"

" Until they are."

" Well! though we get at it in different ways, we agree."

Miltoun leaned his elbow on the mantelpiece, and shading his face with his hand, said :

" You know her story. Is there any way out of that, for her ? "

On Courtier's face was the look which so often came when he was speaking for one of his lost causes—as if the fumes from a fire in his heart had mounted to his head.

" Only the way," he answered calmly, " that I should take if I were you."

" And that ? "

" The law into your own hands."

Miltoun unshaded his face. His gaze seemed to have to travel from an immense distance before it reached Courtier. He answered :

" Yes, I thought you would say that."

CHAPTER XVII

WHEN everything, that night, was quiet, Barbara, her hair hanging loose outside her dressing gown, slipped from her room into the dim corridor. With bare feet thrust into fur-crowned slippers which made no noise, she stole along looking at door after door. Through a long Gothic window, uncurtained, the mild moonlight was coming. She stopped just where that moonlight fell, and tapped. There came no answer. She opened the door a little way, and said:

"Are you asleep, Eusty?"

There still came no answer, and she went in.

The curtains were drawn, but a chink of moonlight peering through fell on the bed. This was empty. Barbara stood uncertain, listening. In the heart of that darkness there seemed to be, not sound, but, as it were, the muffled soul of sound, a sort of strange vibration, like that of a flame noiselessly licking the air. She put her hand to her heart, which beat as though it would leap through the thin silk covering. From what corner of the room was that mute tremor coming? Stealing to the window, she parted the curtains, and stared back into the shadows. There, on the far side, lying on the floor with his arms pressed tightly round his head and his face to the wall, was Miltoun. Barbara let fall the curtains, and stood breathless, with such a queer sensation in her breast as she had never felt; a sense of something outraged—of scarred pride. It was gone at once, in a rush of pity. She stepped forward quickly in the darkness, was visited by fear, and stopped. He had seemed absolutely himself all the evening. A little more talkative, perhaps, a little more caustic than usual. And now to find him like this! There was no great share of reverence in Barbara, but what little she possessed had always been kept for her eldest brother. He had impressed her, from a child, with his aloofness, and she had been proud of kissing him because he never seemed to let anybody else do so. Those caresses, no doubt, had the savour of conquest; his face had been the undiscovered land for her lips. She loved him as one loves that which ministers to one's pride; had for him, too, a touch of motherly protection,

as for a doll that does not get on too well with the other dolls;
and withal a little unaccustomed awe.

Dared she now plunge in on this private agony? Could she
have borne that anyone should see herself thus prostrate? He
had not heard her, and she tried to regain the door. But a
board creaked; she heard him move, and flinging away her fears,
said: "It's me! Babs!" and dropped on her knees beside him.
If it had not been so pitch dark she could never have done that.
She tried at once to take his head into her arms, but could
not see it, and succeeded indifferently. She could but stroke his
arm continually, wondering whether he would hate her ever
afterwards, and blessing the darkness, which made it all seem
as though it were not happening, yet so much more poignant
than if it had happened. Suddenly she felt him slip away from
her, and getting up, stole out. After the darkness of that room,
the corridor seemed full of grey filmy light, as though dream-
spiders had joined the walls with their cobwebs, in which innumerable white moths, so tiny that they could not be seen,
were struggling. Small eerie noises crept about. A sudden
frightened longing for warmth, and light, and colour came to
Barbara. She fled back to her room. But she could not sleep.
That strange mute unseen vibration in the unlighted room—
like the noiseless licking of a flame at the air; the touch of
Miltoun's hand, fiery hot against her cheek and neck; the whole
tremulous dark episode, possessed her through and through.
Thus had the wayward force of Love chosen to manifest itself
to her in all its wistful violence. At this first sight of the red
flower of passion her cheeks burned; up and down her, between
the cool sheets, little hot cruel shivers ran; she lay, wide-eyed,
staring at the ceiling. She thought of the woman whom he so
loved, and wondered if she too were lying sleepless, flung down
on a bare floor, trying to cool her forehead and lips against a
cold wall.

Not for hours did she fall asleep, and then dreamed of running desperately through fields full of tall spiky asphodel-like
flowers, and behind her was running herself.

In the morning she dreaded to go down. Could she meet
Miltoun now that she knew of the passion in him, and he knew
that she knew it? She had her breakfast brought upstairs. Before she had finished Miltoun himself came in. He looked more
than usually self-contained, not to say ironic, and only remarked:
"If you're going to ride you might take this note for me over

to old Haliday at Wippincott." By his coming she knew that
he was saying all he ever meant to say about that dark incident.
And sympathising completely with a reticence which she herself felt to be the only possible way out for both of them, Barbara looked at him gratefully, took the note and said: "All
right!"

Then, after glancing once or twice round the room, Miltoun
went away.

He left her restless, divested of the cloak "of course," in a
strange mood of questioning, ready as it were for the sight of
the magpie wings of Life, and to hear their quick flutterings.
Talk jarred on her that morning, with its sameness and attachment to the facts of the present and the future, its essential
concern with the world as it was—she avoided all companionship
on her ride. She wanted to be told of things that were not, yet
might be, to peep behind the curtain, and see the very spirit of
mortal happenings escaped from prison. And this was all so
unusual with Barbara, whose body was too perfect, too sanely
governed by the flow of her blood not to revel in the moment
and the things thereof. She knew it was unusual. After her
ride she avoided lunch, and walked out into the lanes. But
about two o'clock, feeling very hungry, she went into a farmhouse, and asked for milk. There, in the kitchen, like young
jackdaws in a row with their mouths a little open, were the
three farm boys, seated on a bench gripped to the alcove of
the great fire-way, munching bread and cheese. Above their
heads a gun was hung, trigger upwards, and two hams were
mellowing in the smoke. At the feet of a black-haired girl, who
was slicing onions, lay a sheep dog of tremendous age, with
nose stretched out on paws,.and in his little blue eyes a gleam
of approaching immortality. They all stared at Barbara. And
one of the boys, whose face had the delightful look of him who
loses all sense of other things in what he is seeing at the moment, smiled, and continued smiling, with sheer pleasure. Barbara drank her milk, and wandered out again; passing through
a gate at the bottom of a steep, rocky tor, she sat down on a
sunwarmed stone. The sunlight fell greedily on her here, like
an invisible swift hand touching her all over, and specially
caressing her throat and face. A very gentle wind, which dived
over the tor tops into the young fern, stole down at her, spiced
with the fern sap. All was warmth and peace, and only the
cuckoos on the far thorn trees—as though stationed by the Wist-

ful Master himself—were there to disturb her heart. But all
the sweetness and piping of the day did not soothe her. In
truth, she could not have said what was the matter, except that
she felt so discontented, and, as it were, empty of all but a sort
of aching impatience with—what exactly she could not say. She
had that rather dreadful feeling of something slipping by which
she could not catch. It was so new to her to feel like that—
for no girl was less given to moods and repinings. And all the
time a sort of contempt for this soft and almost sentimental feeling made her tighten her lips and frown. She felt distrustful
and sarcastic towards a mood so subversive of that fetish
" Hardness," to the unconscious worship of which she had been
brought up. To stand no sentiment or nonsense either in herself or others was the first article of faith; not to slop-over anywhere. So that to feel as she did was almost horrible to Barbara. Yet she could not get rid of the sensation. With sudden
recklessness she tried giving herself up to it entirely. Undoing
the scarf at her throat, she let the air play on her bared neck,
and stretched out her arms as if to hug the wind to her; then,
with a sigh, she got up, and walked on. And now she began
thinking of " Anonyma "; turning her position over and over.
The idea that anyone young and beautiful should thus be clipped
off in her life, roused her impatient indignation. Let them try
it with her! They would soon see! For all her cultivated
" hardness," Barbara really hated anything to suffer. It seemed
to her unnatural. She never went to that hospital where Lady
Valleys had a ward, nor to their summer camp for crippled
children, nor to help in their annual concert for sweated workers,
without a feeling of such vehement pity that it was like being
seized by the throat. Once, when she had been singing to them,
the rows of wan, pinched faces below had been too much for her;
she had broken down, forgotten her words, lost memory of the
tune, and just ended her performance with a smile, worth more
perhaps to her audience than those lost verses. She never
came away from such sights and places without a feeling
of revolt amounting almost to rage; and she only continued
to go because she dimly knew that it was expected of
her not to turn her back on such things, in her section of
Society.

But it was not this feeling which made her stop before Mrs.
Noel's cottage; nor was it curiosity. It was a quite simple
desire to squeeze her hand.

"Anonyma" seemed taking her trouble as only those women who are no good at self-assertion can take things—doing exactly as she would have done if nothing had happened; a little paler than usual, with lips pressed rather tightly together.

They neither of them spoke at first, but stood looking, not at each other's faces, but at each other's breasts. At last Barbara stepped forward impulsively and kissed her.

After that, like two children who kiss first and then make acquaintance, they stood apart, silent, faintly smiling. It had been given and returned in real sweetness and comradeship, that kiss, for a sign of womanhood making face against the world; but now that it was over, both felt a little awkward. Would that kiss have been given if Fate had been auspicious? Was it not proof of misery? So Mrs. Noel's smile seemed saying, and Barbara's smile unwillingly admitting. Perceiving that if they talked it could only be about the most ordinary things, they began speaking of music, flowers, and the queerness of bees' legs. But all the time, Barbara, though seemingly unconscious, was noting with her smiling eyes, the tiny movements, by which one woman can tell what is passing in another. She saw a little quiver tighten the corner of the lips, the eyes suddenly grow large and dark, the thin blouse desperately rise and fall. And her fancy, quickened by last night's memory, saw this woman giving herself up to the memory of love in her thoughts. At this sight she felt a little of that impatience which the conquering feel for the passive, and perhaps just a touch of jealousy.

Whatever Miltoun decided, that would this woman accept! Such resignation, while it simplified things, offended the part of Barbara which rebelled against all inaction, all dictation, even from her favourite brother. She said suddenly:

"Are you going to do nothing? Aren't you going to try and free yourself? If I were in your position, I would never rest till I'd made them free me."

But Mrs. Noel did not answer; and sweeping her glance from that crown of soft dark, hair, down the soft white figure, to the very feet, Barbara cried:

"I believe you are a fatalist."

Soon after that, not knowing what more to say, she went away. But walking home across the fields, where full summer was swinging on the delicious air, and there was now no bull but only red cows to crop short the "milk-maids" and buttercups, she suffered from this strange revelation of the strength of softness and passivity—as though she had seen in the white figure of " Anonyma," and heard in her voice, something from beyond, symbolic, inconceivable, yet real.

CHAPTER XVIII

LORD VALLEYS, relieved from official pressure by subsidence of the war scare, had returned for a long week-end. To say that he had been intensely relieved by the news that Mrs. Noel was not free, would be to put it mildly. Though not old-fashioned, like his mother-in-law, in regard to the mixing of the castes, prepared to admit that exclusiveness was out of date, to pass over with a shrug and a laugh those numerous alliances by which his order were renewing the sinews of war, and indeed in his capacity of an expert, often pointing out the dangers of too much in-breeding—yet he had a peculiar personal feeling about his own family, and was perhaps a little extra sensitive because of Agatha; for Shropton, though a good fellow, and extremely wealthy, was only a third baronet, and had originally been made of iron. It was inadvisable to go outside the inner circle where there was no material necessity for so doing. He had not done it himself. Moreover there was a sentiment about these things!

On the morning after his arrival, visiting the kennels before breakfast, he stood chatting with his head man, and caressing the wet noses of his two favourite pointers, with something of the feeling of a boy let out of school. Those pleasant creatures, cowering and quivering with pride against his legs and turning up at him their yellow Chinese eyes, gave him that sense of warmth and comfort which visits men in the presence of their hobbies. With this particular pair, inbred to the uttermost, he had successfully surmounted a great risk. It was now touch and go whether he dared venture on one more cross to the original strain, in the hope of eliminating the last clinging of liver colour. It was a gamble—and it was just that which rendered it so vastly interesting.

. A small voice diverted his attention; he looked round and saw little Ann. She had been in bed when he arrived the night before, and he was therefore the newest thing about.

She carried in her arms a guinea-pig and began at once:

" Grandpapa, Granny wants you. She's on the terrace; she's talking to Mr. Courtier. I like him—he's a kind man. If I put my guinea-pig down, will they bite it? Poor darling—they shan't! Isn't it a darling!"

Lord Valleys, twirling his moustache, regarded the guinea-pig without favour; he had rather a dislike for all senseless kinds of beasts.

Pressing the guinea-pig between her hands, as it might be a concertina, little Ann jigged it gently above the pointers, who, wrinkling horribly their long noses, gazed upwards, fascinated.

"Poor darlings, they want it—don't they? Grandpapa!"

"Yes."

"Do you think the next puppies will be spotted quite all over?"

Continuing to twirl his moustache, Lord Valleys answered:

"I think it is not improbable, Ann."

"Why do you like them spotted like that? Oh! they're kissing Sambo—I *must* go!"

Lord Valleys followed her, his eyebrows a little raised.

As he approached the terrace his wife came towards him. Her colour was deeper than usual, and she had the look, higher and more resolute, special to her when she had been opposed. In truth she had just been through a passage of arms with Courtier, who, as the first revealer of Mrs. Noel's situation, had become entitled to a certain confidence on this subject. It had arisen from what she had intended as a perfectly natural and not unkind remark, to the effect that all the trouble had come from Mrs. Noel not having made her position clear to Miltoun from the first.

He had at once grown very red.

"It's easy, Lady Valleys, for those who have never been in the position of a lonely woman, to blame her."

Unaccustomed to be withstood, she had looked at him intently:

"I am the last person to be hard on a woman for conventional reasons. But I think it showed lack of character."

Courtier's reply had been almost rude.

"Plants are not equally robust, Lady Valleys. Some, as we know, are actually sensitive."

She had retorted with decision:

"If you like to so dignify the simpler word 'weak.'"

He had become very rigid at that, biting deeply into his moustache.

"What crimes are not committed under the sanctity of that

creed 'survival of the fittest,' which suits the book of all you
fortunate people so well!"

Priding herself on her restraint, Lady Valleys answered:

"Ah! we must talk that out. On the face of them, your
words sound a little unphilosophic, don't they?"

He had looked straight at her with a queer, unpleasant smile;
and she had felt at once disturbed and angry. It was all very
well to pet and even to admire these original sort of men, but
there were limits. Remembering, however, that he was her guest,
she had only said:

"Perhaps after all we had better not talk it out"; and
moving away, she heard him answer: "In any case, I'm certain
Audrey Noel never wilfully kept your son in the dark; she's
much too proud."

Though ruffled, she could not help liking the way he stuck up
for this woman; and she threw back at him the words:

"You and I, Mr. Courtier, must have a good fight some
day!"

She went towards her husband conscious of the rather pleasurable sensation which combat always roused in her.

These two were very good comrades. Theirs had been a love
match, and making due allowance for human nature beset by
opportunity, had remained, throughout, a solid and efficient
alliance. Taking, as they both did, such prominent parts in
public and social matters, the time they spent together was
limited, but productive of mutual benefit and reinforcement.
They had not yet had an opportunity of discussing their sons'
affair; and, slipping her hand through his arm, Lady Valleys
drew him away from the house.

"I want to talk to you about Miltoun, Geoff."

"H'm!" said Lord Valleys; "yes. The boy's looking worn.
Good thing when this election's over."

"If he's beaten and hasn't something new and serious to con-
centrate himself on, he'll fret his heart out over that woman."

Lord Valleys meditated a little before replying.

"I don't think that, Gertrude. He's got plenty of spirit."

"Of course! But it's a real passion. And, you know, he's not
like most boys, who'll take what they can."

She said this rather wistfully.

"I'm sorry for the woman," mused Lord Valleys; "I really
am."

"They say this rumour's done a lot of harm."

"Our influence is strong enough to survive that."

"It'll be a squeak; I wish I knew what he was going to do. Will you ask him?"

"You're clearly the person to speak to him," replied Lord Valleys. "I'm no hand at that sort of thing."

But Lady Valleys, with genuine discomfort, murmured:

"My dear, I'm so nervous with Eustace. When he puts on that smile of his I'm done for, at once."

"This is obviously a woman's business; nobody like a mother."

"If it were only one of the others," muttered Lady Valleys: "Eustace has that queer way of making you feel lumpy."

Lord Valleys looked at her askance. He had that kind of critical fastidiousness which a word will rouse into activity. Was she lumpy? The idea had never struck him.

"Well, I'll do it, if I must," sighed Lady Valleys.

When after breakfast she entered Miltoun's "den," he was buckling on his spurs preparatory to riding out to some of the remoter villages. Under the mask of the Apache chief, Bertie was standing, more inscrutable and neat than ever, in a perfectly tied cravatte, perfectly cut riding breeches, and boots worn and polished till a sooty glow shone through their natural russet. Not specially dandified in his usual dress, Bertie Carádoc would almost sooner have died than disgrace a horse. His eyes, the sharper because they had only half the space of the ordinary eye to glance from, at once took in the fact that his mother wished to be alone with "old Miltoun," and he discreetly left the room.

That which disconcerted all who had dealings with Miltoun was the discovery made soon or late, that they could not be sure how anything would strike him. In his mind, as in his face, there was a certain regularity, and then—impossible to say exactly where—it would shoot off and twist round a corner. This was the legacy no doubt of the hard-bitten individuality, which had brought to the front so many of his ancestors; for in Miltoun was the blood not only of the Carádocs and FitzHarolds, but of most other prominent families in the kingdom, all of whom, in those ages before money made the man, must have had a forebear conspicuous by reason of qualities, not always fine, but always poignant.

And now, though Lady Valleys had the audacity of her physique, and was not customarily abashed, she began by speaking of politics, hoping her son would give her an opening. But he gave her none, and she grew nervous. At last, summoning all her coolness, she said:

"I'm dreadfully sorry about this affair, dear boy. Your father told me of your talk with him. Try not to take it too hard."

Miltoun did not answer, and silence being that which Lady Valleys habitually most dreaded, she took refuge in further speech, outlining for her son the whole episode as she saw it from her point of view, and ending with these words:

"Surely it's not worth it."

Miltoun heard her with his peculiar look, as of a man peering through a vizor. Then smiling, he said:

"Thank you"; and opened the door.

Lady Valleys, without quite knowing whether he intended her to do so, indeed without quite knowing anything at the moment, passed out, and Miltoun closed the door behind her.

Ten minutes later he and Bertie were seen riding down the drive.

CHAPTER XIX

THAT afternoon the wind, which had been rising steadily, brought a flurry of clouds up from the South-West. Formed out on the heart of the Atlantic, they sailed forward, swift and fleecy at first, like the skirmishing white shallops of a great fleet; then, in serried masses, darkened the sun. About four o'clock they broke in rain, which the wind drove horizontally with a cold whiffling murmur. As youth and glamour die in a face before the cold rains of life, so glory died on the moor. The tors, from being uplifted wild castles, became mere grey excrescences. Distance failed. The cuckoos were silent. There was none of the beauty that there is in death, no tragic greatness —all was moaning and monotony. But about seven the sun tore its way back through the swathe, and flared out. Like some huge star, whose rays were stretching down to the horizon, and up to the very top of the hill of air, it shone with an amazing murky glamour; the clouds splintered by its shafts, and tinged saffron, piled themselves up as if in wonder. Under the sultry warmth of this new great star, the heather began to steam a little, and the glitter of its wet unopened bells was like that of innumerable tiny smoking fires. The two brothers were drenched as they cantered silently home. Good friends always, they had never much to say to one another. For Miltoun was conscious that he thought on a different plane from Bertie; and Bertie grudged even to his brother any inkling of what was passing in his spirit, just as he grudged parting with diplomatic knowledge, or stable secrets, or indeed anything that might leave him less in command of life. He grudged it, because in a private sort of way it lowered his estimation of his own stoical self-sufficiency; it hurt something proud in the withdrawing-room of his soul. But though he talked little, he had the power of contemplation—often found in men of decided character, with a tendency to liver. Once in Nepal, where he had gone to shoot, he had passed a month quite happily with only a Ghoorka servant who could speak no English. To those who asked him if he had not been horribly bored, he had always answered: "Not a bit; did a lot of thinking."

With Miltoun's trouble he had the professional sympathy of a brother and the natural intolerance of a confirmed bachelor. Women were to him very kittle-cattle. He distrusted from the bottom of his soul those who had such manifest power to draw things from you. He was one of those men in whom some day a woman might awaken a really fine affection; but who, until that time, would maintain the perfectly male attitude to the entire sex, and, after it, to all the sex but one. Women were, like Life itself, creatures to be watched, carefully used, and kept duly subservient. The only allusion therefore that he made to Miltoun's trouble was very sudden.

"Old man, I hope you're going to cut your losses."

The words were followed by undisturbed silence. But passing Mrs. Noel's cottage Miltoun said:

"Take my horse on; I want to go in here." . . .

She was sitting at her piano with her hands idle, looking at a line of music. She had been sitting thus for many minutes, but had not yet taken in the notes.

When Miltoun's shadow blotted the light by which she was seeing so little, she gave a slight start, and got up. But she neither went towards him, nor spoke. And he, without a word, came in and stood by the hearth, looking down at the empty grate. A tortoise-shell cat which had been watching swallows, disturbed by his entrance, withdrew from the window beneath a chair.

This silence, in which the question of their future lives was to be decided, seemed to both interminable; yet, neither could end it.

At last, touching his sleeve, she said: "You're wet!"

Miltoun shivered at that timid sign of possession. And they again stood in silence broken only by the sound of the cat licking its paws.

But her faculty for dumbness was stronger than his, and he had to speak first.

"Forgive me for coming; something must be settled. This rumour——"

"Oh! that!" she said. "Is there anything I can do to stop the harm to you?"

It was the turn of Miltoun's lips to curl. "God! no; let them talk!"

Their eyes had come together now, and, once together, seemed unable to part.

Mrs. Noel said at last:

" Will you ever forgive me? "

" What for—it was my fault."

" No, I should have known you better."

The depth of meaning in those words—the tremendous and subtle admission they contained of all that she had been ready to do, the despairing knowledge in them that he was not, and never had been, ready to " bear it out even to the edge of doom " —made Miltoun wince away.

" It is not from fear—believe that, anyway."

" I do."

There followed another long, long silence. But though so close that they were almost touching, they no longer looked at one another. Then Miltoun said:

" There is only to say good-bye, then."

At those clear words spoken by lips which, though just smiling, failed so utterly to hide his misery, Mrs. Noel's face became colourless as her white gown. But her eyes, which had darkened, seemed, from the sheer lack of all other colour, to have drawn into them the whole of her vitality; to be pouring forth a proud and mournful reproach.

Shivering, and crushing himself together with his arms, Miltoun walked towards the window. There was not the faintest sound from her, and he looked back. She was following him with her gaze. He threw his hand up over his face, and went quickly out. Mrs. Noel stood for a little while where he had left her; then, sitting down once more at the piano, began again to con over the line of music. And the cat stole back to the window to watch the swallows. The sunlight was dying slowly on the top branches of the lime-tree; a drizzling rain began to fall.

CHAPTER XX

CLAUD FRESNAY, Viscount Harbinger, was, at the age of thirty-one, perhaps the least encumbered peer in the United Kingdom. Thanks to an ancestor who had acquired land, and departed this life one hundred and thirty years before the town of Nettle-fold was built on a small portion of it, and to a father who had died in his son's infancy, after judiciously selling the said town, he possessed a very large income independently of his landed interests. Tall and well-built, with handsome, strongly-marked features, he gave at first sight an impression of strength —which faded somewhat when he began to talk. It was not so much the manner of his speech—with its rapid slang, and its way of turning everything to a jest—as the feeling it produced, that the brain behind it took naturally the path of least re-sistance. He was in fact one of those personalities who are often enough prominent in politics and social life, by reason of their appearance, position, assurance, and of a certain energy, half genuine, and half mere inherent predilection for short cuts. Certainly he was not idle, had written a book, travelled, was a Captain of Yeomanry, a Justice of the Peace, a good cricketer, and a constant and glib speaker. It would have been unfair to call his enthusiasm for social reform spurious. It was real enough in its way, and did certainly testify that he was not altogether lacking either in imagination or good-heartedness. But it was over and overlaid with the public-school habit—that peculiar, extraordinarily English habit, so powerful and beguil-ing that it becomes a second nature stronger than the first— of relating everything in the Universe to the standards and prejudices of a single class. Since practically all his intimate associates were immersed in it, he was naturally not in the least conscious of this habit; indeed there was nothing he deprecated so much in politics as the narrow and prejudiced outlook, such as he had observed in the Nonconformist, or labour politician. He would never have admitted for a moment that certain doors had been banged-to at his birth, bolted when he went to Eton, and padlocked at Cambridge. No one would have denied that there was much that was valuable in his standards—a high level of honesty, candour, sportsmanship, personal cleanliness, and self-reliance, together with a dislike of such cruelty as had been officially (so to speak) recognized as cruelty, and a sense of public service to a State run by and for the public schools; but it would have required far more originality than he possessed ever to look at Life from any other point of view than that from which he had been born and bred to watch Her. To fully understand Harbinger, one must, and with unprejudiced eyes and brain, have attended one of those great cricket matches in which he had figured conspicuously as a boy, and looking down from some high impartial spot have watched the ground at lunch time covered from rope to rope and stand to stand with a marvellous swarm, all walking in precisely the same manner, with precisely the same expression on their faces, under precisely the same hats—a swarm enshrining the greatest identity of creed and habit ever known since the world began. No, his environment had not been favourable to originality. Moreover he was naturally rapid rather than deep, and life hardly ever left him alone or left him silent. Brought into contact day and night with people to whom politics were more or less a game; run after everywhere; subjected to no form of discipline—it was a wonder that he was so serious as he was. Nor had he ever been in love, until, last year, during her first season, Barbara had, as he might have expressed it—in the case of another—"bowled him middle stump." Though so deeply smitten, he had not yet asked her to marry him—had not, as it were, had time, nor perhaps quite the courage, or conviction. When he was near her, it seemed impossible that he could go on longer without knowing his fate; when he was away from her it was almost a relief, because there were so many things to be done and said, and so little time to do or say them in. But now, during this fortnight, which, for her sake, he had devoted to Miltoun's cause, his feeling had advanced beyond the point of comfort.

He did not admit that the reason of this uneasiness was Courtier, for, after all, Courtier was, in a sense, nobody, and "an extremist" into the bargain, and an extremist always affected the centre of Harbinger's anatomy, causing it to give off a peculiar smile and tone of voice. Nevertheless, his eyes, whenever they fell on that sanguine, steady, ironic face, shone with a sort of cold inquiry, or were even darkened by the shade of fear. They met seldom, it is true, for most of his day was spent in motoring and speaking, and most of Courtier's in writing and riding, his leg being still too weak for walking. But once or twice in the smoking room late at night, he had embarked on some bantering discussion with the champion of lost causes; and very soon an ill-concealed impatience had crept into his voice. Why a man should waste his time, flogging dead horses on a journey to the moon, was incomprehensible! Facts were facts, human nature would never be anything but human nature! And it was peculiarly galling to see in Courtier's eye a gleam, to catch in his voice a tone, as if he were thinking: 'My young friend, your soup is cold!'

On a morning after one of these encounters, seeing Barbara sally forth in riding clothes, he asked if he too might go round the stables, and started forth beside her, unwontedly silent, with an odd feeling about his heart, and his throat unaccountably dry.

The stables at Monkland Court were as large as many country houses. Accommodating thirty horses, they were at present occupied by twenty-one, including the pony of little Ann. For height, perfection of lighting, gloss, shine, and purity of atmosphere they were unequalled in the county. It seemed indeed impossible that any horse could ever so far forget himself in such a place as to remember that he was a horse. Every morning a little bin of carrots, apples, and lumps of sugar, was set close to the main entrance, ready for those who might desire to feed the dear inhabitants.

Reined up to a brass ring on either side of their stalls with their noses towards the doors, they were always on view from nine to ten, and would stand with their necks arched, ears pricked and coats gleaming, wondering about things, soothed by the faint hissing of the still busy grooms, and ready to move their noses up and down the moment they saw someone enter.

In a large loose-box at the end of the north wing Barbara's favourite chestnut hunter, all but one saving sixteenth of whom had been entered in the stud book, having heard her footstep, was standing quite still with his neck turned. He had been crumping up an apple placed amongst his feed, and his senses struggled between the lingering flavour of that delicacy, and the perception of a sound with which he connected carrots. When she unlatched his door, and said " Hal," he at once went towards his manger, to show his independence, but when she said: " Oh! very well! " he turned round and came towards her. His eyes, which were full and of a soft brilliance, under thick chestnut lashes, explored her all over. Perceiving that her carrots were not in front, he elongated his neck, let his nose stray round her waist, and gave her gauntletted hand a nip with his lips. Not tasting carrot, he withdrew his nose, and snuffled. Then stepping carefully so as not to tread on her foot, he bunted her gently with his shoulder, till with a quick manœuvre he got behind her and breathed low and long on her neck. Even this did not smell of carrots, and putting his muzzle over her shoulder against her cheek, he slobbered a very little. A carrot appeared about the level of her waist, and hanging his head over, he tried to reach it. Feeling it all firm and soft under his chin, he snuffled again, and gave her a gentle dig with his knee. But still unable to reach the carrot, he threw his head up, withdrew, and pretended not to see her. And suddenly he felt two long substances round his neck, and something soft against his nose. He suffered this in silence, laying his ears back. The softness began puffing on his muzzle. Pricking his ears again, he puffed back a little harder, with more curiosity, and the softness was withdrawn. He perceived suddenly that he had a carrot in his mouth.

Harbinger had witnessed this episode, oddly pale, leaning against the loose-box wall. He spoke, as it came to an end :

" Lady Babs ! "

The tone of his voice must have been as strange as it sounded to himself, for Barbara spun round.

" Yes ?"

" How long am I going on like this ? "

Neither changing colour nor lowering her eyes, she regarded him with a faintly inquisitive interest. It was not a cruel look, had not a trace of mischief, or sex malice, and yet it frightened him by its serene inscrutability. Impossible to tell what was going on behind it. He took her hand, bent over it, and said in a low voice :

" You know what I feel ; don't be cruel to me ! "

She did not pull away her hand ; it was as if she had not thought of it.

" I am not a bit cruel."

Looking up, he saw her smiling.

" Then—Babs ! "

His face was close to hers, but Barbara did not shrink back. She just shook her head ; and Harbinger flushed up.

" Why ? " he asked ; and as though the enormous injustice

of that rejecting gesture had suddenly struck him, he dropped her hand.

"Why?" he said again, sharply.

But the silence was only broken by the cheeping of sparrows outside the round window, and the sound of the horse, Hal, munching the last morsel of his carrot. Harbinger was aware in his every nerve of the sweetish, slightly acrid, husky odour of the loose-box, mingling with the scent of Barbara's hair and clothes. And rather miserably, he said for the third time:

"Why?"

But folding her hands away behind her back, she answered gently:

"My dear, how should I know why?"

She was calmly exposed to his embrace if he had only dared; but he did not dare, and went back to the loose-box wall. Biting his finger, he stared at her gloomily. She was stroking the muzzle of her horse; and a sort of dry rage began whisking and rustling in his heart. She had refused him—Harbinger! He had not known, had not suspected how much he wanted her. How could there be anybody else for him, while that young, calm, sweet-scented, smiling thing lived, to make his head go round, his senses ache, and to fill his heart with longing! He seemed to himself at that moment the most unhappy of all men.

"I shall not give you up," he muttered.

Barbara's answer was a smile, faintly curious, compassionate, yet almost grateful, as if she had said:

'Thank you—who knows?'

And rather quickly, a yard or so apart, and talking of horses, they returned to the house.

It was about noon, when, accompanied by Courtier, she rode forth.

The Sou-Westerly spell—a matter of three days—had given way before radiant stillness; and merely to be alive was to feel emotion. At a little stream running beside the moor under the wild stone man the riders stopped their horses, just to listen, and inhale the day. The far sweet chorus of life was turned to a most delicate rhythm; not one of those small mingled pipings of streams and the lazy air, of beasts, men, birds, and bees, jarred out too harshly through the garment of sound enwrapping the earth. It was noon—the still moment—but this hymn to the sun, after his too long absence, never for a moment ceased to be murmured. And the earth wore an under-robe of scent, delicious, very finely woven of the young fern sap, heather buds, larch-trees not yet odourless, gorse just going brown, drifted wood-smoke, and the breath of hawthorn. Above Earth's twin vestments of sound and scent, the blue enwrapping scarf of air, that wistful wide champaign, was spanned only by the wings of Freedom.

After that long drink of the day, the riders mounted almost in silence to the very top of the moor. There again they sat quite still on their horses, examining the prospect. Far away to South and East lay the sea, plainly visible. Two small groups of wild ponies were slowly grazing towards each other on the hillside below.

Courtier said in a low voice:

"'Thus will I sit and sing; watching our two herds mingle together, and below us the far, divine, cerulean sea.'"

And, after another silence, looking steadily in Barbara's face, he added:

"Lady Barbara, I am afraid this is the last time we shall be alone together. While I have the chance, therefore, I must do homage. You will always be the fixed star for my worship. But your rays are too bright; I shall worship from afar. From your seventh Heaven, therefore, look down on me with kindly eyes, and do not quite forget me."

Under that speech, so strangely compounded of irony and fervour, Barbara sat very still, with glowing cheeks.

"Yes," said Courtier, "only an immortal must embrace a goddess. Outside the purlieus of Authority I shall sit cross-legged, and prostrate myself three times a day."

But Barbara answered nothing.

"In the early morning," went on Courtier, "leaving the dark and dismal homes of Freedom I shall look towards the Temples of the Great; there with the eye of faith I shall see you."

He stopped, for Barbara's lips were moving.

"Don't hurt me, please."

Courtier leaned over, took her hand, and put it to his lips.

"We will now ride on. . . ."

That night at dinner Lord Dennis, seated opposite his great-niece, was struck by her appearance.

'A very beautiful child!' he thought, 'a most lovely young creature!'

She was placed between Courtier and Harbinger. And the

old man's still keen eyes carefully watched those two. Though attentive to their neighbours on the other side, they were both of them keeping the corner of an eye on Barbara and on each other. The thing was transparent to Lord Dennis, and a smile settled in that nest of gravity between his white peaked beard and moustaches. But he waited, the instinct of a fisherman bidding him to neglect no piece of water, till he saw the child silent and in repose, and watched carefully to see what would rise. Although she was so calmly, so healthily eating, her eyes stole round at Courtier. This quick look seemed to Lord Dennis perturbed, as if something were exciting her. Then Harbinger spoke, and she turned to answer him. Her face was calm now, faintly smiling, a little eager, provocative in its joy of life. It made Lord Dennis think of his own youth. What a splendid couple! If Babs married young Harbinger there would not be a finer pair in all England. His eyes travelled back to Courtier. Manly enough! They called him dangerous! There *was* a look of effervescence, carefully corked down—might perhaps be attractive to a girl! To his essentially practical and sober mind, a type like Courtier was puzzling. He liked the look of him, but distrusted his ironic expression, and that appearance of blood to the head. A fellow—no doubt—who would ride off on his ideas, humanitarian! To Lord Dennis, there was something queer about humanitarians. They offended, perhaps, his dry and precise sense of form. They were always looking out for cruelty or injustice; seemed delighted when they found it—swelled up, as it were, when they scented it, and since there was a good deal about, were never quite of normal size. Men who lived for ideas were, in fact, to one for whom facts sufficed, always a little worrying! A movement from Barbara brought him back to actuality. Was the possessor of that crown of hair and those divine young shoulders the little Babs who had ridden with him in the Row? Time was certainly the Devil! Her eyes were searching for something; and following the direction of that glance, Lord Dennis found himself observing Miltoun. What a difference between those two! Both no doubt in the great trouble of youth, which sometimes, as he knew too well, lasted on almost to old age. It was a curious look the child was giving her brother, as if asking him to help her. Lord Dennis had seen in his day many young creatures leave the shelter of their freedom and enter the house of the great lottery; many, who had drawn a prize and thereat lost forever the coldness of life;

many too, the light of whose eyes had faded behind the shutters
of that house, having drawn a blank. The thought of "little"
Babs on the threshold of that inexorable saloon, filled him with
an eager sadness; and the sight of the two men watching for her,
waiting for her, like hunters, was to him distasteful. In any
case, let her not, for Heaven's sake, go ranging as far as that
red fellow of middle age, who might have ideas, but had no
pedigree; let her stick to youth and her own order, and marry
the young man, confound him, who looked like a Greek god,
of the wrong period, having grown a moustache. He remembered her words the other evening about these two and the
different lives they lived. Some romantic notion or other was
working in her! And again he looked at Courtier. A Quixotic
type—the sort that rode slap-bang at everything! All very well
—but not for Babs! She was not like the glorious Garibaldi's
glorious Anita! It was truly characteristic of Lord Dennis—
and indeed of other people—that to him champions of Liberty
when dead were far dearer than champions of Liberty when
living. Yes, Babs would want more, or was it less, than just a
life of sleeping under the stars for the man she loved, and the
cause he fought for. She would want pleasure, and not too much
effort, and presently a little power; not the uncomfortable after-
fame of a woman who went through fire, but the fame and power
of beauty, and Society prestige. This fancy of hers, if it were a
fancy, could be nothing but the romanticism of a young girl.
For the sake of a passing shadow, to give up substance? It
wouldn't do! And again Lord Dennis fixed his shrewd glance
on his great-niece. Those eyes, that smile! Yes! She would
grow out of this. And take the Greek god, the dying Gaul—
whichever that young man was!

CHAPTER XXI

It was not till the morning of polling day itself that Courtier left Monkland Court. He had already suffered for some time from bad conscience. For his knee was practically cured, and he knew well that it was Barbara, and Barbara alone, who kept him staying there. The atmosphere of that big house with its army of servants, the impossibility of doing anything for himself, and the feeling of hopeless insulation from the vivid and necessitous sides of life, galled him greatly. He felt a very genuine pity for these people who seemed to lead an existence as it were smothered under their own social importance. It was not their fault. He recognised that they did their best. They were good specimens of their kind; neither soft nor luxurious, as things went in a degenerate and extravagant age; they evidently tried to be simple—and this seemed to him to heighten the pathos of their situation. Fate had been too much for them. What human spirit could emerge untrammelled and unshrunken from that great encompassing host of material advantage? To a Bedouin like Courtier, it was as though a subtle, but very terrible tragedy was all the time being played before his eyes; and in the very centre of this tragedy was the girl who so greatly attracted him. Every night when he retired to that lofty room, which smelt so good, and where, without ostentation, everything was so perfectly ordered for his comfort, he thought:

' My God, *to-morrow* I'll be off!'

But every morning when he met her at breakfast his thought was precisely the same, and there were moments when he caught himself wondering: 'Am I falling under the spell of this existence—am I getting soft?' He recognised as never before that the peculiar artificial "hardness" of the patrician was a brine or pickle, in which, with the instinct of self-preservation, they deliberately soaked themselves, to prevent the decay of their overprotected fibre. He perceived even in Barbara—a sort of sentiment-proof overall, a species of mistrust of the emotional or lyrical, a kind of contempt of sympathy and feeling. And every day he was more and more tempted to lay rude hands on this garment; to see whether he could not make her catch fire, and flare up with some emotion or idea. In spite of her tan-

606

talising, youthful self-possession, he saw that she felt this longing in him, and now and then he caught a glimpse of a streak
of recklessness in her which lured him on.

And yet, when at last he was saying good-bye on the night
before polling day, he could not flatter himself that he had really
struck any spark from her. Certainly she gave him no chance
at that final interview, but stood amongst the other women,
calm and smiling, as if determined that he should not again
mock her with his ironical devotion.

He got up very early the next morning, intending to pass
away unseen. In the car put at his disposal, he found a small
figure in a holland frock, leaning back against the cushions so
that some sandalled toes pointed up at the chauffeur's back.
They belonged to little Ann, who in the course of business had
discovered the vehicle before the door. Her sudden little voice
under her sudden little nose, friendly but not too friendly, was
comforting to Courtier.

"Are you going? I can come as far as the gate."

"That is lucky."

"Yes. Is that all your luggage?"

"I'm afraid it is.'"

"Oh! It's quite a lot, really, isn't it?"

"As much as I deserve."

"Of course *you* don't have to take guinea-pigs about with
you?"

"Not as a rule."

"I always do. There's great-Granny!"

There certainly was Lady Casterley, standing a little back
from the drive, and directing a tall gardener how to deal with
an old oak-tree. Courtier alighted, and went towards her to say
good-bye. She greeted him with a certain grim cordiality.

"So you are going! I am glad of that, though you quite
understand that I like you personally."

"Quite!"

Her eyes gleamed maliciously.

"Men who laugh like you are dangerous, as I've told you
before!"

Then, with great gravity, she added:

"My granddaughter will marry Lord Harbinger. I mention
that, Mr. Courtier, for your peace of mind. You are a man of
honour; it will go no further."

Courtier, bowing over her hand, answered:

" He will be lucky."

The little old lady regarded him unflinchingly.

" He will, sir. Good-bye ! "

Courtier smilingly raised his hat. His cheeks were burning. Regaining the car, he looked round. Lady Casterley was busy once more exhorting the tall gardener. The voice of little Ann broke in on his thoughts:

" I hope you'll come again. Because I expect I shall be here at Christmas; and my brothers will be here then, that is, Jock and Tiddy, not Christopher because he's young. I *must* go now. Good-bye ! Hallo, Susie ! "

Courtier saw her slide away, and join the little pale adoring figure of the lodge-keeper's daughter.

The car passed out into the lane.

If Lady Casterley had planned this disclosure, which indeed she had not, for the impulse had only come over her at the sound of Courtier's laugh, she could not have devised one more effectual, for there was deep down in him all a wanderer's very real distrust, amounting almost to contempt, of people so settled and done for, as were aristocrats, and all a man of action's horror of what he called—" puking and muling." The pursuit of Barbara with any other object but that of marriage had naturally not occurred to one who had little sense of conventional morality, but much self-respect; and a secret endeavour to cut out Harbinger, ending in a marriage whereat he would figure as a sort of pirate, was quite as little to the taste of a man not unaccustomed to think himself as good as other people.

He caused the car to deviate up the lane that led to Aubrey Noel's, hating to go away without a hail of cheer to that ship in distress.

She came out to him on the verandah. From the clasp of her hand, thin and faintly browned—the hand of a woman never quite idle—he felt that she relied on him to understand and sympathise; and nothing so awakened the best in Courtier as such mute appeals to his protection. He said gently:

" Don't let them think you're down; " and, squeezing her hand hard : " Why should you be wasted like this ? It's a sin and shame ! "

But he stopped in what he felt to be an unlucky speech at sight of her face, which without movement expressed so much more than his words. He was protesting as a civilised man; her face was the protest of Nature, the soundless declaration of beauty wasted against its will, beauty that was life's invitation to the embrace which gave life birth.

"I'm clearing out, myself," he said: "You and I, you know, are not good for these people. No birds of freedom allowed!"

Pressing his hand, she turned away into the house, leaving Courtier gazing at the patch of air where her white figure had stood. He had always had a special protective feeling for Audrey Noel, a feeling which with but little encouragement might have become something warmer. But since she had been placed in her anomalous position he would not for the world have brushed the dew off her belief that she could trust him. And now that he had fixed his own gaze elsewhere, and she was in this bitter trouble, he felt on her account the rancour that a brother feels when Justice and Pity have conspired to flout his sister. The voice of Frith the chauffeur roused him from gloomy reverie.

"Lady Barbara, sir!"

Following the man's eyes, Courtier saw against the skyline on the tor above Ashman's Folly, an equestrian statue. He stopped the car at once, and got out.

He reached her at the ruin, screened from the road, by that divine chance which attends on men who take care that it shall. He could not tell whether she knew of his approach, and he would have given all he had, which was not much, to have seen through the stiff grey of her coat, and the soft cream of her body, into that mysterious cave, her heart. To have been for a moment, like Ashman, done for good and all with material things, and living the white life where are no barriers between man and woman. The smile on her lips so baffled him, puffed there by her spirit, as a first flower is puffed through the surface of earth to mock at the spring winds. How tell what it signified! Yet he rather prided himself on his knowledge of women, of whom he had seen something. But all he found to say was:

"I'm glad of this chance."

Then suddenly looking up, he found her strangely pale and quivering.

"I shall see you in London!" she said; and, touching her horse with her whip, without looking back, she rode away over the hill.

Courtier returned to the moor road, and getting into the car, muttered:

"Faster, please, Frith!" . . .

CHAPTER XXII

POLLING was already in brisk progress when Courtier arrived in Bucklandbury; and partly from a not unnatural interest in the result, partly from a half-unconscious clinging to the chance of catching another glimpse of Barbara, he took his bag to the hotel, determined to stay for the announcement of the poll. Strolling out into the High Street he began observing the humours of the day. The bloom of political belief had long been brushed of the wings of one who had flown the world's winds. He had seen too much of more vivid colours to be capable now of venerating greatly the dull and dubious tints of blue and yellow. They left him feeling extremely philosophic. Yet it was impossible to get away from them, for the very world that day seemed blue and yellow, nor did the third colour of red adopted by both sides afford any clear assurance that either could see virtue in the other; rather, it seemed to symbolise the desire of each to have his enemy's blood. But Courtier soon observed by the looks cast at his own detached, and perhaps sarcastic, face, that even more hateful to either side than any antagonist, was the philosophic eye. Unanimous was the longing to heave half a brick at it whenever it showed itself. With its d——d impartiality, its habit of looking through the integument of things, to see if there might be anything inside, he felt that they regarded it as the real adversary—the eternal foe to all the little fat "facts," which, dressed up in blue and yellow, were swaggering and staggering, calling each other names, wiping each other's eyes, blooding each other's noses. To these little solemn delicious creatures, all front and no behind, the philosophic eye, with its habit of looking round the corner, was clearly detestable. The very yellow and very blue bodies of these roistering small warriors with their hands on their tin swords and their lips on their tin trumpets, started up in every window and on every wall confronting each citizen in turn, persuading him that they and they alone were taking him to Westminster. Nor had they apparently for the most part much trouble with electors, who, finding uncertainty distasteful, passionately desired to be assured that the country could at once be saved by little yellow facts or little blue facts, as the case might be; who had, no doubt, a dozen other good reasons for being on the one side or the other; as, for instance, that their father had been so before them; that their bread was buttered yellow or buttered blue; that they had been on the other side last time; that they had thought it over and made up their minds; that they had innocent blue or naïve yellow beer within; that his lordship was the man; or that the words proper to their mouths were " Chilcox for Bucklandbury "; and, above all, the one really creditable reason, that, so far as they could tell with the best of their intellect and feelings, the truth at the moment was either blue or yellow.

The narrow high street was thronged with voters. Tall policemen stationed there had nothing to do. The certainty of all, that they were going to win, seemed to keep everyone in good humour. There was as yet no need to break anyone's head, for though the sharpest lookout was kept for any signs of the philosophic eye, it was only to be found—outside Courtier—in the perambulators of babies, in one old man who rode a bicycle waveringly along the street and stopped to ask a policeman what was the matter in the town, and in two rather green-faced fellows who trundled barrows full of favours both blue and yellow.

But though Courtier eyed the " facts " with such suspicion, the keenness of everyone about the business struck him as really splendid. They went at it with a will. Having looked forward to it for months, they were going to look back on it for months. It was evidently a religious ceremony, summing up most high feelings; and this seemed to one who was himself a man of action, natural, perhaps pathetic, but certainly no matter for scorn.

It was already late in the afternoon when there came debouching into the high street a long string of sandwichmen, each bearing before and behind him a poster containing these words beautifully situated in large dark blue letters against a pale blue ground:

" NEW COMPLICATIONS
DANGER NOT PAST
VOTE FOR MILTOUN AND THE GOVERNMENT
AND SAVE THE EMPIRE "

Courtier stopped to look at them with indignation. Not only did this poster tramp in again on his cherished convictions about

Peace, but he saw in it something more than met the unphilosophic eye. It symbolised for him all that was catch-penny in
the national life—an epitaph on the grave of generosity, unut-
terably sad. Yet from a Party point of view what could be more
justifiable? Was it not desperately important that every blue
nerve should be strained that day to turn yellow nerves, if not
blue, at all events green, before night fell? Was it not perfectly
true that the Empire could only be saved by voting blue? Could
they help a blue paper printing the words, " New complications,"
which he had read that morning? No more than the yellows
could help a yellow journal printing the words " Lord Miltoun's
Evening Adventure." The only business of blues was to win,
ever fighting fair. The yellows had not fought fair, they never
did, and one of their most unfair tactics was the way they had
of always accusing the blues of unfair fighting, an accusation
truly ludicrous! As for truth! That which helped the world
to be blue, was obviously true; that which didn't, as obviously
not. There was no middle policy! The man who saw things
neither blue nor yellow was a softy, and no proper citizen. And
as for giving the yellows credit for sincerity—the yellows never
gave them credit! But though Courtier knew all that, this poster
seemed to him particularly damnable, and he could not for the
life of him resist striking one of the sandwich-boards with his
cane. The resounding thwack startled a butcher's pony standing
by the pavement. It reared, and bolted forward, with Courtier,
who had naturally seized the rein, hanging on. A dog dashed
past. Courtier tripped and fell. The pony, passing over, struck
him on the head with a hoof. For a moment he lost consciousness; then coming to himself, refused assistance, and went to
his hotel. He felt very giddy, and, after bandaging a nasty
cut, lay down on his bed.

Miltoun, returning from that necessary exhibition of himself,
the crowning fact, at every polling centre, found time to go and
see him.

" That last poster of yours! " Courtier began at once.

" I'm having it withdrawn."

" It's done the trick—congratulations—you'll get in! "

" I knew nothing of it."

" My dear fellow, I didn't suppose you did."

" When there is a desert, Courtier, between a man and the
sacred city, he doesn't renounce his journey because he has to
wash in dirty water on the way. But the mob—how I loathe it! "

There was such pent-up fury in those words as to astonish even one whose life had been passed in conflict with majorities.

"I hate its mean stupidities, I hate the sound of its voice, and the look on its face—it's so ugly, it's so little. Courtier, I suffer purgatory from the thought that I shall scrape in by the votes of the mob. There is sin in using this creature and I am expiating it."

To this strange outburst, Courtier at first made no reply.

"You've been working too hard," he said at last, "you're off your balance. After all, the mob's made up of men like you and me."

"No, Courtier, the mob is *not* made up of men like you and me. If it were it would not be the mob."

"It looks," Courtier answered gravely, "as if you had no business in this galley. I've always steered clear of it myself."

"You follow your feelings. I have not that happiness."

So saying, Miltoun turned to the door.

Courtier's voice pursued him earnestly.

"Drop your politics—if you feel like this about them; don't waste your life following whatever it is you follow; don't waste hers!"

But Miltoun did not answer.

It was a wondrous still night, when, a few minutes before twelve, with his forehead bandaged under his hat, the champion of lost causes left the hotel and made his way toward the Grammar School for the declaration of the poll. A sound as of some monster breathing guided him, till, from a steep empty street he came in sight of a surging crowd, spread over the town square, like a dark carpet patterned by splashes of lamplight. High up above that crowd, on the little peaked tower of the Grammar School, a brightly lighted clock face presided; and over the passionate hopes in those thousands of hearts knit together by suspense the sky had lifted, and showed no cloud between them and the purple fields of air. To Courtier descending towards the square, the swaying white faces, turned all one way, seemed like the heads of giant wild flowers in a dark field, shivered by wind. The night had charmed away the blue and yellow facts, and breathed down into that throng the spirit of emotion. And he realised all at once the beauty and meaning of this scene—expression of the quivering forces, whose perpetual flux, controlled by the Spirit of Balance, was the soul of the world. Thousands of hearts with the thought of self lost in one overmastering excitement!

An old man with a long grey beard, standing close to his elbow, murmured:

" 'Tis anxious work—I wouldn't ha' missed this for anything in the world."

" Fine, eh? " answered Courtier.

" Aye," said the old man, " *'tis* fine. I've not seen the like o' this since the great year—forty-eight. There they are—the aristocrats! "

Following the direction of that skinny hand Courtier saw on a balcony Lord and Lady Valleys, side by side, looking steadily down at the crowd. There too, leaning against a window and talking to someone behind, was Barbara. The old man went on muttering, and Courtier could see that his eyes had grown very bright, his whole face transfigured by intense hostility; he felt drawn to this old creature, thus moved to the very soul. Then he saw Barbara looking down at him, with her hand raised to her temple to show that she saw his bandaged head. He had the presence of mind not to lift his hat.

The old man spoke again.

" You wouldn't remember forty-eight, I suppose. There was a feeling in the people then—we would ha' died for things in those days. I'm eighty-four," and he held his shaking hand up to his breast, " but the spirit's alive here yet! God send the Radical gets in! " There was wafted from him a scent as of potatoes.

Far behind, at the very edge of the vast dark throng, some voices began singing: " 'Way down upon the Swanee ribber." The tune floated forth, ceased, spurted up once more, and died.

Then, in the very centre of the square a stentorian baritone roared forth: " Should auld acquaintance be forgot! "

The song swelled, till every kind of voice, from treble to the old Chartist's quavering bass, was chanting it; here and there the crowd heaved with the movement of linked arms. Courtier found the soft fingers of a young woman in his right hand, the old Chartist's dry trembling paw in his left. He himself sang loudly. The grave and fearful music sprang straight up into the air, rolled out right and left, and was lost among the hills. But it had no sooner died away than the same huge baritone yelled: " God save our gracious King! " The stature of the

crowd seemed at once to leap up two feet, and from under that
platform of raised hats rose a stupendous shouting.

'This,' thought Courtier, 'is religion!'

They were singing even on the balconies; by the lamplight he
could see Lord Valleys' mouth not opened quite enough, as
though his voice were just a little ashamed of coming out, and
Barbara with her head flung back against the pillar, pouring out
her heart. No mouth in all the crowd was silent. It was as
though the soul of the English people were escaping from its
dungeon of reserve, on the pinions of that chant.

But suddenly, like a shot bird closing wings, the song fell
silent and dived headlong back to earth. Out from under the
clock-face had moved a thin dark figure. More figures came
behind. Courtier could see Miltoun. A voice far away cried:
"Up, Chilcox!" A huge: "Hush!" followed; then such a
silence, that the sound of an engine shunting a mile away could
be heard plainly.

The dark figure moved forward, and a tiny square of paper
gleamed out white against the black of his frock-coat.

"Ladies and gentlemen. Result of the Poll: Miltoun—Four
thousand eight hundred and ninety-eight. Chilcox—Four thousand eight hundred and two."

The silence seemed to fall to earth, and break into a thousand
pieces. Through the pandemonium of cheers and groaning,
Courtier with all his strength forced himself towards the balcony. He could see Lord Valleys leaning forward with a broad
smile; Lady Valleys passing her hand across her eyes; Barbara
with her hand in Harbinger's, looking straight into his face. He
stopped. The old Chartist was still beside him, tears rolling
down his cheeks into his beard.

Courtier saw Miltoun come forward, and stand, unsmiling,
deathly pale.

PART II

CHAPTER I

At three o'clock in the afternoon of the nineteenth of July little Ann Shropton commenced the ascent of the main staircase of Valleys House, London. She climbed slowly, in the very middle, an extremely small white figure on those wide and shining stairs, counting them aloud. Their number was never alike two days running, which made them attractive to one for whom novelty was the salt of life.

Coming to that spot where they branched, she paused to consider which of the two flights she had used last, and unable to remember, sat down. She was the bearer of a message. It had been new when she started, but was already comparatively old, and likely to become older, in view of a design now conceived by her of travelling the whole length of the picture gallery. And while she sat maturing this plan, sunlight flooding through a large window drove a white refulgence down into the heart of the wide polished space of wood and marble, whence she had come. The nature of little Ann habitually rejected fairies and all fantastic things, finding them quite too much in the air, and devoid of sufficient reality and " go "; and this refulgence, almost unearthly in its travelling glory, passed over her small head and played strangely with the pillars in the hall, without exciting in her any fancies or any sentiment. The intention of discovering what was at the end of the picture gallery absorbed the whole of her essentially practical and active mind. Deciding on the left-hand flight of stairs, she entered that immensely long, narrow, and—with blinds drawn—rather dark saloon. She walked carefully, because the floor was very slippery here, and with a kind of seriousness due partly to the darkness and partly to the pictures. They were indeed, in this light, rather formidable, those old Carádocs, black, armoured creatures, some of them, who seemed to eye with a sort of burning, grim, defensive greed the small white figure of their descendant passing along between them. But little Ann, who knew they were only pictures, maintained her course steadily, and every now and

then, as she passed one who seemed to her rather uglier than
the others, wrinkled her sudden little nose. At the end, as she
had thought, appeared a door. She opened it, and passed on to
a landing. There was a stone staircase in the corner, and there
were two doors. It would be nice to go up the staircase, but it
would also be nice to open the doors. Going towards the first
door, with a little thrill, she turned the handle. It was one of
those rooms, necessary in houses, for which she had no great
liking; and closing this door rather loudly she opened the other
one, finding herself in a chamber not resembling the rooms
downstairs, which were all high and nicely gilded, but more like
where she had lessons, low, and filled with books and leather
chairs. From the end of the room which she could not see, she
heard a sound as of someone kissing something, and instinct had
almost made her turn to go away when the word: "Hallo!"
suddenly opened her lips. And almost directly she saw that
Granny and Grandpapa were standing by the fireplace. Not
knowing quite whether they were glad to see her, she went forward and began at once:

"Is this where you sit, Grandpapa?"

"It is."

"It's nice, isn't it, Granny? Where does the stone staircase
go to?"

"To the roof of the tower, Ann."

"Oh! I have to give a message, so I *must* go now."

"Sorry to lose you."

"Yes; good-bye!"

Hearing the door shut behind her, Lord and Lady Valleys
looked at each other with a dubious smile.

The little interview which she had interrupted, had arisen
in this way.

Accustomed to retire to this quiet and homely room, which
was not his official study where he was always liable to the attacks of secretaries, Lord Valleys had come up here after lunch
to smoke and chew the cud of a worry.

The matter was one in connection with his Pendridny estate,
in Cornwall. It had long agitated both his agent and himself,
and had now come to him for final decision. The question
affected two villages to the north of the property, whose inhabitants were solely dependent on the working of a large quarry,
which had for some time been losing money.

A kindly man, he was extremely averse to any measure which

would plunge his tenants into distress, and especially in cases where there had been no question of opposition between himself and them. But, reduced to its essentials, the matter stood thus: Apart from that particular quarry the Pendridny estate was not only a going, but even a profitable concern, supporting itself and supplying some of the sinews of war towards Valleys House and the racing establishment at Newmarket and other general expenses; with this quarry still running, allowing for the up-keep of Pendridny, and the provision of pensions to super-annuated servants, it was rather the other way.

Sitting there, that afternoon, smoking his favourite pipe, he had at last come to the conclusion that there was nothing for it but to close down. He had not made this resolution lightly; though, to do him justice, the knowledge that the decision would be bound to cause an outcry in the local, and perhaps the Na-tional, Press, had secretly rather spurred him on to the resolve than deterred him from it. He felt as if he were being dictated to in advance, and he did not like dictation. To have to deprive these poor people of their immediate living was, he knew, a good deal more irksome to him than to those who would certainly make a fuss about it, his conscience was clear, and he could dis-count that future outcry as mere Party spite. He had very honestly tried to examine the thing all round; and had reasoned thus: If I keep this quarry open, I am really admitting the principle of pauperisation, since I naturally look to each of my estates to support its own house, grounds, shooting, and to contribute towards the support of this house, and my family, and racing stable, and all the people employed about them both. To allow any business to be run on my estates which does not contribute to the general upkeep, is to protect and really pauperise a portion of my tenants at the expense of the rest; it must therefore be false economics and a secret sort of socialism. Further, if logically followed out, it might end in my ruin, and to allow that, though I might not personally object, would be to imply that I do not believe that I am by virtue of my tradi-tions and training, the best machinery through which the State can work to secure the welfare of the people. . . .

When he had reached that point in his consideration of the question, his mind, or rather perhaps, his essential self, had not unnaturally risen up and said: Which is absurd!

Impersonality was in fashion, and as a rule he believed in thinking impersonally. There was a point, however, where the possibility of doing so ceased, without treachery to oneself, one's order, and the country. And to the argument which he was quite shrewd enough to put to himself, sooner than have it put by anyone else, that it was disproportionate for a single man by a stroke of the pen to be able to dispose of the livelihood of hundreds whose senses and feelings were similar to his own— he had answered: "If *I* didn't, some plutocrat or company would—or, worse still, the State!" Co-operative enterprise being, in his opinion, foreign to the spirit of the country, there was, so far as he could see, no other alternative. Facts were facts and not to be got over!

Notwithstanding all this, the necessity for the decision made him sorry, for if he had no great sense of proportion, he was at least humane.

He was still smoking his pipe and staring at a sheet of paper covered with small figures when his wife entered. Though she had come to ask his advice on a very different subject, she saw at once that he was vexed, and said:

"What's the matter, Geoff?"

Lord Valleys rose, went to the hearth, deliberately tapped out his pipe, then held out to her the sheet of paper.

"That quarry! Nothing for it—must go!"

Lady Valleys' face changed.

"Oh, no! It will mean such dreadful distress."

Lord Valleys stared at his nails. "It's putting a drag on the whole estate," he said.

"I know, but how could we face the people—I should never be able to go down there. And most of them have such enormous families."

Since Lord Valleys continued to bend on his nails that slow, thought-forming stare, she went on earnestly:

"Rather than that I'd make sacrifices. I'd sooner Pendridny were let than throw all those people out of work. I suppose it *would* let."

"Let? Best woodcock shooting in the world."

Lady Valleys, pursuing her thoughts, went on:

"In time we might get the people drafted into other things. Have you consulted Miltoun?"

"No," said Lord Valleys shortly, "and don't mean to—he's too unpractical."

"He always seems to know what he wants very well."

"I tell you," repeated Lord Valleys, "Miltoun's no good in a matter of this sort—he and his ideas throw back to the Middle Ages."

Lady Valleys went closer, and took him by the lapels of his collar.

" Geoff—really, to please me; some other way! "

Lord Valleys frowned, staring at her for some time; and at last answered:

" To please you—I'll leave it over another year."

" You think that's better than letting? "

" I don't like the thought of some outsider there. Time enough to come to that if we must. Take it as my Christmas present."

Lady Valleys, rather flushed, bent forward and kissed his ear.

It was at this moment that little Ann had entered.

When she was gone, and they had exchanged that dubious look, Lady Valleys said:

" I came about Babs. I don't know what to make of her since we came up. She's not putting her heart into things."

Lord Valleys answered almost sulkily:

" It's the heat probably—or Claud Harbinger." In spite of his easy-going parentalism, he disliked the thought of losing the child whom he so affectionately admired.

" Ah! " said Lady Valleys slowly, " I'm not so sure."

" How do you mean? "

" There's something queer about her. I'm by no means certain she hasn't got some sort of feeling for that Mr. Courtier."

" What! " said Lord Valleys, growing most unphilosophically red.

" Exactly! "

" Confound it, Gertrude, Miltoun's business was quite enough for one year."

" For twenty," murmured Lady Valleys. " I'm watching her. He's going to Persia, they say."

" And leaving his bones there, I hope," muttered Lord Valleys. " Really, it's too much. I should think you're all wrong, though."

Lady Valleys raised her eyebrows. Men were very queer about such things! Very queer and worse than helpless!

" Well," she said, " I must go to my meeting. I'll take her, and see if I can get at something," and she went away.

It was the inaugural meeting of the Society for the Promotion of the Birth Rate, over which she had promised to preside. The scheme was one in which she had been prominent from the start, appealing as it did to her large and full-blooded nature. Many movements, to which she found it impossible to refuse her name, had in themselves but small attraction; and it was a real comfort to feel something approaching enthusiasm for one branch of her public work. Not that there was any academic consistency about her in the matter, for in private life amongst her friends she was not narrowly dogmatic on the duty of wives to multiply exceedingly. She thought imperially on the subject, without bigotry. Large, healthy families, in all cases save individual ones! The prime idea at the back of her mind was—National Expansion! Her motto, and she intended if possible to make it the motto of the League was: *" De l'audace, et encore de l'audace!"* It was a question of the full realisation of the nation. She had a true, and in a sense touching belief in " the flag," apart from what it might cover. It was her idealism. "You may talk," she would say, " as much as you like about directing national life in accordance with social justice! What does the nation care about social justice? The thing is much bigger than that. It's a matter of sentiment. We must expand!"

On the way to the meeting, occupied with her speech, she made no attempt to draw Barbara into conversation. That must wait. The child, though languid, and pale, was looking so beautiful that it was a pleasure to have her support in such a movement.

In a little dark room behind the hall the Committee were already assembled, and they went at once on to the platform.

CHAPTER II

UNMOVED by the stare of the audience, Barbara sat absorbed in moody thoughts.

Into the three weeks since Miltoun's election there had been crowded such a multitude of functions that she had found, as it were, no time, no energy to know where she stood with herself. Since that morning in the stable, when he had watched her with the horse Hal, Harbinger had seemed to live only to be close to her. And the consciousness of his passion gave her a tingling sense of pleasure. She had been riding and dancing with him, and sometimes this had been almost blissful. But there were times too, when she felt—though always with a certain contempt of herself, as when she sat on that sunwarmed stone below the tor—a queer dissatisfaction, a longing for something outside a world where she had to invent her own starvations and simplicities, to make-believe in earnestness.

She had seen Courtier three times. Once he had come to dine, in response to an invitation from Lady Valleys worded in that charming, almost wistful style, which she had taught herself to use to those below her in social rank, especially if they were intelligent; once to the Valleys House garden party; and, next day, having told him what time she would be riding, she had found him in the Row, not mounted, but standing by the rail just where she must pass, with that look on his face of mingled deference and ironic self-containment, of which he was a master. It appeared that he was leaving England; and to her questions why, and where, he had only shrugged his shoulders. Up on this dusty platform, in the hot bare hall, facing all those people, listening to speeches whose sense she was too languid and preoccupied to take in, the whole medley of thoughts, and faces round her, and the sound of the speakers' voices, formed a kind of nightmare, out of which she noted with extreme exactitude the colour of her mother's neck beneath a large black hat, and the expression on the face of a Committee man to the right, who was biting his fingers under cover of a blue paper. She realised that someone was speaking amongst the audience, casting forth, as it were, small bunches of words. She could see

623

him—a little man in a black coat, with a white face which kept jerking up and down.

"I feel that this is terrible," she heard him say; "I feel that this is blasphemy. That we should try to tamper with the greatest force, the greatest and the most sacred and secret— force, that—that moves in the world, is to me horrible. I cannot bear to listen; it seems to make everything so small!" She saw him sit down, and her mother rising to answer.

"We must all sympathise with the sincerity and to a certain extent with the intention of our friend in the body of the hall. But we must ask ourselves: Have we the right to allow ourselves the luxury of private feelings in a matter which concerns the national expansion. We must not give way to sentiment. Our friend in the body of the hall spoke—he will forgive me for saying so—like a poet, rather than a serious reformer. I am afraid that if we let ourselves drop into poetry, the birth rate of this country will very soon drop into poetry too. And that I think it is impossible for us to contemplate with folded hands. The resolution I was about to propose when our friend in the body of the hall——"

But Barbara's attention had wandered off again into that queer medley of thoughts, and feelings, out of which the little man had so abruptly roused her. Then she realised that the meeting was breaking up, and her mother saying:

"Now, my dear, it's hospital day. We've just time."

When they were once more in the car, she leaned back very silent, watching the traffic.

Lady Valleys eyed her sidelong.

"What a little bombshell," she said, "from that small person! He must have got in by mistake. I hear Mr. Courtier has a card for Helen Gloucester's ball to-night, Babs."

"Poor man!"

"*You* will be there," said Lady Valleys dryly.

Barbara drew back into her corner.

"Don't tease me, Mother!"

An expression of compunction crossed Lady Valleys' face; she tried to possess herself of Barbara's hand. But that languid hand did not return her squeeze.

"I know the mood you're in, dear. It wants all one's pluck to shake it off; don't let it grow on you. You'd better go down to Uncle Dennis to-morrow. You've been overdoing it."

Barbara sighed.

"I wish it *were* to-morrow."

The car had stopped, and Lady Valleys said:

"Will you come in, or are you too tired? It always does them good to see you."

"You're twice as tired as me," Barbara answered; "of course I'll come."

At the entrance of the two ladies, there rose at once a faint buzz and murmur. Lady Valleys, whose ample presence radiated suddenly a business-like and cheery confidence, went to a bed-side and sat down. But Barbara stood in a thin streak of the July sunlight, uncertain where to begin, amongst the faces turned towards her. The poor dears looked so humble, and so wistful, and so tired. There was one lying quite flat, who had not even raised her head to see who had come in. That slumbering, pale, high-cheek-boned face had a frailty as if a touch, a breath, would shatter it; a wisp of the blackest hair, finer than silk, lay across the forehead; the closed eyes were deep sunk; one hand, scarred almost to the bone with work, rested above her breast. She breathed between lips which had no colour. About her, sleeping, was a kind of beauty. And there came over the girl a queer rush of emotion. The sleeper seemed so apart from everything there, from all the formality and stiffness of the ward. To look at her swept away the languid, hollow feeling with which she had come in; it made her think of the tors at home, when the wind was blowing, and all was bare, and grand, and sometimes terrible. There was something elemental in that still sleep. And the old lady in the next bed, with a brown wrinkled face and bright black eyes brimful of life, seemed almost vulgar beside such remote tranquillity, while she was telling Barbara that a little bunch of heather in the better half of a soap-dish on the window-sill had come from Wales, be-cause, as she explained: "My mother was born in Stirling, dearie; so I likes a bit of heather, though I never been out o' Bethnal Green meself."

But when Barbara again passed, the sleeping woman was sit-ting up, and looked but a poor ordinary thing—her strange fragile beauty all withdrawn.

It was a relief when Lady Valleys said:

"My dear, my Naval Bazaar at five-thirty; and while I'm there you must go home and have a rest, and freshen yourself up for the evening. We dine at Plassey House."

The Duchess of Gloucester's Ball, a function which no one

could very well miss, had been fixed for this late date owing to the Duchess's announced desire to prolong the season and so help the hackney cabmen; and though everybody sympathised, it had been felt by most that it would be simpler to go away, motor up on the day of the Ball, and motor down again on the following morning. And throughout the week by which the season was thus prolonged, in long rows at the railway stations, and on their stands, the hackney cabmen, unconscious of what was being done for them, waited, patient as their horses. But since everybody was making this special effort, an exceptionally large, exclusive, and brilliant company reassembled at Gloucester House.

In the vast ballroom over the medley of entwined revolving couples, punkahs had been fixed, to clear and freshen the languid air, and these huge fans, moving with incredible slowness, drove a faint refreshing draught down over the sea of white shirt-fronts and bare necks, and freed the scent from innumerable flowers.

Late in the evening, close by one of the great clumps of bloom, a very pretty woman stood talking to Bertie Carádoc. She was his cousin, Lily Malvezin, sister of Geoffrey Winlow, and wife of a liberal peer, a charming creature, whose pink cheeks, bright eyes, quick lips, and rounded figure, endowed her with the prettiest air of animation. And while she spoke she kept stealing sly glances at her partner, trying as it were to pierce the armour of that self-contained young man.

" No, my dear," she said in her mocking voice, " you'll never persuade me that Miltoun is going to catch on. *Il est trop intransigeant.* Ah! there's Babs!"

For the girl had come gliding by, her eyes wandering lazily, her lips just parted; her neck, hardly less pale than her white frock; her face pale, and marked with languor, under the heavy coil of her tawny hair; and her swaying body seeming with each turn of the waltz to be caught by the arms of her partner from out of a swoon.

With that immobility of lips, learned by all imprisoned in Society, Lily Malvezin murmured:

" Who's that she's dancing with? Is it the dark horse, Bertie?"

Through lips no less immobile Bertie answered:

" Forty to one, no takers."

But those inquisitive bright eyes still followed Barbara, drift-

ing in the dance, like a great water-lily caught in the swirl of a
mill pool; and the thought passed through that pretty head:

'She's hooked him. It's naughty of Babs, really!' And
then she saw leaning against a pillar another whose eyes also
were following those two; and she thought: 'H'm! Poor Claud
—no wonder he's looking like that. Oh! Babs!'

By one of the statues on the terrace Barbara and her partner
stood, where trees, disfigured by no gaudy lanterns, offered the
refreshment of their darkness and serenity.

Wrapped in her new pale languor, still breathing deeply from
the waltz, she seemed to Courtier too utterly moulded out of
loveliness. To what end should a man frame speeches to a
vision! She was but an incarnation of beauty imprinted on
the air, and would fade out at a touch—like the sudden ghosts
of enchantment that came to one under the blue, and the starlit
snow of a mountain night, or in a birch wood and wistful golden!
Speech seemed but desecration! Besides, what of interest was
there for him to speak of in this world of hers, so bewildering
and so glibly assured—this world that was like a building, whose
every window was shut and had a blind drawn down. A building that admitted none who had not sworn, as it were, to believe it the world, the whole world, and nothing but the world,
outside which were only the rubbled remains of what had built
it. This world of Society, in which he felt like one travelling
through a desert, longing to meet a fellow-creature!

The voice of Harbinger behind them said:

" Lady Babs! "

Long did the punkahs waft their breeze over that brave-hued
wheel of pleasure, and the sound of the violins quaver and wail
out into the morning. Then quickly, as the spangles of dew
vanish off grass when the sun rises, all melted away; and in the
great rooms were none but flunkeys presiding over the polished
surfaces like flamingoes by some lakeside at dawn.

CHAPTER III

A BRICK dower-house of the Fitz-Harolds, just outside the little seaside town of Nettlefold, sheltered the tranquil days of Lord Dennis. In that south-coast air, sanest and most healing in all England, he aged very slowly, taking little thought of death, and much quiet pleasure in his life. Like the tall old house with its high windows and squat chimneys, he was marvellously self-contained. His books, for he somewhat passionately examined old civilisations, and described their habits from time to time with a dry and not too poignant pen in a certain old-fashioned magazine; his microscope, for he studied infusoria; and the fishing boat of his friend John Bogle, who had long perceived that Lord Dennis was the biggest fish he ever caught; all these, with occasional visitors, and little runs to London, to Monkland, and other country houses, made up the sum of a life which, if not desperately beneficial, was uniformly kind and harmless, and, by its notorious simplicity, had a certain negative influence not only on his own class but on the relations of that class with the country at large. It was commonly said in Nettlefold, that he was a gentleman; if they were all like him there wasn't much in all this talk against the Lords. The shop people and lodging-house keepers felt that the interests of the country were safer in his hands than in the hands of people who wanted to meddle with everything for the good of those who were only anxious to be let alone. A man too who could so completely forget he was the son of a Duke, that other people never forget it, was the man for their money. It was true that he had never had a say in public affairs; but this was overlooked, because he could have had it if he liked, and the fact that he did not like, only showed once more that he was a gentleman.

Just as he was the one personality of the little town against whom practically nothing was ever said, so was his house the one house which defied criticism. Time had made it utterly suitable. The ivied walls, and purplish roof lichened yellow in places, the quiet meadows harbouring ponies and kine, reaching from it to the sea—all was mellow. In truth it made all the other houses of the town seem shoddy—standing alone beyond them, like its master, if anything a little too æsthetically remote from common wants.

He had practically no near neighbours of whom he saw any-thing, except once in a way young Harbinger three miles distant at Whitewater. But since he had the faculty of not being bored with his own society, this did not worry him. Of local charity, especially to the fishers of the town, whose winter months were nowadays very bare of profit, he was prodigal to the verge of extravagance, for his income was not great. But in politics, be-yond acting as the figure-head of certain municipal efforts, he took little or no part. His Toryism indeed was of the mild order, that had little belief in the regeneration of the country by any means but those of kindly feeling between the classes. When asked how that was to be brought about, he would answer with his dry, slightly malicious, suavity, that if you stirred hornets' nests with sticks the hornets would come forth. Having no land, he was shy of expressing himself on that vexed question; but if resolutely attacked would give utterance to some such sentiment as this: " The land's best in our hands on the whole, but we want fewer dogs-in-the-manger among us."

He had, as became one of his race, a feeling for land, tender and protective, and could not bear to think of its being put out to farm with that cold Mother, the State. He was ironical over the views of Radicals or Socialists, but disliked to hear such people personally abused behind their backs. It must be con-fessed, however, that if contradicted he increased considerably the ironical decision of his sentiments. Withdrawn from all chance in public life of enforcing his views on others, the natural aristocrat within him was forced to find some expres-sion.

Each year, towards the end of July, he placed his house at the service of Lord Valleys, who found it a convenient centre for attending Goodwood.

It was on the morning after the Duchess of Gloucester's Ball, that he received this note:

"VALLEYS HOUSE.

" DEAREST UNCLE DENNIS,

" May I come down to you a little before time, and rest? London is so terribly hot. Mother has three functions still to stay for, and I shall have to come back again for our last eve-ning, the political one—so I don't want to go all the way to

Monkland; and anywhere else, except with you, would be rackety. Eustace looks so seedy. I'll try and bring him, if I may. Granny is terribly well.

" Best love, dear, from your

" BABS."

The same afternoon she came, but without Miltoun, driving up from the station in a fly. Lord Dennis met her at the gate; and, having kissed her, looked at her somewhat anxiously, caressing his white peaked beard. He had never yet known Babs sick of anything, except when he took her out in John Bogle's boat. She was certainly looking pale, and her hair was done differently —a fact disturbing to one who did not discover it. Slipping his arm through hers he led her out into a meadow still full of buttercups, where an old white pony, who had carried her in the Row twelve years ago, came up to them and rubbed his muzzle against her waist. And suddenly there rose in Lord Dennis the thoroughly discomforting and strange suspicion that, though the child was not going to cry, she wanted time to get over the feeling that she was. Without appearing to separate himself from her, he walked to the wall at the end of the field, and stood looking at the sea.

The tide was nearly up; the South wind driving over it brought to him the scent of the sea-flowers, and the crisp rustle of little waves swimming almost to his feet. Far out, where the sunlight fell, the smiling waters lay white and mysterious in July gaze, giving him a queer feeling. But Lord Dennis, though he had his moments of poetic sentiment, was on the whole quite able to keep the sea in its proper place—for after all it was the English Channel; and like a good Englishman he recognised that if you once let things get away from their names, they ceased to be facts, and if they ceased to be facts, they became —the devil! In truth he was not thinking much of the sea, but of Barbara. It was plain that she was in trouble of some kind. And the notion that Babs could find trouble in life was extraordinarily queer; for he felt, subconsciously, what a great driving force of disturbance was necessary to penetrate the hundred folds of the luxurious cloak enwrapping one so young and fortunate. It was not Death; therefore it must be Love; and he thought at once of that fellow with the red moustaches. Ideas were all very well—no one would object to as many as you liked, in their proper place—the dinner-table, for example. But to fall in love, if indeed it were so, with a man who not only had ideas, but an inclination to live up to them, and on them, and on nothing else, seemed to Lord Dennis *outré*.

She had followed him to the wall, and he looked at her dubiously.

" To rest in the waters of Lethe, Babs? By the way, seen anything of our friend Mr. Courtier? Very picturesque—that Quixotic theory of life!" And in saying that, his voice (like so many refined voices which have turned their backs on speculation) was triple-toned—mocking at ideas, mocking at itself for mocking at ideas, yet showing plainly that at bottom it only mocked at itself for mocking at ideas, because it would be, as it were, crude not to do so.

But Barbara did not answer his question, and began to speak of other things. And all that afternoon and evening she talked away so lightly that Lord Dennis, but for his instinct, would have been deceived.

That wonderful smiling mask—the inscrutability of Youth— was laid aside by her at night. Sitting at her window, under the moon, " a gold-bright moth slow-spinning up the sky," she watched the darkness hungrily, as though it were a great thought into whose heart she was trying to see. Now and then she stroked herself, getting strange comfort out of the presence of her body. She had that old unhappy feeling of having two selves within her. And this soft night full of the quiet stir of the sea, and of dark immensity, woke in her a terrible longing to be at one with something, somebody, outside herself. At the Ball last night the " flying feeling " had seized on her again; and was still there—a queer manifestation of her streak of recklessness. And this result of her contacts with Courtier, this *cacoethes volandi,* and feeling of clipped wings, hurt her—as being forbidden hurts a child.

She remembered how in the housekeeper's room at Monkland there lived a magpie who had once sought shelter in an orchid-house from some pursuer. As soon as they thought him wedded to civilisation, they had let him go, to see whether he would come back. For hours he had sat up in a high tree, and at last come down again to his cage; whereupon, fearing lest the rooks should attack him when he next took this voyage of discovery, they clipped one of his wings. After that the twilight bird, though he lived happily enough, hopping about his cage and the terrace which served him for exercise yard, would seem at times restive and frightened, moving his wings as if flying in spirit, and sad that he must stay on earth.

So, too, at her window Barbara fluttered her wings; then, getting into bed, lay sighing and tossing. A clock struck three; and seized by an intolerable impatience at her own discomfort, she slipped a motor coat over her night-gown, put on slippers, and stole out into the passage. The house was very still. She crept downstairs, smothering her footsteps. Groping her way through the hall, inhabited by the thin ghosts of would-be light, she slid back the chain of the door, and fled towards the sea. She made no more noise running in the dew, than a bird following the paths of air; and the two ponies, who felt her figure pass in the darkness, snuffled, sending out soft sighs of alarm amongst the closed buttercups. She climbed the wall over to the beach. While she was running, she had fully meant to dash into the sea and cool herself, but it was so black, with just a thin edging scarf of white, and the sky was black, bereft of lights, waiting for the day!

She stood, and looked. And all the leapings and pulsings of flesh and spirit slowly died in that wide dark loneliness, where the only sound was the wistful breaking of small waves. She was well used to these dead hours—only last night, at this very time, Harbinger's arm had been round her in a last waltz! But here the dead hours had such different faces, wide-eyed, solemn; and there came to Barbara, staring out at them, a sense that the darkness saw her very soul, so that it felt little and timid within her. She shivered in her fur-lined coat, as if almost frightened at finding herself so marvellously nothing before that black sky and dark sea, which seemed all one, relentlessly great. And crouching down, she waited for the dawn to break.

It came from over the Downs, sweeping a rush of cold air on its wings, flighting towards the sea. With it the daring soon crept back into her blood. She stripped, and ran down into the dark water, fast growing pale. It covered her jealously, and she set to work to swim. The water was warmer than the air. She lay on her back and splashed, watching the sky flush. To bathe like this in the half-dark, with her hair floating out, and no wet clothes clinging to her limbs, gave her the joy of a child doing a naughty thing. She swam out of her depth, then scared at her own adventure, swam in again as the sun rose.

She dashed into her two garments, climbed the wall, and

scurried back to the house. All her dejection, and feverish uncertainty were gone; she felt keen, fresh, terribly hungry, and
stealing into the dark dining-room, began rummaging for food.
She found biscuits, and was still munching, when in the open
doorway she saw Lord Dennis, a pistol in one hand and a lighted
candle in the other. With his carved features and white beard
above an old blue dressing-gown, he looked impressive, having
at the moment a distinct resemblance to Lady Casterley, as
though danger had armoured him in steel.

"You call this resting!" he said, dryly; then, looking at her
drowned hair, added: "I see you have already entrusted your
trouble to the waters of Lethe."

But without answer Barbara vanished into the dim hall and
up the stairs.

CHAPTER IV

WHILE Barbara was swimming to meet the dawn, Miltoun was
bathing in those waters of mansuetude and truth which roll from
wall to wall in the British House of Commons.

In that long debate on the Land question, for which he had
waited to make his first speech, he had already risen nine times
without catching the Speaker's eye, and slowly a sense of unreality was creeping over him. Surely this great Chamber, where
without end rose the small sound of a single human voice, and
queer mechanical bursts of approbation and resentment, did not
exist at all but as a gigantic fancy of his own! And all these
figures were figments of his brain! And when he at last spoke,
it would be himself alone that he addressed! The torpid air
tainted with human breath, the unwinking stare of the countless
lights, the long rows of seats, the queer distant rounds of pale
listening flesh perched up so high, they were all emanations of
himself! Even the coming and going in the gangway was but
the coming and going of little wilful parts of him! And rustling
deep down in this Titanic creature of his fancy was the murmuration of his own unspoken speech, sweeping away the puff
balls of words flung up by that far-away, small, varying voice.

Then, suddenly all that dream creature had vanished; he was
on his feet, with a thumping heart, speaking.

Soon he had no tremors, only a dim consciousness that his
words sounded strange, and a queer icy pleasure in flinging them
out into the silence. Round him there seemed no longer men,
only mouths and eyes. And he had enjoyment in the feeling
that with these words of his he was holding those hungry mouths
and eyes dumb and unmoving. Then he knew that he had
reached the end of what he had to say, and sat down, remaining
motionless in the centre of a various sound, staring at the back
of the head in front of him, with his hands clasped round his
knee. And soon, when that little far-away voice was once more
speaking, he took his hat, and glancing neither to right nor left,
went out.

Instead of the sensation of relief and wild elation which fills
the heart of those who have taken the first plunge, Miltoun had
nothing in his deep dark well but the waters of bitterness. In

truth, with the delivery of that speech he had but parted with what had been a sort of anodyne to suffering. He had only put the fine point on his conviction, of how vain was his career now that he could not share it with Audrey Noel. He walked slowly towards the Temple, along the riverside, where the lamps were paling into nothingness before that daily celebration of Divinity, the meeting of dark and light.

For Miltoun was not one of those who take things lying down; he took things desperately, deeply, and with revolt. He took them like a rider riding himself, plunging at the dig of his own spurs, chafing and wincing at the cruel tugs of his own bitt; bearing in his friendless, proud heart all the burden of struggles which shallower or more genial natures shared with others.

He looked hardly less haggard, walking home, than some of those homeless ones who slept nightly by the river, as though they knew that to lie near one who could so readily grant oblivion alone could save them from seeking that consolation. He was perhaps unhappier than they, whose spirits, at all events, had long ceased to worry them, having oozed out from their bodies under the foot of Life.

Now that Audrey Noel was lost to him, her loveliness and that indescribable quality which made her lovable, floated before him, the very torture-flowers of a beauty never to be grasped—yet, that he could grasp, if he only would! That was the heart and fervour of his suffering. To be grasped if he only would! He was suffering, too, physically from a kind of slow fever, the result of his wetting on the day when he last saw her. And through that latent fever, things and feelings, like his sensations in the House before his speech, were all as it were muffled in a horrible way, as if they all came to him wrapped in a sort of flannel coating, through which he could not cut. And all the time there seemed to be within him two men at mortal grips with one another; the man of faith in divine sanction and authority, on which all his beliefs had hitherto hinged, and a desperate warm-blooded hungry creature. He was very miserable, craving strangely for the society of someone who could understand what he was feeling, and, from long habit of making no confidants, not knowing how to satisfy that craving.

It was dawn when he reached his rooms; and, sure that he would not sleep, he did not even go to bed, but changed his clothes, made himself some coffee, and sat down at the window which overlooked the flowered courtyard.

In Middle Temple Hall a Ball was still in progress, though the glamour from its Chinese lanterns was already darkened and gone. Miltoun saw a man and a girl, sheltered by an old fountain, sitting out their last dance. Her head had sunk on her partner's shoulder; their lips were joined. And there floated up to the window the scent of heliotrope, with the tune of the waltz that those two should have been dancing. This couple so stealthily enlaced, the gleam of their furtively turned eyes, the whispering of their lips, that stony niche below the twittering sparrows, so cunningly sought out—it was the world he had abjured! When he looked again, they—like a vision seen—had stolen away and gone; the music too had ceased, there was no scent of heliotrope. In the stony niche crouched a stray cat watching the twittering sparrows.

Miltoun went out, and turning into the empty Strand, walked on without heeding where, till towards five o'clock he found himself on Putney Bridge.

He rested there, leaning over the parapet, looking down at the grey water. The sun was just breaking through the heat haze; early waggons were passing, and already men were coming in to work. To what end did the river wander up and down; and a human river flow across it twice every day? To what end were men and women suffering? Of the full current of this life Miltoun could no more see the aim, than that of the wheeling gulls in the early sunlight.

Leaving the bridge he made towards Barnes Common. The night was still ensnared there on the gorce bushes grey with cobwebs and starry dewdrops. He passed a tramp family still sleeping, huddled all together. Even the homeless lay in each other's arms!

From the Common he emerged on the road near the gates of Ravensham; turning in there, he found his way to the kitchen garden, and sat down on a bench close to the raspberry bushes. They were protected from thieves, but at Miltoun's approach two blackbirds flustered out through the netting and flew away.

His long figure resting so motionless impressed itself on the eyes of a gardener, who caused a report to be circulated that his young lordship was in the fruit garden. It reached the ears of Clifton, who himself came out to see what this might mean. The old man took his stand in front of Miltoun very quietly.

" You have come to breakfast, my lord? "

" If my grandmother will have me, Clifton."

" I understood your lordship was speaking last night."

" I was."

" You find the House of Commons satisfactory, I hope."

" Fairly, thank you, Clifton."

" They are not what they were in the great days of your grandfather, I believe. He had a very good opinion of them. They vary, no doubt."

" *Tempora mutantur.*"

" That is so. I find quite a new spirit towards public affairs. The ha'penny Press; one takes it in, but one hardly approves. I shall be anxious to read your speech. They say a first speech is a great strain."

" It is rather."

" But *you* had no reason to be anxious. I'm sure it was beautiful."

Miltoun saw that the old man's thin sallow cheeks had flushed to a deep orange between his snow-white whiskers.

" I have looked forward to this day," he stammered, " ever since I knew your lordship—twenty-eight years. It is the beginning."

" Or the end, Clifton."

The old man's face fell in a look of deep and concerned astonishment.

" No, no," he said; " with your antecedents, never."

Miltoun took his hand.

" Sorry, Clifton—didn't mean to shock you."

And for a minute neither spoke, looking at their clasped hands as if surprised.

" Would your lordship like a bath—breakfast is still at eight. I can procure you a razor."

When Miltoun entered the breakfast room, his grandmother, with a copy of the *Times* in her hands, was seated before a grape fruit, which, with a shredded wheat biscuit, constituted her first meal. Her appearance hardly warranted Barbara's description of " terribly well "; in truth she looked a little white, as if she had been feeling the heat. But there was no lack of animation in her little steel-grey eyes, nor of decision in her manner.

" I see," she said, " that you've taken a line of your own, Eustace. I've nothing to say against that; in fact, quite the contrary. But remember this, my dear, however you may change, you mustn't wobble. Only one thing counts in that place, hitting the same nail on the head with the same hammer all the time. You aren't looking at all well."

Miltoun, bending to kiss her, murmured:

"Thanks, I'm all right."

"Nonsense," replied Lady Casterley. "They don't look after you. Was your mother in the House?"

"I don't think so."

"Exactly. And what is Barbara about? She ought to be seeing to you."

"Barbara is down with Uncle Dennis."

Lady Casterley set her jaw; then looking her grandson through and through, said:

"I shall take you down there this very day. I shall have the sea to you. What do you say, Clifton?"

"His lordship does look pale."

"Have the carriage, and we'll go from Clapham Junction. Thomas can go in and fetch you some clothes. Or, better, though I dislike them, we can telephone to your mother for a car. It's very hot for trains. Arrange that, please, Clifton!"

To this project Miltoun raised no objection. And all through the drive he remained sunk in an indifference and lassitude which to Lady Casterley seemed in the highest degree ominous. For lassitude, to her, was the strange, the unpardonable, state. The little great lady—casket of the aristocratic principle—was permeated to the very backbone with the instinct of artificial energy, of that alert vigour which those who have nothing socially to hope for are forced to develop, lest they should decay and be again obliged to hope. To speak honest truth, she could not forbear an itch to run some sharp and foreign substance into her grandson, to rouse him somehow, for she knew the reason of his state, and was temperamentally out of patience with such a cause for backsliding. Had it been any other of her grandchildren she would not have hesitated, but there was that in Miltoun which held even Lady Casterley in check, and only once during the four hours of travel did she attempt to break down his reserve. She did it in a manner very soft for her—was he not of all living things the hope and pride of her heart? Tucking her little thin sharp hand under his arm, she said quietly:

"My dear, don't brood over it. That will never do."

But Miltoun removed her hand gently, and laid it back on the dusty rug, nor did he answer, or show other sign of having heard.

And Lady Casterley, deeply wounded, pressed her faded lips together, and said sharply:

" Slower, please, Frith ! "

CHAPTER V

It was to Barbara that Miltoun unfolded, if but little, the trouble of his spirit, lying that same afternoon under a ragged tamarisk hedge with the tide far out. He could never have done this if there had not been between them the accidental revelation of that night at Monkland; nor even then perhaps had he not felt in this young sister of his the warmth of life for which he was yearning. In such a matter as love Barbara was the elder of these two. For, besides the motherly knowledge of the heart peculiar to most women, she had the inherent woman-of-the-worldliness to be expected of a daughter of Lord and Lady Valleys. If she herself were in doubt as to the state of her affections, it was not as with Miltoun, on the score of the senses and the heart, but on the score of her spirit and curiosity, which Courtier had awakened and caused to flap their wings a little. She worried over Miltoun's forlorn case; it hurt her, too, to think of Mrs. Noel eating her heart out in that lonely cottage. A sister so good and earnest as Agatha had ever inclined Barbara to a rebellious view of morals, and disinclined her altogether to religion. And so, she felt that if those two could not be happy apart, they should be happy together, in the name of all the joy there was in life!

And while her brother lay face to the sky under the tamarisks, she kept trying to think of how to console him, conscious that she did not in the least understand the way he thought about things. Over the fields behind, the larks were hymning the promise of the unripe corn; the foreshore was painted all colours, from vivid green to mushroom pink; by the edge of the blue sea little black figures stooped, gathering samphire. The air smelled sweet in the shade of the tamarisk; there was ineffable peace. And Barbara, covered by the network of sunlight, could not help impatience with a suffering which seemed to her so corrigible by action. At last she ventured:

"Life is short, Eusty!"

Miltoun's answer, given without movement, startled her.

"Persuade me that it is, Babs, and I'll bless you. If the singing of these larks means nothing, if that blue up there is a morass of our invention, if we are pettily creeping on furthering nothing, if there's no purpose in our lives, persuade me of it, for God's sake!"

Carried suddenly beyond her depth, Barbara could only put out her hand, and say: "Oh! don't take things so hard!"

"Since you say that life is short," Miltoun muttered, with his smile, "you shouldn't spoil it by feeling pity! In old days we went to the Tower for our convictions. We can stand a little private roasting, I hope; or has the sand run out of us altogether?"

Stung by his tone, Barbara answered in rather a hard voice: "What we *must* bear, we must, I suppose. But why should we *make* trouble? That's what I can't stand!"

"O profound wisdom!"

Barbara flushed.

"I love Life!" she said.

The galleons of the westering sun were already sailing in a broad gold fleet straight for that foreshore where the little black stooping figures had not yet finished their toil, the larks still sang over the unripe corn—when Harbinger, galloping along the sands from Whitewater to Sea House, came on that silent couple walking home to dinner.

It would not be safe to say of this young man that he readily diagnosed a spiritual atmosphere, but this was the less his demerit, since everything from his cradle up had conspired to keep the spiritual thermometer of his surroundings at 60 in the shade. And the fact that his own spiritual thermometer had now run up so that it threatened to burst the bulb, rendered him less likely than ever to see what was happening with other people's. Yet he did notice that Barbara was looking pale, and—it seemed —sweeter than ever. With her eldest brother he always somehow felt ill at ease. He could not exactly afford to despise an uncompromising spirit in one of his own order, but he was no more impervious than others to Miltoun's caustic, thinly-veiled contempt for the commonplace; and having a full-blooded belief in himself—usual with men of fine physique, whose lots are so cast that this belief can never or almost never be really shaken— he greatly disliked the feeling of being a little looked down on. It was an intense relief, when, saying that he wanted a certain magazine, Miltoun strode off into the town.

To Harbinger, no less than to Miltoun and Barbara, last night had been bitter and restless. The sight of that pale swaying figure, with the parted lips, whirling round in Courtier's arms, had clung to his vision ever since the Ball. During his own last dance with her he had been almost savagely silent; only by a great effort restraining his tongue from mordant allusions to that 'prancing, red-haired fellow,' as he secretly called the champion of lost causes. In fact, his sensations then and since had been a revelation, or would have been if he could have stood apart to see them. True, he had gone about next day with his usual cool, offhand manner, because one naturally did not let people see, but it was with such an inner aching and rage of want and jealousy as to really merit pity. Men of his physically big, rather rushing, type, are the last to possess their souls in patience. Walking home after the Ball he had determined to follow her down to the sea, where she had said, so maliciously, that she was going. After a second almost sleepless night he had no longer any hesitation. He must see her! After all, a man might go to his own "place" with impunity; he did not care if it were a pointed thing to do. Pointed! The more pointed the better! There was beginning to be roused in him an ugly stubbornness of male determination. She should not escape him!

But now that he was walking at her side, all that determination and assurance melted to perplexed humility. He marched along by his horse with his head down, just feeling the ache of being so close to her and yet so far; angry with his own silence and awkwardness, almost angry with her for her loveliness, and the pain it made him suffer. When they reached the house, and she left him at the stable-yard, saying she was going to get some flowers, he jerked the beast's bridle and swore at it for its slowness in entering the stable. He was terrified that she would be gone before he could get into the garden; yet half afraid of finding her there. But she was still plucking carnations by the box hedge which led to the conservatories. And as she rose from gathering those blossoms, before he knew what he was doing, Harbinger had thrown his arm around her, held her as in a vice, kissed her unmercifully.

She seemed to offer no resistance, her smooth cheeks growing warmer and warmer, even her lips passive; but suddenly he recoiled, and his heart stood still at his own outrageous daring. What had he done? He saw her leaning back almost buried in the clipped box hedge, and heard her say with a sort of faint mockery: "Well!"

He would have flung himself down on his knees to ask for

pardon but for the thought that someone might come. He muttered hoarsely: " By God, I was mad ! " and stood glowering in sullen suspense between hardihood and fear. He heard her say, quietly:

" Yes, you were—rather."

Then seeing her put her hand up to her lips as if he had hurt them, he muttered brokenly:

" Forgive me, Babs ! "

There was a full minute's silence while he stood there, no longer daring to look at her, beaten all over by his emotions. Then, with bewilderment, he heard her say:

" I didn't mind it—for once ! "

He looked up at that. How could she love him, and speak so coolly ! How could she not mind, if she did not love him ! She was passing her hands over her face and neck and hair, repairing the damage of his kisses.

" Now shall we go in ? " she said.

Harbinger took a step forward.

" I love you so," he said; " I will put my life in your hands, and you shall throw it away."

At those words, of whose exact nature he had very little knowledge, he saw her smile.

" If I let you come within three yards, will you be good ? "

He bowed; and, in silence, they walked towards the house.

Dinner that evening was a strange, uncomfortable meal. But its comedy, too subtly played for Miltoun and Lord Dennis, seemed transparent to the eyes of Lady Casterley; for, when Harbinger had sallied forth to ride back along the sands, she took her candle and invited Barbara to retire. Then, having admitted her granddaughter to the apartment always reserved for herself, and specially furnished with practically nothing, she sat down opposite that tall, young, solid figure, as it were taking stock of it, and said:

" So you are coming to your senses, at all events. Kiss me ! "

Barbara, stooping to perform this rite, saw a tear stealing down the carved fine nose. Knowing that to notice it would be too dreadful, she raised herself, and went to the window. There, staring out over the dark fields and dark sea, by the side of which Harbinger was riding home, she put her hand up to her lips, and thought for the hundredth time:

' So that's what it's like ! '

CHAPTER VI

THREE days after his first, and as he promised himself, his last Society Ball, Courtier received a note from Audrey Noel, saying that she had left Monkland for the present, and come up to a little flat on the riverside not far from Westminster.

When he made his way there that same July day, the Houses of Parliament were bright under a sun which warmed all the grave air emanating from their counsels of perfection. Courtier passed by dubiously. His feelings in the presence of those towers were always a little mixed. There was not so much of the poet in him as to cause him to see nothing there at all save only some lines against the sky, but there *was* enough of the poet to make him long to kick something; and in this mood he wended his way to the riverside.

Mrs. Noel was not at home, but since the maid informed him that she would be in directly, he sat down to wait. Her flat, which was on the first floor, overlooked the river, and had evidently been taken furnished, for there were visible marks of a recent struggle with an Edwardian taste which, flushed from triumph over Victorianism, had filled the rooms with early Georgian remains. On the only definite victory, a rose-coloured window seat of great comfort and little age, Courtier sat down, and resigned himself to doing nothing with the ease of an old soldier.

To the protective feeling he had once had for a very graceful, dark-haired child, he joined not only the championing pity of a man of warm heart watching a woman in distress, but the impatience of one, who, though temperamentally incapable of feeling oppressed himself, rebelled at sight of all forms of tyranny affecting others.

The sight of the grey towers, still just visible, under which Miltoun and his father sat, annoyed him deeply; symbolising to him, Authority—foe to his deathless mistress, the sweet, invincible lost cause of Liberty. But presently the river, bringing up in flood the unbound water that had bathed every shore, touched all sands, and seen the lighting and fading of each mortal star, so soothed him with its soundless hymn to Freedom,

644

that Audrey Noel coming in with her hands full of flowers, found him sleeping firmly, with his mouth shut.

Noiselessly putting down the flowers, she waited for his awakening. That sanguine visage, with its prominent chin, flaring moustaches, and eyebrows raised rather V-shaped above his closed eyes, wore an expression of cheery defiance even in sleep; and perhaps no face in all London was so utterly its obverse, as that of this dark, soft-haired woman, delicate, passive, and tremulous with pleasure at sight of the only person in the world from whom she felt she might learn of Miltoun, without losing her self-respect.

He woke at last, and manifesting no discomfiture, said:

" It was like you not to wake me."

They sat for a long while talking, the riverside traffic drowsily accompanying their voices, the flowers drowsily filling the room with scent; and when Courtier left, his heart was sore. She had not spoken of herself at all, but had talked nearly all the time of Barbara, praising her beauty and high spirit; growing pale once or twice, and evidently drinking in with secret avidity every allusion to Miltoun. Clearly, her feelings had not changed, though she would not show them! Courtier's pity for her became wellnigh violent.

It was in such a mood, mingled with very different feelings, that he donned evening clothes and set out to attend the last gathering of the season at Valleys House, a function which, held so late in July, was perforce almost perfectly political.

Mounting the wide and shining staircase, that had so often baffled the arithmetic of little Ann, he was reminded of a picture entitled " The Steps to Heaven," in his nursery four-and-thirty years before. At the top of this staircase, and surrounded by acquaintances, he came on Harbinger, who nodded curtly. The young man's handsome face and figure appeared to Courtier's jaundiced eye more obviously successful and complacent than ever; so that he passed him by with a frown and manœuvred his way towards Lady Valleys, whom he could perceive stationed, like a general, in a little cleared space, where to and fro flowed constant streams of people, like the rays of a star. She was looking her very best, going well with great and highly-polished spaces; and she greeted Courtier with a special cordiality of tone, which had in it, besides kindness towards one who must be feeling a strange bird, a certain diplomatic quality, compounded of desire, as it were, to "warn him off," and fear of saying something that might irritate and make him more dangerous. She had heard, she said, that he was bound for Persia; she hoped he was not going to try and make things more difficult there; then with the words: "So good of you to have come!" she became once more the centre of her battlefield.

Perceiving that he was finished with, Courtier stood back against a wall and watched. Thus isolated, he was like a solitary cuckoo contemplating the gyrations of a flock of rooks. Their motions seemed a little meaningless to one so far removed from all the fetishes and shibboleths of Westminster. He heard them discussing Miltoun's speech, the real significance of which apparently had only just been grasped. The words "doctrinaire," "extremist," came to his ears, together with the saying "a new force." People were evidently puzzled, disturbed, not pleased— as if some star not hitherto accounted for had suddenly appeared among the proper constellations.

Searching this crowd for Barbara, Courtier had all the time an uneasy sense of shame. What business had he to come amongst these people so strange to him, just for the sake of seeing her! What business had he to be hankering after this girl at all, knowing in his heart that he could not stand the atmosphere she lived in for a week, and that she was utterly unsuited to any atmosphere that he could give her; to say nothing of the unlikelihood that he could flutter the pulses of one half his age!

A voice behind him said: "Mr. Courtier!"

He turned, and there was Barbara.

"I want to talk to you about something serious. Will you come into the picture gallery?"

When at last they were close to a family group of Georgian Carádocs, and could as it were shut out the throng sufficiently for private speech, she began:

"Miltoun's so horribly unhappy; I don't know what to do for him. He's making himself ill!"

And she suddenly looked up in Courtier's face. She seemed to him very young, and touching, at that moment. Her eyes had a gleam of faith in them, like a child's eyes, as if she relied on him to straighten out this tangle, to tell her not only about Miltoun's trouble, but about all life, its meaning, and the secret of its happiness. And he said gently:

"What can I do? Mrs. Noel is in Town. But that's no good,

unless——" Not knowing how to finish this sentence, he was silent.

"I wish I were Miltoun," she muttered.

At that quaint saying, Courtier was hard put to it not to take hold of the hands so close to him. This flash of rebellion in her had quickened all his blood. But she seemed to have seen what had passed in him, for her next speech was chilly.

"It's no good; stupid of me to be worrying you."

"It is quite impossible for you to worry me."

Her eyes, lifted suddenly from her glove, looked straight into his.

"Are you really going to Persia?"

"Yes."

"But I don't want you to, not yet!" and turning suddenly, she left him.

Strangely disturbed, Courtier remained motionless, consulting the grave stare of the group of Georgian Carádocs.

A voice said:

"Good painting, isn't it?"

Behind him was Lord Harbinger. And once more the memory of Lady Casterley's words; the memory of the two figures with joined hands on the balcony above the election crowd; all his latent jealousy of this handsome young Colossus, his animus against one whom he could, as it were, smell out to be always fighting on the winning side; all his consciousness too of what a lost cause his own was, his doubt whether he were honourable to look on it as a cause at all, flared up in Courtier, so that his answer was a stare. On Harbinger's face, too, there had come a look of stubborn violence slowly working up towards the surface.

"I said: 'Good, isn't it?' Mr. Courtier."

"I heard you."

"And you were pleased to answer?"

"Nothing."

"With the civility which might be expected of your habits."

Coldly disdainful, Courtier answered:

"If you want to say that sort of thing, please choose a place where I can reply to you," and turned abruptly on his heel.

But he ground his teeth as he made his way out into the street.

In Hyde Park the grass was parched and dewless under a sky whose stars were veiled by the heat and dust haze. Never had

Courtier so bitterly wanted the sky's consolation—the blessed sense of insignificance in the face of the night's dark beauty, which, dwarfing all petty rage and hunger, made men part of its majesty, exalted them to a sense of greatness.

CHAPTER VII

IT was past four o'clock the following day when Barbara issued from Valley House on foot; clad in a pale buff frock, chosen for quietness, she attracted every eye. Very soon entering a taxi-cab, she drove to the Temple, stopped at the Strand entrance, and walked down the little narrow lane into the heart of the Law. Its votaries were hurrying back from the Courts, streaming up from their Chambers for tea, or escaping desperately to Lord's or the Park—young votaries, unbound as yet by the fascination of fame or fees. And each, as he passed, looked at Barbara, with his fingers itching to remove his hat, and a feeling that this was She. After a day spent amongst precedents and practice, after six hours at least of trying to discover what chance A had of standing on his right, or B had of preventing him, it was diffi-cult to feel otherwise about that calm apparition—like a golden slim tree walking. One of them, asked by her the way to Mil-toun's staircase, preceded her with shy ceremony, and when she had vanished up those dusty stairs, lingered on, hoping that she might find her visitee out, and be obliged to return and ask him the way back. But she did not come, and he went sadly away, disturbed to the very bottom of all that he owned in fee simple.

In fact, no one answered Barbara's knock, and discovering that the door yielded, she walked through the lobby past the clerk's den, converted to a kitchen, into the sitting-room. It was empty. She had never been to Miltoun's rooms before, and she stared about her curiously. Since he did not practise, much of the proper gear was absent. The room indeed had a worn carpet, a few old chairs, and was lined from floor to ceiling with books. But the wall space between the windows was occu-pied by an enormous map of England, scored all over with figures and crosses; and before this map stood an immense desk, on which were piles of double foolscap covered with Miltoun's neat and rather pointed writing. Barbara examined them, puckering up her forehead; she knew that he was working at a book on the land question, but she had never realised that the making of a book required so much writing. Papers, too, and Blue Books littered a large bureau on which stood bronze busts of Æschylus and Dante.

'What an uncomfortable place!' she thought. The room, indeed, had an atmosphere, a spirit, which depressed her horribly. Seeing a few flowers down in the court below, she had a longing to get out to them. Then behind her she heard the sound of someone talking. But there was no one in the room; and the effect of this disrupted soliloquy, which came from nowhere, was so uncanny, that she retreated to the door. The sound, as of two spirits speaking in one voice, grew louder, and involuntarily she glanced at the busts. They seemed quite blameless. Though the sound had been behind her when she was at the window, it was again behind her now that she was at the door; and she suddenly realised that it was issuing from a bookcase in the centre of the wall. Barbara had her father's nerve, and walking up to the bookcase she perceived that it had been affixed to, and covered, a door that was not quite closed. She pulled it towards her, and passed through. Across the centre of an unkempt bedroom Miltoun was striding, dressed only in his shirt and trousers. His feet were bare, and his head and hair dripping wet; the look on his thin dark face went to Barbara's heart. She ran forward, and took his hand. This was burning hot, but the sight of her seemed to have frozen his tongue and eyes. And the contrast of his burning hand with this frozen silence, frightened Barbara horribly. She could think of nothing but to put her other hand to his forehead. That too was burning hot!

"What brought you here?" he said.

She could only murmur:

"Oh! Eusty! Are you ill?"

Miltoun took hold of her wrists.

"It's all right, I've been working too hard; got a touch of fever."

"So I can feel," murmured Barbara. "You ought to be in bed. Come home with me."

Miltoun smiled. "It's not a case for leeches."

The look of his smile, the sound of his voice, sent a shudder through her.

"I'm not going to leave you here alone."

But Miltoun's grasp tightened on her wrists.

"My dear Babs, you will do what I tell you. Go home, hold your tongue, and leave me to burn out in peace."

Barbara sustained that painful grip without wincing; she had regained her calmness.

"You *must* come! You haven't anything here, not even a cool drink."

"My God! Barley water!"

The scorn he put into those two words was more withering than a whole philippic against redemption by creature comforts. And, feeling it dart into her, Barbara closed her lips tight. He had dropped her wrists, and again begun pacing up and down; suddenly he stopped:

> "'The stars, sun, moon all shrink away,
> A desert vast, without a bound,
> And nothing left to eat or drink,
> And a dark desert all around.'

You should read your Blake, Audrey."

Barbara turned quickly, and went out frightened. She passed through the sitting-room and corridor on to the staircase. He was ill—raving! The fever in Miltoun's veins seemed to have stolen through the clutch of his hands into her own veins. Her face was burning, she thought confusedly, breathed unevenly. She felt sore, and at the same time terribly sorry; and withal there kept rising in her the gusty memory of Harbinger's kiss.

She hurried down the stairs, turned by instinct down-hill and found herself on the Embankment. And suddenly, with her inherent power of swift decision, she hailed a cab, and drove to the nearest telephone office.

CHAPTER VIII

To a woman like Audrey Noel, born to be the counterpart and complement of another, whose occupations and effort were inherently divorced from the continuity of any stiff and strenuous purpose of her own, the uprooting she had voluntarily undergone was a serious matter.

Bereaved of the faces of her flowers, the friendly sighing of her lime-tree, the wants of her cottagers; bereaved of that busy monotony of little home things which is the stay and solace of lonely women, she was extraordinarily lost. Even music for review seemed to have failed her. She had never lived in London, so that she had not the refuge of old haunts and habits, but had to make her own—and to make habits and haunts required a heart that could at least stretch out feelers and lay hold of things, and her heart was not now able. When she had struggled with her Edwardian flat, and laid down her simple routine of meals, she was as stranded as ever was convict let out of prison. She had not even that great support, the necessity of hiding her feelings for fear of disturbing others. She was planted there, with her longing and grief, and nothing, nobody, to take her out of herself. Having wilfully embraced this position, she tried to make the best of it, feeling it less intolerable, at all events, than staying on at Monkland, where she had made that grievous and unpardonable error—falling in love.

This offence, on the part of one who felt within herself a great capacity to enjoy and to confer happiness, had arisen—like the other grievous and unpardonable offence, her marriage—from too much disposition to yield herself to the personality of another. But it was cold comfort to know that the desire to give and to receive love had twice over left her—a dead woman. Whatever the nature of those immature sensations with which, as a girl of twenty, she had accepted her husband, in her feeling towards Miltoun there was not only abandonment, but the higher flame of self-renunciation. She wanted to do the best for him, and had not even the consolation of the knowledge that she had sacrificed herself for his advantage. All had been taken out of her hands! Yet with characteristic fatalism she did not feel rebellious. If it were ordained that she should, for fifty, perhaps sixty years, repent in sterility and ashes that first error of her girlhood, rebellion was, none the less, too far-fetched. If she rebelled, it would not be in spirit, but in action. General principles were nothing to her; she lost no force brooding over the justice or injustice of her situation, but merely tried to digest its facts.

The whole day, succeeding Courtier's visit, was spent by her in the National Gallery, whose roof, alone of all in London, seemed to offer her protection. She had found one painting, by an Italian master, the subject of which reminded her of Miltoun; and before this she sat for a very long time, attracting at last the gouty stare of an official. The still figure of this lady, with the oval face and grave beauty, both piqued his curiosity, and stimulated certain moral qualms. She was undoubtedly waiting for her lover. No woman, in his experience, had ever sat so long before a picture without ulterior motive; and he kept his eyes well opened to see what this motive would be like. It gave him, therefore, a sensation almost amounting to chagrin when coming round once more, he found they had eluded him and gone off together without coming under his inspection. Feeling his feet a good deal, for he had been on them all day, he sat down in the hollow which she had left behind her; and against his will found himself also looking at the picture. It was painted in a style he did not care for; the face of the subject, too, gave him the queer feeling that the gentleman was being roasted inside. He had not been sitting there long, however, before he perceived the lady standing by the picture, and the lips of the gentleman in the picture moving. It seemed to him against the rules and he got up at once, and went towards it; but as he did so, he found that his eyes were shut, and opened them hastily. There was no one there.

From the National Gallery, Audrey had gone into an A.B.C. for tea, and then home. Before the Mansions was a taxi-cab, and the maid met her with the news that "Lady Caradog" was in the sitting-room.

Barbara was indeed standing in the middle of the room with a look on her face such as her father wore sometimes on the racecourses, in the hunting field, or at stormy Cabinet Meetings; a look both resolute and sharp. She spoke at once:

"I got your address from Mr. Courtier. My brother is ill. I'm afraid it'll be brain fever, I think you had better go and see him at his rooms in the Temple; there's no time to be lost."

To Audrey everything in the room seemed to go round; yet all her senses were preternaturally acute, so that she could distinctly smell the mud of the river at low tide. She said, with a shudder:

"Oh! I will go; yes, I will go at once."

"He's quite alone. He hasn't asked for you; but I think your going is the only chance. He took me for you. You told me once you were a good nurse."

"Yes."

The room was steady enough now, but she had lost the preternatural acuteness of her senses, and felt confused. She heard Barbara say: "I can take you to the door in my cab," and murmuring: "I will get ready," went into her bedroom. For a moment she was so utterly bewildered that she did nothing. Then every other thought was lost in a strange, soft, almost painful delight, as if some new instinct were being born in her; and quickly, but without confusion or hurry, she began packing. She put into a valise her own toilet things; then flannel, cotton-wool, eau de Cologne, hot-water bottle, Etna, shawls, thermometer, everything she had which could serve in illness. Changing to a plain dress, she took up the valise and returned to Barbara. They went out together to the cab. The moment it began to bear her to this ordeal at once so longed-for and so terrible, fear came over her again, so that she screwed herself into the corner, very white and still. She was aware of Barbara calling to the driver: "Go by the Strand, and stop at a poulterer's for ice!" And, when the bag of ice had been handed in, heard her saying: "I will bring you all you want—if he is really going to be ill."

Then, as the cab stopped, and the open doorway of the staircase was before her, all her courage came back.

She felt the girl's warm hand against her own, and grasping her valise and the bag of ice, got out, and hurried up the steps.

CHAPTER IX

On leaving Nettlefold, Miltoun had gone straight back to his rooms, and begun at once to work at his book on the land question. He worked all through that night—his third night without sleep, and all the following day. In the evening, feeling queer in the head, he went out and walked up and down the Embankment. Then, fearing to go to bed and lie sleepless, he sat down in his armchair. Falling asleep there, he had fearful dreams, and awoke unrefreshed. After his bath, he drank coffee, and again forced himself to work. By the middle of the day he felt dizzy and exhausted, but utterly disinclined to eat. He went out into the hot Strand, bought himself a necessary book, and after drinking more coffee, came back and again began to work. At four o'clock he found that he was not taking in the words. His head was burning hot, and he went into his bedroom to bathe it. Then somehow he began walking up and down, talking to himself, as Barbara had found him.

She had no sooner gone, than he felt utterly exhausted. A small crucifix hung over his bed, and throwing himself down before it, he remained motionless with his face buried in the coverlet, and his arms stretched out towards the wall. He did not pray, but merely sought rest from sensation. Across his half-hypnotised consciousness little threads of burning fancy kept shooting. Then he could feel nothing but utter physical sickness, and against this his will revolted. He resolved that he would not be ill, a ridiculous log for women to hang over. But the moments of sickness grew longer and more frequent; and to drive them away he rose from his knees, and for some time again walked up and down; then, seized with vertigo, he was obliged to sit on the bed to save himself from falling. From being burning hot he had become deadly cold, glad to cover himself with the bedclothes. The heat soon flamed up in him again; but with a sick man's instinct he did not throw off the clothes, and stayed quite still. The room seemed to have turned to a thick white substance like a cloud, in which he lay enwrapped, unable to move hand or foot. His sense of smell and hearing had become unnaturally acute; he smelled the distant streets, flowers, dust, and the leather of his books, even the scent left by Barbara's clothes, and a curious odour of river mud. A clock struck six, he counted each stroke; and instantly the whole world seemed full of striking clocks, the sound of horses' hoofs, bicycle bells, people's footfalls. His sense of vision, on the contrary, was absorbed in consciousness of this white blanket of cloud wherein he was lifted above the earth, in the midst of a dull incessant hammering. On the surface of the cloud there seemed to be forming a number of little golden spots; these spots were moving, and he saw that they were toads. Then, beyond them, a huge face shaped itself, very dark, as if of bronze, with eyes burning into his brain. The more he struggled to get away from these eyes, the more they bored and burned into him. His voice was gone, so that he was unable to cry out, and suddenly the face marched over him.

When he recovered consciousness his head was damp with moisture trickling from something held to his forehead by a figure leaning above him. Lifting his hand he touched a cheek; and hearing a sob instantly suppressed he sighed. His hand was gently taken; he felt kisses on it.

The room was so dark, that he could scarcely see her face—his sight too was dim; but he could hear her breathing and the least sound of her dress and movements—the scent too of her hands and hair seemed to envelop him, and in the midst of all the acute discomfort of his fever, he felt the band round his brain relax. He did not ask how long she had been there, but lay quite still, trying to keep his eyes on her, for fear of that face, which seemed lurking behind the air, ready to march on him again. Then feeling suddenly that he could not hold it back, he beckoned, and clutched at her, trying to cover himself with the protection of her breast. This time his swoon was not so deep; it gave away to delirium, with intervals when he knew that she was there, and by the shaded candle light could see her in a white garment, floating close to him, or sitting still with her hand on his; he could even feel the faint comfort of the ice cap, and of the scent of eau de Cologne. Then he would lose all consciousness of her presence, and pass through into the incoherent world, where the crucifix above his bed seemed to bulge and hang out, as if it must fall on him. He conceived a violent longing to tear it down, which grew till he had struggled up in bed and wrenched it from off the wall. Yet a mysterious consciousness of her presence permeated even his darkest journeys into the strange land; and once she seemed to be with him, where a strange light showed them fields and trees, a dark line of moor, and a bright sea, all whitened, and flashing.

Soon after dawn he had a long interval of consciousness, and took in with a sort of wonder her presence in the low chair by his bed. So still she sat in a white loose gown, pale from watching, her eyes immovably fixed on him, her lips pressed together, and quivering at his faintest motion. He drank in desperately the sweetness of her face, which had so lost remembrance of self.

CHAPTER X

BARBARA gave the news of her brother's illness to no one else, common sense telling her to run no risk of disturbance. Of her own initiative, she brought a doctor, and went down twice a day to hear reports of Miltoun's progress.

As a fact, her father and mother had gone to Lord Dennis, for Goodwood, and the chief difficulty had been to excuse her own neglect of that favourite Meeting. She had fallen back on the half-truth that Eustace wanted her in Town; and, since Lord and Lady Valleys had neither of them shaken off a certain uneasiness about their son, the pretext sufficed.

· It was not until the sixth day, when the crisis was well past and Miltoun quite free from fever, that she again went down to Nettlefold.

On arriving she at once sought out her mother, whom she found in her bedroom, resting. It had been very hot at Goodwood.

Barbara was not afraid of her—she was not, indeed, afraid of anyone, except Miltoun, and in some strange way a little perhaps of Courtier; yet, when the maid had gone, she did not at once begin her tale. Lady Valleys, who at Goodwood had just heard details of a Society scandal, began a carefully expurgated account of it suitable to her daughter's ears—for some account she felt she must give to somebody.

"Mother," said Barbara suddenly, "Eustace has been ill. He's out of danger now, and going on all right." Then, looking hard at the bewildered lady, she added: "Mrs. Noel is nursing him."

The past tense in which illness had been mentioned, checking at the first moment any rush of panic in Lady Valleys, left her confused by the situation conjured up in Barbara's last words. Instead of feeding that part of man which loves a scandal, she was being fed, always an unenviable sensation. A woman did not nurse a man under such circumstances without being everything to him, in the world's eyes. Her daughter went on:

"I took her to him. It seemed the only thing to do—since
658

it's all through fretting for her. Nobody knows, of course,
except the doctor, and—Stacey."

"Heavens!" muttered Lady Valleys.

"It has saved him."

The mother instinct in Lady Valleys took sudden fright.
"Are you telling me the truth, Babs? Is he really out of
danger? How wrong of you not to let me know before!"

But Barbara did not flinch; and her mother relapsed into
rumination.

"Stacey is a cat!" she said suddenly. The expurgated details of the scandal she had been retailing to her daughter had
included the usual maid. She could not find it in her to enjoy
the irony of this coincidence. Then, seeing Barbara smile, she
said tartly:

"I fail to see the joke."

"Only that I thought you'd enjoy my throwing Stacey in,
dear."

"What! You mean she doesn't know?"

"Not a word."

Lady Valleys smiled.

"What a little wretch you are, Babs!" Maliciously she
added: "Claud and his mother are coming over from Whitewater, with Bertie and Lily Malvezin; you'd better go and
dress"; and her eyes searched her daughter's so shrewdly, that
a flush rose to the girl's cheeks.

When she had gone, Lady Valleys rang for her maid again,
and relapsed into meditation. Her first thought was to consult
her husband; her second that secrecy was strength. Since no
one knew but Barbara, no one had better know.

Her astuteness and experience comprehended the far-reaching
probabilities of this affair. It would not do to take a single false
step. If she had no one's action to control but her own and
Barbara's, so much the less chance of a slip. Her mind was a
strange medley of thoughts and feelings, almost comic, wellnigh tragic; of worldly prudence, and motherly instinct; of
warm-blooded sympathy with all love-affairs, and cool-blooded
concern for her son's career. It was not yet too late perhaps to
prevent real mischief; especially since it was agreed by everyone that the woman was no adventuress. Whatever was done,
they must not forget that she had nursed him—saved him, Barbara had said! She must be treated with all kindness and consideration.

Hastening her toilette, *she* in turn went to her daughter's room.

Barbara was already dressed, leaning out of her window towards the sea.

Lady Valleys began almost timidly:

"My dear, is Eustace out of bed yet?"

"He was to get up to-day for an hour or two."

"I see. Now, would there be any danger if you and I went up and took charge over from Mrs. Noel?"

"Poor Eusty!"

"Yes, yes! But, exercise your judgment. Would it harm him?"

Barbara was silent. "No," she said at last, "I don't suppose it would, now; but it's for the doctor to say."

Lady Valleys exhibited a manifest relief.

"We'll see him first, of course. Eustace will have to have an ordinary nurse, I suppose, for a bit."

Looking stealthily at Barbara, she added:

"I mean to be very nice to *her;* but one mustn't be romantic, you know, Babs."

From the little smile on Barbara's lips she derived no sense of certainty; indeed she was visited by all her late disquietude about her young daughter, by all the feeling that she, as well as Miltoun, was hovering on the verge of some folly.

"Well, my dear," she said, "I am going down."

But Barbara lingered a little longer in that bedroom where ten nights ago she had lain tossing, till in despair she went and cooled herself in the dark sea. Her last little interview with Courtier stood between her and a fresh meeting with Harbinger, whom at the Valleys House gathering she had not suffered to be alone with her. She came down late.

That same evening, out on the beach road, under a sky swarming with stars, the people were strolling—folk from the towns, down for their fortnight's holiday. In twos and threes, in parties of six or eight, they passed the wall at the end of Lord Dennis's little domain; and the sound of their sparse talk and laughter, together with the sighing of the young waves, was blown over the wall to the ears of Harbinger, Bertie, Barbara, and Lily Malvezin, when they strolled out after dinner to sniff the sea. The holiday-makers stared dully at the four figures in evening dress looking out above their heads; they had other things than these to think of, becoming more and more silent as the night grew dark. The four young people too were rather silent. There was something in this warm night, with its sighing, and its darkness, and its stars, that was not favourable to talk, so that presently they split into couples, drifting a little apart.

Standing there, gripping the wall, it seemed to Harbinger that there were no words left in the world. Not even his worst enemy could have called this young man romantic; yet that figure beside him, the gleam of her neck and her pale cheek in the dark, gave him perhaps the most poignant glimpse of mystery that he had ever had. His mind, essentially that of a man of affairs, by nature and by habit at home amongst the material aspects of things, was but gropingly conscious that here, in this dark night, and the dark sea, and the pale figure of this girl whose heart was dark to him and secret, there was perhaps something—yes, something—which surpassed the confines of his philosophy, something beckoning him on out of his snug compound into the desert of divinity. If so, it was soon gone in the aching of his senses at the scent of her hair, and the longing to escape from this weird silence.

"Babs," he said, "have you forgiven me?"

Her answer came, without turn of head, natural, indifferent: "Yes—I told you so."

"Is that all you have to say to a fellow?"

"What shall we talk about—the running of Casetta?"

Deep down within him Harbinger uttered a noiseless oath. Something sinister was making her behave like this to him! It was that fellow—that fellow! And suddenly he said:

"Tell me this——" then speech seemed to stick in his throat. No! If there were anything in *that*, he preferred not to hear it. There was a limit!

Down below, a pair of lovers passed, very silent, their arms round each other's waists.

Barbara turned and walked away towards the house.

CHAPTER XI

THE days when Miltoun was first allowed out of bed were a time of mingled joy and sorrow to her who had nursed him. To see him sitting up, amazed at his own weakness, was happiness, yet to think that he would be no more wholly dependent, no more that sacred thing, a helpless creature, brought her the sadness of a mother whose child no longer needs her. With every hour he would now get farther from her, back into the fastnesses of his own spirit. With every hour she would be less his nurse and comforter, more the woman he loved. And though that thought shone out in the obscure future like a glamorous flower, it brought too much wistful uncertainty to the present. She was very tired, too, now that all excitement was over—so tired that she hardly knew what she did or where she moved. But a smile had become so faithful to her eyes that it clung there above the shadows of fatigue, and kept taking her lips prisoner.

Between the two bronze busts she had placed a bowl of lilies of the valley; and every free niche in that room of books had a little vase of roses to welcome Miltoun's return.

He was lying back in his big leather chair, wrapped in a Turkish gown of Lord Valleys'—on which Barbara had laid hands, having failed to find anything resembling a dressing-gown amongst her brother's austere clothing. The perfume of lilies had overcome the scent of books, and a bee, dusky adventurer, filled the room with his pleasant humming.

They did not speak, but smiled faintly, looking at one another. In this still moment, before passion had returned to claim its own, their spirits passed through the sleepy air, and became entwined, so that neither could withdraw that soft, slow, encountering glance. In mutual contentment, each to each, close as music to the strings of a violin, their spirits clung—so lost, the one in the other, that neither for that brief time seemed to know which was self.

In fulfilment of her resolution, Lady Valleys, who had returned to Town by a morning train, started with Barbara for the Temple about three in the afternoon, and stopped at the doctor's

662

on the way. The whole thing would be much simpler if Eustace were fit to be moved at once to Valleys House; and with much relief she found that the doctor saw no danger in this course. The recovery had been remarkable—touch and go for bad brain fever—just avoided! Lord Miltoun's constitution was extremely sound. Yes, he would certainly favour a removal. His rooms were too confined in this weather. Well nursed—decidedly! Oh, yes! Quite! And the doctor's eyes became perhaps a trifle more intense. Not a professional, he understood. It might be as well to have another nurse, if they were making the change. They would have this lady knocking up. Just so! Yes, he would see to that. An ambulance carriage he thought advisable. That could all be arranged for this afternoon—at once—he himself would look to it. They might take Lord Miltoun off just as he was; the men would know what to do. And when they had him at Valleys House, the moment he showed interest in his food, down to the sea—down to the sea! At this time of year nothing like it! Then with regard to nourishment, he would be inclined already to shove in a leetle stimulant, a thimbleful perhaps four times a day with food—not without—mixed with an egg, with arrowroot, with custard. A week would see him on his legs, a fortnight at the sea make him as good a man as ever. Overwork—burning the candle—a leetle more would have seen a very different state of things! Quite so, quite so! Would come round himself before dinner, and make sure. His patient might feel it just at first! He bowed Lady Valleys out; and when she had gone, sat down at his telephone with a smile flickering on his clean-cut lips.

Greatly fortified by this interview, Lady Valleys rejoined her daughter in the car; but while it slid on amongst the multitudinous traffic, signs of unwonted nervousness began to start out through the placidity of her face.

"I wish, my dear," she said suddenly, "that someone else had to do this. Suppose Eustace refuses!"

"He won't," Barbara answered; "she looks so tired, poor dear. Besides——"

Lady Valleys gazed with curiosity at that young face, which had flushed pink. Yes, this daughter of hers was a woman already, with all a woman's intuitions. She said gravely:

"It was a rash stroke of yours, Babs; let's hope it won't lead to disaster."

Barbara bit her lips.

"If you'd seen him as I saw him! And, what disaster! Mayn't they love each other, if they want?"

Lady Valleys swallowed a grimace. It was so exactly her own point of view. And yet——!

"That's only the beginning," she said; "you forget the sort of boy Eustace is."

"Why can't the poor thing be let out of her cage?" cried Barbara. "What good does it do to anyone? Mother, if ever, when I am married, I want to get free, I will!"

The tone of her voice was so quivering, and unlike the happy voice of Barbara, that Lady Valleys involuntarily caught hold of her hand and squeezed it hard.

"My dear sweet," she said, "don't let's talk of such gloomy things."

"I mean it. Nothing shall stop me."

But Lady Valleys' face had suddenly become rather grim.

"So we think, child; it's not so simple."

"It can't be worse, anyway," muttered Barbara, "than being buried alive as that wretched woman is."

For answer Lady Valleys only murmured:

"The doctor promised that ambulance carriage at four o'clock. What am I going to say?"

"She'll understand when you look at her. She's that sort."

The door was opened to them by Mrs. Noel herself.

It was the first time Lady Valleys had seen her in a house, and there was real curiosity mixed with the assurance which masked her nervousness. A pretty creature, even lovely! But the quite genuine sympathy in her words: "I am truly grateful. You must be quite worn out," did not prevent her adding hastily: "The doctor says he must be got home out of these hot rooms. We'll wait here while you tell him."

And then she saw that it was true; this woman was the sort who understood.

Left in the dark passage, she peered round at Barbara.

The girl was standing against the wall with her head thrown back. Lady Valleys could not see her face; but she felt all of a sudden exceedingly uncomfortable, and whispered:

"Two murders and a theft, Babs; wasn't it 'Our Mutual Friend'?"

"Mother!"

"What?"

"Her face! When you're going to throw away a flower, it looks at you!"

"My dear!" murmured Lady Valleys, thoroughly distressed, "what things you're saying to-day!"

This lurking in a dark passage, this whispering girl—it was all queer, unlike an experience in proper life.

And then through the reopened door she saw Miltoun, stretched out in a chair, very pale, but still with that lcok about his eyes and lips, which of all things in the world had a chastening effect on Lady Valleys, making her feel somehow incurably mundane.

She said rather timidly:

"I'm so glad you're better, dear. What a time you must have had! It's too bad that I knew nothing till yesterday!"

But Miltoun's answer was, as usual, thoroughly disconcerting.

"Thanks, yes! I have had a perfect time—and have now to pay for it, I suppose."

Held back by his smile from bending to kiss him, poor Lady Valleys fidgeted from head to foot. A sudden impulse of sheer womanliness caused a tear to fall on his hand.

When Miltoun perceived that moisture, he said:

"It's all right, Mother. I'm quite willing to come."

Still wounded by his voice, Lady Valleys hardened instantly. And while preparing for departure she watched the two furtively. They hardly looked at one another, and when they did, their eyes baffled her. The expression was outside her experience, belonging as it were to a different world, with its faintly smiling, almost shining, gravity.

Vastly relieved when Miltoun, covered with a fur, had been taken down to the carriage, she lingered to speak to Mrs. Noel.

"We owe you a great debt. It might have been so much worse. You mustn't be disconsolate. Go to bed and have a good long rest." And from the door, she murmured again: "He will come and thank you, when he's well."

Descending the stone stairs, she thought: "'Anonyma'— 'Anonyma'—yes, it was quite the name." And suddenly she saw Barbara come running up again.

"What is it, Babs?"

Barbara answered:

"Eustace would like some of those lilies." And, passing Lady Valleys, she went on up to Miltoun's chambers.

Mrs. Noel was not in the sitting-room, and going to the bed-room door, the girl looked in.

She was standing by the bed, drawing her hand over and over the white surface of the pillow. Stealing noiselessly back, Barbara caught up the bunch of lilies, and fled.

CHAPTER XII

MILTOUN, whose constitution had the steel-like quality of Lady Casterley's, had a very rapid convalescence. And, having begun to take an interest in his food, he was allowed to travel on the seventh day to Sea House in charge of Barbara.

The two spent their time in a little summer-house close to the sea; lying out on the beach under the groynes; and, as Miltoun grew stronger, motoring and walking on the Downs.

To Barbara, keeping a close watch, he seemed tranquilly enough drinking in from Nature what was necessary to restore balance after the struggle and breakdown of the past weeks. Yet she could never get rid of a queer feeling that he was not really there at all; to look at him was like watching an uninhabited house that was waiting for someone to enter it.

During a whole fortnight he did not make a single allusion to Mrs. Noel, till, on the very last morning, as they were watching the sea, he said with his queer smile:

"It almost makes one believe her theory, that the old gods are not dead. Do you ever see them, Babs; or are you, like me, obtuse?"

Certainly about those lithe invasions of the sea-nymph waves, with ashy, streaming hair, flinging themselves into the arms of the land, there was the old pagan rapture, an inexhaustible delight, a passionate soft acceptance of eternal fate, a wonderful acquiescence in the untiring mystery of life.

But Barbara, ever disconcerted by that tone in his voice, and by this quick dive into the waters of unaccustomed thought, failed to find an answer.

Miltoun went on:

"She says, too, we can hear Apollo singing. Shall we try?"

But all that came was the sigh of the sea, and of the wind in the tamarisk.

"No," muttered Miltoun at last, "she alone can hear it."

And Barbara saw once more on his face that look, neither sad nor impatient, but as of one uninhabited and waiting.

She left Sea House next day to rejoin her mother, who, having been to Cowes, and to the Duchess of Gloucester's, was back in Town waiting for Parliament to rise, before going off

to Scotland. And that same afternoon the girl made her way
to Mrs. Noel's flat. In paying this visit she was moved not so
much by compassion, as by uneasiness, and a strange curiosity.
Now that Miltoun was well again, she was seriously disturbed
in mind. Had she made a mistake in summoning Mrs. Noel to
nurse him?

When she went into the little drawing-room Audrey was sitting in the deep-cushioned window-seat with a book on her
knee; and by the fact that it was open at the index, Barbara
judged that she had not been reading too attentively.   She
showed no signs of agitation at the sight of her visitor, nor any
eagerness to hear news of Miltoun. But the girl had not been
five minutes in the room before the thought came to her: 'Why!
She has the same look as Eustace!' She, too, was like an empty
tenement; without impatience, discontent, or grief—waiting!
Barbara had scarcely realised this with a curious sense of dis-
composure, when Courtier was announced. Whether there was
in this an absolute coincidence or just that amount of calculation which might follow on his part from receipt of a note
written from Sea House—saying that Miltoun was well again,
that she was coming up and meant to go and thank Mrs. Noel—
was not clear, nor were her own sensations; and she drew over
her face that armoured look which she perhaps knew Courtier
could not bear to see. His face, at all events, was very red when
he shook hands. He had come, he told Mrs. Noel, to say good-
bye. He was definitely off next week. Fighting had broken
out; the revolutionaries were greatly outnumbered. Indeed, he
ought to have been there long before!

Barbara had gone over to the window; she turned suddenly,
and said:

"You were preaching peace two months ago!"

Courtier bowed.

"We are not all perfectly consistent, Lady Barbara. These
poor devils have a holy cause."

Barbara held out her hand to Mrs. Noel.

"You only think their cause holy because they happen to be
weak. Good-bye, Mrs. Noel; the world is meant for the strong,
isn't it?"

She intended that to hurt him; and from the tone of his
voice, she knew it had.

"Don't, Lady Barbara; from your mother, yes; not from
you!"

"It's what I believe. Good-bye!" And she went out.

She had told him that she did not want him to go—not yet; and he was going!

But no sooner had she got outside, after that strange outburst, than she bit her lips to keep back an angry, miserable feeling. He had been rude to her, she had been rude to him; that was the way they had said good-bye! Then, as she emerged into the sunlight, she thought: 'Oh! well; he doesn't care, and I'm sure I don't!'

She heard a voice behind her.

"May I get you a cab?" and at once the sore feeling began to die away; but she did not look round, only smiled, and shook her head, and made a little room for him on the pavement.

But though they walked, they did not at first talk. There was rising within Barbara a tantalising devil of desire to know the feelings which really lay behind that deferential gravity, to make him show her how much he really cared. She kept her eyes demurely lowered, but she let the glimmer of a smile flicker about her lips; she knew too that her cheeks were glowing, and for that she was not sorry. Was she not to have any—any—was he calmly to go away—without—— And she thought: 'He shall say something! He shall show me, without that horrible irony of his!'

She said suddenly:

"Those two are just waiting—something will happen!"

"It is probable," was his grave answer.

She looked at him then—it pleased her to see him quiver as if that glance had gone right into him; and she said softly:

"And I think they will be quite right."

She knew those were reckless words, nor cared very much what they meant; but she knew the revolt in them would move him. She saw from his face that it had; and after a little pause, said:

"Happiness is the great thing," and with soft, wicked slowness: "Isn't it, Mr. Courtier?"

But all the cheeriness had gone out of his face, which had grown almost pale. He lifted his hand, and let it drop. Then she felt sorry. It was just as if he had asked her to spare him.

"As to that," he said: "the rough, unfortunately, has to be taken with the smooth. But life's frightfully jolly sometimes."

"As now?"

He looked at her with firm gravity, and answered:

"As now."

A sense of utter mortification seized on Barbara. He was too strong for her—he was quixotic—he was hateful! And, determined not to show a sign, to be at least as strong as he, she said calmly:

"Now I think I'll have that cab!"

When she was in the cab, and he was standing with his hat lifted, she looked at him in a way peculiar to women, so that he did not realise that she had looked.

CHAPTER XIII

WHEN Miltoun came to thank her, Audrey Noel was waiting in the middle of the room, dressed in white, her lips smiling, her dark eyes smiling, still as a flower on a windless day.

In that first look passing between them, they forgot everything but happiness. Swallows, on the first day of summer, in their discovery of the bland air, can neither remember that cold winds blow, nor imagine the death of sunlight on their feathers, and, flitting hour after hour over the golden fields, seem no longer birds, but just the breathing of a new season—swallows were no more forgetful of misfortune than were those two. His gaze was as still as her very self; her look at him had in it the quietude of all emotion.

When they sat down to talk it was as if they had gone back to those days at Monkland, when he had come to her so often to discuss everything in heaven and earth. And yet, over that tranquil eager drinking-in of each other's presence, hovered a sort of awe. It was the mood of morning before the sun has soared. The dew-grey cobwebs enwrapped the flowers of their hearts—yet every prisoned flower could be seen. And he and she seemed looking through that web at the colour and the deepdown forms enshrouded so jealously; each feared too much to unveil the other's heart. They were like lovers who, rambling in a shy wood, never dare stay their babbling talk of the trees and birds and lost bluebells, lest in the deep waters of a kiss their star of all that is to come should fall and be drowned. To each hour its familiar—and the spirit of that hour was the spirit of the white flowers in the bowl on the window-sill above her head.

They spoke of Monkland, and Miltoun's illness; of his first speech, his impressions of the House of Commons; of music, Barbara, Courtier, the river. He told her of his health, and described his days down by the sea. She, as ever, spoke little of herself, persuaded that it could not interest even him; but she described a visit to the opera; and how she had found a picture in the National Gallery which reminded her of him. To all these trivial things and countless others, the tone of their voices —soft, almost murmuring, with a sort of delighted gentleness—

671

gave a high, sweet importance, a halo that neither for the world would have dislodged from where it hovered.

It was past six when he got up to go, and there had not been a moment to break the calm of that sacred feeling in both their hearts. They parted with another tranquil look, which seemed to say: 'It is well with us—we have drunk of happiness.'

And in this same amazing calm Miltoun remained after he had gone away, till about half-past nine in the evening, he started forth, to walk down to the House. It was now that sort of warm, clear night, which in the country has firefly magic, and even over the Town spreads a dark glamour. And for Miltoun, in the delight of his new health and well-being, with every sense alive and clean, to walk through the warmth and beauty of this night was sheer pleasure. He passed by way of St. James's Park, treading down the purple shadows of plane-tree leaves into the pools of lamplight, almost with remorse—so beautiful, and as if alive, were they. There were moths abroad, and gnats, born on the water, and scent of new-mown grass drifted up from the lawns. His heart felt light as a swallow he had seen that morning, swooping at a grey feather, carrying it along, letting it flutter away, then diving to seize it again. Such was his elation, this beautiful night! Nearing the House of Commons, he thought he would walk a little longer, and turned westward to the river. On that warm evening the water, without movement at turn of tide, was like the black, snake-smooth hair of Nature streaming out on her couch of Earth, waiting for the caress of a divine hand. Far away on the further bank throbbed some huge machine, not stilled as yet. A few stars were out in the dark sky, but no moon to invest with pallor the gleam of the lamps. Scarcely anyone passed. Miltoun strolled along the river wall, then crossed, and came back in front of the Mansions where she lived. By the railing he stood still. In the sitting-room of her little flat there was no light, but the casement window was wide open, and the crown of white flowers in the bowl on the window-sill still gleamed out in the darkness like a crescent moon lying on its face. Suddenly, he saw two pale hands rise one on either side of that bowl, lift it, and draw it in. And he quivered, as though they had touched him. Again those two hands came floating up; they were parted now by darkness; the moon of flowers was gone, in its place had been set handfuls of purple or crimson blossoms. And a puff of warm air rising quickly out of the night drifted their scent of cloves into his face, so that he held his breath for fear of calling out her name.

Again the hands had vanished—through the open window there was nothing to be seen but darkness; and such a rush of longing seized on Miltoun as stole from him all power of movement. He could hear her playing now. The murmurous current of that melody was like the night itself, sighing, throbbing, languorously soft. It seemed that in this music she was calling him, telling him that she, too, was longing; her heart, too, empty. It died away; and at the window her white figure appeared. From that vision he could not, nor did he try to shrink, but moved out into the lamplight. And he saw her suddenly stretch out her hands to him, and withdraw them to her breast. Then all save the madness of his longing deserted Miltoun. He ran down the little garden, across the hall, up the stairs.

The door was open. He passed through. There, in the sitting-room, where the red flowers in the window scented all the air, it was dark, and he could not at first see her, till against the piano he caught the glimmer of her white dress. She was sitting with hands resting on the pale notes. And falling on his knees, he buried his face against her. Then, without looking up, he raised his hands. Her tears fell on them covering her heart, which throbbed as if the passionate night itself were breathing in there, and all but the night and her love had stolen forth.

CHAPTER XIV

On a spur of the Sussex Downs, inland from Nettlefold, stands a beech-grove. The traveller who enters it out of the heat and brightness, takes off the shoes of his spirit before its sanctity; and, reaching the centre, across the clean beech-mat, he sits refreshing his brow with air, and silence. For the flowers of sunlight on the ground under those branches are pale and rare, no insects hum, the birds are almost mute. And close to the border-trees are the quiet, milk-white sheep, in congregation, escaping from noon heat. Here, above fields and dwellings, above the ceaseless network of men's doings, and the vapour of their talk, the traveller feels solemnity. All seems conveying divinity—the great white clouds moving their wings above him, the faint longing murmur of the boughs, and in far distance, the sea. And for a space his restlessness and fear know the peace of God.

So it was with Miltoun when he reached this temple, three days after that passionate night, having walked for hours, alone and full of conflict. During those three days he had been borne forward on the flood tide; and now, tearing himself out of London, where to think was impossible, he had come to the solitude of the Downs to walk, and face his new position.

For that position he saw to be very serious. In the flush of full realisation, there was for him no question of renunciation. She was his, he hers; that was determined. But what, then, was he to do? There was no chance of her getting free. In her husband's view, it seemed, under no circumstances was marriage dissoluble. Nor, indeed, to Miltoun would divorce have made things easier, believing as he did that he and she were guilty, and that for the guilty there could be no marriage. She, it was true, asked nothing but just to be his in secret; and that was the course he knew most men would take, without further thought. There was no material reason in the world why he should not so act, and maintain unchanged every other current of his life. It would be easy, usual. And, with her faculty for self-effacement, he knew she would not be unhappy. But conscience, in Miltoun, was a terrible and fierce thing. In the delirium of his illness it had become that Great Face which had

marched over him. And, though during the weeks of his re-
cuperation, struggle of all kind had ceased, now that he had
yielded to his passion, conscience, in a new and dismal shape, had
crept up again to sit above his heart. He must and would let
this man, her husband, know; but even if that caused no open
scandal, could he go on deceiving those who, if they knew of
an illicit love, would no longer allow him to be their representa-
tive? If it were known that she was his mistress, he could no
longer maintain his position in public life—was he not therefore in honour bound, of his own accord, to resign it? Night
and day he was haunted by the thought: How can I, living in
defiance of authority, pretend to authority over my fellows?
How can I remain in public life? But if he did not remain in
public life, what was he to do? That way of life was in his
blood; he had been bred and born into it; had thought of
nothing else since he was a boy. There was no other occupation
or interest which could hold him for a moment—he saw very
plainly that he would be cast away on the waters of existence.

So the battle raged in his proud and twisted spirit, which took
everything so hard—his nature imperatively commanding him
to keep his work and his power for usefulness; his conscience
telling him as urgently that if he sought to wield authority, he
must obey it.

He entered the beech-grove at the height of this misery, flaming with rebellion against the dilemma which Fate had placed
before him; visited by gusts of resentment against a passion,
which forced him to pay the price, either of his career, or of
his self-respect; gusts, followed by remorse that he could so
for one moment regret his love for that tender creature. The
face of Lucifer was not more dark, more tortured, than Miltoun's
face in the twilight of the grove, above those kingdoms of the
world, for which his ambition and his conscience fought. He
threw himself down among the trees; and, stretching out his
arms, by chance touched a beetle trying to crawl over the grass-
less soil. Some bird had maimed it. He took the little creature
up. The beetle truly could no longer work, but it was spared
the fate lying before himself. The beetle was not, as he would
be, when his power of movement was destroyed, conscious of
his own wasted life. The world would not roll away down there.
He would still see himself cumbering the ground, when his
powers were taken from him. This thought was torture. Why
had he been suffered to meet her, to love her, and to be loved

by her? What had made him so certain from the first moment, if she were not meant for him? If he lived to be a hundred, he would never meet another. Why, because of his love, must he bury the will and force of a man? If there were no more coherence in God's scheme than this, let him too be incoherent! Let him hold authority, and live outside authority! Why stifle his powers for the sake of a coherence which did not exist! That would indeed be madness greater than that of a mad world!

There was no answer to his thoughts in the stillness of the grove, unless it were the cooing of a dove, or the faint thudding of the sheep issuing again into sunlight. But slowly that stillness stole into Miltoun's spirit. 'Is it like this in the grave?' he thought. 'Are the boughs of those trees the dark earth over me? And the sound in them the sound the dead hear when flowers are growing, and the wind passing through them? And is the feel of this earth how it feels to lie looking up for ever at nothing? Is life anything but a nightmare, a dream; and is not this the reality? And why my fury, my insignificant flame, blowing here and there, when there is really no wind, only a shroud of still air, and these flowers of sunlight that have been dropped on me! Why not let my spirit sleep, instead of eating itself away with rage; why not resign myself at once to wait for the substance, of which this is but the shadow!'

And he lay scarcely breathing, looking up at the unmoving branches setting with their darkness the pearls of the sky.

'Is not peace enough?' he thought. 'Is not love enough? Can I not be reconciled, like a woman? Is not that salvation, and happiness? What is all the rest, but "sound and fury, signifying nothing"?'

And as though afraid to lose his hold of that thought, he got up and hurried from the grove.

The whole wide landscape of field and wood, cut by the pale roads, was glimmering under the afternoon sun. Here was no wild, wind-swept land, gleaming red and purple, and guarded by the grey rocks; no home of the winds, and the wild gods. It was all serene and silver-golden. In place of the shrill wailing pipe of the hunting buzzard-hawks half lost up in the wind, invisible larks were letting fall hymns to tranquillity; and even the sea—no adventuring spirit sweeping the shore with its wing —seemed to lie resting by the side of the land.

CHAPTER XV

WHEN on the afternoon of that same day Miltoun did not come, all the chilly doubts which his presence alone kept away, crowded thick and fast into the mind of one only too prone to distrust her own happiness. It could not last—how could it?

His nature and her own were so far apart! Even in that giving of herself which had been such happiness, she had yet doubted; for so much in him was to her mysterious. All that he loved in poetry and nature, had in it something craggy and culminating. The soft and fiery, the subtle and harmonious, seemed to leave him cold. He had no particular love for all those simple natural things, birds, bees, animals, trees, and flowers, which seemed to her precious and divine.

Though it was not yet four o'clock she was already beginning to droop like a flower that wants water. But she sat down to her piano, resolutely, till tea came; playing on and on with a spirit only half present, the other half of her wandering in the Town, seeking for Miltoun. After tea she tried first to read, then to sew, and once more came back to her piano. The clock struck six; and as if its last stroke had broken the armour of her mind, she felt suddenly sick with anxiety. Why was he so long? But she kept on playing, turning the pages without taking in the notes, haunted by the idea that he might again have fallen ill. Should she telegraph? What good, when she could not tell in the least where he might be? And all the unreasoning terror of not knowing where the loved one is, beset her so that her hands, in sheer numbness, dropped from the keys. Unable to keep still, now, she wandered from window to door, out into the little hall, and back hastily to the window. Over her anxiety brooded a darkness, compounded of vague growing fears. What if it were the end? What if he had chosen this as the most merciful way of leaving her? But surely he would never be so cruel? Close on the heels of this too painful thought came reaction; and she told herself that she was a fool. He was at the House; something quite ordinary was keeping him. It was absurd to be anxious! She would have to get used to this now. To be a drag on him would be dreadful. Sooner than that she would rather—yes—rather he never came

677

back! And she took up her book, determined to read quietly till he came. But the moment she sat down her fears returned with redoubled force—the cold sickly horrible feeling of uncertainty, of the knowledge that she could do nothing but wait till she was relieved by something over which she had no control. And in the superstition that to stay there in the window where she could see him come, was keeping him from her, she went into her bedroom. From there she could watch the sunset clouds wine-dark over the river. A little talking wind shivered along the houses; the dusk began creeping in. She would not turn on the light, unwilling to admit that it was really getting late, but began to change her dress, lingering desperately over every little detail of her toilette, deriving therefrom a faint, mysterious comfort, trying to make herself feel beautiful. From sheer dread of going back before he came, she let her hair fall, though it was quite smooth and tidy, and began brushing it. Suddenly she thought with horror of her efforts at adornment—by specially preparing for him, she must seem presumptuous to Fate. At any little sound she stopped and stood listening—save for her hair and eyes, as white from head to foot as a double narcissus flower in the dusk, bending towards some faint tune played to it somewhere out in the fields. But all those little sounds ceased, one after another—they had meant nothing; and each time, her spirit returning within the pale walls of the room, began once more to inhabit her lingering fingers. During that hour in her bedroom she lived through years. It was dark when she left it.

CHAPTER XVI

WHEN Miltoun at last came it was past, nine o'clock.

Silent, but quivering all over, she clung to him in the hall; and this passion of emotion, without sound to give it substance, affected him profoundly. How terribly sensitive and tender she was! She seemed to have no armour. But though so stirred by her emotion, he was none the less exasperated. She incarnated at that moment the life to which he must now resign himself—a life of unending tenderness, consideration, and passivity.

For a long time he could not bring himself to speak of his decision. Every look of her eyes, every movement of her body, seemed pleading with him to keep silence. But in Miltoun's character there was an element of rigidity, which never suffered him to diverge from an objective once determined.

When he had finished telling her, she only said:

"Why can't we go on in secret?"

And he felt with a sort of horror that he must begin his struggle over again. He got up, and threw open the window. The sky was dark above the river; the wind had risen. That restless murmuration, and the width of the night with its scattered stars, seemed to come rushing at his face. He withdrew from it, and leaning on the sill looked down at her. What flower-like delicacy she had! There flashed across him the memory of a drooping blossom, which, in the Spring, he had seen her throw into the flames, with the words: "I can't bear flowers to fade, I always want to burn them." He could see again those waxen petals yield to the fierce clutch of the little red creeping sparks, and the slender stalk quivering, and glowing, and writhing to blackness like a live thing. And, distraught, he began:

"I can't live a lie. What right have I to lead, if I can't follow? I'm not like our friend Courtier who believes in Liberty. I never have, I never shall. Liberty? What is Liberty? But only those who conform to authority have the right to wield authority. A man is a churl who enforces laws, when he himself has not the strength to observe them. I will not be one of whom it can be said: 'He can rule others, himself——!'"

"No one will know."

679

Miltoun turned away.

"I shall know," he said; but he saw clearly that she did not understand him. Her face had a strange, brooding shut-away look, as though he had frightened her. And the thought that she could not understand, angered him.

He said, stubbornly: "No, I can't remain in public life."

"But what has it to do with politics? It's such a little thing."

"If it had been a little thing to me, should I have left you at Monkland, and spent those five weeks in purgatory before my illness? A little thing!"

She exclaimed with sudden fire:

"Circumstances *are* the little thing; it's love that's the great thing."

Miltoun stared at her, for the first time understanding that she had a philosophy as deep and stubborn as his own. But he answered cruelly:

"Well! the great thing has conquered me!"

And then he saw her looking at him, as if, seeing into the recesses of his soul, she had made some ghastly discovery. The look was so mournful, so uncannily intent that he turned away from it.

"Perhaps it is a little thing," he muttered; "I don't know. I can't see my way. I've lost my bearings; I must find them again before I can do anything."

But as if she had not heard, or not taken in the sense of his words, she said again:

"Oh! don't let us alter anything; I won't ever want what you can't give."

And this stubbornness, when he was doing the very thing that would give him to her utterly, seemed to him unreasonable.

"I've had it out with myself," he said. "Don't let's talk about it any more."

Again, with a sort of dry anguish, she murmured:

"No, no! Let us go on as we are!"

Feeling that he had borne all he could, Miltoun put his hands on her shoulders, and said:

"That's enough!"

Then, in sudden remorse, he lifted her, and clasped her to him.

But she stood inert in his arms, her eyes closed, not returning his kisses.

CHAPTER XVII

On the last day before Parliament rose, Lord Valleys, with a light heart, mounted his horse for a gallop in the Row. Though she was a blood mare he rode her with a plain snaffle, having the horsemanship of one who has hunted from the age of seven, and been for twenty years a Colonel of Yeomanry. Greeting affably everyone he knew, he maintained a frank demeanour on all subjects, especially of Government policy, secretly enjoying the surmises and prognostications, so pleasantly wide of the mark, and the way questions and hints perished before his sphinx-like candour. He spoke cheerily too of Miltoun, who was " all right again," and " burning for the fray " when the House met again in the autumn. And he chaffed Lord Malvezin about his wife. If anything—he said—could make Bertie take an interest in politics, it would be she. He had two capital gallops, being well known to the police. The day was bright, and he was sorry to turn home. Falling in with Harbinger, he asked him to come back to lunch. There had seemed something different lately, an almost morose look, about young Harbinger; and his wife's disquieting words about Barbara came back to Lord Valleys with a shock. He had seen little of the child lately, and in the general clearing up of this time of year had forgotten all about the matter.

Agatha, who was still staying at Valleys House with little Ann, waiting to travel up to Scotland with her mother, was out, and there was no one at lunch except Lady Valleys and Barbara herself. Conversation flagged; for the young people were extremely silent, Lady Valleys was considering the draft of a report which had to be settled before she left, and Lord Valleys himself was rather carefully watching his daughter. The news that Lord Miltoun was in the study came as a surprise, and somewhat of a relief to all. To an exhortation to bring him in to lunch, the servant replied that Lord Miltoun had lunched, and would wait.

" Does he know there's no one here? "

" Yes, my lady."

Lady Valleys pushed back her plate, and rose:

" Oh, well! " she said, " I've finished."

Lord Valleys also got up, and they went out together, leaving Barbara, who had risen, looking doubtfully at the door.

Lord Valleys had recently been told of the nursing episode, and had received the news with the dubious air of one hearing something about an eccentric person, which, heard about any-one else, could have had but one significance. If Eustace had been a normal young man his father would have shrugged his shoulders, and thought: 'Oh, well! There it is!' As it was, he had literally not known what to think. And now, crossing the saloon which intervened between the dining-room and the study, he said to his wife uneasily:

"Is it this woman again, Gertrude—or what?"

Lady Valleys answered with a shrug:

"Goodness knows, my dear."

Miltoun was standing in the embrasure of a window above the terrace. He looked well, and his greeting was the same as usual.

"Well, my dear fellow," said Lord Valleys, "*you're* all right again evidently—what's the news?"

"Only that I've decided to resign my seat."

Lord Valleys stared.

"What on earth for?"

But Lady Valleys, with the greater quickness of women, divining already something of the reason, had flushed a deep pink.

"Nonsense, my dear," she said; "it can't possibly be neces-sary, even if——" Recovering herself, she added dryly:

"Give us some reason."

"The reason is simply that I've joined my life to Mrs. Noel's, and I can't go on as I am, living a lie. If it were known I should obviously have to resign at once."

"Good God!" exclaimed Lord Valleys.

Lady Valleys made a rapid movement. In the face of what she felt to be a really serious crisis between these two utterly different creatures of the other sex, her husband and her son, she had dropped her mask and become a genuine woman. Un-consciously both men felt this change, and in speaking, turned towards her.

"I can't argue it," said Miltoun; "I consider myself bound in honour."

"And then?" she asked.

Lord Valleys, with a note of real feeling, interjected:

"By Heaven! I did think you put your country above your private affairs."

"Geoff!" said Lady Valleys.

But Lord Valleys went on:

"No, Eustace, I'm out of touch with your view of things altogether. I don't even begin to understand it."

"That is true," said Miltoun.

"Listen to me, both of you!" said Lady Valleys: "You two are altogether different; and you must not quarrel. I won't have that. Now, Eustace, you *are* our son, and you have got to be kind and considerate. Sit down, and let's talk it over."

And motioning her husband to a chair, she sat down in the embrasure of a window. Miltoun remained standing. Visited by a sudden dread, Lady Valleys said:

"Is it—you've not—there isn't going to be a scandal?"

Miltoun smiled grimly.

"I shall tell this man, of course, but you may make your minds easy, I imagine; I understand that his view of marriage does not permit of divorce in any case whatever."

Lady Valleys sighed with an utter and undisguised relief.

"Well, then, my dear boy," she began, "even if you *do* feel you must tell him, there is surely no reason why it should not otherwise be kept secret."

Lord Valleys interrupted her:

"I should be glad if you would point out the connection between your honour and the resignation of your seat," he said stiffly.

Miltoun shook his head.

"If you don't see already, it would be useless."

"I do not see. The whole matter is—is unfortunate, but to give up your work, so long as there is no absolute necessity, seems to me far-fetched and absurd. How many men are there into whose lives there has not entered some such relation at one time or another? This idea would disqualify half the nation." His eyes seemed in that crisis both to consult and to avoid his wife's, as though he were at once asking her endorsement of his point of view, and observing the proprieties. And for a moment in the midst of her anxiety, her sense of humour got the better of Lady Valleys. It was so funny that Geoff should have to give himself away; she could not for the life of her help fixing him with her eyes.

"My dear," she murmured, "you underestimate—three-quarters, at the very least!"

But Lord Valleys, confronted with danger, was growing steadier.

"It passes my comprehension," he said, "why you should want to mix up sex and politics at all."

Miltoun's answer came very slowly, as if the confession were hurting his lips:

"There is—forgive me for using the word—such a thing as one's religion. I don't happen to regard life as divided into public and private departments. My vision is gone—broken— I can see no object before me now in public life—no goal—no certainty."

Lady Valleys caught his hand:

"Oh! my dear," she said, "that's too dreadfully puritanical!" But at Miltoun's queer smile, she added hastily: "Logical—I mean."

"Consult your common sense, Eustace, for goodness' sake," broke in Lord Valleys. "Isn't it your simple duty to put your scruples in your pocket, and do the best you can for your country with the powers that have been given you?"

"I have no common sense."

"In that case, of course, it may be just as well that you should leave public life."

Miltoun bowed.

"Nonsense!" cried Lady Valleys. "You don't understand, Geoffrey. I ask you again, Eustace, what will you do afterwards?"

"I don't know."

"You will eat your heart out, of course."

"Quite possibly."

"If you can't come to a reasonable arrangement with your conscience," again broke in Lord Valleys, "for Heaven's sake give her up, like a man, and cut all these knots."

"I beg your pardon, sir!" said Miltoun icily.

Lady Valleys laid her hand on his arm. "You must allow us a little logic too, my dear. You don't seriously imagine that she would wish you to throw away your life for her? I'm not such a bad judge of character as that."

She stopped before the expression on Miltoun's face.

"You go too fast," he said; "I may become a free spirit yet."

To this saying, which seemed to her cryptic and sinister, Lady Valleys did not know what to answer.

"If you feel, as you say," Lord Valleys began once more, "that the bottom has been knocked out of things for you by this—this affair, don't, for goodness' sake, do anything in a hurry. Wait! Go abroad! Get your balance back! You'll find the thing settle itself in a few months. Don't precipitate matters; you can make your health an excuse to miss the Autumn session."

Lady Valleys chimed in eagerly:

"You really are seeing the thing out of all proportion. What is a love-affair? My dear boy, do you suppose for a moment anyone would think the worse of you, even if they knew? And really not a soul need know."

"It has not occurred to me to consider what they would think."

"Then," cried Lady Valleys, nettled, "it's simply your own pride."

"You have said."

Lord Valleys, who had turned away, spoke in an almost tragic voice:

"I did not think that on a point of honour I should differ from my son."

Catching at the word honour, Lady Valleys cried suddenly:

"Eustace, promise me, before you do anything, to consult your Uncle Dennis."

Miltoun smiled.

"This becomes comic," he said.

At that word, which indeed seemed to them quite wanton, Lord and Lady Valleys turned on their son, and the three stood staring, perfectly silent. A little noise from the doorway interrupted them.

CHAPTER XVIII

LEFT by her father and mother to the further entertainment of Harbinger, Barbara had said:

"Let's have coffee in here," and passed into the withdrawing room.

Except for that one evening, when together by the sea wall they stood contemplating the populace, she had not been alone with him since he kissed her under the shelter of the box hedge. And now, after the first moment, she looked at him calmly, though in her breast there was a fluttering, as if an imprisoned bird were struggling ever so feebly against that soft and solid cage. Her last jangled talk with Courtier had left an ache in her heart. Besides, did she not know all that Harbinger could give her?

Like a nymph pursued by a faun who held dominion over the groves, she, fugitive, kept looking back. There was nothing in that fair wood of his with which she was not familiar, no thicket she had not travelled, no stream she had not crossed, no kiss she could not return. His was a discovered land, in which, as of right, she would reign. She had nothing to hope from him but power, and solid pleasure. Her eyes said: 'How am I to know whether I shall not want more than you; feel suffocated in your arms; be surfeited by all that you will bring me? Have I not already got all that?'

She knew, from his downcast gloomy face, how cruel she seemed, and was sorry. She wanted to be good to him, and said almost shyly:

"Are you angry with me, Claud?"

Harbinger looked up.

"What makes you so cruel?"

"I am not cruel."

"You *are*. Where is your heart?"

"Here!" said Barbara, touching her breast.

"Ah!" muttered Harbinger; "*I'm* not joking."

She said gently:

"Is it as bad as that, my dear?"

But the softness of her voice seemed to fan the smouldering fires in him.

"There's something behind all this," he stammered, "you've no right to make a fool of me!"

"And what is the something, please?"

"That's for you to say. But I'm not blind. What about this fellow Courtier?"

At that moment there was revealed to Barbara a new acquaintance—the male proper. No, to live with him would not be quite lacking in adventure!

His face had darkened; his eyes were dilated, his whole figure seemed to have grown. She suddenly noticed the hair which covered his clenched fists. All his suavity had left him. He came very close.

How long that look between them lasted, and of all there was in it, she had no clear knowledge; thought after thought, wave after wave of feeling, rushed through her. Revolt and attraction, contempt and admiration, queer sensations of disgust and pleasure, all mingled—as on a May day one may see the hail fall, and the sun suddenly burn through and steam from the grass.

Then he said hoarsely:

"Oh! Babs, you madden me so!"

Smoothing her lips, as if to regain control of them, she answered:

"Yes, I think I have had enough," and went out into her father's study.

The sight of Lord and Lady Valleys so intently staring at Miltoun restored her self-possession.

It struck her as slightly comic, not knowing that the little scene was the outcome of that word. In truth, the contrast between Miltoun and his parents at this moment was almost ludicrous.

Lady Valleys was the first to speak.

"Better comic than romantic. I suppose Barbara may know, considering her contribution to this matter. Your brother is resigning his seat, my dear; his conscience will not permit him to retain it, under certain circumstances that have arisen."

"Oh!" cried Barbara: "but surely——"

"The matter has been argued, Babs," Lord Valleys said shortly; "unless you have some better reason to advance than those of ordinary common sense, public spirit, and consideration for one's family, it will hardly be worth your while to reopen the discussion."

Barbara looked up at Miltoun, whose face, all but the eyes, was like a mask.

"Oh, Eusty!" she said, "you're not going to spoil your life like this! Just think how I shall feel."

Miltoun answered stonily:

"You did what you thought right; as I am doing."

"Does *she* want you to?"

"No."

"There is, I should imagine," put in Lord Valleys, "not a solitary creature in the whole world except your brother himself who would wish for this consummation. But with him such a consideration does not weigh!"

"Oh!" sighed Barbara; "think of Granny!"

"I prefer not to think of her," murmured Lady Valleys.

"She's so wrapped up in you, Eusty. She always has believed in you intensely."

Miltoun sighed. And, encouraged by that sound, Barbara went closer.

It was plain enough that, behind his impassivity, a desperate struggle was going on in Miltoun. He spoke at last:

"If I have not already yielded to one who is naturally more to me than anything, when she begged and entreated, it is because I feel this in a way you don't realise. I apologise for using the word comic just now, I should have said tragic. I'll enlighten Uncle Dennis, if that will comfort you; but this is not exactly a matter for anyone, except myself." And, without another look or word, he went out.

As the door closed, Barbara ran towards it; and, with a motion strangely like the wringing of hands, said:

"Oh, dear! Oh! dear!" Then, turning away to a bookcase, she began to cry.

This ebullition of feeling, surpassing even their own, came as a real shock to Lady and Lord Valleys, ignorant of how strung-up she had been before she entered the room. They had not seen Barbara cry since she was a tiny girl. And in face of her emotion any animus they might have shown her for having thrown Miltoun into Mrs. Noel's arms, now melted away. Lord Valleys, especially moved, went up to his daughter, and stood with her in that dark corner, saying nothing, but gently stroking her hand. Lady Valleys, who herself felt very much inclined to cry, went out of sight into the embrasure of the window.

Barbara's sobbing was soon subdued.

"It's his face," she said: "And why? Why? It's so unnecessary!"

Lord Valleys, continually twisting his moustache, muttered: "Exactly! He makes things hard for himself!"

"Yes," murmured Lady Valleys from the window, "he was always uncomfortable, like that. I remember him as a baby. Bertie never was."

And then the silence was only broken by the little angry sounds of Barbara blowing her nose.

"I shall go and see mother," said Lady Valleys, suddenly: "The boy's whole life may be ruined if we can't stop this. Are you coming, child?"

But Barbara refused.

She went to her room, instead. This crisis in Miltoun's life had strangely shaken her. It was as if Fate had suddenly revealed all that any step out of the beaten path might lead to, had brought her sharply up against herself. To wing out into the blue! See what is meant! If Miltoun kept to his resolve, and gave up public life, he was lost! And she herself! The fascination of Courtier's chivalrous manner, of a sort of innate gallantry, suggesting the quest of everlasting danger—was it not rather absurd? And—was she fascinated? Was it not simply that she liked the feeling of fascinating him? Through the maze of these thoughts, darted the memory of Harbinger's face close to her own, his clenched hands, the swift revelation of his dangerous masculinity. It was all a nightmare of scaring queer sensations, of things that could never be settled. She was stirred for once out of all her normal conquering philosophy. Her thoughts flew back to Miltoun. That which she had seen in their faces, then, had come to pass! And picturing Agatha's horror, when she came to hear of it, Barbara could not help a smile. Poor Eustace! Why did he take things so hardly? If he really carried out his resolve—and he never changed his mind—it would be tragic! It would mean the end of everything for him!

Perhaps now he would get tired of Mrs. Noel. But she was not the sort of woman a man would get tired of. Even Barbara in her inexperience felt that. She would always be too delicately careful never to cloy him, never to exact anything from him, or let him feel that he was bound to her by so much as a hair. Ah! why couldn't they go on as if nothing had hap-

pened? Could nobody persuade him? She thought again of
Courtier. If he, who knew them both, and was so fond of Mrs.
Noel, would talk to Miltoun, about the right to be happy, the
right to revolt? Eustace ought to revolt! It was his duty.
She sat down to write; then, putting on her hat, took the note
and slipped downstairs.

CHAPTER XIX

THE flowers of summer in the great glass house at Ravensham were keeping the last afternoon-watch when Clifton summoned Lady Casterley with the words:

"Lady Valleys in the white room."

Since the news of Miltoun's illness, and of Mrs. Noel's nursing, the little old lady had possessed her soul in patience; often, it is true, afflicted with poignant misgivings as to this new influence in the life of her favourite, affected too by a sort of jealousy, not to be admitted, even in her prayers, whch, though regular enough, were perhaps somewhat formal. Having small liking now for leaving home, even for Catton, her country place, she was still at Ravensham, where Lord Dennis had come up to stay with her as soon as Miltoun had left Sea House. But Lady Casterley was never very dependent on company. She retained unimpaired her intense interest in politics, and still corresponded freely with prominent men. Of late, too, a slight revival of the June war scare had made its mark on her in a certain rejuvenescence, which always accompanied her contemplation of national crises, even when such were a little in the air. At blast of trumpet her spirit still leaped forward, unsheathed its sword, and stood at the salute. At such times, she rose earlier, went to bed later, was far less susceptible to draughts, and refused with asperity any food between meals. She wrote too with her own hand letters which she would otherwise have dictated to her secretary. Unfortunately the scare had died down again almost at once; and the passing of danger always left her rather irritable. Lady Valleys' visit came as a timely consolation.

She kissed her daughter critically; for there was that about her manner which she did not like.

"Yes, of course I am well!" she said. "Why didn't you bring Barbara?"

"She was tired!"

"H'm! Afraid of meeting me, since she committed that piece of folly over Eustace. You must be careful of that child, Gertrude, or she will do something silly herself. I don't like the way she keeps Claud Harbinger hanging in the wind."

Her daughter cut her short:

"There is bad news about Eustace."

Lady Casterley lost the little colour in her cheeks; lost, too, all her superfluity of irritable energy.

"Tell me, at once!"

Having heard, she said nothing; but Lady Valleys noticed with alarm that over her eyes had come suddenly the peculiar filminess of age.

"Well, what do you advise?" she asked.

Herself tired, and troubled, she was conscious of a quite unwonted feeling of discouragement before this silent little figure, in the silent white room. She had never before seen her mother look as if she heard Defeat passing on its dark wings. And moved by sudden tenderness for the little frail body that had borne her so long ago, she murmured almost with surprise:

"Mother, dear!"

"Yes," said Lady Casterley, as if speaking to herself, "the boy saves things up; he stores his feelings—they burst and sweep him away. First his passion; now his conscience. There are two men in him; but this will be the death of one of them." And suddenly turning on her daughter, she said:

"Did you ever hear about him at Oxford, Gertrude? He broke out once, and ate husks with the Gadarenes. You never knew. Of course—you never have known anything of him."

Resentment rose in Lady Valleys, that anyone should know her son better than herself; but she lost it again looking at the little figure, and said, sighing:

"Well?"

Lady Casterley murmured:

"Go away, child; I must think. You say he's to consult Dennis? Do you know *her* address? Ask Barbara when you get back and telephone it to me." And at her daughter's kiss, she added grimly:

"I shall live to see him in the saddle yet, though I *am* seventy-eight."

When the sound of her daughter's car had died away, she rang the bell.

"If Lady Valleys rings up, Clifton, don't take the message, but call me." And seeing that Clifton did not move she added sharply: "Well?"

"There is no bad news of his young lordship's health, I hope!"

" No."

" Forgive me, my lady, but I have had it on my mind for some time to ask you something."

And the old man raised his hand with a peculiar dignity, seeming to say: 'You will excuse me that for the moment I am a human being speaking to a human being.'

" The matter of his attachment," he went on, " is known to me; it has given me acute anxiety, knowing his lordship as I do, and having heard him say something singular when he was here in July. I should be grateful if you would assure me that there is to be no hitch in his career, my lady."

The expression on Lady Casterley's face was strangely compounded of surprise, kindliness, defence, and impatience as with a child.

" Not if I can prevent it, Clifton," she said shortly; " in fact, you need not concern yourself."

Clifton bowed.

" Excuse me mentioning it, my lady "; a quiver ran over his face between its long white whiskers, " but his young lordship's career is more to me than my own."

When he had left her, Lady Casterley sat down in a little low chair—long she sat there by the empty hearth, till the daylight was all gone.

CHAPTER XX

Not far from the dark-haloed indeterminate limbo where dwelt that bugbear of Charles Courtier, the great Half-Truth Authority, he himself had a couple of rooms at fifteen shillings a week. Their chief attraction was that the great Half-Truth Liberty had recommended them. They tied him to nothing, and were ever at his disposal when he was in London; for his landlady, though not bound by agreement so to do, let them in such a way, that she could turn anyone else out at a week's notice. She was a gentle soul, married to a socialistic plumber twenty years her senior. The worthy man had given her two little boys, and the three of them kept her in such permanent order that to be in the presence of Courtier was the greatest pleasure she knew. When he disappeared on one of his nomadic missions, explorations, or adventures, she enclosed the whole of his belongings in two tin trunks and placed them in a cupboard which smelled a little of mice. When he reappeared the trunks were reopened, and a powerful scent of dried rose-leaves would escape. For, recognising the mortality of things human, she procured every summer from her sister, the wife of a market gardener, a consignment of this commodity, which she passionately sewed up in bags, and continued to deposit year by year in Courtier's trunks. This, and the way she made his toast —very crisp—and aired his linen—very dry, were practically the only things she could do for a man naturally inclined to independence, and accustomed from his manner of life to fend for himself.

At first signs of his departure she would go into some closet or other, away from the plumber and the two marks of his affection, and cry quietly; but never in Courtier's presence did she dream of manifesting grief—as soon weep in the presence of death or birth, or any other fundamental tragedy or joy. In face of the realities of life she had known from her youth up the value of the simple verb " *sto—stare*—to stand fast."

And to her Courtier was a reality, the chief reality of life, the focus of her aspiration, the morning and the evening star.

The request, then—five days after his farewell visit to Mrs. Noel—for the elephant-hide trunk which accompanied his rovings, produced her habitual period of seclusion, followed by her habitual appearance in his sitting-room bearing a note, and some bags of dried rose-leaves on a tray. She found him in his shirt sleeves, packing.

" Well, Mrs. Benton; off again!"

Mrs. Benton, plaiting her hands, for she had not yet lost something of the look and manner of a little girl, answered in her flat, but serene voice:

" Yes, sir; and I hope you're not going anywhere very dangerous this time. I always think you go to such dangerous places."

" To Persia, Mrs. Benton, where the carpets come from."

" Oh! yes, sir. Your washing's just come home."

Her, apparently cast-down, eyes stored up a wealth of little details; the way his hair grew, the set of his back, the colour of his braces. But suddenly she said in a surprising voice:

" You haven't a photograph you could spare, sir, to leave behind? Mr. Benton was only saying to me yesterday, we've nothing to remember him by, in case he shouldn't come back."

" Here's an old one."

Mrs. Benton took the photograph.

" Oh!" she said; " you can see who it is." And holding it perhaps too tightly, for her fingers trembled, she added:

" A note, please, sir; and the messenger boy is waiting for an answer."

While he read the note she noticed with concern how packing had brought the blood into his head. . . .

When, in response to that note, Courtier entered the well-known confectioner's called Gustard's, it was still not quite tea-time, and there seemed to him at first no one in the room save three middle-aged women packing sweets; then in the corner he saw Barbara. The blood was no longer in his head; he was pale, walking down that mahogany-coloured room impregnated with the scent of wedding-cake. Barbara, too, was pale.

So close to her that he could count her every eyelash, and inhale the scent of her hair and clothes—to listen to her story of Miltoun, so hesitatingly, so wistfully told, seemed very like being kept waiting with the rope already round his neck, to hear about another person's toothache. He felt this to have been unnecessary on the part of Fate! And there came to him perversely the memory of that ride over the sun-warmed heather, when he had paraphrased the old Sicilian song: " Here will I sit and sing." He was a long way from singing now; nor was there love in his arms. There was instead a cup of tea; and in his nostrils the scent of cake, with now and then a whiff of orange-flower water.

"I see," he said, when she had finished telling him: "'Liberty's a glorious feast!' You want me to go to your brother, and quote Burns? You know, of course, that he regards me as dangerous."

"Yes; but he respects and likes you."

"And I respect and like him," answered Courtier.

One of the middle-aged females passed, carrying a large white card-board box; and the creaking of her stays broke the hush.

"You have been very sweet to me," said Barbara, suddenly.

Courtier's heart stirred, as if it were turning over within him; and gazing into his teacup, he answered:

"All men are decent to the evening star. I will go at once and find your brother. When shall I bring you news?"

"To-morrow at five I'll be at home."

And repeating, "To-morrow at five," he rose.

Looking back from the door, he saw her face puzzled, rather reproachful, and went out gloomily. The scent of cake, and orange-flower water, the creaking of the female's stays, the colour of mahogany, still clung to his nose and ears, and eyes; but within him it was all dull baffled rage. Why had he not made the most of this unexpected chance; why had he not made desperate love to her? A conscientious fool! And yet—the whole thing was absurd! She was so young! God knew he would be glad to be out of it. If he stayed he was afraid that he would play the fool. But the memory of her words: "You have been very sweet to me!" would not leave him; nor the memory of her face, so puzzled, and reproachful. Yes, if he stayed he would play the fool! He would be asking her to marry a man double her age, of no position but that which he had carved for himself, and without a rap. And he would be asking her in such a way that she might possibly have some little difficulty in refusing. He would be letting himself go. And she was only twenty—for all her woman-of-the-world air, a child! No! He would be useful to her, if possible, this once, and then clear out!

CHAPTER XXI

WHEN Miltoun left Valleys House he walked in the direction of Westminster. During the five days that he had been back in London he had not yet entered the House of Commons. After the seclusion of his illness, he still felt a yearning, almost painful, towards the movement and stir of the town. Everything he heard and saw made an intensely vivid impression. The lions in Trafalgar Square, the great buildings of Whitehall, filled him with a sort of exultation. He was like a man who, after a long sea voyage, first catches sight of land, and stands straining his eyes, hardly breathing, taking in one by one the lost features of that face. He walked on to Westminster Bridge, and going to an embrasure in the very centre, looked back.

It was said that the love of those towers passed into the blood. It was said that he who had sat beneath them could never again be quite the same. Miltoun knew that it was true —desperately true, of himself. In person he had sat there but three weeks, but in soul he seemed to have been sitting there hundreds of years. And now he would sit there no more! An almost frantic desire to free himself from this coil rose up within him. To be held a prisoner by that most secret of all his instincts, the instinct for authority! To be unable to wield authority because to wield authority was to insult authority. God! It was hard! He turned his back on the towers, and sought distraction in the faces of the passers-by.

Each of these, he knew, had his struggle to keep self-respect! Or was it that they were unconscious of struggle or of self-respect, and just let things drift? They looked like that, most of them! And all his inherent contempt for the average or common welled up while he watched them. Yes, they looked like that! Ironically, the sight of those from whom he had desired the comfort of compromise, served instead to stimulate that part of him which refused to let him compromise. They looked soft, soggy, without pride or will, as though they knew that life was too much for them, and had shamefully accepted the fact. They so obviously needed to be told what they might do, and which way they should go; they would accept orders as they accepted their work, or pleasures. And the thought that

697

he was now debarred from the right to give them orders, rankled in him furiously. They, in their turn, glanced casually at his tall figure leaning against the parapet, not knowing how their fate was trembling in the balance. His thin, sallow face, and hungry eyes gave one or two of them perhaps a feeling of interest or discomfort; but to most he was assuredly no more than any other man or woman in the hurly-burly. That dark figure of conscious power struggling in the fetters of its own belief in power, was a piece of sculpture they had neither time nor wish to understand, having no taste for tragedy—for witnessing the human spirit driven to the wall.

It was five o'clock before Miltoun left the Bridge, and passed, like an exile, before the gates of Church and State, on his way to his uncle's Club. He stopped to telegraph to Audrey the time he would be coming to-morrow afternoon; and, on leaving the Post-Office, noticed in the window of the adjoining shop some reproductions of old Italian masterpieces, amongst them one of Botticelli's "Birth of Venus." He had never seen that picture; and, remembering that she had told him it was her favourite, he stopped to look at it. Averagely well versed in such matters, as became one of his caste, Miltoun had not the power of letting a work of art insidiously steal the private self from his soul, and replace it with the self of all the world; and he examined this far-famed presentment of the heathen goddess with aloofness, even irritation. The drawing of the body seemed to him crude, the whole picture a little flat and Early; he did not like the figure of the Flora. The golden serenity, and tenderness, of which she had spoken, left him cold. Then he found himself looking at the face, and slowly, but with uncanny certainty, began to feel that he was looking at the face of Audrey herself. The hair was golden and different, the eyes grey and different, the mouth a little fuller; yet—it was her face, the same oval shape, the same far-apart, arched brows, the same strangely tender, elusive spirit. And, as though offended, he turned and walked on. In the window of that little shop was the effigy of her for whom he had bartered away his life— the incarnation of passive and entwining love, that gentle creature, who had given herself to him so utterly, for whom love, and the flowers, and trees, and birds, music, the sky, and the quick-flowing streams, were all-sufficing; and who, like the goddess in the picture, seemed wondering at her own existence. He had a sudden glimpse of understanding, strange indeed in one who had so little power of seeing into others' hearts. Ought she ever to have been born into a world like this? But the flash of insight yielded quickly to that sickening consciousness of his own position, which never left him now. Whatever else he did, he must get rid of that malaise! But what could he do in that coming life? Write books? What sort of books could he write? Only such as expressed his views of citizenship, his political and social beliefs. As well remain sitting and speaking beneath those towers! He could never join the happy band of artists, those soft and indeterminate spirits, for whom barriers had no meaning, content to understand, interpret, and create. What should he be doing in that gallery? The thought was inconceivable. A career at the Bar—yes, he might take that up; but to what end? To become a judge! As well continue to sit beneath those towers! Too late for diplomacy. Too late for the Army; besides, he had not the faintest taste for military glory. Bury himself in the county like Uncle Dennis, and administer one of his father's estates? It would be death. Go amongst the poor? For a moment he thought he had found a new vocation. But in what capacity—to order their lives, when he himself could not order his own; or, as a mere conduit pipe for money, when he believed that charity was rotting the nation to its core? At the head of every avenue stood an angel or devil with drawn sword. And then there came to him another thought. Since he was being cast forth from Church and State, could he not play the fallen spirit like a man—be Lucifer, and destroy! And instinctively he at once saw himself returning to those towers, and beneath them crossing the floor; joining the revolutionaries, the Radicals, the freethinkers, scourging his present Party, the party of authority and institutions. The idea struck him as supremely comic, and he laughed out loud in the street. . . .

The Club which Lord Dennis frequented was in St. James's untouched by the tides of the waters of fashion—steadily swinging to its moorings in a quiet backwater, and Miltoun found his uncle in the library. He was reading a volume of Burton's travels, and drinking tea.

"Nobody comes here," he said, "so, in spite of that word on the door, we shall talk. Waiter, bring some more tea, please."

Impatiently, but with a sort of pity, Miltoun watched Lord Dennis's urbane movements, wherein old age was, pathetically, trying to make each little thing seem important, if only to the doer. Nothing his great-uncle could say would outweigh the warning of his picturesque old figure! To be a bystander; to see it all go past you; to let your sword rust in its sheath, as this poor old fellow had done! The notion of explaining what he had come about was particularly hateful to Miltoun; but since he had given his word, he nerved himself with secret anger, and began:

"I promised my mother to ask you a question, Uncle Dennis. You know of my attachment, I believe?"

Lord Dennis nodded.

"Well, I have joined my life to this lady's. There will be no scandal, but I consider it my duty to resign my seat, and leave public life alone. Is that right or wrong according to your view?"

Lord Dennis looked at his nephew in silence. A faint flush coloured his brown cheeks. He had the appearance of one travelling in mind over the past.

"Wrong, I think," he said, at last.

"Why, if I may ask?"

"I have not the pleasure of knowing this lady, and am therefore somewhat in the dark; but it appears to me that your decision is not fair to her."

"That is beyond me," said Miltoun.

Lord Dennis answered firmly:

"You have asked me a frank question, expecting a frank answer, I suppose?"

Miltoun nodded.

"Then, my dear, don't blame me if what I say is unpalatable."

"I shall not."

"Good! You say you are going to give up public life for the sake of your conscience. I should have no criticism to make if it stopped there."

He paused, and for quite a minute remained silent, evidently searching for words to express some intricate thread of thought.

"But it won't, Eustace; the public man in you is far stronger than the other. You want leadership more than you want love. Your sacrifice will kill your affection; what you imagine is *your* loss and hurt, will prove to be this lady's in the end."

Miltoun smiled.

Lord Dennis continued very dryly and with a touch of malice:

"You are not listening to me; but I can see quite well that

the process has begun already underneath. There's a curious streak of the Jesuit in you, Eustace. What you don't want to see, you won't look at."

" You advise me, then, to compromise? "

" On the contrary, I point out that you will be compromising if you try to keep both your conscience and your love. You will be seeking to have it both ways."

" That is interesting."

" And you will find yourself having it neither," said Lord Dennis sharply.

Miltoun rose. " In other words, you, like the others, recommend me to desert this lady who loves me, and whom I love. And yet, Uncle, they say that in your own case——"

But Lord Dennis had risen, too, having lost all the appanage and manner of old age.

" Of my own case," he said bluntly, " we won't talk. I don't advise you to desert anyone; you quite mistake me. I advise you to know yourself. And I tell you my opinion of you—you were cut out by Nature for a statesman, not a lover! There's something dried-up in you, Eustace; I'm not sure there isn't something dried-up in all our caste. We've had to do with forms and ceremonies too long. We're not good at taking the lyrical point of view."

" Unfortunately," said Miltoun, " I cannot, to fit in with a theory of yours, commit a baseness."

Lord Dennis began pacing up and down. He was keeping his lips closed very tight.

" A man who gives advice," he said at last, " is always something of a fool. For all that, you have mistaken mine. I am not so presumptuous as to attempt to enter the inner chamber of your spirit. I have merely told you that, in my opinion, it would be more honest to yourself, and fairer to this lady, to compound with your conscience, and keep both your love and your public life, than to pretend that you were capable of sacrificing what I know is the stronger element in you for the sake of the weaker. You remember the saying—Democritus, I think ἦθος ἀνθρώπῳ δαίμων (each man's nature or character is his fate or god). I commend it to you."

For a full minute Miltoun stood without replying, then said:

" I am sorry to have troubled you, Uncle Dennis. A middle policy is no use to me. Good-bye!" And without shaking hands, he went out.

CHAPTER XXII

In the hall someone rose from a sofa, and came towards him. It was Courtier.

"Run you to earth at last," he said; "I wish you'd come and dine with me. I'm leaving England to-morrow night, and there are things I want to say."

There passed through Miltoun's mind the rapid thought: 'Does he know?' He assented, however, and they went out together.

"It's difficult to find a quiet place," said Courtier; "but this might do."

The place chosen was a little hostel, frequented by racing men, and famed for the excellence of its steaks. And as they sat down opposite each other in the almost empty room, Miltoun thought: 'Yes, he does know! Can I stand any more of this?' He waited almost savagely for the attack he felt was coming.

"So you are going to give up your seat?" said Courtier.

Miltoun looked at him for some seconds, before replying:

"From what town crier did you hear that?"

But there was that in Courtier's face which checked his anger; its friendliness was transparent.

"I am about her only friend," Courtier proceeded earnestly; "and this is my last chance—to say nothing of my feeling towards you, which, believe me, is very cordial."

"Go on, then," Miltoun muttered.

"Forgive me for putting it bluntly. Have you considered what her position was before she met you?"

Miltoun felt the blood rushing to his face, but he sat still, clenching his nails into the palms of his hands.

"Yes, yes," said Courtier, "but that attitude of mind—you used to have it yourself—which decrees for women either living death, or the spiritual adultery of continuing abhorred marriage relations, makes my blood boil. And I say you had the right fundamentally to protest against them, not only in words but deeds. You did protest, I know; but this present decision of yours is a climb down, as much as to say that your protest was wrong."

Miltoun rose from his seat. "I cannot discuss this," he said.

702

"For her sake, you must. If you give up your public work, you'll spoil her life a second time."

Miltoun again sat down. At the word "must" a steely feeling had come to his aid; his eyes began to resemble the old Cardinal's. "Your nature and mine, Courtier," he said, "are too far apart; we shall never understand each other."

"Never mind that," answered Courtier. "Admitting those two alternatives to be horrible, which you never would have done unless the facts had been brought home to you personally——"

"That," said Miltoun icily, "I deny your right to say."

"Anyway, you do admit them—if you believe you had not the right to rescue her, on what principle do you base that belief?"

Miltoun placed his elbow on the table, and leaning his chin on his hand, regarded the champion of lost causes without speaking. There was such a turmoil going on within him that with difficulty he could force his lips to obey him.

"By what right do you ask me that?" he said at last. He saw Courtier's face grow scarlet, and his fingers twisting furiously at those flame-like moustaches; but his answer was as steadily ironical as usual.

"Well, I can hardly sit still, my last evening in England, without lifting a finger, while you immolate a woman to whom I feel like a brother. I'll tell you what your principle is: Authority, unjust or just, desirable or undesirable, must be implicitly obeyed. To break a law, no matter on what provocation, or for whose sake, is to break the commandment——"

"Don't hesitate—say, of God."

"Of an infallible fixed Power. Is that a true definition of your principle?"

"Yes," said Miltoun, between his teeth, "I think so."

"Exceptions prove the rule."

"Hard cases make bad law."

Courtier smiled: "I knew you were coming out with that. I deny that they do with this law, which is altogether behind the times. You had the right to rescue this woman."

"No, Courtier, if we must fight, let us fight on the naked facts. I have not rescued anyone. I have merely stolen sooner than starve. That is why I cannot go on pretending to be a pattern. If it were known, I could not retain my seat an hour; I can't take advantage of an accidental secrecy. Could you?"

Courtier was silent; and with his eyes Miltoun pressed on him, as though he would despatch him with that glance.

"I could," said Courtier at last. "When this law, by enforcing spiritual adultery on those who have come to hate their mates, destroys the sanctity of the married state—the very sanctity it professes to uphold, you must expect to have it broken by reasoning men and women without their losing self-respect."

In Miltoun there was rising that vast and subtle passion for dialectic combat, which was of his very fibre. He had almost lost the feeling that this was his own future being discussed. He saw before him in this sanguine man, whose voice and eyes had such a white-hot sound and look, the incarnation of all that he temperamentally opposed.

"That," he said, "is devil's advocacy. I admit no individual as judge in his own case."

"Ah! Now we're coming to it. By the way, shall we get out of this heat?"

They were no sooner in the cooler street, than the voice of Courtier began again:

"Distrust of human nature, fear—it's the whole basis of action for men of your stamp. You deny the right of the individual to judge, because you've no faith in the essential goodness of men; at heart you believe them bad. You give them no freedom, you allow them no consent, because you believe that their decisions would move downwards, and not upwards. Well, it's the whole difference between the aristocratic and the democratic view of life. As you once told me, you hate and fear the crowd."

Miltoun eyed that steady sanguine face askance.

"Yes," he said, "I do believe that men are raised in spite of themselves."

"You're honest. By whom?"

Again Miltoun felt rising within him a sort of fury. Once for all he would slay this red-haired rebel; he answered with almost savage irony:

"Strangely enough, by that Being to mention whom you object—working through the medium of the best."

"High-Priest! Look at that girl slinking along there, with her eye on us; suppose, instead of withdrawing your garment, you went over and talked to her, got her to tell you what she really felt and thought, you'd find things that would astonish you. Men have something splendid in them. And they're raised, sir, by the aspiration that's in all of them. Haven't you ever noticed that public sentiment is always in advance of the Law?"

"And you," said Miltoun, "are the man who is never on the side of the majority?"

The champion of lost causes uttered a short laugh.

"Not so logical as all that," he answered. "The wind still blows; and Life's not a set of rules hung up in an office. Let's see, where are we?" They had been brought to a standstill by a group on the pavement in front of the Queen's Hall: "Shall we go in, and hear some music, and cool our tongues?"

Miltoun nodded, and they went in.

The great lighted hall, filled with the faint bluish vapour from hundreds of little rolls of tobacco leaf, was crowded from floor to ceiling.

Taking his stand among the straw-hatted throng, Miltoun heard that steady ironical voice behind him:

"*Profanum vulgus!* Come to listen to the finest piece of music ever written! Folk whom *you* wouldn't trust a yard to know what was good for them! Deplorable sight, isn't it?"

He made no answer. The first slow notes of the seventh Symphony of Beethoven had begun to steal forth across the bank of flowers; and, save for the steady rising of that bluish vapour, as it were incense burnt to the god of melody, the crowd had become deathly still, as though one mind, one spirit, possessed each pale face inclined towards that music rising and falling like the sighing of the winds, that welcome from death the freed spirits of the beautiful.

When the last notes had died away, he turned and walked out.

"Well," said the voice behind him, "hasn't that shown you how things swell and grow; how splendid the world is?"

Miltoun smiled.

"It has shown me how beautiful the world can be made by a great man."

And suddenly, as if the music had loosened some band within him, he began to pour forth words:

"Look at the crowd in this street, Courtier, which of all crowds in the whole world can best afford to be left to itself; secure from pestilence, earthquake, cyclone, drought, from extremes of heat and cold, in the heart of the greatest and safest

city in the world; and yet—see the figure of that policeman!
Running through all the good behaviour of this crowd, however
safe and free it looks, there is, there always must be, a central
force holding it together. Where does that central force come
from? From the crowd itself, you say. I answered: No.
Look back at the origin of human States. From the beginnings
of things, the best man has been the unconscious medium of
authority, of the controlling principle, of the divine force; he
felt that power within him—physical, at first—he used it to
take the lead, he has held the lead ever since, he must always
hold it. All your processes of election, your so-called democratic apparatus, are only a blind to the inquiring, a sop to the
hungry, a salve to the pride of the rebellious. They are merely
surface machinery, they cannot prevent the best man from
coming to the top; for the best man stands nearest to the
Deity, and is the first to receive the waves that come from Him.
I'm not speaking of heredity. The best man is not necessarily
born in my class, and I, at all events, do not believe he is any
more frequent there than in other classes."

He stopped as suddenly as he had begun.

"You needn't be afraid," answered Courtier, "that I take
you for an average specimen. You're at one end, and I at the
other—and very likely both wide of the golden mark. But the
world is not ruled by power, and the fear which power produces,
as you think; it's ruled by love. Society is held together by
the natural decency in man, by fellow-feeling. The democratic
principle, which you despise, at root means nothing at all but
that. Man left to himself is on the upward lay. If it weren't
so, do you imagine for a moment your 'boys in blue' could
keep order? A man knows unconsciously what he can and what
he can't do, without losing his self-respect. He sucks that
knowledge in with every breath. Laws and authority are not the
be-all and end-all, they are conveniences, machinery, conduit
pipes, main roads. They're not of the structure of the building
—they're only scaffolding."

Miltoun lunged out with the retort:

"Without which no building could be built."

Courtier parried.

"That's rather different, my friend, from identifying them
with the building? They are things to be taken down as fast
as ever they can be cleared away, to make room for an edifice
which begins on earth, not in the sky. All the scaffolding of

law is merely there to save time, to prevent the temple, as it mounts, from losing its way, and straying out of form."

"No," said Miltoun, "no! The scaffolding, as you call it, is the material projection of the architect's conception, without which the temple does not and cannot rise; and the architect is God, working through the minds and spirits most akin to Himself."

"We are now at the bed-rock," cried Courtier. "Your God is outside this world. Mine within it."

"And never the twain shall meet!"

In the ensuing silence Miltoun saw that they were in Leicester Square—all quiet, before the theatres had disgorged; quiet yet waiting, with the lights, like yellow stars low-driven from the dark heavens, clinging to the white shapes of music-halls and cafés, and a sort of flying glamour blanching the still foliage of the plane trees.

"A 'whitely wanton'—this Square!" said Courtier: "Alive as a face; no end to its queer beauty! And, by Jove, if you go deep enough, you'll find goodness even here."

"And the vileness—you would ignore!" Miltoun answered.

He felt weary all of a sudden, anxious to get to his rooms, unwilling to continue this battle of words, which brought him no nearer to relief. It was with strange lassitude that he heard the voice still speaking:

"We must make a night of it, since to-morrow we die. . . . You would curb licence from without—I from within. When I get up and when I go to bed, when I draw a breath, see a face, or a flower, or a tree—if I didn't feel that I was looking on the Deity, I believe I should quit this palace of varieties, from sheer boredoom. You, I understand, can't look on your God, unless you withdraw into some high place. Isn't it a bit lonely there?"

But Miltoun did not answer, so that they walked on in silence; till suddenly he broke out:

"You talk of tyranny! What tyranny could equal this tyranny of your freedom? What tyranny in the world like that of this 'free' vulgar, narrow street, with its hundred journals, teeming like ants' nests, to produce—what? In the entrails of that creature of your freedom, Courtier, there is room neither for exaltation, discipline, nor sacrifice; there is room only for commerce, and licence."

There was no answer for a moment; and from those tall houses, whose lighted windows he had apostrophised, Miltoun turned away towards the river. "No," said the voice, "for all its faults, the wind blows in that street, and there's a chance for everything. By God, I would rather see a few stars struggle out in a black sky than any of your perfect artificial lighting."

And suddenly it seemed to Miltoun that he could never free himself from the echoes of that voice—it was not worth while to try. "We are repeating ourselves," he said, dryly.

The river's black water was making stilly, slow recessional under a half-moon. Beneath the cloak of night the chaos on the far bank, the forms of cranes, high buildings, jetties, the bodies of some sleeping barges, a million queer dark shapes, were invested with emotion. All was religious out there, all beautiful, all strange. And over this great quiet friend of man, lamps— those humble flowers of night—were throwing down the faint continual glamour of fallen petals; and a sweet-scented wind stole along from the West, very slow as yet, bringing in advance the tremor and perfume of the innumerable trees and fields which the river had loved as she came by.

A murmur that was no true sound, but like the whisper of a heart to a heart, accompanied this voyage of the dark water.

Then a small blunt skiff manned by two rowers came by under the wall, with the thudding and creak of oars.

"So 'To-morrow we die'?" said Miltoun: "You mean, I suppose, that 'public life' is the breath of my nostrils, and I must die, because I give it up?"

Courtier nodded.

"Am I right in thinking, it was my young sister who sent you on this crusade?"

Courtier did not reply.

"And so," Miltoun went on, looking him through and through; "to-morrow is to be your last day, too? Well, you're right to go. *She* is not an ugly duckling, who can live out of the social pond; she'll always want her native element. And now, we'll say good-bye! Whatever happens to us both, I shall remember this evening." Smiling, he put out his hand: "*Moriturus te saluto.*"

CHAPTER XXIII

COURTIER sat in Hyde Park waiting for five o'clock.

The day had recovered somewhat from a grey morning, as though the glow of that long hot summer were too burnt-in on the air to yield to the first assault. The sun, piercing the crisped clouds, darted its beams at the mellowed leaves, and showered to the ground their delicate shadow stains. The first, too early, scent from leaves about to fall, penetrated to the heart. And sorrowful shrill birds were tuning their little autumn pipes, blowing into them fragments of Spring odes to Liberty.

Courtier thought of Miltoun and his mistress. By what a strange fate had those two been thrown together; to what end was their love coming? The seeds of grief were already sown; what flower of darkness, or of tumult would come up? He saw her again as a little, grave, considering child, with her soft eyes, set wide apart under the dark arched brows, and the little tuck at the corner of her mouth that used to come when he teased her. And to that gentle creature who would sooner die than force anyone to anything, had been given this queer lover; this aristocrat by birth and nature, with the dried fervent soul, whose every fibre had been bred and trained in and to the service of Authority; this rejecter of the Unity of Life; this worshipper of an old God! A God that stood, whip in hand, driving men to obedience. A God that even now Courtier could conjure up staring at him from the walls of his nursery. The God his own father had believed in. A God of the Old Testament, knowing neither sympathy nor understanding. Strange that He should be alive still: that there should still be thousands who worshipped Him. Yet, not so very strange, if, as they said, man made God in his own image! Here indeed was a curious mating of what the philosophers would call the will to Love, and the will to Power!

A soldier and his girl came and sat down on a bench close by. They looked askance at this trim and upright figure with the fighting face; then, some subtle thing informing them that he was not of the disturbing breed called officer, they ceased to regard him, abandoning themselves to dumb and inexpressive

709

felicity. Arm in arm, touching each other, they seemed to Courtier very jolly, having that look of living entirely in the moment, which always especially appealed to one whose blood ran too fast to allow him to speculate much upon the future or brood much over the past.

A leaf from the bough above him, loosened by the sun's kisses, dropped, and fell yellow at his feet. The leaves were turning very soon!

It was characteristic of this man, who could be so hot over the lost causes of others, that, sitting there within half an hour of the final loss of his own cause, he could be so calm, so almost apathetic. This apathy was partly due to the hopelessness, which Nature had long perceived, of trying to make him feel oppressed, but also to the habits of a man incurably accustomed to carrying his fortunes in his hand, and that hand open. It did not seem real to him that he was actually going to suffer a defeat, to have to confess that he had hankered after this girl all these past weeks, and that to-morrow all would be wasted, and she as dead to him as if he had never seen her. No, it was not exactly resignation, it was rather sheer lack of commercial instinct. If only this had been the lost cause of another person. How gallantly he would have rushed to the assault, and taken her by storm! If only he himself could have been that other person, how easily, how passionately could he not have pleaded, letting forth from him all those words, which had knocked at his teeth ever since he knew her, and which would have seemed so ridiculous and so unworthy, spoken on his own behalf. Yes, for that other person he could have cut her out from under the guns of the enemy; he could have taken her that fairest prize.

And in queer, cheery-looking apathy—not far removed perhaps from despair—he sat, watching the leaves turn over and fall, and now and then cutting with his stick at the air, where autumn was already riding. And, if in imagination he saw himself carrying her away into the wilderness, and with his devotion making her happiness to grow, it was so far a flight, that a smile crept about his lips, and once or twice he snapped his jaws.

The soldier and his girl rose, passing in front of him down the Row. He watched their scarlet and blue figures, moving slowly towards the sun, and another couple close to the rails, crossing those receding forms. Very straight and tall, there was something exhilarating in the way this new couple swung along, holding their heads up, turning towards each other, to exchange words or smiles. Even at that distance they could be seen to be of high fashion; in their gait was the almost insolent poise of those who are above doubts and cares, certain of the world and of themselves. The girl's dress was tawny brown, her hair and hat too of the same hue, and the pursuing sunlight endowed her with a hazy splendour. Then, Courtier saw who they were—that couple!

Except for an unconscious grinding of his teeth, he made no sound or movement, so that they went by without seeing him. Her voice, though not the words, came to him distinctly. He saw her hand slip up under Harbinger's arm and swiftly down again. A smile, of whose existence he was unaware, settled on his lips. He got up, shook himself, as a dog shakes off a beating, and walked away, with his mouth set very firm.

CHAPTER XXIV

LEFT alone among the little mahogany tables of Gustard's, where the scent of cake and of orange-flower water made happy all the air, Barbara had sat for some minutes, her eyes cast down—as a child from whom a toy has been taken contemplates the ground, not knowing precisely what she is feeling. Then, paying one of the middle-aged females, she went out into the Square. There a German band was playing Delibes' "Coppélia"; and the murdered tune came haunting her, a ghost of incongruity.

She went straight back to Valleys House. In the room where three hours ago she had been left alone after lunch with Harbinger, her sister was seated in the window, looking decidedly disturbed. In fact, Agatha had just spent an awkward hour. Chancing, with little Ann, into that confectioner's where she could best obtain a particularly gummy sweet which she believed wholesome for her children, she had been engaged in purchasing a pound, when looking down, she perceived Ann standing stock-still, with her sudden little nose pointed down the shop, and her mouth opening; glancing in the direction of those frank, enquiring eyes, Agatha saw to her amazement her sister and a man whom she recognised as Courtier. With a readiness which did her complete credit, she placed a sweet in Ann's mouth, and saying to the middle-aged female: "Then you'll send those, please. Come, Ann!" went out. Shocks never coming singly, she had no sooner reached home, than from her father she learned of the development of Miltoun's love affair. When Barbara returned, she was sitting, unfeignedly upset and grieved; unable to decide whether or no she ought to divulge what she herself had seen, but withal buoyed-up by that peculiar indignation of the essentially domestic woman, whose ideals have been outraged.

Judging at once from the expression of her face that she must have heard the news of Miltoun, Barbara said:

"Well, my dear Angel, any lecture for me?"

Agatha answered coldly:

"I think you were quite mad to take Mrs. Noel to him."

712

"The whole duty of woman," murmured Barbara, "includes a little madness."

Agatha looked at her in silence.

"I can't make you out," she said at last; "you're not a fool!"

"Only a knave."

"You may think it right to joke over the ruin of Miltoun's life," murmured Agatha; "I don't."

Barbara's eyes grew bright; and in a hard voice she answered:

"The world is not your nursery, Angel!"

Agatha closed her lips very tightly, as who should imply: "Then it ought to be!" But she only answered:

"I don't think you know that I saw you just now in Gustard's."

Barbara eyed her for a moment in amazement, and began to laugh.

"I see," she said; "monstrous depravity—poor old Gustard's!" And still laughing that dangerous laugh, she turned on her heel and went out.

At dinner and afterwards that evening she was very silent, having on her face the same look that she wore out hunting, especially when in difficulties of any kind, or if advised to "take a pull." When she got away to her own room she had a longing to relieve herself by some kind of action that would hurt someone, if only herself. To go to bed and toss about in a fever—for she knew herself in these thwarted moods—was of no use! For a moment she thought of going out. That would be fun, and hurt them, too; but it was difficult. She did not want to be seen, and have the humiliation of an open row. Then there came into her head the memory of the roof of the tower, where she had once been as a little girl. She would be in the air there, she would be able to breathe, to get rid of this feverishness. With the unhappy pleasure of a spoiled child taking its revenge, she took care to leave her bedroom door open, so that her maid would wonder where she was, and perhaps be anxious and make them anxious. Slipping through the moonlit picture gallery on to the landing, outside her father's sanctum, whence rose the stone staircase leading to the roof, she began to mount. She was breathless, when, after that unending flight of stairs, she emerged on to the roof at the extreme northern end of the big house, where, below her, was a sheer drop of a hundred feet. At first she stood, a little giddy, grasping the rail that ran round that garden of lead, still absorbed in her brooding rebellious thoughts. Gradually she lost consciousness of everything save the scene before her. High above all neighbouring houses, she was almost appalled by the majesty of what she saw. This night-clothed city, so remote and dark, so white-gleaming and alive, on whose purple hills and valleys grew such myriad golden flowers of light, from whose heart came this deep incessant murmur—could it possibly be the same city through which she had been walking that very day! From its sleeping body the supreme wistful spirit had emerged in dark loveliness, and was low flying down there, tempting her. Barbara turned round, to take in all that amazing prospect, from the black glades of Hyde Park, in front, to the powdery white ghost of a church tower, away to the East. How marvellous was this city of night! And as, in presence of that wide darkness of the sea before dawn, her spirit had felt little and timid within her—so it felt now, in face of this great, brooding, beautiful creature, whom man had made. She singled out the shapes of the Piccadilly hotels, and beyond them the palaces and towers of Westminster and Whitehall; and everywhere the inextricable loveliness of dim blue forms and sinuous pallid lines of light, under an indigo-dark sky. Near at hand, she could see plainly the still-lighted windows, the motor-cars gliding by, far down, even the tiny shapes of people walking; and the thought that each of them meant someone like herself, seemed strange.

Drinking of this wonder-cup, she began to experience a queer intoxication, and lost the sense of being little; rather she had the feeling of power, as in her dream at Monkland. She too, as well as this great thing below her, seemed to have shed her body, to be emancipated from every barrier—floating deliciously identified with air. She seemed to be one with the enfranchised spirit of the city, drowned in perception of its beauty. Then all that feeling went and left her frowning, shivering, though the wind from the West was warm. Her whole adventure of coming up here seemed bizarre, ridiculous. Very stealthily she crept down, and had reached once more the door into the picture gallery, when she heard her mother's voice say in amazement: "That you, Babs?" And turning, saw her coming from the doorway of the sanctum.

Of a sudden very cool, with all her faculties about her, Barbara only stood looking at Lady Valleys, who said with hesitation:

"Come in here, dear, a minute, will you?"

In that room resorted to for comfort, Lord Valleys was standing with his back to the hearth, and an expression on his face that wavered between vexation and decision. The doubt in Agatha's mind whether she should tell or no, had been terribly resolved by little Ann, who in a pause of conversation had announced: "We saw Auntie Babs and Mr. Courtier in Gustard's, but we didn't speak to them."

Upset by the events of the afternoon, Lady Valleys had not shown her usual *savoir faire*. She had told her husband. A meeting of this sort in a shop celebrated for little save its wedding cakes was in a sense of no importance; but, being both disturbed already by the news of Miltoun, it seemed to them nothing less than sinister, as though the heavens were in league for the demolition of their house. To Lord Valleys it was peculiarly mortifying, because of his real admiration for his daughter, and because he had paid so little attention to his wife's warning of some weeks back. In consultation, however, they had only succeeded in deciding that Lady Valleys should talk with her. Though without much spiritual insight, both these two had a certain cool judgment; and they were fully alive to the danger of thwarting Barbara. This had not prevented Lord Valleys from expressing himself strongly on the "confounded unscrupulousness of that fellow," and secretly forming his own plan for dealing with this matter. Lady Valleys, more deeply conversant with her daughter's nature, and by reason of femininity more lenient towards the other sex, had not tried to excuse Courtier, but had thought privately: 'Babs *is* rather a flirt.' For she could not altogether help remembering herself at the same age.

Summoned thus unexpectedly, Barbara, her lips very firmly pressed together, took her stand coolly enough by her father's writing-table.

Seeing her suddenly appear, Lord Valleys instinctively relaxed his frown; his experience of men and things, his thousands of diplomatic hours, served to give him an air of coolness and detachment which he was very far from feeling. In truth he would rather have faced a hostile mob than his favourite daughter in such circumstances. His tanned face with its crisp grey moustache, his whole head indeed took on, unconsciously, a more than ordinarily soldier-like appearance. His eyelids drooped a little, his brows rose slightly.

She was wearing a blue wrap over her evening frock, and he seized instinctively on that indifferent trifle to begin this talk.

"Ah! Babs, have you been out?"

Alive to her very finger-nails, with every nerve tingling, but showing no sign, Barbara answered:

"No; on the roof of the tower."

It gave her a malicious pleasure to feel the real perplexity beneath her father's dignified exterior. And detecting that covert mockery, Lord Valleys said dryly:

"Star-gazing?"

Then, with that sudden resolution peculiar to him, as though he were bored with having to delay and temporise, he added:

"Do you know, I doubt whether it's wise to make appointments in confectioners' shops when Ann is in London."

The dangerous little gleam in Barbara's eyes escaped his vision but not that of Lady Valleys, who said at once:

"No doubt you had the best of reasons, my dear."

Barbara curled her lip inscrutably. Indeed, had it not been for the scene they had been through that day with Miltoun, and for their very real anxiety, both would have seen, then, that while their daughter was in this mood, least said was soonest mended. But their nerves were not quite within control; and with more than a touch of impatience Lord Valleys ejaculated:

"It doesn't appear to you, I suppose, to require any explanation?"

Barbara answered:

"No."

"Ah!" said Lord Valleys: "I see. An explanation can be had no doubt from the gentleman whose sense of proportion was such as to cause him to suggest such a thing."

"He did not suggest it. I did."

Lord Valleys' eyebrows rose still higher.

"Indeed!" he said.

"Geoffrey!" murmured Lady Valleys, "I thought *I* was to talk to Babs."

"It would no doubt be wiser."

In Barbara, thus for the first time in her life seriously reprimanded, there was at work the most peculiar sensation she had ever felt, as if something were scraping her very skin—a sick, and at the same time devilish, feeling. At that moment she could have struck her father dead. But she showed nothing, having lowered the lids of her eyes.

"Anything else?" she said.

Lord Valleys' jaw had become suddenly more prominent.

"As a sequel to your share in Miltoun's business, it is peculiarly entrancing."

"My dear," broke in Lady Valleys very suddenly, "Babs will tell me. It's nothing, of course."

Barbara's calm voice said again:

"Anything else?"

The repetition of this phrase in that maddening cool voice almost broke down her father's sorely tried control.

"Nothing from you," he said with deadly coldness. "I shall have the honour of telling this gentleman what I think of him."

At those words Barbara drew herself together, and turned her eyes from one face to the other.

Under that gaze, which for all its cool hardness, was so furiously alive, neither Lord nor Lady Valleys could keep quite still. It was as if she had stripped from them the well-bred mask of those whose spirits, by long unquestioning acceptance of themselves, have become inelastic, inexpansive, commoner than they knew. In fact a rather awful moment! Then Barbara said:

"If there's nothing else, I'm going to bed. Good-night!"

And as calmly as she had come in, she went out.

When she had regained her room, she locked the door, threw off her cloak, and looked at herself in the glass. With pleasure she saw how firmly her teeth were clenched, how her breast was heaving, how her eyes seemed to be stabbing herself. And all the time she thought:

'Very well! My dears! Very well!'

CHAPTER XXV

In that mood of rebellious mortification she fell asleep. And, curiously enough, dreamed not of him whom she had in mind been so furiously defending, but of Harbinger. She fancied herself in prison, lying in a cell fashioned like the drawing-room at Sea House; and in the next cell, into which she could somehow look, Harbinger was digging at the wall with his nails. She could distinctly see the hair on the back of his hands, and hear him breathing. The hole he was making grew larger and larger. Her heart began to beat furiously; she awoke.

She rose with a new and malicious resolution to show no sign of rebellion, to go through the day as if nothing had happened, to deceive them all, and then——! Exactly what "and then" meant, she did not explain even to herself.

In accordance with this plan of action she presented an un-troubled front at breakfast, went out riding with little Ann, and shopping with her mother afterwards. Owing to this news of Miltoun the journey to Scotland had been postponed. She parried with cool ingenuity each attempt made by Lady Valleys to draw her into conversation on the subject of that meeting at Gustard's, nor would she talk of her brother; in every other way she was her usual self. In the afternoon she even volun-teered to accompany her mother to old Lady Harbinger's in the neighbourhood of Prince's Gate. She knew that Harbinger would be there, and with the thought of meeting that other at "five o'clock," had a cynical pleasure in thus encountering him. It was so complete a blind to them all! Then, feeling that she was accomplishing a masterstroke, she even told him, in her mother's hearing, that she would walk home, and he might come if he cared. He did care.

But when once she had begun to swing along in the mellow afternoon, under the mellow trees, where the air was sweetened by the South-West wind, all that mutinous, reckless mood of hers vanished, she felt suddenly happy and kind, glad to be walking with him. To-day too he was cheerful, as if deter-mined not to spoil her gaiety; and she was grateful for this. Once or twice she even put her hand up and touched his sleeve,

718

calling his attention to birds or trees, friendly, and glad, after all those hours of bitter feelings, to be giving happiness. When they parted at the door of Valleys House, she looked back at him, with a queer, half-rueful smile. For, now the hour had come!

In a little unfrequented ante-room, all white panels and polish, she sat down to wait. The entrance drive was visible from here; and she meant to encounter Courtier casually in the hall. She was excited, and a little scornful of her own excitement. She had expected him to be punctual, but it was already past five; and soon she began to feel uneasy, almost ridiculous, sitting in this room where no one ever came. Going to the window, she looked out.

A sudden voice behind her, said:

"Auntie Babs!"

Turning, she saw little Ann regarding her with those wide, frank, hazel eyes. A shiver of nerves passed through Barbara.

"Is this your room? It's a nice room, isn't it?"

She answered:

"Quite a nice room, Ann."

"Yes. I've never been in here before. There's somebody just come, so I must go now."

Barbara involuntarily put her hands up to her cheeks, and quickly passed with her niece into the hall. At the very door the footman William handed her a note. She looked at the superscription. It was from Courtier. She went back into the room. Through its half-closed door the figure of little Ann could be seen, with her legs rather wide apart, and her hands clasped on her low-down belt, pointing up at William her sudden little nose. Barbara shut the door abruptly, broke the seal, and read:

"DEAR LADY BARBARA,

"I am sorry to say my interview with your brother was fruitless.

"I happened to be sitting in the Park just now, and I want to wish you every happiness before I go. It has been the greatest pleasure to know you. I shall never have a thought of you that will not be my pride; nor a memory that will not help me to believe that life is good. If I am tempted to feel that things are dark, I shall remember that you are breathing this same mortal air. And to beauty and joy I shall take off my hat with

the greater reverence, that once I was permitted to walk and talk
with you. And so, good-bye, and God bless you.

        "Your faithful servant,
                "CHARLES COURTIER."

Her cheeks burned, quick sighs escaped her lips; she read the
letter again, but before getting to the end could not see the
words for mist. If in that letter there had been a word of complaint or even of regret! She could not let him go like this,
without good-bye, without any explanation at all. He should
not think of her as a cold, stony flirt, who had been merely stealing a few weeks' amusement out of him. She would explain
to him at all events that it had not been that. She would make
him understand that it was not what he thought—that something in her wanted—wanted——! Her mind was all confused.
'What was it?' she thought: 'What did I do?' And sore
with anger at herself, she screwed the letter up in her glove,
and ran out. She walked swiftly down to Piccadilly, and crossed
into the Green Park. There she passed Lord Malvezin and a
friend strolling up towards Hyde Park Corner, and gave them a
very slight bow. The composure of those two precise and well-
groomed figures sickened her just then. She wanted to run, to
fly to this meeting that should remove from him the odious
feelings he must have, that she, Barbara Carádoc, was a vulgar
enchantress, a common traitress and coquette! And his letter
—without a syllable of reproach! Her cheeks burned so, that
she could not help trying to hide them from people who passed.
   As she drew nearer to his rooms she walked slower, forcing
herself to think what she should do, what she should let him do!
But she continued resolutely forward. She would not shrink
now—whatever came of it! Her heart fluttered, seemed to stop
beating, fluttered again. She set her teeth; a sort of desperate
hilarity rose in her. It was an adventure! Then she was
gripped by the feeling that had come to her on the roof. The
whole thing was bizarre, ridiculous! She stopped, and drew
the letter from her glove. It might be ridiculous, but it was
due from her; and closing her lips very tight, she walked on. In
thought she was already standing close to him, her eyes shut,
waiting, with her heart beating wildly, to know what she would
feel when his lips had spoken, perhaps touched her face or hand.
And she had a sort of mirage vision of herself, with eyelashes
resting on her cheeks, lips a little parted, arms helpless at her

sides. Yet, incomprehensibly, his figure was invisible. She discovered then that she was standing before his door.

She rang the bell calmly, but instead of dropping her hand, pressed the little bare patch of palm left open by the glove to her face, to see whether it was indeed her own cheek flaming so.

The door had been opened by some unseen agency, disclosing a passage and flight of stairs covered by a red carpet, at the foot of which lay an old, tangled, brown-white dog full of fleas and sadness. Unreasoning terror seized on Barbara; her body remained rigid, but her spirit began flying back across the Green Park, to the very hall of Valleys House. Then she saw coming towards her a youngish woman in a blue apron, with mild, reddened eyes.

"Is this where Mr. Courtier lives?"

"Yes, miss." The teeth of the young woman were few in number and rather black, and Barbara could only stand there saying nothing, as if her body had been deserted between the sunlight and this dim red passage, which led to—what?

The woman spoke again:

"I'm sorry if you was wanting him, miss, he's just gone away."

Barbara felt a movement in her heart, like the twang and quiver of an elastic band, suddenly relaxed. She bent to stroke the head of the old dog, who was smelling her shoes. The woman said:

"And, of course, I can't give you his address, because he's gone to foreign parts."

With a murmur, of whose sense she knew nothing, Barbara hurried out into the sunshine. Was she glad? Was she sorry? At the corner of the street she turned and looked back; the two heads, of the woman and the dog, were there still, poked out through the doorway.

A horrible inclination to laugh seized her, followed by as horrible a desire to cry.

CHAPTER XXVI

By the river the West wind, whose murmuring had visited Courtier and Miltoun the night before, was bringing up the first sky of autumn. Slow-creeping and fleecy grey, the clouds seemed trying to overpower a sun that shone but fitfully even thus early in the day. While Audrey Noel was dressing, sunbeams danced desperately on the white wall, like little lost souls with no to-morrow, or gnats that wheel and wheel in brief joy, leaving no footmarks on the air. Through the chinks of a side window covered by a dark blind, some smoky filaments of light were tethered to the back of her mirror. Compounded of trembling grey spirals, so thick to the eye that her hand felt astonishment when it failed to grasp them, and like zestful ghosts busy about their affairs, they brought a moment's distraction to a heart not happy. For how could she be happy, her lover away from her now thirty hours, without having overcome with his last kisses the feeling of disaster which had settled on her when he told her of his resolve. Her eyes had seen deeper than his; her instinct had received a message from Fate.

To be the dragger-down, the destroyer of his usefulness; to be not the helpmate, but the clog, not the inspiring sky, but the cloud. And because of a scruple which she could not understand! She had no anger with that unintelligible scruple; but her fatalism, and her sympathy had followed it out into his future. Things being so, it could not be long before he felt that her love was maiming him; even if he went on desiring her, it would be only with his body. And if, for this scruple, he were capable of giving up his public life, he would be capable of living on with her after his love was dead! This thought she could not bear. It stung to the very marrow of her nerves. And yet surely Life could not be so cruel as to have given her such happiness meaning to take it from her! Surely her love was not to be only a summer's day; his love but an embrace, and then—for ever nothing!

This morning, fortified by despair, she admitted her own beauty. He would, he *must* want her more than that other life, at the very thought of which her face darkened. That other life so hard, and far from her! So loveless, formal, and yet—to

722

him so real, so desperately, accursedly real! If he must indeed give up his career, then surely the life they could live together would make up to him—a life among simple and sweet things, all over the world, with music and pictures, and the flowers and all Nature, and friends who sought them for themselves, and in being kind to everyone, and helping the poor and the unfortunate, and loving each other! But he did not want that sort of life! What was the good of pretending that he did? It was right and natural he should want to use his powers! To lead and serve! She would not have him otherwise. With these thoughts hovering and darting within her, she went on twisting and coiling her dark hair, and burying her heart beneath lace and silk. She noted too, with her usual care, two fading blossoms in the bowl of flowers on her dressing-table, and, removing them, emptied out the water and refilled the bowl.

Before she left her bedroom the sunbeams had already ceased to dance, the grey filaments of light were gone. Autumn sky had come into its own. Passing the mirror in the hall which was always rough with her, she had not courage to glance at it. Then suddenly a woman's belief in the power of her charm came to her aid; she felt almost happy—surely he must love her better than his conscience! But that confidence was very tremulous, ready to yield to the first rebuff. Even the friendly fresh-cheeked maid seemed that morning to be regarding her with compassion; and all the innate sense, not of " good form," but of form, which made her shrink from anything that should disturb or hurt another, or make anyone think she was to be pitied, rose up at once within her; she became more than ever careful to show nothing even to herself. So she passed the morning, mechanically doing the little useful things. An overpowering longing was with her all the time, to get him away with her from England, and see whether the thousand beauties she could show him would not fire him with love of the things she loved. As a girl she had spent nearly three years abroad. And Eustace had never been to Italy, nor to her beloved mountain valleys! Then, the remembrance of his rooms at the Temple broke in on that vision, and shattered it. No Titian's feast of gentian, tawny brown, and alpenrose could intoxicate the lover of those books, those papers, that great map. And the scent of leather came to her now as poignantly as if she were once more flitting about noiselessly on her business of nursing. Then there rushed through her again the warm wonderful sense that had been with her all those precious days—of love knowing secretly of its approaching triumph and fulfilment; the delicious sense of giving every minute of her time, every thought, and movement; and all the sweet unconscious waiting for the divine, irrevocable moment when at last she would give herself and be his. The remembrance too of how tired, how sacredly tired she had been, and of how she had smiled all the time with her inner joy of being tired for him.

The sound of the bell startled her. His telegram had said the afternoon! She determined to show nothing of the trouble darkening the whole world for her, and drew a deep breath, waiting for his kiss.

It was not Miltoun, but Lady Casterley.

The shock sent the blood buzzing into her temples. Then she noticed that the little figure before her was also trembling; drawing up a chair, she said: " Won't you sit down? "

The tone of that old voice, thanking her, brought back sharply the memory of her garden at Monkland, bathed in the sweetness and shimmer of summer, and of Barbara standing at her gate towering above this little figure, which now sat there so silent, with very white face. Those carved features, those keen, yet veiled eyes, had too often haunted her thoughts; they were like a bad dream come true.

" My grandson is not here, is he? "

Audrey shook her head.

" We have heard of his decision. I will not beat about the bush with you. It is a disaster—for me a calamity. I have known and loved him since he was born, and I have been foolish enough to dream dreams about him. I wondered perhaps whether you knew how much we counted on him. You must forgive an old woman's coming here like this. At my age there are few things that matter, but they matter very much."

And Audrey thought: ' And at my age there is but one thing that matters, and *that* matters worse than death.' But she did not speak. To whom, to what should she speak? To this hard old woman, who personified the world? Of what use, words?

" I can say to you," went on the voice of the little figure, which seemed so to fill the room with its grey presence, " what I could not bring myself to say to others; for you are not hard-hearted."

A quiver passed up from the heart so praised to the still lips. No, she was not hard-hearted! She could even feel for this old woman from whose voice anxiety had stolen its despotism.

"Eustace cannot live without his career. His career is himself, he must be doing, and leading, and spending his powers. What he has given you is not his true self. I don't want to hurt you, but the truth is the truth, and we must all bow before it. I may be hard, but I can respect sorrow."

To respect sorrow! Yes, this grey visitor could do that, as the wind passing over the sea respects its surface, as the air respects the surface of a rose, but to penetrate to the heart, to _understand_ her sorrow—_that_ old age could not do for youth! As well try to track out the secret of the twistings in the flight of those swallows out there above the river, or to follow to its source the faint scent of the lilies in that bowl! How should she know what was passing in here—this little old woman whose blood was cold? And Audrey had the sensation of watching someone pelt her with the rind and husks of what her own spirit had long devoured. She had a longing to get up, and take the hand, the chill, spidery hand of age, and thrust it into her breast, and say: "Feel that, and cease!"

But, withal, she never lost her queer dull compassion for the owner of that white carved face. It was not her visitor's fault that she had come! Again Lady Casterley was speaking.

"It is early days. If you do not end it now, at once, it will only come harder on you presently. You know how determined he is. He will not change his mind. If you cut him off from his work in life, it will but recoil on you. I can only expect your hatred, for talking like this, but believe me, it's for your good, as well as his, in the long run."

A tumultuous heart-beating of ironical rage seized on the listener to that speech. Her good! The good of a corpse that the breath is just abandoning; the good of a flower beneath a heel; the good of an old dog whose master leaves it for the last time! Slowly a weight like lead stopped all that fluttering of her heart. If she did not end it at once! The words had now been spoken that for so many hours, she knew, had lain unspoken within her own breast. Yes, if she did not, she could never know a moment's peace, feeling that she was forcing him to a death in life, desecrating her own love and pride! And the spur had been given by another! The thought that someone —this hard old woman of the hard world—should have shaped in words the hauntings of her love and pride through all those ages since Miltoun spoke to her of his resolve; that someone else should have to tell her what her heart had so long known it must do—this stabbed her like a knife! This, at all events, she could not bear!

She stood up, and said:

"Please leave me now! I have a great many things to do, before I go."

With a sort of pleasure she saw a look of bewilderment cover that old face; with a sort of pleasure she marked the trembling of the hands raising their owner from the chair; and heard the stammering in the voice: "You are going? Before—before he comes? You—you won't be seeing him again?" With a sort of pleasure she marked the hesitation, which did not know whether to thank, or bless, or just say nothing and creep away. With a sort of pleasure she watched the flush mount in the faded cheeks, the faded lips pressed together. Then, at the scarcely whispered words: "Thank you, my dear!" she turned, unable to bear further sight or sound. She went to the window and pressed her forehead against the glass, trying to think of nothing. She heard the sound of wheels—Lady Casterley had gone. And then, of all the awful feelings man or woman can know, she experienced the worst: She could not cry!

At this most bitter and deserted moment of her life, she felt strangely calm, foreseeing clearly, exactly, what she must do, and where go. Quickly it must be done, or it would never be done! Quickly! And without fuss! She put some things together, sent the maid out for a cab, and sat down to write.

She must do and say nothing that could excite him, and bring back his illness. Let it all be sober, reasonable! It would be easy to let him know where she was going, to write a letter that would bring him flying after her. But to write the calm reasonable words that would keep him waiting and thinking, till he never again came to her, broke her heart.

When she had finished and sealed the letter, she sat motionless with a numb feeling in hands and brain, trying to realise what she had next to do. To go, and that was all!

Her trunks had been taken down already. She chose the little hat that he liked best, and over it fastened her thickest veil. Then, putting on her travelling coat and gloves, she looked in the long mirror, and seeing that there was nothing more to keep her, lifted her dressing bag, and went down.

Over on the embankment a child was crying; and the passionate screaming sound, broken by the gulping of tears, made her cover her lips, as though she had heard her own escaped soul wailing out there.

She leaned out of the cab to say to the maid:

" Go and comfort that crying, Ella."

Only when she was alone in the train, secure from all eyes, did she give way to desperate weeping. The white smoking rolling past the windows was not more evanescent than her joy had been. For she had no illusions—it was over! From first to last —not quite a year! But even at this moment, not for all the world would she have been without her love, gone to its grave, like a dead child that evermore would be touching her breast with its wistful fingers.

CHAPTER XXVII

Barbara, returning from her visit to Courtier's deserted rooms, was met at Valleys House with the message: Would she please go at once to Lady Casterley?

When, in obedience, she reached Ravensham, she found her grandmother and Lord Dennis in the white room. They were standing by one of the tall windows, apparently contemplating the view. They turned indeed at sound of Barbara's approach, but neither of them spoke or nodded. Not having seen her grandmother since before Miltoun's illness, Barbara found it strange to be so treated; she too took her stand silently before the window. A very large wasp was crawling up the pane, then slipping down with a faint buzz.

Suddenly Lady Casterley spoke.

" Kill that thing! "

Lord Dennis drew forth his handkerchief.

" Not with that, Dennis. It will make a mess. Take a paper knife."

" I was going to put it out," murmured Lord Dennis.

" Let Barbara with her gloves."

Barbara moved towards the pane.

" It's a hornet, I think," she said.

" So he is! " said Lord Dennis, dreamily.

" Nonsense," murmured Lady Casterley, " it's a common wasp."

" I know it's a hornet, Granny. The rings are darker."

Lady Casterley bent down; when she raised herself she had a slipper in her hand.

" Don't irritate him! " cried Barbara, catching her wrist. But Lady Casterley freed her hand.

" I will," she said, and brought the sole of the slipper down on the insect, so that it dropped on the floor, dead. " He has no business in here."

And, as if that little incident had happened to three other people, they again stood silently looking through the window.

Then Lady Casterley turned to Barbara.

" Well, have you realised the mischief that you've done? "

728

"Ann!" murmured Lord Dennis.

"Yes, yes; she is your favourite, but that won't save her. This woman—to her great credit—I say to her great credit— has gone away, so as to put herself out of Eustace's reach, until he has recovered his senses."

With a sharp-drawn breath Barbara said:

"Oh! poor thing!"

But on Lady Casterley's face had come an almost cruel look.

"Ah!" she said: "Exactly. But, curiously enough, I am thinking of Eustace." Her little figure was quivering from head to foot: "This will be a lesson to you not to play with fire!"

"Ann!" murmured Lord Dennis again, slipping his arm through Barbara's.

"The world," went on Lady Casterley, "is a place of facts, not of romantic fancies. You have done more harm than can possibly be repaired. I went to her myself. I was very much moved. If it hadn't been for your foolish conduct——"

"Ann!" said Lord Dennis once more.

Lady Casterley paused, tapping the floor with her little foot. Barbara's eyes were gleaming.

"Is there anything else you would like to squash, dear?"

"Babs!" murmured Lord Dennis; but, unconsciously pressing his hand against her heart, the girl went on.

"You are lucky to be abusing me to-day—if it had been yesterday——"

At these dark words Lady Casterley turned away, her shoe leaving little dull stains on the polished floor.

Barbara raised to her cheek the fingers which she had been so convulsively embracing. "Don't let her go on, uncle," she whispered, "not just now!"

"No, no, my dear," Lord Dennis murmured, "certainly not —it is enough."

"It has been your sentimental folly," came Lady Casterley's voice from a far corner, "which has brought this on the boy."

Responding to the pressure of the hand, back now at her waist, Barbara did not answer; and the sound of the little feet retracing their steps rose in the stillness. Neither of those two at the window turned their heads; once more the feet receded, and again began coming back.

Suddenly Barbara, pointing to the floor, cried:

"Oh! Granny, for Heaven's sake, stand still; haven't you squashed the hornet enough, even if he did come in where he hadn't any business?"

Lady Casterley looked down at the débris of the insect.

"Disgusting!" she said; but when she next spoke it was in a less hard, more querulous voice.

"That man—what was his name—have you got rid of him?"

Barbara went crimson.

"Abuse my friends, and I will go straight home and never speak to you again."

For a moment Lady Casterley looked almost as if she might strike her grand-daughter; then a little sardonic smile broke out on her face.

"A creditable sentiment!" she said.

Letting fall her uncle's hand, Barbara cried:

"In any case, I'd better go. I don't know why you sent for me."

Lady Casterley answered coldly:

"To let you and your mother know of this woman's most unselfish behaviour; to put you on the *qui vive* for what Eustace may do now; to give you a chance to make up for your folly. Moreover to warn you against——" she paused.

"Yes?"

"Let me——" interrupted Lord Dennis.

"No, Uncle Dennis, let Granny take her shoe!"

She had withdrawn against the wall, tall, and as it were, formidable, with her head up. Lady Casterley remained silent.

"Have you got it ready?" cried Barbara: "Unfortunately he's flown!"

A voice said:

"Lord Miltoun."

He had come in quietly and quickly, preceding the announcement, and stood almost touching that little group at the window before they caught sight of him. His face had the rather ghastly look of sunburnt faces from which emotion has driven the blood; and his eyes, always so much the most living part of him, were full of such stabbing anger, that involuntarily they all looked down.

"I want to speak to you alone," he said to Lady Casterley.

Visibly, for perhaps the first time in her life, that indomitable little figure flinched. Lord Dennis drew Barbara away, but at the door he whispered:

"Stay here quietly, Babs; I don't like the look of this."

Unnoticed, Barbara remained hovering.

The two voices, low, and so far off in the long white room, were uncannily distinct, emotion charging each word with preternatural power of penetration; and every movement of the speakers had to the girl's excited eyes a weird precision, as of little figures she had once seen at a Paris puppet show. She could hear Miltoun reproaching his grandmother in words terribly dry and bitter. She edged nearer and nearer, till, seeing that they paid no more heed to her than if she were an attendant statue, she had regained her position by the window.

Lady Casterley was speaking.

"I was not going to see you ruined before my eyes, Eustace. I did what I did at very great cost. I did my best for you."

Barbara saw Miltoun's face transfigured by a dreadful smile —the smile of one defying his torturer with hate. Lady Casterley went on:

"Yes, you stand there looking like a devil. Hate me if you like—but don't betray us, moaning and moping because you can't have the moon. Put on your armour, and go down into the battle. Don't play the coward, boy!"

Miltoun's answer cut like the lash of a whip.

"By God! Be silent!"

And weirdly, there was silence. It was not the brutality of the words, but the sight of force suddenly naked of all disguise —like a fierce dog let for a moment off its chain—which made Barbara utter a little dismayed sound. Lady Casterley had dropped into a chair, trembling. And without a look Miltoun passed her. If their grandmother had fallen dead, Barbara knew he would not have stopped to see. She ran forward, but the old woman waved her away.

"Go after him," she said, "don't let him go alone."

And infected by the fear in that wizen voice, Barbara flew.

She caught her brother as he was entering the taxi-cab in which he had come, and without a word slipped in beside him. The driver's face appeared at the window, but Miltoun only motioned with his head, as if to say: Anywhere, away from here!

The thought flashed through Barbara: 'If only I can keep him in here with me!'

She leaned out, and said quietly:

" To Nettlefold, in Sussex—never mind your petrol—get more
on the road. You can have what fare you like. Quick! "
The man hesitated, looked in her face, and said:
" Very well, Miss. By Dorking, ain't it? "
Barbara nodded.

CHAPTER XXVIII

THE clock over the stables was chiming seven when Miltoun and Barbara passed out of the tall iron gates, in their noisy, swift-moving world, which smelled faintly of petrol. Though the cab was closed, light spurts of rain drifted in through the open windows, refreshing the girl's hot face, relieving a little her dread of this drive. For, now that Fate had been really cruel, now that it no longer lay in Miltoun's hands to save himself from suffering, her heart bled for him; and she remembered to forget herself. The immobility with which he had received her intrusion, was ominous. And though silent in her corner, she was desperately working all her woman's wits to discover a way of breaking into the house of his secret mood. He appeared not even to have noticed that they had turned their backs on London, and passed into Richmond park.

Here the trees, made dark by rain, seemed to watch gloomily the progress of this whirring-wheeled red box, unreconciled even yet to such harsh intruders on their wind-scented tranquillity. And the deer, pursuing happiness on the sweet grasses, raised disquieted noses, as who should say: Poisoners of the fern, defilers of the trails of air!

Barbara vaguely felt the serenity out there in the clouds, and the trees, and wind. If it would but creep into this dim, travelling prison, and help her; if it would but come, like sleep, and steal away dark sorrow,, and in one moment make grief—joy. But it stayed outside on its wistful wings; and that grand chasm which yawns between soul and soul remained unbridged. For what could she say? How make him speak of what he was going to do? What alternatives indeed were now before him? Would he sullenly resign his seat, and wait till he could find Audrey Noel again? But even if he did find her, they would only be where they were. She had gone, in order not to be a drag on him—it would only be the same thing all over again! Would he then, as Granny had urged him, put on his armour, and go down into the fight? But that indeed would mean the end, for if she had had the strength to go away now, she would surely never come back and break in on his life a second time. And a grim thought swooped down on Barbara. What if he

733

resigned everything! Went out into the dark! Men did sometimes—she knew—caught like this in the full flush of passion.
But surely not Miltoun, with his faith! "If the lark's song
means nothing—if that sky is a morass of our invention—if we
are pettily creeping on, furthering nothing—persuade me of it,
Babs, and I'll bless you." But had he still that anchorage, to
prevent him slipping out to sea? This sudden thought of death
to one for whom life was joy, who had never even seen the
Great Stillness, was very terrifying. She fixed her eyes on the
back of the chauffeur, in his drab coat with the red collar,
finding some comfort in its stolidity. They were in a taxicab,
in Richmond Park! Death—incongruous, incredible death! It
was stupid to be frightened! She forced herself to look at
Miltoun. He seemed to be asleep; his eyes were closed, his
arms folded—only a quivering of his eyelids betrayed him.
Impossible to tell what was going on in that grim waking sleep,
which made her feel that she was not there at all, so utterly did
he seem withdrawn into himself!

He opened his eyes, and said suddenly:

"So you think I'm going to lay hands on myself, Babs?"

Horribly startled by this reading of her thoughts, Barbara
could only edge away and stammer:

"No; oh, no!"

"Where are we going in this thing?"

"Nettlefold. Would you like him stopped?"

"It will do as well as anywhere."

Terrified lest he should relapse into that grim silence, she
timidly possessed herself of his hand.

It was fast growing dark; the cab, having left the villas of
Surbiton behind, was flying along at great speed among pine
trees and stretches of heather gloomy with faded daylight.

Miltoun said presently, in a queer, slow voice: "If I want, I
have only to open that door and jump. You who believe that
'to-morrow we die'—give me the faith to feel that I can free
myself by that jump; and out I go!" Then, seeming to pity
her terrified squeeze of his hand, he added: "It's all right,
Babs; we shall sleep comfortably enough in our beds to-night."

But, so desolate to the girl was his voice, that she hoped now
for silence.

"Let us be skinned quietly," muttered Miltoun, "if nothing
else. Sorry to have disturbed you."

Pressing close up to him, Barbara murmured:

" If only—— Talk to me!"

But Miltoun, though he stroked her hand, was silent.

The cab, moving at unaccustomed speed along these deserted roads, moaned dismally; and Barbara was possessed now by a desire which she dared not put in practice, to pull his head down, and rock it against her. Her heart felt empty, and timid; to have something warm resting on it would have made all the difference. Everything real, substantial, comforting, seemed to have slipped away. Among these flying dark ghosts of pine trees—as it were the unfrequented borderland between two worlds—the feeling of a cheek against her breast alone could help muffle the deep disquiet in her, lost like a child in a wood.

The cab slackened speed, the driver was lighting his lamps; and his red face appeared at the window.

" We'll 'ave to stop here, miss; I'm out of petrol. Will you get some dinner, or go through?"

" Through," answered Barbara.

While they were passing the little town, buying their petrol, asking the way, she felt less miserable, and even looked about her with a sort of eagerness. Then when they had started again, she thought: 'If I could get him to sleep—the sea will comfort him!' But his eyes were staring, wide-open. She feigned sleep herself; letting her head slip a little to one side, causing small sounds of breathing to escape. The whirring of the wheels, the moaning of the cab joints, the dark trees slipping by, the scent of the wet fern drifting in, all these must surely help! And presently she felt that he was indeed slipping into darkness —and then—she felt nothing.

When she awoke from the sleep into which she had seen Miltoun fall, the cab was slowly mounting a steep hill, above which the moon had risen. The air smelled strong and sweet, as though it had passed over leagues of grass.

'The Downs!' she thought; 'I must have been asleep!'

In sudden terror, she looked round for Miltoun. But he was still there, exactly as before, leaning back rigid in his corner of the cab, with staring eyes, and no other signs of life. And still only half awake, like a great warm sleepy child startled out of too deep slumber, she clutched and clung to him. The thought that he had been sitting like that, with his spirit far away, all the time that she had been betraying her watch in sleep, was dreadful. But to her embrace there was no response, and awake indeed now, ashamed, sore, Barbara released him, and turned her face to the air.

Out there, two thin, dense-black, long clouds, shaped like the wings of a hawk, had joined themselves together, so that nothing of the moon showed but a living brightness imprisoned, like the eyes and life of a bird, between those swift sweeps of darkness. This great uncanny spirit, brooding malevolent over the high leagues of moon-wan grass, seemed waiting to swoop, and pluck up in its talons, and devour, all that intruded on the wild loneness of these far-up plains of freedom. Barbara almost expected to hear coming from it the lost whistle of the buzzard hawks. And her dream came back to her. Where were her wings—the wings which in sleep had borne her to the stars; the wings which would never lift her—waking—from the ground? Where too were Miltoun's wings? She crouched back into her corner; a tear stole up and trickled out between her closed lids—another and another followed. Faster and faster they came. Then she felt Miltoun's arm round her, and heard him say: "Don't cry, Babs!" Instinct telling her what to do she laid her head against his chest, and sobbed bitterly. Struggling with those sobs, she grew less and less unhappy—knowing that he could never again feel quite so desolate, as before he tried to give her comfort. It was all a bad dream, and they would soon wake from it! And they would be happy; as happy as they had been before—before these last months! And she whispered:

"Only a little while, Eusty!"

.   .   .   .

CHAPTER XXIX

OLD LADY HARBINGER dying in the early February of the following year, the marriage of Barbara with her son was postponed till June.

Much of the wild sweetness of spring still clung to the high moor borders of Monkland on the early morning of the wedding day.

Barbara was already up and dressed for riding when her maid came to call her; and noting Stacey's astonished eyes fix themselves on her boots, she said:

"Well, Stacey?"

"It'll tire you."

"Nonsense; I'm not going to be hung."

Refusing the company of a groom, she made her way towards the stretch of high moor where she had ridden with Courtier a year ago. Here over the short, as yet unflowering, heather, there was a mile or more of level galloping ground. She mounted steadily, and her spirit rode, as it were, before her, longing to get up there among the peewits and curlew, to feel the crisp, peaty earth slip away under her, and the wind drive in her face, under that deep blue sky. Carried by this warm-blooded sweetheart of hers, ready to jump out of his smooth hide with pleasure, snuffling and sneezing in sheer joy, whose eye she could see straying round to catch a glimpse of her intentions, from whose lips she could hear issuing pleasant bitt-music, whose vagaries even seemed designed to startle from her a closer embracing—she was filled with a sort of delicious impatience with everything that was not this perfect communing with vigour.

Reaching the top, she put him into a gallop. With the wind furiously assailing her face and throat, every muscle crisped, and all her blood tingling—this was a very ecstasy of motion!

She reigned in at the cairn whence she and Courtier had looked down at the herds of ponies. It was the merest memory now, vague and a little sweet, like the remembrance of some exceptional spring day, when trees seem to flower before your eyes, and in sheer wantonness exhale a scent of lemons. The ponies were there still, and in distance the shining sea. She sat thinking of nothing, but how good it was to be alive. The fullness and sweetness of it all, the freedom and strength! Away to the West over a lonely farm she could see two buzzard hawks hunting in wide circles. She did not envy them—so happy was she, as happy as the morning. And there came to her suddenly the true, the overmastering longing of mountain tops.

" I must," she thought; " I simply must! "

Slipping off her horse she lay down on her back, and at once everything was lost except the sky. Over her body, supported above solid earth by the warm, soft heather, the wind skimmed without sound or touch. Her spirit became one with that calm freedom. Transported beyond her own contentment, she no longer even knew whether she was joyful.

The horse Hal, attempting to eat her sleeve, aroused her. She mounted him, and rode down. Near home she took a short cut across a meadow, through which flowed two thin bright streams, forming a delta full of lingering " milkmaids," mauve marsh orchis, and yellow flags. From end to end of this long meadow, so varied, so pied with trees and stones, and flowers, and water, the last of the Spring was passing.

Some ponies, shyly curious of Barbara and her horse, stole up, and stood at a safe distance, with their noses dubiously stretched out, swishing their lean tails. And suddenly, far up, following their own music, two cuckoos flew across, seeking the thorn-trees out on the moor. While she was watching the arrowy birds, she caught sight of someone coming towards her from a clump of beech-trees, and suddenly saw that it was Mrs. Noel!

She rode forward flushing. What dared she say? Could she speak of her wedding, and betray Miltoun's presence? Could she open her mouth at all without rousing painful feeling of some sort? Then, impatient of indecision, she began:

" I'm so glad to see you again. I didn't know you were still down here."

" I only came back to England yesterday, and I'm just here to see to the packing of my things."

" Oh! " murmured Barbara. " You know what's happening to me, I suppose? "

Mrs. Noel smiled, looked up, and said: " I heard last night. All joy to you! "

A lump rose in Barbara's throat.

" I'm so glad to have seen you," she murmured once more;

"I expect I ought to be getting on," and with the word, "Good-bye," gently echoed, she rode away.

But her mood of delight was gone; even the horse Hal seemed to tread unevenly, for all that he was going back to that stable which ever appeared to him desirable ten minutes after he had left it.

Except that her eyes seemed darker, Mrs. Noel had not changed. If she had shown the faintest sign of self-pity, the girl would never have felt, as she did now, so sorry and upset.

Leaving the stables, she saw that the wind was driving up a huge, whit, shining cloud. 'Isn't it going to be fine after all!' she thought.

Re-entering the house by an old and so-called secret stairway that led straight to the library, she had to traverse that great dark room. There, buried in an armchair in front of the hearth she saw Miltoun with a book on his knee, not reading, but looking up at the picture of the old Cardinal. She hurried on, tip-toeing over the soft carpet, holding her breath, fearful of disturbing the queer interview, feeling guilty, too, of her new knowledge, which she did not mean to impart. She had burnt her fingers once at the flame between them; she would not do so a second time!

Through the window at the far end she saw that the cloud had burst; it was raining furiously. She regained her bedroom unseen. In spite of her joy out there on the moors, this last adventure of her girlhood had not been all success; she had again the old sensations, the old doubts, the dissatisfaction which she had thought dead. Those two! To shut one's eyes, and be happy—was it possible! A great rainbow, the nearest she had ever seen, had sprung up in the park, and was come to earth again in some fields close by. The sun was shining out already through the wind-driven bright rain. Jewels of blue had begun to star the black and white and golden clouds. A strange white light—ghost of Spring passing in this last violent outburst—painted the leaves of every tree; and a hundred savage hues had come down like a motley of bright birds on moor and fields.

The moment of desperate beauty caught Barbara by the throat. Its spirit of galloping wildness flew straight into her heart. She clasped her hands across her breast to try and keep that moment. Far out, a cuckoo hooted—and the immortal call passed on the wind. In that call all the beauty, and colour, and rapture of life seemed to be flying by. If she could only seize and ever-more have it in her heart, as the buttercups out there imprisoned the sun, or the fallen raindrops on the sweetbriars round the windows enclosed all changing light! If only there were no chains, no walls, and finality were dead!

Her clock struck ten. At this time to-morrow! Her cheeks turned hot; in a mirror she could see them burning, her lips scornfully curved, her eyes strange. Standing there, she looked long at herself, till, little by little, her face lost every vestige of that disturbance, became solid and resolute again. She ceased to have the galloping wild feeling in her heart, and instead felt cold. Detached from herself she watched, with contentment, her own calm and radiant beauty resume the armour it had for that moment put off.

After dinner that night, when the men left the dining-hall, Miltoun slipped away to his den. Of all those present in the little church he had seemed most unemotional, and had been most moved. Though it had been so quiet and private a wedding, he had resented all cheap festivity accompanying the passing of his young sister. He would have had that ceremony in the little dark disused chapel at the Court; those two, and the priest alone. Here, in this half-pagan little country church smothered hastily in flowers, with the raw singing of the half-pagan choir, and all the village curiosity and homage—everything had jarred, and the stale aftermath sickened him. Changing his swallow-tail to an old smoking jacket, he went out on to the lawn. In the wide darkness he could rid himself of his exasperation.

Since the day of his election he had not once been at Monkland; since Mrs. Noel's flight he had never left London. In London and work he had buried himself; by London and work he had saved himself! He had gone down into the battle.

Dew had not yet fallen, and he took the path across the fields. There was no moon, no stars, no wind; the cattle were noiseless under the trees; there were no owls calling, no night-jars churring, the fly-by-night chafers were not abroad. The stream alone was alive in the quiet darkness. And at Miltoun followed the wispy line of grey path cleaving the dim glamour of daisies and buttercups, there came to him the feeling that he was in the presence, not of sleep, but of eternal waiting. The sound of his footfalls seemed desecration. So devotional was that hush, burning the spicy incense of millions of leaves and blades of grass.

Crossing the last stile he came out, close to her deserted cottage, under her lime-tree, which on the night of Courtier's adventure had hung blue-black round the moon. On that side, only a rail, and a few shrubs confined her garden.

The house was all dark, but the many tall white flowers, like a bright vapour rising from earth, clung to the air above the beds. Leaning against the tree Miltoun gave himself to memory.

From the silent boughs which drooped round his dark figure, a little sleepy bird uttered a faint cheep; a hedgehog, or some small beast of night, rustled away in the grass close by; a moth flew past, seeking its candle flame. And something in Miltoun's heart took wings after it, searching for the warmth and light of his blown candle of love. Then, in the hush he heard a sound as of a branch ceaselessly trailed through long grass, fainter and fainter, more and more distinct; again fainter, but nothing could he see that should make that homeless sound. And the sense of some near but unseen presence crept on him, till the hair moved on his scalp. If God would light the moon or stars, and let him see! If God would end the expectation of this night, let one wan glimmer down into her garden, and one wan glimmer into his breast! But it stayed dark, and the homeless noise never ceased. The weird thought came to Miltoun that it was made by his own heart, wandering out there, trying to feel warm again. He closed his eyes and at once knew that it was not his heart, but indeed some external presence, unconsoled. And stretching his hands out he moved forward to arrest that sound. As he reached the railing, it ceased. And he saw a flame leap up, a pale broad pathway of light blanching the grass.

And, realising that she was there, within, he gasped. His finger-nails bent and broke against the iron railing without his knowing. It was not as on that night when the red flowers on her windowsill had wafted their scent to him; it was no sheer overpowering rush of passion. Profounder, more terrible, was this rising up within him of yearning for love—as if, now defeated, it would nevermore stir, but lie dead on that dark grass beneath those dark boughs. And if victorious—what then? He stole back under the tree.

He could see little white moths travelling down that path of lamplight; he could see the white flowers quite plainly now, a pale watch of blossoms guarding the dark sleepy ones; and he stood, not reasoning, hardly any longer feeling; stunned, battered by struggle. His face and hands were sticky with the honey-due, slowly, invisibly distilling from the lime-tree. He bent down and felt the grass. And suddenly there came over him the certainty of her presence. Yes, she was there—out on the verandah! He could see her white figure from head to foot; and, not realising that she could not see him, he expected her to utter some cry. But no sound came from her, no gesture; she turned back into the house. Miltoun ran forward to the railing. But there, once more, he stopped—unable to think, unable to feel; as it were abandoned by himself. And he suddenly found his hand up at his mouth, as though there were blood there, to be staunched, escaped from his heart.

Still holding that hand before his mouth, and smothering the sound of his feet in the long grass, he crept away.

CHAPTER XXX

IN the great glass house at Ravensham, Lady Casterley stood close to some Japanese lilies, with a letter in her hand. Her face was very white, for it was the first day she had been allowed down after an attack of influenza; nor had the hand in which she held the letter its usual steadiness. She read:

"MONKLAND COURT.

"Just a line, dear, before the post goes, to tell you that Babs has gone off happily. The child looked beautiful. She sent you her love, and some absurd message—that you would be glad to hear she was perfectly safe, with both feet firmly on the ground."

A grim little smile played on Lady Casterley's pale lips: Yes, indeed, and time too! The child had been very near the edge of the cliffs! Very near committing a piece of romantic folly! That was well over! And raising the letter again, she read on:

"We were all down for it, of course, and come back to-morrow. Geoffrey is quite cut up. Things can't be what they were without our Babs. I've watched Eustace very carefully, and I really believe he's safely over that affair at last. He is doing extraordinarily well in the House just now. Geoffrey says his speech on the Poor Law was head and shoulders the best made."

Lady Casterley let fall the hand which held the letter: Safe? Yes, he was safe! He had done the right—the natural thing! And in time he would be happy! He would rise now to that pinnacle of desired authority which she had dreamed of for him, ever since he was a tiny thing, ever since his little thin brown hand had clasped hers in their wanderings amongst the flowers, and the furniture of tall rooms. But, as she stood—crumpling the letter, grey-white as some small resolute ghost, among her tall lilies filling with their scent the great glass house—shadows flitted across her face. Was it the fugitive noon sunshine? Or was it some glimmering perception of the old Greek saying—"Character is Fate;" some sudden sense of the universal truth that all are in bond to their own natures, and what a man has most desired shall in the end enslave him?

1909-10